Praise for

American Wife

NAMED ONE OF THE BEST BOOKS OF THE YEAR BY

Amazon • *Chicago Tribune* • *Entertainment Weekly* • National Public Radio • *People* • *Rocky Mountain News* • *St. Louis Post-Dispatch* • *The New York Times Book Review* • *The Washington Post Book World* • *Time*

"Curtis Sittenfeld is an amazing writer, and *American Wife* is a brave and moving novel about the intersection of private and public life in America. Ambitious and humble at the same time, Sittenfeld refuses to trivialize or simplify people, whether real or imagined." —RICHARD RUSSO

"Sittenfeld installs herself deep within the psyche of the tight-lipped wife of the president and emerges with an evenhanded, compassionate look at her mind and heart. . . . Powerfully intimate. Grade: A."

—*The Washington Post Book World*

"A sparkling, sprawling novel . . . a ridiculously gifted writer . . . Sittenfeld has harnessed her talents perfectly in *American Wife*, producing an exhilarating epic infused with humor, pain and hope." —*BookPage*

"A well-researched book that imagines what lies behind that placid facade of the first lady . . . Ms. Sittenfeld was not out to sensationalize but sympathize. The portraits of Laura and W.—known as Alice and Charlie Blackwell here—are trenchant and make you like them more."

—MAUREEN DOWD, *The New York Times*

"A gripping epic of public and private lives. A gem." —*Good Housekeeping*

"*American Wife* reveals how difficult it can be, living this American life with its dreams of power and prosperity, to be true to yourself. . . . Sittenfeld hits all the hot spots: daughterhood, sex, money, career, marriage, motherhood. . . . Alice's life has something in it for every American female."

—*Los Angeles Times*

"Audacious . . . Sittenfeld's imagination knows no bounds." —*People*

"Showing that she's grown immensely even since her bestselling debut, Sittenfeld now claims her spot as one of a new generation's greatest novelists."

—*BUST*

"[Sittenfeld] writes in the sharp, realistic tradition of Philip Roth and Richard Ford—clear, unpretentious prose; metaphors so spot-on you barely notice them. Sittenfeld may have lifted the set pieces from a real woman's life, but in the process she has created a wise and insightful character who is entirely her own." —*Time Out New York*

"The novel is a gift, a sweeping exploration of a woman's odyssey from obscurity to fame and the painful decisions she must make along the way."

—*The Miami Herald*

"We love Sittenfeld. We love her wry, razor-sharp observations. We love her funny, straightforward honesty. . . . An empathetic, fascinating, and gorgeously written story about a thirty-year marriage. We devoured it in one night." —*Boston* magazine

"If you've ever wondered, while watching President Bush cavorting through the minefields of foreign policy and public opinion, 'What must Laura be thinking?' novelist Curtis Sittenfeld has written the book for you."

—*The Dallas Morning News*

"A big, thick, juicy steak of a book, a page-turner . . . a moving and often powerful imaginative experiment." —REBECCA TRAISTER, Salon.com

"My favourite book of the year." —KATE ATKINSON

"[Sittenfeld] can be lauded for writing a complex, undeniably fascinating portrait of the woman behind the perfectly coiffed hair and fresh coat of lipstick." —*Washington City Paper*

"A masterful highbrow-lowbrow mash-up that satisfies as ass-kicking literary fiction and juicy gossip simultaneously." —*Radar*

"The novel, Sittenfeld's most fully realized yet, artfully evokes the painful reverberations of the past." —*The New Yorker*

"A broad, deep and utterly convincing account of a straightforward, serious middle-class American girl . . . A portrait of a woman and a marriage that brings the reader as close to the probable essence of the outgoing president as any other novelist, or any biographer, is likely to get." —*The Oregonian*

"Endearing and poignant, humorous and enlightening, *American Wife* is a must-read for Sittenfeld fans—and a good first read for would-be converts." —Fredericksburg *Free-Lance Star*

"Immensely readable. It's a nuanced portrait of a woman in a singularly fascinating position." —*The Plain Dealer*

"Curtis Sittenfeld is one of our best contemporary chroniclers of class and caste. . . . Sittenfeld invents a deep, messy, sympathetic life for a public person whose surface is all we'll ever know." —*St. Petersburg Times*

"A remarkable piece of work, nuanced and persuasive as a portrait of a decent woman navigating her contradictions and the buffetings of fate."

—*Houston Chronicle*

"With *American Wife,* Curtis Sittenfeld has deftly crossed an extraordinarily high wire. . . . I read *American Wife* in just two or three delicious sittings, struck by the granular clarity of the author's descriptions and the down-to-earth believability of the story, bewitched by the charming, frustrating woman at the center of it." —ANA MARIE COX, *The New York Observer*

"Vastly entertaining . . . An intelligent, well-crafted, psychologically astute novel." —*The New York Sun*

"A perfect political fairy tale . . . an audacious, engrossing novel that belongs on a shelf with Jonathan Franzen's *The Corrections* or Michael Chabon's *The Amazing Adventures of Kavalier & Clay*. By combining questions of politics with an intense focus on one woman's psychology, Sittenfeld has created something that feels new, and necessary." —Bloomberg.com

"Convincing and complex . . . In prose that is unadorned, strong in detail yet presented in an engaging, matter-of-fact way, Sittenfeld flexes her skills as a writer. Rather than ghostwrite a version of what has already been conveyed by the media many times over, she creates characters who are less thinly veiled stand-ins than full, engaging personalities. Even the most partisan readers should enjoy the storytelling." —*Nashville Scene*

"What a remarkable (and brave) thing: a compassionate, illuminating and beautifully rendered portrait of a fictional Republican first lady with a life and husband very much like our actual Republican first lady's. Curtis Sittenfeld has written a novel as impressive as it is improbable."

—KURT ANDERSEN

"[Sittenfeld] succeeds in creating a memorable and sympathetic heroine. . . . Nimble . . . wickedly hilarious."

—MICHIKO KAKUTANI, *The New York Times*

"Just as she did in *Prep,* Sittenfeld masterfully deflates the middle-class fairy tale—rose gardens and all." —*Marie Claire*

"Bold . . . convincing, thoroughly riveting . . . What [Sittenfeld] does here, in prose as winning as it is confident, is to craft out of the first-person narrative a compelling, very human voice, one full of kindness and decency. And, as if making the Bush-like couple entirely sympathetic is not enough of a feat in itself, she also provides many rich insights into the emotional ebb and flow of a long-term marriage." —*Booklist* (starred)

"It is not easy to write fiction inspired by current events, especially if those events involve politics. The stage is too grand, the spotlight too bright. Our public life already is ridiculously flagrant, far too obvious and overwrought for good fiction. And so, all too often, political novels descend from satire into cheap farce. Such books can be entertaining and sometimes cathartic but usually not very nourishing. *American Wife* is something else entirely—the opposite of a political satire, in fact—with a languorous pace and a fierce literary integrity: Alice and Charlie are complete creations, unique in their humanity—Alice especially. She is the quirky and (usually) reliable narrator. This is the story of her inner life, a place that only fiction can go." —JOE KLEIN, *Time*

ALSO BY CURTIS SITTENFELD

The Man of My Dreams

Prep

AMERICAN WIFE

Curtis Sittenfeld

AMERICAN WIFE

A Novel

RANDOM HOUSE TRADE PAPERBACKS | NEW YORK

2009 Random House Trade Paperback Edition

Published in the United States by Random House Trade Paperbacks, an imprint of The Random House Publishing Group, a division of Random House, Inc., New York.

RANDOM HOUSE TRADE PAPERBACKS and colophon are trademarks of Random House, Inc.

RANDOM HOUSE READER'S CIRCLE and colophon is a registered trademark of Random House, Inc.

Originally published in hardcover in the United States by Random House, an imprint of The Random House Publishing Group, a division of Random House, Inc., in 2008.

Grateful acknowledgment is made to the following for permission to reprint previously published material:

SONY/ATV MUSIC PUBLISHING AND ALFRED PUBLISHING CO., INC: Excerpt from "Lonesome Town" by Baker Knight, copyright © 1958 (renewed) by Sony/ATV Songs LLC, EMI Unart Catalog, Inc., and Matragun Music, Inc., EMI. All rights assigned to EMI Catalogue Partnership. All rights controlled and administered by EMI Unart Catalog, Inc., and Sony/ATV Music Publishing. Reprinted by permission of Sony/ATV Music Publishing, 8 Music Square West, Nashville, TN 37203 and Alfred Publishing Co., Inc.

VIKING PENGUIN, A DVISION OF PENGUIN YOUNG READERS GROUP, A MEMBER OF PENGUIN GROUP (USA) INC.: Excerpt from *Madeline* by Ludwig Bemelmans, copyright © 1939 by Ludwig Bemelmans and copyright renewed 1967 by Madeleine Bemelmans and Barbara Bemelmans Marciano. All rights reserved. Used by permission of Viking Penguin, a Division of Penguin Young Readers Group, a Member of Penguin Group (USA) Inc., 375 Hudson Street, New York, NY 10014.

Grateful acknowledgment is made to *Time* magazine for permission to reprint "Q&A: Curtis Sittenfeld" from the September 2, 2008, issue, copyright © 2008 by Time, Inc. Reprinted through the courtesy of the editors of *Time* magazine.

Library of Congress Cataloging-in-Publication Data
Sittenfeld, Curtis.
American wife: a novel / Curtis Sittenfeld.
p. cm.
ISBN 978-0-8129-7540-6
1. Presidents' spouses—United States—Fiction. 2. Women librarians—Fiction. I. Title.
PS3619.I94A8 2008
813'.6—dc22 2008008175

Printed in the United States of America

www.randomhousereaderscircle.com

4 6 8 9 7 5

For Matt Carlson,
my American husband

CONTENTS

American Wife is a work of fiction loosely inspired by the life of an American first lady. Her husband, his parents, and certain prominent members of his administration are recognizable. All other characters in the novel are products of the author's imagination, as are the incidents concerning them.

AMERICAN WIFE

PROLOGUE

June 2007, the White House

HAVE I MADE terrible mistakes?

In bed beside me, my husband sleeps, his breathing deep and steady. Early in our marriage, really in the first weeks, when he snored, I'd say his name aloud, and when he responded, I'd apologetically request that he turn onto his side. But it didn't take long for him to convey that he'd prefer if I simply shoved him; no conversation was necessary, and he didn't want to be awakened. "Just roll me over," he said, and grinned. "Give me a good hard push." This felt rude, but I learned to do it.

Tonight, though, he isn't snoring, so I cannot blame my insomnia on him. Nor can I blame the temperature of the room (sixty-six degrees during the night, seventy degrees during the day, when neither of us spends almost any time here). A white-noise machine hums discreetly from its perch on a shelf, and the shades and draperies are drawn to keep us in thick darkness. There are always, in our lives now, security concerns, but these have become routine, and more than once I've thought we must be far safer than a typical middle-class couple in the suburbs; they have a burglar alarm, or perhaps a Jack Russell terrier, a spotlight at one exterior corner of the house, and we have snipers and helicopters, armored cars, rocket launchers and sharpshooters on the roof. The risks for us are greater, yes, but the level of protection is incomparable—absurd at times. As with so much else, I tell myself it is our positions that are being deferred to, that we are simply symbols; who we are as individuals hardly matters. It would embarrass me otherwise to think of all the expense and effort put forth on our behalf. If not us, I repeat to myself, then others would play this same role.

For several nights, I've had trouble sleeping. It's not going to bed in the first place that's the challenge: I feel all the normal stages of weariness, the lack of focus that becomes more pronounced with each half hour past ten o'clock, and when I climb beneath the covers, usually a little after eleven, sometimes my husband is still in the bathroom or looking over a last few papers, talking to me from across the room, and I drift away. When he comes to bed, he cradles me, I rise back out from the sea of sleep, we say "I love you" to each other, and in the blurriness of this moment, I believe that something essential is still ours; that our bodies in darkness are what's true and most everything else—the exposure and the obligations and the controversies—is fabrication and pretense. When I wake around two, however, I fear the reverse.

I am not sure whether waking at two is better or worse than waking at four. On the one hand, I have the luxury of knowing that eventually, I'll fall back to sleep; on the other hand, the night seems so long. Usually, I've been dreaming of the past: of people I once knew who are now gone, or people with whom my relationship has changed to the point of unrecognizability. There is so much I've experienced that I never could have imagined.

Did I jeopardize my husband's presidency today? Did I do something I should have done years ago? Or perhaps I did both, and that's the problem—that I lead a life in opposition to itself.

PART I

1272 Amity Lane

IN 1954, THE summer before I entered third grade, my grandmother mistook Andrew Imhof for a girl. I'd accompanied my grandmother to the grocery store—that morning, while reading a novel that mentioned hearts of palm, she'd been seized by a desire to have some herself and had taken me along on the walk to town—and it was in the canned-goods section that we encountered Andrew, who was with his mother. Not being of the same generation, Andrew's mother and my grandmother weren't friends, but they knew each other the way people in Riley, Wisconsin, did. Andrew's mother was the one who approached us, setting her hand against her chest and saying to my grandmother, "Mrs. Lindgren, it's Florence Imhof. How are you?"

Andrew and I had been classmates for as long as we'd been going to school, but we merely eyed each other without speaking. We both were eight. As the adults chatted, he picked up a can of peas and held it by securing it between his flat palm and his chin, and I wondered if he was showing off.

This was when my grandmother shoved me a little. "Alice, say hello to Mrs. Imhof." As I'd been taught, I extended my hand. "And isn't your daughter darling," my grandmother continued, gesturing toward Andrew, "but I don't believe I know her name."

A silence ensued during which I'm pretty sure Mrs. Imhof was deciding how to correct my grandmother. At last, touching her son's shoulder, Mrs. Imhof said, "This is Andrew. He and Alice are in the same class over at the school."

My grandmother squinted. "*Andrew,* did you say?" She even turned her head, angling her ear as if she were hard of hearing, though I knew she wasn't. She seemed to willfully refuse the pardon Mrs. Imhof had offered, and I wanted to tap my grandmother's arm, to tug her over so her face was next to mine and say, "Granny, he's a *boy*!" It had never occurred to me that Andrew looked like a girl—little about Andrew Imhof had occurred to me at that time in my life—but it was true that he had unusually long eyelashes framing hazel eyes, as well as light brown hair that had gotten a bit shaggy over the summer. However, his hair was long only for that time and for a boy; it was still far shorter than mine, and there was nothing feminine about the chinos or red-and-white-checked shirt he wore.

"Andrew is the younger of our two sons," Mrs. Imhof said, and her voice contained a new briskness, the first hint of irritation. "His older brother is Pete."

"Is that right?" My grandmother finally appeared to grasp the situation, but grasping it did not seem to have made her repentant. She leaned forward and nodded at Andrew—he still was holding the peas—and said, "It's a pleasure to make your acquaintance. You be sure my granddaughter behaves herself at school. You can report back to me if she doesn't."

Andrew had said nothing thus far—it was not clear he'd been paying enough attention to the conversation to understand that his gender was in dispute—but at this he beamed: a closed-mouth but enormous smile, one that I felt implied, erroneously, that I was some sort of mischief-maker and he would indeed be keeping his eye on me. My grandmother, who harbored a lifelong admiration for mischief, smiled back at him like a conspirator. After she and Mrs. Imhof said goodbye to each other (our search for hearts of palm had, to my grandmother's disappointment if not her surprise, proved unsuccessful), we turned in the opposite direction from them. I took my grandmother's hand and whispered to her in what I hoped was a chastening tone, "*Granny.*"

Not in a whisper at all, my grandmother said, "You don't think that child looks like a girl? He's downright pretty!"

"Shhh!"

"Well, it's not his fault, but I can't believe I'm the first one to make that mistake. His eyelashes are an inch long."

As if to verify her claim, we both turned around. By then we were thirty feet from the Imhofs, and Mrs. Imhof had her back to us, leaning toward a shelf. But Andrew was facing my grandmother and me. He still was smiling slightly, and when my eyes met his, he lifted his eyebrows twice.

"He's flirting with you!" my grandmother exclaimed.

"What does 'flirting' mean?"

She laughed. "It's when a person likes you, so they try to catch your attention."

Andrew Imhof liked me? Surely, if the information had been delivered by an adult—and not just any adult but my wily grandmother—it had to be true. Andrew liking me seemed neither thrilling nor appalling; mostly, it just seemed unexpected. And then, having considered the idea, I dismissed it. My grandmother knew about some things, but not the social lives of eight-year-olds. After all, she hadn't even recognized Andrew as a boy.

IN THE HOUSE I grew up in, we were four: my grandmother, my parents, and me. On my father's side, I was a third-generation only child, which was greatly unusual in those days. While I certainly would have liked a sibling, I knew from an early age not to mention it—my mother had miscarried twice by the time I was in first grade, and those were just the pregnancies I knew about, the latter occurring when she was five months along. Though the miscarriages weighted my parents with a quiet sadness, our family as it was seemed evenly balanced. At dinner, we each sat on one side of the rectangular table in the dining room; heading up the sidewalk to church, we could walk in pairs; in the summer, we could split a box of Yummi-Freez ice-cream bars; and we could play euchre or bridge, both of which they taught me when I was ten and which we often enjoyed on Friday and Saturday nights.

Although my grandmother possessed a rowdy streak, my parents were exceedingly considerate and deferential to each other, and for years I believed this mode to be the norm among families and saw all other dynamics as an aberration. My best friend from early girlhood was Dena Janaszewski, who lived across the street, and I was constantly shocked by what I perceived to be Dena's, and really all the Janaszewskis', crudeness and volume: They hollered to one another from between floors and out windows; they ate off one another's plates at will, and Dena and her two younger sisters constantly grabbed and poked at one another's braids and bottoms; they entered the bathroom when it was occupied; and more shocking than the fact that her father once said *goddamn* in my presence—his exact words, entering the kitchen, were "Who took my goddamn hedge clippers?"—was the fact that neither Dena, her mother, nor her sisters seemed to even notice.

In my own family, life was calm. My mother and father occasionally disagreed—a few times a year he would set his mouth in a firm straight line, or the corners of her eyes would draw down with a kind of wounded disappointment—but it happened infrequently, and when it did, it seemed unnecessary to express aloud. Merely sensing discord, whether in the role of inflictor or recipient, pained them enough.

My father had two mottoes, the first of which was "Fools' names and fools' faces often appear in public places." The second was "Whatever you are, be a good one." I never knew the source of the first motto, but the second came from Abraham Lincoln. By profession, my father worked as the branch manager of a bank, but his great passion—his hobby, I suppose you'd say, which seems to be a thing not many people have anymore unless you count searching the Internet or talking on cell phones—was bridges. He especially admired the majesty of the Golden Gate Bridge and once told me that during its construction, the contractor had arranged, at great expense, for an enormous safety net to run beneath it. "That's called employer responsibility," my father said. "He wasn't just worried about profit." My father closely followed the building of both the Mackinac Bridge in Michigan—he called it the Mighty Mac—and later, the Verrazano-Narrows Bridge, which, upon completion in 1964, would connect Brooklyn and Staten Island and be the largest suspension bridge in the world.

My parents both had grown up in Milwaukee and met in 1943, when my mother was eighteen and working in a glove factory, and my father was twenty and working at a branch of Wisconsin State Bank & Trust. They struck up a conversation in a soda shop, and were engaged by the time my father enlisted in the army. After the war ended, they married and moved forty-five miles west to Riley, my father's mother in tow, so he could open a branch of the bank there. My mother never again held a job. As a housewife, she had a light touch—she did not seem overburdened or cranky, she didn't remind the rest of us how much she did—and yet she sewed many of her own and my clothes, kept the house meticulous, and always prepared our meals. The food we ate was acceptable more often than delicious; she favored pan-broiled steak, or noodle and cheese loafs, and she taught me her recipes in a low-key, literal way, never explaining why I needed to know them. Why *wouldn't* I need to know them? She was endlessly patient and a purveyor of small, sweet gestures: Without commenting, she'd leave pretty ribbons or peppermint candies on my bed or, on my bureau, a single flower in a three-inch vase.

My mother was the second youngest of eight siblings, none of whom we saw frequently. She had five brothers and two sisters, and only one of her sisters, my Aunt Marie, who was married to a mechanic and had six children, had ever come to Riley. When my mother's parents were still alive, we'd drive to visit them in Milwaukee, but they died within ten days of each other when I was six, and after that we'd go years without seeing my aunts, uncles, and cousins. My impression was that their houses all were small and crowded, filled with the squabbling of children and the smell of sour milk, and the men were terse and the women were harried; in a way that was not cruel, none of them appeared to be particularly interested in us. We visited less and less the older I got, and my father's mother never went along, although she'd ask us to pick up schnecken from her favorite German bakery. In my childhood, there was a relieved feeling that came over me when we drove away from one of my aunt's or uncle's houses, a feeling I tried to suppress because I knew even then that it was unchristian. Without anyone in my immediate family saying so, I came to understand that my mother had chosen us; she had chosen our life together over one like her siblings', and the fact that she'd been able to choose made her lucky.

Like my mother, my grandmother did not hold a job after the move to Riley, but she didn't really join in the upkeep of the house, either. In retrospect, I'm surprised that her unhelpfulness did not elicit resentment from my mother, but it truly seems that it didn't. I think my mother found her mother-in-law entertaining, and in a person who entertains us, there is much we forgive. Most afternoons, when I returned home from school, the two of them were in the kitchen, my mother paused between chores with an apron on or a dust rag over her shoulder, listening intently as my grandmother recounted a magazine article she'd just finished about, say, the mysterious murder of a mobster's girlfriend in Chicago.

My grandmother never vacuumed or swept, and only rarely, if my parents weren't home or my mother was sick, would she cook, preparing dishes notable mostly for their lack of nutrition: An entire dinner could consist of fried cheese or half-raw pancakes. What my grandmother did do was read; this was the primary way she spent her time. It wasn't unusual for her to complete a book a day—she preferred novels, especially the Russian masters, but she also read histories, biographies, and pulpy mysteries—and for hours and hours every morning and afternoon, she sat either in the living room or on top of her bed (the bed would be made, and she would be fully dressed), turning pages and smoking Pall Malls. From early on, I understood that the household view of my grandmother, which is to say my parents' view, was not simply that she was both smart and frivolous but that her smartness and her frivolity were intertwined. That she could tell you all about the curse of the Hope Diamond, or about cannibalism in the Donner Party—it wasn't that she ought to be ashamed, exactly, to possess such knowledge, but there was no reason for her to be proud of it, either. The tidbits she relayed were interesting, but they had little to do with real life: paying a mortgage, scrubbing a pan, keeping warm in the biting cold of Wisconsin winters.

I'm pretty sure that rather than resisting this less than flattering view of herself, my grandmother shared it. In another era, I imagine she'd have made an excellent book critic for a newspaper, or even an English professor, but she'd never attended college, and neither had my parents. My grandmother's husband, my father's father, had died early, and as a young widow, my grandmother had gone to work in a ladies' dress shop, waiting on Milwaukee matrons who, as she told it, had money but not taste. She'd held this job until the age of fifty—fifty was older then than it is now—at which point she'd moved to Riley with my newlywed parents.

My grandmother borrowed the majority of the books she read from the library, but she bought some, too, and these she kept in her bedroom on a shelf so full that every ledge contained two rows; it reminded me of a girl in my class, Pauline Geisseler, whose adult teeth had grown in before her baby teeth fell out and who would sometimes, with a total lack of self-consciousness, open her mouth for us at recess. My grandmother almost never read aloud to me, but she regularly took me to the library—I read and reread the Laura Ingalls Wilder books, and both the Nancy Drew and the Hardy Boys series—and my grandmother often summarized the grown-up books she'd read in tantalizing ways: *A well-bred married woman falls in love with a man who is not her husband; after her husband learns of the betrayal, she has no choice but to throw herself in the path of an oncoming train . . .*

Such plots infused my grandmother's bedroom with an atmosphere of intrigue enhanced by her few but carefully chosen belongings, my favorite of which was a bust of Nefertiti that rested on her bureau. The bust had been given to my grandmother by her friend Gladys Wycomb, who lived in Chicago, and it was a replica of the ancient Egyptian one by the sculptor Thutmose. Nefertiti wore a black headdress and a jeweled collar, and she gazed forward with great composure. Her name, my grandmother explained, translated as "the beautiful woman has come."

Beside the bust were framed pictures: a photograph of my grandmother as a girl in a white dress, standing next to her parents in 1900 (so very long ago!); one of my parents at their wedding in which my father wore his army uniform and my mother wore a double-breasted sheath dress (though the photo was black and white, I knew because I'd asked my mother that her dress was lavender); a photo of my grandmother's deceased husband, my grandfather, whose name had been Harvey and who was caught here squinting into the sun; and finally, one of me, my class picture from second grade, in which I was smiling a bit frantically, my hair parted in the center and pulled into pigtails.

Beyond her books, her photos, the Nefertiti bust, and her perfume bottle and cosmetics, my grandmother's bedroom was actually rather plain. She slept, as I did, on a single bed, hers covered by a yellow spread on which she heaped plaid blankets in the winter. There was little on her walls, and her bedside table rarely held anything besides a lamp, a book, a clock, and an ashtray. Yet this was the place, smelling of cigarette smoke and Shalimar perfume, that seemed to me a passageway to adventure, the lobby of adulthood. In my grandmother's lair, I sensed the experiences and passions of all the people whose lives were depicted in the novels she read.

I don't know if my grandmother was consciously trying to make me a reader, too, but she did allow me to pick up any of her books, even ones I had small hope of understanding (I began *The Portrait of a Lady* at the age of nine, then quit after two pages) or ones my mother, had she known, would have forbidden (at the age of eleven, I not only finished *Peyton Place* but immediately reread it). Meanwhile, my parents owned almost no books except for a set of maroon-spined *Encyclopaedia Britannica*s we kept in the living room. My father subscribed to Riley's morning and evening newspapers, *The Riley Citizen* and *The Riley Courier,* as well as to *Esquire,* though my grandmother seemed to read the magazine more thoroughly than he did. My mother didn't read, and to this day I'm not sure if her disinclination was due to a lack of time or interest.

Because I was the daughter of a bank manager, I believed us to be well off; I was past thirty by the time I realized this was not a view any truly well-off American would have shared. Riley was in the exact center of Benton County, and Benton County contained two competing cheese factories: Fassbinder's out on De Soto Way, and White River Dairy, which was closer to the town of Houghton, though plenty of people who worked at White River still lived in Riley because Riley, with nearly forty thousand residents, had far more attractions and conveniences, including a movie theater. Many of my classmates' parents worked at one of the factories; other kids came from small farms, a few from big farms—Freddy Zurbrugg, who in third grade had laughed so hard he'd started crying when our teacher used the word *pianist,* lived on the fourth largest dairy farm in the state—but still, being from town seemed to me infinitely more sophisticated than being from the country. Riley was laid out on a grid, flanked on the west by the Riley River, with the commercial area occupying the south section of town and the residential streets heading north up the hill. As a child, I knew the names of all the families who lived on Amity Lane: the Weckwerths, whose son, David, was the first baby I ever held; the Noffkes, whose cat, Zeus, scratched my cheek when I was five, drawing blood and instilling in me a lifelong antipathy for all cats; the Cernochs, who in hunting season would hang from a tree in their front yard the deer they'd shot. Calvary Lutheran Church, which my family attended, was on Adelphia Street; my elementary school and junior high, located on the same campus, were six blocks from my house; and the new high school—completed in 1948 but still referred to as "new" when I started there in 1959—was the largest building in town, a grand brick structure supported in the front by six massive Corinthian columns and featured on postcards sold at Utzenstorf's drugstore. All of what I thought of as Riley proper occupied under ten square miles, and then in every direction around us were fields and prairies and pastures, rolling hills, forests of beech and sugar maple trees.

Attending school with children who still used outhouses, or who didn't eat food that wasn't a product of their own land and animals, did not make me haughty. On the contrary, mindful of what I perceived as my advantages, I tried to be extra-polite to my classmates. I couldn't have known it at the time, but far in the future, in a life I never could have anticipated for myself, this was an impulse that would serve me well.

FOR A FEW years, I hardly thought of that day at the grocery store with my grandmother, Andrew Imhof, and his mother. The two people who, in my opinion, ought to have been embarrassed by it—my grandmother, for making the error about Andrew's gender, and Andrew, for having the error made about him (if any of our classmates had caught wind of it, they'd have mocked him relentlessly)—seemed unconcerned. I continued going to school with Andrew, but we rarely spoke. Once in fourth grade, before lunch, he was the person selected by our teacher to stand in front of the classroom and call up the other students to get in line; this was a ritual that occurred multiple times every day. First Andrew said, "If your name begins with B," which meant his friend Bobby could line up right behind him, and the next thing Andrew said was "If you're wearing a red ribbon in your hair." I was the only girl that day who was. Also, I was facing forward when Andrew called this out, a single ponytail gathered behind my head, meaning he must have noticed the ribbon earlier. He hadn't said anything, he hadn't yanked on it as some of the other boys did, but he'd noticed.

And then in sixth grade, my friend Dena and I were walking one Saturday afternoon from downtown back to our houses, and we saw Andrew coming in the other direction, riding his bicycle south on Commerce Street. It was a cold day, Andrew wore a parka and a navy blue watch cap, and his cheeks were flushed. He was sailing past us when Dena yelled out, "Andrew Imhof has great balls of fire!"

I looked at her in horror.

To my surprise, and I think to Dena's, Andrew braked. The expression on his face when he turned around was one of amusement. "What did you just say?" he asked. Andrew was wiry then, still shorter than both Dena and me.

"I meant like in the song!" Dena protested. "You know: 'Goodness, gracious . . .' " It was true that while her own mother was an Elvis fan, Dena's favorite singer was Jerry Lee Lewis. The revelation the following spring that he'd married his thirteen-year-old cousin, while alarming to most people, would only intensify Dena's crush, giving her hope; should things not work out between Jerry Lee and Myra Gale Brown, Dena told me, then she herself would realistically be eligible to date him by eighth grade.

"Did you come all the way here on your bike?" Dena said to Andrew. The Imhofs lived on a corn farm a few miles outside of town.

"Bobby's cocker spaniel had puppies last night," Andrew said. "They're about the size of your two hands." He was still on the bike, standing with it between his legs, and he held his own hands apart a few inches to show how small; he was wearing tan mittens. I had not paid much attention to Andrew lately, and he seemed definitively older to me—able, for the first time that I could remember, to have an actual conversation instead of merely smiling and sneaking glances. In fact, conscious of his presence in a way I'd never been before, I was the one who seemed to have nothing much to say.

"Can we see the puppies?" Dena asked.

Andrew shook his head. "Bobby's mother says they shouldn't be touched a lot until they're older. Their feet and noses are real pink."

"I want to see their pink noses!" Dena cried. This seemed a little suspect to me; the Janaszewskis had a boxer to whom Dena paid negligible attention.

"They hardly do anything now but eat and sleep," Andrew said. "Their eyes aren't even open."

Aware that I had not contributed to the conversation so far, I extended a white paper bag in Andrew's direction. "Want some licorice?" Dena and I had been downtown on a candy-buying expedition.

"Andrew," Dena said as he removed his mittens and stuck one hand in the bag, "I heard your brother scored a touchdown last night."

"You girls weren't at the game?"

Dena and I shook our heads.

"The team's real good this year. One of the offensive linemen, Earl Yager, weighs two hundred and eighty pounds."

"That's disgusting," Dena said. She helped herself to a rope of my licorice though she'd bought some of her own. "When I'm in high school, I'm going to be a cheerleader, and I'm going to wear my uniform to school every Friday, no matter how cold it is."

"What about you, Alice?" Andrew gripped the handles of his bicycle, angling the front wheel toward me. "You gonna be a cheerleader, too?" We looked at each other, his eyes their greenish-brown and his eyelashes ridiculously long, and I thought that my grandmother may have been right after all—even if Andrew wasn't flirting with you, his eyelashes were.

"Alice will still be a Girl Scout in high school," Dena said. She herself had dropped out of our troop over the summer, and while I was leaning in that direction, I officially remained a member.

"I'm going to be in Future Teachers of America," I said.

Dena smirked. "You mean because you're so smart?" This was a particularly obnoxious comment; as Dena knew, I had wanted to be a teacher since we'd been in second grade with Miss Clougherty, who was not only kind and pretty but had read *Caddie Woodlawn* aloud to us, which then became my favorite book. For years, Dena and I had pretended we were teachers who coincidentally both happened to be named Miss Clougherty, and we'd gotten Dena's sisters, Marjorie and Peggy, to be our students. As with Girl Scouts, playing school was an activity Dena had lost interest in before I did.

Dena turned back to Andrew. "Tell Bobby to let us come over and play with his puppies. We promise to be gentle."

"You can tell him yourself." Andrew pulled on his mittens and set his feet back on the pedals of his bicycle. "See you girls later."

THAT MONDAY, DENA wrote Andrew a note. *What is your favorite food?* the note said. *What is your favorite season? Who do you like better, Ed Sullivan or Sid Caesar?* And, like an afterthought: *Who is your favorite girl in our class?*

She didn't mention the note before delivering it, but when a few days had passed without a response, she was too agitated not to tell me. Hearing what she'd done made me agitated, too, like we were preparing to sprint against each other and she'd taken off before I knew the race had started. But I wasn't sure feeling this way was within my rights—why shouldn't Dena write Andrew a note?—so I said nothing. Besides, as three and then four days passed and Andrew sent no reply, my distress turned into sympathy. I was as relieved as Dena when at last a lined piece of notebook paper, folded into a hard, tiny square, appeared in her desk.

Mashed potatoes, it said in careful print.

Summer.

I do not watch those shows, prefer Spin and Marty on The Mickey Mouse Club.

Sylvia Eberbach, also Alice.

Sylvia Eberbach was the smallest girl in the sixth grade, a factory worker's daughter with pale skin and blond hair who, when I look back, I suspect had dyslexia; in English class, whenever the teacher made her read aloud, half the students would correct her. Alice, of course, was me. Surely, to this day, Andrew's answers represent the most earnest, honest document I have ever seen. What possible incentive did he have for telling the truth? Perhaps he didn't know any better.

Dena and I read his replies standing in the hall after lunch, before the bell rang for class. Seeing that line—*Sylvia Eberbach, also Alice*—felt like such a gift, a promise of a nebulously happy future; all the agitation that had consumed me after learning Dena had sent the letter went away. Me—he liked me. I didn't even mind sharing his affection with Sylvia. "Should I keep the note?" I said. This was logical, my ascent over Dena clear and firm. But she gave me a sharp look and pulled away the piece of paper. By the end of the school day, which was less than two hours later, I learned not from Dena herself but from Rhonda Ostermann, whose desk was next to mine, that Andrew and Dena were going steady. And indeed as I left the school building to go home, I saw them standing by the bus stop, holding hands.

When I approached them—Andrew rode the bus, but Dena and I walked to and from school together—Dena said, "Greetings and salutations, Alice." Clearly, she was delighted with herself. Andrew nodded at me. I looked for a sign that he was Dena's hostage, being held against his will, or at least that he felt conflicted. But he seemed amiable and content. What had happened to *Sylvia Eberbach, also Alice?*

Improbably, Dena and Andrew remained a couple for the next four years. A pubescent couple, granted, meaning there may have been no one besides me who took them seriously. But they continued holding hands in public, and they were permitted by their parents to meet for hamburgers and milk shakes at Tatty's. Andrew was quiet, though not silent, around Dena. The three of us sometimes went to the movies at the Imperial Theater, and once in seventh grade it happened that he sat between us—usually, Dena sat in the middle—and before the curtain opened, Dena got up to buy popcorn. During those few minutes when she was gone, Andrew and I said precisely nothing to each other, and for the entire time, I thought, *It is really the two of us who are together. Not Andrew and Dena. Andrew and me. I know it, and he knows it, and anyone who would look over at us now would know it, too.* I felt that we were under a kind of spell, and when Dena returned, the spell broke; his energy shifted back to her. Certainly he never gave any proof that I was still one of his two favorite girls. I searched for it, I waited, and it didn't come. In eighth grade, Dena fell while running across the pavement behind the school, and he licked the blood off her palms. For weeks, thinking of that made me feel like a chute had opened in my stomach and my heart was descending through it.

One afternoon in the beginning of our sophomore year in high school, Andrew unceremoniously broke up with Dena; he said football practice made him too tired to have a girlfriend. He was six feet tall by then, was a JV kicker for the Benton County Central High School Knights, and wore his once-shaggy hair in a crew cut. At that point, I stopped talking to him altogether. This was less out of loyalty to Dena—Andrew and I did still smile mildly at each other in the halls—than due to simple logistics, the fact that I had no classes with him. Our high school was bigger than our elementary or junior high schools had been, drawing kids who came from as much as an hour away.

During the years Dena and Andrew had been together, I'd often marveled at both the swiftness and randomness of their coupling. Ostensibly, he'd had no interest in Dena, and hours later, he'd become hers. It seemed to be a lesson in something, but I wasn't sure what—an argument for aggression, perhaps, for the bold pursuit of what you wanted? Or proof of most people's susceptibility to persuasion? Or just confirmation of their essential fickleness? After I'd read Andrew's note, was I supposed to have immediately marched up to him and staked my claim? Had my faith in our pleasantly murky future been naive, had I been passive or a dupe? These questions were of endless interest to me for several years; I thought of them at night after I'd said my prayers and before I fell asleep. And then, once high school started, I became distracted. By the time Dena and Andrew broke up (she seemed insulted more than upset, and the insult soon passed), I had, somewhere along the way, stopped dwelling on the two of them and on what hadn't happened with Andrew and me. When I did think of it, fleetingly, it seemed ridiculous; if the events behind us held any lessons, they were about how silly young people were. Dena and Andrew's supposed love affair, my own yearnings and confusion—they all came to seem like nothing more than the backdrop of our childhood.

EVERY YEAR, THE day after Christmas, my grandmother took the train to visit her old friend Gladys Wycomb in Chicago, and every summer, my grandmother returned to Chicago for the last week in August. In the winter of 1962, when I was a junior, my grandmother announced at dinner one evening in November that this Christmas she wanted me to accompany her—her treat. It would be a kind of cultural tour, the ballet and the museums, the view from a skyscraper. "Alice is sixteen, and she's never been to a big city," my grandmother said.

"I've been to Milwaukee," I protested.

"Precisely," my grandmother replied.

"Emilie, that's a lovely idea," my mother said, while at the same time, my father said, "I'm not sure it'll work this year. It's rather short notice, Mother."

"All we need to do is book another train ticket," my grandmother said. "Even an old bird like myself is capable of that."

"Chicago is cold in December," my father said.

"Colder than here?" My grandmother's expression was dubious.

No one said anything.

"Or is there some other reason you're reluctant to have her go?" My grandmother's tone was open and pleasant, but I sensed her trickiness, the way she was bolder than either of my parents.

Another silence sprang up, and at last my father said, "Let me consider this."

In the mornings, my family's routines were staggered: My father usually had left for the bank by the time I came downstairs—I'd find sections of *The Riley Citizen* spread over the table, my mother at the sink washing dishes—and my grandmother would still be asleep when I took off for school. But that next morning, I hurried downstairs right after my alarm clock rang, still in my nightgown, and said to my father, "I could buy my own train ticket so Granny doesn't have to pay."

My allowance was three dollars a week, and in the past few years, I'd saved up over fifty dollars; I kept the money in an account at my father's bank.

My father, who was seated at the table, glanced toward my mother; she was standing by the stove, tending to the bacon. They exchanged a look, and my father said, "I didn't realize you were so keen on seeing Chicago."

"I just thought if the ticket was the reason—"

"We'll talk about it at dinner," my father said.

Every evening, the grace my father recited before we ate was "Come, Lord Jesus, be our guest, and let these gifts to us be blessed. O give thanks unto the Lord, for He is good, and His mercy endures forever." Then the rest of us said "Amen." That night, as soon as we'd raised our bowed heads, my father said, "My concern about Alice traveling to Chicago with you, Mother, is the imposition it creates for Gladys, so I've called and made a reservation for you both to stay at a hotel called the Pelham. You'll be my guests for the week."

As if she, too, were hearing this offer for the first time, my mother exclaimed, "Isn't that generous of Daddy!" In a normal voice, she added, "Alice, pass the creamed broccoli to your grandmother."

"My colleague Mr. Erle used to live in Chicago," my father said. "According to him, the Pelham is a very fine place, and it's in a safe neighborhood."

"You're aware that Gladys has an enormous apartment with several spare bedrooms?" It was hard to tell whether my grandmother was irritated or amused.

"Granny, we just don't know Mrs. Wycomb the way you do," my mother said. "We'd feel forward presuming on her."

"Doctor," my grandmother said. "Dr. Wycomb. Not Mrs. And Phillip, you know her well enough to realize she'll still insist on having us over."

"Gladys Wycomb is a doctor?" I said.

Once again, my parents exchanged a look. "I don't see that having dinner with her once or twice would be a problem," my father said.

"What's she a doctor of?" I asked.

All three of them turned toward me. "Female problems," my

mother said, and my father said, "This isn't appropriate conversation for the dinner table."

"She was the eighth woman in the state of Wisconsin to earn her medical degree," my grandmother said. "I don't know about you, but as someone who can hardly read a thermometer, I take my hat off to that."

I HAD GROWN up hearing Gladys Wycomb's name—given my grandmother's biannual journeys, Gladys Wycomb was, in my mind, less a person than a destination, faraway yet not entirely unfamiliar—but it was only with the introduction of my own trip to Chicago that I realized how little I knew about her. A few hours later, my mother came to say good night while I was reading an Agatha Christie novel in bed, and I asked, "Why doesn't Dad like Dr. Wycomb?"

"Oh, I wouldn't say he doesn't like her." My mother had been standing over me and had already kissed my forehead, but now she sat on the edge of the bed, setting her hand where my knees were beneath the covers. "Dr. Wycomb has known Daddy since he was a little boy, and she can be a bit bossy. She thinks everyone should share her opinions. I guess you wouldn't remember her visits here because the first was when you were just a baby, and the next one might have been when you were four or five, but there was something that happened on the second visit, a discussion about Negroes—should they have rights, and that sort of thing. Dr. Wycomb was very keen on the subject, as if she wanted us to disagree with her, and we just thought, for heaven's sakes, there aren't any Negroes *in* Riley." This was literally true, that not one black person lived in our entire town. I'd seen black people—as a child, I'd once been captivated as we drove by a restaurant outside which stood a mother, father, and two little girls my age in pink dresses—but that had been in Milwaukee.

"Do *you* dislike her?" I asked.

"Oh, no. No. She's a formidable woman, but I don't dislike her, and I don't think Daddy does, either. It's more that we all realized it might be simpler for Granny to go there than for Dr. Wycomb to come here." My mother patted my knee. "But I'm glad they're friends, because I know Dr. Wycomb was a real comfort to your granny after your grandfather died." This had happened when my father was two years old; his own father, a pharmacist, had had a heart attack one afternoon at work and dropped dead at the age of thirty-three. Just the idea of my father as a two-year-old pinched at my heart, but the idea of him as a two-year-old with a dead father was devastating.

My mother stood then and kissed my forehead a second time. "Don't stay up too late," she said.

THOUGH MY CULTURAL enrichment had been the justification for our trip, the train had scarcely left the Riley station when it emerged that my grandmother's overriding goal in Chicago was to buy a sable stole from Marshall Field's. She'd seen an advertisement for it in *Vogue,* she confided, and she'd written a letter to the store asking them to save one in size small.

"If I'd been clever, I'd have ordered it a month ago and worn it to church on Christmas Eve," she said.

"Does Dad know you're buying it?"

"He'll know when he sees me in it, won't he? And I'll look so ravishing that I'm sure he'll be thrilled." We were sitting side by side, and she winked. "I have some savings, Alice, and it's not a crime to treat yourself. Now, let me put some lipstick on you."

I puckered my mouth. When she was finished, she held up my chin and gazed at me. "Beautiful," she said. "You'll be the belle of Chicago." Personally, I did not consider myself beautiful, but in the last few years, I had begun to suspect that I was probably pretty. I stood five feet five, with a narrow waist and enough bosom to fill out a B-cup bra. My eyes were blue and my hair chestnut-brown and shiny; I wore it chin-length and curled toward my cheeks with a wispy fringe of bangs. Being attractive felt, more than anything, like a relief—I imagined life was harder for girls who weren't pretty.

Our train ride was just over two hours, and at Union Station in Chicago, we were met by a woman I did not recognize at first as Dr. Gladys Wycomb; absurdly, I think I'd expected her to have a stethoscope around her neck. After she and my grandmother embraced, my grandmother stood next to Dr. Wycomb and set one arm on her back. "A legend in her own time," my grandmother said, and Dr. Wycomb said, "Hardly. Shall we go have a drink?"

They seemed to me an unlikely pair of friends, at least with regard to appearance: Dr. Wycomb was a bit heavy in a way that suggested strength, and her handshake had almost hurt. She had short gray hair and wore white cat's-eye glasses and a black gabardine coat over a gray tweed suit; her shoes were black patent-leather pumps with low heels and perfunctory bows. My grandmother, meanwhile, always proud of her style and slimness (her tiny wrists and ankles were a particular source of pleasure to her), was especially decked out for our city visit. We'd given ourselves manicures the day before, and she'd gone to Vera's in downtown Riley to have her hair dyed and set. Under a tan cashmere coat, she wore a chocolate-brown wool suit—the collar was velvet, the skirt fell just below her knee—complemented by matching brown crocodile pumps and a brown crocodile handbag. So prized were these accessories that she'd bestowed on them the nickname "my crocs," and the reference was understood by all other family members; in fact, a few weeks earlier, before we'd crossed our snowy street to get to the Janaszewskis' Christmas party, I'd been amused to hear my father say, "Mother, I urge you to wear boots outside and change into your crocs at their house." To meet Dr. Wycomb, I also was dressed up, outfitted in a kilt, green tights, saddle shoes, and a green wool sweater over a blouse; on the collar, I wore a circle pin, even though Dena had recently told me it was a sign of being a virgin.

Outside the train station was a chaos of people and cars, the sidewalks swarming, the traffic in the street jerking and honking, and the buildings around us were the tallest I had ever seen. As we approached a beige Cadillac, I was surprised when a driver in a black cap emerged from it, took our bags, and opened the doors for us; being a lady doctor was, it seemed, a lucrative profession. The three of us sat in the backseat, Dr. Wycomb behind the driver, my grandmother in the middle, me on the right side. "We need to make a stop, if you don't mind," my grandmother said to Dr. Wycomb. "The Pelham at Ohio and Wabash.

Phillip got it into his head that Alice and I together would be burdensome to you—you can see that Alice is very unruly and belligerent—so he made us a reservation, which of course we'll cancel."

"Oh, for crying out loud," Dr. Wycomb said. "Does he really see me as such a corrupting influence?"

"We hope that's what you are!" At this, my grandmother turned and kissed Dr. Wycomb on the cheek. I knew that kiss, the lightness of her lips, the scent of Shalimar that floated ahead of her as she approached. When she'd settled against the seat again, my grandmother said, "Don't we?" and patted my hand. Unsure what to say, I laughed.

Dr. Wycomb leaned forward and said, "When your father was a boy, he'd remove all his clothes before making a bowel movement."

"Oh, Gladys, she doesn't want to hear about this."

"But it's instructive. It captures a certain . . . rigidity, I suppose, that Phillip has always shown. He'd remove his clothes, and when he was seated on the john, he'd shut his eyes tightly and press his hands over his ears. That was the only way he could eliminate."

My grandmother made a face and fanned the air in front of her, as if mere words had brought the stench of a bathroom into the car.

"Am I telling the truth, Emilie?" Dr. Wycomb asked.

"The truth," my grandmother said, "is overrated."

"Your grandmother was my landlady," Dr. Wycomb said to me. "Has she ever mentioned that?"

"It was scarcely as formal as you make it sound," my grandmother said.

"In medical school, I was poor as a church mouse," Dr. Wycomb said. "I lived in a terrible attic belonging to a terrible family—"

"The Lichorobiecs," my grandmother interrupted. "Doesn't that *sound* like the name of a terrible family? Mrs. Lichorobiec felt she'd been wronged by mankind."

"She refused to let me keep food in the attic because she said it would attract animals," Dr. Wycomb said. "She wouldn't let me keep food in the pantry, either, because she said there wasn't space. This was nonsense, but what could I do? Luckily, your grandmother, who lived next door, took pity and invited me to have my meals at their house."

"I thought you'd starve otherwise," my grandmother said. "I've always been slender, but Gladys was positively skeletal. Just a bag of bones, and big dark circles under her eyes."

"A bag of bones," Dr. Wycomb repeated, and chortled. She leaned forward again, and when our eyes met, she said, "Can you imagine?" In fact, I'd been thinking the same thing, but I smiled in what I hoped was a neutral and unrevealing way. "And then your poor grandfather died," she continued. "What year was that, Emilie? Was that '24?"

"It was '25."

"And your grandmother was ready to move, but I said, 'Let's think this through. If I'm champing at the bit to get away from the Lichorobiecs, and you'd just as soon stay in this house where you're all settled . . .' And so I became your grandmother's tenant, and we had some wonderful times."

"When the Depression hit, you can bet I was thankful to have Gladys," my grandmother said. "Being a widow, I certainly couldn't have gotten by on my salary at Clausnitzer's. Speaking of spending beyond your means"—she pulled the *Vogue* ad from her purse and unfolded it—"have you ever seen more gorgeous sable?"

Dr. Wycomb laughed. "Alice, your grandmother is the only person in this country who became *less* frugal following the Depression."

"If it's all about to vanish at any moment, why not have some fun? And tell me that's not stunning. The gloss on it, it's absolutely—Mmh." My grandmother shook her head appreciatively.

"Are you a clothes horse as well, Alice?" Dr. Wycomb's voice was laced with affection for my grandmother.

"Oh, she's far less shallow than I am," my grandmother said. "Straight A's every semester—imagine my disappointment." In fact, while my parents did not seem to have strong feelings about whether I attended college, my grandmother was the one who'd told me that doing so would give me a leg up.

"Is that right?" Dr. Wycomb said. "All A's?"

"I got an A-minus in home ec," I admitted. The reason why was that on the final project, for which Dena, Nancy Jenzer, and I were partners, we had prepared Hawaiian meatballs in class, and Dena dropped the bowl of Oriental sauce on the floor.

"Are you interested in the sciences?" Dr. Wycomb asked me, but before I could answer, we'd pulled over in front of a maroon awning that said THE PELHAM on it in white cursive.

"Gladys, you stay here and we'll just be a moment," my grandmother said. "Alice, come in with me."

Although we left our suitcases in the car, it wasn't until we were inside that I fully understood: We weren't, as my grandmother had claimed to Dr. Wycomb, canceling our reservation. We were checking in, then walking back out and riding away in Dr. Wycomb's car. My grandmother did not explain this to me, but when the woman behind the reception desk said, "A view of the lake would cost you just six dollars more a day," my grandmother replied, "We'll be fine in the room we have." She also said we wouldn't need a porter. I was not a person who openly challenged others, and besides, I considered myself an ally of my grandmother. That was why, after we'd retraced our steps through the Pelham's dim lobby and climbed back in the car, I said nothing when she told Dr. Wycomb, "All taken care of, and they didn't give us a bit of trouble." I couldn't understand the reason for our double deception—lying to my father about where we were staying, lying to Dr. Wycomb about canceling the reservation—but I knew that good manners meant accommodating the person you were with. My grandmother assumed my loyalty, and this, surely, is the reason she got it.

IN THE TRAIN station, when Dr. Wycomb had suggested having a drink, I'd imagined she meant at a restaurant, but instead, we drove to her apartment on Lake Shore Drive, then rode an elevator to the seventh floor; an elevator operator wore a uniform not unlike the driver's and nodded once, saying "Dr. Wycomb" just before pressing the button. With no additional exchange of words, we rose, and when the elevator stopped, we stepped into a hallway lined with gold fabric for wallpaper—not glittery gold but subtly shiny brocade with unshiny fleurs-de-lis appearing at tasteful intervals.

The elevator operator carried our bags inside the apartment. The room where I was to stay featured twin beds separated by a white marble table, and on the table sat a lamp with a large base of raspberry-colored ribbed glass; also, there was an actual suitcase stand on which the operator set my suitcase. At first I'd thought to decline when the man had offered to carry our bags, but when my grandmother had accepted, I had, too. Then I wondered if she ought to tip him, which she didn't. Her room, connected to mine by a bathroom we'd share, had a canopy bed, the canopy itself silvery-blue silk shantung gathered in the center around a mirror the size of a Ritz cracker.

In the living room was a mix of modern and old-fashioned funiture: two low, geometric white couches, an antique-looking gold-leaf chair, a revolving walnut bookcase, and many prints and paintings, some of them abstract, hung close together on the walls. Dr. Wycomb asked a maid in a black dress and a white apron for a Manhattan. My grandmother held up her index and middle fingers: "And two old-fashioneds."

Dr. Wycomb glanced at me through her cat's-eye glasses. "Would you prefer a hot cocoa, Alice?"

"She'll take an old-fashioned," my grandmother said. To the maid, she said, "With brandy, not whiskey."

"Oh, Myra knows." Dr. Wycomb laughed. "Don't forget, I'm from Wisconsin, too, Emilie." When the maid left the room, Dr. Wycomb said, "Myra and I have quite a rivalry going. She's a White Sox fan, while I root for the Cubs. Do you follow baseball, Alice?"

"Not really," I admitted.

"We'll convert you yet. Last season, I'm afraid Myra had more to gloat about, but with Ron Santo, the Cubs just might have a chance this year."

When Myra returned with the drinks, my grandmother held up her glass and said, "Gladys, I'd like to propose a toast. To you, my dear, for being a world-class hostess and a true friend."

Dr. Wycomb raised her own glass. "And I turn it back and say to both of you—to the Lindgren women, Emilie and Alice."

The two of them looked at me expectantly. "To baseball," I said. "To 1963."

"Hear, hear." Dr. Wycomb nodded emphatically.

"To a wonderful time together in Chicago," my grandmother said.

The three of us clinked our glasses.

DR. WYCOMB, IT turned out, had taken several days' vacation to be our hostess. Our first order of business was for my grandmother to acquire her sable stole, which, as by then I had intuited would happen, Dr. Wycomb paid for with no discussion. Over the next several days, we bundled up and toured the city together, visiting the Art Institute, Shedd Aquarium (I was appalled and transfixed by a ten-foot alligator), and the Joffrey Ballet, where we took in an afternoon performance of *La Fille Mal Gardée* and where Dr. Wycomb, I observed, fell deeply asleep. At the Prudential building, my stomach dropped as we rode the elevator forty floors—when the building had opened in 1955, its elevators had been the world's fastest—and on the forty-first-floor public observation deck, I thought how much my father would have enjoyed the view. Even though I wore a hat, scarf, and mittens, it was unbearably cold in the wind, and I stayed outside under a minute before retreating. My grandmother and Dr. Wycomb did not venture onto the observation deck at all. In the evenings, we ate heavy dinners prepared and served by Myra: braised veal chops with prunes, or lamb and turnips.

That Sunday, Dr. Wycomb went to the hospital to check on her patients, and after she'd left the apartment, my grandmother and I caught a cab to the Pelham. We climbed the steps to the third floor—the building was five stories, with no elevator—and found in our room a double bed and not much else. Breathing heavily from the stairs, my grandmother threw back the coverlet, mussed the sheets, filled a glass with water from the bathroom sink, and set the glass on the windowsill. Then she stood at the window, which looked onto the gray backside of another building. It was seven degrees that day and so overcast I was tempted to lie on the bed and take a nap. "I'm being a little silly, aren't I?" my grandmother said.

I shrugged, still unable to bring myself to ask about our duplicitousness.

"It's not as if your father will ring the management to see if our room looks inhabited," my grandmother said. This was true—due to the expense, my father avoided making long-distance calls. The rare times when he did make them, he shouted uncharacteristically, as if raising the volume of his voice would enable a second cousin in Iowa to hear him better.

"Did Dr. Wycomb ever have a husband?" I asked.

"Gladys is a suffragette. She always says she couldn't have been a doctor if she'd married and had children, and I'm sure she's right. Shall we go warm up with some tea?"

A block away, we found a café, mostly empty, where we were seated at a small table. My grandmother scanned the menu. "Have you ever had an éclair?" When I shook my head, she said, "We'll split one. They're bad for your figure but quite delicious."

"Is Dr. Wycomb friends with Negroes?"

"Who told you that?" My grandmother scrutinized me.

It seemed unfair to pinpoint my mother. "I just was wondering, since a lot of them live in Chicago," I said. I had at that time only the slightest awareness of the protests and sit-ins occurring in other parts of the country; my main reminder of race came from Dena, who was not allowed by her father to listen to records by black musicians and therefore liked for me to play Chubby Checker or the Marvelettes when she came over.

"Dr. Wycomb supports desegregation, as do I, as should you," my grandmother said. "That just means they can eat and live and go to school where we do. But if you're talking about socializing, Gladys spends more time with Jews than Negroes. Jews often become doctors, you know." My grandmother still was looking at me closely and apropos of nothing, it seemed, she said, "You don't have a beau, do you?"

"No," I said, but I could feel my face heating. A month before, just after Thanksgiving, Dena and I had spent a Saturday night sledding on Bony Ridge with two senior boys, Larry Nagel and Robert Beike. Robert was the one who'd invited Dena, and Dena had brought me. In the inside pocket of his down coat, Larry had tucked a flask of bourbon that we passed around. More than once I'd sipped my grandmother's old-fashioneds—she'd sometimes give me the maraschino cherry—but this was the first time I'd tasted alcohol away from home. And though I felt a wave of guilt, I knew I couldn't refuse the bourbon without seeming to the boys and Dena like what I was: a goody-goody. So I had drunk from the flask each of the four times it came to me, and though it didn't taste good, it made me warm and relaxed. Prior to meeting up with Larry and Robert, I'd been jittery, but I began to feel calm and amused. At one point, at the bottom of the hill, Dena and I scurried to a grove of trees, pulled down our snow pants, and urinated into the snow, giggly and unself-conscious. "Write your name in yellow," Larry called to us. At the end of the night, the boys walked us back to our houses, and from across the street, I could see Dena and Robert on her porch, kissing deeply. For several minutes, Larry stood a few feet away from me—at one point, under his breath, he said, "If they don't watch out, their tongues will freeze"—but after Robert and Dena pulled apart and Robert called in a shouting whisper, "We've gotta go, Nagel," Larry zoomed toward me without warning, his mouth on mine, his lips cold but his tongue warm. The entire kiss lasted about eight seconds and involved much head and neck movement, as if Larry were participating in a pie-eating contest, but instead of a pie, there was my face. Then he was off our stoop, headed up Amity Lane with Robert, and as soon as they were sufficiently far away, Dena and I met in the middle of the street, clutching each other, trying not to scream. "You two were *making out,*" she hissed. Until Larry had kissed me, I had not necessarily thought I wanted him to, but after he had, I was glad. In the four weeks since then, Robert and Dena had gone on actual dates, but Larry and I had only passed in the halls at school, acknowledging each other vaguely.

In the café, my grandmother said, "You should have a beau. When I last went to see Dr. Ziemniak, he showed me a picture of Roy, who seems to be growing into a handsome fellow." Dr. Ziemniak was our dentist.

"Roy Ziemniak is short," I said.

"Aren't we picky? Eugene Schwab, then." The Schwabs lived two doors down from us.

"Eugene goes out with Rita Sanocki."

"Not Irma and Morris's daughter?"

I nodded.

"I've always thought she has a piggy face."

"Granny!"

"You called Roy Ziemniak short, my dear. And I don't mean to be cruel about Rita, but you must know what I'm referring to. It's her eyes and nose." The waitress arrived then to take our order, and when she was gone, my grandmother said, "I'd had two marriage proposals by the time I was your age. It's time for you to start dating."

"WE'VE FOUND A gentleman for you," Dr. Wycomb announced the next evening at dinner. We were having rack of lamb, buttered rolls, and artichokes—another food I'd never tasted, and one Dr. Wycomb apparently ordered once a year in a crate from California. My grandmother had shown me how to remove the leaves and dip them in butter, how to daintily skim off the meat with my front teeth. "Marvin Benheimer is the son of a colleague of mine, a gastroenterologist," Dr. Wycomb was saying to me. "He's in his second year at Yale University, and he's very tall. He'll pick you up tomorrow at seven."

"What fun," my grandmother said.

"He'll pick me up *here*? Tomorrow?"

"It's New Year's Eve," my grandmother said. "We thought it would be a treat for you after spending all week with two old ladies."

"I like spending time with the two of you."

"You don't have to marry him, Alice," my grandmother said. "Just consider it practice. It's important to know how to behave in a range of social situations."

I couldn't tell my grandmother that she was underestimating me—I may not have been on any actual dates, but Larry Nagel was not even the first person I'd kissed. At Pauline Geisseler's fourteenth birthday party in ninth grade, when we'd played post office, Bobby Sobczak had picked me, and then it became my turn and I picked Rudy Kuesto. Both of them had tasted like peanuts because that was one of Pauline's party snacks.

"You shouldn't worry," Dr. Wycomb said. "Marvin is an upstanding young man. He'll take you to dinner, then bring you to the Palmer House, where your grandmother and I will be having a drink with his parents, and we'll all ring in the New Year together. That doesn't sound so dreadful, does it?"

Before I could respond, my grandmother set down her fork and beamed. "That sounds perfect," she said.

HE HAD ON a coat and tie, and I wore the kilt and blouse I'd worn on the train from Riley, but not the circle pin or the green wool sweater. "It's manly," my grandmother had said about the sweater when I appeared in the living room to show her and Dr. Wycomb the outfit, and though I protested that I'd be cold, she said it would be a short walk to the restaurant. Marvin visited with my grandmother and Dr. Wycomb before we left; when Myra asked what he'd like to drink, he said, "I'll take a Miller, if you've got it," then added, in the same tone of unjustified enthusiasm that the announcer used in the ads, "The champagne of bottled beers!" In this moment, I could feel my grandmother not making eye contact with me, refusing to concede what I'd been nearly certain of right away—that Marvin possessed little appeal.

When we stood to leave, Dr. Wycomb said, "Here's a key, just in case, and I've written down my address and telephone number, should there be any sort of emergency." She handed me a small square of paper.

"Gladys, they'll be three blocks away," my grandmother said. "And Marvin has no prison record, at least none that he's mentioned."

"Dr. Wycomb knows I'm as squeaky clean as they come," Marvin said, and everyone chuckled. But I had an unsettled feeling in my stomach; it had come over me while I brushed my hair in the bathroom, and it hadn't gone away when I'd met Marvin, even after I'd realized there was no reason to be intimidated by him. As she helped me put on my coat, my grandmother whispered, "So he's a bit of a horse's ass, but remember: practice." In the elevator down to the lobby, I couldn't help asking, "How tall are you?" and Marvin said, "Six-five," in a way that implied both that he was asked often and that he never grew tired of answering.

The restaurant was called Buddy's, which had made me imagine it would not be fancy, that we might even be overdressed. But it *was* fancy, and we were some of the youngest people there. Someone took our coats on our arrival, and the maître d' led us to the dining room, which was dimly lit, with heavy curtains and large wingback chairs at the tables.

After we'd sat, Marvin said, "To be honest, when my father told me I had to do this, I thought you'd be a dog, but you're pretty darn cute."

Uncertainly, I said, "Thanks."

"Don't be insulted—I wouldn't be telling you if you *were* a dog."

"Oh," I said. "Okay."

"You're still in high school, aren't you?" When I nodded, he said, "Well, I advise you to stay away from Bryn Mawr. Of all the Seven Sisters, the girls there are the biggest ding-a-lings."

"Who are the seven sisters?"

He looked at me as if trying to decide whether I was joking or serious. Then, not unkindly, he said, "You really are from a small town. They're the female counterparts of the Ivies. Radcliffe goes with Harvard, Barnard goes with Columbia, and so on. In New Haven, our sister school is Vassar, though they're a solid hour and a half away."

"I want to go to Ersine Teachers College in Milwaukee," I said. "It's all girls, so maybe it's a sister school—I don't know."

"It's not a *Seven* Sisters school."

"Yeah, I don't think it is. I don't know, though."

"No," he said. "It's definitely not."

That unsettled feeling from before—it still hadn't gone away. It was now accompanied by a heat that was spreading through my body, collecting in my cheeks and neck.

"If I order for both of us, I'm sure they'll bring you a drink," he said.

"Water is fine." I touched my fingertips to my face and, as I'd expected, my skin was burning. "Excuse me for a second." The bathroom was also fancy: An attendant, a black girl who looked not much older than I, was sitting by the sink, and every stall had a wooden door that went all the way up to the ceiling; inside the stall, the fixture holding the toilet paper was gold. As my mother had taught me, I placed a strip of paper on either side of the seat before I sat down, and when I was finished urinating, I leaned forward with my elbows on my knees, covering my face with my hands. It was not that I definitely would throw up, but the possibility existed. Was I really such a social coward?

Though I didn't think I cared what Marvin thought of me, perhaps my body knew more than my mind.

Conscious of the attendant out by the sink, I forced myself to stand, flush, and fix my clothes. I washed my hands, and when the woman passed me a towel, I said—I'd seen the dish of coins—"I'm sorry, but I left my purse at the table."

When I returned to the dining room, Marvin said, "I took the liberty of ordering an hors d'oeuvre. How do you feel about escargot?"

"That's fine." I had, of course, never tasted them, though I knew what they were, and they sounded awful. When the waiter brought the small white bowl filled with brown globs in a pool of melted butter, I had to look away. For a main course, Marvin asked for fricassee of rabbit—smirking, he added, "With apologies to Mr. Bugs Bunny"—and I asked for steak; it seemed like something that wouldn't hold surprises, it would be straightforward, and I could take three bites, then push the rest around my plate.

Marvin leaned intently across the table. "Here's a moral dilemma for you. You've built a bomb shelter in your backyard, and your neighbors haven't. When the Soviets attack, you hightail it to your shelter, but your neighbors come around begging for food and water. What do you do?"

"What?" I said.

"Alice, do you follow current affairs? And I don't mean what hat Jackie Kennedy is wearing this week and who designed her dress."

"Sometimes I read the newspaper." One of my organs had just done a somersault inside my stomach, which was distracting enough that Marvin's condescension didn't really offend me.

"You shoot 'em dead," he said. "That's what you do. If your neighbors didn't plan ahead, their survival isn't your responsibility."

This was when the waiter arrived with our entrées, and my steak was a lump of brown meat still attached to the bone, accompanied by menacingly glistening peas and carrots, and a baked potato bulging at the seams. I knew I couldn't eat any of it; I couldn't touch it.

"The thing no one realizes about Khrushchev—" Marvin began, and I said, "I'm sorry, but I don't feel very well. I need to leave."

"Now?" Marvin looked bewildered.

"I'm sorry." I stood. "Please stay. I'll be fine getting back to Dr. Wycomb's."

"Are you sure?"

"Both our meals shouldn't go to waste. I'm so sorry." I hurried through the restaurant and retrieved my coat from the coat-check man, who spoke as he passed it to me, but I walked outside without replying. I was dizzy and scalding hot, focused only on not letting the horrible churning inside me erupt into something public and visible. If I could just get back to Dr. Wycomb's empty apartment, I could sit on the bathroom floor next to the toilet, and it would all emerge in an orderly fashion; this moment would pass with no one watching.

Walk forward over the sidewalk, I thought, and as I repeated the phrase in my head, it seemed, in my unsteadiness and desperation, to be a palindrome I was inside of, a purgatory of nausea. It was brutally cold outside, which at first was an improvement over the restaurant but quickly became its own misery. Then, miraculously, I'd reached Dr. Wycomb's building. The doorman nodded as I went in, and the elevator attendant also seemed to recognize me. "Happy New Year," he said, and I did not respond, again aware of the rudeness of my silence yet afraid to open my mouth.

The gold silk wallpaper then, the hallway, the door to Dr. Wycomb's apartment, my hands shaking as I turned the key she'd given me. There was music playing when I entered the apartment—it was jazz and it was loud—and this was why, in spite of my nausea, I did not immediately step from the foyer into the hall leading to the bedrooms. Having believed the apartment would be vacant on my return, I was surprised and curious (could Myra be playing this noisy music? But no, she'd gone home late that afternoon), so I stepped instead into the living room, and just before I crossed the threshold, I heard my grandmother's laughter, and just after I heard her laughter, I saw her sitting on Dr. Wycomb's lap, kissing Dr. Wycomb on the lips.

Dr. Wycomb was dressed in a burgundy silk bathrobe; my grandmother was wearing a beige bra and a beige half-slip trimmed with lace. She was facing Dr. Wycomb, and their mouths were open a little and their eyes were closed, and the kiss went on for several seconds and had not yet stopped when I backed out, so stunned that briefly, my shock outweighed my queasiness. I had to leave the apartment; there was no alternative. And so I did, handling the door as carefully and quietly as possible. In the hall, my nausea came roaring back, and by the time I knew what I was doing, I'd already done it. On either side of the elevator were large metallic vases, almost three feet high, with red bows tied around them and Christmas greens emerging artfully from their centers. Approaching the nearer vase, I pushed aside the greens and then I vomited—hideously, pungently, gloriously—into the vase's depths.

FOR A LONG time, I remained crumpled on the carpeted floor, spent. I knew I ought to move, to either go downstairs to the lobby or knock on the door and wait for my grandmother or Dr. Wycomb to let me back in the apartment, but neither of these options was appealing. Instead, curled up in my kilt and coat by the elevator, I began to doze. I think about an hour had passed, though it could have been much shorter or longer, by the time the elevator attendant found me. He was the one who knocked on the apartment door, and when Dr. Wycomb answered, I felt like a truant. "She got sick out here," the attendant said. "Now, I don't know who's cleaning it up, but I've got an elevator to run tonight."

Dr. Wycomb's gaze had jumped to my face.

"Maybe I ate something bad," I murmured.

"Thank you, Teddy," Dr. Wycomb said to the attendant. "I'll take care of the situation." She guided me inside, calling, "Emilie, Alice has come back early."

"Was he that objectionable?" My grandmother's voice grew louder as she approached us. "Alice, you really ought to give—" Then she saw me and said, "Good Lord, you look ghastly." She was fully dressed, I noted, wearing her brown suit.

"She's vomited, and I suspect she also has a fever and is dehydrated," Dr. Wycomb said. Together, they tucked me into bed and took my temperature—102, apparently—and Dr. Wycomb said, "It's important for you to have fluids. Emilie, get her some ginger ale from the pantry."

When my grandmother brought the glass to me, I took a few sips—it was sweet and fizzy—and promptly fell asleep, this time far more deeply than I had in the hallway. When I next awakened, it was close to four in the morning, according to the small round clock on the marble table, and my grandmother was sleeping in the other bed. The third time I awakened, it was light out, I was the only one in the room, and I could smell coffee. I rose to use the toilet, and when I returned from the bathroom, my grandmother was waiting for me, smoking a cigarette. "You certainly know how to bring in the new year in style," she said.

"I'm sorry if I made you miss going to that hotel last night."

"If Marvin's parents are anything like their offspring, you spared us. I must say that for a sick girl, you chose the best place to be in all of Chicago. You have the city's finest physician at your beck and call."

I climbed back into bed, and for the rest of the day, I emerged only when I needed to go to the bathroom; I didn't even bathe. Beneath the covers, I alternately shivered and sweated, my body aching, and they took my temperature at intervals. "This just needs to run its course," Dr. Wycomb said. "You'll feel like yourself in another day or two."

"Oh, I bet she'll be well by tomorrow," my grandmother said. "Don't you suppose, Alice?" We were scheduled to take the train back to Riley late the next morning.

"Let's not decide now," Dr. Wycomb said.

Around eight that night, when my grandmother brought me two aspirin and a fresh glass of water, she said, "I'm sure your parents would rather have you home slightly under the weather than late. If we stay another night here, there'll be calls back and forth. We'll have to change the tickets, and your father will get out of sorts."

More like there would be explanations required. There'd be shuttling between Dr. Wycomb's apartment and the Pelham, the pretense of extending a reservation for a room where we'd never slept. This chain of lies enabling my grandmother to press her lips against the lips of another woman, an old woman, a not even attractive woman—and then I couldn't stand to think about it anymore, the fragment of a moment, that weird disturbing glimpse.

I said nothing, and my grandmother said, "Get some rest. Our train isn't until eleven, so we'll have plenty of time to pack in the morning."

After I'd closed my eyes, I heard her stand, and I was not sure whether I was dreaming or actually speaking when I mumbled, "I don't even know why you brought me."

"Brought you where?" my grandmother said, and then I knew I'd spoken aloud. "To Chicago?"

I rolled over. "What?"

My grandmother's expression was shrewd and alert. She watched me for a few seconds. "You were talking in your sleep," she finally said.

MY TEMPERATURE RIGHT before we left for the train station was just over a hundred degrees, but the truth was that by the time we passed Dodsonville, which was the stop before Riley, I felt almost normal. My parents greeted us excitedly. "Did you go to the top of a skyscraper?" my mother asked. "Was it wonderful?"

In the car, my father said to my grandmother, "It was very good of you to take Alice," and this seemed a type of apology.

"The house was so quiet without you two," my mother said. "I even started to read one of Granny's magazines."

My grandmother smiled over at me, and I almost smiled back, but then I remembered and turned my face to look out the window.

DENA CALLED THE next day. "You need to come over," she said, and she sounded tearful. "It's an emergency."

"What happened?"

"Just come."

I was standing in the kitchen, and after I hung up the phone, I pulled on my coat and hurried outside. Across the street, I knocked on the Janaszewskis' front door—their doorbell had been broken since 1958—but I was too cold and concerned to wait, so I turned the knob and let myself in. "Hello?" I called.

In the living room, Dena's sisters, Marjorie and Peggy, were squabbling over whose turn it was to play a record. Peggy glanced at me, said, "Dena's upstairs," and returned to the disagreement.

On the second floor, the door to the room Dena and Marjorie shared was open, but the room appeared vacant. Tentatively, I said, "Dena?"

A hand emerged from beneath one of the twin beds and waved at me. I squatted, then leaned forward so I was on my knees, and lifted the dust ruffle. "What's wrong?" I said. "Should I come under there?"

"I've ruined my life." Dena's voice was loose and watery from crying.

I rolled over so I, too, was on my back, then I inched beneath the bed. Immediately, I could feel dust in my throat. There also were a few unidentifiable objects—shoes, maybe, and old toys—that I had to push out of the way before I was next to her. "What happened?" I asked.

She swallowed and then said mournfully, "I shaved my sideburns."

"But you don't have sideburns."

"Yeah, *now* I don't."

I grabbed a fistful of dust ruffle and held it up so daylight would show under the bed. "I can't see anything," I said. "You have to come out." I scooted away, and after a minute, she followed.

When she was sitting upright on the floor, her shoulders against the bed, her face was red and blotchy, her eyes were wet, and her hair, which was lighter brown than mine but styled the same way, was sticking up in the back like a little girl's. She reached for a mirror that was resting on the carpet shiny side down. I knew this mirror well, having spent a large portion of my life gazing into it, often at the same time as Dena. The reflective part was about the size of an actual face, with a dull pink plastic backing and handle. Holding the mirror up in front of her, Dena turned to the side, her eyes focused grimly on the spot around her ear.

"I still don't know what you're talking about," I said.

"Well, first I cut them, but they looked funny, so then I used a razor."

I came in closer and rubbed the tip of my index finger over the area in question. "You did a good job. It's completely smooth. Turn to the other side." When she did, I touched the skin there, too. "It's fine," I said.

"But think about when it grows back. I'll have stubble. Alice, I'll have a five o'clock shadow!"

"You can just shave again."

"Every day for the rest of my life?"

"Nobody will notice," I said. "I promise."

"Robert thinks hairy girls are like monkeys. You know how Mary Hafliger—"

"Dena, don't," I said. "She can't help it." Mary Hafliger, who I was in Spirit Club with, had dark, thick hair on her forearms, and I had heard it discussed among both our male and female classmates.

"She can too help it," Dena said. "At the least, she could bleach it."

"Mary's nice," I said. "Remember those pipe-cleaner Santa Clauses we were selling before Christmas? She glued all their beards on individually, and it took her about a week."

Dena grinned. "Yeah, I'll bet she glued on their beards." Dena had made good on her preadolescent plan of becoming a cheerleader, and Spirit Club members ranked well below cheerleaders in our school hierarchy. More than once, she had encouraged me to trade up—if I tried out for cheerleading, she would put in a good word for me—but I had no desire to yell and leap in front of other people.

Dena was still holding the mirror, looking at herself, and, idly, she pursed her lips. Her teariness seemed to have departed. Then she set the mirror back on the carpet and whispered, "I'm only half a virgin."

"What do you mean?"

"Close the door." She gestured toward it, and when I had, Dena said, "I let Robert put it in partway."

"You don't have to do what he says, Dena. He should respect you."

"Why do you think he doesn't?" She smirked.

On prior occasions, I knew Dena had let Robert place his hand inside her skirt or pants, though not inside her underwear, or at least this was what she'd claimed. These reports from the field had struck me as exciting but very dangerous. As our home ec teacher, Mrs. Anderson, had told us, some men, once aroused, could not control themselves. There was also one's reputation to consider, and most significantly, there was the risk of pregnancy. Certain girls at Benton County Central High were rumored to have had sex—what people said about Cindy Pawlak was not only that she'd done it but that she'd done it with multiple people, most scandalously with the junior high bus driver, a married man who lived in Houghton—and there were girls, usually country girls, who got pregnant and dropped out of school and then, if they were lucky, got married. Also, there was a girl in the class ahead of ours named Barbara Grob, a cheerleader with blond hair who'd supposedly decided the previous spring to go live with cousins in Eau Claire but everyone knew she was having a baby at a convent and giving it up for adoption; she'd returned to school looking drawn and heavy and had not attempted to rejoin the cheer squad. And yet, even if sex wasn't unheard of, I hadn't expected Dena to *really* do it; I'd expected her to teeter on the edge, bragging and teasing, without slipping over.

"Don't you want to save it for marriage?" I said. This was my plan, and it seemed perfectly reasonable given that we'd likely be married within a few years. In Riley, even girls who went to college often were brides before they graduated, and if you got to twenty-five without a wedding, you were staring down spinsterhood. Ruth Hofstetter, who worked at the fabric store where my mother and I bought material for our clothes, was twenty-eight and had no beau, and whenever we left the store, my mother and I would talk about how sad it was, especially because Ruth was kind and pretty.

"It's a little late for that," Dena said. "There's hardly a difference between partway and all the way."

"Do you think you'll marry Robert?"

"I might."

"Dena, if you marry someone else, he'll figure it out when you don't bleed on your wedding night."

She scoffed. "Not everyone bleeds." She picked up the mirror again and looked into it. "You don't know anything."

I HAD BEEN avoiding my grandmother, but one afternoon in early February, my mother was at the grocery store when I came home from school, and my grandmother was sitting in the living room, smoking and reading a novel by Wilkie Collins. I hung my book bag by the door and went into the kitchen to make a snack, and my grandmother followed me. As I pulled honey from the cupboard—I was planning to spread it on toast—she said, "You've been awfully moody since we returned from Chicago. Is there anything about the trip you'd like to discuss?"

"No," I said.

"No more questions about Dr. Wycomb?"

I shook my head.

The room was silent, and then my grandmother said, "I won't claim I've never in my life done anything I'm ashamed of, but I haven't done anything for a good while. If not everyone would agree with the decisions I've made, that's fine. What other people think has never made a situation right or wrong."

In this moment, I detested my grandmother. She was such a hypocrite, I thought—pretending to be bold and frank as she distorted the truth and implicated me in her distortions. Standing with my back to the stove, I glared at her.

"People are complicated," she continued, "and the ones who aren't are boring."

"Then maybe I'm boring."

We looked at each other, and in a genuinely sad voice, she said, "Maybe you are."

ROBERT BEIKE AND Dena had officially been boyfriend and girlfriend for several months by the time the junior-senior prom rolled around that May, and Dena had decided in March that Larry Nagel ought to ask me. A few weeks before prom, this had come to pass; when I emerged from the chemistry classroom late one morning, he was standing in the hallway, his arms folded. We made eye contact, and I was pretty sure I knew why he was there. I'd been walking beside my friend Betty Bridges, and I murmured to her, "Go ahead and I'll catch up."

When she was gone, Larry said in a not particularly warm tone, "Are you going to prom?"

"I think so," I said.

"Want to go together?"

"Sure."

"Okay," he said, and his tone remained flat. "See you around." He then headed up the hall, which happened to be the same direction I was going, but since it didn't seem to occur to him that we might travel together, or continue the conversation, I held back, letting him disappear. To be fair, I couldn't expect him to be shocked or thrilled that I'd accepted when the entire scenario had been choreographed by Dena. Had I been shocked or thrilled that he'd asked? But I hoped I'd see more flashes of the sweetly impulsive boy who'd kissed me on the stoop, and in a way, his usual coolness made his capacity for sweetness even sweeter. Surely at some point on the night of prom, there'd be further evidence of it.

My mother sewed my dress from a pattern I found in *Mademoiselle*—it was green, with a sweetheart neckline and tulle skirt—and I planned to wear it with white gloves that went above my elbows and made me feel, in both good and bad ways, like the queen of England. A few hours before prom, I discovered a paper bag on my bureau containing a green headband that was an almost identical shade to the dress. I bounded downstairs with the headband in my hand. In the kitchen, my mother was putting a casserole in the oven. "Thank you so much," I said. "It matches perfectly."

She smiled. "I hope you have a wonderful time." She closed the oven door, and impulsively, I hugged her—I felt closer to her now that I steered clear of my grandmother. Because of my position in Spirit Club, I'd been responsible for bringing two hundred cupcakes to school that morning, which would serve as prom refreshments. The night before, my mother had stayed up with me until midnight, applying yellow frosting.

A little later, as my parents and grandmother were finishing dinner, I came downstairs, still barefoot but with the gloves and headband on, to model the dress. When I entered the dining room, they applauded. "Curtsy," my grandmother commanded, and because it was more when we were alone together that things between us seemed strained—in the presence of my parents, their obliviousness negated the tension—I complied. Really, how could I not? It was a spring night; next door, Mr. Noffke was mowing his lawn, and the smell of cut grass wafted through our dining room windows.

Then, to my astonishment, my father stood, extended his hand, and said, "May I have this dance?"

"Oh, let me put on music!" My mother hurried into the living room to turn on the radio, and big-band music—it sounded like Glenn Miller—became audible.

My father raised our arms so they made an arch above my head, and he twirled me beneath it. Over the music, my mother said, "Alice, the dress really flatters your figure."

My father held me lightly, prompting me to turn and sway, and he said, "Stand up straight. Even short fellows prefer girls with good posture because it's a sign of confidence."

I set my shoulders back and lifted my chin.

"Dip her!" my grandmother called, and my mother immediately said, "Don't hurt your back, Phillip."

As the saxophones on the radio soared, I felt myself swooshing down, and I heard my mother and grandmother clapping again. It may just have been the blood that had rushed to my head when I was near the floor, or the emotion of the music, but in this moment I loved my family, including my grandmother, so greatly that I felt I might weep. They were so kindhearted and good to me, I was so lucky, and even then I sensed luck's fragility.

When I was upright again, my father said softly, so my grandmother and mother couldn't hear, "You're a very pretty girl. Don't let your date take advantage of you tonight."

ROBERT AND LARRY and Dena and I ate dinner at Tatty's. This was Riley tradition, to get all dressed up in your finery and then go have a greasy hamburger, and, remembering stories of girls who ended up in tears well before they got to prom, their silk dresses splattered with ketchup or relish, I took care to fold my white gloves into my purse and spread three separate napkins across my lap. Robert had driven us, and sitting in the backseat next to Larry, I'd first felt my optimism for the night dimming when Larry made one perfunctory attempt to affix my corsage to my dress and then held out the pale pink rose and said, "Can you just do this yourself?" From Tatty's, we drove to school, where the gym was hot and loud and crowded, which seemed to me exactly how it ought to be. The yellow and blue streamers crisscrossed above our heads, and the yellow-and-blue-frosted cupcakes were being consumed enthusiastically—I scanned to see how mine were faring, though with all of them lined up on tables against the wall, I couldn't tell my own apart from anyone else's—and a cover band from Madison called the Little Brothers, four men in tuxedos, were standing onstage playing "Who Put the Bomp."

"Hey, Alice," Robert said.

I looked at him.

He grinned lasciviously. "Larry's really excited to dance with you."

Both Dena and Larry laughed, and I felt a lurching panic that Dena had, via Robert, made some promise to Larry about my physical availability for the evening. Dena and Robert had by then had sex six times—once for each month of dating, as she explained, although half the times were retroactive. She told me she didn't want to do it too frequently because then it wouldn't be as special. Also, she said that his knowing he might or might not get it made Robert dote on her more; the week before, he'd bought her a stuffed white poodle that came with its own miniature fake-gold bone.

When Larry and I started dancing, he did not, to my relief, immediately try groping me. In fact, he was a good dancer, a better dancer than I was, and we stayed out there as one song ended and another began, and then another and another. The songs were all fast, and in the middle of "The Watusi," he shouted into my ear, "Robert has some—" He mimed drinking from a flask. "We're meeting in the parking lot."

"But there're teachers everywhere."

"No one will see us in Robert's car."

"I need to check on my cupcakes."

He shrugged. "Suit yourself."

As he walked away, I saw that Dena and Robert, who had been dancing close to us, were already near the doors of the gym. I headed to the refreshment table, where Betty Bridges was helping scoop punch, and I was still several feet away when I felt a hand on my forearm. I turned, and Andrew Imhof was standing beside me. "Would you like to dance?"

"Sure." Then I recognized the first notes of Ricky Nelson's "Lonesome Town" and I said, "Oh, but it's a slow song."

He smiled. "Does that matter?"

"No, I guess not," I said, but I wondered, was it bad manners to slow-dance with someone other than your date?

As we walked together back to the dance floor, I felt an immediate and unexpected awareness of how we appeared—a sense that if people looked at us, they might form an impression. What that impression would be was harder to say.

We found a space in the forest of couples and faced each other. After a second's hesitation, I set my left hand on his right shoulder, he set his right hand on my lower back, and we clasped our free hands together, held high. I was wearing my gloves.

"Who's your date?" I asked.

"Bess Coleman." He gestured with his chin, and I saw that Bess was dancing beneath a basketball hoop with Fred Zurbrugg, one of Andrew's close friends.

"Are you and Bess . . . ?" Later, I thought that if I'd consciously been interested in Andrew that night, I wouldn't have been so direct.

He shook his head. "You're here with Larry, huh?"

"Dena set us up, but I'm beginning to wonder about her skills as a matchmaker."

Andrew laughed. "Yeah, you're definitely way too good for Nagel."

We both were quiet, and then Andrew said, "Do you remember when your grandma thought I was a girl?"

"I had no idea you knew!"

"After she said to my mom, 'Your daughter sure is pretty,' it wasn't very hard to figure out."

"She never said that," I protested.

"Close."

"It was only because—"

"I know." He covered both of his eyes—both sets of eyelashes—with his right hand and shook his head. "I wouldn't wish them on my worst enemy. My brother says Max Factor should hire me to model mascara, and he doesn't mean that as a compliment."

"I'm sure he's just jealous," I said.

Onstage a member of the band was singing solo: " 'Goin' down to lonesome town / Where the broken hearts stay . . .' "

"What I said before, I didn't mean Larry's a bad guy." Andrew's tone had become more serious. "He's just not who I'd picture you with."

I could sense what Dena would say in this situation, what probably a lot of girls would say: Who *would* you picture me with? But it was so nice to rest in the moment without pushing it further, to feel its possibilities rather than its limitations. Later, I remembered thinking that I knew then Andrew would become my boyfriend, but that it wasn't as if I were realizing it for the first time. Hadn't I always known, for my whole life? And therefore, what was the hurry? Experiencing other people was almost a thing we *ought* to do before we were joined to each other.

"Have you eaten any of the cupcakes?" I asked.

"Yeah, they're pretty good. There's potato chips over there, too."

"I made some of the cupcakes," I said. "Not the blue ones, but the ones with yellow icing."

"I *thought* that tasted like it came from the kitchen of Alice Lindgren!" he said, and I lightly slapped his arm. "No, it was delicious," he said. "Really."

We both were smiling, and after a beat, he said, "If you want to, you can put your head on my shoulder."

I hesitated. "Am I tall enough?" Obviously, this was not my only hesitation.

"You don't have to," he said. "Just if you want to."

When I did, we were body to body in a way we hadn't been before. I could feel the heat of him, the solidity, and a calmness came over me; it made the conversation we'd been having seem like nothing, the words were nothing, they were raindrops or confetti, and holding on to each other was real.

When the song ended, we stepped apart, and then Bobby Sobczak approached Andrew, and I made my way to Betty Bridges at the refreshment table. Ten minutes had passed when Dena materialized, her cheeks flushed and liquor on her breath. "Were you dancing with Andrew?" she asked, and she sounded not quite accusatory but almost—she was forceful and intensely curious.

I was under the impression that she'd been outside all this time, which meant someone else must have already told her. "When you all left, I guess he saw me standing by myself," I said. "He probably felt sorry for me."

But I knew that wasn't true. At one point, near the end of the song, Andrew had inhaled deeply, and I'd been pretty sure he was smelling my hair.

THAT AUGUST, MY grandmother returned to Chicago to visit Gladys Wycomb, and my father, mother, and I packed our suitcases and ourselves into our sedan—it was a turquoise 1956 Chevy Bel Air, with a silver hood ornament shaped like a paper airplane—and we drove north through Wisconsin to Michigan's Upper Peninsula to visit the Mackinac Bridge, aka the Mighty Mac. As we approached the St. Ignace side, my father, who'd driven the entire way up to this point, pulled over and switched places with my mother so he'd be free to look around as we crossed the bridge. It went on and on, over rough blue water, and on the other side, my mother turned around and we drove back, heading north. It was a toll bridge costing fifty cents, which wasn't much, but still, it was an uncharacteristic indulgence on my father's part. We parked on the shores of St. Ignace, my mother and I wearing jackets even though it was summer, and my father shook his head happily. "Imagine all the concrete, steel, and cables running for five miles over water," he said. "That's a remarkable feat of engineering."

The sky beyond the bridge held curvy cirrus clouds, and in the air you could feel fall's approach. Back in Riley, it was still hot.

"Shall we stroll for a bit?" my father asked.

We walked along an esplanade. At intervals, coin-operated binoculars sat atop poles, and my father paused at several of them, though I couldn't really see how the view would change much from one to the next. "Before they built the bridge, it used to take people an hour to get across by ferry," he said. "But sometimes there was such backup you'd have to wait ten or twelve hours before there was room for your car."

I nodded, while inside I was thinking of the announcement I'd make. *Granny is having an affair with Dr. Wycomb,* I would say. Briefly, I had believed she wouldn't return to Chicago now that I knew her secret. Or maybe she didn't realize I knew. But she had to, otherwise she'd have demanded more explanation for my sullenness.

"Can you imagine having the patience to wait twelve hours?" my mother was saying.

Should I have guessed about my grandmother? I had read *The Well of Loneliness* at the age of fourteen, pulling it down from her shelf and returning it with slight confusion at the idea of two women falling in love, but not enough to ask her about it. Anyhow, that book had been set decades ago, and in England. For my own grandmother, the grandmother living in my house, who used the same bar of soap in the bathroom that I did, whose jewelry and high heels I'd dressed up in as a little girl—for her to be in a homosexual relationship didn't make sense. She'd been married, she'd had a child! And even if it was true, why hadn't she been more careful to prevent me from becoming party to her secret? She was making me choose between her and my parents, and what sort of choice was that? In a way, I had always loved her more deeply, I had loved her most, but I had thought she and I were conspiring to conceal this hurtful fact.

We were passing another set of binoculars, and my father stooped and peered into them. When he rejoined us, he took my mother's hand, and I could sense the buoyancy of his enthusiasm.

For the next three nights, we stayed in a motel in St. Ignace, all of us in one room. The motel was called Three Breezes and had a pool in which my father swam laps, though my mother and I found it too cold. On the day we hiked the sand dunes of Lake Michigan, I thought, *I will tell them in fifteen minutes. In another fifteen minutes. When we're back in the car.* The day after that, we took the ferry to Mackinac Island, where we rode in a horse-drawn carriage, ate fudge, and had lunch at a restaurant in the Grand Hotel. "Maybe you'll come back someday for your honeymoon," my mother said, and she squeezed my knee beneath the table. *They are having an affair,* I thought, *and Dr. Wycomb is giving her lavish presents, and maybe she's even giving her money.*

During our last dinner in St. Ignace, my parents drank two bottles of wine between them, and later, my father convinced my mother to swim with him in the motel pool, the sky dark but the pool lit up. From the room, I could hear them giggling. I went to sleep, and the next morning, I opened my eyes and thought, *They already know.* I listened to them sleeping in the bed across from mine, my mother's deep breathing and my father's quiet snores, as if even when asleep, he was trying to be polite. *They already know,* I thought, *and if they don't, it's because they've chosen not to.* Surely that accounted for my father's initial resistance to my accompanying my grandmother to Chicago the previous winter. I would say nothing, I realized, because it wasn't necessary, it wasn't my place. I was glad then that I had not previously been able to express the words.

And really, what has stayed with me from that vacation as much as my own suspicious, petty agonizing is my father on the esplanade just after our arrival. The wind blew his hair, and he was fidgety with delight, straining to explain to my mother and me exactly why the Mighty Mac was so impressive. I wondered at the time—I wonder still—if that was the happiest my father had ever been.

IT TOOK LONGER, but we drove home via the southern route: once more across the Mighty Mac (this time I was allowed to take the wheel), then down through the lower part of Michigan, curving southwest through the edge of Indiana and northwest into Illinois, where, at a train station in Bolingbrook, thirty miles outside Chicago, we picked up my grandmother. She and I sat together in the backseat, but she seemed to have given up on me months before and was reading *Anna Karenina.* "That's the second time, isn't it?" my mother asked, and my grandmother said a little tartly, "It's the fourth."

Then we were back in Wisconsin, a place that in late summer is thrillingly beautiful. When I was young, this was knowledge shared by everyone around me; as an adult, I've never stopped being surprised by how few of the people with whom I interact have any true sense of the states between Pennsylvania and Colorado. Some of these people have even spent weeks or months working in such states, but unless they're midwesterners, too, to them the region is nothing but polling numbers and caucuses, towns or cities where they stay in hotels whose bedspreads are glossy maroon and brown on the outside and pilly on the inside, whose continental breakfasts are packaged doughnuts and cereal from a dispenser, whose fitness centers are a single stationary bike and a broken treadmill. These people eat dinner at Perkins, and then they complain about the quality of the restaurants.

Admittedly, the area possesses a dowdiness I personally have always found comforting, but to think of Wisconsin specifically or the Midwest as a whole as anything other than beautiful is to ignore the extraordinary power of the land. The lushness of the grass and trees in August, the roll of the hills (far less of the Midwest is flat than outsiders seem to imagine), that rich smell of soil, the evening sunlight over a field of wheat, or the crickets chirping at dusk on a residential street: All of it, it has always made me feel at peace. There is room to breathe, there is a realness of place. The seasons are extreme, but they pass and return, pass and return, and the world seems far steadier than it does from the vantage point of a coastal city.

Certainly picturesque towns can be found in New England or California or the Pacific Northwest, but I can't shake the sense that they're *too* picturesque. On the East Coast, especially, these places—Princeton, New Jersey, say, or Farmington, Connecticut—seem to me aggressively quaint, unbecomingly smug, and even xenophobic, downright paranoid in their wariness of those who might somehow infringe upon the local charm. I suspect this wariness is tied to the high cost of real estate, the fear that there might not be enough space or money and what there is of both must be clung to and defended. The West Coast, I think, has a similar self-regard—all that talk of proximity to the ocean *and* the mountains—and a beauty that I can't help seeing as show-offy. But the Midwest: It is quietly lovely, not preening with the need to have its attributes remarked on. It is the place I am calmest and most myself.

THE WEEKEND BEFORE my senior year of high school, I emerged from Jurec Brothers' butcher shop late in the afternoon on Saturday, carrying a pound of ground beef my mother had asked me to pick up, when I heard the salutatory honk of a nearby car horn. I turned my head to see a mint-green Ford Thunderbird with a white roof; leaning out the passenger window, tanned and smiling, was Andrew Imhof. I waved as I stepped off the curb, moving between two parked cars. When I was closer, I could see that beyond Andrew, driving, was his brother, Pete; the car was a two-seater.

"Welcome back," Andrew said.

"How'd you know I was gone?"

"After you weren't at Pine Lake the other night, I thought you might be sick, but Dena said—not that Dena and I are—I just ran into her there—"

"Not that he's feeding at her trough again," Pete said. "He wants to make that perfectly clear." Pete leaned over the steering wheel and grinned sarcastically. He was four years older; after high school, he'd gone on to the University of Wisconsin at Madison, and presumably, he'd graduated the previous June. He and Andrew didn't look much alike: They had the same hazel eyes, but Pete didn't have Andrew's impossible eyelashes, and where Andrew was lean and fair, Pete was meaty and had darker hair. He looked like an adult man, and not a terribly appealing one.

Andrew rolled his eyes good-naturedly in the direction of his brother and said to me, "Ignore him. You were in Michigan, huh?"

"My dad wanted to see the Mackinac Bridge, and then we went to Mackinac Island. They don't have any cars there, only carriages."

"Where goeth the horses, so goeth the shit," Pete said. "Am I right?"

"Pretend he's not there," Andrew said.

"It sounds like a lot of people were at Pine Lake," I said. "Dena told me it was the most fun she'd had all summer."

"Really?" Andrew looked amused. "It was mostly just Bobby challenging anyone who'd listen to a chicken fight. The real party will be next weekend at Fred's, have you heard about that? If it gets below seventy-five degrees, we're making a bonfire."

Pete leaned forward again. "And Andrew promises he'll roast you a nice big wiener. This has been a fascinating conversation, but I've got places to go, little brother. You and Alice want to wrap things up?"

Andrew shook his head again, and Pete revved the engine. "Sorry,"

Andrew said to me. "See you on Tuesday at school. Hey, pretty cool we'll finally be seniors, huh?"

I smiled. "The great class of '64."

The mint-green Thunderbird pulled away, and as I walked home carrying the ground beef for my mother, an unexpected energy seized me, spurred by a jumble of fresh thoughts: how good Andrew looked, tanned from the summer sun; how weird it was that Pete Imhof knew my name; how excited I felt for the start of school, for new classes and the perks of being the oldest students; and how much I hoped it fell below seventy-five degrees on Saturday so they'd build the bonfire at Fred's party and I could stand next to it, braced by that wall of heat against my body, watching the leap of the flames, being reminded, as I always was by fires, that they were alive and so was I.

WHEN I SAW Andrew over the next few days, sitting a couple rows ahead of me in the bleachers at the assembly that first morning back, or pulling books out of his locker in a crowded hall between classes, there was little chance of us talking, or even making eye contact, and I didn't try. I was always with Dena or another friend, or he was with guys from football, and I felt like what I had to say to him, I could say only when we were alone. It wasn't even that I *knew* what I wanted to say, but surely, if we found ourselves with no one else around, I'd be able to come up with something.

All that week, I had the sense that we were making our way toward each other—even when we passed outside the science classrooms, headed in opposite directions, I had this sense—and I was not surprised on Thursday afternoon when, half an hour after the final bell of the day had rung, I walked out of the library and saw him coming from the gym, dressed for football practice in a jersey and those shortened pants, holding his helmet in his right hand. Looking back, I find it hard to trust my memory of this episode, hard to believe I'm not infusing it with meaning it didn't contain at the time. It was a sunny afternoon (as it turned out, the temperature would not fall below seventy-five degrees that Saturday, or for another few weeks), and the cicadas were buzzing and the trees and grass were green, and we were walking toward each other, he was squinting against the sun, we both were smiling, and I loved him, I loved him completely, and I knew that he loved me back. I could feel it. That moment—inside it, I could anticipate the thing I most wanted and I could be beyond it, it had happened already, and I was ensconced in the rich reassurance of knowing it was certain and definite.

Or maybe this is only what I think now. But it was all we ever had! Approaching each other, him from the gym, me from the library—this was when I walked down the aisle and he was waiting, this was when we made love, it was every anniversary, every reunion in an airport or train station, every reconciliation after a quarrel. This was the whole of our lives together.

It seemed like the natural thing to do when we were in front of each other would have been to embrace, but we didn't. It is a great regret, though not, certainly, my greatest. We stood there with the roiling energy of not hugging between us, and he said, "Sorry about my brother the other day," gesturing over his shoulder as if perhaps Pete were nearby. "I hope he didn't offend you."

"No, he's funny, but you two seem very different."

"Wait, I'm *not* funny?"

"No, you're funny, too," I said. "You're both funny."

"That's very diplomatic—I appreciate it. You coming to the game tomorrow?"

"I'll be selling popcorn." Working at the refreshment stand was one of my Spirit Club duties. "I heard you're starting this year," I said.

"Well, I waited long enough." He laughed a little in a self-effacing rather than bitter way. "No one would mistake me for Pete, that's for sure."

This was true—before we'd gotten to high school, Andrew's brother had been a star running back for the Knights—but I said, "No, you look very tough in your football gear." Immediately, hearing myself, I began to blush.

"Yeah?" Andrew was watching me. "Do I look like I could protect you?"

We both were smiling; every reference one of us made the other would get, every remark was a joke or a compliment, and I suddenly thought, *Flirting.*

Then—I couldn't help it—I said, "Why did you go steady with Dena?"

"Because I was eleven years old." He still was smiling. "I didn't know better."

"But you *kept* going steady with her. For four years!"

"Were you jealous?"

"I thought it was"—I paused—"odd."

"When Dena was my girlfriend," he said, "it meant I got to spend time around you."

Was he teasing? "If that's true, it's not very nice to Dena," I said.

"Alice!" He seemed both amused and genuinely concerned that he'd displeased me.

I looked at the ground. What was I trying to express, anyway? The important thing I'd been planning all week to say when Andrew and I were alone—it was eluding me.

"What about this?" he said. "What if I try to be nicer from now on?"

Looking up, I said, "I'll try to be nicer, too."

He laughed. "You've always been nice." There was a pause, and then he asked, "Is that a heart?" He reached forward and lifted the silver pendant on my necklace, holding it lightly, the tips of his fingers grazing the hollow of my clavicle.

"My grandmother gave it to me for my sixteenth birthday," I said.

"It's pretty." He set the pendant back against my neck. "I should probably go to practice so I don't get yelled at. If I don't see you tomorrow after the game, you'll be at Fred's on Saturday, right?"

I nodded. "Will it be more a party where people come on time or later?"

"I'll leave my house about seven-thirty. You should come then, too." Andrew was unusually direct, especially for a boy in high school; I think it came from an understated confidence. When I got to college, the guys and girls seemed to play such games, the girl waiting a certain number of days to return a phone call, or the guy calling only after the girl didn't talk to him at a party or he saw her out with someone else. But maybe, unlike those boys and girls in college, Andrew genuinely liked me. Then I think no, maybe he didn't. Maybe, because of what occurred later, I invented for us a great love; I have been granted the terrible privilege of deciding what would have happened with no one left to contradict me. And maybe I am absolutely wrong.

After we said goodbye, I turned around, watching for a second as he walked toward the bleachers beyond which were the track and the football field: his light brown hair, his moderately broad shoulders further broadened by shoulder pads, his tan golden-haired calves emerging from those pants that stopped well before his ankles. When you are a high school girl, there is nothing more miraculous than a high school boy.

And despite my concerns that I am manipulating the past, whenever I doubt that Andrew had feelings for me and that those feelings would have grown over time, that we had finally reached an age when something real could unfold between us, I think back to him examining my necklace, holding the pendant and asking what it was. That was obviously just an excuse to touch me. After all, everyone knows what a heart is.

THAT EVENING, I was washing dishes with my mother after dinner when there was a knock on the front door. My father and grandmother were playing Scrabble in the living room, and I heard my father answer the door and then say, "Hello there, Dena."

"Offer her some peach cobbler," my mother said, and Dena, entering the kitchen, said, "No thank you, Mrs. Lindgren. We just ate, too." To me, Dena mouthed, *I need to talk to you.*

"Mom, may I be excused?" I said.

As soon as we were upstairs in my bedroom, Dena folded her arms and said, "If you try to get Andrew to be your boyfriend, I'll never forgive you."

I closed the door and sat in the rocking chair in the corner. Sitting there made me feel like a visitor in my own room; my parents had given me the chair when I entered high school, thinking I'd use it to read in, but when I read, I always laid in bed. Dena was leaning against the bureau.

"Andrew's not my boyfriend," I said.

"But you want him to be. Nancy saw you flirting with him in front of the library after school."

How could I deny it? Even in the moment, I'd realized that was exactly what I was doing.

"And I already know you two danced at prom."

"I didn't think you still liked him," I said.

"It doesn't matter. If you're my friend, you won't steal a guy who belonged to me."

"Dena, Andrew's not a pair of shoes."

"So it's true you're going after him?"

I looked away.

"I could get him back if I wanted," she said. "He still carries a torch for me."

Given my conversation with Andrew earlier in the day, this seemed unlikely, but I didn't underestimate Dena—she'd once before surprised me with her ability to turn Andrew's head.

Carefully, I said, "You haven't dated him for two years, and now you have Robert. You don't even mention Andrew anymore."

"You mean every day I'm supposed to say, 'I sure wonder what he's up to! Hmm, I hope Andrew's happy right now!'—that's what I should tell you?" Color had risen in her cheeks, an outraged pink, and it was her very sincerity, her righteousness, that got to me.

"Dena, *you* took him from me! And you know it. In sixth grade, you wrote that stupid letter, and even though he said he liked me, you bullied him into being your boyfriend. How do you think I felt all that time? But I kept being your friend, and now it's my turn."

Dena glared at me. "You shall not covet your neighbor's house," she said angrily. "You shall not covet your neighbor's wife, or male or female slave, or ox, or donkey, or anything that belongs to your neighbor."

I never entirely trusted Dena's religiosity—the Janaszewskis were Catholic, but I knew their attendance at church was spotty. I said, "I'm no guiltier of coveting than you."

Dena took a step toward the door, but before she left, she gave me one last dirty look. "You and Andrew are alike," she said. "You're both quiet but selfish."

DE SOTO WAY heads north from Riley and intersects with Farm Road 177 about five miles outside of town. Saturday, September 7, 1963, was a clear night. I wore a pale blue felt skirt and a white blouse with a Peter Pan collar, and I carried with me a light pink cardigan mohair sweater. I also wore light pink lipstick, lily-of-the-valley perfume (I had bought it at Marshall Field's when my grandmother bought her sable stole, my main souvenir from the trip to Chicago), and my heart pendant necklace. Under normal circumstances, I'd have driven out to Fred Zurbrugg's house with Dena and Nancy Jenzer—Nancy was the only one of the three of us who had her own car, a white Studebaker Lark—but in light of recent developments, I was borrowing my parents' sedan.

I was pretty sure I looked the best I ever had. I was wearing the unprecedented combination of my favorite skirt, my favorite top, and my favorite piece of jewelry. After dinner with my parents and grandmother, I had tweezed my eyebrows, shaved my legs, and painted my nails. Getting dressed, I had listened to a Shirelles record—sometimes I would almost physically crave the song "Soldier Boy"—and I'd felt when I stood in front of the mirror over my bureau as if the music were building inside me; I was storing it up, and later in the night, I'd use it. In a strange way, my fight with Dena added to rather than detracted from the energy of the evening, amplifying the anticipatory hum in the air.

When I appeared in the living room, my mother said, "Don't you look nice," and they all turned toward me. My mother, father, and grandmother were playing bridge with our neighbor, Mrs. Falke, who was a widow, like my grandmother, but a few years younger.

"Who's the fellow?" my grandmother asked.

"It's just a regular back-to-school party," I said. "There'll be a bonfire."

"I see." I could tell my grandmother didn't believe me, but where the understanding that passed between us in this moment once would have been sympathetic, it now contained a note of antagonism. Nevertheless, I kissed them all on the cheek one by one, even Mrs. Falke, because by the time I'd done everybody else, it felt rude to bypass her.

"You know your curfew," my father said, and I replied, "Eleven o'clock."

"Have fun," my mother called as I stepped out the front door.

In the car, I changed the radio from my father's preferred station, which featured big-band music, to mine, on which Roy Orbison's "Dream Baby" was playing. I backed out of the driveway, first setting my arm around the passenger-side seat, as my father had taught me, which always gave me the sense that I was trying to embrace a phantom. It was getting dark, but full darkness hadn't yet set in.

I wondered if Andrew and I would kiss that night, if we'd slip away from the other people, perhaps go for a walk in the apple orchard near Fred's family's farmhouse. I suspected there would be alcohol at the party, but if it were offered to me, I wouldn't accept—I didn't want Andrew to think I was trashy. At the same time, I was glad I'd kissed those other boys, Bobby and Rudy in ninth grade, Larry the previous winter and then again when he'd walked me to the door after prom, both of us seeming to recognize that we would never speak again but kissing anyway, maybe for that very reason. Now, when a kiss mattered, I wouldn't be wholly unprepared.

I couldn't imagine Andrew trying to take advantage of me, or talking afterward with other boys; I trusted him. And would *he* be the person I eventually gave my virginity to, not anytime soon but if we got married, or possibly even if we were engaged, because wasn't that almost the same? This line of thought made my mind jump to Dena and how I'd greet or not greet her at the party. I would be polite, I decided. I would try to catch her eye, and if she seemed receptive, I'd say hello. But if she looked away sulkily, I would say nothing and let time pass before calling her the following week. I didn't want to have any sort of public conflict—no doubt if we did, it would be terrifically entertaining to our classmates and probably serve as the defining event of the evening, but how mortifying.

And this was what I was pondering, this was the subject my skittering, fickle mind had landed upon, when I breezed through the intersection of De Soto Way and Farm Road 177 and collided loudly with a blur of pale metal. Very quickly, it had already happened. I was lying on my back on the gravel road; my door had flown open, I'd been thrown about eight feet from the car, and shards of glass were sprinkled around me. It was dark by then, the sun had set perhaps half an hour earlier, and I lay there, first confused and then so startled and upset that I had difficulty catching my breath. The collision (how had it occurred, where had the other car come from?) had been a squealing boom accompanied by the shatter of windshields, and now my car and the other one were making creaking, whirring noises of adjustment. Oddly, my radio was still playing—the song was "Venus in Blue Jeans." The other car must have been making a right turn from Farm Road 177 onto De Soto Way, I thought, because when I lifted my head, I saw that the hood of my parents' Bel Air was smashed up against the driver's door. I was in the middle of the road, I realized; I needed to move. I tried to prop myself up on my elbows, and a searing pain shot through my left arm. I leaned my weight on my right arm and dragged myself around the back of the sedan, trying to avoid the glass; the road had no shoulder, and a shallow ditch ran along it, so there wasn't really anywhere to go. Something was dripping from my left temple, and when I wiped at it, blood coated my fingers.

It was not until I saw the farmer and his wife approaching that I sat up, though I felt too weak to call to them. The farmer was a stout white-haired man in overalls, not running but lumbering along in a quick way, and his wife was a few yards behind him in a housedress. They had heard the collision and had called for an ambulance, the farmer said. When he asked what had happened, we all turned to look at the cars, the mess of metal and broken glass, and this was when I realized two things: that the other car was a mint-green Ford Thunderbird and that there was a slumped, unmoving figure in the driver's seat.

I could hear the rise of my own hysteria, a panicked kind of panting—was it him or was it not him?—and the farmer spoke to his wife, and then his wife was crouching, her arms were around me, and she was saying, "Honey, when the ambulance comes, they'll take care of that fellow." I believe they thought I was babbling nonsensically, but the wife understood first. Raising her head, she said softly to her husband, "She thinks she might know him. She says they're classmates."

There were two ambulances that came, ambulances in those days being just police-cruiser station wagons fitted in the back to hold stretchers, a single flashing red light on the top. As I was raised on the stretcher, I saw, shockingly and unmistakably: It *was* him. His head hung at a strange angle, but it was him. Inside the ambulance, while I cried uncontrollably, one nurse took my pulse and examined me as another nurse and two police officers attended to the Thunderbird. The farmer's wife appeared at the rear of my ambulance and said she'd call my parents if I told her their name and number. Then she sighed and said, "Honey, they put that stop sign where it's so hard to see that it was only a matter of time." The ambulances were parked south of the accident, and I raised myself, peering out the window and noticing for the first time the sign she was referring to. It was in a field to the right of the road—it had been my stop sign.

My ambulance left before the other one, and though I did not yet understand everything, I knew that it was very bad, that it was far worse than I'd realized even in the seconds following the collision: The other driver was Andrew, and the accident was my fault. I sensed, though no one would tell me until we'd reached the hospital and my parents had met us, that he was dead. I turned out to be correct. The cause of death was a broken neck.

I THINK OF this time as an oyster in a shell. Not pried open and nakedly displayed—that hideous pale flesh lined in black around the edges and hued purple, stretched over the oyster's insides, the mucus and feces and colorless blood—but not tightly closed, either. It is open a few centimeters. You can look if you choose; it would not be difficult to open further. But the oyster is rancid, there's no need. Everyone knows what's in there.

For any question, the answer is of course. How would *you* feel if you killed another person? And if, further, you were a seventeen-year-old girl and the person you killed was the boy you thought you were in love with? Of course I wished it had been me instead. Of course I thought of taking my own life. Of course I thought I would never know peace or happiness again, I would never be forgiven, I *should* never be forgiven. Of course.

To open the oyster shell—it is an agonizing pain. I am haunted by what I did, and yet I can hardly stand to think about the specifics. There were so many terrible moments, a lifetime of terrible moments, really, which is not the same as a terrible lifetime. But surely, surely, the moments right after it happened were the worst.

If I said now that not a day passes when I don't think of the accident, of Andrew, it would be both true and not true. Occasionally, days go by when his name is nowhere on my tongue or in my mind, when I do not recall him walking away from me toward football practice in his jersey, his helmet at his side. Yet all the time, the accident is with me. It flows in my veins, it beats along with my heart, it is my skin and hair, my lungs and liver. Andrew died, I caused his death, and then, like a lover, I took him inside me.

MY PARENTS DIDN'T understand that night at the hospital, at first, that it was my fault; they thought the blame was shared. They arrived as the doctor was wrapping my left wrist in a putty-colored bandage that seemed embarrassing in its inconsequentiality, less a true injury than a plea for leniency from others. I also received twenty-five milligrams of Librium and a bandage on my left temple, and a nurse dabbed translucent yellow ointment on the cuts on my arms and legs.

I was the one who told my parents there had been a stop sign, that Andrew had had the right of way. My mother and father were wearing what they'd been wearing when I'd left the house under an hour before, my father in a twill shirt tucked into trousers, my mother in a belted shirtwaist dress, and I thought of having made them jump up from their card game, of how I'd been in their presence so very recently. The shift in events seemed bizarre and bewildering; it all had happened far too fast.

In the empty waiting room, when a police officer confirmed to us that Andrew had died, my mother gasped, my father took her hand, and none of us said a word. The officer asked me a few questions about the accident, including how fast I'd been driving (I had not been speeding), and then he spoke alone to my father. They were still speaking when Mr. and Mrs. Imhof arrived and were escorted away; his mother's wails were audible all the way down the hall. My father concluded his conversation with the police officer and said, "Dorothy, we're taking her home."

"Should she talk to his parents?" my mother asked.

"For now, leave them be," my father said.

In the parking lot, I saw that my parents had borrowed the Janaszewskis' station wagon. We rode home in silence (what must they have been thinking during this drive?), and on Amity Lane, my father dropped my mother and me off in front of our house and drove across the street to return the keys. My grandmother had already come out to the front stoop—this was unusual, she rarely even stood when you came home and found her reading on the living room couch—and she said, "Thank goodness you're all right."

My mother, in a curter tone than I'd ever heard, said, "Emilie, we need to get inside."

My grandmother followed us back in. "I take it the car was wrecked?" In my peripheral vision, I saw my mother shake her head: *Do not ask.* Then I saw that Mrs. Falke was still there, sitting at the card table smoking, and she said, "Alice, you've had us on pins and needles. Now, what have you done to your arm?" and my mother said, "Go upstairs, Alice."

I didn't look at my grandmother or Mrs. Falke as I left the room. I'd stopped crying after the nurse had given me the Librium, but my throat was still raw, and my eyes felt scrubbed out, my cheeks puffy. Decades later, I had a friend named Jessica who was much younger than I, and I once told her about the night I hit Andrew Imhof's car. I almost never discussed it with anyone, but Jessica and I were very close, and it was around the anniversary of the accident, always a difficult time. Jessica couldn't believe that I had come home from the hospital and gone up to my bedroom, that my parents and grandmother had left me alone. It was such a different time, though, there was so much less talk of feelings, and of course we were so unprepared; it was not the type of tragedy for which there was a script.

I entered my room without turning on the lights, removed my shoes, and climbed under the covers with my skirt and blouse still on (the cardigan sweater I never saw again—I must have left it in the car). It was impossible: I had caused another person's death? And the person whose death I'd caused was Andrew, Andrew Imhof was dead because of me? There were things I worried about, tests, and the tension with my grandmother, and sometimes, when it occurred to me, Khrushchev bombing the United States. But this? It was, in all ways, impossible.

And I thought, *Andrew*. His smile and eyelashes, his hazel eyes, his tanned calves, my head against his chest at last spring's prom. He had always liked me, he had never hidden it—the Dena years, I thought, didn't really count, and why had I pretended they had?—and I had felt his recognition of me. People recognized you or they didn't, and it was unrelated to knowing you. Knowing you could just be your name or the street you lived on, your father's job. Recognizing you was understanding you had thoughts in your head, finding the same things funny or excruciating, remembering what you'd said months or even years after you'd said it. Andrew had always been kind to me, he had always noticed me. Who else in my life was that true of beyond my immediate family?

So why, when Andrew had offered his attention and affection since childhood, since well before Dena had staked her claim to him, why had I waited, holding him off? And I *had* held him off, I knew it now, and I'd known it when I was doing it. I'd been passive and ambivalent, I'd imagined that we had plenty of time. Then I thought that if he'd become my boyfriend earlier, we'd have gone to the party together; I would not have been driving alone.

The confusing part, the sickening part, was the double calamity. If Andrew had been killed in a car accident in which I was not involved, it still would have felt to me like a devastating loss. Or if I had hit the car of a person I didn't know and the person had died, that, too, would have been a devastation. But both—both at once were unbearable. He was gone from me *and* I had caused it. In my life now, every year or so in a newspaper or magazine, I come across reports of similarly coincidental misfortunes: two brothers die on the same road on the same evening in separate motorcycle accidents, or a husband and wife, each in their own car, have a head-on collision. "How bizarre" is the tone of such articles, how interesting and unlikely. What are the odds! To me, these stories don't seem interesting, and they don't seem unlikely.

I DID NOT attend his funeral, nor did my parents. I didn't return to school for a week, and then I did return, and very few people said anything to me that was either kind or unkind. An article about Andrew's death had run on the front page of *The Riley Citizen,* but I didn't know this at the time—my parents hid it from me, and many years passed before I was prompted by outside forces to read it. At school, there was no public acknowledgment, even in my absence, though after I graduated the following spring I learned the yearbook had been dedicated to Andrew. But even this was restrained, just a page that said IN MEMORIAM with a photo, his name, and the dates of his life: ANDREW CHRISTOPHER IMHOF, 1946–1963. Mrs. Schaub, my tenth-grade English teacher, slipped me a card and a copy of a Shakespeare sonnet, the one that starts "That time of year thou mayest in me behold / When yellow leaves, or none, or few, do hang," and I was not exactly sure what I was supposed to take from it. I could manage only to skim her note, and I saw the phrase "very difficult time for you" in Mrs. Schaub's loopy blue cursive, the same handwriting in which she'd praised my papers on *Beowulf* and *Canterbury Tales.* That was what I still wanted, to be treated as a regular student, to *be* regular—not this fraught goodwill, or the surreptitiously curious glances of my classmates, or the outright animosity, though that was rare. On my second day back at school, I passed Karl Ciesla, a former football teammate of Andrew's, in the hall, and he murmured, "There's a reason girls shouldn't be allowed to get a license."

But generally, there was an aura around me, and I knew it: a stunned, ashamed haze that made me both piteous and unapproachable. I think this was why almost no one besides Karl expressed their anger, though surely some people were angry with me. Also, I had years of being a good girl to trade on, a credit history of pleasantness. Once during the week I'd stayed home, I'd been at the kitchen table, trying to eat a tuna sandwich my mother had fixed for lunch, and I had stiffened in my seat, panicked by a horrifying thought: What if people suspected I'd done it on purpose? That I had wanted, in some crazy fashion, to keep him for myself, or that he'd spurned me and I was seeking revenge? But no one seemed to think this, or at least no one accused me—there had been, after all, no obvious link between Andrew and me other than that we were classmates.

Really, almost no one said anything, no one suggested I see a counselor, not even my grandmother, who was a reader of Freud and Jung. The Sunday morning after the accident, my mother had knocked on my door and said, "Daddy thinks it's all right for you to miss church, but we'll pray for Andrew, just you and me." I let her lead the prayer (the scab on my left elbow hurt when I bent my arms), but the lack of comfort I drew from it was my first indication that I'd begun to lose my faith. The next evening, Monday, my father came into my room and said, "I went to see Mr. Imhof, and there aren't going to be any charges pressed, not by them or the county. Mr. Imhof is an honorable man, and we're very lucky." I was sitting at my desk, and soberly, he patted my shoulder. But I was less grateful for this news than startled to learn charges against me had been a possibility; so dumbfounded was I by everything else that I hadn't considered it.

This was just about all either of my parents ever said on the topic of the accident. A consensus seemed to have been reached among everyone in Riley, including my own family members, that the best thing was simply not to mention it at all.

ONE PERSON WAS direct with me. At the end of that first day back at school, when I went to drop off books in my locker before going home, Dena was waiting. Unsure what I was in store for, I stopped a few feet short of her.

"I'm so sorry I made you drive to the party alone," she said, and she burst into tears.

"Dena—" We stepped into each other's arms, we clung to each other, and her tears fell on my neck and shirt.

"I know he liked you better," she blubbered, "he always liked you better, and if you'd ridden with Nancy and me, it never would have happened."

I took a step back so I could see her; her face was red and smeary. "It wasn't your fault," I said. Already, in the privacy of my mind, I had considered her culpability and ruled against it. No matter what events had led up to that moment in the car, I was the one who'd run the stop sign.

"I just can't picture him, you know"—she paused then whispered —"*dead.*"

Instantly, an image came to me of that strange angle of his head, his face obscured. Why hadn't I gone to him, why hadn't I climbed through the passenger window and across the seat and wrapped my arms around him when he'd been so alone there, amid the broken glass and ruined metal? There are many ways I tortured myself in the subsequent months and years, and one of them was wondering if he'd still been alive then, and if he had, whether human touch, my touch, could have saved him. But I do not think this way any longer. If I'd climbed in the car and he'd still died, I'd have been convinced that that, too, had been a mistake.

To Dena, I said, "Are people mad at me?"

"Robert thinks your family should move away, but he's an idiot. I told him he should move away."

Robert thought my family should move away? He had graduated the previous spring and was working at White River Dairy.

"What else have people said?" I asked.

Dena sniffled. "You don't have a tissue, do you?"

I did; I pulled it from my bag and passed it to her.

After she'd blown her nose, she said, "When I found out, I thought the police were going to arrest me. I was so scared, I made Marjorie sleep in my bed."

"I never even told anyone about our fight," I said. "Dena, really, that isn't why it happened."

She bit her lip, clearly trying to suppress more tears. "I just shouldn't have gotten in the way of him being your boyfriend," she said. "But I didn't think I *could* stop it, and that's the only reason I tried."

I NO LONGER attended church with my parents and grandmother. I had stayed in bed that Sunday following the accident, and then the next Sunday as well, and after that, it seemed they never expected me to return at all. In fact, and it was a painful notion to consider, my absence might have made churchgoing easier for them; the other parishioners wouldn't stare, or if they did, they'd do so less intently. On the last Sunday in September, I waited until my parents and grandmother had left, then pulled the envelope I'd already sealed from my desk drawer and walked out the front door. I had not driven since the accident, and I had never driven this car—it was a newer model and a different color of the Chevy Bel Air. The day my father had brought it home, which had been the week after the accident, I'd heard my mother say, her voice anxious, "Black, Phillip?" and he sounded very tired when he replied, "Dorothy, it was what they had."

It was a cool gray fall morning, and I drove out of town under twenty miles an hour, my heart jolting against my chest and my hands shaking. I could never have another accident, I realized; I would always have to be extremely careful. The streets were quiet and empty because everyone was at church—including, I presumed, Andrew's parents, who were Catholic. The emptiness was calming. By the time I picked up De Soto Way, I felt confident enough to press my foot more heavily against the accelerator. I wasn't at the speed limit—though I hadn't been speeding before the accident, I'd never speed for the rest of my life—but I was close enough to the limit that a car behind me would not have honked. Luckily, there wasn't a car behind me, and I was alone in a way I hadn't been since the accident, alone in a way I no longer could be at home. Even when I was by myself in my room, with the door shut, there was someone on the other side of the door—my mother or father or grandmother, individually or in combination—and that person or those people knew. They might be sympathetic, but they still knew that I was in there and that I had done something hideous, however inadvertently. In other parts of the house, they walked and breathed and sighed and shifted, and their presence was always a question, even if they weren't speaking, even if they were consciously refraining from asking me anything: *Are you going to come out of your room? Are you crying right now, or not crying? When will enough time have passed that this misfortune won't hide in every corner and wait beneath every conversation, including the conversations that seem at first to be about something else?* Obviously, they weren't really asking these questions, which meant I didn't need to answer. And I was willing to fake it, willing already to pretend I was fine, that life was close to normal. I didn't want them to carry my burden but preferred for it to be condensed and only mine, a knapsack of distress. Out on the road, though, beside the bur oak trees and silver maples, the hickories and elms, I felt a gratitude for my own insignificance. I was nothing but a nameless, foolish girl. The Wisconsin land, scraped and rearranged by glaciers, accosted by tornadoes, drenched and dried out and drenched again—it didn't care what I had done.

I knew I'd need to stay neutrally focused as I approached Farm Road 177, and I repeated to myself, *Turn right, turn right, turn right,* the world reduced to two words, and then I did turn, and the site of the accident was behind me. I had driven past it without weeping or hyperventilating, without even slowing down. From there, I had to concentrate on finding the Imhofs' driveway—I'd been out at their house once, for Andrew's birthday party in second or third grade—and after a mile, I saw it, a black mailbox with a red metal flag, recently harvested cornfields flanking the narrow driveway.

The house was white with green shutters; it seemed a house where you'd have an unremarkably happy childhood. A swing hung unmoving on the front porch, and a red barn sat a few dozen yards back, chickens waddling in front of its open double doors. No cars were visible, only a decrepit red pickup truck of the sort farm families kept for driving around their own land but didn't use on the roads. Holding the envelope, I walked up three steps to the porch. I set the envelope between the screen door and the wooden door and hoped neither Mr. nor Mrs. Imhof would step on it as they entered the house. *I will never be able to express to you how sorry I am,* I had written on the card. *I know that I have caused you great pain. If there was anything in the world I could do to change what happened, I would.* I had written five drafts of the note; one had included the line *I will spend the rest of my life trying to make up for my actions,* but I'd cut that part because I feared it emphasized that I had a life still to live. *This pendant is something of mine Andrew once told me he liked, so I thought it might comfort you to have it,* I had written in conclusion, and this was the reason I was delivering the note rather than mailing it; I'd removed the silver heart from its chain before inserting it in the envelope.

I was not quite back to the car when I heard a sound behind me, the lift and release of a door opening, and I whirled around mostly in terror and also, just a little, in hope; under my surprise and alarm was the irrational idea that it might be Andrew himself. Even when I was facing the house again, the difficulty of seeing the features of the figure behind the screen prolonged this glimmering impossibility. And then I realized it was Pete Imhof. Of course it wasn't Andrew.

He didn't open the screen door right away, but stood there for several beats, watching me, I suppose. I was pretty sure he wasn't wearing a shirt. At last, pointing, I called out, "I left a note." And then, absurdly, with my palm against my chest, "It's Alice Lindgren."

He pushed the screen door open, and because it seemed like I ought to, I walked toward him, reclimbing the steps, standing before him on the porch. He was indeed shirtless—he was wearing light brown corduroys, no socks, and no shoes—and though I tried to avert my eyes, I noticed the dark hair covering his chest. It was heavier around his nipples, which were broad and ruddy, and it thickened in a line down his sternum to his navel, and then down farther, where he had a pinch of flesh hanging over the waist of his pants. His arms were also lined with dark hair, except at the tops, where he was visibly muscular. My father, who was the only man I'd seen shirtless on a regular basis, including the previous summer at the motel pool in St. Ignace, was muscular, too—at five-nine, he had a compact muscularity—but his chest was white and almost hairless.

"My parents aren't here," Pete said. "They're at church." His face was stubbly and puffy. I had thought often of Mr. and Mrs. Imhof during the last few weeks, but the truth was that I had hardly considered Pete.

I hadn't even been sure that he still lived in Riley, though I realized in this moment that the car I'd plowed into had most likely been his.

"I thought—" I hesitated. "It seemed like it would be better if I came when they weren't around. I'm sorry if I woke you up." And then, predictably, there was the silent echo of the bigger apology I owed him: *I'm sorry I killed your brother.*

"You didn't wake me up," Pete said.

I looked down (there even was dark hair on his bare toes) and then up again at his eyes, hazel, like Andrew's. "I'm sorry," I said, and we held each other's gaze, and then I said, "for what I did," and to keep from crying, I looked down and pressed together my thumbs and forefingers. I couldn't cry in front of an Imhof.

"Everyone knows that," Pete said.

I looked up.

"Everyone knows you're sorry." His voice was neither harsh nor compassionate; it was matter-of-fact. And though I don't think he doubted my sincerity, I felt a wish to convince him of it that seemed in itself insincere. "You don't have to write my parents a letter," he said. "They already know. My mother feels bad for you."

"Should I take it with me?"

He shrugged. We both were silent for almost a minute. Finally, he said, "Are you waiting for me to invite you in?" I was about to say no when he added, "You can do what you want," and he turned and walked back into the house. I followed him. Not by a lot but by a little bit, it seemed less awkward than just leaving.

No lights were on inside, and as we passed a dim living room, I observed a stone fireplace, a settee covered in navy blue velvet, and an old-looking upright piano. A wooden staircase with a shiny banister rose from the first-floor hall, but we took a second staircase, cramped and carpeted, that we entered from the kitchen. At the top of the steps were two doors, one closed and one open, and in the room with the open door was the first lit lamp I'd seen in the entire house. It was a small room with a large bureau, a little desk, a single bed (this was unmade, the white sheets and brown spread rumpled at its foot, a paperback book open and facedown against the mattress), and a nightstand on which rested the lamp and an ashtray.

As he sat on the bed, I stayed in the doorway and pointed. "I read that." The book was *Atlas Shrugged.*

"It's interesting, but it's too long," he said.

"Yeah, I wouldn't say it was my favorite."

He was looking at me, not speaking. Then he patted the space on the bed next to him and said, "Why don't you come over here?"

I swallowed and stepped forward. It is important for me to say that I was complicit—I had followed him into the house and up the stairs. None of it was premeditated, but I was complicit. When we were sitting next to each other, I don't think more than a second or two had passed before his mouth was on mine, his hungry, pushy, wet, sour mouth, moving in a way that seemed too desperate to be called kissing, and no more than a few seconds had passed after that before he set his fingers firmly around my right breast, squeezing and releasing and squeezing again. Although his desire was stronger than mine, and his strength was greater—although he was already shirtless—I was not afraid. What I felt was enormous relief. I'd been trying so hard these past few weeks to prop myself up, to act the way I was supposed to and try to take the first small steps toward compensating for my terrible error, and now I was only submitting. I wasn't being watched or talked about or gently queried, not condemned or accommodated. I was being asked for something, something wrong, which another person wanted, and I could give it to him.

He had reached beneath my blouse and under my bra, and because it seemed that the buttons on the blouse might pop otherwise, I unfastened them. When I wore nothing on top, he pushed me down on the mattress, straddled me, and leaned forward to roll his face between my breasts, pressing them against his cheeks and licking my nipples, his stubble rubbing not unpleasantly over my skin, and the more he grabbed and thrashed, the more the grabbing and thrashing seemed to stir rather than satisfy his desire. He pulled off my pants and underwear at the same time—I was wearing blue jeans, and he had to unbutton and unzip them first—and then I was naked except for my socks, which were white with lace trim. He tugged me upward and flipped me over, and when he said, "No, you have to be on your knees," it was the first time either of us had spoken in several minutes.

I have never described this to another person, I would never. And in today's world, where nineteen-year-old girls on reality shows kiss each other for the entertainment of male onlookers, where women on network television climb into hot tubs in string bikinis, the globes of their fake breasts bobbing merrily—in this world, perhaps it wouldn't seem so shocking. But it was 1963, I was a high school senior, and I had not known this sexual position existed, had never heard the fittingly coarse phrase *doggy-style.* I wasn't sure what Pete and I were doing, wasn't sure it *was* sex, and then after a few minutes of his pumping, I felt his surge inside me, and I knew it must have been. He pressed his hand against the side of my thigh, prompting me to lie down. When I did, he lay flat on top of me, and I could feel his sticky erection shrink up.

We stayed like that, both of us facing the mattress: his head over my left shoulder, beside my head; his chest to my back; his flaccid penis in the split of my buttocks; his legs against my legs. His body was heavy and warm, and my mind was blank, and there was only his welcome weight, like a shield that covered me completely.

Unsurprisingly, it had hurt somewhat, and it had been hasty, and there had not been the physical release for me that there had been for him; I was so naive that I didn't know there could have been. Also, it had been ill-advised. None of that mattered. Lying on my stomach against the mattress, I could not see his face next to mine, but I could see the fingertips of his hand grazing my shoulder, and I could smell his skin, like sautéed onions and soap. So this was what it was to lie unclothed in the arms of a young man.

Another minute passed before abruptly, Pete rolled off me. When he rose, the entire back of my body was exposed in his bedroom, beside the lamp, at noon on a Sunday, and I instinctively turned over and pulled up the sheet. He stood naked before me, his dark body hair and impassive expression. "My parents will be home," he said. "You need to leave."

EVEN BY THE time I was back on De Soto Way, it seemed shocking and inexplicable. I'd had *sex* with Andrew's brother? Forty minutes before, I'd been a virgin with a condolence note, and then Pete Imhof had been inserting his penis into me from behind and I'd resisted not at all? I'd practically invited it! As I drove into town, I'd have thought I'd imagined the whole scene except for the indisputable leaking between my legs.

And yet I felt far lighter than I had driving out. Presumably, I had betrayed people—my parents and grandmother, maybe Andrew—but that wasn't how I felt. It was more like something had been awry, a phone off the hook, a sink of dirty dishes, and what I'd done was to clean it up and set it right.

At home, I parked the car and entered the house, and when I appeared in the dining room, my mother exclaimed, "There you are!" She was already standing and walking toward me, setting her hands on my shoulders. They were eating Sunday lunch, lamb and green beans and biscuits.

"We were concerned," my father said. "We didn't know where you'd gone."

"I had to run an errand."

"Next time leave a note," my father said. "Dorothy, let her sit so she can eat."

I longed to go upstairs and take a bath, but that would seem suspicious; I'd already showered that morning. Taking my place at the table, I wondered if Pete's fluid had seeped through my underwear and stained the back of my jeans.

"What was your errand?" my grandmother asked.

There was a long silence. "For school," I said. Another silence descended—they seemed to do that more often now, or maybe I just noticed them more—and then my mother said, "Alice, the Frick girls sang 'A Mighty Fortress Is Our God' today. Such beautiful voices." No one responded, and my mother added, "Do you know, Cecile told me the girls hope to perform at the state fair next summer."

"Fools' names and fools' faces often appear in public places," my father said. Although he repeated this expression frequently—the most recent time had been when Mr. Janaszewski won three rounds of bingo in a row at St. Ann's, and his photo ran the next day on the front page of *The Riley Citizen*—performing at the state fair did not strike me as all that unseemly.

"Well, I don't think it's definite," my mother said.

I knew I should help out—my mother was trying—but I'd been gripped by a paralyzing awareness of a smell coming from inside me, a sour salty odor I had never been exposed to yet recognized immediately.

"I went to school with a girl who had a gorgeous voice," my grandmother said. "Leona Stromberg."

My grandmother set her knife and fork side by side on the edge of her plate, though she'd eaten less than half her food. She lit a Pall Mall as she talked. "When she sang, she was so good it gave you goose bumps. One summer, this must have been in '09 or '10, the circus came to town. She convinces someone to give her an audition, and what I always heard is they didn't hire her for her voice as much as her looks, which is a shame. Not that she wasn't pretty, too, but she had a real gift, and I take it they used her more as a magician's assistant. In any event, she leaves Milwaukee with the circus—she's about eighteen—and she travels this way and that, hither and yon. One night the circus is performing in Baltimore, and what happens in the middle of the show but a tiger bites off her nose."

"Oh my word," my mother said.

"Is this appropriate for the table?" my father asked.

"We're all adults." My grandmother winked at me, something she had not done in a long while. "Now, by this time, I forgot to mention, she's changed her name. No more Leona Stromberg. Instead, she goes by Mimi Étoile—'Étoile' is French for 'star.' *Parlez-vous Français?*" She was looking at me. I shook my head. An image of Pete Imhof appeared in my brain like a flare, and I did my best to ignore him. "Me, neither," my grandmother said. "But back to our heroine. Mimi née Leona has no nose, which means no more performing. You don't want to remind the audience of the circus's dark side, after all. Now, you'd think she was out of luck. She doesn't have savings, she isn't married, she's far from home. But the circus owner goes to fire her, and lo and behold they fall in love. Her face is covered with bandages, but that just forces him to listen more attentively to her exquisite voice. He's years older than she is, in his fifties, but he courts her and makes her his noseless bride. They lived happily ever after, so far as I know."

"That's a very peculiar story," my father said.

"Did she keep traveling with the circus?" my mother asked.

"For a little while, but soon he bought her a house in Denver, and he stayed there, too, when the circus didn't need him. Eventually, because remember, he was no youngster, he sold the circus and joined Mimi year-round. The weather in Denver is quite temperate, apparently, even though it's near the mountains."

I swallowed my last bite of green beans. "May I be excused?"

"Sweetheart, there's butterscotch tapioca," my mother said.

"I have a history test tomorrow." I stood and kept speaking as I backed out of the room, so that that would seem like the reason I was still facing them. "I need to study."

In my bedroom, I changed underpants. I didn't know what to do with the soiled pair—I didn't want to risk leaving them in the laundry basket in the corner of my room and having my mother find them—so I balled them up and set them in the back of my sock drawer. In the bathroom, before urinating, I wiped a wad of toilet paper between my legs, and the wad came away with a clear, filmy smear. The second time I wiped myself, I wet the toilet paper first. Then I flushed both wads, as if destroying the evidence could undo the act.

LATE THE NEXT afternoon, when my father was still at work, my grandmother was in the living room smoking and reading *Vogue,* and my mother and I were preparing dinner, I walked to the edge of the living room. "Mom wants to know if you want the cheese sauce on your broccoli or on the side."

My grandmother looked up. "On the side will be fine."

I didn't move immediately. "Was that story about Mimi Étoile true?"

My grandmother regarded me. "If it were," she said at last, "don't you think it'd be awfully interesting?"

THAT WEDNESDAY MORNING, as I ate oatmeal in the kitchen, my mother said, "Spirit Club meets this afternoon, doesn't it, sweetie?" And though I had not attended a meeting since the accident, I went because of the willed brightness of her tone, the way she thought—it was touching, really—that if we spoke cheerily, it might mean I hadn't killed Andrew.

It was an ordinary meeting, with a forty-five-minute argument over whether the GO BENTON KNIGHTS banner for Friday's football game against Houghton North High should be unfurled at morning assembly or withheld until the actual game; I did not speak at all except to vote yea for opening the banner at assembly. Spirit Club was composed of sixteen girls and one boy, a slim, excitable sophomore named Peter Smyth who was obsessed with Elizabeth Taylor and who would, at any opportunity, impersonate her in her role as a call girl in *BUtterfield 8*.

The next day, I was leaving the cafeteria after lunch when Mary Hafliger, the Spirit Club president, approached me. "Can I speak with you in private?" she asked.

I nodded, and we walked from the noisy cafeteria outside to the faculty parking lot. It was a sunny day, and the leaves on the trees at the parking lot's edge were red and gold.

"This is hard to tell you," she said, "but we think you shouldn't be in Spirit Club anymore."

I was stunned and also not surprised at all. I expected censure in general, but I was never prepared for it in the moment.

I swallowed. "That's fine."

"I knew you would understand," she said. "It's just that you make people sad."

I thought of having defended Mary's hairy forearms to Dena the previous spring, and then I wondered, had I made people sad at the meeting the day before? It had consisted of nothing but bickering and, at random intervals, Peter Smyth announcing, " 'Mama, face it. I was the slut of all time!' "

But could I really fault Mary? I was Mimi Étoile, I realized suddenly, I was the girl whose nose had been bitten off by a tiger, and now I reminded cheerful people of life's sorrow. Or no, maybe I wasn't Mimi, because she had gone on to find her happy ending. Besides, it had only been her nose.

THE NEXT TIME was after school that Friday. He was in the rusty red pickup I'd seen at the Imhofs' farm, and he'd parked near campus and was sitting in the driver's seat. When I was right beside the pickup, he said in a low voice, "Alice." I turned, recognized him, said nothing, and climbed in the truck. We didn't speak until after we'd made a right into his family's driveway. I was surprised; without consciously knowing I'd thought that far ahead, I'd assumed we'd go somewhere secluded, that we might even use the bed of the truck.

"But what about your—" I began, and he said, "They're spending the weekend with my aunt and uncle in Racine."

In the house, I followed Pete up the stairs; I felt purposeful and not nervous. The first round was like before, both of us on our hands and knees, him behind me. But after we collapsed onto the mattress, we eventually ended up turning over, so we were on our backs next to each other, then he was on his side facing me; because he was taller, his mouth was near the top of my head. This repositioning all took a long time, and we spoke very little. We still were lying like that when he began running his fingers back and forth across the concave dip between my hip bones, his hand dropping progressively lower after each round-trip. When he got where he'd been going, I flinched, which wasn't the same as not wanting to be touched. He stilled his hand, but he didn't lift it away, and he didn't say anything. He was waiting, perhaps, for me to protest. When I didn't, he proceeded. I shut my eyes. At first my gasps were shallow and quiet, but they grew deeper and louder, and this might have been mortifying if I were still me, if the world still existed, but I wasn't and it didn't. I'd open my eyes and see an off-white ceiling, the tops of brown-and-yellow-plaid curtains, and then I'd close my eyes and go back into the roiling blackness of outer space, comets, and asteroids, and then I'd open my eyes again—ceiling, curtains—and the difference was as great as if I'd been sitting at my desk in homeroom one moment and then I'd turned around and found the Great Wall of China stretched out before me. It was not clear whether he rolled onto me or I pulled him, but at some point he was in me again, we were face-to-face, grinding and colliding, and I was gripping his buttocks, and it happened at the same time for both of us, I raised my legs and curled them around his back to pull him as close to me as possible, to make him be as far inside. In retrospect, this whole time period with Pete is so clouded with sorrow and regret that I try not to think of it; sometimes still, it can make me wince. And yet I confess to slight amusement that what happened for us that day in his bedroom, the synchronicity of timing, has never once happened in decades of marriage to a man I love dearly.

Lying there with Pete Imhof, his weight on me as our breathing and our heartbeats slowed, I thought how there was nothing else, nothing on any topic that any person could say. This was the only thing more powerful than grief.

DENA HAD REALIZED that Andrew's death was an act of God. She told me this while I sat on her bed watching her apply makeup before meeting people at Tatty's on Saturday night. Several times, she had invited me to go, but I'd declined, and she'd said, "You have to quit thinking about him. Andrew was an angel taken from us too soon, but it's not for us to ask why."

Because she'd been having trouble sleeping, she told me, her mother had arranged for her to meet with their priest, and Father Krauss had helped her see that it was all part of God's plan. "You should talk to your pastor," she said.

I said nothing, and then she said, "You're looking at my sideburn stubble, aren't you?"

"I wasn't looking at anything."

"Nancy said I should just grow them out, but how many months will that take? Three?"

I hadn't told Dena about Andrew's brother, and I couldn't. It was not a juicy tidbit, not even a moral quandary for us to debate; it was unspeakable.

"Your sideburns look fine," I said.

WHEN MY FAMILY walked to Calvary Lutheran that Sunday, I drove back to the Imhofs' farm. I knocked on the door, and Pete took so long to answer that I decided he wasn't home, but I knocked once more anyway, for thoroughness. The previous night, the temperature had dropped to the low forties, and I wore a coat.

When he opened the door, he said, "That was stupid of you to come out here. What if my parents were home?"

"You said they went to Racine."

"I didn't say when they were coming back."

"Should I leave?"

He gave me a surly look. "If you're already here, you might as well come inside." He turned and headed back toward the kitchen, and as I had both times before, I followed him.

In addition to scrambling what had to be five or six eggs, he was frying sausage and toasting two pieces of bread, and as I watched, he poured himself a glass of orange juice. When he'd assembled all the food on a plate, he sat at the kitchen table, so I sat, too. I took off my coat, folding it and setting it on the chair next to me. Neither of us spoke until Pete had finished his food. He leaned back, folded his arms, and looked at me.

"Should we go upstairs?" I asked. Although it was a forward question, it seemed so obvious this was the next step that to say anything else would have been disingenuous. Besides, once we were in his bed, undressed and entangled, I knew the dull hostility of his mood would recede.

But he ignored my suggestion and said, "What are your hopes and dreams, Alice? Think you'll stay in Riley forever?"

"I don't know."

"I'd never stay here," he said. "I'm moving to Milwaukee or Chicago to make something of myself."

I was, of course, too young to know there's no surer sign of a man who won't make something of himself than his repeated assertions that he will, and I also was bewildered by why we were having this conversation. The wish to go upstairs was like a bar of gold hovering vertically inside my chest. "I went to Chicago with my grandmother," I said.

"Yeah? Congratulations." Though his comment had its desired effect—it made me feel foolish—I couldn't tell if it meant Pete himself had or hadn't been. "I could take over the farm, but farming is for chumps," he continued. "I had to get up at six this morning to feed the chickens. You break your back in the fields, live at the mercy of the weather, and for what? I'm looking for a white-collar job, business or banking. Andy liked it here, but I never understood why."

We both were quiet. I don't think he'd meant to mention his brother, I think he'd temporarily forgotten my connection to Andrew or perhaps he'd even forgotten Andrew's death.

All this time, there had been no light on in the kitchen, and we sat there in the gloomy quiet. In an unfriendly voice, he said, "Come here." I stood and walked around the table. He was wearing the same tan corduroys from before and a sweater with wide black and red stripes. "Get on your knees," he said.

When I was kneeling in front of him, I said, "Like this?"

Sarcastically, he said, "Pretend you're in church."

He held my gaze as he unbuttoned his pants, unzipped them, and slid them to his ankles along with his white jockey shorts. His penis looked shockingly small, but he took my hand and brought it toward him and said, "Move it around and rub it," and soon his erection had sprung to life. "Come in closer," he said. "Now put it in your mouth." Even as he spoke, he was cupping my head with one hand, pulling me in.

Years before, in sixth grade, my classmate Roy Ziemniak, our dentist's son, had described this act to Dena and me, and I hadn't known whether to believe him. He had apparently been telling the truth.

I gagged twice in the first minute, and then I tried to keep a rhythm, up and down, and I thought, *I'll count to twenty-five,* and I made sure to count with Mississippis in between so real seconds were passing: *One Mississippi, two Mississippi . . .* Above me, I could hear Pete sighing increasingly deeply. After thirty-four seconds, I raised my head. His eyes were closed, but he opened them quickly, and his voice sounded half sleepy and half desperate—it did not sound cruel—when he said, "No, you have to finish."

When I'd resumed, I began to cry. I didn't want him to notice, and I don't think he did, preoccupied as he was; there was a lot of wetness down there already because I was drooling from not swallowing. When at last he erupted into my mouth, I quickly pulled back my head, and most of it dribbled onto his pale, hairy thighs. There was only a little I wiped from the edge of my lips, a tiny bit that might have gone down my throat. He leaned over to pull up his jockey shorts and trousers, and

I bent my head, my tears flowing rapid and hot and unobstructed. Perhaps thirty more seconds had passed when he said, "Are you *crying?*"

I'd been sitting with my knees forward and my rear end balanced against my heels, and I shifted then so my rear end was on the floor and my knees were a tent. I crossed my arms, leaned my face into them, and wept so hard my shoulders shook.

"What's wrong with you?" I heard Pete say.

When I looked up, he towered over me. A minute before, he'd been sitting and I'd been kneeling, but he'd gone higher when I went lower. Our eyes met, and I could feel my face contract (it would have been so different with Andrew; I would have wanted to make him feel good, and afterward he'd have held and kissed me). I said, "I know there's nothing I can do to make it up to you or your parents, but I miss him, too."

"You don't think the two of you were in love, do you?" The fury in Pete's tone told me not to answer. "That he was your boyfriend?"

I did not reply, but I had stopped crying and gone on a kind of bodily alert. I suddenly knew I would be leaving this house very soon, and the likelihood was slim that I would ever come back.

"My brother wasn't your boyfriend," Pete said.

I wiped my eyes, I tucked my hair behind my ears. As I stood, I held on to a chair.

"Did you hear me?" Pete said. "He wasn't your boyfriend." As I pulled on my coat, it occurred to me that he might try to bar my exit. "What you just did," he said, "only whores do that, and my brother would never have dated a whore."

I walked out of the kitchen, down the hall past the living room and front staircase. Pete followed me, but when I reached the door, he stayed over ten feet back. I grasped the doorknob, turning it, and he said, "See, you can't even defend yourself. That's what a whore you are."

That this ugliness had arisen so quickly between us—it could only mean it had been there all along. I looked back at him and said the one thing I knew was true. I said, "I'm sorry it wasn't me instead of him."

IT WAS THEN in my life that I entered a twilight in which all I tried to do was move forward. I saw how, with Pete, I'd been trying to fix the situation—I'd been trying in a perverse way, but trying all the same—and now I understood that the situation was unfixable. That, in fact, I'd made it worse. And it wasn't as if I could take consolation in the idea that I'd been martyring myself: I'd mostly liked it when Pete touched my body, I'd liked the physical aspect (he had been a naked, hairy man five years older than I was, stroking me in ways he ought not to have tried and I ought not to have allowed—of course it had been exciting) and I'd also liked the plot of it, wondering what would happen next, thinking about something that was close to Andrew without having to think about his death. But the end result had turned out to be rancor, rancor on top of tragedy, as well as new and incriminating secrets, misbehaviors that would further hurt the people who knew me if they learned of them. The solution was to retreat, to shut down, and doing so did not require effort. Rather, it was the opposite of effort—capitulation.

I went to school, and I continued to turn in all my work, most of which I completed in study hall; after sophomore year, study hall was optional, and in the past, I'd spent it in the gym with Dena, sitting on the bleachers while boys in penny loafers shot baskets, ducking when the balls came threateningly close. In the evenings, I watched television or played cards with my family just enough so they wouldn't think I'd stopped watching television or playing cards with them, and at meals, I talked enough so they wouldn't worry that I was on the brink of doing something rash and destructive, which I wasn't. I didn't have the energy.

I tried to read novels, once my most reliable refuge, but even when I was immersed in sixteenth-century Scotland or contemporary Manhattan, I could always feel the dread of my own life at the edge of the page, an incoming tide. Sometimes the dread simply washed right over me, and there was nothing I could do to prevent it. It was worst in the morning, when I first awakened. I'd feel sick, literally nauseated, and occasionally, if I was still, it would pass. But more often I'd have to hurry to the bathroom, where I'd vomit into the toilet bowl and then try not to cry. It would be five-fifteen, five-twenty, and it would seem impossible that the day had gone wrong already.

At night, I'd lie on my bed with the lights on and my eyes shut, and

I'd listen to "Lonesome Town," and I'd feel the song steadying me, cradling me, the way another person can hold you in water when you are nearly weightless. "You can buy a dream or two / To last you all through the years," Ricky Nelson sang. "And the only price you pay / Is a heart full of tears." I'd fiddle with the silver necklace I'd been wearing that afternoon outside the library; though a part of me wished I hadn't given the heart pendant to Andrew's parents, the fact that I was bothered by its absence seemed a sign that I'd made the right decision.

ONE MORNING IN early November, I emerged from the bathroom after throwing up—it was not yet six o'clock—and found my grandmother standing in the unlit hall, specter-like in her pink satin bathrobe and white slippers. "Were you sick in there?"

"I'm fine," I said softly. "My stomach hurt, but now I feel better."

She scrutinized me. "It's not a way to stay thin, you know. It's an old trick that lots of girls try, but it's bad for your teeth and makes your cheeks swell. Before long, you'll look like a chipmunk."

"Granny, I didn't make myself throw up on purpose."

"If you're worried about gaining weight, it would be much more ladylike to smoke. Cigarettes curb your appetite at the same time that they burn calories."

I knew cigarettes were bad for you—Mr. Frisch had told us in biology—but I didn't want to argue with her.

My grandmother reached out and held her thumb and forefinger around my chin, so I couldn't look anywhere except at her. Since eighth grade, I'd been taller than she was, but she usually wore heels that eliminated the discrepancy in our heights. Now I was gazing down on her. "Don't punish yourself," she said. "It never makes anything better."

ONCE I WAS at school, amid the noise and all the people hurrying toward obligations that didn't really matter, I'd often wonder if I wouldn't have been better off staying home, if I shouldn't drop out altogether. But home was no better, just bad in a different way. Gradually, I came to understand that I needed to leave Riley, to go to college and not come back. And I needed to enroll somewhere other than Ersine Teachers College in Milwaukee, which had fewer than twelve hundred young women in the whole school. It was too likely, in such a small community, that my story would get out, someone there would know someone from Riley, or one of my high school classmates would also enroll. I suppose it's a mark of my provincialism at the time that I thought applying to the University of Wisconsin in Madison was a radical move. The school had an undergraduate and graduate population of more than twenty thousand; this, I thought, would surely be enough in which to get lost.

THE SECOND TIME my grandmother caught me vomiting, she didn't wait in the hall; she sat on my bed paging through the copy of *The Rise of Silas Lapham* that she'd found on my nightstand. Her voice was raspy with morning as she said, "Close the door." When I had, she said, "That was very foolish of me before, wasn't it? Thinking you were trying to lose weight."

I stood by the bureau and said nothing.

"We'll go to Chicago, and we'll have it taken care of. Next week, likely. I need to make a few calls. You can do as you see fit, but I'd advise against saying anything to your parents. I just can't imagine what purpose it would serve."

I felt an impulse then to express incomprehension, except that I did comprehend. At night, when I listened to "Lonesome Town," I knew. She was right.

"Isn't it—" I hesitated. "Isn't it illegal?"

"Certainly, and it happens all the time. You can't legislate human nature."

"You don't think that I should have it?"

Quietly, she said, "I think it would kill you. If circumstances were different, I would say, 'Go live at a girls' home in Minnesota, go to California.' But you don't have the strength. You'll be strong again, but you're not strong now."

As she spoke, I could feel my lips curling out, the tears welling in my eyes. I whispered, "I'm sorry for disappointing you."

"Come sit by me," she said, and when I did, she rubbed my back, the palm of her hand sweeping over the white cotton of my nightgown. After a moment, she said, "We have to make mistakes. It's how we learn compassion for others." She paused. "You don't need to tell me whose it is. That doesn't matter."

WE TOOK THE bus rather than the train. At my grandmother's instruction, I had gone to school as if it were a normal day, but before the end of first period, I'd been summoned to the principal's office, where my grandmother awaited me. We walked quickly to the bus station, rode the bus to Chicago—"I'm sure there's someone who does it in Riley, too," my grandmother said, "but I'd have to ask around, and I don't want people talking"—and from the bus station on Broad Street, we took a taxi to the hospital. As directed by my grandmother, I had not eaten or drunk since the night before, and in the taxi, my stomach turned, filled with nothing but anxiety. "I've given your name as Alice Warren," my grandmother said. "Just as a precaution." Warren was her own maiden name.

"You don't think I'll get arrested, do you?"

"You won't get arrested," my grandmother said.

"And the doctor won't use dirty tools?"

My grandmother looked at me strangely. "I thought you understood that Gladys is performing the procedure. That's why we've come here."

My grandmother was not permitted in the operating room. I wore a blue hospital gown, and when I lay on the table, the nurse had me set my feet in metal stirrups. "The doctor wants to talk to you before we put you under anesthesia," the nurse said, and ten or twelve minutes had passed before Dr. Wycomb appeared in a white coat. She squeezed my hand, and the warmth of her grip made me realize how cold I was.

"I know this is difficult, Alice," she said. "It will be over before you know it, though, and you'll recover quickly. The way a D and C works is that I'll expand the entrance of your uterus, and I'll use a very thin instrument for the curettage. You might experience cramps and spotting for several days—you'll want to use sanitary napkins—but you'll be able to walk out of here."

I nodded, feeling faint. I did not even know then what *curettage* meant, but back in Riley, I looked it up; the dictionary definition was *scraping.*

"If any problems arise in the next days or weeks, it's important that you call me," Dr. Wycomb said. "Your grandmother has my telephone number." She was not distant—she still held my hand—but she was crisp and professional in a way that made me understand she was probably very good at her job.

"One more thing: I'll leave these items with Emilie, and I want you to get them from her when you're home. You need not discuss them with her." Dr. Wycomb reached into a small brown paper bag I hadn't noticed and extracted an object I didn't recognize, a white rubber dome that she handed to me along with a capped tube, also white. "Fill the diaphragm with spermicide before you insert it," she said. "Then push the diaphragm deep into your vagina so it walls off your cervix. Make sure to practice a few times before you're in a situation where you need it and remember that spermicide alone isn't effective—if your friends suggest otherwise, they're wrong."

Once, it would have been unthinkable, unendurable, to listen to my grandmother's friend use the words *spermicide* and *vagina.* But by then so much had happened that was unthinkable and unendurable, and furthermore, the words themselves were overshadowed by the larger implication of her comments.

"It won't happen again," I said. "I'm not—" I wanted to say, *I really am the girl I seemed to be last winter,* but surely, the necessity of making such an assertion would undermine it.

"This is a conversation about health, not morality," Dr. Wycomb said. "Once a person engages in sexual intercourse, the likelihood of remaining sexually active is high." She patted my forearm. "I'm very sorry about the automobile accident," she said, and then she called for the nurse.

WHEN I EMERGED from the fog of anesthesia, I was in a different room—I opened my eyes, closed them, opened them again—and my grandmother was sitting beside me reading. I blinked several times, my mind blurry. "Should I write Dr. Wycomb a thank-you note?" I asked.

"I don't think that's necessary." My grandmother set a bookmark between two pages and closed the book. "She's coming by to check on you, though, if you'd like to thank her in person. How are you feeling?"

"What time is it?"

"It's after two. You've been sleeping for nearly an hour."

"Isn't my mother— Won't she expect me home?"

"I told her I was meeting you after school to take you shopping. Alice, if you'd like to tell them, that's your decision."

"I'll never tell them," I said, which proved to be true.

When Dr. Wycomb came into the recovery room, I still was loopy. I said, "I hope you don't go to prison because of me."

Dr. Wycomb and my grandmother exchanged glances, and Dr. Wycomb said, "This is a very common procedure, Alice. You were my third this week."

BACK IN RILEY, I could hardly make eye contact with my parents. *Whatever you are, be a good one,* I had grown up hearing my father say, and oh, how I had failed him, how I'd failed them all. On the weekends, when Mrs. Falke came over to play bridge with my parents and grandmother, I'd stand in the upstairs hall listening to the slap and turn of their cards, and they seemed to me like children.

I bled for a few days, and then I stopped. I was not even sore, not really. When an image or a feeling of Andrew or Pete came into my mind—they came at different moments, for different reasons—I'd try to suppress it. I waited for time to pass.

On November 22, a Friday, I was walking out of the cafeteria after lunch, just behind a few other students, when a sophomore named Joan Skryba and a junior named Millie Devon came toward us, running and crying. Though they were shouting, they were nearly incoherent. I couldn't understand at first, and when I finally did, I still wasn't sure I had because it seemed so unlikely—the president of the United States? President Kennedy? Then someone else, a boy, emerged from the cafeteria behind us and said the same thing, and everyone was talking at once, and a girl next to me whom I wasn't friends with at all, Helen Pajak, took my hand and gripped it tightly. It wasn't until I saw Mrs.

Moore, my math teacher, weeping openly that I knew it was true: A little over an hour before, President Kennedy had been shot in Dallas.

Everything felt suspended; in the remaining classes that afternoon, we spoke of nothing else, but people were no longer excitable. We all were simply stunned. And then, an hour or so later, we heard he had died, and if President Kennedy had just been assassinated, what would happen next? What sense or logic was there, which rules still existed in the world? Normally, at the end of the day and especially on a Friday, the hall containing our lockers was filled with yells and laughter and slamming metal, but that afternoon it was quiet.

I did not cry for him, not then or ever, though I, like everyone, found the television coverage mesmerizing. That evening was the only time I can recall my family watching television while we ate dinner; we carried our plates into the living room. Everything was canceled, in Riley and everywhere else, sports events and plays, and restaurants and stores and movie theaters were closed, and you hardly saw a car on the street. Really, there was nothing to do but wonder at what had happened. Over the next few days, seeing the picture in the newspaper of Lyndon Johnson being sworn in on *Air Force One* by Sarah Hughes, watching the surreal footage of Lee Harvey Oswald getting shot at the police headquarters by Jack Ruby, listening to Johnson's address on Thanksgiving—"From this midnight of tragedy we shall move toward a new American greatness," he told us—my parents and grandmother seemed as stupefied as I was.

But this is the truth: I had admired Kennedy, I'd thought he was smart and handsome and full of vigor. And yet with his death, I felt a grim relief. I wasn't *happy;* certainly not. But something had occurred that was so dreadful, it eclipsed the dreadfulness of what I had caused. Not in my opinion, it didn't, but in everyone else's; it made what I'd done seem small. And I knew it immediately that afternoon at school. This was a death far bigger and worse than Andrew's, and it had nothing to do with me; there was no part of it that was my fault. If this was not absolution, it was as close as I would get.

To this day, I remain deeply ashamed of my reaction. In all my life, I have admitted what I felt that afternoon to just one person.

PART II

3859 Sproule Street

When I was twenty-seven, the month after Simon Törnkvist and I broke up, I decided that if I wasn't married by the time I turned thirty, I would buy a house alone. Although I told no one, keeping this idea in the back of my mind provided reassurance; it made my life seem less like something I was waiting for and more like something I was planning. When I drove around Madison, I'd sometimes think, *A place like that.* Three bedrooms at the most, a yard but not a large one, on a street with tall trees. Also, not a house on a corner, because those seemed too exposed. As a librarian at Theodora Liess Elementary School, I earned eight hundred and thirty-three dollars a month after taxes, and as soon as I'd made my decision, I began to put away two hundred dollars from each paycheck in a savings account; I deposited the money at my neighborhood branch of Wisconsin State Bank & Trust on the last Saturday morning of every month.

I'm not sure exactly when I would have called a realtor—the day I turned thirty? The day after? My plan had never gotten that specific—but it didn't turn out to be anywhere close, because it was two months before my birthday, in February 1976, that my father died. Like his own father, he had a heart attack, and although my father made it into his fifties—two decades longer than my grandfather had lived—this seemed to me even then to be a dubious reprieve. Now, of course, it does not seem like a reprieve at all.

It snowed the day of my father's funeral, and my mother, grandmother, and I all tried, for one another's sakes and because we were midwestern, to be stoic; my mother either was or pretended to be greatly preoccupied by whether the black crepe dress I had bought at Prange's was warm enough. Back at the house, we visited awkwardly with my mother's siblings and their spouses, none of whom I'd seen in years. Other members of Calvary Lutheran dropped by, and my father's coworkers at the bank, all of them bearing flowers or food (mostly casseroles, though the assistant manager brought a whole ham). Then they were gone and a quiet descended, amplified by the snow that had fallen.

I needed to drive back to Madison that Sunday evening—I'd arranged to have a substitute for three days the previous week, but the next morning, I was due at school again—and my mother walked me to my car, hugging herself against the cold. When I was settled in the driver's seat, she motioned for me to roll down the window and said, "Fasten your seat belt," and I said, "It's fastened already." As I pulled away from her, away from the house where I'd grown up, I was alone at last, and I began to sob. By the time I reached the highway, a new snow flurry had started, and though it didn't accumulate into anything, it was my father's directions for driving in the snow that I thought of: *Go slowly. Stay well behind the car in front of you. If you skid, turn in to the skid.* When I unlocked the door to my apartment in Madison—I was living then on the second floor of a house on Sproule Street—I could hear the phone ringing, and when I answered, it was, as I'd known it would be, my mother, who'd no doubt been calling every ten minutes for the last hour to see if I'd arrived yet. My upper back, between my shoulders, ached from the tension of the drive and from everything else.

In the year and a half since my father's death, I had gone back to Riley most weekends to check in on my mother and grandmother. Usually, I'd pull into the driveway shortly before lunch on Saturday, and I'd once brought them a pizza, but instead of relieving my mother of the burden of cooking, as I'd intended, it appeared to make her agitated. So these days I brought only myself and sometimes some laundry, and the three of us sat in the dining room eating meals that had already started to seem old-fashioned to me: meat loaf and mashed potatoes, shepherd's pie. I always planned to leave on Sunday after church (with no discussion, I had begun attending again after my father's funeral, though it was for my mother's sake, and I never went on the weekends I remained in Madison), but then thinking of saying goodbye, picturing them sitting in the living room that evening, my mother needlepointing in front of *60 Minutes* and my grandmother reading, always made me far too sad and I ended up staying a second night, sleeping again in my old bed. The next morning, if it was during the school year, I'd have to take off around six o'clock to get back to Madison and change clothes before work. Interstate 94 would be dark and mostly empty, me and a bunch of eighteen-wheelers.

It was, I suppose, for all these reasons that I had not started looking for a house to buy until the summer of 1977. My realtor turned out to be a woman named Nadine Patora who was lively, zaftig, and over a decade my senior. Given the modesty of the houses I was considering—I'd pay forty thousand dollars at the absolute most—she treated me with more patience than I had any right to expect. By early July, we'd looked at more than thirty places, and there was only one I'd seriously considered, a little brick one-story in the Nakoma neighborhood, but after thinking it over for a few days, I hadn't made a bid. I wanted a house I really loved, one I'd be happy to stay in forever and sink endless energy into, rather than one that was merely adequate. Otherwise, why not keep renting? "I bet you're just as picky with men," Nadine said, smiling mischievously as we drove one Sunday afternoon to an open house.

I laughed. "I guess that would explain why I'm still single."

"No, it's good." Nadine leaned over and patted my knee. She was divorced, with two teenage daughters. "Take it from someone who settled for the first thing that came down the pike."

Most of the houses we looked at sounded quite appealing in the MLS listings Nadine showed me, but I'd know from the minute I stepped into them, and sometimes from the outside, that they weren't right: The windows were too small, or the kitchen cabinets depressed me, or a sour smell hung in the rooms, and I didn't want to run the risk of assuming it would vanish along with the current owner. And so when Nadine called me the Thursday after the Fourth of July and said, "I've found your new home," I honestly didn't believe her.

It was a two-bedroom bungalow on a street called McKinley, not quite as pretty as where I lived presently, but it was unlikely I could afford to buy in my current neighborhood. And McKinley did have a pleasant energy, I thought as soon as Nadine and I turned on to it, passing a man walking a dog, two children in bathing suits darting through a sprinkler. The house we parked in front of was white-shingled with a narrow porch and, as I saw when we went inside, a living room that had window seats, and a kitchen that was small and old-fashioned but very light. Even before I consciously thought I might like to live in it, I found myself imagining where I'd place various pieces of furniture, wondering whether my round breakfast table would fit in the kitchen, or which wall I'd put my headboard against in the master bedroom upstairs. The house was empty—there was a convoluted story I half listened to Nadine tell about the owner having moved to Tennessee six months before but putting the house on the market only this week. I peeked behind the shower curtain and opened all the closets; I walked down to the basement. The clincher was a little oak cabinet in the second-floor hallway, shoulder-high, with a clasp that you turned shut. It was about the size of a medicine cabinet you'd find behind a bathroom mirror but slightly deeper—too small to keep linens or cleaning supplies or anything truly practical. It seemed a place to store love letters, secret charms or trinkets.

Back in Nadine's car, I said, "I want it."

"Aren't we decisive all of a sudden."

"You were right," I said. "It's perfect."

"All right, then." Nadine seemed amused. "If you're sure you wouldn't like to sleep on it first, how much are you offering?"

The asking price was thirty-eight thousand, four hundred. "Thirty-seven?" I said uncertainly.

She shook her head. "Thirty-two. You'll go up, he'll come down, you'll meet in the middle." She glanced at her watch—it was a little before five on Thursday afternoon. "You want to give him twenty-four hours?"

"Are we allowed to make him decide that quickly?"

"If you'd rather, we can say forty-eight."

"No, twenty-four would be great. I just don't want to be pushy." In fact, twenty-four hours was preferable; I was driving to Riley on Saturday, and I strongly wished to avoid being on the phone with Nadine in front of my mother or grandmother. I hadn't told them I was hoping to buy a place because I was afraid my mother would try to give me money, which I doubted she could afford after my father's death. My plan was to tell them when it was all finished, when rather than just mentioning the possibility, I could invite them to Madison, show them the actual house, and call it mine. The three of us would sit on the front porch drinking lemonade, I thought—well, assuming I bought some outdoor chairs.

"Pushy, my fanny!" Nadine was saying. "You're offering this man money. Now, the likelihood is that negotiations *will* go through the weekend, but I'll see what I can do." She punched my shoulder lightly. "Kind of exciting, huh? Cross your fingers, babycakes."

THAT NIGHT, ABOUT twenty minutes after I'd turned out the light for bed, the phone rang, and I thought immediately that it might be Nadine, with an answer already, but when I picked up the receiver, a far more familiar female voice said, "Don't you dare think of skipping the Hickens' barbecue."

"Dena, I thought you had a date tonight, or I'd have called to tell you I made an offer on a house."

"You finally found one that meets your exacting standards? Hot damn—let's go see it!"

"Not now," I said quickly. "We'd be arrested for prowling." By this point, I was seated at the kitchen table—the kitchen was where I kept my phone—wearing my white sleeveless nightgown. I'd been sleeping in the living room pretty much since school had let out in June. It was not yet ten-thirty, I noted on the wall clock, which meant I really couldn't scold Dena for calling late. She already mocked my early bedtime, and my usual defense—that I had to get up in the morning to be at school—wouldn't cut it, given that it was summer. "It's on McKinley Street," I said. "Maybe we can go by tomorrow, although I don't want to jinx it before I hear back."

Dena sighed extravagantly. "You have no sense of fun. Speaking of which, I ran into Kathleen Hicken at Eagle, and she said you told her you're going home this weekend. Alice, you can't make me socialize with those people by myself. Rose Trommler hates me."

"Don't be ridiculous."

"All those women are fat, and their husbands are boring."

"First of all, that's not true, but if you really feel that way, why are you so intent on going?"

"I have to," Dena said. "Charlie Blackwell will be there, and I'm planning to seduce him."

I laughed. "I'm sure you'll be just fine without me."

"Charlie *Blackwell,*" she said. "As in *the* Blackwells."

"Oh, Dena, do you really want to be mixed up with that family?" The Blackwells, as everyone from Wisconsin knew, had made their fortune in meat products. (There were several plants near Milwaukee, and it was said you could now buy a package of Blackwell sausage at any grocery store in the country—not, I thought, that you'd necessarily want to. It was what I'd grown up eating, but as an adult, I found it rather greasy.) Harold Blackwell, this generation's paterfamilias, had served as Wisconsin's governor from '59 to '67 and then made an unsuccessful presidential bid in '68. A week after a rally at UW in which a young woman named Donna Ann Keske, a sophomore from Racine, was paralyzed from the chest down when police used force to break up the demonstration, Governor Blackwell appeared on *Face the Nation* and called Vietnam protestors "unwashed and uneducated," thereby demonstrating a tin ear that would have been unfortunate under normal circumstances but was downright callous during a time of such tumult. Though Blackwell was a Republican and from Wisconsin, even my father wouldn't have supported him had he not dropped out of the presidential race after the New Hampshire primary: He had a disdainful air, as if he didn't trust the average person to be smart enough to vote for him. Now he was out of politics—I had the dim sense he was head of some university, though I couldn't have said which—but one of his sons, of whom there were four, had been elected to Congress from Milwaukee the year before. "You know," I said, "if Charlie is the Blackwell brother I'm thinking of, then Jeanette and Frank tried to set me up with him a couple years ago. But maybe it was a different brother."

"They tried to set you up with him and you said no?" Dena sounded incredulous.

"I was dating Simon." The truth was that I probably would have declined anyway—money and Republicans and sausage did not strike me as a particularly tempting combination.

"Ed is the one who's a congressman, but Charlie's also about to run," Dena said. "North of here, I think around Houghton. It's still a secret, but Kathleen told me he'll announce his candidacy in the spring. Don't you think I deserve to be married to a powerful man?"

"Absolutely."

When she spoke again, Dena sounded less confident. "Alice, the Hickens and all those people are so judgmental. The only reason Kathleen invited me is that I'm friends with you. I need you there for moral support."

Dena had been married—her ex-husband was an older man, an ad executive who was already twice divorced when she met him while working as a flight attendant for TWA. They'd lived in Kansas City in the late sixties and early seventies, and in 1975, having had no children, they, too, divorced. Dena had moved to Madison then and used the money from her settlement to open a store on State Street that sold clothes and accessories to fashionable coeds: bell-bottoms and pantsuits and miniskirts, sheer scarves and velvety handbags, crocheted shawls, ambiguously ethnic baubles. Entering the store—it was called D's—never failed to make me feel very old, and while the merchandise was not really to my taste, I usually bought something.

My inappropriate sartorial purchases aside, having Dena in town was a real joy, especially since almost everyone I'd once been close to from college had gotten married. And it wasn't that you couldn't be friends with a married woman, but you weren't friends in the same way, she didn't have the same freedom in her schedule, especially not after she had children, and even before that, she didn't need you; you needed friendship, and friendship to her was auxiliary, extra.

But Dena and I would phone each other four times a day, including a minute after we'd just hung up if one of us remembered something we'd forgotten to say: "What's the name of that guy at Salon Styles who cut your hair last time?" Or "When you come over tonight, will you bring the Carpenters' album?" She'd swing by to show me her outfit before a date, or she'd call and say, "I'm in the mood for a movie," and ten minutes later, we'd meet at the Majestic. We went for long walks together on Sunday mornings—Dena no longer attended church, either, and we called these walks our constitutionals, which made them sound a little more like a respectable substitute for prayer—and we'd regularly meet for dinner, after which she'd suggest having a drink and be gravely disapproving of my need to go home and sleep. She dated much more frequently than I did; she told me once that she'd gotten a prescription for the pill the first week she was hired at TWA, the summer we graduated from high school, and she hadn't been off it since. As for my own dating habits, people I knew often tried to set me up, and sometimes I went to be a good sport, but on a Saturday night, I tended to be just as happy attending a play with a female friend—Dena also teased me for my friendship with Rita Alwin, a French teacher at Liess Elementary who was black and older than our mothers—or even staying in and reading. People like the Hickens, whom I saw every month or two, formed a kind of secondary social circle: I'd been sorority sisters at the University of Wisconsin with a lot of the wives in these couples, I'd gone to fraternity formals with a few of the husbands (one starry night beside Lake Mendota, in the spring of our junior year, Wade Trommler had drunkenly announced that he considered me the ideal girl), and we'd remained in touch after graduation as they all paired off and had children. Admittedly, my enthusiasm for spending time with them fluctuated with my tolerance for being pecked at about my single status. It always amazed me that married people thought they could say an illuminating thing to you on the topic, as if you were scarcely aware, until they pointed it out, of being unwed.

"Dena, I'm sorry," I said, "but I already told Kathleen Hicken I can't come. My mother and grandmother are expecting me."

"Go home Sunday," Dena said. "What's the difference if it's summer?"

"You don't need me at the party," I said. "Wear your halter dress, and Charlie Blackwell won't be able to take his eyes off you."

"Listen," Dena said. "This isn't negotiable. I'll pick you up Saturday at five-thirty."

"I thought the barbecue started at five."

"We're arriving fashionably late. We'll toast to you becoming landed gentry."

SO FAR, THAT summer had been an especially nice one. The grief I felt about my father's death was milder after a year and a half, without the rawness of surprise. Plus, I was filled with purpose, and not just in looking for a house; there was also my library project.

I had graduated from the University of Wisconsin in 1968, taught for two years—I taught third-graders, an especially boisterous age—then returned to the university to get my master's in library science. What I'd realized while teaching was that the part of the school day I loved most was reading period: *Charlotte's Web, Harold and the Purple Crayon, Blueberries for Sal,* the kids sitting cross-legged on the floor, their eyes wide, their bodies leaning forward with anticipation. If I could be a librarian, I decided, it would be like reading period lasting forever. After I'd earned my master's degree in 1972, I went to work at Liess Elementary, and five years later, at the age of thirty-one, I was still there.

My project that summer was this: I was creating ten large papier-mâché figures of characters from children's books, among them Eloise; the mother and baby rabbits from *The Runaway Bunny;* and Mr. Sneeze from the *Mr. Men* series (I'd used chicken wire to fashion the triangular points of Mr. Sneeze's oversize head). I'd had the idea the previous fall when I saw a little girl on my street dressed as Pippi Longstocking for Halloween. In the spring, I'd written to publishers asking for permission—I suppose I could have gotten away with not doing so, but the idea of being a librarian who infringed on copyrighted material made me shudder—and in early June, I'd bought the materials. By the time school opened after Labor Day, I planned to have all the characters displayed on the library's shelves, or, in the case of the *Paddle-to-the-Sea* figure in his canoe, hanging over the entrance.

I'd been surprised by the scope of the project—I had thought it would take only a couple weeks—but the longer it lasted, the more absorbed I became. At first I'd worked in my living room, but the characters began taking up so much space, and I didn't want anyone who might come over (mostly, this meant Dena) to see them before I was finished, so I'd covered the floor of my bedroom and even the bed with butcher paper, then started sleeping on the living room couch. When I was working, I wore a denim skirt and old shirts of my father's, often dropping globs of the flour and water mixture on myself, and perspiring because I didn't have an air conditioner.

Every morning, before it got hot, I'd cut through campus and walk along Lake Mendota, the sun sparkling on the water, the waves lapping lightly at the shore (walks by myself weren't constitutionals—they were just walks), and then I'd come back and work until lunch, or until long after that if Nadine didn't have any houses to show me. During my walks, and sometimes in the middle of the night, I'd suddenly have an idea about, say, how to create more realistic eyebrows for Maurice Sendak's "I don't care" Pierre (by snipping up a black wig, because when I painted on the eyebrows, they just looked flat). Early in the evening, I'd stop working and make a corn-and-tomato salad, or broil a pork chop, and after dinner, I'd perch on the windowsill of the bedroom and drink a beer and admire my progress. I hadn't mentioned the project to anyone, and sometimes I worried that the other teachers might find it odd or excessive, but when I thought of the children entering the library on the first day of school, I felt excited.

NADINE CALLED EARLY Friday afternoon. "The seller counteroffered—you interested in going up to thirty-five and a half?"

If I were putting down 20 percent, which was what I had told the loan officer at the bank I probably could do, that would mean seventy-one hundred dollars. "Okay," I said.

"Jeez Louise, you're way too easy. Don't you want to complain just a little?"

I laughed. "I want the house."

"All righty. Stand by."

She called me back twenty minutes later and said, "Let me be the first to congratulate you on becoming a homeowner."

I yelped.

"Why don't you come by my office now to sign the papers, and I'd recommend calling the inspector before the end of the day. Can I make one more suggestion?"

"Sure," I said.

"Buy yourself a bottle of champagne. You've got a lot to look forward to."

DENA PICKED ME up the next afternoon for the Hickens' barbecue, but first we drove to McKinley Street. In the car, Dena sang, " 'Home, home on the range, where the deer and the antelope play . . .' " When I pointed to where she should park, the house was both different and the same as I remembered—it was more vivid somehow, more *real*. There was a spruce tree in the yard, and the grass was deep green; the house was a white box, the wooden front-porch floor peeling maroon. There wasn't a garage, just a driveway that was two concrete lines separated by a strip of grass. The knowledge that all of this would belong to me was overwhelming and exhilarating. I didn't yet have keys, but Dena insisted on peering into the windows and wandering into the backyard, which sloped.

"It's cute, right?" I said.

Dena nodded vigorously and sang, " 'Where seldom is heard a discouraging word / And the skies are not cloudy all day.' "

Although we were late to the barbecue, Charlie Blackwell was later, and Dena and I were already out back, sitting side by side on a picnic bench in the grass, when he emerged from the kitchen at the rear of the house and appeared on the deck holding a six-pack in each hand. He was wearing Docksiders without socks, fraying khaki shorts, a belt with a rectangular silver buckle, and a faded pink button-down shirt that I could tell, even from several yards away, had once been good quality. He held the six-packs up near his ears, shook them—a stupid thing to do with beer, I thought—and called out to the yard at large, "*Hello* there, boys and girls!"

About fifteen of us were present, and several men approached him at once, Cliff Hicken slapping him on the back. Charlie opened one of the beers he'd brought, and after he popped the top, some fizzed up and he pressed his mouth against the side of the can and slurped the cascading foam. Then he said something, and when he and the other men burst into laughter, his was the loudest. Under my breath, I said to Dena, "He's perfect for you."

"I don't have lipstick on my teeth, do I?" She turned to me, baring her incisors.

"You look great," I said. She waited ten minutes, so as not to be too obvious, and I watched as she crossed the yard and offered herself up, like a gift, to Charlie Blackwell. The day before, I had been in the public library and looked for mentions of Charlie in news articles—long before the arrival of the Internet, I prided myself on my ability to find information, my golden touch with reference books and microfiche—and although I'd turned up little about Charlie himself beyond his status as a former governor's son, I'd learned that if he really was running in the district that contained Houghton, as Dena had claimed, he'd be up against an incumbent of forty years.

When Dena was gone, Rose Trommler, who was sitting on the opposite side of the picnic bench next to Jeanette Werden, said, "Dena Cimino is sure a piece of work." Cimino was Dena's surname now; she was no longer a Janaszewski.

As if I'd misunderstood Rose's meaning, I nodded and said, "Dena's the most entertaining person I know. She's been exactly the same since we were in kindergarten."

Rose and I were drinking white wine; Jeanette was six months pregnant and not drinking. Rose leaned forward. "I shouldn't say this, but doesn't she sometimes drive you crazy?" Rose and her husband lived next door to the Hickens; we'd been in Kappa Alpha Theta together in college, and she wasn't a bad person, but she was quite a gossip.

"No more than I probably drive her crazy," I said lightly.

"She's practically throwing herself at Charlie Blackwell," Jeanette said. "I wonder if we should warn him."

I looked directly at her. "About what?" I asked in a neutral voice, and neither she nor Rose said anything. "I bet he can take care of himself," I added.

"Alice, how about you?" Rose dunked a potato chip in a bowl of onion dip. "You must have your eye on someone special."

"Not really." I smiled to show that I didn't mind. The irony was, I honestly didn't mind, or not in the way they imagined. In my least charitable moments, I'd think about these women, *It's not that I couldn't have married your husbands; it's that I didn't want to.* But it was a rare married woman who was able to believe that a single woman had any choice in the matter of her own singleness. I shifted on the bench. "Jeanette, am I right that you and Frank were in Sheboygan for the Fourth of July? That must have been wonderful."

"Well, the way Frank's mother scolded Katie and Danny, you'd think she'd never been around children before." Jeanette shook her head. "Just a broken record of 'Put that down, quit running around,' when why were we there but for them to run around? And Frank was one of six growing up, but he claims she was even-tempered back then."

"That's hard," I said.

"Oh, but you're lucky having the company of other adults, Jeanette," Rose said. "When Wade and I took the kids up to La Crosse, he spent so much time fishing, I felt like a widow. I said to him, 'Wade, if you're not careful, your son won't remember his daddy's face.' "

Jeanette chuckled, and so did I, to be pleasant, though the remark made me think of my mother and grandmother—actual widows—and of how much I'd have preferred to be at the house in Riley with them instead of sitting with these two women. Or I'd rather have been working on my papier-mâché characters—I was halfway through Babar (the tricky part was his trunk) and hadn't started on Yertle the Turtle—or I'd rather have been sitting alone with a pen and a pad of paper, figuring out plans for my house.

"Alice, am I right that you haven't had a serious beau since that tall fellow?" Rose said. "Remind me of his—"

"Simon." Again, I tried to smile agreeably, and then I did it, I gave her what I was sure she wanted—some admission of failure on my part—because I hoped it would get her to drop the subject. "I guess I'm in a dry spell," I said.

"Frank has a real good-looking coworker at the DA's office," Jeanette said.

"Jeanette, that's not nice to set up Alice with a felon," Rose said.

Jeanette swatted her. "You know that isn't what I mean. He's another lawyer, and he owns a super place over in Orchard Ridge. You wouldn't mind an iguana, would you?"

"I'm not sure if I'm the reptile type." I stood. "I'm just getting a bit more wine. Do either of you need anything?"

"When you come back, remind me to tell you about the new principal at Katie's school," Jeanette said. "He's a big, tall fellow, and he has the shortest little Chinese wife."

I nodded several times and held up my empty glass, as if to offer proof that I wasn't walking away because I found them intolerable.

On the deck, I passed Dena and Charlie Blackwell just as Dena set her fingertips on his forearm. *Good for her,* I thought. Once inside the house, I used the first-floor powder room, and on my way out, I almost collided with Tanya, the older of the Hickens' two daughters.

She held up a hardcover book. "Will you read this to me?" It was *Madeline's Rescue,* the one where Madeline falls in the Seine and is saved by a dog.

I looked around. There were a few adults in the kitchen, including Kathleen Hicken, Tanya's mother, but we were out of their view, and I doubted anyone would notice my absence. "Sure," I said.

We sat on the living room couch, Tanya next to me. She was a fair-haired little girl with a bob and large brown eyes. "Do you know my name?" I asked. "I'm Miss Alice. And you're Tanya, aren't you?"

She nodded.

"And how old are you?" I asked.

"Five and one quarter."

"Five and one quarter! Does that mean your birthday is in April?"

"It's April twenty-third," she said. "Lisa's birthday is January fourth, but she's only two years old." Lisa was the Hickens' other daughter.

"My birthday's in April, too," I said. "It's on the sixth, seventeen days before yours." I opened the book and began reading: " 'In an old house in Paris that was covered with vines—' " I paused. Tanya had squirmed closer to me, as if hopeful that she might be able to climb inside the book. It was an impulse I understood well. "I bet you know what comes next," I said, and I repeated, " 'In an old house in Paris that was covered with vines—' "

"—'Lived twelve little girls in two straight lines,' " Tanya said.

" 'They left the house at half past nine / In two straight lines, in rain or shine. / The smallest one was—' "

"—'Madeline,' " Tanya cried.

I turned the page, which featured an illustration of Madeline falling over the bridge. "Uh-oh," I said.

"She doesn't drown," Tanya told me reassuringly.

We kept reading, and when we got to the next page, Tanya added, "They name the dog Genevieve."

She continued to inject these comments, either editorial or explanatory—"The fat lady is mean," "Genevieve has puppies"—and when we'd gotten to the end, she said, "Will you read it again?"

I glanced at my watch. "All right, and then I should go back out and talk to the grown-ups. Your daddy's grilling the meat for dinner, isn't he?"

"I'm having fish sticks with tartar sauce."

"Doesn't that sound fancy," I said.

As if comforting me, helping me to not be intimidated, Tanya said, "No, tartar sauce is like mayonnaise," and I decided that I liked her even more.

We had neared the end of our second run-through of *Madeline's Rescue* when Charlie Blackwell appeared in the archway of the living room. I looked up, made eye contact with him, smiled, and continued reading. It didn't seem that what Tanya and I were doing required explanation, and besides, I believed that the secret of interacting with children—or it appeared to be a secret, based on the behavior of some parents—was that all you did was talk to them in a normal way. You didn't let yourself be distracted by someone else, you didn't perform above their heads, using them as a prop, nor did you coddle and indulge them. You paid attention, but not inordinately.

He didn't leave, though. I could feel him standing there watching us, and when we got to the last page, he set down his beer can and applauded. This applause concealed the sound of Tanya farting, which I was glad for, because she seemed self-aware enough, despite her age, that farting in front of a tall, unfamiliar man might have embarrassed her. "I have to go potty," she murmured, and slid off the couch, darting around Charlie Blackwell in the threshold.

"I scare her off?" He had a bit of a drawl, not the flat Wisconsin accent but something at once twangier and more educated.

"I think she had somewhere to go," I said.

"Then I guess you just lost your excuse for hiding out." He took a sip of beer and grinned.

"I'm not hiding out. We were reading a story."

"Is that right?" He was undeniably handsome, but his bearing was cocky in a way I didn't like: He was just over six feet, athletic-looking, and a little sunburned, with thick, dry, wavy light brown hair of the sort that wouldn't move if he shook his head. He also had mischievous eyebrows and a hawk nose with wide nostrils, as if he was flaring them at all times. This lent him an air of impatience that I imagined enhanced his stature in the view of some people—implying that he had other, more interesting places to go, that his attention to you would be limited.

"Sometimes I find that the company of children compares favorably to the company of adults," I said wryly.

"Touché." He didn't seem at all offended—he still was grinning—but I immediately felt remorseful because I knew I'd been rude.

"Or maybe it's that I don't always have much to say around adults," I said.

"Not having much to say doesn't stop most people." His expression was impish. "Not me, anyway."

His self-mockery caught me off guard, and I smiled. As I stood, planning to return to the backyard, I said, "I should introduce myself. I'm Alice Lindgren."

"Oh, I know who you are. You think I'd forget the name of a girl who refuses to go on a date with me?"

"I didn't—" I paused, flustered. "That was years ago. I was involved with someone. It wasn't personal."

"I thought maybe you'd heard some terrible rumor. Or, better yet, some terrible truth." He grinned; clearly, he was accustomed to being considered charming.

"If there are terrible truths about you circulating, you might want to take care of them before running for office." I could have played it cool and pretended I didn't know who he was, but I didn't see the point. Everyone at the barbecue knew who he was, whether or not we'd met him before. And he knew we knew; otherwise, he'd have introduced himself when I had.

"Before I run for office, huh?" he said. "Word travels fast."

"Madison is a pretty small town."

"Yet we've never met until now. How do you explain *that*?"

I shrugged. "Have you lived here that long? I was under the impression— Isn't your family more from Milwaukee?"

"Au contraire, mademoiselle. I'm a Madison native. Went to kindergarten and first grade at Duncan Country Day and came back for part of eighth grade."

"Oh, I teach at Liess," I said. "I'm the librarian."

"Aha! I thought you showed authority when you were reading. Cliff and Kathleen's little girl knew just who to ask, huh?"

"Now do you believe I wasn't hiding out?"

"There was a boy on my street growing up who went to Liess," Charlie said. "Norm Barker, but we called him Ratty. He was a good kid. Real pale face and pink, quivery nose, but a good kid. I don't think I've laid eyes on the guy since 1952."

"I suspect the school has changed since Ratty's time."

Charlie grinned. "You mean it's not lily-white anymore?"

"Not exactly." There was a silence, and I suppose it was to fill it—it was in the interest of preventing Charlie from implying that Liess's non-lily-whiteness was a bad thing (I didn't know if he would imply this, but I didn't want to run the risk)—that I announced, "I bought a house yesterday."

He raised his eyebrows. "No kidding? Just you, not . . . ?" Not at all surreptitiously, he glanced at the ring finger of my left hand.

I ignored the question. "It's on McKinley. If you know where Roney's Hardware is, it's behind that a couple streets."

"Congratulations—way to get yourself a little piece of the American dream." He held up his own left hand, high-five-style; to slap it required walking toward him, which, a little self-consciously, I did. Our hands hit firmly, a satisfying slap, and he said, "It's in decent shape? The pipes and the roof and all that jazz?"

"It seems all right, although the inspector hasn't gone through yet." I tapped my knuckles against the wall. "Knock on wood."

"You run into any problems, I'd be happy to take a look." He paused. "Not that I know a damn thing about house maintenance, but I'm trying to impress you. Is it working?"

Although I laughed, I felt a clenching in my stomach. No. This barbecue was about Dena's interest in Charlie Blackwell, not mine.

And then he said, "How about if you let me take you out for dinner next week to celebrate life, liberty, and the pursuit of the ten percent mortgage rate—you free Tuesday?"

"Oh, the rate isn't nearly that bad anymore," I said. "It's closer to seven percent."

"What, the other fellow's still in the picture?" His voice remained game, but I could tell he was rattled that I hadn't immediately accepted his invitation—I could tell by the way the corners of his smile collapsed a little. "You want me to challenge him to a duel, that's what you're trying to say?"

I had no desire to hurt Charlie Blackwell's feelings. I attempted to sound as sincere as possible when I said, "Unfortunately, I have a busy few weeks coming up—lots of lesson plans."

"You can't do better than that? Lesson plans in July, hell, that's on the order of needing to wash your hair."

"It's not you," I said. "It's really not." We were standing a few feet apart, and I was tempted to set my palm on his cheek. He was more vulnerable, less smug, than I had initially thought. Then I did close the space between us, but all I touched was his elbow, through his pink oxford shirt. This close to him, I could sense his clean soapy warmth, the way he smelled of beer and summer. I tilted my head. "Should we go back to the party?"

I HAD THOUGHT I'd leave shortly after the food was served, but we started a game of charades that was lengthy and quite a lot of fun and, just before my team's last turn, Dena pressed up against me, her lips at my ear, and said, "I'm gonna be sick." I pulled her arm around my neck and placed my own arm at her waist, and I walked us briskly into the house; at the two steps leading up to the deck, she stumbled a little, and I hoped that the other guests were preoccupied by the game. It was after nine o'clock, still over eighty degrees and only now getting dark. The mosquitoes were out, but Kathleen Hicken had lit a few citronella candles that were semi-successfully keeping them at bay.

In the first-floor bathroom, I lifted the toilet seat and said, "Lean over it." Already, Dena had arranged herself so she was supine on the floor, her head as far from the bowl as possible. "Come on, Dena," I said. "You need to cooperate."

"How is it we're thirty-one years old and neither of us has a husband or children?" she slurred. "I was supposed to have *three* children by now. Mindy and Alexander and— What was I planning to call the other one?"

"I don't remember," I said.

"Don't *tell* me that." She was as petulant as my students, the first- or second-graders, when it had been too long since their last snack. "You do remember!"

"Tracy?" I said.

"Tracy's not a special name."

"Dena, if you're going to throw up, you need to lean over the toilet. Can you take my hand and I'll lift you?" Dena hadn't gone up for charades in several turns, but even so, if she was this drunk, I was surprised not to have noticed outside. In an uncharacteristic act of compliance, she raised both her arms, and I tugged on them until she was sitting up. "Scoot your behind forward," I said.

"You haven't even been married once," she said.

"You know what, Dena, I'm all right with that."

She looked at me, her eyes glassy. "But you've been pregnant. Do you ever wish you'd kept the baby?" It had been only a couple of years earlier that I'd finally told Dena about my long-ago abortion; she was the first person I'd ever mentioned it to, and she seemed to see it as considerably less significant than I did. She said, "At TWA, I knew a girl who had three."

In the Hickens' bathroom, I said, "Dena, do you want me to help you here or not?"

"Did I ever tell you, when you were dating Simon, I used to picture him having a really long, thin penis. Because, you know, he was such a long, thin person."

This was not actually inaccurate, but I wasn't going to give her the satisfaction of saying so.

"Have you ever noticed," she continued, "that every time we see Rose Trommler, she's either gained or lost twenty pounds?"

"She does look a little heavy tonight," I admitted.

"It's like Superman going into the phone booth. She walks out of the room a size six, and she walks back in a size twelve." Dena belched then, and I was crouched so near her that it was a warm, sour wind on my face.

"Come on, Dena! Be considerate. Should I wait outside?"

"Here it comes," she said, and at last she did lean properly over the toilet bowl. We both were quiet.

Perhaps a minute had passed, and I said, "It's Theresa. That's your other daughter's name. I just remembered."

Dena seemed about to respond, but instead, she belched again, a smaller belch that seemed unequal as a harbinger to the monstrous chunky gush that erupted from inside her. I held her hair back and looked away as she finished retching. Working with children had made me less squeamish—they were constantly presenting their grubby hands to you, having accidents—but at some point, disgusting was still disgusting. Especially with an adult woman.

I flushed the toilet, and when the water had resettled, Dena spat a few times into it. Her voice was matter-of-fact, already more sober, when she said, "Charlie Blackwell doesn't like me." She stood, turned on the faucet, cupped one hand beneath the stream, and brought her hand to her mouth. When she'd swallowed, she said, "He seems like a guy you'd meet on the East Coast more than someone from around here. Real full of himself."

"I just talked to him briefly," I said.

"Another Saturday night down the crapper, huh?" She almost but didn't quite smile.

"This isn't the time to analyze your life," I said. "Let me thank the Hickens and I'll drive us home."

"I need to lie down." She opened the bathroom door, and I followed her into the living room. The Madeline book was still on the sofa, and

I moved it to an ottoman. I would have preferred for us to leave instead of me waiting while Dena passed out, which I felt reflected badly on both of us.

But Kathleen Hicken seemed practically tickled when I found her in the kitchen and told her that Dena wasn't feeling well and was resting. "Must be the sign of a successful party," Kathleen said.

"I'll give her half an hour," I said.

"Oh, jeez, leave her until morning." Kathleen waved a hand through the air. "You don't want to wrestle her into bed by yourself."

"Really?" I bit my lip. "If you honestly don't mind, then I can walk home tonight and give her car keys to you so she has them tomorrow."

"Well, she won't need an alarm clock." Kathleen smiled as she wiped down the counter with a rag. "The girls will make sure she's awake before the rooster crows."

IN THE YARD, the party seemed to be breaking up. Most people were standing, some had already taken off, and I joined the other women who were carrying in the bone-laden paper plates, the bowls of chips and empty wineglasses and beer cans. A few minutes later, when I went to thank Kathleen before leaving, I said, "Are you sure about Dena?" and she said, "Alice, don't give it a thought."

I thanked Cliff, too, collected my bag, peeked in at Dena—she was lying on her side, snoring—and walked out the front door; I lived about three quarters of a mile west of the Hickens. I had gone half a block when I heard quick footsteps behind me. I turned, and over my shoulder, I saw Charlie Blackwell. "Got somewhere better to be?" he asked.

"I'm pretty sure things were winding down," I said.

"Fair enough. Can I offer you a ride?"

It *was* buggy out. I tried to scrutinize his face, which, in the glow cast by the streetlight a few yards away, was both flushed and sallow.

"How many drinks have you had?" I asked.

"You're certainly direct."

Since high school, I had never ridden in a car with a driver who might be so much as tipsy. "You know what?" I said. "I'll walk. But it was nice to meet you." When I turned around again, Charlie stayed beside me.

"You've at least got to let me escort you. There's only so much rejection a fellow can withstand in one night, Alice."

We continued walking, and he said, "I take it you're not afraid of the dark?"

I gave him a sidelong glance. "Are you joking?"

"I'll tell you a secret, but you've got to promise not to repeat it. You promise?" Without waiting for my reply, he said, "I'm *terrified* of the dark. Scares the living bejesus out of me. My parents have a place up in Door County, and I'd rather chew off my own leg than spend the night there alone."

"What are you so afraid of?"

"That's just it—you have no idea what's out there! But hey, you know what? I'm not scared right now, and it's because you're beside me. Dainty as you are, you seem extraordinarily capable. If something terrible befell us, I'm sure you'd take care of it."

"Do you always lavish compliments on women you hardly know?"

"Hardly know you? Good God, I thought we were old friends by now." He brought his hand to his heart as if wounded, then made a rapid recovery. "Here's what I've got: Number one, you just bought a house by yourself, which means you're independent and financially solvent. Number two, you're already getting your school papers together even though it's July, which means you're responsible. Or you're a liar, but I'm giving you the benefit of the doubt." He was raising one finger for each point. "Number three, you're a crackerjack charades player." This was untrue; my enactment of *The Sound of Music* had been particularly abysmal. "Number four, either you have a boyfriend but are pretending not to because of your overpowering attraction to me, or you don't have a boyfriend and are letting me down easy. Whichever it is, these are challenges I'm willing to surmount. In conclusion, I know all about you." As we walked, I could feel Charlie looking at me, grinning. "I understand you, I sense a long and happy future for the two of us, and I'm sure you sense it, too. Oh, but you have to like baseball—you like baseball?"

"I wouldn't say I'm a die-hard fan."

"You will be." Charlie swung an imaginary bat through the air. "The Brewers are finally pulling it together. A lot of young talent on the team, and you mark my words, this could be a winning season."

"Truthfully," I said, "the only reason I went to the Hickens' party tonight was to help Dena catch your eye."

"Dena?" He sounded puzzled. "You mean the divorcée?"

"Who told you that? No, never mind—you're as bad as Rose and Jeanette. Dena's a wonderful person. She was a flight attendant for more than five years, and she's traveled the country."

"Yet she still hasn't learned to hold her liquor."

"She didn't have much to eat," I said. "That's why."

"I'll tell you what," he said. "You can look at her face and know she's done some hard living, but who am I to throw stones? She seemed like a perfectly nice girl. But she does not, if you catch my meaning, strike me as marriage material for a rising star of the Republican Party."

His arrogance was really rather extraordinary; it was amusing, and it was also irritating. "I'm a registered Democrat," I said. "That's something you might want to include in your dossier on me. And I have to say that you're remarkably confident for someone who's about to run against a forty-year incumbent."

Rather than being insulted, Charlie appeared delighted. "I always appreciate someone who's done her research. You know who does seem like ideal wife material?" He pointed toward me.

"You're ridiculous," I said.

"How is it that a woman as—as *lovely* as you hasn't been snapped up by now?"

"Maybe I don't want to be snapped up," I said. "Did that occur to you?" Needless to say, I wanted it very much: I wanted to get married and sleep in a bed with a man at night, I wanted to hold his hand while walking downtown, to prepare the meals for him that were too much trouble for one person—roast beef, and lasagna. I wanted children, and I knew I would be a good mother, not perfect but good, and I'd already decided I wouldn't let my daughters have hair longer than chin-length because I'd seen in my students how it made them vain, the maintenance of one's locks as a family project. Still, despite all this, it felt gratifying to lie to Charlie Blackwell.

"Don't tell me you're one of those feminists," he said. "You couldn't be, because you're too pretty."

I stared at him. "That's not even worth dignifying, and frankly, I'm not sure why my romantic status is your business."

"Oh, it's most definitely my business. It's my business because I'm bewitched by you."

Part of the reason he was frustrating was that his comments were so close to what I wanted to hear from a man, but I wanted them to be real. I yearned for genuine emotion, not this banter and jest.

When we arrived in front of the house where I lived, Charlie said, "I think you ought to invite me in for a cup of coffee. There's a rumor that I'm drunk."

I shook my head in exasperation and let him follow me into the small entry hall and up the carpeted stairs to the second floor. He stood behind me as I unlocked the door to my apartment. In the kitchen, I went to turn on the coffeemaker when he said, "You got any beer? Because if it's all the same to you, I'd prefer it."

I pulled two cans of Pabst from the refrigerator and passed him one. When we'd pulled the tabs off, he tipped his can toward mine. "To Alice," he said. "A woman of beauty, virtue, and outstanding taste in alcohol."

"Has anyone ever told you you're relentless?" I asked, and then I watched in horror as he walked out of the kitchen, down the hall, and toward the bedroom where I worked on my book characters.

"Please don't go in—" I started to say, but he was well ahead of me and obviously not listening. Besides, the door to the room was open. When I caught up with him, he was standing in the room's center, turning to look at the papier-mâché figures one by one.

"They're for the library where I work," I said, and my voice was loud in the silence. I couldn't imagine how he'd react to the characters or even how I wanted him to. He was not, I reminded myself, the intended audience. He was quiet for a full minute, and then, in a completely serious tone, he said, "These are amazing."

I swallowed.

"I recognize Ferdinand." He pointed to the bull with flowers woven around his horns. "And that's Mike Mulligan and his steam shovel, Mary Anne."

"They're not exactly to scale," I said.

"I was madly in love with Mary Anne." He grinned. "I just knew they'd be able to dig that cellar in one day. Oh, and Eloise—I always thought she was a pain in the ass."

"Girls like her more than boys."

"Who's that?" He motioned with his chin toward the corner of the room, where bright green leaves—I'd cut them from a bolt of lurid silk fabric—hung atop a brown trunk.

"*The Giving Tree,*" I said. "It's a book published when we were in high school, assuming— Well, how old are you?"

"Thirty-one," he said. "Class of 1964."

"Me, too. That's the year *The Giving Tree* came out. It's my favorite book. I've probably read it seventy times, and the end still always makes me cry." Just describing the book, I could hear my voice thickening with emotion, and I felt embarrassed.

"Why would you want to cry seventy times?" Charlie said, but his tone was sweet, not mocking. He gestured to his right. "Who's the Chinaman?"

"That's Tikki Tikki Tembo. He's a boy who falls down a well, and everyone who tries to get help for him has to repeat his name, which is really long. Tikki Tikki Tembo is actually the short version. His whole name is— Trust me, it's long."

"Now you have to say it."

"Really?"

He nodded.

I took a breath. I rarely talked about my job when I was out on dates—though this was not, of course, a date. "Tikki Tikki Tembo-no sa rembo-chari bari ruchi-pip peri pembo," I said, and when I finished, we were smiling at each other.

"One more time," he said. I complied, and he said, "That's most impressive."

I bowed.

"Those kids you teach must be nuts about you," he said.

"Well, I'm no fool. Students start rebelling against their teachers in junior high, but in elementary school, they're fighting to sit on your lap."

He regarded me—he was still in the center of the room, and I was just inside the door—and the only way I can describe the expression on his face is to say it was one of enchantment; I had no idea why, but Charlie Blackwell found me enchanting. And I recognized, with a pang that was at once sorrow, remorse, and the first stirring of hope, that it was a way no one had looked at me since Andrew Imhof. In the last fourteen years, I had been on plenty of dates, I'd been in relationships, I'd even been proposed to, but there was nobody I'd enchanted.

"Alice, what would you do if I kissed you right now?" Charlie said.

We looked at each other, and the room was filled with shyness and promise. After a long time, I said, "If you want to find out, I guess you'll have to try."

I'D MET SIMON Törnkvist at a shoe store when I was twenty-six; he was buying clogs, and I was buying Dr. Scholl's sandals. He was six-four and slender, wore John Lennon–style glasses with gold frames and round lenses, and had floppy blond hair, a wispy blond beard, a droopy left eye contiguous to a scar running from the outer tip of his cheekbone to below his ear, and an amputated left hand. His injuries were from Vietnam, which I guessed before he told me. Because he'd been left-handed, his writing looked childish; this was something I learned later.

As we sat in the store waiting for the salesman to return with shoes, I remarked on the unseasonably warm March weather. After we'd made our purchases, we stood on the sidewalk outside the store, continuing to talk. Perhaps ten minutes passed, and then he held up his left arm. He wore a long-sleeved rust-colored velour shirt, and the sleeve was folded under his elbow and pinned at his shoulder. He said, "Does this bother you?"

"No," I said.

"Then would you like to see a movie sometime?"

We went to *The Godfather,* and I made sure to sit on his right side, in case he wanted to hold my hand, but he didn't try. Afterward, we ate dinner at a pub on Doty Street, and he said he'd found the movie overrated, though he did not explain in what way. He was a year younger than I was—this surprised me, because upon meeting people, I had a silly tendency to think of those who were shorter than I was as younger and those who were taller as older—and he was working as the dispatcher for a plumbing company while taking classes at the university. He hadn't decided on a major yet but was inclined, he said, toward philosophy or political science. He had grown up on a pea farm outside Oshkosh.

I didn't find our conversation very interesting, but the entire time, I felt a sort of internal shuddering, as if my ribs were about to collapse and I had to concentrate fiercely to hold them aright. I recognized this sensation for what it was: physical attraction. Simon drove me home (I had wondered if he might have on his steering wheel what we'd called, growing up, a "necker's knob"—Dena's grandfather, who'd lost his right hand in a tractor accident, had had one—but Simon did not and was a perfectly competent driver with one hand), and outside my apartment I scooted across the seat and kissed his cheek. I had never made the first move, but the fact that Simon was a little younger emboldened me.

He seemed surprised but receptive, and we curled toward each other, he wrapped his right arm around me, and I hoped he would set his left arm on me, too, the stub, but he did not. I know now—I didn't know it then, but years later, I read an article—that there are amputee fetishists, and while denying such an inclination in myself feels rather defensive, I sincerely don't think that's what it was. I recognize in retrospect that I wouldn't have been attracted to him if not for his injuries. But it wasn't the injuries, per se. It was that if he set his handless arm on my back, it would be an act of trust, he would make himself vulnerable in order to be closer to me, and it would give me the opportunity to show I was worthy of the risk he'd taken. Unjudgmentally, I would care for him.

The question he'd asked outside the shoe store notwithstanding, Simon himself didn't appear all that self-conscious about his wounds. He also had scars, as I discovered over our next several dates, on the left side of his chest. In Phuoc Long Province, in the early winter of 1970, his company had been ambushed, and he had been hit by a rocket-propelled grenade. He was matter-of-fact about this, as about most everything; he referred more than once to the Vietnam War as "a bill of goods," but he expressed his political views infrequently and succinctly. He was certainly not the first person I knew to have fought in Vietnam. More than a dozen boys from my class at Benton County Central High School had gone over, and Bradley Skilba had been killed in Tay Ninh in September 1968; in 1969 Yves Haakenstad had come home in a wheelchair, paralyzed below the waist; Randall Larson had died northeast of Katum in 1970. Sometimes I thought of how things might have been different if Andrew Imhof had gone over also—not an impossibility—and if it had been in Vietnam that he had died instead of at the intersection of De Soto Way and Farm Road 177. Probably it would have been easier for his family, I imagined; it would have felt like an honorable tragedy and not just a waste. Clearly, it would have been easier for me, without the suffocating guilt. But I'd still miss him, he'd still be gone, and in some ways, it would be worse to know it had happened in another country, that he'd been so far from home; in the end, it didn't really seem a better sadness.

The first few times Simon and I had sex, it was flushed and protracted and new and exciting. Since Pete Imhof, I had slept only with Wade Trommler, whom I'd dated for two years in college; although we'd broken up when I turned down his marriage proposal the summer before we were seniors, I would always be grateful to Wade for his kindness and tenderness, for being so different from Pete. In the time since Wade, I had gone on dates here and there, and I'd often been able to sense when certain fellows would have asked me out, had I given them encouragement. But these men seemed to me, as Wade had, mostly innocent, boyish.

During my senior year in high school, I'd stopped thinking of marriage as my birthright. It wasn't just that I no longer considered myself inherently deserving or that I no longer believed I was looked after by the universe. It was also that I would not want to marry a man unless I could show myself to him truly—I had no interest in tricking anyone—but I couldn't imagine showing myself to most men, revealing myself as someone more complicated than I seemed. If thinking of the exertion and explanations that would require discouraged me, it also made me calm. I didn't work myself up, as other women I knew did, panicking over finding Mr. Right. I accepted that the years to come would unfold in their way, that I could control only a few aspects of them. To remain alone did not seem to me a terrible fate, no worse than being falsely joined to another person.

Then I met Simon, who was a variation I hadn't anticipated. He represented neither solitude nor phony bliss but some third possibility, a redemptive coupling. I thought this had to be the next best thing to being accepted completely—to completely accept someone else. I still partly agree with this notion, though the rest of what I thought about Simon, about my own capacity to take care of him, I now see as vain and wrongheaded.

We dated for eleven months, during which time we lived a mile and a half apart and saw each other twice a week. I was busy teaching, he was taking classes and working at the plumbing company, but that should have been another sign: It wasn't that I was consciously unwilling to turn my schedule upside down for him, more that the thought never occurred to me. Although he had a younger sister who was married and a younger brother who was mentally retarded and lived with his parents on the farm, I didn't ever meet anyone in his family. I did, however, after about three months, take him to have Sunday lunch in Riley. At the end of the visit, though the subject of Vietnam had not come up, my father—himself a veteran—shook his hand and said, "Young men like you are a credit to this country." In the car back to Madison, Simon said, "Your father is painfully naive."

Was I some kind of automaton? That's what I wonder now, not just about that moment when I didn't respond, but about all my time with Simon. But it appeared to be a relationship, it had all the contours and rituals, so who was to say it wasn't? I made dinner for him Wednesdays, we went to a movie every Saturday night at the Majestic (he was the only person I knew besides my friend Rita Alwin, the French teacher, whom I never had to convince to see a foreign film), and following the movie, we went back to my place and had sex before he drove home around midnight. After the first few episodes, I did not climax regularly with Simon, but I attributed the erraticness more to an early abundance of excitement on my part than to a subsequent failure on his. We soon became used to each other, and if he was grumpy, then his grumpiness was a guiding force; to accommodate him was an opportunity. And I didn't think this because of generational notions about gender, not really. I thought it because I was me, because he was him.

My parents seemed pleased. My mother wouldn't bring herself to ask directly when we might get engaged, but she'd say, "Do you think if Daddy could help Simon get a job at the bank, would he be interested in that?" Or "Ginny Metzger told me that Arlette found a wedding dress with real lacework for seventy dollars at a bridal shop in Milwaukee." Meanwhile, all my grandmother said was "He's like Mr. Lloyd, isn't he?" This was a reference to the licentious one-armed art teacher in *The Prime of Miss Jean Brodie,* and I knew it meant Simon had made an unfavorable impression on my grandmother. I did not realize how unfavorable for several months.

At Christmas that year—it was 1973—I was ironing a shirt in my grandmother's room while she sat on her bed reading when she said, "You simply can't marry that friend of yours." She wasn't even looking at me as she spoke.

I turned. "You mean Simon?"

"He's a wet blanket."

I was taken aback. "Granny, he's been through a lot."

She shook her head. "I'm not saying he hasn't known difficulty, but I'll bet he was a wet blanket even when he was a boy."

"Are you suggesting I end things with him?"

My grandmother considered the question, then said, "I suppose I am."

I was silent.

"With Dena down in Kansas City, who'll give you a piece of their mind if I don't?" my grandmother said. "Don't be offended. I'm only thinking of your best interest."

"Maybe you don't want me to get married," I said, and the part I did not say was *to a man.* My grandmother and I never discussed Gladys

Wycomb, not even before or after my grandmother's visits to Chicago. Following everything that had happened in the fall of 1963, my grandmother and I had wordlessly made peace—there was much I was indebted to her for—and over time, our interactions had returned to normal. But it was a normality that sometimes had to be attended to and guarded. I tried to be less judgmental, more deferential and considerate, than I had been as a teenager, and the very fact of my trying was evidence that things between us would never again be effortless.

"Why would I not want you to marry?" My grandmother scoffed. "That's absurd. Marriage is no picnic, but it compares favorably to the alternative. I'll tell you what the problems are with your beau. There are two."

I felt torn, tempted to stop her before she could go any further, and also extremely curious to know what she thought.

"First," she said, "he's dull. He's not lively. Now, plenty of women marry dull men, but your Simon isn't kind, either, and that's a terrible combination. Marrying a man who's dull and nice is fine, or a man who's cruel but fascinating—some people have an appetite for that. But marrying a man who's ponderous *and* unkind is a recipe for unhappiness."

As I listened to her, I felt my face flushing, and it wasn't from the iron. "You scarcely know him," I said.

"I'm a keen observer of human behavior. You dote on that young man, and he's a cold fish. Listen—if you choose to marry him, I'll sit in the church smiling, because I'll know it's a decision you made with your eyes wide open. But if I'd never said a word, I'd wonder if I could have prevented a great deal of heartache."

"Well, you can't be held responsible now." I used a light tone, I meant to show I was willing to forgive her harsh remarks, but apparently, she didn't yet wish to be forgiven.

"It's very clear to me that this is about the Imhof boy," she said. "You want to trade a dead boy for an injured man, and if I thought it would work, I'd let you try. It isn't immoral. But it's unrealistic. Misfortunes don't cancel each other out."

I thought, of course, that she was wrong about Simon. I thought it almost completely, then less so as days passed and her words continued to echo in my head; I remembered them one evening after dinner at an Italian restaurant, when I stood on tiptoe to kiss Simon before we climbed in the car, and he turned his head and said, "Your breath is too garlicky."

Still, we continued to spend time together twice a week, and on a Wednesday night a month before our one-year anniversary, as I dished creamed chicken onto plates at my apartment, I said, "Do you ever think of us getting married?"

The chicken was steaming, and Simon had removed his glasses and was rubbing at the lenses with a napkin. He said, "Not really."

I knew right away that both the conversation and our relationship were over, but the situation seemed to demand that I persist.

"Even though we've been dating for almost a year?"

"I don't know if I believe in marriage." He put his glasses back on. "It seems like a doomed institution. But I do know I definitely don't want children."

I'm not sure what expression I made in this moment (as much as I felt disappointed and caught off guard, I also felt just plain stupid—shouldn't I have found this out about him months earlier, shouldn't I have done my research?), but Simon said, "I take it you do want kids."

"Simon, I'm a teacher. I wouldn't work with them if I didn't enjoy being around them."

He set his hand on mine. "Let's talk about this another time."

Two weeks later, over the phone, he said, "I'm not sure we're compatible in the long term," and I said, "I think you might be right." In this way, we completed perhaps the most bloodless breakup of all time. When I was home next, my grandmother said, "I know in my bones you made the right decision." Because I didn't want her to see me as pitiable, I simply nodded, never revealing that the decision had hardly been mine.

WITH CHARLIE AT my apartment until late the night before, I had gotten so little sleep that by the time I arrived in Riley early Sunday afternoon, I was giddy and guilt-ridden and exhausted; a headache had formed in a band above my eyes.

I noticed that my mother's car, a cream-colored Ford Galaxie, wasn't in the driveway. When I let myself in to the house, my grandmother was seated on the living room couch—my skinny, ageless grandmother, sustained on a diet of nicotine and literature—and she offered her cheek to me to kiss. "I think your mother has a secret," she said.

"A good or bad one?"

My grandmother's features formed an expression of both concentration and confusion, the sort you'd make if you were tasting a spice whose name you couldn't remember. "I believe she might be having a romance with Lars Enderstraisse."

"Mr. Enderstraisse the mailman?"

"He's a decent-looking fellow. A bit portly, but he probably doesn't eat right, living on his own."

"You think Mom is *dating* Mr. Enderstraisse? Since when?" Mr. Enderstraisse had worked at the post office on Commerce Street since I was a child; he was a kind-seeming man with a walrus mustache and a rotund midsection.

"There's no need to work yourself up," my grandmother said. "Your mother is a mature woman, and she deserves to enjoy herself."

"But how certain are you?"

"She's been having lengthy phone conversations that she takes upstairs—to thwart my attempts at eavesdropping, I can only assume. And she runs mysterious errands. When I ask where she's been, she's quite vague."

"How does Mr. Enderstraisse figure into this?"

"That's where she is now. He has shingles, or so Dorothy claims, and she's taken him some cold soup."

"But if you know where she is, that's not a mysterious errand."

My grandmother frowned. "Don't sass me."

"I just meant—" I paused. "Granny, I might be having a romance, too."

She perked up immediately.

"But Dena had dibs on the guy first, so I have no idea what to do. I really like him, even though I just met him last night."

"Oh my word." My grandmother crossed one leg over the other. "Bring me an iced tea, if you would, and then you can tell me the whole story."

I poured iced tea for both of us from the pitcher in the refrigerator, carried the glasses back to the living room, and summarized the events of the previous night, skimming over Dena's intoxication and Charlie's extended visit to my apartment; I tried to imply, without saying it outright, that we'd bade each other farewell after he'd walked me home. I was genuinely uncertain what my grandmother's reaction would be, given her fondness for Dena. Never a particular Dena fan when I was growing up, my grandmother had developed a soft spot for her the summer I'd graduated from college. This was 1968, and my grandmother had announced to me one afternoon that she'd like to try marijuana; she was hearing a lot about it. I hadn't previously tried pot myself, and without enthusiasm, I'd approached Dena when she was next in town—as a stewardess, she could fly free into Milwaukee, then come to visit me in Madison or go home to Riley—and the time after that, when my parents were at a fish fry, the three of us sat in my grandmother's bedroom, smoking a joint. "While I'm having trouble seeing what all the fuss is about," my grandmother said, "I'm very grateful to you girls for satisfying my curiosity." When the joint was gone, she lit a normal cigarette.

After I finished my description of meeting Charlie, my grandmother took a sip of her iced tea. "That certainly is awkward for you and Dena."

"Do you think I shouldn't see him again?"

She set the glass down on a cork coaster on the end table. "I wouldn't rush to a decision. See how the situation evolves."

"I don't even know if he'll call, but meeting him made me feel hopeful—I can't really describe it."

"He was good company," my grandmother said.

Was it that simple? And if it was, why did it feel so rare? From outside, I heard the approach of my mother's car.

"Don't breathe a word about Lars Enderstraisse." My grandmother pinched her thumb and forefinger together and ran them across her mouth. "Zip your lip."

THAT NIGHT, MY grandmother had gone upstairs by eight P.M., and my mother and I sat in front of *The Six Million Dollar Man,* though neither of us was really watching: She was needlepointing an eyeglasses case, and I was flipping through my grandmother's latest issue of *Vogue.* During a commercial break, I turned to her. "Mom, if you ever want to start dating—"

Before I could go further, she said, "Where on earth did you get that idea?"

"I'm not saying you should or shouldn't, but if you did—if you feel like you're ready—no one will disapprove."

"Alice, think how your father would feel to hear you talk like that." She set down her needlepoint and walked out of the room, and as I was wondering how deeply I'd offended her, she returned with her left hand clenched in a fist. When she'd sat beside me again, she uncurled her fingers, revealing a gold brooch. "Can you sell this for me?"

It was shaped like a tree branch, the leaves encrusted with tiny diamonds, and one small round garnet—meant to resemble an apple, or perhaps a berry—hung down. I had never seen it before.

"It belonged to my mother, but I don't have any use for it," she said.

"It must be nice to have as a keepsake, though." My mother seemed to have so few tangible ties to her family that it was hard to understand why she'd get rid of one. She passed me the brooch, and I touched the garnet with my fingertip; it was cool and smooth. "You could wear it to church on Christmas," I said, and without warning, my mother burst into tears. "Mom, what's wrong?" I set my hand on her back. I had not seen my mother cry since shortly after my father's death.

"I've made such a mess of things," she said.

"What are you talking about?"

"I had a misapprehension from the beginning. But you want to give a young person the benefit of the doubt, and I thought it could be an opportunity to create a nest egg not just for Granny and me but for you, too, because you work so hard at the school. And he said the annual returns get up to three hundred percent."

"Who's he? Start at the beginning." Although an anxious tingle had risen on my skin, I felt that it was important for one of us to remain calm. "I want to help you, Mom, but I need to understand what's happened."

"It's a fellow about your age. He came by, and he was very nice, very intelligent."

"So you gave him some money?" I strove to keep emotion from my voice.

"I made a dreadful mistake." The tears seized her again, and I said, "Mom, it's okay. We'll sort it out. I just have to ask, how much did you give him?"

"From your father—from his insurance—" Her voice was shaky.

The tingling had turned into goose bumps covering my entire body. "Money from Dad's life insurance policy?" I asked, and she nodded. "Did you give him all of it?"

"Oh, honey, I wouldn't do that."

"Then how much?" It was astonishing to me that I sounded as neutral as I did.

"Originally, he asked for ten thousand dollars, but I told him I wouldn't recruit other investors. I said, 'I don't know about finances, and I won't pretend I do.' He said if I made a double investment, he'd make an exception for me, because most people have to recruit."

"So you gave him twice as much money?"

Tears pooled again in her eyes, and she said, "Alice, I'm so ashamed. I don't know what on earth I was thinking—I just—"

"Mom, please don't get upset. I'm wondering, was there anything you were buying? Was it stock, or real estate, or some kind of product?"

"It was an investment fund."

"I can't help thinking," I said slowly, "could it have been a pyramid scheme?"

"Oh, certainly not." For the first time in several minutes, my mother's tone was firm. "No, no. It was an investment fund, and the money would come back when new members joined."

"So maybe it still *will* make money—"

She was shaking her head. "He couldn't get enough people to join, but he had to pay the administrative costs."

"Who is this guy? This sounds incredibly fishy to me."

"I know, honey. I wish I didn't make the double investment, but if I'd encouraged my friends to do it, oh, I would feel so much worse now."

"So besides what's left of Dad's life insurance policy, are there other savings you have?"

"Heavens, Alice, Granny and I won't end up on the street, if that's what you're worried about. If worse comes to worst, we can take out a home equity loan. You know Daddy's bank will give us the most favorable rate, although to spare him the embarrassment, I'd have half a mind to go somewhere else. Oh, he'd be appalled at what I've done."

A home equity loan? I still couldn't figure out what she had left in savings, nor did I know how much their monthly expenses were, but I feared that if I forced my mother to provide numbers, it would undo her.

"You can't beat yourself up," I said. "You were trying to take care of you and Granny, and that's exactly what Dad would want you to do."

"He was such a responsible man. Do you know I get half his pension every month, and when I'm sixty-two, I'll get his social security as well?" This would be in 1987, which seemed so far away that it provided me with little comfort. "You mustn't mention anything to your grandmother," my mother was saying. "At her age, we can't have her worrying."

"Fine, but it sounds like this investment guy should go to prison. I know you're embarrassed, but I think you should report him."

An expression crossed my mother's face in this moment, a look of fake innocence I had never seen on her.

"We don't—" I hesitated. "We don't know him, do we?"

"Honey, that hardly matters."

"Mom, you need to tell me who it was."

"Riley is such a small town, and you know how people talk," she said, and I thought of having made a similar observation to Charlie Blackwell about Madison. But it was truer, much truer, of Riley. "After we sell the brooch, we'll see where that leaves us," my mother continued. "It's Victorian, you know, which means it's valuable. If I can make up some of what I lost, we'll pretend it never happened."

"Mom, who did you invest the money with?"

She did not seem angry at all, which was more than I could say for myself; she just seemed sad and tired. "I don't want to get anyone in trouble, do you understand? You can't tell a soul. I'm sure he didn't mean harm, but he was inexperienced, and he got ahead of himself." She seemed to consider a few more rationalizations, but in the end, she simply said, "It was Pete Imhof."

AFTER A FITFUL night in my childhood bed, I ate the bacon and eggs my mother prepared for breakfast, and we did not acknowledge our conversation of the night before; my grandmother was still asleep upstairs. When I finished breakfast, I read *The Riley Citizen,* and as soon as my mother left the kitchen, I leaped up and opened the drawer where she kept the phone book. He was listed, his number and an address on Parade Street. A few minutes later, I took off on foot; I told my mother that, driving into Riley the previous afternoon, I'd seen a blouse I liked in one of the windows downtown.

Given that it was a Monday, my going over there before five o'clock, when he'd be at work, didn't seem to serve much purpose, but I was so agitated that I was reluctant to be around my mother or grandmother. I'd walk by his place first, I thought, figure out exactly where it was, and then return in the afternoon to try to catch him before I left town. If I didn't speak to him, I'd need to stay another night, which I wasn't keen to do; among other reasons, I couldn't help wondering if Charlie Blackwell would call, and if he did, I wanted to be in Madison. (Courtship before the widespread use of answering machines, before voice mail or e-mail—how quaint it seems now.)

When thoughts of Charlie came to me, as they had repeatedly in the last twenty-four hours, I'd have the feeling of a pat of butter melting in a hot pan. Our initial kiss had lasted for several minutes, and eventually, we'd ended up sitting on the couch and then lying on it, me on my back with my head on the armrest, and him on top of me. We had talked and talked and kissed and kissed, his mouth warm and wet and familiar and new, and sometimes we'd just looked at each other, our faces ridiculously close together, and smiled. We both were old enough to know how unlikely this was to last or become anything genuine, but that probably made us enjoy it more, the awareness that it might only be these few hours. Lying beneath him, I felt tremendously happy.

Just past midnight, he said, "I think I'd better leave in the next five minutes, before I abandon my gentlemanly act and try to seduce you."

Although we both had on all our clothes, my bra had come unfastened along the way, and as he spoke, he had an erection. And certainly we could sleep together, people did that now, it was 1977. A diaphragm (not the one given to me by Gladys Wycomb but a newer version) sat inside a toiletry case in the cabinet beneath my bathroom sink, unused since Simon. But this was the first time in my life I'd been tempted to have sex with a man the night we met, and I was only half tempted—it would be like leapfrogging over the normal stages of getting acquainted. Besides, Dena would never speak to me again.

A little reluctantly, I said, "Maybe you should kiss me good night and ask if I'm free later this week."

"Hold on a second." He feigned shock. "You mean to tell me you can squeeze in a date in between all the library preparation?"

"That's not very nice." I turned my head to the side, glancing back at him from under my eyelashes. "I wanted to accept when you asked me out earlier. I just thought I shouldn't because of Dena."

"I'm glad you reconsidered." When I turned my head again, he was grinning, and the force of his grin was almost enough to obliterate the idea of Dena's wrath.

But he didn't ask me out again before he left, we didn't make a firm plan, and as soon as he was gone, I wished we had. I didn't specifically think that I liked Charlie Blackwell, but it was the same as wondering where to put my furniture in the house on McKinley before realizing I wanted the house itself. Except, I thought now, how could I buy a house when my mother's financial situation had become so precarious? Wouldn't I be better off keeping my money in savings in case the problem was even worse than I thought?

And what about Dena? As I headed east on Commerce Street, away from the Riley River, my betrayal of her seemed far starker without Charlie present to distract me. I needed to talk to her. First I needed to think of what to say, then I needed to talk to her. No, first I needed to figure out what was happening with Charlie, if he was nothing but a flirt, or if we really would see each other again, then I needed to think of what to say to Dena, *then* I needed to talk to her.

Walking up Commerce, I passed Jurec Brothers' butcher shop, Grady's Tavern, and Stromond's bakery, where, if you were under the age of twelve, they gave you a free sugar cookie in the shape of a dog bone. In the space that had once been occupied by the fabric shop, there was now a Chinese restaurant—a Chinese restaurant in Riley!—and I had heard that Ruth Hofstetter, the comely fabric-shop clerk whose single status into her late twenties had confused and saddened my mother and me, had later become the shop's proprietress before selling it altogether when she married a widowed farmer in Houghton. Ruth was probably in her early forties now, I thought, and the age difference between us struck me as significantly smaller than when I was in high school and she was twenty-seven or twenty-eight. It had occurred to me recently that I could marry a man in his forties or even his fifties, as I was pretty sure Ruth had, especially if I didn't marry anytime soon. And this seemed not so much objectionable as impossibly hard to fathom. How could you, if it was your first wedding, marry an old man? How could you still carry within yourself the you of your girlhood, your ideas of satin dresses and white lilies, yet be joined to a groom with fleshy hands, age spots, thinning gray hair? Dick Cimino had been forty-eight when Dena had married him, though in her case, that had sort of been the point, May-December, a sugar daddy to bestow on her gifts and attention.

The answer to how Ruth had done it, I supposed, was that she was older, too; if you married an older man, *you* were older, and you looked older. You were not so different from him. Or, inversely, he carried inside him a younger self, his droops and wrinkles felt like a costume.

Where Commerce crossed Colway Avenue, I could feel a shift in the neighborhood. Not that it was seedy, none of Riley was truly seedy, but there were more houses here with peeling paint, ratty indoor furniture on their front porches. The sun had gone behind a cloud, but it was still hot.

I turned onto Parade Street, checking the numbers. His address was a two-story structure with gray vinyl siding; it clearly had been built as apartments without ever having been a house. My heart beat rapidly as I tried the main door, which was not locked, and then I was standing in an entryway with gray walls, a blue linoleum floor, and a wooden staircase covered by a clear plastic runner. The hall smelled of old cigarette smoke. His door was along the left wall of the first floor, and I thought before I rang the bell that he would be home after all, because if you lived in a place this dingy, you probably didn't have a job, and then I thought that was a snobby observation on my part and no doubt incorrect, and then he opened the door.

He seemed surprised, but in a faintly amused way, to find me standing there. "Alice Lindgren," he said. "It's been a long time."

Although I was nervous, I was angry, too, and my anger guided me. "How could you?" I blurted out.

He actually smiled, which infuriated me more. He was wearing a white tank top, cutoff jeans, and flip-flops, and he had grown a dark, dense beard and gained perhaps forty pounds since I'd seen him last. (Once, getting milk shakes at Tatty's with Betty Bridges when I was home from college, I'd spotted him across the restaurant, sitting at the counter with his back to us, and I had hardly moved or spoken until he left half an hour later. Other than that, I had not laid eyes on him in nearly fourteen years.)

He ambled to the couch where it seemed he'd been sitting before—the television beside me was on, showing *The Price Is Right* (Pete Imhof watched *The Price Is Right*?), and on the coffee table in front of the couch was an incomplete *Riley Citizen* crossword puzzle with an uncapped pen lying sideways atop it and an ashtray, the smoke still rising from a just-stubbed cigarette. Only after he'd lit a fresh one, inhaled, and released smoke through his nostrils did he say, "Business deals go south all the time."

"Pete, it was clearly a scam!"

"Since when are you an expert on asset management?" He looked indignant, and for the first time, it occurred to me that this hadn't been intentional. He had gone to my mother because, presumably, he'd heard my father had died, he'd guessed she'd have received an inheritance, and he'd been trying to raise money for this scheme. But he really might have thought it would turn out to be profitable. Perhaps it hadn't been just to spite me.

"Whatever it was," I said, "you don't involve vulnerable people in a risky venture. My mother needs that money to live off, and to support my eighty-two-year-old grandmother."

"Alice, I lost out, too. Thirty-five grand, in fact, which is a lot more than anyone else."

"You need to repay my mother." I tried to sound firm and persuasive.

He snorted. "You can't squeeze blood from a turnip."

"Then find some other way to fix the situation."

"If I hear of an opportunity in the future she might be interested in—"

"Don't even think about contacting her again."

"You seem to be having trouble making up your mind." I glared at him, and he added, "Why don't you relax?" He extended the pack of cigarettes to me—they were Camels—and I shook my head. "If you'd prefer a beer, I've got plenty," he said. "It's early in the day, but I don't judge."

I folded my arms in front of my chest.

"Hey, I see you're not wearing a wedding ring," he said. "You still single?"

I stared at him, and my rage was like a storm inside me, a hurricane of fury. I thought of him calling me a whore that day at his family's house; it was a memory I'd never forgotten but one I tried to store as far back in my mind as possible.

"I can think of something that might take the edge off." He was smirking. "Be fun for both of us."

"You're repulsive," I said.

"That's not what you used to think." He smiled, and when I didn't return the smile, his expression grew sour. "Forget about the money, Alice. Your mother's a grown woman, married her whole life to a banker, for Christ's sake. That deal had a lot of potential, but not enough people came on board, and we had to cut our losses."

"That isn't satisfactory," I said.

We looked unpleasantly at each other, and he shook his head. "You have some nerve, I gotta say. What are you really accusing me of here, fucking over your family? When you of all people should understand that mistakes happen."

It was his ace card. And hadn't I, in my way, forced it? Because then the situation could, at core, be my fault instead of his, and I could feel guilt instead of anger. And wasn't guilt much more ladylike, didn't it fit me far more comfortably? Yes, no matter what Pete Imhof did or said, no matter how manipulative or crude, I would always have done worse. This knowledge was what prevented me from upending his coffee table, from throwing his ashtray across the room or clawing his face. As I left his apartment, all I said was "Never come near any of us."

I MADE IT a few blocks before I began to cry, and I was so worried about being seen by someone I knew that I immediately ducked into the narrow alley between two houses; presumably, I was trespassing. I stood there, leaning against one house's white aluminum siding, and my shoulders shook, and I was grateful for the blasting noise of an air-conditioning unit above my head. It wasn't even that I believed I didn't deserve to be punished; sure, I deserved it. Almost fourteen years had passed since the evening I'd slammed my car into Andrew Imhof's—the dread that gathered in me every late August, as September approached, would come in a few weeks, as reliable in its annual arrival as dogwood blossoms or fireflies—and Andrew would still be dead, and I would still be shocked by the enormity of my mistake. Andrew would always be dead, and I would always be shocked. It never went away.

And the problems that had arisen for me in the last forty-eight hours, my mother losing twenty thousand dollars while I unexpectedly found myself drawn to a man Dena was interested in—what right did

I have to complain about either situation? On the whole, I was far more lucky than unlucky. But it was hard not to wonder what I could have done differently, how I could have prevented this sequence of events. I went out of my way to be considerate and responsible; it wasn't as if I didn't care what people thought or how they felt.

Don't, I told myself. *Don't be self-pitying. You're fine.* The tears had begun drying up—really, the older I got, the less I cried in either frequency or duration. *Be practical. Think of which steps you need to take, address each problem on its own without lumping them together. You have not committed a new wrong toward Andrew; it is only the same wrong arising again. You can't undo anything; you have to live your life forward, trying not to cause additional unhappiness.* Immediately, it was clear to me that I couldn't go through with my purchase of the house on McKinley and that even if Charlie did call, I couldn't see him again; there were my solutions, and they hadn't been remotely difficult to figure out.

I swallowed, wiped my eyes with a tissue from my purse, and stepped out from between the houses. Long ago, I had become my own confidante.

I HADN'T DECIDED ahead of time to do so—I'd had the dim notion that I'd go to a store that sold estate jewelry—but on 94 heading into Madison, after I'd passed the third billboard for the same pawnshop, I pulled off. It surprised me that the proprietor was a woman or that, at any rate, it was a woman behind the counter that afternoon. The aisles were cramped with television sets and stereos, with motorcycles and leather jackets and, on a shelf behind glass, a large jade Buddha.

My mother had given me the brooch by itself, not even wrapped in brown paper, and as I passed it to the woman, I immediately wished I'd waited and put it first in one of the three or four small velvet jewelry boxes I'd acquired over the years (they always seemed too nice to throw away). That surely would have given the brooch a classier aura.

"I'd like to sell this," I said. I thought it best to speak as little as possible, lest I reveal my ignorance of pawn lingo. I was the only customer in the shop, so at least I didn't have an audience.

The woman was about my mother's age, wearing several bracelets and rings (her nails were long and dark red) and a large silver cross on a silver chain. Her hair was a brassy shade, short but voluminous, and her voice was deep and friendly. "Hot as blazes out there, huh?" she said as she inspected the brooch.

"Wisconsin in July," I said agreeably. *Please,* I thought. *Please, please, please.*

She was peering at the brooch through a magnifying glass. "I'm taking my granddaughter swimming this evening, I bet you the beach is packed. I'll give you ninety bucks for it."

I blinked. She looked up, and I tried to compose my face in a normal way.

"Really, you don't think—" I paused. "I'm pretty sure it's Victorian." Standing there next to an oversize television set, I sounded ridiculous even to myself.

"Ninety bucks," the woman repeated, and she seemed a degree less friendly. Surely she had heard countless stories of financial woe; flintiness was a quality that would serve her well.

I took back the brooch. "I'd like to think about it."

"Offer's good till eight tonight. After that, bring it in, and it gets reappraised."

"Thank you for your help." And then, because I didn't want to seem desperate or resentful, because I didn't want to *be* desperate or resentful, I added before I stepped outside again, "Enjoy swimming."

I CALLED NADINE from my kitchen, and when I'd identified myself, she said, "How's tricks?"

"I feel terrible doing this," I began. "I'm so sorry, especially after how hard you worked to help me find the right house, but can we retract the bid? We can, right? That's legal? And the seller just keeps the earnest money?" I had put down five hundred dollars for this—not nothing, but a good deal less than a down payment and a monthly mortgage would be.

"Are you pulling my leg?" Nadine asked.

What I felt most aware of in this moment, far more than the loss of the house, was the social awkwardness of reneging on a person who'd been good to me. Equally powerfully, I felt a fear that I wouldn't be able to renege, that it was already too late.

"Alice, everyone has second thoughts." Nadine sounded upbeat. "Here's what I want you to do. Make a list of your concerns, and we'll go through them together and see if they check out. Buying a house is a big step, but I know you'll be happy as a clam."

"I can't buy the house," I said. "Something has come up."

"Are you worried about the inspection?" Nadine asked.

"It's not this house. I can't buy any house."

For a long, excruciating moment, Nadine was silent. Then she said, "You know, there are some nutso clients out there, but I never thought you were one of them."

"I'm sincerely grateful for your help," I said. I did not consider telling her the reason for my change of heart—it would have been a violation of my mother's privacy—but I decided that later in the week, I would write Nadine a note. That would make the situation at least a little better. "I'm wondering if there's a penalty besides the earnest money. Do I need to pay you any sort of fee?"

"Nope." Her voice was cold in a way I had never heard. "You're free to walk away. All you gave was your word."

I WAS IN my apartment working on Babar—he wore a papier-mâché green suit and red bow tie, a yellow papier-mâché crown—and I was delighted with how he'd turned out, except for the not insignificant problem that the weight of his trunk made his whole head fall forward, as if he were asleep. My solution was to attach a weight to a string around his neck; the weight, which in this trial run was a can of chicken noodle soup from my cupboard, would be hidden behind his back, but unfortunately, the string was still visible and looked like a very small noose. Maybe a better solution, I thought, would be to attach some sort of wire loop to the back of his head (I could set him against a wall so the children wouldn't see it) and then to run a hook from the wall to the loop. As I considered all this, there unfolded in my mind a simultaneous consideration of Charlie Blackwell and how he hadn't called yet and how, if he didn't call at all, it would be insulting—it would show he hadn't really been interested in me, he'd just been hoping to spend the night—but it would also make things far simpler; I wouldn't have to explain to him why we couldn't see each other again. Either way, I had decided not to say anything about him to Dena. To confess would be indulgent, an attempt to absolve myself more than to enlighten her. As my brain skipped among Babar and Charlie and Dena, the phone rang and my heart seized a little (*Charlie?*), but when I answered, it was Dena who said, "If you come over tonight, I'll make ratatouille. I have an eggplant that's about to turn against me."

"What can I bring?" I asked.

"I never say no to a bottle of wine. Shit, I have a customer. Let me call you in a second."

A few minutes later, the phone rang again. "Red goes better with ratatouille, right?" I said.

There was a pause, and then Charlie said, "Alice?"

I felt dual surges of pleasure and anxiety. "Sorry—I was expecting someone else."

"Should I call you back?"

"No—no, I mean—" I paused. "I can talk now, if you can."

"Well, I did call you." He sounded amused.

There was a silence, and at the same time, he said, "What's up?" and I said, "I'm working on Bab—" We both paused, to let the other reply first.

Finally, he said, "So I had a thought about our plans tonight."

We had plans tonight? It *was* Tuesday, the night he'd first suggested, but hadn't I declined that invitation, and hadn't he neglected to offer another?

"I'm thinking the Gilded Rose," he continued. "I have a speaking engagement up in Waupun, so if you don't mind, let's make it on the late side. Eight-thirty all right with you?"

The Gilded Rose was the fanciest restaurant in Madison, practically the only fancy restaurant, and I had never been; my friend Rita, who'd been taken there by her nephew and his wife, had told me they had a shrimp cocktail for five dollars. "Charlie, I can't go out with you," I said.

"Haven't we been through this already?"

"I had a chance to think about it, and it's not that you aren't appealing or that I'm not—" I paused, but there wasn't much reason not to be frank with him, especially if it would spare his feelings. "It's not that I'm not attracted to you. But Dena is my best friend, and this would be unfair to her."

"That's the most ridiculous thing I've ever heard."

I had expected him to agree, or at least to see this as an argument not worth having. I was making myself seem neurotic, and why would he persist with someone who showed her neuroses so quickly? But his utter dismissal of my concerns wasn't insulting; on the contrary, it gave me a lift of happiness, a hope that he might be right. This hope ran against my certainty that he was not.

"I met your friend about ten minutes before I met you," he said. "If she thinks she staked some kind of claim on me, she's crazy, and if you believe her, you're even crazier than she is."

"Charlie, questioning a woman's sanity probably isn't the most effective way of wooing her," I said. He laughed, an embarrassed laugh. "But I bet our paths will cross again," I continued, "so how about if we say goodbye as friends?"

"You know the last time I invited a girl to the Gilded Rose?" He still didn't sound annoyed; he sounded determined. "Never. I'm a stingy dude, but that's how hard I'm trying to win you over."

"I'm flattered, Charlie, I really—"

"Okay, how about this," he interrupted. "Forget dinner. Come to my speech. It won't be a date, it'll be a civic field trip."

"Your speech tonight?"

"It's one of those Lions Club gigs. Didn't you mention that you enjoy listening to people who have nothing to say?"

"Is this because you're running for Congress?"

"Who says I'm running for Congress? This is how rumors get started, sweetheart." He was all breeziness and good cheer; when I was talking to him, the world did not seem like such a complicated place. "I promise it won't be a date," he said. "We'll have a lodge full of septuagenarian farmers chaperoning us."

"Are women even allowed at those things?"

"You kidding me? The Lions love their Lionesses. I gotta go up early and talk with a few folks, so if you're okay meeting there, the address is 2726 Oak Street, right off Waupun's main drag. Speech starts at seven." I could hear him grinning. "Earplugs are optional."

THAT AFTERNOON, I went by a store near the capitol that sold not only estate jewelry but also antiques. I felt more comfortable there than I had at the pawnshop, but the man behind the counter—he was about sixty, a thin fellow with a thin mustache and exaggerated inflections that made me almost sure he was homosexual—offered me seventy-five dollars for my mother's brooch.

"But it's real, isn't it?" I said. Here, I was less shy of showing my ignorance about jewelry resale.

"It's fourteen-carat," he said. "It contains more base metal than gold. I'd guess it's Victorian."

At the pawnshop, my unrealistic sense of hope, my hunch that the brooch probably couldn't solve my mother's financial problems but my lack of certainty that this was so—they had made me vulnerable, priming me for disappointment. This time my expectations were low. I wouldn't try to convince this man of anything.

UPON HANGING UP after my conversation with Charlie, I'd called Dena and asked if we could postpone the ratatouille until the following night—I'd claimed I'd forgotten that I had prior plans with Rita Alwin—and Dena had said, "Okay, but I'm warning you that the eggplant's best days are behind it." I tried to justify the lie by telling myself that when we'd been on the phone earlier, she'd hardly given me the chance to confirm that I could come. But this felt like a weak defense, and I was uneasy as I showered and applied mascara and lipstick. My mood lifted in the car, though—Jimmy Buffett was on the radio, and it really was a nice time for driving, the evening sun a fuzzy gold medallion over the fields.

The Waupun Lions Club was a low brick building that shared a parking lot with a title company. When I walked inside just before seven, about forty people were sitting in sixty chairs, and most members of the audience were in the rows farther from the front. (Something I was to learn quickly is that a turnout's success can always be judged proportionally. It is better to have twenty-five people and twenty chairs than a hundred and fifty people and six hundred chairs. Though now, I also must confess, the idea of a public audience of either twenty-five or a hundred and fifty makes me quite nostalgic.) I sat halfway back in an aisle seat, and when Charlie saw me—he was standing in front by the podium, wearing a blue-and-white-seersucker jacket, khaki pants, a wide-collared white shirt, and a fat red-and-brown-striped tie—he gestured for me to come closer. In as unobvious a way as I could manage, I shook my head. He tilted his head—*Why not?*—and I had a flashing realization of how little we knew each other. If he thought I was a person who'd want to sit in the front row or, heaven forbid, a person who'd like to be singled out in any way during a speech, then he had no sense of me whatsoever.

He was introduced by a gentleman who identified himself as the club president, and upon my hearing Charlie's biography, I was also reminded of how little I knew him; as the summary of his degrees and accomplishments gained momentum, it occurred to me that I didn't have the slightest idea what his job was, or whether gearing up to run for Congress was a job by itself. He had graduated from Princeton University in 1968, I learned, and worked from '68 to '73 in the hospitality industry out west. Then he'd gone on to the Wharton School of the University of Pennsylvania, graduating in 1975. (*Business school?* I thought.) For the last two years, he'd been executive vice president of Blackwell Meats, where he oversaw product management and sales (so he did have a job) and was currently making his home in Houghton. But wait a second—Houghton?

Charlie stood before the podium and adjusted the microphone. "Those of us in Wisconsin's Sixth District are a strong citizenry," he said. "We are a self-reliant people, a salt-of-the-earth people, proud but not prideful, forward-looking but respectful of the past."

I turned my head to the left, scanning the faces in my row. How could anyone mistake this for anything other than a campaign speech? Not that, as a campaign speech, it was bad. He wasn't electrifying, but he seemed confident and intelligent, and—I could admit it now—he was remarkably good-looking. "It is no secret that we face challenges," he was saying. "Our state needs more jobs, more comprehensive health care, fewer expenses for working families. These have long been priorities for all Blackwells, and they are important priorities for me."

When he was finished, questions came from a few men (except for two grandmotherly types, the audience was all men), but it was a typical midwestern audience, polite and deferential. Even the most potentially confrontational question—"How about if you drum up some jobs by opening a Blackwell factory here in Waupun?"—seemed to be meant as a joke or was, at any rate, met with laughter. I stayed in my seat until the lodge had cleared out, leaving only Charlie, the club president who'd introduced him, another man who began folding up the chairs, and a younger man who was standing next to Charlie. From my purse, I pulled the book I was reading—*Rabbit Redux,* which I had started the night before—and after a few minutes, the young man approached me. When he was still a few feet away, he stuck out his hand. "Hank Ucker. You must be Marian the Librarian."

"Alice Lindgren," I said, standing to accept his handshake. I didn't acknowledge the Marian reference—I heard them often, usually from men and especially from men I'd just met. The references tended, of course, to be accompanied by allusions to buns, glasses, and frigidity that concealed sexual wildness.

Hank Ucker gestured toward my Updike novel. "I've always enjoyed a good animal story."

In fact, *Rabbit Redux* was about a man in Pennsylvania whose marriage has foundered, but I did not correct him. Hank Ucker was shorter than Charlie, an inch or so taller than I was, with a receding hairline, intelligent and slightly squinty eyes behind tortoiseshell glasses, a large upturned nose, and the beginning of a double chin. Although I assumed he, too, was about thirty, he was one of those men who looked like he'd been born middle-aged; indeed, over the decades to come, his appearance would change little, and in his fifties, he was almost babyfaced. "A fine speech on the part of our friend Blackwell," he said. "Wouldn't you agree?"

"Will you be working on his campaign?" I asked.

Mock-oblivious, Hank Ucker said, "What campaign?"

I hesitated.

"I'm kidding," he said. "Although we're keeping a lid on it for now, the better to make a bang when it's official. You haven't been married before, have you?"

I blinked at him.

"I ask because you're so beautiful," he added, and the absence of any flirtatious energy behind the comment was striking. "I'd imagine a woman like you has many suitors."

"Are *you* married, Mr. Ucker?"

"Hank, please, and yes, I am." He held up the back of his left hand and wiggled his fingers, showing off a gold band. "The Mrs. and I just celebrated our fifth anniversary."

"Congratulations."

"It's an institution I highly recommend, or maybe you've experienced firsthand its myriad pleasures?" He said this jovially—he *was* jovial, he was practically cherubic—but he also came across as entirely calculating. In a tone just as cheerful as his, I said, "I'm *almost* certain I haven't been married," and this was when Charlie came up behind Hank, setting both hands on Hank's shoulders for a three-second massage.

"Don't listen to a word this man says," Charlie said, and then I could tell that he was deciding whether to kiss me on the cheek, trying to figure out if it would be too forward or public. Instead, he took my hand and squeezed it. Slowly, not showily, I pulled my hand away from his.

As the three of us began walking toward the front doors of the lodge, I said, "I enjoyed your speech."

Charlie shrugged. "Could have been better, could have been worse. Might've helped if the audience wasn't comatose." We still were just inside the lodge, and across the room, the club president was unplugging the microphone. I wondered, as Charlie did not seem to, if he could hear us.

"This is all warm-up, Alice," Hank said, pushing the lodge door open. "Think tonight times a thousand, and that ought to give you some idea."

Charlie elbowed me lightly. "Don't bother, Ucks. She's not easily impressed."

Standing in the parking lot, Hank said, "An honor meeting you, Alice." He took my right hand and kissed the back of it. This was both aggressive and parodic, though I wasn't sure what it was a parody of.

Charlie tossed Hank a set of keys. "Talk in the morning, big guy?"

"You know where to find me," Hank said. He walked a few feet away, then turned back. "In case you're worried, Alice, Harry and Janice get back together at the end."

I must have looked at him blankly, because he pointed toward the novel I still was carrying outside my purse and said, "*Redux* is a more mature work than *Rabbit, Run,* but frankly, I found both books self-indulgent."

"You'd know about self-indulgence, huh, Ucks?" Charlie said as Hank headed to his car. Then, as if something had just occurred to him, Charlie said to me, "Hey, you know what? Looks like I need a ride."

I rolled my eyes. "Well, I heard you don't really live in Madison, so I'm not sure I'd know where to take you."

"Oh, that." Charlie waved his arm through the air. "Obviously, you've got to live in the district you're running in, so Hank found me a rental in Houghton. My place in Madison's in my brother's name."

"Very sneaky."

"Nah, pretty standard, actually. So there's a burger joint between here and Beaver Dam that's out of this world—you a girl that eats bacon cheeseburgers?"

"This is sounding a lot like a date, Charlie."

He grinned. "Not at all. Just two adults of different sexes out on a summer evening, having a conversation."

As Charlie spoke, Hank was pulling out of the parking lot, and he honked once. "Your campaign manager or whatever he is just gave away the ending of my book," I said. "Do you realize that?"

Charlie made a fake-menacing expression. "Oh man, Hank's in deep shit now. Tomorrow I'll show *him* which way is up."

"Seriously," I said. "There was no reason for that."

"He was just toying with you. He probably wants to talk to you about books—he's superbly well read—but he's too clumsy to say so. As for those of us less intellectually inclined—" Charlie took my hand again, and this time I let him. "How 'bout a burger?"

THE RESTAURANT WAS called Red's, and the pine walls were covered in a cheap shiny finish, the seats in our booth black vinyl, the table scratched with initials and declarations of love or enmity. "The onion rings here are stellar," Charlie said. "If I get an order, are you in?"

I generally steered clear of both onion rings and french fries—I watched my weight—but I nodded, knowing that when they came, I'd be too keyed up to eat more than a few.

Our waitress was over fifty and wore a name tag that said EVELYN. "Thanks, sweetheart," Charlie said as she set down two plastic glasses of ice water. After we'd ordered, he said, "You gonna make that burger rare like I like it? Full of flavor?"

The waitress smiled indulgently. "I'll tell the cook."

When she was gone, I said, "Do you know her?"

"In these parts, Alice, I know everyone." He was grinning his Charlie grin. "Okay, I've never seen her in my life. But I bet you dollars to doughnuts if I told her I was running for office, I could win her vote by the end of dinner."

"Then I guess it's too bad you're being secretive. Did you put Hank up to asking me if I'd been married before?"

Charlie whistled. "Boy, he really cuts to the chase. I definitely didn't put him up to anything of the kind." I actually believed Charlie—he seemed to be someone who found his own flaws endearing and thus concealed nothing. "I imagine he was vetting you to see if you're acceptable to date a congressional candidate. He doesn't understand that the question is whether I'm good enough to date *you.* I probably should have warned you about him—he's not a master of subtlety, but honest to God, he's absolutely brilliant. Twenty-seven years old, graduated first in his law school class at UW, and the guy was weaned on the Wisconsin Republican Party. You can't imagine anyone more devoted. He started interning when he was sixteen, seventeen, and after he graduated college Phi Beta Kappa, he became an assistant to my dad."

"Are you two friends?"

"He's not who I call to have a beer with, and that's only partly because he's a teetotaler. But we've begun to log a lot of hours together, and he holds up. He's a quality guy, and the sharpest mind. I'll bring in the big guns as the race heats up, but I'm not sure there's a more talented strategist out there than Ucks. He's spectacular at thinking through the big picture, anticipating attacks from the other side—I'll be sure to get a lot of nepotism crap, and his thing is, address it and move on. We control the agenda."

The waitress brought our beers—Charlie had ordered a Miller, so I had, too—and Charlie knocked his bottle toward mine. "Cheers."

"So what are the other questions that would determine whether or not I'm fit to go out with a congressional candidate?" I asked. "Hypothetically, of course."

He took a long sip of beer. "There's the problem of your party affiliation." He still seemed mischievous, though, not really serious. "Why are you a Democrat, anyway? I mean, Jimmy Carter—how can you stand that peanut-growing goofball?"

"He compares pretty favorably to Nixon."

Charlie shook his head. "Nixon is out of the picture. New day, new order."

"I think it's standard for public school teachers to be Democrats," I said. "You'd be surprised how many of my students have to get free lunches."

"I assume these are the kids of the black welfare mothers moving in from Chicago?"

"That doesn't seem like a very nice way to put it."

"You just have a soft heart," Charlie said. "That's why you think you're a Dem. You'll get older, come into some money, and see where you stand then."

"Aren't we the same age?"

"But I grew up around all this. I've been thinking about it longer."

"I'm not a Democrat because I haven't thought about the issues," I said. "I'm a Democrat because I have."

"Holy cats, woman, you ever thought of writing speeches? You're not convincing me, but a lot of people would eat that shit up. Pardon my French."

"You know, I grew up in Riley, right near Houghton," I said. "Houghton High was our rival. So if you need to know anything about the place you allegedly live, I might be able to help you, but only if you quit mocking my political party."

"In that case, I don't have to explain to you why I live there in name only," he said. "I go once a week, collect mail, make sure a raccoon hasn't destroyed the place, and get the hell back out of Dodge."

"If it's so awful, you could have picked somewhere else."

Charlie shook his head. "Sixth District extends up to Appleton, but we have factories in the north, so that's taken care of. Down south is Alvin Wincek's stronghold, where we gotta focus. See, you're lucky you grew up in Riley instead of Houghton—Meersman is your rep, right? There's a good Republican team player for you, Bud Meersman."

"I've never voted in Riley," I said. "The first time I was eligible was in '68, and I registered in Madison."

"Please don't say you voted for Humphrey."

"Charlie, I'm a Democrat," I said. "Of course I did."

"It's people like you that cost my dad the race," Charlie said, and though there were several reasons I could have pointed to that Governor Blackwell hadn't been elected president in '68—he hadn't even been one of the final three Republican candidates—it did not seem that Charlie was completely kidding.

The waitress appeared carrying red oval plastic baskets, the food nestled inside them in waxed paper. "You see if that's to your liking," she said, and Charlie replied, "I'm sure it will be, Miss Evelyn."

As I sliced my burger in half, I said, "So why'd you go to school in the East?"

"Are you referring to my *Ivy League education*?" He pronounced the words in a mincing way. "Believe me, it's worse than Princeton and Penn. First, I was shipped off to boarding school—a little place called Exeter that's basically a breeding ground for snobs. It's in New Hampshire, my mother grew up in Boston, and she's still enamored with the East Coast way of life—you can take the girl out of Massachusetts, et cetera, et cetera. So we all did our time at Exeter, then four years at Old Nassau, as the cognoscenti call Princeton, then Wharton. I made some terrific friends, and I did learn a thing or two in spite of my best efforts, but make no mistake, New England trust-funders are not my people. It's all very *Mimsy, won't you pass the gin and tonic,* very cold and fake. You go to one of their weddings—I was a groomsman for a fellow from New Canaan—and it's the most uptight affair this side of a funeral. That ain't my style."

"But if you were the son of the governor, I'd think you grew up belonging to the Madison Country Club and all that."

Charlie scoffed. "The Madison Country Club is for parvenus, sweetheart. The Maronee Country Club is where those in the know belong. It's north of Milwaukee."

"Is that a joke?"

"What?" His expression was defensive but lightheartedly so, how he might have looked if he'd been accused of eating the last cookie in the jar.

"Listen to yourself," I said. "Forget your classmates at Princeton—*you're* the snob."

"There's nothing wrong with separating the wheat from the chaff, and I'm not saying on an economic basis. That's the Ivy League mentality—did your daddy join such-and-such eating club, was your grandma a DAR? Those are just labels. But surely you don't deny that some people are quality and some aren't."

"I have no idea what you even mean by that." I think I might have turned against him in that moment, at least a little and maybe more, but he furrowed his brow, grinned, and said, "Yeah, neither do I."

He took a bite of his burger. Unlike me, he had not cut it in half but held the bun with both hands, and he was plowing through it with alacrity. "I suppose I'm a hypocrite like anyone else," he said. "But to give a guy a split personality, nothing compares to having your dad become governor when you're in eighth grade. I'm not complaining, mind you. I couldn't be prouder of him. But you're royalty at public events, you're a bull's-eye target in the locker room, then you go away to boarding school, and when people hear you're from Wisconsin, they think you were raised in a barn. My first week at Exeter, I had a fellow ask me, I kid you not, if I'd grown up with electricity. Now, the prejudice I faced ultimately bolstered my pride in where I come from and who I am, but that said, am I about to join a bowling team with Bob the mechanic? Probably not." He leered. "At least not until I've officially declared my candidacy and a photographer from *The Houghton Gazette* is there to document it. Really, though—" He leaned forward. "I'm not an elitist. You believe me, don't you?"

"I'm not sure what to believe."

A look of sincere worry crossed his face, and his sincerity won me back. I was pretty sure Charlie's views were not unlike those of the other men who'd been at the Hickens' barbecue. The difference was that Charlie was so open about his. I said, "I bet that when you were a tormented eighth-grade boy, you were awfully cute."

His grin reappeared immediately. "Damn straight I was. How's that burger working out for you?"

"It's delicious." He'd polished his off, and I wasn't yet through my first half.

"I have an idea," Charlie said. "It just occurred to me. You want to hear it?"

"Sure."

"I'll go settle the tab. Then we head back to Madison—I'm happy to drive. We go to your apartment, we take off all our clothes, we get in bed, and I show you that Republicans do know a little something about a little something." He paused. "After you're finished eating, of course."

Had I expressed shock or distaste, it would have been disingenuous—enough had happened in my life already that was far more shocking and distasteful than a sexual proposition. And besides, he'd sounded so boyish, so sweet, even. Then, too, I suppose I might have feigned offense not because I really was offended but because I wanted him to think I was, for propriety's sake. But this seemed silly. I was thirty-one. To hell with my concerns about leapfrogging over the stages of acquaintanceship, to hell with making an argument—the argument against dating Charlie—that I didn't want to win. No, I wasn't completely certain about him, and yes, this would strain my friendship with Dena. But the responsibility and caution that I'd tried to employ for so long—since the accident, though in some ways even before that—hadn't served me well, especially lately. Plus, Charlie was an incredibly handsome man. I *wanted* to take off all my clothes and climb in bed with him.

I set down my cheeseburger. "I'm finished eating."

BACK AT MY apartment, Pierre and Mr. Sneeze were reclining on my bed, and crouching near them was the baby rabbit from *The Runaway Bunny,* whom I'd outfitted in fish garb. (The mother rabbit was in the living room, awaiting her fishing rod and waders.) I carefully set the figures on the floor by the wall, and when I turned around, Charlie was shirtless and unfastening his pants. "What?" he said. "Did you think I was kidding?"

"Let me at least put on a record." As I walked past him, I swatted at the side of his head without making contact, though I did note (subtly, I hoped) that his bare chest was muscular, tan, and had some but not too much light brown hair. In the living room, I first reached for a John Denver album, then remembered Denver had supported President Carter. I imagined Charlie might think I was trying to make a point and instead put on Stevie Wonder.

A short hall led from the living room to my bedroom, and as I headed back down it, Charlie stood completely naked in the bedroom doorway, his arms folded across his chest, his grin huge. As I approached, he unfolded his arms, opened them, and took me in, he rubbed my back and kissed the top of my head, and in return, I kissed his bare shoulder—it was dotted with beige freckles—and we found each other's mouths, then each other's tongues, and his penis flicked toward me a few times before hardening into an erection. It is a pleasantly uneven thing to embrace a man while he is naked and you are clothed, and I could smell his skin, I could taste the beer from dinner, and I was the one who lifted my shirt above my head and let it drop on the floor. He leaned forward and buried his face in my breasts; he didn't unfasten my bra but simply pushed down the cups.

Soon all my clothes were off, too, we were rolling on the bed, I'd wrapped my legs around him, and I took his erection in my hand and guided him into me, and it felt so elemental, so necessary, for us to be joined like this and then it was like awakening abruptly, and I gripped his arms and said, "Wait, my diaphragm is in the—"

"No, I have protection. We're fine." It was in his wallet, which was inside his pants on the floor, and as I watched him retrieve the condom, I was already too dazed to feel self-conscious about staring. His butt was small in the way that I always forgot a lot of men's were; how could he possibly be an unscrupulous politician with such a cute little butt? Back in bed, he knelt on the mattress—I was lying flat, and he was above me—and perhaps it sounds crude to say that this was the moment I knew I could love him, when I saw his penis. With men in my past, the penis had seemed to me an odd creature, both comic and forlorn. But I felt a great devotion to Charlie when I first got a look at his, the ruddy-hued upward-pointing shaft, its swollen veins and cap-like tip. All of it was so completely *of* him, and I felt how there was no part of his body I wouldn't want to touch, no way I wouldn't allow him to touch me.

When he'd rolled the condom on, he straddled my waist and lowered his body down and thrust into me again, and he murmured, "I can't believe anything that feels this good is legal," and I said, "I'm really happy you're here right now," and he groaned against my neck. He came a few minutes later, collapsing onto me, and we both were quiet, I hugged him without speaking, and after a few more minutes, he lifted his head so we could see each other and said, "I meant to hold on a little longer, but you're this goddess with these amazing, luscious breasts—"

"*Charlie.*" This was the first moment of the evening I did feel embarrassment.

"Do you not know that you have luscious breasts?"

I clamped my hand over his mouth.

When he pulled my hand off, he said, "Now your turn. I'm a rightie, so for maximum dexterity, it's better if I go this way." He nodded left with his chin and rolled off me.

"You don't have to," I said.

"Alice, I aim for total customer satisfaction."

"I'm not sure—I just don't—"

"You've had an orgasm before, haven't you? It's fine if you haven't, although if that's the case, you've been seriously shortchanged."

"No, I have," I said. "Just not, you know, every time."

"That's unacceptable. It's a simple biological function."

"Aren't you enlightened."

"Hey, I've read *Fear of Flying.* I know all about the zipless you-know-what."

"I appreciate—" I hesitated. How long I took had become an issue toward the end of my relationship with Simon; sometimes he'd given up. "I'm glad you want to try," I said. "But I'm afraid it might not work, and I don't want to spoil what's been a really fun evening."

"Clearly, you have no idea how talented I am in this department."

I turned my head so we were making full eye contact. "Not tonight."

He drew his eyebrows together. "I don't understand how someone can turn down the—"

"Charlie, I don't feel like it," I said, and I knew there was an edge in my voice.

Neither of us spoke until he said tentatively, "Want to hear the other information I've gathered for your dossier?"

We had been under a spell, and the spell had broken. I didn't want to be cold to him, but I also didn't want to feign merriment. I said, "Maybe later."

"No, it's all positive. I've been updating my file over the course of the night." His voice was warm and conciliatory. "I'll start at the beginning: Alice Marie Lindgren, born April 6, 1946. Beloved only daughter of Phillip and Dorothy, granddaughter of—hmm— You might need to give me a hint."

"Emilie." I made sure to sound nicer, too—if he was trying, so could I. Also, I was surprised and flattered to hear him reciting these facts. Although I had revealed them during the hours we'd spent lying on the couch in my living room the previous Saturday night, I hadn't expected he'd remember, partly because he'd been drinking and partly because we'd been talking idly.

"Honor-roll student and all-around good girl," he continued. "What religion are you, by the way?"

"My family is Lutheran, but I only go to church when I'm with them."

"You don't go to church? Mon dieu, I was bedded by an atheist!"

"Oh, please," I said, and Charlie snuggled in to me.

"Moving on. University of Wisconsin class of 1968—summa cum laude?"

I shook my head. "Magna, but given that you're the one who went to Princeton, I'm not sure why you think I'm so smart."

He grinned. "Let's just say I wasn't known around campus for my straight A's. Luckily, this is about you, not me. After college, you teach third grade at— Give me a little help on this one, too."

"Harrison Elementary," I said. "But I doubt I told you before, so I won't deduct points."

"Frequent reader of *The Giving Tree,* equally frequent crier. No, I'm teasing—I took a look at it, and I see why you're a fan. And not too many big words for a knucklehead like me." He'd sought out *The Giving Tree* in the three days since we'd seen each other last? I was astonished. (Later it emerged that he hadn't actually bought it, he'd read the whole thing standing in the bookstore—but still.)

"Then a master's back at UW," he was saying, "then Theodora Liess Elementary, where our heroine presently remains, dazzling children during the school year with her charm and good looks and spending the summers constructing large, brightly colored cardboard animals."

"Papier-mâché, but that was very impressive overall."

"Wait, there's one more entry in the dossier." He squinted at his palm, pretending to read. " 'Now being wooed by a strapping young politico. Doesn't know it yet but is about to fall madly in love.' "

"Oh, really? Is that what it says?" I grabbed for his hand, and he pulled it away.

"These are classified documents, Miss Lindgren, and you don't have clearance." He turned and kissed me on the lips, and at first the kiss was a distraction, and then it was what both of us were paying all our attention to, the push and retreat of each other's mouths.

Charlie was wrong, though; I did know, I knew already, that I was falling in love.

I MET DENA at her store. I was the one who'd suggested lunch, thinking I could get my confession over with, that by the time we saw each other that evening for our belated ratatouille, this conversation would be finished and behind us, but I realized as soon as I walked into D's that I'd made a mistake. The store was crowded with customers, and Dena was buzzing with a tense, pleased preoccupation. As we left, she said to the girl behind the counter, "If Joan Dorff doesn't pick up the corduroy handbag by one, call her and say we can't keep holding it."

We walked to a nearby sandwich place, and when we opened the menus, I said, "By the way, my treat."

"Shit, if I'd known, I'd have suggested the Gilded Rose. Are we celebrating your home ownership?"

It seemed early in the lunch to bring up the real reason. But maybe I was worrying too much, maybe it would only be a brief awkwardness.

Dena said, "Before I forget, I saw this great couch at Second Time Around that you should buy for your new living room. It's three hundred bucks, but I know the owner, and I bet I can talk her down."

"Dena, I went on a date with Charlie Blackwell," I said.

Immediately, her eyes narrowed.

I pressed on. "At the party, you said you didn't really like him." In fact, she had said she thought he didn't like her, but the two weren't so far off, and this seemed the more diplomatic version. "Obviously, this wasn't my plan, but we just— I guess we clicked. I would have thought before I got to know him that you'd be more compatible, but it turns out—" I seemed to be losing traction. "Our friendship is so important to me, Dena, and that's why I'm being honest. I realize that—"

She cut me off. "You didn't sleep with him, did you?"

I hesitated.

"You've got to be kidding." She exhaled disgustedly. "It's like me being interested in a guy automatically makes you interested. You've always been jealous."

"That's not true at all."

"How do you explain it, then? Because this isn't the first time."

Don't say it, Dena, I thought. *Please, for both of our sakes.* I swallowed. "If I didn't feel a true sense of connection with Charlie, I wouldn't have let things progress. But when I'm with him—" It was impossible, I realized. I couldn't justify my behavior without sounding like I was gloating.

"What, are you planning to marry him?"

"I don't think it's beyond the realm of possibility," I said, and I suspect I was as surprised as Dena. Not that I wasn't dimly, dimly aware of having considered it, but I would never have guessed I'd risk uttering the thought aloud. Quickly, I added, "We're still getting to know each other."

"Is it because he's rich?"

"Of course not! I've never even— We haven't talked about money. I'm not sure he *is* that rich."

"He is," Dena said. "He's loaded."

"His family, maybe, but—"

"No." Her voice was flat. "Him. All of them."

The waitress approached, and Dena held up her palm. "I'm not staying." The waitress looked at me.

"Give us a minute?" I said, and she nodded and walked away. "Dena, don't leave. Or leave if you feel like you need to, but please let's not have this be some ugly thing between us. You're my closest friend."

She was shaking her head. "Once you've been divorced, you know that walking away from a marriage is a lot harder than walking away from a friendship."

"But I've known you longer than Dick did," I said, which sounded slightly pathetic even to my own ears.

"The last time you pulled this crap, we were teenagers, and what did we know about anything?" Dena said. "But we're adults, which means this is who you really are—a person who goes after the man your best friend is interested in." I almost wished she were ranting, but she hadn't raised her voice at all. "I'm sick of your fakeness," she said. "You've always gotten to be the good girl, so go be a congressman's wife, you know? Spend all your time with the Trommlers and the

Hickens and those other uptight couples. Let Charlie buy you jewelry and cars." Though we'd never ordered, we both had set our napkins on our laps; she crumpled hers, dropped it on the table, and stood. "I hope he gives you everything you want."

Sitting there after she left, I felt a mild embarrassment at having been abandoned, and also an incredulity at how extreme her reaction had been; it was what I'd feared but hadn't really expected. And then, less close to the surface than these emotions but perhaps more profound, I felt one more: a great gratitude that she, like Pete Imhof, had never mentioned Andrew by name.

ON MY NEXT visit to Riley, I didn't tell my mother or grandmother that I wouldn't be staying over until we were nearly finished with lunch. With as little fanfare as possible, I said, "I made some plans in Madison tonight, so I think I'll take off this afternoon." It was a hot Saturday, and we had just finished chicken-salad sandwiches.

"Really, this afternoon?" my mother said, and my grandmother said, "What sort of plans?" Since my father's death, I had never come home without spending the night.

I gave my grandmother a look—presumably, she could have guessed the plans involved Charlie, and she also could have guessed that if I wanted to be more specific, I would have—and I said, "Just some people getting together on the Terrace." This, at least, was true: I'd be meeting a bunch of Charlie's friends for the first time.

When my mother rose to clear the plates, my grandmother gripped my wrist, holding me back. As soon as my mother was in the kitchen, my grandmother murmured, "She made a Vienna torte for dessert tonight on your account."

"Oh, I didn't realize— No, I can stay then," I said.

My mother came back into the dining room, and my grandmother said, "Dorothy, it sounds like your daughter has a new beau."

"Oh my goodness." It was my mother, not me, who blushed in this moment.

"It's not official yet." I shot my grandmother an irritated look. "But his name is Charlie, he grew up in Madison and Milwaukee, and I met him through Kathleen Hicken and her husband, remember them?" Volunteering this information was a subterfuge, a way of not volunteering the more noteworthy details of Charlie's upbringing or his current congressional aspirations. I was uncertain what my family's reaction would be when I did share the news, given my father's maxim about fools' names and fools' faces. Also, as I sat there, it occurred to me that I had no idea of my mother's political leanings. I'd always known that my grandmother was a Democrat and my father a Republican, but I wasn't sure my mother voted.

My grandmother said, "A little companionship can be wonderful. Don't you think, Dorothy?"

My mother, still standing, lifted the iced-tea pitcher. "He sounds appealing, Alice," she said, and she disappeared again into the kitchen. When she turned on the water, my grandmother whispered, "I was trying to give her an entrée to talk about Lars Enderstraisse."

"Granny, I really doubt they're involved." I, too, was whispering. "Whatever Mom's mystery errands are, I'm pretty sure they don't have to do with him."

"You think you're the only one being wooed?" My grandmother chuckled, and, speaking at a normal volume, said, "Someone has an awfully high opinion of herself."

MY GRANDMOTHER AND I read in the living room that afternoon, she on the couch and I in the chair, and when I went to find my mother, she was weeding tomato plants in the backyard.

"If it's all right, I think I will stay for dinner," I said. "My friends aren't meeting until around nine o'clock." This was a lie, but my mother's face lit up.

"Oh, I'm delighted. We're having a dessert I know you like."

Watching her—she was on her knees, wearing a white terry-cloth hat—I felt colliding surges of affection and guilt. Why had I not told Charlie from the start that I wouldn't be free tonight? Our schedules were flexible, we could go out during the upcoming week. But the truth was that I didn't want to stay in Riley. The pulls of familial love and obligation could not, for the moment, compete with the promise of early-relationship sex. Starlight and beer and our twisting, naked bodies—that was what I wanted, not a seat at a dining room table with two old women eating breaded veal cutlets and Vienna torte. If infatuation was making me selfish, it was not, I supposed, that I'd previously been exempt from a capacity for it; it was more that I hadn't ever been infatuated, or at least not in a good long time.

I squatted next to her. "The tomatoes look nice."

My mother set a bunch of weeds on the pile. "Honey, Dena must have told you about Marjorie. Lillian is having a fit."

I tried to make a noncommittal expression. Of course Dena hadn't told me about Marjorie, who was one of her two younger sisters.

"You know how that family is, though," my mother said. "The girls have always been so strong-willed. Mack could be such a disciplinarian, Lillian compensated by being lenient, and it was feast or famine for the girls." The last I'd heard of Marjorie Janaszewski, she'd gotten involved with David Geisseler, the younger brother of our former classmate Pauline Geisseler; David already had two children with a woman whom he hadn't married, and he and Marjorie were bartenders together at the Loose Caboose on Burlington Street. "I can't fault Lillian for worrying, though," my mother said.

All this time I had been carrying an envelope—it was unsealed, unwritten on—and I held it out to my mother. "That was a good idea about selling the brooch," I said. "I took it to an antiques store."

"Oh, bless your heart." Without looking inside, she folded the envelope and inserted it in the pocket of her skirt.

I had to bite my tongue to keep from saying *Be careful with that.* The closest I came, straining to sound casual, was "It turns out it was pretty valuable."

"That's wonderful," she said vaguely. "Alice, I was having some trouble with hornworms feeding on the tomatoes, and Mrs. Falke told me to plant marigolds, and they've worked beautifully. Mrs. Falke's very modest, but she has quite a green thumb."

I closed my eyes, and briefly, the house on McKinley, the porch and the window seats and the secret cupboard, appeared in my mind, but then I opened my eyes, and my mother was pulling weeds from the soil, my steadfast and kindhearted mother in her white terry-cloth hat, and the house went away. The check was for seventy-one hundred dollars—a great deal less than my mother had given to Pete Imhof, and exactly the amount I'd have put toward a down payment.

IT WAS AFTER midnight by the time Charlie and I left the Terrace. His friends, it turned out, were a lot like the crowd at the Hickens' barbecue, and in fact there was some overlap: Will Werden, who was Frank Werden's first cousin, was there with his wife, Gayle, and as soon as Charlie introduced me to everyone two of the other women and I realized we'd met a few years before at a baby shower. Ten of us were there in total, all couples, and the other couples all were married except for Charlie's stockbroker friend Howard and his girlfriend, Petal, a twenty-one-year-old who'd graduated from the university two months before. "How long ago do you think she made *that* name up?" one of the baby-shower women—her own name was Anne—whispered to me, rolling her eyes. "We don't know where Howard gets them." This was an extension of friendship on Anne's part that I gratefully accepted, though later, I talked to Petal (it wasn't her fault that she was a decade younger than the rest of us), and she was perfectly intelligent; she'd double-majored in art history and Italian. At the end of the night, Anne pulled me aside and said, "Charlie is *smitten* with you." I laughed, because it was easier than saying anything. Even Will Werden nudged me at one point and said, "I didn't know you and Blackwell there were an item." Again, I only smiled.

There'd been a bit of shifting over the course of the night, people getting up to use the restroom or the parents in the group checking in by pay phone with their babysitters, but most of the time Charlie and I had sat side by side, and even when we were both talking to other people, I felt his attention: his hand on my knee or at the small of my back, the quickness with which he'd turn if I said his name or tapped his arm. Every so often he'd lean in and say, "You okay?" Or "Hanging in there?" It was probably seventy degrees, a perfect summer night, and Lake Mendota was mostly blackness with a few wavering reflected lights.

And then we were bidding everyone goodbye—another couple left at the same time we did—and as we walked around Memorial Union to where Charlie had parked on Gilman Street, he took my hand. As if our fingers were acting independently of us, down there far below the conversation, we adjusted them so they were interlocked. "Your friends are nice," I said.

We reached Charlie's car, a gray Chevy Nova hatchback, and I said, "How about if I drive?" I had carefully nursed one glass of beer.

Charlie passed me the keys, and as I was turning on the ignition, he said, "Look over here." When I did, he leaned forward and kissed me. Then he said, "I've been wanting to do that all night." I turned the ignition back off, tilting my head toward his, and we kissed some more, we wrapped our arms around each other, and I was happy that we were alone, just us, holding each other tight. It wasn't that I hadn't enjoyed being on the Terrace—I had—but suddenly, it was as if all the talk had been the part we had to get through in order to arrive at this reward.

Charlie pulled back an inch. "So I haven't forgotten about what I owe you. Let's go to my place."

Confused, I said, "You don't owe me anything." And then I understood—he was grinning—and I said, "Oh, that."

"I'm not taking no for an answer. You've got to claim what's rightfully yours."

And even though, as I drove, I felt stirrings of nervous anticipation, I also wanted to just stay forever in this limbo; I'd have been content to drive all the way to Canada, knowing that something wonderful would happen when we got there.

It was the first time I'd been to Charlie's apartment, and what I noticed immediately was that he'd left nearly all his lights on. His place was both smaller and less furnished than mine, and the living room seemed mostly like a repository for sports equipment: a brown leather bag of golf clubs leaning against one wall and, in a messy pile, a baseball bat, gloves, tennis racquets, a soccer ball, and the first lacrosse stick I'd ever seen. There was a large television set, a sizable stereo, a black bean bag, and a French baroque sofa complete with cabriole legs and covered in burgundy mohair. (I would learn that he'd acquired the sofa by raiding his parents' basement in Milwaukee, which was where his paternal grandmother's belongings had been stored untouched since her death seventeen years before.) Nothing hung on the walls, and a five-ledge bookshelf had two empty ledges. Of the remaining three, one contained books, one contained gewgaws, and one contained photos in frames: his father in a tuxedo and his mother in a sparkly red gown, looking into each other's eyes; Charlie and three men I assumed to be his brothers, standing in a row in blazers; him and another guy in plaid jackets, crouched over the body of a dead buck with blood trickling from its mouth, Charlie grinning as the other man bent his head to kiss the buck's antlers; Charlie at twenty or twenty-one clutching a BLACKWELL FOR PRESIDENT sign. On the next ledge, the one holding books, were a dictionary, a biography of Willie Mays, best-sellers such as Peter Benchley's *The Deep* and, yes, *Fear of Flying,* and a smattering of the sort of titles one reads in undergraduate literature courses: *Paradise Lost, A Midsummer Night's Dream,* Goethe's *Faust.* Resting on the final shelf were a signed baseball, a beer stein, several shot glasses, a paperweight of a black-and-orange enamel shield, and a chartreuse rubber snake.

I noticed all of this, I took it in quickly, and I didn't really care. So he was a bachelor—of course he was, otherwise he wouldn't be dating me. The space actually was clean, not dusty or cluttered. The bedroom was empty except for a mattress on top of box springs with no frame. The sheets were blue-and-white striped, pulled tidily up to the pillows, and a ceiling fan was already running. In the doorway of the bedroom, Charlie kissed me again, and then he walked me backward, maneuvering me onto the bed. When I was lying on my back, he stood above me grinning. "That's much better."

I was wearing my denim skirt and a maroon tunic with orange and pink flowers. He leaned over and used both hands to lift the tunic from around my waist and push it above my bra and over my shoulders. Being undressed like this made me feel, in a strangely nice way, like a child: watched over and taken care of. My bra was next to go, and when he'd tossed it somewhere behind my head, he gazed down at me, lying in the light of his bedroom—attached to the ceiling fan, sticking out from its center, was a bare bulb—and he said, "I can't believe how beautiful you are." He leaned forward and kissed one nipple and then the other, slowly and methodically, first with his lips closed, then opening his mouth to suck in a manner that seemed respectful, almost reverent.

Next he unbuttoned my denim skirt, unzipped the zipper, and I arched my back to help him slide it off; this, too, he tossed aside. I was wearing pink cotton underpants, and he stuck his thumb inside the elastic waistband, snapping it lightly against my hipbone and grinning. "Hi, pink," he said.

"Hi," I said back, and as we looked at each other, I felt what I'd felt the times I'd laid beneath him at my apartment: sprawling, enormous happiness. What I most wanted was exactly the same as what was about to happen. Which forces had conspired to make me so unreasonably lucky?

He ran his forefinger from my navel straight down over the front of my underwear, slowing above my pubic bone, and when he got to the cleft, the cotton fabric beneath his finger was damp, and he said, "Looks like someone's enjoying herself."

I reached up; he had so little fat on his stomach that I could slip my hand into his boxer shorts without unfastening his pants. His erection was hot and stiff, and when I brushed my fingers over the tip, he inhaled, but then he drew back, shaking his head. "This is about you. We'll get to me later."

"It can be about both of us." I was touching him from outside his pants now, and he shook his head and nudged my hand away.

This was when he pulled down my underwear—they got caught for a second around my ankles before I kicked them off—and then I was naked on his blue-and-white-striped sheets and he was crouching over me, tanned and masculine in a yellow oxford shirt, his flared nostrils, his slight hint of stubble, his light brown hair, and his smile, his perfect smile, and I felt a total, unfettered attraction to him. He bent his head to kiss my sternum, my navel and belly, my pubic bone, the tops of my thighs, and then he dropped to his knees on the floor and used his elbows to spread my legs, to open me up, and he brought his face in and was licking me, he was licking me firmly and repeatedly, and it seemed both difficult to believe (Charlie Blackwell's face burrowed between my legs?) and also entirely inevitable: beyond logic and language and decorum. Possibly, I thought, I had lived my life up to now in order to be licked by this man. I could hear myself cooing—I was leaning on my elbows with my feet near the floor, and he was kneeling, with his arms beneath my thighs—and he began to flick his tongue rapidly, almost thrashing it, in a focused spot. His cheeks between my thighs, his bobbing head, and his earnest assiduous lapping—very quickly, it was too much to bear, and I gasped and cried out. It was like tremors, and I felt my thighs clenching around his head, and when he came up a few seconds later and kissed my forehead, I said, "I hope I didn't suffocate you," and he said, "I can't think of a better way to go." Then he whispered, his mouth against my ear, "I really want to be inside you right now," and as soon as he'd rolled on the condom, I encircled him with my legs, and he slid into me. He didn't make much noise when he came, his breathing just thickened and slowed a little, and we both were still. Lying there, I felt a peaceful kind of sleepiness come over me. I could have gone to bed right then, without brushing my teeth or washing my face, without changing positions. Not that I would; instead, I'd leave within the hour and return alone to my own apartment. To have sex with a man was one thing, but to spend the night with him was another—even if my personal sense of etiquette had become outdated, I had difficulty disregarding it.

Against my neck, Charlie said, "We should do this every day for the rest of our lives." Then he said, "I can feel you smiling."

ALL AT ONCE we were spending vast amounts of time together. In my apartment, I moved the papier-mâché characters into the living room so he and I could lie on my bed, and though I didn't let him stay over, he ended up leaving at a later hour each night—one or two, sometimes three. Because we often fell asleep after making love, I started setting my alarm clock for two, and when it beeped, Charlie would groan and say, "For the love of God, woman, make that thing stop," and then we'd curl in to each other and fall back asleep, and after twenty or thirty minutes, I'd wake with a start and push at his torso, saying, "You really have to go now," and he'd pretend to cower, covering his head and groaning, "I'm being exiled! The queen is banishing me from the castle!"

Several times he said, "Don't you think it'd be nice to wake up together? And we can make some morning mischief that no one but us needs to know about?" But the fact that I felt it was improper for us to stay over at each other's apartments was really our only point of dissent. He was very easy to be around, very comfortable, in a way that surprised me. With Simon, if we had gone to kiss each other and our mouths missed, he'd pretend it hadn't happened; he wouldn't acknowledge if one of our stomachs rumbled. With Charlie, everything was out in the open. Once, after dinner, when we were watching television in his living room, he stuck his hand beneath my shirt to rub my belly, and when I shook my head and said, "I have a stomachache," he said, "Go ahead and let one rip if you need to. I'll still think you're the prettiest girl in all of Madison." I didn't do it—I couldn't have, I'd sooner have tap-danced in Calvary Lutheran Church—but he apparently felt no such inhibition. A few days later, I walked into the kitchen after him, smelled an earthily unpleasant odor, and said, "Did you just—?"

"I can't remember, but probably." He grinned. "In my family, we call that tooting your own horn."

He was so appealing to me, and so confident of his own appeal in a way that was boyishly endearing rather than arrogant. He always wanted to snuggle, he even used the word *snuggle,* which I'd never heard a man do. The night I made us halibut in aspic for dinner, he did the dishes afterward, and when he finished, he came into the living room, where I was lying on the couch reading. Wordlessly, he lifted away my book and lay flat on top of me, then said, "Aren't you going to put your arms around your man?"

At his apartment, we always grilled out, making either hamburgers or steaks (I had not realized the evening we'd gone to Red's that we were having one of the two dinners Charlie most preferred). His refrigerator was largely empty but held a few items that all belonged to the same category: ketchup; mustard; relish; packs of hamburger buns that he never closed properly after their first use, causing them to go stale; and a shelf of beer. Meanwhile, his freezer was filled to capacity with multiple packages of Blackwell-brand boneless strip steaks and ground beef. His apartment was on the first floor, and he kept a three-legged black kettle charcoal grill on a patch of pavement in the backyard and usually accessed it by climbing out his kitchen window rather than walking through the front of the house and around the side. I'd perch on a stool in the kitchen while he climbed in and out, tending to the meat, and when dinner was ready, we carried our plates to the living room, sat on the couch, and watched baseball. I knew plenty of women wouldn't have considered this a pleasant arrangement, but I liked how the game made conversation easy, how we could talk or comfortably not talk, and Charlie seemed especially sweet when he was explaining a play: "That was a great save, because when the ball's coming directly at you, it's harder to tell how deep it is." Or "He bunted foul with two strikes, so that's why it's an out."

Charlie ate breakfast every morning at a diner on Atwood Avenue, and he encouraged me to meet him there, but I was afraid, should we run into anyone we knew, that it would look like we'd spent the night together. ("Then I guess we might as well," he'd joked, but I had come of age before sexual liberation really took hold, there'd been curfews in place when I'd started college—ten on weeknights, midnight on weekends—and men weren't allowed in our rooms in the sorority. I'd had trouble entirely shaking the propriety of that time.) Besides, I had work to do during the day: I wanted to finish the papier-mâché characters by the time back-to-school faculty meetings started in late August, and as the weeks passed, I really was beginning my lesson plans. I prided myself on being a librarian who didn't just rehash the same material year after year, and this year I was especially excited about a new book called *Sadako and the Thousand Paper Cranes,* which I planned to use with the fourth-graders as an entry point into a unit on origami.

As for Charlie's schedule, he described this time as the calm before the storm—he used the expression repeatedly, both with me and with other people. I was hesitant to ask him much about his impending congressional run because the topic made me skittish, and it also didn't seem entirely real. Did he actually want to live most of the year in Washington, D.C., to sit in an office building on Capitol Hill debating policy, casting votes on the House floor? Restless, joking, athletic, spontaneous Charlie? It seemed like he'd be acting out a role in a play. And of course, if he were elected (it was unlikely, but if he were), what would happen to us?

For his job at Blackwell Meats, he did not, as far as I could tell, go to the company headquarters on the outskirts of Milwaukee more than twice a week. He did drive to Milwaukee regularly, but more often it was to play midday golf or tennis with one of his brothers, preceded by lunch with Hank Ucker and prospective donors to his war chest: lawyers from large firms, the CEO of an outboard motor company, men Charlie referred to as stuffed shirts. I once asked a little tentatively if he considered his job at the meat company full-time, and without hesitating, he said, "Alice, here's an insight I'll give you into who I am. Being a Blackwell is my full-time job."

In the late afternoons or on the weekends when, increasingly, I skipped my trips to Riley, Charlie and I would go swimming at BB Clarke Beach ("You should wear a bikini," he said the first time we went, when he saw my red-and-white-striped one-piece) and then we'd go play badminton at the Hickens' house or meet up on the Terrace with Howard and his latest young thing—he had already moved on from Petal—and Howard and Charlie would go through several pitchers of beer (Charlie would always drive there, I'd always drive back), and then Charlie and I would go home and grill. We'd never made it to the Gilded Rose, we hadn't even discussed it again. I didn't mind.

The way I'd felt in Charlie's presence, ever since leaving the Hickens' barbecue, was as if I were suspending disbelief. Our compatibility seemed so improbable that at first dating him struck me as some combination of amusing and mildly irresponsible. Once, late on a Sunday afternoon the previous May, I had run into Maggie Stenta, one of Liess's first-grade teachers, at the food co-op where I belonged, and we'd started chatting while Maggie's children ran wild in the aisles. "Listen, do you want to come over?" Maggie had said. "We're just having sloppy joes." Though I'd drawn up a list of other errands I needed to run, I accepted the invitation, which meant following Maggie back to her house, where I proceeded to forget my milk in a bag in the backseat of my car. Inside, Maggie said, "Do you want some sangria? We had people over last night, and it'll go bad if we don't drink it." We sat on chairs in the yard, Maggie's kids were jumping on a trampoline—the older one, Jill, was my student—and Maggie's husband was inside on the second floor, and Maggie yelled at him, "Can you fix dinner, Bob?

I don't have the energy," and then her neighbor, a woman named Gloria, came over and said she was pretty sure she'd seen a lizard run under her living room couch—"Not a big one, maybe four inches," she explained—and this seemed to delight Maggie, so we went over and were tipping up the couch, and then the lizard scampered out—it was olive-colored—and into a vent in the floor, and Maggie decided what we needed was a net, which neither household had, so we left the children with Maggie's husband and walked to a hardware store that he'd told us would be closed and indeed was. On our return, Maggie said good-naturedly, "Have you ever seen kids more badly behaved than mine?" We went back to Gloria's house and looked around in the basement, which was outrageously cluttered, but we saw no sign of the lizard. By then it was seven o'clock, I had prep work for my classes the next day, I was tipsy from sangria (I ended up calling a taxi two hours later), and no doubt the milk in my car had gone bad. But what I felt that afternoon and evening was what I felt around Charlie all the time: *This is not my real life. There are other things I should be doing. I'm enjoying myself.*

IN MID-AUGUST, I was getting a haircut at Salon Styles—I had just settled into the chair after being shampooed—when Richard, the man who cut my hair, said, "Did you hear about Elvis?"

"I don't think so."

"He died. They were saying on the radio it was a heart attack, but it sounds to me like the old hound dog had a fondness for the pharmaceuticals."

In the large mirror I was facing, I could see my own eyes widen. "He wasn't that old, was he?"

"Forty-two." Richard had parted my wet hair in the middle, and he took hold of chunks on either side, holding out the hair by the tips. "How many inches are we taking off today?"

THAT EVENING, AS soon as I knew she'd be home from work, I dialed Dena's number. The friendliness in her voice when she answered the phone, before she knew it was me, broke my heart a little.

"It's Alice," I said. "I was thinking about you today because of— I'm sure you know Elvis died, and do you remember when your mom took us to see *Jailhouse Rock* the night it opened, and then she made us peanut-butter-and-banana sandwiches afterward?" Dena didn't respond immediately, and I added, "Is your mom really upset?"

"I haven't talked to her."

"Well, I just was thinking about your family." I paused. "Dena, I miss you. I'm sorry and I miss you."

She was silent. Then she said, "Are you still seeing him?"

"I understand why you're angry at me, obviously, but this shouldn't ruin our friendship. I didn't set out to spite you."

"So you are still seeing him?"

"Dena, you've dated a lot more men than I have. It just seems like— Well, you're so pretty and dynamic, and I'm a hundred percent confident that you'll meet someone you really click with. You'll be *glad* you didn't end up with Charlie."

"It must be nice to be clairvoyant." Her tone was dry.

"What I have with him, it's not like anything I've experienced in the past," I said. "I wouldn't be cavalier about our friendship, but this just feels different."

"That's what you called to tell me?"

I was sitting at my kitchen table, and I looked down at the place mat, orange vinyl with a butterfly motif, and I knew Dena wouldn't forgive me. Still, I said, "Is your sister all right? A few weeks ago, my mom mentioned—"

"Alice, just stop," she said. "Okay? Stop it."

"If you change your mind—" I began.

She cut me off. "Leave me alone. That's all I want from you."

THE FOLLOWING EVENING, as we were standing in line at the co-op, Charlie turned and said, "Wait—didn't you buy a house?"

I froze, but only for a second or two. "It didn't pass the inspection."

"What was the problem?"

"A beam in the basement had shifted, and the whole foundation was unstable." Nadine had once told me about other clients who'd made an offer on a house where the inspection had revealed this exact problem. The lie made me uncomfortable, but how could I explain to Charlie the chain of events that had led me to change my mind—how could I tell him about my mother and the investment scam before he met her and saw for himself that she was not flighty or flaky, and how could I possibly explain my family's relationship to Pete Imhof? I had never told either Wade Trommler or Simon Törnkvist about Andrew; particularly with Wade, I'd wondered if he'd find out on his own because I wasn't the only person from Riley living in Madison, but as far as I knew, he hadn't.

"That's a bummer," Charlie was saying.

"I guess it wasn't meant to be." We had reached the front of the line, and I began unloading our purchases. I had decided to make lentil salad to go with our steak that night, and Charlie had come with me to the co-op; apparently, he had never been inside, and as we'd entered, he'd said, "I had my suspicions you were a hippie."

I set down the lentils and garlic and feta cheese, the walnuts and olive oil and fresh dill. Charlie was not looking at me when he said, "How much do you think it would cost to fix the foundation?"

"Oh—" I hesitated. We were, I sensed, approaching a delicate topic with many complicated subtopics. Two days earlier, at Charlie's apartment, when I had carried my plate of steak from the kitchen into the living room, I had noticed on the living room table a typed check made out to Charles Blackwell for twenty thousand dollars. But it also was from Charles Blackwell—his name was printed in the upper-left-hand corner. I had never seen a check for anywhere close to that amount, and I couldn't imagine what it was for, or what it meant that it was both to and from him. I did not touch it but scooted back on the couch, waiting for him to join me. When he did, carrying his own plate, he sat, flipped the check over without acknowledging it, and we continued the conversation we'd been having in the kitchen.

In the co-op, I said, "Fixing the foundation would probably be as much as buying the whole house. It's not worth it." The cashier started ringing us up, and behind us, the next customer was setting down her items. She was a slender woman around our age, wearing a short-sleeved blouse and a wraparound skirt, and she had the freckles and bright red hair that people never seem to like in themselves but that I'd always found quite charming.

"Was that your dream house, or were you so-so about it?" Charlie asked.

Trying to remain composed, I said, "I was so-so." I couldn't continue this conversation much longer, or I would start to cry. Not because losing the house had been devastating—I honestly hadn't thought about it that much—but because this all felt so fraught and strange. If I said *Please do buy the house for me, if you wouldn't mind,* would Charlie agree to it? I noticed then that the red-haired woman was buying the food you eat when you live alone: a box of cereal, a few apples, a plastic container of plain yogurt. As we waited for the cashier to tally our total, Charlie said, "I'm looking forward to our hippie salad," and he leaned in and kissed my neck.

With an abrupt clarity, I saw how I had been launched into another category. I had been the red-haired woman; for a decade of my adult life, I had bought cereal and yogurt, I'd stood near couples and watched them nuzzle, and now I was part of such a couple. And I would not be launched back, I was nearly certain. But I recognized her life, I knew it so well! I wanted to clasp her freckled hand, to say to her—surely we understood some shared code (or surely not, surely she'd have thought me preposterous)—*It's good on the other side, but it's good on your side, too. Enjoy it there. The loneliness is harder, and the loneliness is the biggest part; but some things are easier.*

A FEW MONTHS back, Rita Alwin and I had bought tickets to see *Romeo and Juliet* at a small experimental theater, and when we went that week, we realized the experimental part was that all the actors were nude for the entire play. They also were not particularly skilled performers. Rita and I kept glancing at each other and giggling, and at intermission, she said, "Think we've seen enough?"

We went to get a glass of wine at a bar around the corner, and sitting across from me, Rita said, "Something's different about you."

"I got a haircut." I jokingly fluffed it. My hair was chin-length then, still thick and dark (I took secret pride in not having needed to pluck a single strand of gray), and I had it feathered a bit on the sides. I'd been told the previous spring that I resembled Sabrina on *Charlie's Angels,* but this was an observation I'd found alarming more than flattering because it came from a third-grade girl.

"It isn't your hair," Rita said. "It's more like a glow." She leaned in. "Are you in *love*?"

"What? No. No, but I'm a little sunburned." Then I said, "Well, I'm seeing this guy named Charlie."

"I knew it!" Rita was sixty and had never been married, and though she was attractive, she didn't seem to date. She had known about Simon, but I rarely mentioned to her the more casual setups I found myself on—it struck me as tedious when women ceaselessly discussed their romantic entanglements. "Bring him to the back-to-school picnic," Rita said. "What's he like?"

"He's cute and funny and— I don't know, he's fun. He's really cute."

Rita reached out and patted my forearm. I was surprised by how excited she seemed. She said, "I knew it would happen for you."

I WOULDN'T HAVE thought it possible, but Charlie's place in Houghton made his Madison apartment seem like a triumph of interior design. I accompanied him there one Friday afternoon for no particular reason—because now we were going everywhere together—and discovered that he'd rented, or Hank Ucker had rented for him, a unit in a soulless four-story complex a few blocks from downtown. Charlie's was a two-bedroom with a galley kitchen, brown wall-to-wall carpet, beige drapes, a wheat-colored sectional sofa flecked with small blue and red zigzags, and a low glass coffee table. An unplugged television sat on the floor in a corner. The closets were bare, the cupboards were empty, and there was no soap in either bathroom, no towels, no dish towels in the kitchen, not even napkins or tissues; there was a full container of dish soap at the kitchen sink, and when I washed my hands with it after using the toilet, Charlie thrust out his midsection and said, "Dry them on me." As I rubbed my palms against the oxford fabric, he said, "Oh boy, now you're turning me on."

"Why do you need two bedrooms if you never even stay here?"

"Eventually, some reporter will come sniffing around." Charlie grinned. "A one-bedroom might look suspicious, like I'm just renting a place here to establish my eligibility in the district. I would hate to seem like a cynical politician to the good folks of Houghton."

"We should go shopping," I said.

"That's what you women always say."

I made a face at him, and he said, "I'm kidding. Maj has promised to spruce up the place before I move in, but if you're that keen to add your feminine touch, be my guest." Maj was apparently what Charlie and his brothers called their mother—short for Her Majesty. And she actually liked the nickname, Charlie claimed; he'd said he couldn't remember when it had started but probably when his oldest brother was in high school and Charlie was in fourth or fifth grade. I asked what they called their father, and as if no other possibility had ever occurred to him, Charlie said they called him Dad, though he did add that the grandchildren called him Pee-Paw; they called their grandmother Grandmaj.

"I'm talking about shopping for soap, which some people would consider hygienic rather than decorative," I said. "This place is depressing, and it doesn't need to be. It's depressing, and it seems fraudulent."

"It *is* fraudulent." He leaned forward and kissed me.

"Charlie, if you're running for Congress in this district, you should spend time here. There are worse places in the world to live than Houghton."

"You think they've considered that as the town motto?"

"Believe it or not, I'm trying to be helpful." I looked around. "I'll make a deal with you. We settle you in for real. We go buy sheets and towels and food—not anything that will spoil, but a few items to keep in the cupboard. And then we can spend the night here." We still hadn't spent an entire night together, which felt increasingly silly on my part.

Charlie said, "How about if we snuggle first and then go shopping?"

"I'm not snuggling on a bed with no sheets."

"You drive a hard bargain, Lindy." Lindy was Charlie's new nickname for me, an abbreviation of my surname. "You're not secretly on the payroll for the Houghton Chamber of Commerce, are you?"

But we were smiling at each other, and this was the thing about Charlie—that my impatience with him was always tinged with, if not overshadowed by, amusement. That he entertained me, that I enjoyed trying to cajole him. I felt like I really could help him, that my organization and calmness complemented his energy and humor, and vice versa.

"If I am on their payroll," I said, "I'll never tell you."

WE DID MAKE love late that afternoon, though we ended up using the sofa, because even after we'd bought sheets, I'd wanted to wash them before making up the bed. "Who does that?" Charlie said, and I said, "Everyone."

He furrowed his brow. "But they're brand-new."

Naked on the sofa, he had stroked me until there was that warm rapid internal uncoiling, and then he'd plunged into me, and when we were finished, we lay there, the sweat that had risen on our skin drying, and I said, "Poor Hank Ucker will probably sit on this sofa someday with no idea what's taken place," and Charlie said, "Nothing would please Ucks more. When my mother sits here, on the other hand—"

"Don't even say it. That's so embarrassing."

"You've gotta meet my folks soon," he said. "They're out in Seattle now, but everyone's gathering in Halcyon, up in Door County, for Labor Day. Oh, and Christmas, you gotta come for Christmas. Maj makes a fabulous goose. The trick is to baste it in ginger ale."

My impression was that Charlie's parents were traveling more often than not—technically, they lived in Milwaukee, but they were visiting friends in Denver or Boston, staying in Door County (apparently, there was yet another home, a third one, in Sea Island, Georgia), flying to a university in Virginia for Harold Blackwell to give a speech or to a business conference in Oklahoma City for him to deliver the keynote address. It sounded exhausting to me, though admittedly I was someone who had traveled by plane exactly twice: At the age of twenty, I'd gone with my parents and grandmother to Washington, D.C., and my father and I had climbed the stairs to the top of the Washington Monument while my mother and grandmother rode the elevator; and at the age of twenty-six, before I started saving money for a house, I'd gone with Rita Alwin to London during our spring break, a trip on which we had ridden a double-decker bus and attended performances of *The Merchant of Venice* and *The Mousetrap.* Charlie himself was extremely well traveled. When various places came up in conversation, he'd mention casually, as if it didn't occur to him that another person might be either impressed or put off, that he'd been there: Honolulu and Charleston and Palm Springs, Martha's Vineyard and Dallas and Nashville and New Orleans. Baltimore, he declared, was "filthy." Portland, Oregon, was "a snooze."

"My brother Arthur's starting to guess that something's up," Charlie was saying. "He's been trying to introduce me to a girl for weeks, and the other day I told him to forget it, which was, shall we say"—he grinned—"out of character." Arthur, I had gathered, was the brother Charlie was closest to in both age and friendship; all of his brothers were married. "You'd say no if a fellow asked you out, wouldn't you?" Charlie said.

"Of course. Charlie, I don't sleep with someone lightly."

"No, that's what I thought. Just making sure we're in agreement is all."

"You know, we're very close right now to where *my* family lives," I said. "Maybe we ought to go over there tomorrow."

"You think I'd pass muster with the Lindgren ladies?"

"If you behave yourself."

Charlie laughed. "I shouldn't ask your grandma to pull my finger?"

It was six-thirty by then, and we rose and dressed and made dinner. We'd bought plates, silverware, pots, and pans at Scorilio's, which was Houghton's only department store—I insisted on washing these, too, before we used them—and we'd stopped by the grocery store for spaghetti and marinara sauce and bread. (Charlie had whispered, "You think the other customers are looking at you and thinking what a loose lady you are for staying overnight with your boyfriend?") Back at the apartment, cooking dinner, it all felt very languorous; we brought out the clock radio from the bedroom and tuned it to a jazz station, and in the middle of all of this, a thought solidified itself that had previously occurred to me more than once but always in a shadowy form: the near-certainty that the kiss I had witnessed all those years ago between Gladys Wycomb and my grandmother had been postcoital. I had not recognized it at the time; it had been enough—too much—to view the embrace by itself, without knowing it was either a precursor or a wrap-up to anything else. But in retrospect, it was undeniable: that leisurely, affectionate, spent quality that arises between two people when they're no longer building up to the act but have completed it, that happy relaxation. It's unlikely I would have made such an assertion in the first weeks of my courtship with Charlie, but with age, I have decided that the denouement is the best part. The potentially fraught negotiations of intercourse are replaced with pleasantly shallow concerns: when to get out of bed, or where you left your shirt, or what to eat. Neither of you is trying, any longer, to convince the other to either go through with or delay it; you're not trying to *achieve* anything, and you can simply enjoy each other's company.

AROUND THREE IN the morning, I awoke to find my hand at Charlie's groin. We both were naked beneath the sheet, which he had persuaded me we ought to be on our inaugural night together. He was on his back, and I was on my side next to him, my head on the same pillow, my palm on his upper thigh. I was mortified. But if I moved my hand, would that alert him to the fact that it had been there in the first place? As slowly as I could, I slid my fingers a few inches away, and he stirred, as I'd feared he would. He had one arm set around my back, and without opening his eyes, he turned his head, kissed the part in my hair, and immediately seemed to fall back to sleep.

I lay in the dark with my eyes open. Had I not, in fact, been attempting something? Wondering, if only subconsciously, what I could get away with, what would be indecorous, how much we could casually encroach upon each other? And he either hadn't noticed or had been unfazed. I moved my hand back to where it had been, and I, too, fell asleep again.

WHEN WE ARRIVED at the house in Riley the next day, I knocked on the door, and my grandmother answered wearing an orange sleeveless acrylic dress, sheer panty hose, and orange heels. A skinny white leather belt was cinched around her tiny waist, and her bare arms were painfully scrawny. She looked back and forth between Charlie and me several times—she had to crane her neck—and then she clapped her hands together once and said, "Oh, this'll be *good*!" She held out her cheek for me to kiss.

"This is Charlie," I said. "Charlie, this is my grandmother Emilie Lindgren. Granny, I thought of calling, but we were in the area, and I—"

"My dear, I love surprises." Her voice contained a note of mischief as she added, "I hope you do, too."

The reality was that I had purposely not called ahead, not only because I didn't want to draw attention to the fact that Charlie and I had spent the previous night together in Houghton, but also because I didn't want my mother to feel as if she had to prepare an elaborate meal on short notice. They ate lunch every day at twelve-thirty, and it was a quarter to two as we entered the house.

"Mrs. Lindgren, I've promised your granddaughter I'll be on my best behavior," Charlie said, but before my grandmother could respond, my mother called, "Who is it, Emilie?"

Then my mother walked into the living room, and her eyes widened. "Alice, how lovely, but I wasn't expecting you until next weekend."

"We're just stopping by," I said. "I wanted to introduce you to— This is Charlie. Charlie, my mother."

"Dorothy Lindgren," my mother said, and she and Charlie shook hands. There was an extended silence, and then my mother said, with less enthusiasm than I might have anticipated, "Why don't you two come sit in the other room?"

Had this been a bad idea? It wasn't until we'd entered the dining room, where they didn't usually linger this long after lunch, that I understood: There, sitting at the table, wearing a plaid short-sleeved shirt, sipping from a coffee cup that seemed especially dainty in the grip of such a heavyset man, was Lars Enderstraisse. Without looking at her, I immediately sensed my grandmother gloating; I also sensed my mother's twittery discomfort. "Honey, you know Mr. Enderstraisse," she said. "Lars, you remember my daughter, Alice, and this is her friend— What's your last name, Charlie?"

"Blackwell," I said quickly.

"By all means, call me Lars," Mr. Enderstraisse said.

Charlie and I sat at the chairs without place mats or plates in front of them. "Can I get you two some ham?" my mother said, and I replied, "We already ate. I'm sorry for not calling ahead, but we just were in Houghton." By this point, I very much regretted our decision to arrive unannounced. Another silence descended, and my mother said, "Let me at least get you something to drink."

At the same time, I said, "Oh, we're fine," and Charlie said, "I'll take a beer if you have one."

"I'll help." I stood. "Anyone else?"

"Beer does a real number on Lars's stomach," my grandmother announced authoritatively. Although I may have been the only one to notice, my grandmother was emanating supreme self-satisfaction.

"Bloating, gas, and the like," Mr. Enderstraisse—Lars—affirmed. He spoke genially, and I wondered, was he really dating my mother? I had never seen him not wearing a postal uniform.

"Alice, sit," my mother said, and uncertainly, I complied.

"Alice, I'll bet you haven't heard about the break-in at the Schlingheydes'." My grandmother had turned to Charlie and me. "It's the talk of the neighborhood. Don and Shirley slept through the whole thing, but in the morning, they saw that a kitchen window had been shattered and the television set was gone, along with Shirley's silver. Now, the bizarre bit is that they found half a turkey sandwich left out on the drain board, with just a few bites taken from it and the other half gone. Can you imagine having the presence of mind to fix a snack at the same time you're robbing a house? He'd even spread mayonnaise on the bread."

"When was this?" I asked.

Over her shoulder, my grandmother called into the kitchen, "Dorothy, was it Sunday night?"

"Monday," my mother said as she appeared in the doorway carrying Charlie's beer. "It sounds to me like a very disturbed person."

She passed the beer to Charlie, who said good-naturedly, "Some friends of my folks got robbed one time in the sixties, and the thief left behind a shoe." Charlie had, of course, no idea how irregular Lars Enderstraisse's presence was.

"I hope you've been keeping the doors locked," I said.

"Oh, the Riley PD will catch the fellow in no time." My grandmother's tone was festive. "If Sheriff Culver manages to tear himself away from Grady's Tavern for more than an hour, that burglar won't stand a chance." Without warning, my grandmother said to Charlie, "Now, what is it you've done to earn a visit to Alice's ancestral home?"

"I've won her heart." Charlie grinned, and I felt a nervous curiosity about whether he and my grandmother would like each other. While they shared a certain high-spiritedness, I was not certain it was of the same variety, and sometimes different varieties of a similar tendency were worse than total dissimilarity. Under the table, Charlie took my hand.

"Charlie, are you also a teacher?" my mother asked.

"No, ma'am, I'm in the beef industry." When Charlie squeezed my hand, I wondered if he could tell I was tense. "I divide my time between Houghton, Madison, and Milwaukee."

Did Charlie assume that I'd previously told them who his family was? Given that I hadn't, perhaps I ought to now, when my indirection was on the cusp of turning into an outright lie.

My grandmother lit a cigarette she'd extracted from a pack beside her plate. "You must be paying a pretty penny at the gas pump."

"Charlie, I heard Alice say your surname is Blackwell," Lars Enderstraisse said. "I don't imagine you're a relation to Blackwell sausage or the former governor."

"I should hope not," my grandmother said cheerfully. "What a chokehold that man had on this state!"

In a loud voice, as if I could retroactively cover up her remark, I said, "Harold Blackwell is Charlie's father."

There was a silence, and Charlie was the one who broke it. He said, "Nothing like politics to inspire passionate disagreement, is there?" He smiled—a feeble smile, but he was trying.

"*Your* father is Harold Blackwell?" A confused expression had contorted my mother's features.

"And Charlie's running for Congress next year," I said. "But it's a secret, so don't tell anyone." I glanced over to see if he was irritated, and he appeared to be less than thrilled, though it was hard to say whether this was because of my grandmother's comment or my own lack of discretion. But wasn't it better to get all of it over with at once? Or would this visit be the abrupt death knell of our relationship, the revelation of how little, against the backdrop of my upbringing, we actually had in common?

"Running for Congress—goodness gracious!" my mother said, and I was reminded of my ignorance of her political leanings. "What an exciting time for you."

"I won't announce my candidacy until January," Charlie said. "Frankly, I'll have a tough road ahead of me with an incumbent like Alvin Wincek. But I can honestly say it would be a privilege to serve the people of Wisconsin's Sixth District."

Please don't use your speech voice, I thought. I couldn't even look at my grandmother.

"You're a Republican like your father?" she said, and when I did dare to glance at her, I saw that she was staring unabashedly at Charlie.

"Indeed I am," he said, and his voice contained a jovial defensiveness.

"In a progressive town like Madison, I'd think that would put you out of step with your peers," my grandmother said.

"Appearances can be deceiving." Charlie's tone was still perfectly civil. "The students holding their protests are loud and strident, but the backbone of Madison is hardworking middle-class families."

Both of you, stop it, I wanted to cry out.

"A Republican I really admire is Gerald Ford," my mother said. "What a difficult situation to enter into, and his poor wife, struggling like that with her health."

"Jerry is a loyal foot soldier," Charlie said. "He's a man who knows his strengths and limitations."

There was a pause as we all tried to determine which direction the conversation would go. Charlie seized the reins. "This is a lovely home, Mrs. Lindgren," he said and it was clear that the Mrs. Lindgren he was addressing was not my grandmother but my mother. "How long have you lived here?"

"Oh, mercy, it's been—help me, Emilie—we came here right before Alice was born, so I suppose thirty-one years. Now, Charlie, you must have met Alice's dear friend Dena. Mack and Lillian, Dena's parents, are just across the street, and they moved in not but six months after we did."

"I have met Dena," Charlie said warmly. "She's the life of the party."

"Oh, she's a pistol. Lillian tells me business is booming at her store."

"How's her sister?" I asked.

"I think she's doing better now." My mother smiled. "Charlie, did Alice tell you her father managed Riley's branch of Wisconsin State Bank and Trust?"

Charlie smiled too, but blankly.

"They also have branches in Madison," I said. "There's one at West Washington off the square."

"They're the best bank in the region." My mother nodded fervently. "Are you sure I can't get either of you something to eat? Alice, I made apple kuchen again last night, and you were exactly right about adding sour cream to the dough."

"That I can vouch for," Lars said. "I must say that if I'd known when I woke up this morning I'd end up sitting across from the son of the governor of Wisconsin, I'd have brought along my camera. Everyone at the post office will be tickled pink when I tell them on Monday." Directing his comment at Charlie, he added, "That's where I work, at the one down on Commerce."

I willed myself not to be embarrassed or to give in to adolescent shallowness.

"You'd be surprised that even in a town like Riley, people send their mail to the most unusual of places," Lars was saying. "The other day a gentleman shipped a package all the way to Brussels, Belgium."

"Where Audrey Hepburn was born," my grandmother said.

There was a lull, and Charlie, who appeared neither troubled by nor interested in Lars's employment, said, "Mrs. Lindgren, have I missed my chance at the apple kuchen?"

"Not at all." My mother sprang from her seat. "Alice?"

"None for me, but let me help you," I said.

In the kitchen, a foil-covered pan sat on a burner, and my mother turned on the oven and stuck the pan inside.

"Charlie can eat it cold, Mom."

"But it's so much better warmed up. I just wish we had a little vanilla ice cream left—you don't think I ought to run down to Bierman's?"

"You definitely shouldn't."

"I had no idea he was the son of Harold Blackwell," she said, and then, after a beat, "I know Lars's presence must be quite a surprise. I was in buying stamps one day, and we got to talking—he's a very kind man, Alice."

"No, he seems like it. I'm sorry I didn't call to say we were coming."

"No one will ever replace your father for me." There was a fierceness in her expression, as if she expected that I would not believe her.

"Mom, I think it's fine. It's good for you to, you know, socialize. You two should come to Madison for dinner, either with Granny, or just you and Lars if you want to come when Granny's in Chicago."

My mother appeared confused. "Did Granny tell you she's going to Chicago?"

"Isn't her visit to Dr. Wycomb in the next week or two?"

My mother shook her head. "Granny hasn't visited Gladys Wycomb in years."

I was startled. "Does she not have the energy anymore?"

"Well, she's eighty-two," my mother said. "She's so sharp that it's easy to forget." My mother had picked up her egg timer, and I watched her set it for seven minutes. As she did, she said, "I've been meaning to say, Alice, thank you for selling the brooch. I know we probably didn't get as much as it was worth, but every little bit helps."

WE DID NOT stay long; I think all of us, with the exception of my grandmother, had found the encounter draining. My mother insisted on sending Charlie home with the portion of kuchen he didn't eat, and the five of us stood in the living room exchanging goodbyes. "I can see why Alice speaks so fondly of where she comes from," Charlie said to my mother, and his voice was loud and confident but also distant—it was the way I'd later see him speak to constituents. When my grandmother shook his hand, she said, "I never voted for your father, but I always admired your mother's sense of style. There's a picture I once saw of her in a stunning fox cape."

Charlie was not smiling as he said, "I'll tell her you said so."

In the car, I directed him out of town, and after we reached the highway, neither of us spoke for nearly ten minutes. "I'm sorry if that was awkward," I finally said. "You were a good sport."

He said nothing.

"Are you angry?" I asked.

"You lecture me on how to behave, but you might want to save some of your etiquette lessons for your grandmother."

"Charlie, she's eighty-two years old. And she was joking around."

"You must find her a hell of a lot funnier than I do. You'll give me crap for saying this, but there are quite a few nice Republican girls out there who'd be plenty happy to date me."

"I'm sure that's true."

"If we're going to stay together, I need your support. Running for office puts pressure on a man. I've watched my father go through it, and now my brother, and it ain't easy. It's exhausting. I have to go out there and convince voters that I deserve to be elected, but if I can't even convince the girl I'm dating, how ass-backward is that?"

I was quiet, and then I said, "I would vote for you."

"Lucky for you, I'm not running in your district."

"Do you not believe me that I would?"

He looked over. "Sure, I believe you. Why shouldn't I?"

"Charlie—"

"It's not like you have to put your money where your mouth is." He leered a little. "So to speak."

"You're not being fair."

"Alice, loyalty is everything to my family. There's nothing more important. Someone insults a Blackwell, and that's it. Starting in grade school, kids would think they'd lure me into an argument, or they were just busting my chops—I don't care. I don't try to convince people. I cut them off. So for me to hear your grandmother—"

"I wish she hadn't said that."

"As a public servant, you rally your supporters, and you try to win over the people on the fence, but your detractors, forget it. You'll never get 'em. If you're smart, that's not how you use your time."

We both were quiet, and I said, "What about this: What if we don't talk about the political stuff? Spending time with you this summer has been the most fun I've ever had. It really has. But I don't want to pretend that I believe things I don't. I don't want to stand at a rally chanting slogans." (The number of times I have stood at a rally chanting slogans, chanting onstage, with cameras rolling—years and years ago, I lost count.) "What if I support you not as a politician but as a person?" I continued. "What if we put our differences to one side, you don't try to convince me and I don't try to convince you, and we just appreciate being together? Am I crazy, or is that possible? I can assure you I'll never *tell* anyone if I disagree with you—that's no one's business but ours."

"Let me get this straight," he said. "I'm running for Congress on the Republican ticket, you're a hippie who promises not to admit it in public or around my family, and together we make beautiful music?"

I hesitated. "Something like that."

"And I can't even try to convince you that Jimmy Carter is a pathetic chump?" But his tone had lightened; I didn't need to hear him say we were on the same side again to know we were. "To answer your question," he added, "no, you're not remotely crazy. I've dated crazy girls, and you don't qualify."

"Thank you."

He was looking over at me again. "You're an unusual woman, Alice."

I smiled wryly. "Some might say that you're an unusual man."

"You have a strong sense of yourself. You don't need to prove things to other people."

Did I agree? It had never felt to me like I had a strong sense of myself; it simply felt like I *was* myself.

"I have this image in my head," he was saying. "We're old, older than my parents are now. We're eighty or hell, we're ninety. And we're sitting in rocking chairs on a porch. Maybe we're up in Door County. And we're just really happy to be in each other's company. Can you picture that?"

My heart flared. Was he about to *propose?*

"I don't think I'd ever get sick of you," he said. "I think I'd always find you interesting."

This was when my eyes filled with tears. But I didn't actually cry, and he didn't propose (of course he didn't, we'd been dating for a month) and for another long stretch, neither of us spoke.

We had just pulled onto Sproule Street when I said, "There's something I need to tell you."

"That's an auspicious start to a conversation." He parked in front of my apartment and turned to me, his eyes crinkly, his lips ready to pull into a smile. I knew I had to forge ahead quickly or I'd lose my nerve.

"When I was a senior in high school, I was in an accident," I said. "I was driving, and I hit another car, and the person in the other car died."

"Jesus," Charlie said, and I wondered if telling him was a mistake. Then he reached out to tug me toward him. "Come here."

I put up one arm, holding him off. "There's more. It was a boy I knew. I had a crush on him, and I think he had a crush on me, too. There were never repercussions in the legal sense, but the accident was my fault."

Again, Charlie reached out for me, and I shook my head. "You have to hear all of this. I felt very guilty afterward. I still feel guilty, although I'm not as hard on myself as I was then. But I ended up"—I took a deep breath—"I ended up sleeping with Andrew's brother. That was the boy's name, Andrew Imhof, and his brother was Pete. It was just a few times, and no one knew about it. But I got pregnant, and I had an abortion. My grandmother arranged for a doctor she knew, a friend of hers, to do it. I never told Pete, or my parents, or anyone."

"Alice—" He pulled me in so we were hugging, and this time I let him, and his skin was warm and he smelled exactly the way I'd come to expect him to. Against my neck, he murmured, "I'm so sorry, Lindy."

"I don't know that I'm the one who deserves sympathy."

He drew back so we were making eye contact. "You think I haven't made mistakes?"

"Of that magnitude?"

"As a matter of fact, I thought I got a girl pregnant in college. She missed her period two months in a row, and we were both beside ourselves. She was down at Sweet Briar when I was at Princeton, and I wondered if I could get away with pretending it wasn't mine even though I knew I was the only fellow she'd slept with. When she did finally get her period, I never talked to her again, so how's that for not deserving sympathy?"

"You were young."

"So were you. And people fuck up. We just do. It started with Adam and Eve, and as far as I can tell, there's been a steady flow of human error since. Can I make a suggestion? Let's go inside so I can hold you properly."

"Okay, although as long as I'm telling you everything else— Well, my mother just lost a bunch of money in a pyramid scheme, and the reason I didn't go through with buying the house wasn't because of the inspection, it was because of that. Oh, and I'm pretty sure my grandmother is a lesbian."

To my surprise, Charlie burst out laughing. "Your grand—" He tried to compose himself. "Sorry—it's just—that old girl back there is a muff diver?"

"Watch it, Charlie."

"You have proof?"

"She has a . . . a lady friend. The woman who's the doctor, they've been a couple for years. I think my grandmother has gotten too frail to travel to Chicago to see her, but they're very devoted to each other."

"Bully for her." Charlie seemed genuinely admiring. "Anyone who finds women more attractive than men won't get an argument from me. What else? This is getting juicy."

"I think we've covered it," I said. "No, I guess there's also the fact that Dena isn't speaking to me because I'm dating you. I was right that she's furious." The more I thought about it, the more it seemed Dena's behavior had to reflect her frustration with her own life more than with me—her disappointment at not being married or having children. Perhaps she really had pinned her hopes on Charlie before she'd met him, but this seemed unrealistic on her part, and her anger at me felt excessive.

Charlie waved an arm through the air. "She'll come around." He pulled the key from the ignition. "I'm not cutting off the conversation, but let's continue it inside."

Though I don't know if what he had in mind was sex—it probably was—that's what happened: We stepped through the door of my apartment and he hugged me tightly, and soon we were grabbing and groping, impatient to shake off all the tension and verbiage. There had been too many words, they'd begun to overlap and run together, and now it was just his body on top of mine, his erection inside me, the jolting rhythm of our hips. You feel like a cavewoman saying it, but if there's a better way than sex for restoring equanimity between a couple, I don't know what it is.

After, he spooned me from behind. He said, "I want to take care of you and protect you and always keep you safe," and this time I did start to cry, real tears that streamed down my face.

"I wish you could," I said. "I wish anyone could do that for anyone else."

"Turn around," he said. I complied, and he said, "I love you, Alice." With his thumb, he wiped a tear from beneath the outer corner of my eye.

"I love you, too," I said, and it seemed such an inadequate expression of my affection and gratitude and relief, of my guilt-inflected excitement at all we had to look forward to. How had this happened? And thank goodness it had.

"What you told me in the car, I know that's big stuff," he said. We were facing each other, and he rubbed my hip beneath the sheet. "But from now on, it's smooth sailing. It's all going to be okay."

MY GRANDMOTHER CALLED late the next morning while I was rinsing a paintbrush I'd used on Yertle the Turtle's shell. "Charlie's terrific," she said.

I was stunned. "Are you teasing me?"

"Well, his politics are appalling, but he's been suckling too long at the teat of the conservatives. I'm sure you can coax him over to our way of seeing things."

"Granny, he's running for Congress as a Republican."

"He doesn't have a snowball's chance in hell, my dear. That old coot Wincek has had a lock on the Sixth District since before you were born. Anyway, I suspect it's more a rite of passage in the Blackwell family than a bona fide attempt to win on Charlie's part. Why not let him get it out of his system? But he's mad for you, there's no doubt about that."

"And you liked him apart from the political stuff?"

"He's adorable. Very lively, very well mannered. Oh, he's a real catch, and your mother agrees. At this very moment, she's tidying up your trousseau. Speaking of which—should I say I told you so about your mother and Lars, or would you prefer to say it for me?"

"I think you just did."

"That bit about his bloating and gas, and at the dining room table—it's clearly not Lars's debonair manner that's attracted her, but we shouldn't judge her for wanting to enjoy herself."

"Granny, you baited him."

She laughed. "Well, maybe a little."

"I'm glad you approve of Charlie," I said. *Even,* I thought, *if it's not reciprocated.*

"Alice, you hold on to that young man." My grandmother sounded positively ecstatic. "You've found a keeper."

THE FOLLOWING WEEK, which was the one before school started, I drove my papier-mâché characters to the library. It took two trips to fit them all in my Capri, delicately stacked atop one another. Though no one had seen them besides Charlie, I felt nearly certain that they had turned out the way I'd wanted. Even Babar's head stayed upright once I'd secured it to a hook behind him.

While I was situating Eloise on a shelf, I heard a deep voice say, "Those are real nice, Alice."

"Big Glenn!" This was what we all, teachers and students alike, called Liess's janitor, who was an extremely tall black man in his early seventies; he'd worked at the school for over fifty years. I hurried over and hugged him. "Did you and Henrietta have a good summer?" I had never actually met Big Glenn's wife, though there was a famous pineapple upside-down cake she made that Big Glenn dropped off in the faculty lounge every May, some morning before the end of the school year. It was usually decimated by eight-twenty A.M. as if its consumption were a competitive activity.

"It's sure been peaceful not having the hellions around." Big Glenn smiled.

"You mean the teachers or the students?" He laughed, and I said, "I bet you missed us all."

He stepped forward, his voice lowered. "Don't go repeating this, but I hear Sandy's husband is real sick."

I winced. "Again?" Sandy Borgos taught second grade and was a friendly woman twice my age who knitted during faculty meetings and wore, whenever possible, a beige shawl that she'd made herself. Her husband had been diagnosed with throat cancer two years earlier, though the last I'd heard, he'd been in remission.

"It's in God's hands now," Big Glenn said. "You know about Carolyn, anyone tell you that?" Big Glenn was, among other things, an extremely well-informed source of school gossip.

I shook my head. Carolyn Krawiec worked in the kindergarten and was seven or eight years younger than I was; she'd been at Liess just a short time, and I hardly knew her.

"Not coming back this year," Big Glenn said. "Took up with a new beau and followed him to Cedar Rapids, Iowa." He arched his eyebrows meaningfully. This was always part of the transaction—the eschewal of explicit disapproval in favor of coded glances.

"Wow," I said.

"Must be the real thing." Big Glenn's tone was highly dubious, and I felt a wave of defensiveness. Maybe it *was* the real thing.

"How long ago did she tell Lydia?" Lydia Bianchi was our fifty-five-year-old principal and a woman of whom I was quite fond. She was married but had no children, which led to speculation among her employees—that is to say, us—over whether her childlessness had been a choice or a private disappointment.

"Not more than a week or two," Big Glenn said. "The gentleman is in the pharmaceuticals field, comes up to Madison on a regular basis, so you might think they could have seen each other like that." He shrugged. "I must have forgot the passions of young love."

"Have they hired her replacement?"

"You interested?"

"No way—I'm staying right here in the library." This was when, somewhere inside, I knew that the opposite was true. I would leave. I would go away. If Charlie and I stayed together, if things progressed between us in ways I had not specified to anyone, including myself, since that conversation with Dena at the sandwich place, then my days as a teacher were probably numbered.

Standing there chatting with Big Glenn, I could feel the present moment rushing from me. I would leave soon, I realized, and when I did, in my absence, the other teachers would talk about me, too.

EVERYONE ALWAYS SAID there weren't tornadoes in Madison because of the lakes. The city is an isthmus, a term children who grow up in Madison know from an early age. And while Wisconsin wasn't hit by tornadoes with the regularity of towns in the states south and west of us, we tended to have a few watches a year and perhaps one warning and one real storm. In Riley, when I was a girl, we'd have tornado drills every spring. If we were in class, we filed out and sat Indian-style on the floor in the hall, knee to knee with the students beside us, all of us facing the wall, our heads down and our hands crossed over the crowns of our skulls. If we were outside—the drills happened sometimes at recess, which felt like a great waste—a teacher would lead us to a dip in the grassy hill behind the elementary school, and we'd lie flat on our bellies and join hands, forming an irregular circle or a human flower, our bodies the petals pointing out. In high school, we joked about the absurdity: *That* was supposed to save us? I pictured a net of children blown aloft, straining to hold on to one another.

The tornado watch that happened in late August 1977 was on a Sunday afternoon, and the night before, Charlie and I had gone to a party at the house of a couple he knew named the Garhoffs. I was pretty sure people had been smoking marijuana in the upstairs bathroom, which surprised me—I'd been to parties where there was pot, but the Garhoffs had children who were asleep on the same floor. We left a little after midnight, Charlie came to my apartment for an hour, and he tried to persuade me to let him stay over. "Like in Houghton" was his new argument. "And see, the flames of hell haven't licked us yet."

I declined. I knew that the next morning, he was going with Hank Ucker to a church service in Lomira, followed by a pancake breakfast. I, meanwhile, was greatly looking forward to cleaning my apartment—there were dishes in the sink, several loads of laundry, unpaid bills, everything that you happily neglect in the early stage of a relationship.

On Sunday, I tended to this tidying up for several hours while the sky turned from blue to dark gray. By two P.M., the temperature had dropped at least fifteen degrees since sunrise, and I shut my kitchen and bedroom windows and turned on the radio. A tornado was approaching Lacrosse, apparently, heading southwest, and it wasn't yet clear if it would hit Madison. I called Charlie, and when he answered, I said, "I'm glad you're home safely."

"I am *never* eating another pancake. God almighty, Lindy, those little old ladies refuse to take no for an answer."

"Have you looked outside lately?" I was standing in front of the kitchen sink, which faced the backyard and the rear of the house behind mine. "Even the birds aren't chirping."

"You're not worried, are you?"

I could hear his television, and I said, "Are you watching baseball?"

"The Brew Crew is trouncing the White Sox, thank you very much. Victory tastes even sweeter after our last two losses."

"Would it be annoying if we stay on the phone?" I said. "We don't need to talk."

"Why don't you come over? Or want me to come there?"

"Do you remember that my TV is black and white?"

"Then you come here, and I'll let you rub my tummy."

"I'd rather not drive right now, in case—" I began to say, and outside a pounding rain abruptly started. Then I realized it was not rain but hail.

"Mike Caldwell's the next at bat," Charlie said. "I had my doubts about him, but he's playing a decent game. Steve Brye, on the other hand—" This was when there was a flash of lightning followed by a terrific crack of thunder, and then the sirens went off, that menacing wail.

"I'm going down to the basement, and you should, too," I said. "Please, Charlie, don't keep watching the game."

"You know everything's fine, don't you?" His voice was calm and kind.

"Charlie, turn off the TV."

As if I were headed to the beach, I grabbed a towel and a book (it was *Humboldt's Gift*), and a flashlight as well, and I hurried from my apartment. The door to the basement was behind the stairs in the first-floor hall. There was one other apartment in the house, a first-floor unit belonging to a doctoral student named Ja-hoon Choi, and though I'd waited out tornadoes with him a few times before, his car wasn't in the driveway, so I didn't think he was home. The basement staircase was rickety and wooden, with air between the steps, and there was a bare lightbulb whose string I yanked on when I reached the bottom. Our landlord kept old sailing equipment here, and some outdoor furniture, but for the most part, the space was empty. I unfolded a lawn chair with metal arms and a plaid polyester seat, but it was so rusty and cobwebby that I folded it right back up. Then I just stood there holding the towel, *Humboldt's Gift,* and the flashlight. In the last few minutes, it had become hard to suppress thoughts about the unreliability of luck. *I will not be the one it happens to*—this is what we all believe, what we must believe to make our way in the world each day. *Someone else. Not me.* But every once in a while it *is* you, or someone close enough that it might as well be you. People to whom a terrible thing has never happened trust fate, the notion that what's meant to be will be; the rest of us know better. I pictured a tree crashing through Charlie's living room window, Charlie himself being lifted from the couch, trapped in the spinning air, violently deposited on the street or a roof. It's a phenomenon that seems comic to those who don't live in tornado-prone areas—the flying cow or refrigerator—and even to those of us who live in tornado states, it can be funny during calm times. But it was hailing outside, it was as dark as night, and anxiety clutched me. *It can't happen twice to a person I love,* I thought, but I was not able to convince myself.

Then, over the dropping hail and the squeal of the sirens, I heard a pounding that I eventually realized was coming from the first floor. I did nothing, and then I darted up the steps, expecting to see Ja-hoon Choi through the window in the front door. Instead, I saw Charlie.

I opened the door, saying, "Charlie! My God!" He sauntered in, sopping wet, and I threw my arms around him and said, "You shouldn't have driven over!" When we kissed, his lips were slick.

I pulled him back toward the basement, and when we were safely down there, he gestured at the towel I'd been holding all this time. "That for me?" He rubbed it over his head, and after he pulled it away, he surveyed the basement. "Nice ambience."

"I can't believe you're here."

"There's fallen branches on Williamson, but I bet you anything the tornado bypasses us. This is just a thunderstorm." Even as he said it, the sirens stopped. "See?" He grinned. "God agrees with me."

"Still, it can't have been safe to—"

He put his hand over my mouth, cutting me off. "I thought of something on the way here, but you have to stop scolding me. If I move my hand, will you stop?"

I nodded, and he withdrew his hand.

"I decided we should get married," he said. "No more of this running-through-the-rain shit. We should live in the same place, sleep in the same bed at night, wake up together in the morning, and whenever there's a tornado, I can take care of you and watch baseball at the same time."

We regarded each other. Uncertainly, I said, "You mean— Is this— Are you proposing?"

"It sure feels like it." He grinned, but a little nervously.

I said, "Okay." And then I beamed.

When Charlie took hold of me, he embraced me so tightly my feet left the ground—literally, I mean, not figuratively. And here we were in the basement, the grimy basement: My life was changing, and we stood in the dankest of places. I was still myself, I didn't feel catapulted into a different existence, the room was not aglow. It was only later that this moment would take on its proper burnish. While it was happening, everything felt new and strange and exciting and tenuous, which was the opposite of how it would feel later: weighty and familiar and reassuring. It would in retrospect appear to be a stop on a narrative path that was inevitable, but this is only because most events, most paths, feel inevitable in retrospect.

And so I had lost Dena, and in exchange I had gotten marriage; I'd traded friendship for romance, companionship for a husband. Was this not a reasonable bargain, one most people would make? I'd no longer be that allegedly eccentric, allegedly pitiable never married woman; my very existence would not pose a question that others felt compelled to try answering.

But what amazed me was that I would marry a man I loved; my choices had not turned out to be settling or remaining single. The generic relief of being coupled off was something I could have found by marrying Wade Trommler in 1967, or another man since. The remarkable part was that I'd be getting much more. Charlie was sweet and funny and energetic, he was incredibly attractive—his wrists with light brown hair on the back, his preppy shirts, his grin, and his charisma—and I had waited until the age of thirty-one, I'd sometimes felt like the last one standing, and then I had found somebody who was not perfect but was perfect enough, perfect for me. I was not to be punished, after all. I was to be rewarded, though it was hard to say for what.

It had been six weeks since we'd met.

WE HAD BACK-TO-SCHOOL faculty meetings that Wednesday and Thursday, before Labor Day weekend, and really, we teachers were no different than high school students, sniffing one another out after several months apart, comparing vacations, checking to see who'd gotten thin or tan. During the principal's welcoming speech in the gym, I sat on the bleachers between Rita and Maggie Stenta, the first-grade teacher who'd had me to her house for sloppy joes and sangria the previous spring. As our principal, Lydia Bianchi, described the new schedule for after-school bus duty, Rita leaned over and whispered, "How's your *boyfriend*?"

Maggie turned. "Are you dating someone?"

I shook my head as if I didn't follow or dared not turn my attention from Lydia. Truthfully, I didn't know quite how to talk about Charlie; I did not want to gush or boast. After three days, we still hadn't mentioned our engagement to anyone. We wanted to tell our families first, and because we'd be spending Labor Day weekend in Door County with the Blackwells and would return to Riley the following weekend, it seemed nicer to wait and share the news in person. What his family would make of simultaneously meeting me and finding out I was to be their newest in-law, I couldn't imagine.

Every year, all the teachers were required to watch the same half-hour filmstrip on head lice—it was a source of much grumbling, and I personally was seeing it for the sixth time—and the film was shown that Thursday in the library after lunch. I was walking back from the cafeteria with Rita and was still in the hall when Steve Engel, a science teacher who was six-five, hit his head on the *Paddle-to-the-Sea* canoe hanging in the library doorway. "Cool boat," I heard him say to no one in particular.

After a bit of shifting, I'd found the right place for all the papier-mâché pieces: the Runaway Bunnies and Mike Mulligan and Mary Anne perched on the lower shelves where the youngest children's books were kept; Ferdinand stood guard over the card catalog; the Giving Tree received a place of honor on my desk. A part of me couldn't believe I'd finished all ten of them, especially with the happy distraction of Charlie. I had probably spent two hundred hours total on the project—admittedly, most of those hours had been before Charlie—and I did not doubt that some people would have judged that a colossal waste of time.

When the filmstrip was over, Deborah Kuehl, the ostentatiously organized school nurse who was in charge of showing the film, was explaining the institution of a new no-nits policy. "I can't believe she does this right after lunch," Rita muttered. Although Deborah had a brisk manner, she was generous with her medical expertise and didn't seem to mind when teachers hit her up for advice—she'd peer into your throat and tell you if it looked like strep, or advise you on whether the black fingernail you'd banged in a door needed to be treated for infection.

When Deborah asked if there were any questions, Rita raised her hand. "I just wanted to say, doesn't the library look fabulous? Alice made all the animals herself."

I could feel the teachers in the rows ahead of and behind us look at me.

"While that's very supportive of you, Rita, I was hoping for questions pertaining to the nit policy." Deborah scanned her audience. No one else raised a hand, and she seemed only a little disappointed. Primly but not ungenerously, she said, "The sculptures are indeed a colorful addition to this space. Bravo, Alice, for your creativity."

Rita started clapping, and I murmured, "Rita, please," but it had already caught on. I knew I was blushing.

As it happened, when the children returned to school the following week, they seemed to get a kick out of the characters but also to see them for what they were, which was background decoration. The characters did not wear well that year: Even by the end of the first day, one of Ferdinand's horns had come off, a casualty of a second-grader's overexcitement, and after the sixth-graders' library period, I found a mustache drawn above Eloise's lips (I was pretty sure I knew which two boys had done it). At the conclusion of the school year, I ended up throwing them all out except for the Giving Tree, which I still have; each time I move, I pack it more carefully, as if it is a priceless vase. But I can honestly say I didn't mind the other characters' short lives. I enjoyed making them, and if it's great reverence you're looking for, or earnest expressions of gratitude—well, then you don't work with kids.

What I couldn't have imagined at the time was that the applause after the lice film was the moment of my greatest professional achievement. It was the most public recognition I ever received for being myself rather than an extension of someone else or, even worse, for being a symbol. Thirty-five teachers clapping in an elementary school library is, I realize, a humble triumph, but it touched me. In the years since, I have received great and vulgar quantities of attention, more attention than even the most vain or insecure individual could possibly wish for, and I have never enjoyed it a fraction as much.

THAT NIGHT, CHARLIE and I were eating dinner at his place, sitting on the living room couch with plates on our laps while the Brewers played the Detroit Tigers, and I said, "If we get married in the spring, what about doing it in the Arboretum? Would it upset your parents if we didn't have the ceremony in a church?"

"I knew you were an atheist!" He pointed at me. "Nah, I don't think they'd mind the outdoor thing, but it's gotta be much sooner. I need to be settled in Houghton come January."

"By yourself, do you mean, or with me?"

"That's usually how it works, man and wife under the same roof." Charlie's expression was mischievous. He was barefoot, wearing white shorts and a white polo shirt because he hadn't yet taken a shower after playing tennis with Cliff Hicken that afternoon. "Are you turned on by my virile man scent?" he'd asked when we were standing in the yard grilling hamburgers, and he'd pressed his body against mine and danced a little. Although I'd made a show of holding my nose—it seemed to be what he wanted—I found him cute when he was sweaty; he didn't smell bad to me at all.

"But when would the wedding be?" I said. "January is only five months away, Charlie."

"A wedding's nothing but a party where the lady wears a white dress. Hell, we could have it tomorrow."

"Your sense of romance is really sweeping me off my feet."

"Let's say October," he said. "You free in October?"

I considered it. This was far sooner than I'd imagined, but it was doable. "I don't see why not."

"That's the spirit. We don't want some fancy-schmancy deal, anyway, do we? My brothers and their wives all did those country-club receptions with the receiving-line crap. Well, not John, he married Nan, who's from back east, so they did it at her parents' place in Bar Harbor. Hey, there's an idea for you—what about Halcyon? Plenty of room, lots of beds, and you couldn't ask for a more spectacular setting."

"I'll let you know after I see it tomorrow. But if we do it in October, there might be snow on the ground."

Charlie thought about this for a moment, then said, "Damn your practicality."

I hesitated. "I'll finish out the school year, right? Even when we live in Houghton, I'll just drive back to Madison?"

Charlie shrugged. "If it's important to you."

"I wouldn't feel comfortable resigning in the middle of the year. People do it, but Lydia—our principal—hates when it happens."

"So long as this is your last year at Liess, do what you like. I'll need you around next summer, that's for certain. Being the wife of a candidate is a job in itself, which Maj knows all too well."

"I'll never have to speak in public, will I? I won't have to give speeches?"

He grinned. "Is that a condition of marrying me?"

"Charlie, I can hardly talk at faculty meetings."

"Okay, okay, you never have to give a speech." He was silent for a moment, and when he spoke again, his tone was serious. "I won't win. You understand that, don't you?"

"That's not very optimistic."

"This isn't a fake candidacy, I don't see myself as a straw man. That's not what I'm saying. I'll campaign my heart out. But the numbers aren't there. The focus isn't on getting elected, not yet. It's about putting my name out there, letting people know I'm an adult. I'm a serious person with serious ideas about the state of Wisconsin."

Looking at him, I had the uneasy thought that I could not imagine saying to someone: *I'm a serious person with serious ideas.* I couldn't imagine needing to.

Slowly, I said, "But won't a lot of people be putting a lot of time and money—"

He shook his head. "This is how it works. We're laying a foundation."

"A foundation for what? Are you planning to run for Congress again in two years?"

"I'm keeping my options open. Probably not in two years, no, but down the line, who knows? Maybe a position with the Republican Party, maybe a Senate run. So much of the political process is nothing but timing."

I set down my hamburger. "You sound incredibly cynical."

"I didn't write the rules," Charlie said.

"You seem happy to play by them."

"Dammit, Alice—" He put his hamburger down, too, and moved his plate to the coffee table in front of the couch. The table was shoddy white Formica, and he'd told me with evident pride that he'd gotten it off the sidewalk a few months before, when his neighbors had set it out with their trash. "I thought you were going to support me. Isn't that what you said in the car, or did I misunderstand?"

"Don't you ever just want a regular life? I don't see why it's so much better to be a public figure than a private citizen."

"For one thing, this is about service, not ego. Some people are in it to satisfy their own narcissism, sure, but not the Blackwells. Alice, if you're trying to talk me out of running, we have a serious problem."

"You gave me the impression that this was a onetime thing."

"Meaning you also thought I'd lose. Here you pretend to be aghast at me wasting money on a campaign when you've been counting on the other guy winning."

We both were quiet. "Let's not argue," I said.

He balled up his napkin and tossed it across the room toward the fireplace. When I stole a look at his profile, I saw that his expression was churlish.

"Do you want me to leave?" I asked.

"That might not be a bad idea."

I stood and carried my plate into the kitchen, and my hands were shaking. Were we still engaged? Were we still a couple, even? If we hadn't told anyone we were getting married, we wouldn't need to tell anyone we weren't. Perhaps there had been something vaporous about our relationship all along, something unreal. We could end things and there'd be nothing to explain. If anyone asked, I could simply say that it had fizzled.

Driving back to my own apartment, I thought that maybe it was for the best. Was I really so keen to trade my independence for a boosterish supporting role? Why would I want to sign on for a lifetime of listening to speeches like the one I'd heard him give at the Lions Club in Waupun? Putting aside the question of whether I agreed with his political platform, those types of speeches were just boring. Their repetition and their wheedling undertone and their righteous scorn and their phony clarity—they were so false and silly exactly as they pretended to be honest and important. And Charlie expected me not merely to tolerate his participation in this culture but to be excited about it? Yet would I ever expect him to come sit in the library and listen to me read *Bread and Jam for Frances*?

These thoughts roiled in my brain for over two hours—I was lying in bed, above the covers, reading *Humboldt's Gift*—and then I looked up from the middle of a paragraph on page 402, my certainty disintegrated all at once, and I was left with a feeling of heavy, insistent badness. What Charlie and I had been quarreling about seemed abstract and insubstantial. I could hardly remember the words either of us had used, and I just wanted to be sitting next to him, lying beneath him, my arms around him and his arms around me. He was the opposite of vaporous; everything else was vapor, and he was solid and central. The possibility that we might have broken up was devastating; it was unbearable.

I willed myself not to give in to the temptation to call him—it would be better to wait until the next morning. It was presumptuous to think his anger was on the same time line mine was, to imagine that he'd already have forgiven me, too. And yet if I could call him, if I could make things all right, the relief would be so great that perhaps it was a risk worth taking. In the bathroom, I washed my face and brushed my teeth, and then I tweezed my eyebrows a bit, just to occupy myself. I went back into the bedroom and changed into my sleeveless cotton nightgown. It was ten-twenty, I saw, and I decided that I wouldn't call him before eleven o'clock. I wouldn't even make a definite plan to call him until then; I would leave open the possibility, and if I could restrain myself, I would, but if I couldn't, at eleven I'd think through what I wanted to say.

I lay on my side, with the light on and the window open, and a warm breeze blew in. I tried not to cry. Who cared if I had to sit through speeches about taxes for the next fifty years? Perhaps I could learn to hold a novel in my purse at such an angle that no one would observe me reading it. No, it wouldn't be a narrowing, a stricture, to become Charlie's wife; whenever I was with him, my life felt dense with possibilities, fuller and noisier and far more fun. I had never been a person who believed life was an adventure. To me, it was more a series of obligations, some of which could be quite rewarding and some of which you just gritted your teeth for. But now I saw the case for larks and mischief. Here I was being offered my own personal tour guide in the country of good fortune, and I was stalling as I had once stalled with Andrew Imhof. What was wrong with me?

I nearly leaped from the bed, I hurried into the kitchen, I'd lifted the receiver and begun dialing and then my buzzer rang, and when I flew downstairs and opened the front door, we made eye contact, and without either of us saying anything, we were hugging tightly, and he said, "If you don't want me to run again after this, I won't. Hell, I don't even need to run now," and I said, "Of course you should."

"I promise I won't try to brainwash you," he said. "You can vote for Fidel Castro and I won't bat an eye."

Although I hadn't been crying, when I laughed, it was the kind of deep, gaspy laughter that follows tears.

"Can we decide there won't be ugliness between us?" He was looking down at me, and he set his palms on my cheeks. "Because I can't stand it, I really can't."

I still was giggly with nervous relief. "Charlie, I'm so sorry."

"Obviously, we're still getting to know each other," he said. "No doubt some folks will say we rushed this. But I've never felt more sure of anything. Getting to know you better, the idea of spending all the coming weeks and years together—there's nothing I look forward to more."

"Charlie, I do know you've been raised for this life, and I think it's honorable. You believe in making the world better, and I admire that."

As I said it, it became true. There was a skepticism that I surrendered in this moment, and the surrender was long-lasting; it was practically permanent. There is such a thing as lively debate, and Charlie and I weren't cut out for it—so limited was our appetite for rancor that any taste of it was acrid. We could agree, or we could avoid discussion, and I was good at both; by generation, gender, and geography, and above all, by temperament, I was good at agreement and good at avoidance.

If I were to tell the story of my life (I have repeatedly declined the opportunity), and if I were being honest (I would not be, of course—one never is), I would probably feel tempted to say that standing that night just inside my apartment, me in my nightgown and Charlie in jeans and a red shirt, I made a choice: I chose our relationship over my political convictions, love over ideology. But again, this would be false honesty; it would once more contribute to a narrative arc that is satisfying rather than accurate. My convictions were internal—I'd rarely seen the point in expressing them aloud, and if I had, my entire political outlook could have been summarized by the statement that I felt bad for poor people and was glad abortion had become legal. And so I didn't *choose* anything in this moment. I had met Charlie a matter of weeks before, and already the idea of living without him made me feel like a fish flopping on the sand. To go from being a Democrat to a Republican, or at least to pretend, through smiling obfuscation, that I had—this was a small price to pay for the water washing back over me, allowing me to breathe.

Charlie was grinning.

"What?" I said.

"I just realized." His nostrils flared a little. "We get to have our first makeup sex."

I HAD BOUGHT a basil plant in a small terra-cotta pot to give as a hostess present to Charlie's mother, but we were less than halfway to Halcyon when I began to question my selection. This second-guessing occurred right around the time I came to understand that Halcyon, Wisconsin, was not, as I had previously assumed based on Charlie's passing references, a town. Rather, Halcyon was a row of houses along a seven-hundred-acre eastern stretch of the peninsula that was Door County, and in order to own one of the houses, you had to belong to the Halcyon Club. Apparently, you became a member by being born into one of five families: the Niedleffs, the Higginsons, the deWolfes, the Thayers, and the Blackwells. Charlie's first kiss, he explained cheerfully, had been with Christy Niedleff, when he was twelve and she was fourteen; Sarah Thayer, the matriarch of the Thayer family, was the sister of Hugh deWolfe, the patriarch of the deWolfes; Hugh deWolfe and Harold Blackwell, Charlie's father, had been roommates at Princeton; Emily Higginson was the godmother of Charlie's brother Ed; and those were about all the intramural details I managed to retain, though there were many, many more, and Charlie shared them with increasing zest the closer we got to our destination. The families had purchased the land together in 1943, he said; they each had their own house, their own dock, and everyone took their meals at a jointly owned and maintained club. Oh, and that weekend was the Halcyon Open, the long-standing tennis competition for which a silver trophy vase sat on the mantel in the clubhouse and on whose surface the men's singles and doubles champions' names were engraved each year. Charlie had won singles in 1965, 1966, and 1974, and he and his brother Arthur had won doubles in 1969.

"You eat *all* your meals at a clubhouse?" I said. "Breakfast, lunch, and dinner?"

"The peanut-butter no-bake bars are out of this world," Charlie said. "And the apple pie, it makes you proud to be an American."

"But who cooks? Do you take turns?"

"No, no, there's a staff." His voice was casual—naturally, there was a staff—and I tried to absorb this information quickly and invisibly. Just as I did not think I ought to apologize for having been raised middle-class, I did not think Charlie ought to apologize for or feel self-conscious about his privilege. "Mainly, it's Ernesto and his wife, Mary," he was saying. "Just terrific people, one of those couples that fight like cats and dogs but you know they're crazy for each other. And they always hire a couple of kids from town. One niece of theirs, damned if I can remember her name, but she was— I guess *plentifully endowed* would be a nice way to put it. This has to have been twenty years ago.

She's bending over to set down the French toast every morning, and my eyeballs are popping out of my head. My brothers and I were in pig heaven, let me tell you, until Maj caught wind of what was going on and told Mary she had to buy the niece a better-fitting uniform." Charlie tapped his fingers against the steering wheel; he was in an exceptionally good mood. "What there used to be on Labor Day weekend," he said, "and I guess no one wants to put in the time anymore, but there were annual musicals. Walt Thayer would play the piano, Maj and Mrs. deWolfe would write the lyrics, and I swear I believed I'd have a career on Broadway, which practically gave Maj a coronary, as you can imagine."

"What were the musicals about?"

"Just things that had happened during the summer. We'd stay up here for two and a half, three months a year, so there were hijinks galore, and not only among the kids—the adults cut loose, too. Get a few G and T's in them, and all bets are off. You know those pink flamingos, the lawn ornaments that are popular with white trash?"

When I had been a freshman in high school, our neighbor Mrs. Falke had acquired a pair and set them in her yard. But I merely said, "Uh-huh."

"Well, Billy and Francie Niedleff buy a couple in town and put them in front of our place. After we figure out who did it, Maj wants revenge, so one night under the cover of darkness, she attaches them to the bow of Mr. Niedleff's sloop. Mrs. Niedleff returns them to our yard a few nights later, and they're wearing Cubs baseball caps, these little hats she made out of cardboard, because Dad just hates the Cubs. And so on and so forth for the whole summer, until the shenanigans culminate with Dad going into the lav one night, and what does he find standing in the tub but a real live flamingo." Charlie chuckled. "I tell you, I'm not sure if Dad or the bird was more terrified."

"But what did you do with it—you didn't keep it, did you?"

"Oh, they took him to the zoo down in Green Bay the next day. He managed to take an epic crap before then, but hey, he was in the bathroom. Can you blame him?"

Charlie was still chortling when I said, "Maybe we shouldn't mention our engagement to your family this weekend. Is that all right? We could invite your parents and my mother and grandmother to lunch in Madison and tell them all together."

Charlie turned toward me, grinning. "Having second thoughts?"

"It feels more respectful not to tell either family first," I said. "Plus, it might be too much to say to your parents, 'This is Alice, and by the way, she's my fiancée.' "

"You're not worried they won't like you, are you?"

Not entirely honestly, I said, "No." We were passing tall, skinny white birch trees, and along with my anxiety about the impending introductions, I had started to feel the restlessness that arises when you know you're nearing water but it hasn't yet come into view. The drive from Madison was almost four hours, and it was past three o'clock as we turned onto a series of smaller roads eventually leading to a dirt one, which we bumped along for three miles. Then, at last, I saw Lake Michigan through the trees, still distant but blue and sparkly in the sun. Charlie pulled off the road and drove onto a stretch of lushly green grass dotted with sugar maples, evergreens, and irregularly spaced white-shingled buildings of various sizes. I took the largest one to be the clubhouse.

"Halcyon sweet Halcyon," he said, and he began honking in rapid spurts. He pointed to the big building. "That's the Alamo, which is where Maj and Dad and some of the grandkids sleep. They might put you in there, but it's likelier you'll be in one of those." He was pointing at the smaller cottages. "That's Catfish, and Gin Rummy, and Old Nassau. And you see that one?" He grinned. "Smoked my first joint there, and nearly burned the place to the ground. It's called Itty-Bitty." He stuck his head out the window, and I saw that someone had emerged from the biggest house and was approaching us, someone who strongly resembled Charlie except with darker hair. Charlie drove directly toward this person—he was probably going fifteen miles an hour, not fast but not all that slow, either, given the proximity—and the closer Charlie got, the wider this guy's smile grew. He walked with complete nonchalance, and at the last second, when I was already wincing, Charlie slammed on the brakes, and the guy called out, "You're so chickenshit, Chas!"

Charlie parked the car next to a wood-paneled station wagon—there were five cars pulled up near the back of the house—and the other man approached my door, resting his forearms on the roof while peering down at me through my open window. "So you're the reason none of us have heard from Chasbo in weeks," he said. "Now I see why."

"Back off, perv," Charlie said, and there was a happiness in his tone I had not heard before, not quite like this. "Alice, meet my brother Arthur."

We shook hands through the window. "I admire you," Arthur said. "Not every woman is willing to go out with a retard."

Charlie was out of the car by then, and before I really knew what had happened, he'd tackled Arthur from the side and they were rolling over and over in the grass, tussling and laughing. I opened the car door and stepped out. The smell, that sweet clean smell of northern Wisconsin—it almost made Halcyon seem worthy of its pretentious name. I looked around at the five buildings. I was pretty sure, though Charlie had not explicitly said so, that these structures represented only the Blackwells' property, their compound, and not the entirety of Halcyon, as I'd thought when the houses had first come into view. With my own recent foray into real estate having taught me to think in such terms, I guessed that the largest house was five thousand square feet; three of the others were about eight or nine hundred square feet each; and the last, Itty-Bitty, couldn't have been over two hundred. A bed of periwinkles grew around the base of an elm tree, and the grass was such a rich green that I was tempted to take off my shoes. I walked around the side of the big house. Perhaps twenty feet in front of me, a slate sidewalk was embedded in the grass, and beyond the sidewalk, past a sloping grassy descent of about forty yards, was a narrow rocky beach and then the water. A long dock extended into the lake. At the end of the dock, figures lay on towels and sat in folding chairs. Out in the water, there was a raft off which a person in red swim trunks jumped while I watched.

When I returned to the car, Charlie and Arthur were standing and they walked toward me, panting agreeably. "Tell me, Alice," Arthur said, "is Chasbo's impotence still a problem, or did he get that taken care of?"

"Cured by the same doc who treated your flatulence." Charlie was grinning. "Super fellow."

"Better gaseous than limp," Arthur said, and Charlie replied, "Keep telling yourself that, ass-blaster."

"Alice, be honest," Arthur said. "Was it Chas's silver tongue that won you over?"

Charlie set one arm around Arthur's shoulders. "Everything I know, I learned from my older brother."

They both were grinning the same grin, and Arthur said, "Welcome to Halcyon. You guys want a beer?"

We opened the trunk and carried our things toward the house—"I'm not sure where Maj is putting Alice, but we'll stash her stuff in the Alamo for now," Arthur said—and I held my purse and the basil plant (it now seemed officially cornpone, hippie cornpone), and Arthur took the suitcase I'd bought the previous winter from Dena's shop, which was swirling pink and brown paisley vinyl with pink leather straps. As we reached a screen door at the back of the house, Charlie asked, "Who's around?"

"Let's see . . . Ed and John are out fishing with Joe Thayer, Ginger has a migraine"—Arthur raised his eyebrows dubiously—"Dad and Maj are swimming with the boys and Liza, Jadey, and the baby drove to town to get bug spray—careful, 'cause the mosquitoes are a bitch right now—Uncle Trip is sleeping, and Nan is playing tennis with Margaret. Am I leaving anyone out?"

"Uncle Trip's here?" Charlie said.

Arthur grinned. "Would Labor Day weekend be complete without him?"

At that moment, as Arthur opened the screen door and Charlie and I followed him inside, I may as well have been listening to them speak Portuguese—very few of the names meant anything to me, and it seemed that a tremendous amount of time would have to pass before they did. But I was wrong, and even by the end of the weekend, I could have decoded the summary haltingly but accurately: Ed was the oldest brother, the congressman; Ginger was his wife, prone to migraines or to faking them, depending on whom you believed (either way, there seemed to be a consensus among all the Blackwells besides Ed that Ginger was joyless and rigid, and thus she served, perhaps as they intended, as a cautionary tale for me); the boys were their sons, Harry, age ten, Tommy, age eight, and Geoff, age four; also falling under the heading of "the boys" was Arthur's son, Drew, age three; Jadey was Arthur's wife, and the baby was their eleven-month-old daughter, Winnie; John was the second oldest brother, the husband of Nan; Liza, age nine, was John and Nan's older daughter, and Margaret, age seven, was their younger daughter; Uncle Trip was nobody's uncle but had been the third roommate in the triple shared by Harold Blackwell and Hugh deWolfe at Princeton University in the fall of 1939 and the spring of 1940; and finally, Dad was Harold Blackwell, and Maj was Priscilla Blackwell. Joe Thayer, with whom Ed and John were out fishing (the Blackwells owned five boats: a cutter, a motorboat, two Whitehall rowboats, and a canoe), was, at thirty-six, the oldest child of Walt and Sarah Thayer—the Thayers were another Halcyon family—and was a lawyer in Milwaukee. Joe was also a man whom, eleven years later, at night on the campus of Princeton, I'd find myself kissing on the lips. But this was the least of what I didn't know that afternoon.

We'd entered the big house—the Alamo—through a pantry that led to the kitchen. Both the existence of the kitchen and its lack of fanciness surprised me. The refrigerator was white with rounded corners (it looked to be from the forties and hummed loudly). There was a large gas range with four burners, and an oak table with a greasy finish was pushed against the wall, its other sides flanked by chairs with thin navy blue cushions. On the wall hung a clock with a cream face, black minute and second hands, and a Schlitz logo in the center. What was striking was how full the room seemed—it was stocked like any kitchen for a large family, onions and potatoes in a wire basket hanging from the ceiling, a spice rack next to the stove, boxes of cereal stacked atop the refrigerator, and an open bag of potato chips sitting on the table. I gestured toward the chips. "I thought you ate all your meals at the clubhouse."

"Alice, man cannot live on breakfast, lunch, and dinner alone," Arthur said.

"Only thing the Blackwells are better at than eating is drinking,"

Charlie said. "Speaking of—" He opened the refrigerator and withdrew three cans of beer, passing one each to Arthur and me. After Charlie had snapped the tab on his, he took a long swallow, and when he was finished, he said, "Christ, is it good to be here."

Arthur turned to me. "I assume Chas has gone through the whole plumbing spiel with you."

I looked at Charlie. "Oops," he said, but he was smiling. To Arthur, he said, "I was afraid she wouldn't come."

"I offer a math lesson," Arthur said. "There are now—Chas, is it seventeen Blackwells here? Eighteen? And there's one bathroom, and I don't just mean in this house, I mean in all the houses. Well, Maj and Dad have a half-bath, but that's off limits to everyone but them. What I'm trying to say is, efficiency is appreciated."

I nodded. "Okay."

"The pipes aren't the greatest, so flush early and often," Charlie said.

"If you take a massive crap, let a wire hanger be your friend." Arthur turned his hand sideways and made a slicing gesture.

He didn't shock me; to be fair, I didn't know if he was trying, or if he was just being himself. Arthur struck me as childish, but I didn't mind childishness—it wasn't by accident that I worked at a school—and besides, meeting Charlie's family, I wanted to be a good sport. I said, "Is this the same bathroom where your father came upon the flamingo?"

"You told her about that?" Arthur laughed, shaking his head. "Classic, absolutely classic. You should have heard that thing honking and growling. Who even knew flamingos made noise? Let me give you the grand tour."

The three of us walked from the kitchen into the living room, an enormous open space that contained, against its north wall, the largest fireplace I had ever seen—it was a fireplace I could have stood inside. On the walls above it were mounted animal trophies: High up were a moose and several deer (at least two with six-point antlers), and lower down were trout and salmon, pheasant and wild turkey and a ruffed grouse. In one corner was what I might have taken for the showpiece of the collection—a stuffed black bear standing upright at roughly eight feet, its mouth frozen open in a ferocious growl, a heart-shaped patch of white fur on its chest—except that the beast had been stripped of its gravitas by the placement of a cowboy hat on its head. I wondered, didn't the bear frighten the younger grandchildren?

The furniture in the living room was mismatched and faded, dominated by two white bamboo couches with cushions I suspected had once been red but were now a washed-out dark pink; both couches held a smattering of aquatic-themed throw pillows featuring lighthouses, sailboats, and shells. On a shelf beneath the large bamboo coffee table, board games were stacked in boxes that were also faded and, in some cases, coming apart (I glimpsed Scrabble, Monopoly, and Candy Land, as well as a few jigsaw puzzles). On the front wall, jalousie windows ran vertically from waist height to the ceiling and horizontally from one end of the room to the other. Many of the panes were open, and they revealed a screened-in front porch crowded with wicker furniture on a vast straw rug. At the far end, between the walls, there was strung a hammock in which—it took me a second to notice—a middle-aged man appeared to sleep soundly. Beyond the porch was Lake Michigan.

"Bedrooms are this way." Arthur guided us into a short hallway leading to two smaller rooms. The first had another straw rug, a low king-size bed covered in a white spread, two bedside tables stacked high with hardcover books and papers, and a mirrored dressing table whose light blue paint was chipping. The second room had a double bed on a mint-colored iron frame and a not-new-looking television set propped on the dresser. It wasn't until I saw the two bedrooms on the other side of the house, both of which contained several single beds and were spare except for the clutter of children's toys and small articles of abandoned clothing, that I realized the first bedroom must have belonged to Charlie's parents.

"If it's all right, I'll use the famous bathroom now," I said.

"Thataway." Charlie cocked his head, and as I walked in the direction he was gesturing, Arthur called after me, "Flush early and often."

I found myself in a hallway where old-looking coats and flannel shirts hung on hooks, and carelessly stacked items of household paraphernalia sat above them on a high ledge: a Frisbee and snowshoes, a plastic kite, a copy of the Milwaukee White Pages, a dusty one-gallon metal can of gray wall paint.

Affixed to the outside of the bathroom door was a porcelain oval that said W.C. in fancy script. But this was disingenuous—it was no closet, I realized as I pushed open the door to find a room the size of my family's dining room in Riley. In here were a washer and dryer; a clawfoot tub; an old toilet with a black plastic seat, a chain you pulled for flushing, and a tank situated above the user's head; a small white porcelain sink; a low wooden table near the sink on which sat four mugs with two or three toothbrushes in each of them; a bookshelf with mostly paperback potboilers but also a few hardcovers—*The Confessions of Nat Turner,* a large green copy of Leon Uris's *Trinity;* and a window blocked by a not entirely opaque white cotton voile curtain through which I could see parked cars and hear not just the breeze in the backyard but also the distant cries of the swimmers and sunbathers on the dock. I shut the door and was lifting my skirt—to meet Charlie's family, I had chosen to wear a yellow knit dress with a collar, short sleeves, and a tie belt, along with my blue Dr. Scholl's sandals—when I realized that the door had opened on its own. After a second attempt at closing it, I figured out that it didn't stay put; no lock clicked into place, and the soft wood of the door slid away from the soft wood of the frame. Of course it did. I felt a brief rise of distress (one bathroom for eighteen people! for the next three nights!), but I swallowed it back, pulling *Trinity* and *The Confessions of Nat Turner* from the bookshelf and stacking them on the floor against the door—for all I knew, that was what they were there for. For good measure, I reached behind the curtain and shut the window; there was no screen.

When I reemerged, Charlie and Arthur were in the living room, where Arthur was showing Charlie an article about their brother Ed in *Washingtonian* magazine, a publication with which I was not familiar. "God almighty, is Eddie losing his hair." Charlie held up the magazine for me to see. "I'm giving him grief about that, for sure. Alice, you want to put your swimsuit on?"

"It might be more dignified to meet your parents while I'm still wearing clothes."

Arthur laughed. "If you're looking for dignified, you've come to the wrong place." He walked over to a small table between two white bamboo chairs, and he lifted from it a tarnished silver eight-by-ten picture frame. "I refer you to Exhibit A."

"Oh, boy." Charlie grinned. "You trying to get her to dump me here and now?"

Arthur passed me the frame. On the top, under the clouded silver, a monogram was discernible, the letters PBH, with the bigger B in the middle. The photograph showed a blond woman in a white wedding dress, Arthur in a tuxedo and tails, and fanning out on either side of them, a row of smiling young people; on the bride's side were six women in matching satin pink dresses, and on Arthur's side were six men in tails, the closest one to him being Charlie.

"This is beautiful," I said. "When did you get married?"

"Seventy-one, but that's not the point. Look closer."

"All I can say is, you'd better watch your back," Charlie said. "Not you, Alice."

I was still scanning the photograph. Then I saw, and Arthur saw me see, and he said, "Quite a pair on him, huh? But I guess you already knew that."

In the photo, in front of the place where Charlie's zipper would be, hung a ruddy bulge. It was slightly out of context but unmistakable: He had (or at least I hoped it had been him and not someone else) removed his scrotum from inside his pants and displayed it for the photo.

I glanced at Charlie—really, the Blackwells were exactly like sixth-grade boys at Liess, the ones who'd use a dirty word in earshot of a teacher, waiting for a reaction—and I said mildly, "That's an unusual pose for a picture."

"Took about five years for Jadey to forgive me, but it was worth every minute." Charlie grinned. "No, she knew it was all in good fun."

"My wife is a *huge* admirer of the black-tie nutsack," Arthur said. "And I do mean huge."

Charlie took my hand and squeezed it. "I promise not to do that at our wedding." Arthur chortled—having no idea that we really were engaged—and this was when we heard footsteps on the stairs leading up to the porch and then a voice, a refined, middle-aged female voice, calling out, "Fee-fi-fo-fum, I smell the blood of an interloping girlfriend."

"Do I call your mom Priscilla or Mrs. Blackwell?" I whispered.

Charlie was walking out to the porch with me behind him, and he said, "Hey, Maj, Alice wants to know if she should call you Priscilla or Mrs. Blackwell."

"*Charlie,*" I hissed.

His mother laughed. "It depends," she said. "We'll have to see how much I like Alice."

She had chin-length white hair that was slicked back, its wetness holding it in place in the way it does for only a few minutes after you emerge from water. She wore a navy blue tank swimsuit and a watch and nothing else, not even shoes or a towel. She was nearly six feet, and her legs and chest and shoulders were all both wrinkly and tan; her body was slim and athletic. ("I was field-hockey captain at Dana Hall as well as Holyoke," she mentioned later in the weekend, and I murmured my approval not because I actually was impressed but because I could tell I should be.)

She had not yet glanced in my direction, and she reached out and set her fingers under Charlie's chin—I observed the strange fact of Charlie and his mother not embracing—and after her eyes had roamed over his face, she said in a warm tone, "That haircut makes you look like a Jew."

Without hesitation—sincerely, it seemed—Charlie laughed. "Hey, at least I still have hair, which is more than I can say for your oldest son."

But she had already moved on; with no embarrassment or apology, she was looking me up and down. "Aren't you a little dish."

I stepped forward and extended the terra-cotta planter with the basil in it. "Thank you very much for having me."

"Alice brought you some homegrown marijuana," Charlie said. "Madison's finest."

"It's basil," I said quickly.

Mrs. Blackwell turned to Charlie. "I'll bet you wish it were marijuana," she said, and there was a note of pride in her voice that thickened as she added, addressing me, "My sons are incorrigibly naughty, except for Eddie, who's straight as a ruler. Charlie tells me you're from Riley, so you must know the Zurbrugg family."

I nodded. "I went all through school with Fred." The Zurbruggs were the richest people in Riley, maybe the only rich people—they owned one of the largest dairy farms in the state, and of course it had been Fred's party that I was driving to the night of my accident.

Mrs. Blackwell said, "Ada Zurbrugg's gladiola are the envy of our Garden Club in Milwaukee. We don't know what her trick is. But such a shame about Geraldine, isn't it? She was the most darling child."

"Did something—?" I hesitated. Geraldine was Fred's older sister, and if a great misfortune had befallen her, I wasn't aware of it.

"Well, she's fat as a house!" Mrs. Blackwell exclaimed. "She must weigh two hundred and fifty pounds! It's absolutely tragic."

"I haven't seen her for a few years."

"If ever the bikini should be made illegal . . ." Mrs. Blackwell laughed merrily. "Alice, I'm putting you in Itty-Bitty. Chas, help her settle in, and do explain about the lav." She turned back to me. "Halcyon can be a bit rustic, but I'm sure you don't mind roughing it. Are you a singles or a doubles girl?"

It took me a few seconds to figure out what she was referring to. "Oh, I don't play tennis." I smiled ruefully. "Charlie told me about the tournament, though, and it sounds like a fun tradition."

"If you don't play tennis, what on earth do you do?" She was feigning confusion when I'm sure she wasn't confused at all. Shrewdness emanated from her.

"Well—" I paused. Was her question rhetorical or literal? No one spoke, and I said, "I enjoy reading." For the first time in this exchange, I did not strain to seem positive and sincere; I simply spoke, because I could see already that Priscilla Blackwell was a person who would hate you for trying to convince her you were good enough. She might hate you for not trying, too, but probably less so.

Charlie set one hand on my back. "Alice is a genius," he said. "She's read every book there is." If the statement was absurd, it was also sweet. He added, "I hear Ginger has a migraine?"

Mrs. Blackwell snorted. "Ginger is a patsy." She looked at her watch. "Drinks will be at six sharp, and we'll leave for the clubhouse at seven-twenty." She was looking at me again when she added, "You'll want to change for dinner."

ITTY-BITTY CONTAINED two sets of bunk beds, a mini-refrigerator (Charlie helped himself to another beer from it as soon as we walked inside), and a closet in which nothing hung except bare wire hangers; there was, of course, no bathroom. Of the four mattresses, only one was made up: tightly pulled white sheets, a single pillow in a white pillowcase, a maroon wool blanket folded at the foot of the bed.

Charlie sat on the blanket, hunched forward so he didn't hit his head on the top bunk, as I hung my clothes. "This is ideal," he said. "I was worried she'd put you in with some squawking niece or nephew, but you've got privacy so you can read, sleep in . . ." He grinned. "Entertain midnight visitors."

"Don't count on it." I slid a blouse onto a hanger. "I don't want to risk getting caught by your mom. You've brought other girlfriends to Halcyon, haven't you?"

"Is that code for how many girls have I slept with? You can ask me that."

"It wasn't code, but now that you mention it—"

"Eleven," he said. "Before you, I mean. You're twelve. What about you—how many dudes?"

"Counting you, four." I set my white pumps on the closet floor.

"Really, four?" Charlie seemed surprised.

"What did you think?"

"The brother of the fellow in high school, and me, and—"

"I dated Wade Trommler during college, and a few years ago a guy named Simon."

"*You* made the beast with two backs with Trombone Trommler? You were boned by the Trombone?" Charlie seemed not at all jealous but greatly amused. "That's priceless. Oh, man, Wade has to be, hands down, the dullest man on the planet. Don't get me wrong, he's as nice as they come, but duller than dishwater. How was he?"

"Why do you want to talk about this?" During a recent badminton game at the Hickens', Wade and Charlie had been on the same team, but I no longer thought of Wade as my ex-boyfriend; I simply thought of him as Rose's husband.

"Does that mean he was bad or good?" Charlie asked.

"He was fine," I said. "You're right that he's nice, and you're right that he's dull."

"He was no Charlie Blackwell?"

I walked to Charlie and wrapped my arms around him. He was still sitting, and he nuzzled his face against my chest. "There's only one Charlie Blackwell," I said, and I couldn't help adding, "Thank goodness."

"And this other fellow, Simon who?"

"His last name is Törnkvist. I'm sure you don't know him. He was kind of a hippie and a very serious person."

"What about in the sack?"

"Charlie, come on."

"I'm trying to get a sense of the full Lindy. To move into the future together, we must also honor our past."

I gently tilted his head back so we were looking at each other. "Is that from a speech?"

He smirked. "Maybe."

"I think Simon was haunted by having been in Vietnam," I said.

"Aha." Charlie nodded. "The embittered kind of hippie. Wise of you to move on."

"Don't make light of him," I said. "He's a decent person. You didn't—" I had a hunch about the answer to this question, but I wasn't certain. "You didn't go to Vietnam, did you?"

"Couldn't. Flat feet." Charlie was barefoot, already wearing his swim trunks, and he extended his legs and flexed his feet.

"Did your brothers go?"

"First Ed was in law school, then he'd married Ginger, so he got draft deferments, and it turns out John and Arthur are flat-footed, too. What are the chances, huh?" Charlie grinned. Making air quotes, he said, "Those were my years in the 'hospitality industry'—aka I was a ski bum. I was an instructor in Squaw Valley, and I grew a mountain-man beard, which I'll ask Maj if she has any pictures of, because you have to see it to believe it."

It was strange to have been reminded of Simon while standing in this guest cottage on the Blackwell vacation compound, strange to think how different this place was, surely, from the pea farm where Simon's family lived. He would, I imagined, find the Blackwells indulgent and vulgar and self-satisfied, and they in turn would find him dour and humorless—not that they would ever cross paths. So what did it mean that I could dwell in either camp without much difficulty? Was I mutable, without a fixed identity? I could see the arguments for every side, for and against people like the Blackwells, for and against a person like Simon. Yet it was hard to imagine Charlie's behavior, unlike my own, changing depending on whom he dated; he would always be Charlie. He had told me I had a strong sense of myself, but I wondered then if the opposite was true—if what he took for strength was really a bending sort of accommodation to his ways, if what he saw when he looked at me was the reflection of his own will and personality. I was polite, adequately educated, and adequately pretty, and if I wanted to marry him, it meant he was a worthy person to marry. But no—this line of thought served little purpose. Lots of women would have married Charlie. How pompous to imagine my affirmation determined his standing in some sort of sweeping or official way, how truly laughable to a person like Priscilla Blackwell, who saw me, no doubt, as a humble teacher from a small town. I *was* a humble teacher from a small town. (And then, beneath this conclusion, which was the one I pretended to myself that I had drawn, there lay the conclusion that I actually drew: that I was right after all. While plenty of women indeed would have married Charlie, these were women like Dena, not women like me. I wasn't marrying him for his money or social standing. I was marrying him because I enjoyed his company. And I was, from his point of view, a serious person—he saw me the way I had seen Simon—and it was my seriousness that fundamentally affirmed Charlie, explaining away his playfulness as a superficial distraction, alluding to hidden reservoirs of wisdom and stability. If Charlie Blackwell was really a spoiled lightweight, Alice Lindgren would not have been marrying him; we both needed to believe it. But again, as I said: This is the conclusion I pretended not to have drawn.)

Charlie patted my backside. "Hurry up and put your suit on," he said. "I want to get in a swim before dinner."

TWO HOURS LATER, as I climbed the steps leading to the screened-in porch of the Alamo at a minute to six, I saw that the porch was empty. Naturally, I wondered if I'd gotten the time or place wrong that we were to have drinks, and my apprehension increased when I looked over my shoulder and saw Charlie's brother John walking up the grassy incline from the lake, wearing plaid swim trunks and holding the hand of Margaret, his seven-year-old daughter. As he approached, he made a wincing smile. "We'll do a very quick turnaround," he said to me. "Lightning speed, right, Margaret? Alice, you look lovely." A threadbare towel hung around John's neck, and in his right hand he carried a rubber inner tube. Both he and Margaret had burnt noses and shoulders.

I'd met John and several other Blackwells on the dock that afternoon. Everyone was friendly—the children were busy splashing and playing—and I had trouble remembering who was who except for Harold Blackwell, who, when Charlie and I arrived, was climbing a wooden ladder out of the water. He looked like an older version of the governor I had paid only passing attention to in the newspaper and on television when I was in high school and college, except that instead of wearing a business suit, he wore swim trunks, his gray chest hair clung wetly to his skin, and his nipples were mauve coins; to see the nipples of the former governor was an unsettling experience on which I did my best not to dwell. (I had the thought that Dena would appreciate the awkwardness of this encounter, then I felt a twinge of regret that I wouldn't be able to describe it to her, then I was distracted by meeting the many other Blackwells.) When Charlie introduced us, Harold Blackwell placed both his hands over both of mine. "I can't tell you how delighted we are to have you here," he said, and he didn't seem the way I remembered him from television, which was distant and self-assured and generically middle-aged and generically male. Had time changed him? He possessed an air of kindness that was both sorrowful and authentic—a sad person whose sadness had, of all possible outcomes, made him nice.

I had just opened the screen door onto the porch of the Alamo when a thin, middle-aged black woman in a black dress and a white apron appeared from inside the house, carrying a tray of crab dip and crackers that she set on a large round table. Already there, sitting on the white tablecloth, were bottles of wine, whiskey, brandy, sweet vermouth, and bitters, as well as a silver ice bucket, a lemon, a dish of maraschino cherries, green cocktail napkins, and many glasses—wineglasses and highballs and old-fashioneds—off which the evening sun reflected enchantingly. A plastic cooler filled with ice and cans of Pabst and Schlitz waited adjacent to the table with the lid removed.

"Hello," I said. "I'm Alice Lindgren. I'm Charlie's— I'm a guest of Charlie."

The woman nodded in a not particularly warm way. "What do you want to drink?"

"Am I early?" I asked. "May I help you set up?" On the wicker tables between chairs, I noticed little bowls of peanuts and, separately, Cheetos; also, on closer inspection, I saw that the cocktail napkins featured a yellow ball midbounce and said in white letters TENNIS PLAYERS HAVE NO FAULTS!

The woman said, "You want some white wine, is that what you want?"

"That would be wonderful." When I saw that she was opening a bottle, I wished I'd declined, but it seemed to be too late. She passed the glass to me, and I had just taken a sip when a male voice cried out, "Miss Ruby!" There was a whir in my peripheral vision, a quick-moving human figure, and the woman in the apron was swept off her feet. The figure, it turned out, was Charlie; he had lifted her into a spinning embrace, and as he set her down, the woman glared at him, smoothing her apron, and said, "You don't have an ounce of sense."

Charlie grinned. "Miss Ruby, meet my bride-to-be, Alice Lindgren. Alice, this is my first love, Miss Ruby."

I might have been annoyed by Charlie's disclosure about our engagement—it seemed a violation of our agreement in the car—except that as Miss Ruby and I shook hands, she seemed no more interested in me than she had before Charlie's arrival. Had Charlie introduced other young women to her as his bride-to-be? It was not impossible. "Don't you touch that crab dip, Charlie Blackwell," she snapped, and I saw that he'd dipped his index finger into the crystal bowl beside the wine bottles. Miss Ruby exhaled through her nostrils. "You can't use a knife like a civilized person?"

"It tastes better like this." Charlie licked his finger. "Alice, want a drink?"

I held up my wine.

"Excellent," he said. "And you look ravishing, of course." He leaned in to kiss my lips; clearly, he was in a performative mode. I had seen this a few times in Madison when we were in groups. Sometimes he was charmingly silly but still capable of listening to what you said, and sometimes, particularly when he'd been drinking for several hours, he was wound up into a frenzy of goofiness, deaf to the remarks of anyone who wasn't similarly drunk and wound up. I'd simply ridden out these episodes, waiting until we could go home for the night, sometimes exchanging sympathetic looks with the wives or girlfriends of other men. I didn't want to encourage Charlie, but I also had no desire to tell him how to behave.

"Miss Ruby can verify that this is the only time in family history I've been the first one here," Charlie said. "I didn't want you to think you were in the wrong place, Lindy. Blackwell Standard Time is— What would you say, Miss Ruby, about forty-five minutes behind?"

"Don't be fresh," she said.

Charlie gestured toward her. "This woman took care of me from the day I came home from the hospital, and honest to God, I'd lay down my life for her."

"I'll bet you would," Miss Ruby said as she walked back into the house.

"She's hilarious, right?" Charlie said. "The genuine article." I was not sure I agreed, but immediately, with Miss Ruby having stepped away and an audience of only me, he settled down a little. Still, I could tell that he was geared up for the night ahead. And I couldn't blame him—it was obvious that for the Blackwells, family reunions not only involved competitive sports but were a kind of competitive sport in themselves. Being around the Blackwells (these impressions returned again and again in the years to come) filled me with a jealous wonder at their clannish energy, their confidence, their sheer numbers, and also with a gratitude that I had grown up in a calm and quiet family. So many inside jokes for the Blackwells to keep track of, so many nicknames and references to long-ago incidents, so much one-upmanship: Surely I was not the only one who found it tiring.

Within the next half hour, they all appeared, either from inside the

Alamo or traipsing over from the other cottages, many of them wet-haired, the men in seersucker suits or khaki pants and navy blazers, the women in sundresses, holding the hands of children—little girls in green or pink dresses with smocking across the chest, or hand-stitched balloons or apples, wearing Mary Janes on their feet; little boys in shortalls and white socks that folded down and white saddle shoes.

Drinks were distributed—most of the adults had old-fashioneds, while the children had Shirley Temples or Roy Rogers—and Miss Ruby carried around the crab dip and I met the family members I hadn't met before. It quickly became clear that there was no conversation in which I was required to do much more than nod and laugh. "We're all *so* curious about you," said Nan, the wife of Charlie's brother John, and then she proceeded not to ask me any questions as she and John and Charlie and I stood there for ten minutes. John and Charlie carried the conversation, focusing first on the current quality of fish in the lake and then moving on to whether the Brewers' 1–0 victory over the Detroit Tigers the previous night could be attributed more to the Brewers playing well or the Tigers playing poorly. I didn't mind this; I have always had a soft spot for people who talk a lot because I feel as if they're doing the work for me. I don't usually have a great deal to say—I almost envy people their heated opinions, their vehemence and certainty—and I am perfectly content to listen. There are a few topics of particular interest to me (when another person has just read the same book I have, I enjoy comparing reactions), but I can't bear pretending to have an opinion when I don't. The few times I have pretended in this way have left me with a sour sort of hollowness, a niggling regret.

I subsequently found myself in a conversation with Uncle Trip, also loquacious, who explained that he divided his time—for reasons of business or pleasure, I could not discern—among Milwaukee, Key West, and Toronto. This seemed to me at the time to be the oddest triangle imaginable, but really, for the Blackwells' friends, it proved not to be particularly unusual at all. Milwaukee and Sun Valley, Milwaukee and the Adirondacks, Minneapolis and Cheyenne and Phoenix, Chicago and San Francisco. They sold textiles, or mined ore, or owned a gallery in Santa Fe, or they were consultants—this was before consulting was as common as it is today—or they had just taken a cruise around the Gulf of Alaska, and it had, they reported, been marvelous.

As for the employ of Charlie's brothers, Ed, the oldest, was the congressman; Charlie's second oldest brother, John, was CEO of Blackwell Meats (on the dock that afternoon, Charlie had introduced John as "the sausage king's sausage king"); and Arthur, who was two years older than Charlie, worked for the family company as a lawyer. None of their wives held jobs.

The porch was crowded, and I was discussing Wisconsin's public school superintendent with John, which is to say that John was talking about the time Superintendent Ruka, whom he called Herb, had birdied a long par 4 at the Maronee Country Club, when Liza and Margaret, John's two daughters, scampered between us and disappeared again into the thicket of adult bodies. The younger one, Margaret, returned and tapped my forearm. She was looking up at me with an expression of nervousness, excitement, and secrecy that made me almost certain she had been dispatched by her older sister. "Are you Uncle Chas's girlfriend?"

"Margaret, what do we say when we interrupt a conversation?" John chided.

"Excuse me," Margaret said. "Excuse me, but are you Uncle Chas's girlfriend?"

"I am," I said.

"Do you wear perfume?"

I laughed. "Sometimes."

"Do you know how to do cat's cradle?"

"I do," I said. "Do *you* know how to do cat's cradle?"

"It's Liza's string, but she said if you play, I can, too."

I looked at John. "I believe I've been summoned." John smiled as if embarrassed (I can't imagine he really was, but all the Blackwells understood how endearing a bit of self-deprecation can be—and the more privileged the source, of course, the more endearing the self-deprecation). "You certainly don't have to," he said, then, to Margaret, "What do you say to Miss Lindgren?"

"Thank you, Miss Lindgren," Margaret said as she took my hand and guided me out the screen door and onto the porch steps, where Liza awaited us. A few feet away, their boy cousins were dueling with skinny sticks.

We were on our third iteration of a figure Liza called crab's mouth when the sound of tinkling glass silenced the porch. On my watch, I saw that it was seven-forty. Had the children eaten yet? If not, they were behaving remarkably well. "If you'll permit a doddering old man to say a few words," Harold Blackwell said, and there were hoots and whoops of support; Arthur brought his fingers to his mouth and whistled. Charlie was just inside the screen door, and he poked it open and motioned for me to come up the steps. When I did, slipping in next to him, he took my hand and whispered, "Everything okay?" I nodded.

"What a tremendous pleasure for Priscilla and me to have you all here." Harold Blackwell looked around the porch. "And how blessed we are as a family." Although I was still prepared for his words to sound at least a little fake and canned, I was again struck by how kind and genuine he seemed. "Looking at the group assembled here, I can't tell you how proud it makes me," he said, and I thought he might cry. (I tried to imagine him as a presidential candidate uttering the phrase *unwashed and uneducated,* and it was difficult; already that notion of him was elusive, replaced by this man just a few feet away, his face lined, his hair brown like Charlie's but thin and combed back, the vulnerability of his scalp.) He did not cry. Instead, smiling, he said, "We're so very pleased to meet Alice. A special welcome to you, my dear."

"Hear, hear," Charlie said, and rattled the ice in his cup—he'd been drinking whiskey.

John called out, "Alice, think you can tame the Blackwell bronco?"

"She hasn't been knocked off yet," Charlie said.

"Was that knocked off or knocked *up*?" someone yelled—it seemed like a comment Arthur would make, but it could even have come from Uncle Trip.

"Settle down, fellas," Harold said. "My point is simply that I hope someday all of you will have the opportunity to look out at three generations and feel the love and pride that are in my heart tonight. May God forever bless and protect the Blackwell family, and may the light of His spirit shine through all of us." Here, he held up his glass, and everyone voiced assent; a few people said, "Amen." Conversations had just begun to resume when Arthur loudly cleared his throat, then actually climbed atop a chair. "This seems as good a time as any," he said. "When I heard Chasbo was bringing home a new girl, I wanted to do something in her honor. So I wrote a poem—" At this, the porch erupted into raucous cheers, including from Charlie. Arthur pulled a folded piece of paper from his pocket, looked at it, then refolded it. "I'm pretty sure I've got it memorized."

"Watch out, Shakespeare!" Charlie called.

"All right." Arthur swallowed and nodded once. "Wait, it's a limerick—did I mention that?"

"Just say the friggin' poem," John yelled.

Arthur looked directly at me and smiled.

" 'Nymphomaniacal Alice
Used a dynamite stick as a phallus
They found her vagina
in North Carolina
And bits of her tits down in Dallas.' "

In the ensuing silence, I could hear the lilt of the tiny waves hitting the shore below us, and one of the little boys in the grass out front said, "But it's *mine.*" And then on the porch there was a delighted sort of roaring, and I quickly realized, though I had trouble believing it, that the roar had come from Mrs. Blackwell. Soon everyone else joined in, guffawing and applauding. I was so shocked that I could have cried—they'd have been tears of astonishment, not of sadness or hurt—but I knew that it was very important not to. I kept my head up, smiling in a glazed kind of way. I didn't look at Charlie because I was afraid I'd see a gleeful expression. I wondered, had the children heard? Had Miss Ruby?

"Again!" Mrs. Blackwell cried. "Encore!"

And in case anyone had missed a word, Arthur began, " 'Nymphomaniacal Alice . . .' "

When he'd finished, Mrs. Blackwell, still smiling joyfully, said, "I defy anyone who says I don't have the cleverest sons in Christendom. Arty, you've outdone yourself."

"Far be it from me to offer praise to one of my younger brothers," Ed said, "but that was masterful." (And here Ed was supposed to be the uptight one.)

Uncle Trip nudged me. "It's not every day you get a poem written in your honor, is it?"

I gave a spluttery fake laugh that was the best I could manage.

Charlie and I were still standing side by side, not looking at each other, but I was pretty sure he was grinning while speaking through clenched teeth when he said, "You're horrified, right?"

"Arthur didn't write that." I was barely moving my lips, either. "I first heard it from a boy named Roy Ziemniak in 1956."

Charlie chuckled. "Beg, borrow, or steal," he said. "That's Arthur." Then he said, "You're doing well. I know this isn't easy." He turned to me, and we looked at each other straight on, and his expression wasn't gleeful; it was tentative. His face in that moment was very familiar to me; perhaps this was in contrast to everyone else I'd just met, but I was surprised by the familiarity. Charlie's brown eyes and the crinkles at their corners, his bristly wavy light brown hair, his light pink lips, dry right now, which I had spent a good deal of the last seven weeks pressing my own lips against—his features were comforting. It was much harder not to touch him than it would have been to touch him, to set my palm against his cheek or neck, to lean in and kiss him, to wrap my arms around his body and be hugged back. It was comforting also to know that eventually—if not tonight, then soon, and for a long time to come—I'd again be alone with him and we could talk about everyone else or not even talk but just be together in the aftermath of interacting with these other people. I felt so lucky, it seemed practically a miracle, that of everybody on the porch, he was the person I was paired off with, he was my counterpart. Not Arthur, thank God, or John or Ed, but Charlie—Charlie was the one who was mine. Certainly he could be a joker, too, but I felt that he had a more sympathetic heart than his brothers, that he understood more about the world, about human behavior; Charlie's joking seemed a decision rather than a reflex. (Of course I later wondered: When you are the object of a person's affection, do you naturally credit him with a sympathetic heart and an understanding of the world? Perhaps your impression is right only insofar as it applies to you; in your presence, he is indeed possessed of these qualities for the very reason that you *are* the object of his affection. He is not observant so much as observant of you, not kind so much as kind toward you.)

As Charlie and I regarded each other, surrounded by the chatter and clinking of the Blackwell cocktail hour, it occurred to me that if I had visited Halcyon before he and I had gotten engaged, there was a good chance we would not have done so. In the contexts of our families, the differences between us loomed large. But in this moment it seemed a good thing that I hadn't known what I was getting into; I was glad it was too late.

WE WALKED TO the clubhouse for dinner in a sloppy sort of caravan, and beyond a grove of pine trees, another compound appeared on our right, a grouping of houses whose sizes and layout were similar to those of the Blackwells. Apparently, Charlie's family owned the northernmost plot of land; at the next large house, a throng of men, women, and children was emerging, led by a silver-haired octogenarian who dragged his right foot, leaned on a hooked cane of dark wood, and wore navy blue pants embroidered with little green turtles. "Harold, I won't have you eating all the sweet-potato puffs," he called in a plummy tone, and Harold Blackwell called back, "Wouldn't dream of it, Rumpus!" Or at least this was what I thought Harold said, but I doubted my own ears until I ended up next to this same man in the clubhouse dining room. Four long tables extended north, south, east, and west from the center of the room—they were like a tremendous cross—and the tables were not divided by family, as I'd have imagined (I later realized they couldn't have been, because there were four tables and five families), but rather, by the clucking, seemingly arbitrary instructions of the matriarchs. Mrs. Blackwell directed the grandchildren toward one table, her older sons and their wives to scattered points, and then she turned her attention to Charlie and me. "Chas, go sit by Mrs. deWolfe, because she's dying to hear your theory about Jimmy Connors. Alice, you're right here." She pointed to the second-to-last place at one table. "I find it so tiresome when couples are seated side by side, don't you?" I nodded, unable to remember the last place I'd been that had featured assigned seating. White linen covered the tables, and there were full place settings. The china and silverware all were nice enough, if far from new-looking, but the clubhouse as a whole shared the same worn quality I'd found in the Alamo—the curtains, of forest-green cotton, were faded, the hardwood floor was scratched, the chairs were of the not particularly comfortable wooden sort you might have found with a dormitory desk. A large vase of purple hydrangea sat at the intersection of the four tables, and over the mantel was a handsome oil painting of dark water: Lake Michigan, quite possibly.

When we'd all taken our seats—the men waited for the women, I observed, and the women first seated their children—the man next to me, the wearer of the turtle pants, extended his hand. "Rumpus Higginson," he said.

"Alice Lindgren." As we shook, I felt slightly proud of myself for not laughing, not even smiling or letting my lips twitch. (Two weeks later, back in Madison, I picked up the *Wisconsin State Journal* to find a front-page article about the expansion of Wall Bank—a rival of Wisconsin State Bank & Trust, my father's employer for over thirty years—and a small photo accompanied the article, a photo that was grainy and no larger than a postage stamp but still recognizable to me, of a man identified as Leslie J. Higginson; he was, apparently, the bank's founder. This meant my father surely would have heard of him, though I doubted that my father had ever known he answered to Rumpus.)

We had a first course of vichyssoise served in shallow white bowls with a sprinkling of chives. Over the soup, Rumpus, or Mr. Higginson—really, I had little idea how to address anyone—said, "Have you spent much time in Door County, Allison?"

I did not correct him. "As a matter of fact, I haven't made it here before, but it lives up to its reputation."

"You couldn't buy a better day." Rumpus shook his head. "Absolutely gorgeous."

On being assigned this seat, I had wondered if Mrs. Blackwell might be exiling me, but she had sat across the table and one over (to keep an eye on me? But no, I was being silly). She said then, "Rump, tell me it isn't true about Cecily and Gordon. If they move to Los Angeles, we have no hope of seeing them again."

"Oh, for heaven's sake!" Rumpus protested. "A flight to California is nothing for an inveterate traveler like you, Priscilla."

She shook her head. "The last time I was in Los Angeles, I said to myself, 'Enough is enough.' Terrible traffic, lousy food, and the staff at the Biltmore was appallingly incompetent. It claims to be a world-class city, but I find it quite provincial." I know there are people who would not believe that a person from Wisconsin would dare to make such a remark; they are wrong. Mrs. Blackwell was saying, "I saw Cecily down in Sea Island last March, and I said, 'Cecily, if the two of you even think of defecting to the West Coast, that's the last you'll hear from Harold and me.' "

"It's really Gordon, though, isn't it? I know he's keen to cultivate relationships with Asian investors, which makes it a good deal more convenient . . ."

The conversation proceeded in much this way as we moved on to the main course of broiled chicken. They discussed another couple named the Bancrofts who, I inferred, lived in Milwaukee, were renovating their kitchen, and had had the misfortune of hiring a feckless contractor; they discussed a couple named the LeGrands, whose son was in his second year of medical school at Dartmouth, though Mrs. Blackwell questioned whether he had "the goods"—she tapped her temple—to earn his degree ("His grades at UW were worse than Chas's at Princeton!" she exclaimed); and finally, they discussed a Viennese cellist who had been playing with the Milwaukee Symphony Orchestra for the last several months and staying with Emily and Will Higginson, who were Rumpus's son and daughter-in-law. "The Italians say that houseguests are like fish." Mrs. Blackwell smirked. "After three days, they start to smell." (Of course I quickly calculated that if Charlie and I had arrived on a Friday and were leaving on a Monday, that was no more than three days, was it? Though only I was a guest; Charlie was family.)

During the whole of dinner, I nodded at what seemed to be the appropriate intervals, I smiled when they smiled and laughed when they laughed, I even answered a question about my own taste in music—"Allison, do you prefer the classical or romantic era?" Rumpus inquired, and I said, "I've always enjoyed Mahler's Fifth"—and at the same time, I became first tipsy and then solidly drunk in a way I had never been in my entire life. The waiters and waitresses, most of whom appeared to be about fourteen years old, refilled our wineglasses frequently. On my second trip to the bathroom, I left just as coffee was being served with dessert, and the walls shifted as I walked.

There was a sitting room outside the dining room, and both its walls and those in the halls leading to the bathroom were densely covered with framed photos, the majority of them black-and-white: Halcyon inhabitants holding fish or playing tennis (the latter activity featured action shots and posed ones, with the players crossing their racquets in front of their bodies). One picture was of Mrs. Blackwell gripping the hand of a toddler who might well have been Charlie, standing on the porch of what I believed to be this very building. Mrs. Blackwell had not been beautiful, but she'd been dark-haired and attractive, the skin on her face smooth and unlined, a canny glint in her eye. On my return from the bathroom, I was studying the photo when a woman appeared from nowhere and threw herself into my arms. "I am *so* excited to meet you!" she cried. She spoke in a drawl that, like Charlie's, was vaguely southern.

Even when she'd extracted herself from our nonmutual embrace, she held tightly to my upper arms, looking at me with great enthusiasm. She had white-blond hair pulled back in a ponytail, big front teeth, and tanned skin; she was pretty, but in this moment she was also far too physically close. "And I heard about that *raunchy* poem Arthur wrote, and I am *mortified.* I was with the baby in Gin Rummy, but if I had been there, I would *never* have let him do that. You must think we're the most *disgraceful* family in the entire *world.*"

Then her eyes widened, and I do not exaggerate when I say that she proceeded to shriek. "Oh, you don't even know who I am! Oh my stars!" She began to laugh, bringing a hand to her chest. "I'm Jadey! Arthur's wife! I'm Jadey Blackwell! Oh, Alice, you have to forgive my terrible manners!"

"What a pleasure to meet you." I could hear the expansiveness in my voice, a decidedly unfamiliar tone. "But your husband forgot there's an alternate ending for the limerick." Both the words *alternate* and *limerick* had been daunting to pronounce, and I was proud that I had surmounted them. "What he said was 'And bits of her tits down in Dallas.' But also, it can go 'And her anus in Buckingham Palace.' Did you know you're married to a plagiarizer?"

Jadey peered at me more closely, then whispered. "Oh my Lord, are you *drunk*?" I shook my head, but she was saying, "Oh, I would be, too! Oh, you must be just beside yourself! I can only imagine what this weekend is like for you. They tease you *so much,* don't they? My first year of marriage, I was on the brink of tears the whole time, and I had grown *up* with the Blackwells! Oh, I just hated *all* of them, and after Arthur *made* me marry him, I thought to myself, Jadey, are you crazy? You *knew* that family was a bunch of hooligans!"

Was Jadey crazy? I had been in her company for about a minute, and already, I felt that I could have answered this question accurately.

"Stay *right here,*" she said. "I'm getting Charlie. You poor baby, you're drunk as a skunk."

Because I was indeed drunk, I didn't mind standing there doing nothing; I gazed up at the silver trophy vase sitting on the mantel above the fireplace—it was about a foot tall—and by the time Charlie emerged from the dining room, Jadey just behind him, I was holding the trophy in my arms, squinting down at it. "Where's your name?" I asked Charlie, and he seemed both amused and perturbed.

"Let's put that back where it belongs, sticky fingers." He eased the trophy from my hands and returned it to the mantel, then said to Jadey, "Tell Maj you think Alice has whatever the baby is sick with."

Jadey made a face. "Colic, Chas?"

He waved his hand dismissively. "Make something up. I'm taking her back to Itty-Bitty."

Jadey set her hands on the slopes where my shoulders became my neck; the effect of her standing like this was halfway between a babushka pinching your cheeks and a lover moving in for a kiss. "Alice, we are going to be *best* friends," she said. She dropped her voice. "Ginger and Nan are *no fun.* They mean well, but they're worrywarts. But I heard about you"—she was talking louder again, and more quickly—"and I just knew right away. I said to myself, 'Alice sounds like my kind of girl.' "

What had Jadey heard about me? And when—that day or earlier?—and from whom?

"You seem like a very special person," I said, and Charlie burst into laughter. To Jadey, he said, "She's never like this. Seriously, I've never seen this before."

"She's adorable," Jadey said, and she held the clubhouse door for us as we stepped outside. "Don't let her fall, Chas."

The slate sidewalk was lit only by the stars and the half-moon, and the distance we needed to go seemed significantly greater than it had on the way there. Charlie had one arm across my back and the other hand holding my elbow. "Steady there, party girl," he said. "Was Rump Higginson that bad a dinner companion?"

We were passing the family compound closest to the clubhouse—this one, I'd learned a few hours before, belonged to the Thayers—and I said, "Everyone here is *so* rich."

Charlie laughed but not all that heartily. After a beat, he asked, "You like that?"

"Rich people are bizarre!" I exclaimed. (This was a remark Charlie quoted back to me many times in the years to come.) "I love you, Charlie, but all this fuss about tennis and Princeton and the Biltmore Hotel—if you were the foreman at Fassbinder's, sometimes I think that would be easier."

"You mean Fassbinder's the cheese factory?"

"They make butter, too," I said. "Want to go swimming?"

"I'm not sure that's the best idea."

"You're supposed to be the fun one." I poked him in the ribs. "Good-time Charlie. Are you scared now? Remember when you told me you're scared of the dark?"

"I'm doing my best to keep it together for my blotto girlfriend."

"I know you're scared of the dark, because I wrote it down in my dossier. My *Charlie Van Wyck Blackwell* dossier." I pronounced each of his names lavishly. "And now I can't protect you because I'm"—I thought of Jadey—"drunk as a skunk."

"That you are," Charlie said. "What I'm trying to figure out is if you're a good drunk or a bad one."

"If you let me go swimming," I said, "we'll be naked, and you can put your penis inside me in the water."

"Oh, man!" Charlie said. "Okay, I've decided you should become an alcoholic. You're an excellent drunk."

"It's my first time," I said.

"Sorry, but it's a little late for me to believe that one."

"No, no," I said. "My first time being drunk."

"Well, you seem like a pro."

"No, honestly—I can tell you don't believe me, but I'm telling the truth."

When we reached the Blackwell compound, he said, "The problem is, I don't know how long till the others get back, and if we're splashing around in the lake after Jadey told Maj you were sick—"

"I don't think you're afraid of the dark." I tapped the end of Charlie's nose with my fingertip. "You're afraid of your mother."

He laughed. "You would be, too." I suspect Charlie's own fondness for drinking, his lifetime spent around it, made him especially tolerant of the drunkenness of others. "I'd love to take you up on the whole penis-inside-you offer," he said, "but how about if we go in Itty-Bitty?"

"Let's do it here." I slipped from his arms and lay on the grass. We were in front of the Alamo; Miss Ruby may still have been inside, or she may already have gone for the night to the dormlike building behind the clubhouse where she and the other Halcyon families' maids slept, but either way, I had forgotten about her. The grass was cool, the blades slightly sticky.

"God almighty, woman," Charlie said. "Who *are* you?" He scooped me up and half-carried, half-dragged me across the lawn toward Itty-Bitty. All its lights were off, and he settled me on the bottom bunk before flicking the switch. "I gotta take a whiz," he said. "Don't go anywhere."

I knew he didn't walk back to the Alamo to use the bathroom but stayed somewhere very nearby because I could hear him urinating as I lay in bed. I giggled a little, I thought of teasing him when he returned, I thought of how his penis would feel in my hand. But this was the last thing I thought, because abruptly I fell asleep. As Charlie told me the following day, by the time he reentered Itty-Bitty, I was snoring obliviously.

AROUND FOUR A.M., when the darkness of true night had faded into a pre-sunrise gray, I awakened with a clenching in my stomach and knew I desperately had to use the toilet. It would have been better if I needed to vomit, because that was potentially something you could do outside; this was not. Yet for several minutes more, I lay in agony on the bottom bunk, the prospect of darting across the lawn to the Alamo and then of sitting on the toilet, making rude noises in a house where everyone else was asleep, just a little worse than remaining in discomfort in bed. Before making an early-morning lavatory journey such as this, did one first change into real clothes? Was there some sort of protocol established, and was I expected to guess what it was? When I could stand it no longer, I rose from the bed, realized to my surprise that I was wearing not my nightgown but my dress from the night before—it smelled of food and alcohol—and hurried outside barefoot, the grass cool and dewy. I had feared that the house would be locked, which it wasn't. (I later learned that it was never locked, not even during the winter, when no one came up from month to month; it was only looked in on by a local caretaker. "If vandals want to get in, I'd rather have them use a door than a window," Mrs. Blackwell said wryly, as if she were being a very good sport. It was rarely possible, especially in the early days, for me to guess Mrs. Blackwell's reaction to a particular situation, but no matter what that reaction was, when mine did not match hers, I was left with the feeling that this was the case because I came from a different class. Or at least I knew she would chalk up any disagreement to this discrepancy, and she'd believe it so heartily that it might as well have been true.)

I slipped inside through a back door—not the one off the kitchen, but another one off the hallway leading to the bathroom. As I had expected, the house was completely silent. I shut the bathroom door, knowing this time to push the books against it, and then I sat down, and it felt as if a snake were uncoiling in my stomach—it was uncoiling very quickly—and still I couldn't release it. I wanted to, but I was incapable because I was so anxious about the sounds I'd make. I leaned forward, hugging my sides, trying not to whimper. *They're all asleep,* I told myself, but I was immobilized, and then the snake reared up, baring its fangs and forked tongue, and everything inside me gushed out, a prolonged and mortifying splatter. Recalling the warnings about the fragility of the plumbing, I immediately yanked the flushing chain. But I wasn't finished—I knew I wasn't—and the water in the bowl had not yet resettled when another grotesque gush surged from inside me. How humiliating that I had drunk so much, and also how foolish. (Never since that episode have I had more than two drinks in a single evening.) My belly was empty now, blissfully empty, but still sour and shaky. I wiped myself, then flushed the toilet a second time, and when I stood, when the water had climbed back up the bowl, I saw that mere flushing was not going to suffice; brown smudges clung to the porcelain. Ought I stick my hand in there? I was accustomed to cleaning up after children; it was usually just urine, but the younger ones had accidents regularly, or someone would throw up, and if Big Glenn was otherwise occupied, I'd sprinkle the sawdust on the carpet myself rather than waiting for him. I flushed a third time, and when the water swirled down, I reached in with a wad of toilet paper and wiped at the most egregious clumps and streaks before the water could rise. Then I dropped the toilet paper, flushed a fourth time—was Priscilla Blackwell at this very moment listening to me wreak havoc on her plumbing?—and washed my hands. The soap was a light blue oval, cracked in many places and rubbed down to the thinness of a guitar pick; as I moved my palms against it, it broke in two, and I thought—it came to me so naturally, such a casual reaction—*I hate it here.*

This was the sort of thought I never had, and even in the moment, I felt an immediate reassessment. My upset stomach was no more the Blackwells' fault than a summer storm would have been! (Oh, but how they loved their one toilet, how they loved their faded furniture and mossy, rickety dock, their chipped saucers and tarnished picture frames and hard mattresses. They loved this false, selective form of roughing it, and their own ease with its conventions, and a visitor's potential unease. In the house I'd grown up in, we, too, had had one bathroom, but it had never occurred to anyone in my family to take *pride* in this fact. It did not surprise me at all—by then I understood—when, just a few weeks later, I accompanied Charlie to the Blackwells' house in Milwaukee, their primary residence, which dwarfed even the Alamo; the Milwaukee house was, I suspect, closer to twelve thousand feet, a fieldstone behemoth with a slate roof. It sprawled horizontally, with multiple peaks and chimneys, banks of windows, sections that jutted forward or hung back; the combination of the stones and the sheer size evoked a castle. The front lawn was as green and meticulously mowed as a golf course, the garage held four cars—this usually meant, with household help and visitors and members of the younger generations, that three or four cars were still parked outside in the gravel driveway—and in the back was a pool that they kept at a punitive sixty degrees; Charlie referred to it as "scrotum-shriveling." Inside were hardwood floors and vast Oriental rugs, chandeliers, floor-length draperies, massive furniture, oil paintings of fruit still lifes and skulls, and in the dining room, covering an entire wall, a mural of an English hunting scene: lords and ladies, fields and trees, dogs and birds. Also, there were seven bathrooms. So of course—of course the deprivations of Halcyon tickled them. They loved them as suburban children love sleeping in a tent in their own backyard. But I filed this not-quite-knowledge about the Blackwells, this sub-awareness, in the same place I'd filed my ideas about Charlie marrying me because I lent him credibility: the basement of my mind. It is, I think, a tendency of coastal urbanites more than those of us from the Midwest to believe you need to bring all your impressions to the fore, to dwell on the unpleasant feelings those close to you provoke—to decide these feelings matter, that they are a subject worthy of discussion, perhaps with a therapist, and that you might ride your own ideas toward a resolution, or at the very least spend time comparing them with your peers, who undoubtedly harbor similar sentiments.)

No. I did not hate it here, I did not blame Charlie's family for my upset stomach or for anything else. Hate was such a melodramatic emotion, so blustery and silly. If the Blackwells incited in me a certain skepticism, I was scarcely the first person to have reservations about her prospective in-laws, or about the wealthy.

I reshelved the books and opened the bathroom door slowly, to minimize creaking. As I let myself out the door to the outside, I heard a person coughing, but I had no idea which bedroom the sound came from. I retraced my steps across the wet grass, and just before I entered Itty-Bitty, I glanced to my right, and the lake was flat and gray, a darker gray than the sky, so somber and severe and lovely that my breath caught. No, it was not pretentiousness and affectation that drew the Blackwells here—how unfair of me to presume such a thing. Rather, it was that they recognized the beauty of Halcyon and could afford it. Wouldn't my own parents, had they the same luxuries of time and money, have liked to spend a few months each summer in a place like this?

Or maybe, standing on the steps of Itty-Bitty, I was just more forgiving of the Blackwells because I was tired and wanted to go back to bed. Perhaps it was simple fatigue that made me inclined to surrender to rather than try to extricate myself from the future Charlie and I had begun to plan.

AT BREAKFAST IN the clubhouse a few hours later, Arthur said to me from across the table, "Alice, the word of the day is legs. Please spread the word." Jadey, who was sitting next to him holding the baby, slapped Arthur playfully and said, "She hasn't even had her coffee yet." Jadey made no mention of our interaction the night before, for which I was grateful, though I did detect in her expression a discreet merriment.

Breakfast, I discovered, was a more haphazard affair than dinner, with people appearing and departing at various times, and if you wanted toast or an English muffin or cold cereal, you fixed it yourself from the buffet set out on a long table; only if you wanted eggs or bacon or waffles did you order from the waiter, a pale and skinny teenage boy with an enormous Adam's apple.

Some of the children were already in bathing suits, and several of the adults, in anticipation of the day's competition, were in their tennis whites, the women in pleated skirts so short they would have bordered on the obscene were it not clear that they had been approved at some point in the distant past. Priscilla Blackwell wore one of these minuscule skirts, and very low socks with pink pom-poms on the back of the ankle. (It was 1988 before the Halcyon Board of Overseers—which had its own charter and held as a requirement of membership that you first be male and second be elected, so that two men from each family served for five years at a time—decreed that it was permissible to wear non-white apparel on the Halcyon tennis courts. The dissenters in this decision, foremost among them seventy-six-year-old Billy Niedleff and his middle son, Thaddeus, then forty, continued to grumble about the decline in standards for the next decade.)

When I'd arrived at Halcyon the previous afternoon, I had felt a fear that the weekend would pass slowly, but the opposite proved true. While I did have a splitting headache at breakfast, the pain had dulled by late morning. I spent most of the day sitting on a blanket on the sidelines of the tennis courts, observing the matches, either watching Charlie play or sitting next to him when he wasn't playing. He'd work up a vigorous sweat during his sets, then fill a cup of water from the large thermos by the net, pour the cup over his head, and shake his head like a dog. That morning, when he'd come to Itty-Bitty to find me for breakfast, I'd been awake and dressed, waiting for him, and as he'd entered through the screen door, he'd called, "Where's my favorite lush?" and I'd said, "Charlie, I'm so sorry for my behavior last night," and he'd said, "Only part you have to apologize for is getting me all horned up and then passing out, but I'll take a rain check." He'd leaned in to kiss me, and I'd felt the great relief of dating a man who does not hold a grudge, or at least not toward you (Simon had been the other way). Then he'd said, "Bring your toothbrush to the clubhouse, because Maj already had to call a plumber out this morning for the Alamo toilet, and the guy's trying to work a miracle as we speak. Right now the lead suspect for who took the huge shit is John." I nodded neutrally and—forgive me, John, for my lie of omission—said absolutely nothing.

At the tennis courts, after beating Emily Higginson 7–5, 6–4, Mrs. Blackwell said to me, "I take it a good night's sleep was just what the doctor ordered." I was almost certain that she knew I'd had too much to drink, and I wondered if she knew the clogged toilet was my fault as well, but all I did was murmur my assent.

I had brought a novel to the tennis courts with me—it was *Pale Fire,* which I'd purchased after Nabokov's death earlier in the summer—but because of the sun and the conversation, I didn't end up reading a word. I spent quite a bit of time playing with Jadey and Arthur's baby, Winnie (as a single woman in my early thirties, I was careful not to coo excessively over other people's infants, lest it seem like I was telegraphing my desperation; the necessity of this precaution annoyed me, making me want to defiantly announce that I'd *always* liked babies, since I was a child, but Jadey was the generous kind of mother who acted as if I was doing her a favor by keeping Winnie on my lap). Really, during that day and the next, there were so many conversations and activities and meals, so many changes of clothes, into a swimsuit and out and back in when the suit wasn't quite dry, back into the water (it was the ideal temperature, cool enough to be refreshing but not chilly, the way Lake Michigan often can be), and then we rode the motorboat to the town a few miles over for ice cream, then back to Halcyon, back into a skirt, up to dinner, and suddenly, I realized I'd acquired a tan on my face and arms. On Sunday morning, an Episcopal priest, Reverend Ayrault, arrived at ten to hold a service for the Blackwell family on the porch of the Alamo, complete with Communion; apparently, he had driven from Green Bay solely for this purpose, and afterward he sat beside Mrs. Blackwell at lunch in the clubhouse. "That's nice of him to come all the way up here," I remarked to Charlie, who replied, "Republicans give the good reverend a hard-on."

The winners of the Halcyon Open were awarded their trophies on Sunday afternoon, small cheap gold figures perched on wood bases, about to serve a ball; the silver vase would be engraved later but was presented to, in men's singles, Roger Niedleff, and in men's doubles, Dwight deWolfe and his brother-in-law, Wyman Lawrence. In women's singles, Sarah Thayer had won, and in women's doubles, Priscilla Blackwell and her daughter-in-law Nan. "Roger is such a competitive douche bag," Charlie grumbled as the winners accepted the trophies, followed by twelve-year-old Nina deWolfe playing "The Star-Spangled Banner" on a recorder. Mrs. Blackwell, for her part, gloated magisterially. As we walked back from the tennis courts to the Alamo—a distance of about half a mile—I thought of leaving the next day and felt a flicker of preemptive nostalgia. I was just settling into Halcyon's rhythms.

We were nearing the Alamo when Jadey caught up with us and set her hand on my forearm. "Come wash your hair with me in the lake. I've got twenty minutes before the baby wakes up and all holy hell breaks loose." She jogged toward Gin Rummy, the cottage she and Arthur and their children were staying in, and I glanced quizzically at Charlie.

"You heard her," he said. "Shake a leg."

"She washes her hair *in* the lake?"

"It's to avoid waiting in line for the bathroom."

In fact, the impression I got a few minutes later as Jadey and I stood in the water near the dock, her plastic shampoo bottle set on the top step of the wooden ladder, was that she washed her hair in the lake mostly because she thought washing her hair in the lake was fun. She held her hands up to her head, massaging, until her scalp was covered in white lather. "Remember doing this at summer camp?" she said.

I laughed noncommittally, having never attended summer camp.

"I've been meaning to say, that's the cutest swimsuit," she added. "Is it from Marshall Field's?"

"It's from a store in Madison owned by a friend of mine." Jadey's swimsuit was a Lilly bikini, and mine was red with white stripes. I was not yet aware that Jadey was a superb shopper—she had a sixth sense about when something was about to go on sale or, conversely, when it was worth paying full price because if you waited, it would disappear. It had occurred to me already that Jadey and Dena would have quite liked each other, or else the opposite—as with Charlie and my grandmother, their personalities might have overlapped in just the wrong ways.

"You're lucky your boobs are still so perky," Jadey was saying. "Are you thirty yet?"

"Thirty-one," I said.

"Well, that's no fair! I just turned twenty-seven."

"Look at my crow's-feet, though." I brought my face closer to hers and angled my right eye to the side.

"Is Charlie like Arthur about wanting you to wear sexy underwear?

Arthur tells me to buy these getups that would make a *prostitute* blush. And I say to him, 'Until you have been through the *hell* of childbirth yourself, you cannot *fathom* what has happened to my body. You need to give me five years' peace before I'm *halfway* ready to be a tart again.' "

I laughed, although I was conscious that voices carried on the lake. Furthermore, fifty yards away, one of the Higginsons was swimming laps perpendicular to their dock; I didn't recognize which Higginson it was, but when we'd arrived, he'd paused midstroke to give us a wave.

Jadey and I were standing in water up to our chests, the lake dark blue now, and the sun in the western sky was heavy and yellow. Jadey let herself fall backward, dunking her shoulders and head, and when she reappeared, the shampoo was washed out; the wetness made her blond hair almost gold. She arched onto her back, kicking her feet to stay afloat. "How's Maj treating you? She can be rough, right?"

I raised one finger to indicate a pause, then held my nose as I sank underwater. When I broke the surface, Jadey said, "She wanted a girl, is what they say, but she just kept having boys and finally—"

"Shhh!" I couldn't stand it—not the information, which I was curious about, but the sense that other people, perhaps Mrs. Blackwell herself, might be overhearing the discussion.

Jadey laughed. "You really are a librarian."

"No," I was whispering, and I gestured toward the house. "I'm afraid they can—"

"Gotcha." Jadey nodded, lowering her voice. "That's the theory, anyway, why she doesn't like girls—because she feels *rejected* by them. Do I sound like Sigmund Freud?" She was smiling in a self-deprecating way, and I wondered whether she had picked up the Blackwells' habit of alternate teasing and self-mockery or whether she'd had the habit all along. She'd told me earlier that her parents were friends of the Blackwells, that she'd met Arthur when she was an eighth-grader and he was a senior in high school, though they hadn't started dating until she was in college. She'd also told me—I'd asked—that Jadey was a nickname given at birth by her mother; her real name had been Jane Davenport Aigner, and of course she'd taken Blackwell as a surname when she married Arthur.

"Don't be afraid of Maj, is my point," Jadey said. "Her bark is worse than her bite."

"I wouldn't say I'm afraid of her." I really wasn't. Here in Halcyon, I was on her turf, but the more general notion I kept returning to was that there was something Mrs. Blackwell could bestow, some sort of approval, that did not fundamentally matter to me. It would have mattered to Dena. But all I wanted was adequately pleasant relations. I didn't need to be close to Mrs. Blackwell, didn't need to be one of her favorites. If she *disliked* me, it would be unsettling, but as long as she thought I was fine, that was enough. And over the course of the weekend, I'd had the sense that she was warming to me—late the previous afternoon, before the cocktail hour, she had walked past Charlie and me as we played Scrabble on the porch of the Alamo and had said, "Give him hell, Alice."

Jadey began doing backstroke, thrusting one arm and then the other over her head, and I watched, impressed. I was not a strong swimmer. Although my father had taught me at Pine Lake in Riley, I couldn't do much more than dog-paddle, and I could not have emulated Jadey's backstroke or the smooth, confident slice of that Higginson family member's freestyle.

Jadey flipped forward, coming back toward me. "You're lucky that you're older," she said. "No offense. Just, you know, I was twenty-one when I married Arthur, and I was so easily intimidated. If Maj said boo to me, I'd be crying in the corner. Plus, Arthur used to—" At this point, unmistakably, we heard a baby's wail. Jadey rolled her eyes. "*Never* have children," she said, but already, she was swimming toward the ladder.

"Jadey," I said, and she looked over her shoulder. "Thank you for being so nice about Friday night."

ON SUNDAY EVENING, during the cocktail hour (if there was a day of the week the Blackwells abstained from drinking, I never saw it), I found myself for the first time talking one-on-one to Charlie's brother Ed. Though we had been in the same general space several times in the past few days, I had hardly spoken to him directly. I'd felt aware of not wanting to seek him out just because he was the congressman—not that I secretly *did* want to seek him out, but I most certainly didn't want to seem like I was. But he was the one who approached me on the porch, saying, "I hope you haven't found us overwhelming." (Of course, they took pride in their overwhelmingness, as all families that are both large and happy do.)

"No, I've had a wonderful time," I said.

"I hear you're an elementary school librarian. I confess that I don't read as much as I'd like, but I do think teaching is a wonderful profession for women."

"I imagine your sons are very strong students." I wasn't just trying to ingratiate myself—I'd noticed that Harry, Tommy, and Geoff were all articulate for their ages, and energetic but not wild.

"They're good boys," Ed said. "Ginger has her hands full, but there's never a dull moment." With his thinning hair, Ed bore the strongest resemblance to their father, I realized as he spoke. He also was the only Blackwell who was even slightly pudgy, and he wore glasses. "I'll tell you that raising three sons makes me appreciate Maj even more in retrospect—I don't know how she managed four."

"Do you find it difficult going back and forth between Milwaukee and Washington?" So I'd taken the conversation in this direction after all; I hoped it was not a gauche error.

Ed shook his head. "It's really a privilege," he said. "To serve this country, Alice, what an honor. And my boys know it. When their daddy's not around to tuck them in at night, it isn't easy, but they're proud that he's out there protecting the interests of the people of Wisconsin." As I listened to Ed, it struck me that his use of words that he obviously had used many times did not automatically make them untrue—weren't they true if he believed them? That was my first thought; my second was *Please, please don't let Charlie win the election.*

As if sensing my psychic betrayal of him, Charlie materialized beside us. "Eddie, you in for poker at ten? Gil deWolfe just called."

"Alice, how do you feel about consorting with a gambling man?" Ed pulled his glasses down to the tip of his nose and looked over them with mock seriousness. "Is this something you approve of?"

"The only poker Alice plays is strip poker," Charlie said, and I said, "Charlie!"

Ed laughed, pointing at his brother. "You've got to guard your wallet with this one, or he'll rob you blind. Now, what's this about?" Ed's middle son, Tommy, had approached, in tears, and he announced mournfully, "Drew is hogging the Slinky."

Ed shrugged at Charlie and me. "Duty calls."

"You don't mind if I head over to the deWolfes' for a couple hours after dinner, do you?" Charlie said.

I shook my head. "I need to pack anyway."

"Eager to make your escape?"

"I like your family, Charlie," I said. "They've been really hospitable this weekend—well, besides the limerick, but I've gotten over that."

"You know what? I like you. And I think you look very pretty right now." Charlie leaned in and kissed me on the lips. It was a quick peck, but right away I heard someone cry out, "Look at the lovebirds!" Then John, who was nearby, said, "Good Christ, can you two not keep your hands off each other?"

I stepped back, though we truly hadn't been touching at all inappropriately. The porch grew quiet, and from the other end of it, Uncle Trip called, "Chasbo, now that Alice has seen the kind of stock you come from, think she'll stick around?"

"Hope so," Charlie said, and—I could feel the Blackwells' eyes on me—I smiled stiffly. *Do not cower.* These weren't the words Jadey had used, but that had been the message.

John said, "Alice, if you're not careful, it looks to me like Chas here might pop the question."

There was a silence, a short one, and before someone could fill it with an off-color joke, I said, "Actually—" My voice was hoarse, and I cleared my throat in as genteel a way as I could manage. "Actually, Charlie has already asked me to marry him, and I've accepted."

I might have imagined this part, but I think I heard a gasp—a woman's gasp, which I'm pretty sure was Ginger's. Charlie set his hand on the small of my back, and then Harold, who was standing by the hammock, said, "Golly, that's tremendous. That's just super news. We couldn't be happier for both of you." Soon all the Blackwells were talking at once. "No shit?" Arthur was saying, and he and John were manfully hugging Charlie, and Ed returned to kiss my cheek, and Arthur gave me a noogie and cried, "Welcome to the fam-damily, Al!" Harold leaned around Charlie to pat my hand, then Jadey enveloped me, shouting, "I knew it! I knew it! I told you we'd be best friends, and now it's even better, because we'll be *sisters*!"

I disentangled myself from Jadey's arms when I saw Mrs. Blackwell approaching; I smoothed my hair. The rest of them—they faded around me. That I was not afraid of Mrs. Blackwell was more or less true, at least in the abstract. But it was also true that when she turned her attention to me, I always felt, and not in a positive way, as if we were the only ones in the room and total vigilance were required.

She did not hug or kiss me, she didn't touch me at all. She seemed both amused and dubious as she looked at me for a long moment before speaking. Finally, she said, "What a clever girl you are."

IN THE CAR driving back to Madison, Charlie said, "I'm not angry. I'm really not. In a perfect world, would it have been better if we'd told Maj and Dad first, without everyone else around? Sure, but what's done is done."

"Do you know that your mother is displeased, or do you just think she is?"

"Maj likes to be deferred to." Charlie grinned. "Like all women. Listen, you were the one who wanted to wait and tell our parents together, but everybody was going to find out eventually, so I don't see the big difference." He reached across the seat and squeezed my hand. "If Maj is unhappy about anything, it's how the news broke. She's not unhappy with you."

"I've never had trouble getting along with people," I said. "If she'd prefer a daughter-in-law from a more socially connected family, I don't fault her. That's what she's accustomed to. But I think she'll get used to me, and I don't want you to worry about having to run interference."

A minute had passed when Charlie said, looking straight ahead out the windshield, "Just so you know, I'd choose you over them."

"Don't be ridiculous," I said.

"We could run away to— Where have you always wanted to run away to? In my fantasies, it's Mexico, but I'd probably just get giardia. California might be a safer bet."

"I'm not *that* concerned," I said.

"A little shack on the beach," Charlie said. "We'll sleep in a hammock, live off the conch that I spear, and you'll wear a coconut bra."

What if I'd said yes? Not to the cartoon version but to a real one, a move to another state. Lives that we carved out for ourselves rather than inheriting, distance and space. What would we—would Charlie—have had to prove, away from his family? Could what has happened in the years since have been prevented, could I have prevented it by merely capitulating? Did Charlie have more foresight than I gave him credit for? Perhaps the future appeared with greater clarity to him than it did to me. Or perhaps he was simply bluffing.

"We're from Wisconsin, Charlie," I said. "This is where we belong."

AND THEN SCHOOL had started, that inimitable, unmistakable sound of children crying out and running around before the bell rang in the morning, the checkout cards that I kept on my desk, the careful way the students gripped the pencils to print their names, and the pride of the ones who were just learning cursive. I read *Tico and the Golden Wings* to the first-graders, and *Flowers for Algernon* to the sixth-graders—I believed eleven-year-olds, even if they didn't admit it, still liked to be read aloud to—and the fourth-graders made paper cranes during our origami unit. There were our Monday-morning assemblies, there was recess duty, when I tried to keep the viciousness of the foursquare games in check, and there were lunches in the cafeteria: chili hot dogs and pepperoni pizza and peach halves in syrup, and on alternating Fridays, breakfast for lunch, which the students loved and the teachers hated—French toast, hash browns, sausage links. You'd be finished with this meal at a quarter to twelve, your stomach churning with sugar and starch and cheap meat, and you'd feel like what you most wanted to do was lie down, and then another class would come flying in, frantic about who got to sit in one of the two bean bags during story time, or who was next in line to check out the newest *Encyclo-*

pedia Brown. Every day, when school let out at three o'clock, I felt exhausted and happy.

But here was the difference: Whereas for all the years I'd been working, I'd spent vast amounts of time focused on school during the hours it wasn't in session, I now spent almost none. Once I had stayed in the library until early evening, preparing for the next day, or after the final bell had rung in the afternoon, I'd gone to Rita's classroom to discuss some student I was concerned about—had Rita also noticed the rash on Eugene Demartino's arm, or did she think it seemed like Michelle Vink and Tamara Jones were ganging up on Beth Reibel? But with the start of this school year, I hurried to my car when classes were out, and I experienced mild irritation on the days I had bus duty. I felt the press of my other life, my life with Charlie—I wanted to go to the grocery store to buy food for the dinner we'd eat that night, or go home to straighten up my apartment or shave my legs. If it was a day he had neither met with Hank Ucker nor driven to his job in Milwaukee, well, then I just wanted to spend time with him, to lie together on top of the bedspread on my bed with the warm yellow light of a September afternoon filtering through the window, to luxuriate in what was ours and new and exciting while it still was ours and new and exciting. In the library, I remained energetic and patient with the children. Outside of it, there were times when I left my school bag by the front door to my apartment, or sometimes even in my car, and I didn't open it from the moment I drove away from school until the moment I returned. Instead, I kissed Charlie's lips and his upper arms, his flat abdomen, all his salty skin, and he moved inside me, over and over; I loved to lie beneath him, to receive him. Now that we were engaged, I finally let him stay the night, or I slept at his place, and he was right that it was awfully nice to wake up together. I gave thanks, not for the first time, that being a librarian meant I had no grading to complete.

OUR WEDDING WAS on Saturday, October 8, in Milwaukee; it was at eleven in the morning, held in the front hall of the Blackwells' house, officiated by the Right Reverend Wesley Knull, bishop of the Episcopal Diocese of Milwaukee. There was a luncheon afterward, champagne and lemonade, watercress and egg salad sandwiches with the crusts cut off; these were prepared by Miss Ruby and her daughter, a nineteen-year-old named Yvonne.

When I'd told my mother and grandmother that I was marrying Charlie—I'd taken that trip to Riley without him—my mother had wept with happiness, and my grandmother had, while sitting in a chair, simulated a dance of glee. I had explained later to my mother that the wedding wouldn't cost much because we'd be using the Blackwells' house and their household help; if she wanted to write a check for ninety dollars for champagne, that would be more than enough. I'd settled on this figure by coming up with the lowest possible number that I thought would seem plausible to her. I am not sure how much the wedding really cost the Blackwells, but I let them absorb the expense. I also, in a way that I hoped would discourage questions, admitted to my mother that Dena and I had had a falling-out and she would not be invited to the wedding. Nevertheless, I received a gravy boat from her parents.

Forty-nine guests came: Twenty-nine were Blackwells, twelve were friends of Charlie's (men he knew from Exeter or Princeton or Wharton) and their wives; two were Hank Ucker and his wife; two were Kathleen and Cliff Hicken, who were the only ones we invited from that extended Madison friend group; and four were my mother, my grandmother, our longtime next-door neighbor Mrs. Falke, and my closest friend from Liess, Rita Alwin; Rita proved to be the only black person present besides Miss Ruby and Yvonne. It could have been a much different wedding, a much larger one, but I didn't see the need for it; I didn't yearn to be fussed over. We had no attendants except Liza and Margaret Blackwell, our flower girls, and no dancing, though a harpist played near the buffet. Jadey applied my makeup and styled my hair in an upstairs bedroom before the ceremony, and my dress was a matching skirt and blouse I'd found on the rack at Prange's a few weeks before: white cotton, a blousy V-necked top with a cinched waist and a calf-length skirt that I wore with my white pumps. (When Priscilla Blackwell peered into the bedroom where I was dressing, she exclaimed, "Isn't that a sweet little frock! Why, you look like a pioneer preparing to cross the Great Plains.") I carried a small bouquet of five white lilies; Charlie wore a boutonniere of a single white lily, as did his father; Mrs. Blackwell, my mother, and my grandmother wore corsages.

I walked alone down the aisle, a space created by the rows of white wooden folding chairs that it turned out we didn't need to rent because the Blackwells owned nearly two hundred of them, as well as round folding tables; they kept these stacked in their vast unfinished basement, and the help brought them up for parties and fund-raisers. When I saw Charlie waiting for me by the staircase next to Reverend Knull, I did not feel any sort of epochal emotion; I felt a slight embarrassment to be drawing such attention to myself, to the affection Charlie and I had for each other. What was the reason to declare this so publicly? But the reason was convention, and there are worse rationales. It was necessary, I recognized, for everyone else. As I passed the front row, I saw that my mother and grandmother were beaming. The ceremony was short; afterward, the toasts from Charlie's brothers, a source of worry for me in advance, were crude but in an essentially harmless way.

At the reception, when Charlie was talking to my mother, I went and sat by my grandmother; Mrs. Falke was using the bathroom, and my grandmother was surveying the room, smoking a cigarette. "It's a swell family you've married into," she said. We looked at each other, and she added, "They're lucky to get you."

"May I have a sip?" I gestured toward her glass of champagne on the table, and my grandmother nodded. I said, "Mom told me you haven't been to see Dr. Wycomb for a while, and if it's because of the hassle of the train, I could drive you to Chicago sometime. One of the next few weekends, even. Things will be pretty quiet for me with the wedding behind us."

My grandmother looked startled.

"Not if you don't want me to," I said quickly. "I just thought—"

"If we showed up at Gladys's doorstep, I'm afraid she wouldn't let us in." My grandmother smiled sadly. "She became cross with me years ago."

"Was there—" I hesitated. "Did something happen?" And so we had arrived at the subject I'd studiously avoided for as long as I could, and instead of being gripped by nervousness or distaste, I felt a to-hell-with-it sort of nonchalance; I found myself wondering why I'd invested quite so much energy all this time in evasion.

"Gladys wanted me to move to Chicago," my grandmother said. "After you went away to school, particularly, she'd say, 'What's there for you in Riley?' She couldn't understand, never having had a child or grandchild of her own. She thought I was wasting my twilight years in this square little town when she and I could have a cosmopolitan life together. But I didn't seriously consider it. Your father wouldn't have understood, and if I was to choose between Gladys and my own son, it wasn't much of a choice."

I swallowed. "And then you lost touch?"

"She took up with another friend." My grandmother's expression was wry as she inhaled on her cigarette. "A younger lady, if I'm not mistaken. It would be hard not to be younger than me, but I mean a good deal younger than Gladys, too. Cradle-robbing, isn't that what they call it?"

"I'm sorry, Granny. I'm sorry that—" I paused. *That I was childish about what you wanted in the world. That I was unable to accept a thing that caused no harm, that I acted as if it were shameful because someone somewhere gave me the impression that it was and not because I bothered to consider the situation for myself.* "I'm sorry it turned out like that," I said.

"Well, it's scarcely recent history." She lifted her champagne flute toward me. "Find me something stiffer to drink, would you? Don't Republicans like old-fashioneds?"

"I'm sure I can get somebody to fix one."

As I stood, my grandmother said, "Your new mother-in-law seems like a crafty broad."

"I don't think she approves of me."

My grandmother tapped her cigarette against an ashtray. "You must be doing something right."

AFTERWARD, AS WE pulled out of the driveway, Charlie smacked his hand against his forehead and said sarcastically, "Oh, shit—we forgot to do the dollar dance!" In Riley, if not in Madison, I had attended many weddings where dollar dances occurred; Charlie, I suspected, had never attended one.

We were to stay overnight in a bed-and-breakfast in Waukesha, a Victorian house painted blue-gray. "It looks haunted," Charlie said as we turned up the gravel driveway.

I was the one who had chosen it, based on a recommendation from another teacher, and I replied, "Then you should have picked out someplace else."

"Are you always so grumpy when you get married?" he asked, and we grinned at each other across the front seat.

Around three in the morning, I woke to find Charlie shaking me. "I've gotta take a leak," he said.

I shooed him away. "I'm sleeping."

"Come with me, will you?" The bathroom was outside our room and down the hall about twenty feet. He leaned across me and switched on the light on my nightstand. "Just come. One minute. I'll be fast."

I was covering my eyes with the inside of my elbow. "Turn it off," I said.

"Come on." His tone was both cajoling and whiny. "This place gives me the creeps."

I lifted my arm. "You seriously want me to go with you to the bathroom?"

"Lindy, you've known since the night we met that I'm afraid of the dark. There was no false advertising."

I shook my head, but, just the tiniest bit, I was smiling. In the hall, a night-light stuck into a plug gave off a weak glow, but neither of us could find the main light switch. I walked in front, and when a floorboard creaked, Charlie whispered, "You hear that?" and I whispered back, "Calm down. This house is probably a hundred years old."

In the bathroom, I perched on a low radiator against the wall while he stood over the toilet. After he was finished, he turned and kissed me on the lips. "I knew I married the right woman."

"Wash your hands and let's go back to bed," I said.

WHEN I FELL asleep again, I dreamed, as I had not for many years, of Andrew Imhof. We were in some sort of large, vague, crowded room—the poorly lit auditorium of a school, possibly—and we did not speak or even make eye contact, but I was acutely conscious of every place he moved; really, he was all I paid attention to, though I was pretending otherwise. Then, abruptly, he was gone, and I was deeply disappointed. I had been planning to approach him, I'd known he wanted me to, but I'd put it off so long I'd missed my chance. When I awakened, it was half past six, and our room in the B and B was just getting light; we were sleeping on a high, canopied bed, beneath a patchwork quilt so heavy I had broken into a sweat. The feeling of disappointment stayed with me—that what I wanted was the boy in the dream. Without turning my head to look at Charlie, I knew. Not this. That. Andrew. To be with Andrew would have been utterly natural; everything had been set in place, and I'd needed only to give in. And that feeling of being adored by a handsome boy, that feeling of being seventeen, of life being *about* to happen—how was it all so long ago, how had my path gone this way instead? My sense of disappointment wasn't because I'd had to escort Charlie to the bathroom—that was practically endearing. It was because of everything else: I was now married (*married*) to an aspiring politician from a smug and ribald family, I had a mother-in-law who didn't like me, my husband was a man who basically (I rarely, even in the privacy of my own head, admitted this) did not hold a job. I'd been meant to grow old in Riley; I'd never been meant for ribaldry or riches.

Charlie stirred then, pulling me to him, and when I finally looked at his face, the dream began to dissipate. I rolled toward him, feeling the tops of his feet with the bottoms of my toes, feeling the hair on his calves against the skin of my own legs, and his bony knees—they almost hurt me sometimes, when his legs were bent—and I pressed my torso to his, I huddled beneath his chest and shoulders. I recognized the smell of his skin, and he was handsome; he was not as handsome as Andrew Imhof had been, because Andrew had been a teenager, perfect and golden, but surely, had Andrew lived, he would no longer be handsome the way he'd been then. If what I had with Charlie did not feel as ripe with promise as what I'd had with Andrew—well, of course it didn't. That earlier promise had hinged on never being realized. Charlie and I already knew each other far better than Andrew and I ever had. If Charlie couldn't name the bakery on Commerce Street, or give the reason why Grady's Tavern had caught fire in 1956, if he didn't fully understand where I came from, he understood who I was now—he knew how well done I liked my steak, knew the color of my toothbrush, the expression I made when I realized I'd forgotten to roll up my car windows before it rained. And if I'd been meant to stay in Riley, wouldn't I have? Charlie wasn't the reason I'd moved to Madison—I was the one who'd chosen to go over a decade earlier, and I'd rarely doubted my choice.

There then occurred the first and only paranormal incident of my marriage. Charlie shifted in his sleep, opened his eyes, looked at me, and, without preamble, said, "You have to forgive yourself for killing that boy." (He was the first one who had ever said *killing*—though I had used the word plenty in my own thoughts, no one had used it with me. Years later, that was how people put it in articles and especially on the Internet, but Charlie was the first.) "For your own sake but for mine, too," he was saying, and his voice was hoarse from sleep yet also certain and insistent. "If you don't forgive yourself, you're making that accident too important, you're making *him* too important." Charlie paused. "And I want to be the love of your life."

I was so surprised that I don't recall what I said—probably nothing more than "Okay"—and we fell back to sleep, Charlie first. When we awoke over an hour later, we did not refer to the exchange. We chatted idly, Charlie tried to persuade me to have sex—"We need to consummate this thing pronto"—but I didn't want to until we got home that afternoon because the walls of the B and B were so thin we'd heard the owner sneeze the night before. For breakfast, we went downstairs to eat biscuits and cherry jam. The bewilderment my dream had left behind, that jarring sorrow—they were gone, and now that we were up and dressed, walking around, now that it was an ordinary day, I could see the dream's utter irrationality. I *did* love Charlie; I was extravagantly lucky.

But the dream came back—the truth is that it has come back and come back and come back. For the entirety of my marriage, I would estimate I have dreamed of Andrew Imhof every two or three weeks, almost always as he appeared to me the night of my wedding: present but elusive. He stands nearby, we do not speak, and I am filled with exquisite longing. When I wake, the longing takes more time to fade than the dream itself.

But the dream is also, I have thought, a kind of gift: It allows me to remember Andrew without the memory being overwhelmed by my own sense of guilt. Perhaps Charlie's exculpation had some effect, along with the passage of time. By my wedding night, it had been so many years. I was scarcely the same person I'd been that September evening in high school, and because it was no longer me, exactly, who had crashed the car, I could forgive the girl it had been as I would have been willing, much sooner, to forgive a classmate who'd been driving.

And so the dream was the first time that I experienced our separation not as Andrew's loss but purely as mine. Not as *I am so very sorry for the thing I did to you.* But as *Come back to me. Come back to me because fourteen years have passed, but still I miss you terribly.*

IT WAS THE following spring, in early May, when I ran into my former realtor Nadine Patora. It was a Saturday morning, Charlie was off with Hank dashing from a 4-H dairy conference in Kimberly to a nursing home in Menasha to a diner in Manitowoc, and I was picking through a bin of apples at the farmers' market when I felt the weight of someone staring. I glanced up. Nadine stood directly across the table from me. Unsure what to do, I smiled at her.

"I hear you got married." She nodded at my wedding ring, which was a plain gold band.

I realized I had never written her a note apologizing for backing out of the purchase of the house. I had intended to, but during my courtship with Charlie, I'd forgotten. "Nadine, I'm really sorry about what—"

"I saw the wedding announcement in the paper," she said. "You should have had the courtesy to tell me the truth."

"My decision didn't have anything to do with getting married," I said.

"I don't know what realtor you two went through, but I'll say this: I was good enough to work with when you were a single gal on a tight budget, and I know, even if you don't, that I could have done a first-rate job finding the right house for you and your husband. When you've been in the business as long as I have, you're familiar with lots of areas."

"No, no," I said quickly. "We haven't bought a house. We're renting a place in Houghton."

"There are public records, Alice. I can go on Monday and find out who brokered the deal and how much you paid."

"Honestly," I said. "We're renting."

Nadine pursed her lips. "The former governor's son is running for Congress, and you expect me to believe he lives in some crappy little apartment?"

I DID NOT have another confrontation with Dena, but I am sorry to say this may have been only because I didn't speak to her again before I moved from the city. The day she'd walked out on our lunch, I hadn't thought that our friendship was over, her declarations to the contrary; I'd have guessed that she would forgive me. I still believe this may have been the case but that circumstances—geography, really—kept us apart. If I'd had the nerve to go into her store one day after enough time had passed, or if she'd found a serious boyfriend while I was still in Madison, I think we might have been able to pick up where we left off.

But only once before I moved did I see her, and I lacked the courage to say hello. This was a few months prior to when I ran into Nadine, a dark weekday afternoon in February, and I was coming out of a stationery store on State Street after buying a valentine for Charlie. I saw Dena from across the street, from the back, and my breath caught; I stood there, unmoving, against the brick exterior of the store, until she was all the way up the block. I did not lay eyes on her again for thirty years.

IN NOVEMBER 1978, Charlie lost the Sixth District congressional election to Alvin Wincek, 58 percent to 42 percent. Charlie had done better than people anticipated, but he still hadn't come close. I had given notice to Liess's principal, Lydia Bianchi, the previous spring, and I'd spent the summer and fall riding with Charlie in lawn chairs set in the flatbed of a pickup truck with BLACKWELL FOR CONGRESS signs affixed to the sides. I'd heard him introduce himself to thousands of voters and give the same speech hundreds of times, I'd passed him lozenges when he lost his voice and still kept speaking, I'd held his hand, I'd clapped, I'd eaten onion rings and french fries, I'd clapped again and eaten more onion rings and more french fries, and when Charlie gave his concession speech at the campaign headquarters on election night, we both had cried a little bit, and if our tears were not for exactly the same reasons, they weren't for entirely different ones, either. We had gone together through something big; what we wanted was much more merged than it had been when we were dating.

In February, three months after the election, we bought a house in a northern suburb of Milwaukee—Maronee—and moved in on March 31, 1979. I was five weeks pregnant, which I'd found out at the doctor's office the day before we closed on the house; once we were in our new home, Charlie would scarcely let me unpack a box. We both were thrilled. We had stopped using any form of birth control a few weeks after our wedding, and given that seventeen months had passed since then and I was almost thirty-three, the arrival of my period had become a discouraging event; with increasing frequency, we'd been discussing the possibility of adoption.

The house we bought on Maronee Drive had five bedrooms, and it had cost $163,000. If Nadine had been our realtor, she'd have made almost $5,000, but we'd used a guy named Stuey Patrickson who played squash with Charlie's cousin Jack. We made one bedroom ours, one we designated as a nursery, one was Charlie's office, one was a guest room, and one was a mini-gym for Charlie where he could lift weights; we even had a large mirror installed along the wall, though more often he worked out at the weight room of the Maronee Country Club, whose golf course was across the street. (The weight room was a grim little affair back then, but it became increasingly fancy as the national interest in exercise grew.) Charlie and I did not discuss the possibility—it didn't occur to me, and I don't think it occurred to him, either—that I would also have an office in our new house. The second-floor hallway was spacious, and at one end, near a window, we set a desk where, kept company by my papier-mâché Giving Tree, I paid bills and wrote thank-you notes. I had gotten quite good at writing thank-you notes; after our wedding, we'd received dozens and dozens of gifts from Blackwell family friends whom we hadn't invited to the ceremony. For years, this was how I kept Milwaukee people straight in my head: the LeGrands, who had given us the toaster oven; the Wendorfs, who had given us the white porcelain serving platter.

Charlie and I settled easily into our new life together; the headiness of our courtship passed, but its passage seemed organic rather than lamentable. The rhythms of keeping a house suited me. I had wondered if I would be bored, but there was a lot to do when we moved in, painters and contractors to oversee (we renovated the master bathroom), and I also had a garden to maintain. Every morning after Charlie left for work—he was going to Blackwell Meats four and sometimes five days a week—I'd read for at least an hour, and I had worked long enough to recognize this for the great luxury it was. I admit that early on, I'd sometimes reach the end of a chapter, look up, and be startled by my surroundings; while inside a fictional world, I had forgotten what I'd become, it had slipped my mind that I was a married woman with a house, living with my husband in a suburb of Milwaukee. At these moments, and at others, I'd think of my apartment on Sproule Street, my former students and colleagues, my friendships with Dena and Rita (I had given my mother's brooch to Rita when I quit my job—though it was pretty, it held such unpleasant associations that I'd never have worn it myself). While on balance, I didn't regret the changes that had taken place in my life, I'd feel a small twinge for what was no longer mine.

Charlie and I were newlyweds, and then, very quickly, we were just another married couple, socializing often with his brothers and other couples who belonged to our country club and our church. Charlie usually played squash or tennis after work and brought me flowers once a week. On Sundays, if Harold and Priscilla were in town, we went to their house for dinner—I learned to call them Harold and Priscilla rather than Mr. and Mrs. Blackwell—and we traveled, sometimes with Jadey and Arthur. In our first five years of marriage, we visited Colorado, California, North Carolina, New York, and New Jersey, and I was only slightly disappointed when Charlie decided for us against accompanying his parents to Hawaii. By then our daughter, Ella, was two and quite a handful to take on a plane.

In the early years of our marriage, we were very happy—for most of our marriage, we have been happy, though like all couples, we have experienced bumps. This is not necessarily the story the public wishes to hear, that the good times have greatly outweighed the bad, but it is the true story. The longer we have been together, the more far-fetched our compressed courtship has come to seem. Engaged after six weeks! Married after six more! How impulsive, how bold or foolish. Did we know each other at all? But I think we did. In most ways, I believe we're the same people we were then, though the circumstances of our lives have changed dramatically.

During that initial congressional run and in later elections, when pundits or journalists underestimated Charlie, I could not be surprised; after all, when we'd first met, I had underestimated him, too.

PART III

402 Maronee Drive

BECAUSE WE HAD theater tickets for seven-thirty, Charlie had promised to be home by six-fifteen, and I'd made a chicken marsala we could eat with Ella before we left. But by six-forty, Charlie still wasn't back, and our sitter, a college sophomore named Shannon whom Ella adored, had arrived. I called Charlie's office, where his answering machine picked up, his secretary's voice explaining that he was away or in a meeting. Had he forgotten about the play—it was Chekhov's *The Seagull*—and gone to the country club to play squash or lift weights? Had he gone to a baseball game? It was a Wednesday in May, and though we had season tickets to the Milwaukee Performing Arts Center, we usually went to performances on Friday or Saturday nights.

I checked the paper, and the Brewers were indeed playing at home; they were playing the Detroit Tigers. That was the likeliest explanation for Charlie's absence, but just in case, I called the country club, and the operator connected me to the athletic building, where Tony, the seventy-year-old who tended bar in the oak-paneled lounge between the men's and women's locker rooms, told me he hadn't seen Charlie. This still could mean Charlie had entered the squash courts or the weight room through the side door, or it could mean he'd gone to his parents' house, where he and Arthur liked to watch baseball games together in peace and quiet. Harold and Priscilla had moved to Washington, D.C., in 1986, two years earlier, when Harold was elected chair of the Republican National Committee, but the house was still fully furnished.

I called Jadey—she and Arthur also lived on Maronee Drive, a mile west of us—and their son Drew, who was fifteen, said, "Mom's walking Lucky."

"Is your dad home yet?" I asked.

"He's working late."

When I hung up, it was ten to seven, and it would take a solid twenty-five minutes to get downtown. Shannon and Ella sat at the kitchen table, Ella finishing her dinner. I crossed the kitchen and kissed Ella on her forehead. To both of them, I said, "Upstairs at eight-thirty, lights out at eight-forty-five, and no TV."

"Mommy, your earrings look like thumbtacks," Ella said.

I laughed. The earrings in question were gold, and they did look a little like thumbtacks. I also wore a pale pink suit—a skirt and jacket—and pink Ferragamo pumps. "Make sure to put away Barbie's tea party," I said to Ella, then looked at Shannon. "There's some cooked steak in the fridge if you want to reheat it. We should be home by ten-thirty. I'm stopping by Mr. Blackwell's parents' house, because I think that's where he is, but if he comes here, tell him to meet me downtown."

He wasn't at his parents', though. At first, pulling into the driveway of their castlelike dwelling, I'd noticed lights in the kitchen and thought I'd found him, but when I approached the side door on foot, I saw through a window that it was Miss Ruby; she was cinching the belt of a tan raincoat.

She opened the door for me, and I said, "Charlie's not here, is he?"

"You try the country club?"

"I don't think he's there, either." I glanced at my watch. "We're supposed to go to a play that starts at seven-thirty."

Miss Ruby regarded me impassively. Over the years, I had observed the Blackwells competing for her opprobrium—if she scolded Arthur for, say, setting a glass on the living room table without a coaster, he'd treat it as a minor victory—but this was not a competition in which I wanted to participate. If Miss Ruby was grumpy, she was also an unfailingly hard worker, and on more than one holiday, I'd walked into the kitchen to find her scrubbing dishes at eleven P.M., then I'd returned to the house the following morning and found her setting out breakfast fixings by eight o'clock. Just a few years before, I'd learned she had a bedroom off the kitchen, as well as her own adjacent bathroom, but sleeping at the Blackwells' rather than going home for the night seemed to me more a drawback than a perk of her job.

It was by this point exactly seven, which meant I'd likely miss the start of the play, which meant why bother? I nodded toward the back door. "You're headed out, I take it?"

"Just making sure the house is ready for Mr. and Mrs."

I had forgotten that Harold and Priscilla were coming to town for the weekend, and that in fact we all were due for dinner there Saturday night. I made a mental note to call Priscilla and ask what I could bring.

I gestured to Miss Ruby to walk out in front of me, and almost imperceptibly, she shook her head; I walked out first, and she followed. It was about sixty degrees, the late-May sky darkening, the Blackwells' lawn canopied by trees thick with new leaves. As we crossed the gravel driveway, I realized my car was the only one parked, and I turned to Miss Ruby. "Can I offer you a ride?"

"No, ma'am, I take the bus."

"Then at least let me drive you to your stop. It's on Whitting, isn't it?" A few times, in the late afternoon or early evening, I had driven past her waiting there.

"You don't need to," she said.

"No, I insist." I laughed a little. "I'd like to do *something* worthwhile with my night." When she climbed in the car, I had the distinct sense that she was humoring me.

We drove in silence—the NPR show I'd been listening to had come on with the ignition, and I'd switched it off in case it wasn't to her liking (Charlie referred to the station as National "Pubic" Radio)—and as we were approaching the corner of Montrose Lane and Whitting Avenue, I said, "Would *you* be interested in going to the theater with me? Our tickets are for *The Seagull,* and they'll go to waste otherwise. But please don't feel like you have to—it'll be a bit of a rush to get there." She didn't respond immediately, and I wondered if I should explain the play's plot or author, or if it would be presumptuous to assume Miss Ruby hadn't heard of Chekhov.

"I don't know that I'm dressed right," she finally said, and I looked over, worried that she would have on the black dress that was her uniform—I wouldn't blame her for not wanting to go to a play in a maid's uniform—but I saw that beneath her raincoat, she was wearing red slacks and a black sweater.

"No, you're fine," I said. "I'm a little overdressed, to tell the truth. Have you been to the Performing Arts Center?"

"Jessica went with her school to hear the Christmas carols." Jessica was Miss Ruby's granddaughter, the daughter of Yvonne, and I knew both of them lived with Miss Ruby; Jessica's father was not in the picture. Yvonne had actually helped at a few parties Charlie and I gave early in our marriage, while she was in nursing school, and now she worked downtown in the ER at St. Mary's. Yvonne was a sunnier woman than her mother, and I'd always liked her, and Ella was crazy about Jessica, who was a few years older. On the days Miss Ruby brought her granddaughter to the Blackwells' house, if Jessica was out of school but Yvonne had to work, the two little girls would spend hours playing with Barbies in Priscilla's kitchen. It struck me then that I hadn't seen either Jessica or Yvonne for quite a while, not since before Harold and Priscilla had left for Washington. I said, "Is Jessica still at Harrison Elementary?"

"Yes, ma'am, she is." A bit uncertainly, Miss Ruby added, "I suppose I could go to that play."

I was shocked and delighted, but I intentionally remained low-key. I said, "Wonderful," and then, as I accelerated, "Jessica was always so bright. Am I right in thinking she's about to finish fifth grade?"

"She's in the sixth grade with Mr. Armstrong," Miss Ruby said. "Straight A's on her report card, vice president of the student council, and she's a leader in the youth group at Lord's Baptist."

"That's fabulous," I said. "Where will she go for junior high?"

"She'll be at Stevens."

I made a conscious effort not to react negatively. Stevens was, without a doubt, the worst junior high school in Milwaukee. We lived in the suburbs, and Ella went to private school, to Biddle Academy, but you didn't have to be a faithful reader of *The Milwaukee Sentinel* to know what dire straits the city's public schools were in, and Stevens was in the direst: The year before, a gun that a seventh-grader had brought to school somehow went off between classes, and within the last month, two ninth-graders had been expelled for selling crack. (Ninth-graders! And for God's sake, *crack*. It reminded me why I'd taught younger kids, though I couldn't have fathomed anything like that in the seventies.) "What's Jessica's favorite subject?" I asked.

"I guess it's English, but she's good at everything." Miss Ruby pointed. "You want to save time, you should take Howland Boulevard."

"That's great she's doing so well," I said. "How's Yvonne?"

"Not getting any sleep since the baby came. He sure does like to be held."

"Oh my goodness, I didn't realize Yvonne had had a baby. When was this?"

"Antoine Michael," Miss Ruby said. "Turns two months old on the first of June."

"Miss Ruby, that's so exciting. I would love to see him." I had thought my fondness for babies might be a thing I got out of my system after I had one myself, but it had never passed. I still was fascinated by their tiny fingernails and noses and earlobes, the perfect softness of their skin—they seemed magical, from another planet. When Ella became a toddler and then a child, I loved every new stage, she was always funny and charming and of course infuriating, but I admit that I mourned a little when she was no longer a newborn; that transition had been the hardest. "Maybe Ella and I could swing by some afternoon," I said, and when Miss Ruby didn't respond, I added, "Or let's find a time for your family to come to our house. Would lunch a week from Sunday work? Or"—I didn't know what time the Suttons finished church, so perhaps Sunday wasn't ideal—"what about Monday? Next Monday is Memorial Day, isn't it?"

"I suppose we could come."

"Oh, Ella will be thrilled. Now, is Yvonne—is the baby's father—"

"Clyde, he lives with us, too. He and Yvonne got married back last summer."

"Miss Ruby, I had no idea so much was going on in your life! How did Yvonne and Clyde meet?"

"He's at the hospital, too, down in the cafeteria." Miss Ruby chuckled. "Sold Yvonne her pie and coffee, if that doesn't beat all."

"Good for them."

When we reached the Performing Arts Center, we parked in a lot on Water Street and hurried inside. The ushers were closing the doors of the theater, but we were able to slip in and take our seats as the lights went down. I had never seen *The Seagull,* and I thought it was quite good—the actress playing Madame Arkadina was superb. It was not until the second act that I was overtaken by an uneasy feeling. Where *was* Charlie? Was it safe to assume he was at the baseball game, or could he be somewhere else entirely?

At intermission, I found a pay phone in the lobby, but again there was no answer at his office, and at home, Shannon said she hadn't heard from him. I hovered between irritation and anxiety. The fact was, I had more reason to think he'd simply forgotten about the play, or even purposely avoided it, than I did to think something was wrong. In the last few months, Charlie had accompanied me to the theater increasingly grudgingly, and sometimes we skipped events altogether when I didn't want to see a performance enough to try persuading him. The truth of our lives was that for close to two years, he had been in a bad mood; he was almost always restless and disagreeable.

To a certain extent, Charlie had been restless since I'd met him—he drummed his fingers on the table when he felt we'd stayed too long at a dinner party, he'd murmur to me, "I bet even God has fallen asleep" during sermons at church—but in the past, it had been a restlessness that was physical, situational, rather than existential. His bad mood was different. It wasn't directed *toward* me, but it had become such a constant that the times when he wasn't in its grip were the exceptions.

I'd tried to pinpoint when it had all started, and it seemed to have been around the time he turned forty, in March 1986. To my surprise, he had not wanted a party—he, Ella, and I had celebrated with hamburgers and carrot cake at home—and in the months before and after his birthday, Charlie talked often about his legacy. He'd say, "I just have to wonder what kind of mark I'll make. By the time Granddad Blackwell was my age, he'd founded a company with three dozen employees, and by the time Dad was forty, he'd gone from being the state attorney general to being governor." If I were to be completely candid, I would make the following admission: There were many things about

Charlie that I knew other people might imagine I'd find irritating—his crudeness, his healthy ego, his general squirminess—and I didn't. But his fixation with his legacy (I even grew to hate the word) I found intolerable. It seemed so indulgent, so silly, so *male;* I have never, ever heard a woman muse on her legacy, and I certainly have never heard a woman panic about it. I once, in the most delicate manner possible, expressed this observation about gender to Charlie, and he said, "It's because you're the ones who give birth." I did not find this answer satisfying.

Whatever the source of Charlie's discontent, in late 1986 and the first half of 1987, it had been exacerbated by three quarters in a row of declining profits at Blackwell Meats. There ensued a many-months-long debate about taking the company public, an idea Charlie favored, and his brother John, who was still the CEO, opposed. The five other members of the company's board of directors were Arthur, Harold, Harold's brother, the brother's son, and Harold's sister's husband, and their votes were evenly split, with Harold siding with John. This meant the decision came down to Arthur, who, after much back-and-forth, voted with John and against Charlie. Charlie spared his father and Arthur and saved his anger for John, and the previous November, we'd all experienced a rather strained Thanksgiving, with Priscilla seating John and Charlie as far apart as possible. Although the chill seemed to have thawed in the six months since—John and Charlie saw each other every day at work, after all—Charlie still privately seethed about what he saw as John's ignorance (a particularly sore spot for Charlie was that John had never attended business school), and the rancor was a vivid reminder that if someone else criticized a Blackwell, it wasn't acceptable, but a Blackwell criticizing a Blackwell was just fine. Meanwhile, I had tried not to let the conflict affect my relationship with John's wife, Nan—I invited her to lunch more often than usual, or I'd suggest we drive together to Junior League meetings—and Ella, with no idea that her father and uncle were sparring, was worshipful of her girl cousins: Liza, who had taught me string figures during my first visit to Halcyon, was now twenty and finishing her junior year at Princeton, and Margaret was seventeen and would enter Princeton in the fall.

But Charlie was less and less inclined to participate in family gatherings—he certainly didn't initiate any—and he could be guaranteed to show up for a Blackwell brunch or dinner only if his parents were in town, which wasn't more often than every six weeks. A month before, in April, John and Nan had bought a table for eight at a benefit for the art museum and invited us to sit with them, and Charlie hadn't gone at the last minute; it was a Saturday evening, he'd been drinking heavily while watching a baseball game in the den, and when he came upstairs and saw that I'd hung his tuxedo on the back of our bedroom door, he said, "No way I'm putting on that monkey suit."

"Charlie, it's black-tie," I said, and he said, "Tough titty. I'm wearing what I have on, or you can go without me." I had thought at first that he was kidding, but he'd maintained his refusal to change clothes, which was the same as refusing to go. When I'd asked what I was supposed to tell John and Nan—I knew they'd paid a hundred dollars a plate—he shrugged. "Tell 'em the truth." Instead, I said he'd come down with the stomach flu. When I got home that night, he was still watching television—some police drama—and he smiled impishly and said, "Do you forgive your scoundrel husband?" Because it wasn't worth it not to, I did, but that Monday, I ordered pamphlets from two treatment facilities for alcoholics, one local and one in Chicago. When I showed the pamphlets to Charlie, he said angrily, "Because I didn't want to change my clothes the other night? Are you kidding me? Lindy, get a fucking grip."

At some point during the spring, Charlie's malaise had expanded to include not just his brothers but also his upcoming twentieth reunion at Princeton, which would occur in early June. In advance of the event, he'd received a bonded leather book in which alumni provided updates about their professional and personal lives, and before bed, he'd taken to reading aloud from it in tones of scorn and disbelief: " 'Having made partner at Ellis, Hoblitz, and Carson was an achievement outmatched only by the indescribable pleasure of seeing the sunrise over Maui's Haleakala Crater as Cynthia and I celebrated fifteen years of marriage . . .' I'm telling you, this guy didn't know his asshole from his elbow in college. Oh, *here's* a good one: 'I find it humbling to think that my oncology research literally saves lives . . .' We all knew O'Brien was a homo." I did not find these excerpts or Charlie's editorializing enjoyable, mostly because I'd be trying to read my own book, and they were interruptions. We didn't have to go to the reunion, I pointed out once, eliciting a snappish rebuttal: Of course we had to go! What kind of chump skipped Reunions? (That was what Princetonians called the event—not *the* reunion, just capital-R Reunions.) It was clear that the book had touched a nerve, that while working for a family-owned meat company sufficed in Maronee, at least on good days, Charlie questioned how impressive it sounded in a more national context. Though I tried to be sympathetic to his insecurities, I couldn't shake the feeling that this was, on balance, a rather fortunate problem to have.

In recent weeks, he had been coming home from work later and later and rarely calling to say where he was. Sometimes, it would turn out, he'd been at the country club, sometimes he'd stopped at a bar for a drink (this bothered me most, because it seemed seedy—in Riley, husbands and fathers frequented bars, but they didn't in Maronee), and sometimes he'd driven directly from the office to a Brewers game. The Blackwells had four season tickets, formerly Harold's, which were shared among Charlie and his brothers but often went unused. On these nights, when I asked whom he'd gone with, once it was Cliff Hicken (he and Kathleen, the friends who'd held the backyard cookout where Charlie and I had met, had moved from Madison to Milwaukee three years after we had, when Cliff had taken a job as vice president of a financial advising company), and once Charlie had gone to a game with a younger fellow from work, but several times, it sounded like Charlie had gone alone. He'd arrive home as I was going to bed, and I'd feel simultaneously angry, distressed, and too tired for a confrontation. I'd postpone a real conversation until morning, by which point I didn't have the heart to begin today with what was worst from yesterday. In any case, though he never said as much, I had the sense that on many of these mornings, Charlie was too hungover to do more than force himself out of bed and into the shower.

It had occurred to me that he could be having an affair, but I didn't think he was. We still had sex regularly, if not with the frequency we'd enjoyed early on, and he was, in smaller ways, as affectionate as he'd ever been. In the middle of the night, he'd take my hand and hold it while we slept; the previous week, I'd awakened around three to find him rubbing his feet against mine. When we got up, I'd asked, "Were you playing footsie with me last night?" and he'd said, "Lindy, don't pretend that footsie isn't your favorite game." His ongoing bad mood had not obliterated his usual personality; it was more that it accompanied it, like a sidecar on a motorcycle. And as for the possibility of him having an affair, really, he seemed more preoccupied than secretive.

AT THE END of intermission, I rejoined Miss Ruby in the theater and said, "What do you think?" and she said in a guarded way, "It's interesting." When the play was over and the lights went on, I was approached by several people Charlie and I knew, and when I introduced Miss Ruby to them (instead of calling her Miss Ruby, which felt peculiar in this context, I said, "This is Ruby Sutton"), I could tell some of them wondered who she was; the only person who seemed to recognize her was an older woman named Tottie Gagneaux, who squinted and said, "Aren't you Priscilla's helper?"

Quickly, I said, "Did you know they'll be in town this weekend? They're coming from Arizona, if I'm not mistaken, although it's hard to keep track with how much they travel these days . . ."

It was raining lightly as we left the theater, and Miss Ruby gave me directions to her house. She lived in Harambee, it turned out, in a modest one-story shingle house on a hill, with a steep concrete staircase leading to the door. As I let her out, I could see, at the edges of the curtain in the front window, the flickering blue light of a TV. A figure carrying a baby—Yvonne, obviously—lifted the curtain from one side and peered out the window at my car. "Thanks so much for keeping me company tonight," I said, and Miss Ruby said, "Yes, ma'am." Before she shut the car door, she added, "Good night, Alice." I was nearly certain that in the eleven years since I had met her, it was the first time she'd ever used my name.

DRIVING HOME, I felt an odd, happy lightness. The evening had gone in a different direction than I'd expected, but it seemed like it had been a good direction—while Charlie would have been bored by *The Seagull,* I sensed that Miss Ruby had enjoyed it. When I pulled into our driveway, though, I felt a flicker of doubt. Shannon's car was gone, and after I'd pressed the garage-door opener, I saw Charlie's Jeep Cherokee. Had the baseball game been rained out?

I unlocked the front door, and as soon as I stepped inside, I heard the approach of heavy footsteps. Charlie met me in the hall. "I hope that was a damn good play."

"Is Ella all right?"

"She's fine. I sent Shannon home at nine, and I've been waiting for you ever since."

"I called here and spoke to her at intermission, so you must have gotten in right after that."

"Intermission, huh?" He folded his arms. Whenever he left for work in the morning, and whenever he came home at night, we always hugged and kissed, sometimes repeatedly. So far, we had done neither. In a sarcastic voice, he said, "You get your daily dose of the fine arts?"

I said nothing.

"You didn't maybe wonder where I was?" he added. "Just for a minute or two, while you watched the actors recite their lines?"

"I assumed you were at the ball game. Charlie, I called the country club, I called Arthur and Jadey, I drove over to your parents', and I'm sorry, but this isn't the first time I've been left in the dark on your whereabouts."

"So it didn't cross your mind for even half a second that something might be wrong?"

"*Is* something wrong?"

"I don't know. What do you think?" *You've screwed up,* his expression said, *and I've got all the time in the world to wait for you to realize it.*

Simultaneously, I felt a sincere fear, a bone-deep apprehension, and I felt a surge of resentment. If something was wrong, why was he toying with me? And if something wasn't wrong, the question was the same—why was he toying with me?

"Don't do this," I said. We looked at each other for several seconds, and I did not smile a coddling smile, I did not smile at all. I was willing to coddle Charlie when he thought everyone else was plotting against him, but I wouldn't do so when he acted as if I were plotting, too.

At last, in a surprisingly casual voice, he said, "The company's royally fucked." He turned and walked past the living room and into the back den, and I followed him. (Really, I was not so stern at all—I *would* follow, I *would* coddle, in exchange for the smallest amount of respect and sometimes in exchange for less than respect, for mere neutrality. Had anyone been watching, I probably would have seemed like a doormat, but I believed in picking my battles, and there was rarely anything I wanted more than I didn't want to keep fighting.)

The TV was on, set to the game he apparently hadn't gone to, and on the table in front of the TV were an open bag of Fritos, a half-empty bottle of whiskey, and an old-fashioned glass with an inch of amber liquid in it. Charlie took a seat in the center of the couch, in a spread-out posture that did not invite joining him. I sat in one of the two heavy armchairs on either side of the couch.

Gesturing at the Fritos, I said, "Did you see there's chicken marsala?"

"I had a steak."

He grabbed a throw pillow from beside him, a pillow covered in dark brown corduroy, and clutched it in a way that was so childish it might have been funny or sweet were he not seething. He was looking at the television screen as he said, "Eleven people in Indianapolis puked their guts out after a high school sports banquet Monday night, and what do you suppose was the banquet's entrée? If you guessed chili made with Blackwell ground beef, then ding, ding, ding, you win first prize! Now the USDA has gotten involved, John has decided to do a recall—we're talking, at a minimum, hundreds of thousands of pounds of chuck, maybe millions, in at least five states—and you want to know the best part? I bet you dollars to doughnuts it's not our fault. For all we know, the dipshits in Indiana bought expired meat, but hey, if the big corporation up in Milwaukee can take the fall for it, why not?"

"Charlie, I'm sorry."

He lifted his head. "You and me both. I spent an hour talking to some jackass from the *Sentinel* tonight when I don't give a shit about any of this. I'll grill meat, I'll eat meat, end of story. I'm sick of pretending I care about the integrity of sausage—I didn't go to business school to oversee quality control."

"How are Arthur and John doing?"

"Arthur and John can go fuck themselves."

As he spoke, a player for the Brewers struck out, ending the inning, and Charlie hurled the pillow he'd been holding at the TV. Then he leaned forward, setting his head in his hands, and I stood and went to sit by him. I placed my palm on his back, rubbing it over his white oxford shirt, saying nothing.

With his head still in his hands, he said, "I'm tired of this bullshit."

"I know." I kept rubbing his back. "I know you are."

"I'm this close to quitting. I've had my fill."

"It's fine if you quit," I said, "although I'm sure you'll want to do it as diplomatically as possible." Relatively early in our marriage, I'd had the strange realization that Charlie's income didn't affect our standard of living. It turned out that at the age of twenty-five, Charlie had inherited a trust of seven hundred thousand dollars, and though he'd spent twenty-seven thousand dollars of his own money on his congressional campaign in '78 and a hundred and sixty-three thousand when we bought our house, he'd hardly touched it besides that, and he earned a good salary. With the exception of the precipitous stock-market drop in October 1987, our investments had done well, and there was now in various accounts over a million dollars. I still thought it was important that Charlie hold a job—important for his sense of himself, his ability to give an answer when people asked what he did, and I also couldn't imagine anything more disastrous for our marriage than if we were both in the house all day—but it didn't matter to me what his job was, and I agreed with him that he could probably find something he found more engaging than the meat industry.

Having quit my own job eight months after our wedding, I had contributed a negligible amount to the family pot, and I never lost sight of the fact that *our* money was not exactly ours; I was, however, the one who wrote the checks for all our bills, and I also kept files for the accounts. I sometimes thought back to that check I'd seen for twenty thousand dollars one of the first times I visited Charlie's apartment, how bewildered I'd been by it. Certain things, I now knew, required checks with many zeroes: painting the outside of our house, making a respectable contribution to the annual giving fund at Biddle Academy, acquiring my Volvo station wagon outright, monthly payments being a phenomenon with which Charlie appeared to have little experience.

I suppose it was because the taxes we paid each April on dividends from our investments were greater, even accounting for inflation, than my salary as a teacher had ever been, that I felt it was all right to quietly, and without mentioning it to Charlie, make occasional donations to charities that I suspected would have appealed less to him than they did to me. The donations were in the amount of two or three or, at most, five hundred dollars: I'd read in the paper about an inner-city food pantry, a literacy program, an after-school drop-in center for teens that was in danger of closing, and I'd feel a swelling uneasiness—familiar to me by this point—as I sat in the den or kitchen of our five-bedroom house on Maronee Drive. I'd write a check, send it off, and the uneasiness would subside for a while, until the next time. Although Charlie looked over our finances only once a year, when taxes were due, I did not include my donations in the list of deductions I gave our accountant. Of course, after you make a donation, it seems you remain on an organization's mailing list in perpetuity, and Charlie did once, when rifling through the mail, hold up an envelope from the food pantry and say, "Have you noticed that we get something from them every fucking month?"

In the den, Charlie sat up, and I took the opportunity to lean in and kiss his cheek. He turned his face and kissed me back on the lips, and as we hugged, a sideways sitting hug, the hostility of our encounter in the front hall evaporated. "If you leave the company, what do you think you might like to do instead?" I asked.

"Play first base for the Brewers." He grinned.

"I know I've told you this before, but I've always thought you'd be a wonderful high school baseball coach. You're so knowledgeable, you'd get to be outside, and I'll bet anything the kids would find your enthusiasm infectious."

His grin faded.

"Seriously," I said. "High school positions are competitive, obviously, but if you started at the junior high level—we could even see if any spots are open at Biddle—and then you worked your way up, in a few years, you—"

"Alice, Jesus! Is that really what you think I'm worth?" I glanced down, and he said, "I'm not trying to hurt your feelings, but why don't you try not to hurt mine? Christ almighty, a high school coach—"

I said, "Well, I found working in schools very gratifying."

"Alice, I went to *Princeton.* I went to *Wharton.* I ran for *Congress.*"

I remained quiet.

"It's not that I don't have plenty of options. That isn't the problem," he said. "Dad would be thrilled to have me join him at the RNC, Ed would love it if I came on board as a policy adviser either here or in Washington. The question is, what would be meaningful to me? What would I find most rewarding?" *Please don't say it,* I thought, and he said, "What's the work I can do now that will create the kind of legacy I'll be proud of?"

"I'll fully support you working in Ed's district office, but you know how I feel about moving to Washington."

"Are you saying you won't?"

I sighed. "I won't do it happily. Washington's a long way from Riley, and I just think, in this day and age, Ella's so lucky to have her great-grandmother in her life."

"But she'd get to see Maj and Dad all the time—six of one, half dozen of another, right?"

This was not at all how I saw it, but I said simply, "Your parents are able to travel a lot more easily than my grandmother." My grandmother no longer left the house on Amity Lane, and my mother had had a stair lift installed so that my grandmother didn't need to climb to the second floor. Its seat and back were beige Naugahyde, and sometimes while riding it, my grandmother would wave regally as she ascended, as if she were the queen of England. I had actually lobbied to name Ella after my grandmother, while Charlie had wanted to name her after his mother; we compromised by blending their names and, not for the first time, my mother was more or less ignored.

Charlie took a swallow of whiskey. "I thought my path would be clearer by now, you know? My destiny." Oh, how I hated this talk—

who besides seniors in high school reflected unironically on their destiny?

"Honey, I don't know if such a thing as destiny exists, but I'm pretty sure that if it does, you won't find yours in there." I pointed to the whiskey bottle.

Charlie grinned. "How can we be sure before I've gotten to the bottom?"

I didn't pursue the topic. Instead, I said, "If you want to stay at the company, we'll figure out a way to make it better, and if you want to move on, I know you'll find a position you enjoy. You have a good life, and we have a good life together—we have each other and Ella. Will you try to remember that?"

He was still grinning. "I'm only becoming a high school coach if you become the head cheerleader and you show me your pom-poms."

I leaned in and kissed his cheek. "Don't hold your breath."

I WAS IDLING in the after-school pickup line of cars at Biddle, waiting to get Ella, when a woman knocked on the half-open passenger-side window of my Volvo. The woman was crouching down, and I realized it was Ella's third-grade teacher, Ida Turnau. "Alice, can I talk to you for a sec?" she asked.

Mrs. Turnau was a petite, pink-skinned woman about my age who had a very kind face. (Although I called her Ida when I spoke to her, I always thought of her, and we referred to her at home, as Mrs. Turnau.) I'd gotten to know her because I'd chaperoned a bunch of the class field trips: At a pizza parlor in Menomonee Falls, the children were allowed in the kitchen to make their own individual pizzas; at Old World Wisconsin, they attended a faux temperance rally and watched a demonstration on flax processing, and I'm afraid to say I seemed to find both events considerably more interesting than Ella and her classmates did.

Mrs. Turnau said, "This is awkward, but I saw on the news last night about the beef recall, and I'm wondering, would it be all right if we avoid serving Blackwell hamburgers at the end-of-the-year party? I hate to do this, and I'm sure the problem will be all taken care of by then, but I just know I'll have parents asking." The third-grade party would be held at our house in two weeks.

"Oh, of course," I said. I was tempted to repeat what Charlie had told me—it was unlikely that the contamination had been Blackwell Meats' fault—but there probably wasn't a point. "Absolutely."

"Just so the other parents won't worry," Mrs. Turnau said. The line of cars moved forward a few feet, and she added, "I'll let you go. Nice to see you, Alice."

When she was gone, I realized that the car in front of me was the Volvo of Beverly Heit, whose son was a year ahead of Ella. (I'd heard that the teachers at Biddle called the parents the Volvo Mafia, a nickname in which I personally was complicit. More than once, though, I'd felt the urge, never acted on, to say to Ella's teachers, *I'm one of you! I know I seem like one of them, but really, I'm one of you!*) I honked very lightly, and when I could tell Beverly was looking at me in the rearview mirror, I waved. Beverly waved back, then held up her wrist, tapping her watch: *This is taking forever.* I nodded: *I know!*

As a product of public school, and as a former employee at two of them, I had initially felt a slight resistance to enrolling Ella at Biddle. It wasn't that Charlie and I debated it, because we didn't. Biddle, which started with a prekindergarten Montessori and ran through the twelfth grade, was where all of Ella's cousins either went or had gone, where Charlie's brother John was head of the board of trustees, where Charlie had attended second through eighth grade and Jadey had graduated from in 1967. (Until 1975, the boys' and girls' divisions of the school had been on opposite sides of the campus, now divided between the lower and upper schools.) Even though the public schools in Maronee were extremely well funded, and a far cry from those in the city of Milwaukee, Ella's attendance at Biddle had been a foregone conclusion. Still, I had wondered if the students would be snobby, if the teachers would be overly pleased with themselves. As it turned out, I fell in love with Biddle's white-wood lower school building with the colonnade in front, with its traditions—in third grade, everyone had a Japanese pen pal (Ella's was named Kioko Akatsu), and in fourth grade, all the students, including the boys, cross-stitched a bookmark—and with its quietly hippie-ish leanings: The songs Ella learned in music class and came home singing were "If I Had a Hammer" and "One Tin Soldier" and "Imagine." I could see how not having to follow a curriculum determined by the state allowed the teachers to be more creative, and I was especially looking forward to when Ella would be in fifth grade, and as part of a unit on colonial America, her class would get to dress up, the boys in tricorn hats and jabots and knickers, the girls in dresses that came with aprons and bonnets, and they'd all prepare a feast of stewed corn and apple cider and venison shot by someone's father.

It was another five minutes before my car reached the entrance of the lower school, and as soon as it did, Ella flew into the front seat, her purple backpack falling off one shoulder, a bunch of loose papers in her hand; she thrust them at me before she'd closed her door. "You have to sign the permission slip saying I can go on the Slip 'n Slide even though the party's at our house," she said.

"I *have* to?" I repeated.

She turned and smiled at me—Ella had, without question, the best smile of anyone I had ever known, so lively and mischievous and affectionate—and she said, "I meant, will you please, pretty please, my pretty Mother? Did you bring me graham crackers?" Already, she had found the box between our two seats, and she opened it and began chomping, spilling crumbs down the front of her shirt. *Mother* was a new and ironic term for Ella, not that my nine-year-old daughter had the slightest idea what irony was. But calling me Mother instead of Mommy was something she'd borrowed from her friend Christine, who had worldly and irreverent older sisters. While I wasn't crazy about it, I found it preferable to Ella calling Charlie and me by our first names, which she'd done for a brief time when she was about four, apparently having picked up on the way we addressed each other.

"Can I change the station?" she said, and before I could respond, she'd leaned forward and was twisting the radio dial from NPR to 101.8 FM, causing Bon Jovi's "You Give Love a Bad Name" to erupt into the car. Ella sang loudly along with the chorus: " 'Shot through the heart / And you're to blame . . .' "

Oh, my daughter, my noisy, happy, strong-willed, irrepressible only child—I adored her. One of the things I had not anticipated about motherhood was how entertaining it would be. I'd known from my experience as a librarian that children were often amusing, sometimes outrageously so, but it was different, it was far more fun, when the amusing child was mine, when I spent hours and hours with her on a daily basis, knew her every expression and intonation, each appetite and anxiety and enthusiasm. Her current obsessions included stickers, hopscotch, nail polish (her Aunt Jadey had a much larger supply than I did), Nutter Butter cookies, and Uno, and her fondest wishes were to acquire a Pekingese, which was out of the question because she was allergic to dogs, and to see the movie *Dirty Dancing,* which I had told her I wouldn't allow until she was in seventh grade because it was rated R.

Not infrequently, I was struck by how savvy Ella was, how much more pop-culturally aware than I had been at her age: She had requested a Jane Fonda exercise tape for Christmas (we hadn't given it to her because I didn't want her to become preoccupied with her weight—besides, she already played soccer, squash, and softball); she had encouraged me to "crimp" my hair, saying it would "jazz up" my appearance; and she had asked us at dinner the previous week if it was possible to get AIDS from a toilet seat. Charlie had said, "Not unless you're using the bathroom at Billy Torks's house." This was a reference to Jadey's interior-designer friend, whom Charlie had met only a few times. I'd shot Charlie a look and said to Ella, "You can't, but you still should put toilet paper down before you go, because of other germs."

In the car, Ella and Bon Jovi were still singing, and I said, "Ladybug, turn it down a bit."

She leaned in, her long light brown hair falling forward. Of course my daughter had long hair, coming halfway down her back—I'd been wrong about the one maternal restriction I was sure I'd impose, and even as a very little girl, Ella had protested vehemently when I cut off over an inch or two. Although I'd spent more hours than I cared to think about untangling knots (and once removing grape-flavored gum), I recognized that Ella was very pretty: Along with my blue eyes, she had a dainty upturned nose sprinkled with golden freckles. I was relieved that so far, she appeared largely unaware of her prettiness. When she'd resisted my attempts to cut her hair, it had seemed more an assertion of free will than an act of vanity.

I knew that Ella was a little spoiled, and possibly more than a little. I suppose part of why I wasn't good at saying no to her was that she'd inherited her father's cajoling personality, but another part of it was that we hadn't succeeded in having more children; I'd never been able to get pregnant after her. We'd considered fertility drugs or IVF—this was in the early days of the procedure—but I was wary, concluding that if my body was rejecting pregnancy, perhaps there was a reason, and I ought not to force the situation. I expressed this belief to Charlie, though what I didn't express was a deeper sense that to push for a second child might be greedy, more than I deserved. There was a bittersweet symmetry in having had one abortion and one child; to try so hard for another might have been to press my luck. I'm sure Charlie was disappointed—an only-child family was, to him, an aberration—but beyond a few conversations, he did not insist, and he found as much joy in Ella as I did.

I turned left out of the parking lot, still behind Beverly Heit; the Heits lived about half a mile from us, and I'd probably be following her all the way home. "Ladybug, how was school?" I asked.

"Mrs. Turnau sent Megan to the principal because she wouldn't quit asking people if they wanted a poop sandwich."

"A what?" I said.

"A poop sandwich. Oh, I love this song!" "So Emotional" had come on the radio—a few months back, Ella had bought the new Whitney Houston cassette, the first music she'd ever purchased with her own money—and she leaned forward, turning it up. I reached out and turned off the radio altogether.

"Mommy!"

"Ella, you need to be respectful when someone is talking to you." I glanced over at her. "Now, what on earth is a poop sandwich?"

Ella shrugged. Megan was Megan Thayer, the daughter of Joe and Carolyn, who were another Halcyon family. They had separated in the winter, and I'd heard from Jadey that Carolyn had recently filed for divorce; the rumor was that Carolyn had come into some family money and felt freed to end the marriage. Charlie and I weren't extremely close to either Carolyn or Joe, but we ended up seeing a fair amount of Halcyon people in Milwaukee because, like us, they belonged to the Maronee Country Club, I was in Garden Club and Junior League with the wives, and our children all attended the same school. This meant that on a regular basis, Charlie and I would share a blanket with Carolyn and Joe at one of Ella and Megan's soccer games, or chat with them at a fund-raiser. When the news had broken that they were splitting up, I'd had the impression that most people were shocked, but I really wasn't. Joe was a gentle, slightly dull man thought by many women in Maronee to be quite handsome in a classic way: He was tall and slim, with a long, dignified nose and a full head of gray hair with a wave in front. Meanwhile, Carolyn was a complicated and not particularly happy-seeming woman. The famous story about her was that once when they were hosting a dinner party, she'd brought out the main course, a duck cassoulet, and one of the guests, a fellow named Jerry Greinert who was a good friend of theirs, had said jokingly, "Not that again," and Carolyn had proceeded to throw the serving dish on the floor, turn around, and storm out of the house.

"Can I turn the music back on?" Ella said.

"Not yet. Do people pick on Megan?"

"If you would like to know the answer to that, then you can only find out when I turn on the radio."

"Be nice to her," I said. "When you and Christine are playing at recess, see if she wants to join you." Although Megan and Ella knew each other well—there were only forty-four students in the third grade, plus they spent a good deal of the summer mere houses apart—they had never been real friends. Megan was a tall, broad-shouldered, dark-haired girl, a strong athlete, but she had that overly watchful, overly eager quality that's off-putting to adults and children alike; the previous summer, in Halcyon, she had asked me whether Ella would be having a slumber party for her next birthday, and if so, whether she, Megan, would be invited.

I said to Ella, "But if Megan offers you a poop sandwich, tell her no."

With great exasperation, Ella said, "Mother, I *already* told her no."

"Oh," I said. "Good. But still be nice to her. You have such a big heart, ladybug."

"Can I turn on the radio?"

We were a mile from our house. "Not too loud," I said.

DESPITE THE ONGOING investigation by the USDA, it still wasn't clear how the meat in Indianapolis had come to be contaminated. That evening, Charlie got home from work at a reasonable hour, and out of either habit or defiance he lit the grill. (He still insisted on using a charcoal one for flavor.) I had planned a quick walk with Jadey, and after I called her, we met halfway between our houses and cut onto the golf course's cart path. On the weekend, this route had its risks—about five months before, by the seventh hole, a ball had hit Lily Jones in the shoulder—but I loved the green grass, the groves of pine trees, the spring sky at dusk. Golf balls aside, it was all incredibly calming.

Jadey was wearing white sweatpants, a red T-shirt, and a white sweatband that held back her blond hair; we both had shorter hair now, about chin-length, though hers was more layered than mine. We had just passed the duck pond when she said, "So I've figured out how to get back at Arthur. First I'll lose weight, then I'll have an affair. Want to go on a diet with me?"

"I hope you're kidding."

She lifted her left arm and pinched a bunch of flesh beneath her bicep. "Arthur's right. I mean, who'd want to commit adultery with *that*?"

A few weeks earlier, Arthur had, according to Jadey, announced that she needed to lose weight; since then she'd refused to have sex with him. Although I sided with her, the story felt incomplete. As off-color as Arthur could be, he wasn't cruel, and I couldn't imagine he'd expressed the thought as bluntly as she claimed; I even wondered if he'd been answering a question she'd asked. In the time since I'd met Jadey, it was true she'd gained about thirty pounds, but she was still very pretty. She'd become softer, less girlish, but she *wasn't* a girl, she was thirty-eight years old, and what was wrong with looking the age you were? I myself had gained probably ten pounds in the last decade, mostly weight that I'd never quite lost after Ella's birth, and it seemed like a worthwhile trade-off. I said, "Do I dare ask who it is you're planning to have an affair with?"

"Let's just say all applications will be considered seriously."

"This is a terrible idea, Jadey."

"Oh, come on—don't be the morality police."

"Well, it is a terrible idea morally, but I was thinking logistically. Can you imagine getting a divorce, having to share custody and being apart from Drew and Winnie?" None of Charlie's brothers and their wives had sent their children to boarding school, a precedent that greatly relieved me; I would have fought hard against sending Ella. "Or how about this," I said. "Picture Arthur remarrying."

Jadey shook her head. "I'd slit his throat first. Though wouldn't it be fascinating to know who he'd pick? I've always thought he had a thing for Marilyn Granville."

"She's married."

"So am I."

"You're much cuter than Marilyn," I said.

"I am, aren't I?" Jadey smiled at me sideways, mock-flirtatiously, but then she frowned. "Too bad Arthur doesn't think so."

"Does he know how upset you are?"

"It's been almost a month since he visited the hospitality deck on the S.S. *Jadey,* so he should figure it out soon."

"Has he initiated sex and you've refused?"

"Has he initiated it?" Jadey said. "Alice, is the pope Catholic?"

"And you've said no?"

"Sixteen-year-old virgins say no. I *demur.*"

"Jadey, I just worry. Sex is important in a marriage."

"I don't even miss it. It had gotten so predictable that I felt like we'd already done it before we started—I had to pinch myself to stay awake. I recently realized I've been married to Arthur for almost half my life. Can you believe that? Why didn't someone tell me that twenty-one was way too young to commit to another person?"

"My doctor says you should have sex twice a week."

"And you listen?"

"Well—" Generally, I was less forthcoming than Jadey about topics

I considered private. There was no one I confided in more, but I also was aware that Jadey's greatest asset and her most serious downfall was that she was a talker. Years before, for Christmas, Charlie had given her a pillow he'd found himself and been quite proud of, supposedly modeled on one owned by Alice Roosevelt Longworth. It had a white background and said in green print: IF YOU DON'T HAVE ANYTHING NICE TO SAY, COME SIT BY ME.

Jadey and I had gotten this far into the conversation, though, and it didn't seem fair to be coy, so I said, "I try for once a week."

"Do you *enjoy* it?"

"Sometimes I'm not in the mood beforehand, but I'm still glad after. It makes me feel close to him."

"Do you always, you know, grab the brass ring?"

"Mostly," I said. "Occasionally, I'm just too tired."

"I only can if the kids are out of the house."

"No wonder it's not as fun. Maybe you should buy some books or movies or something."

"You mean *pornography*? Is Alice Blackwell recommending *pornography*?" She adopted a prim tone. "As I live and breathe—"

"Jadey, come on." I nudged her. Two men were about fifty feet away, cruising toward us in a golf cart, and there was a 90 percent chance—such was the Maronee Country Club—that we knew them.

"You two don't use it, do you?" At least she'd lowered her voice a little.

"Charlie looks at magazines once in a while."

"Doesn't that *bother* you?"

I shrugged. "Men tend to be more visual than women."

"Does he take matters into his own hands, so to speak?"

"I suppose."

"You suppose? Well, where's he when he's looking at them, and where are you?"

"Sometimes if he can't fall asleep, he goes into the bathroom." Simultaneously, I felt that we had veered into territory that was none of Jadey's business, and I also felt that being married to a man who every so often looked at pornography, or who masturbated, wasn't a big deal. And yes, Charlie definitely masturbated, he did it to *Penthouse*—he didn't subscribe, but he bought an issue every few months, and while we didn't exactly talk about it, he also didn't try to hide it. It would have horrified me if he left a magazine in the living room, or if Ella found one, but since he was discreet—he kept them in the locked bottom drawer of his nightstand—I didn't mind.

I sometimes got the impression that because of my frequent reading, I was less easily shocked than the people around me, that I knew more factual information—about sex, yes, but also about typhoons or folk dancing or Zoroastrianism. In addition to reading a novel every week or two, I subscribed to *Time, The Economist, The New Yorker,* and *House and Garden,* and if I found an article particularly interesting, I'd see what I could track down about the subject at the Maronee public library.

Jadey was saying, "Don't you feel like him looking at other women is an insult to you?"

"I just assume most men notice other women, and most women notice other men. *You* obviously do."

She laughed. "That's the problem—I can't think of anyone to have an affair with." The golf cart passed by us then, and one of the two men on it called out, "Ahoy, Blackwell ladies!" I recognized them as Sterling Walsh, who owned a real estate development company, and Bob Perkins, who was a good friend of Charlie's brother Ed.

Jadey turned to me and nodded once meaningfully at the back of the golf cart. "Definitely not," I said. "Arthur's much more appealing than either one."

"Are you at least going to support me on my diet? I can never stick to one when I do it by myself."

"You don't need to go on a diet. Just eat sensibly, and we'll walk more often. We should walk in Halcyon, too." Our families both were going for the month of July and into August; Charlie and Arthur would return at intervals to Milwaukee.

"Have you heard of the one where you eat half a grapefruit with every meal?"

"Oh, Jadey, girls in my sorority used to try that, and by the third day, they'd see a grapefruit and gag." But I was struck in this moment by my immense fondness for Jadey. Though her upbringing had been more like Arthur's and Charlie's than like mine—her father had made a fortune as a cement supplier, and she'd been raised in a house as large as Harold and Priscilla's—I still felt that as Blackwell in-laws, we were expats who'd found each other in a foreign country. I said then, "I want to ask you something. Have you ever thought that Charlie drinks too much?"

Jadey furrowed her brow. "The Blackwell boys know how to enjoy themselves—not Ed, but *our* boys do. But no. I mean, what would Chas do drunk that he wouldn't do sober, right? Same with Arthur."

"No, I agree." It was such a relief to hear her say these things—they were almost identical to one side of the argument I'd been having with myself for the last few months. "How much does Arthur drink on an average night? For instance, if you're all having dinner?"

"He has a few beers. Hell, *I* have a few beers. Hell, *Drew* has a few beers. I'm an awful mom, right?" She laughed. "No wonder everyone thinks people from Wisconsin are lushes."

"So Arthur has, what, three beers? Or more?"

"Alice, let's quit dancing around this. How much does Chas drink?"

Slowly, I said, "Well, it's mostly whiskey these days, and I guess about a third of a bottle, but maybe a little less. It's hard to say, because he buys the cases wholesale."

"A third of a bottle every night?"

"I think so."

"And does he *act* drunk?"

"Last week, he banged his forehead coming into the kitchen, like he'd misjudged the width of the doorway. But it's more that he's not in the best mood. He's not mean, but he's discouraged. Don't repeat any of this to Arthur, obviously."

"What, you mean while we're making sweet love?"

"Charlie never plays squash in the morning anymore, he never takes Ella to school," I said. "I don't know if it's because he's hungover or just— I don't know."

"Have you asked him about it?"

"I tell him to go easy, but I wouldn't say he listens."

"Well, I'll watch for anything unusual when we're at Maj and Pee-Paw's on Saturday." Jadey made a face. "Although I guess these aren't normal circumstances with the brouhaha in Indianapolis—if this reassures you at all, Arthur was in the foulest humor when he got home last night."

"Charlie's grilling steaks for dinner as we speak," I said. "Would you eat Blackwell meat right now?"

She nodded. "It wasn't Blackwell. More people would have gotten sick by now, and you can bet we've got guys talking to every ER in the region. The poor people at that sports banquet, huh?" We both were quiet, surrounded by the country club's smooth green grass, a spring breeze rising and carrying with it the smell of soil. Jadey said, "That's the problem with being married to them. We're forced to see how the sausage gets made."

AT DINNER, I did manage to eat the steak, though I wouldn't have said I enjoyed it. Without consulting Charlie, I fixed Ella a peanut-butter sandwich instead—it would have made me far tenser for her to consume Blackwell meat than for me to—and Charlie either didn't notice or chose not to comment. After dinner, Ella took a bath and I washed her hair, a request I was sadly aware that she'd stop making of me in the near future, and then I climbed into bed with her and read aloud from *The Trumpet of the Swan;* for me, this was the sweetest part of every day. Before I turned out the light, Ella summoned Charlie—she shrieked, "Daddy! Daddy, it's time for me to be tucked in!"—and he came as called. About half the time, he'd rile her up more than settle her down, tickling her, dancing, making such outrageous noises or faces that she'd be squealing and jumping on the mattress, but on this night, he was so subdued that she whispered after he'd left, "Is Daddy mad at me?"

I ran my hand over her hair, smoothing it out against the pillowcase. Ella had a ridiculously girlish bedroom, all pink and white (we'd let her pick it out), and she had a double bed, which seemed indulgent for a third-grader, but it was actually the bed I'd had before I married Charlie. "Daddy's not mad," I said. The phone rang then, and I heard Charlie answer it.

"Can I rent *Dirty Dancing* this weekend?" Ella asked.

"You can rent *Dirty Dancing* when you're in seventh grade."

"Mommy, it's not really dirty just because that's what it's called."

I leaned in and kissed her forehead. "Time to go to sleep, sweetheart."

WHEN I ENTERED the den, I was startled to find Hank Ucker sitting in an armchair, watching the ball game with Charlie. Without standing, Hank bowed in his seat. "The maternal glow positively emanates from you, Alice," he said. "You call to mind a Renaissance Madonna."

"I see her more like the trampy singer Madonna," Charlie said, and grinned. "Come here, baby." When I stood beside him, he affectionately patted my rear.

"Hank, I didn't realize we'd have the pleasure of your company tonight," I said. "May I offer you something to eat or drink?" It was almost nine o'clock, so I wondered how long he planned to stay. As far as I knew, Hank still lived in Madison. Though I hadn't seen him for a few years, I'd heard he'd left his position as chief of staff for the minority leader of the Wisconsin State Senate to help run the U.S. Senate campaign of a Republican from Fond du Lac, a man who initially hadn't seemed to have much of a shot but in recent weeks had pulled ahead of the incumbent in several polls.

"A glass of ice water would be superb," Hank said.

Charlie, who was drinking whiskey, chuckled. "Still living life in the fast lane, I see."

Hank smiled his slow, untrustworthy smile. "As ever."

I slipped away to the kitchen, filled a glass for Hank, and when I returned to the den, they were talking about Sharon Olson, the incumbent against whom Hank's candidate was running. "A shame that had to come out about her taste for men of the Negro persuasion," Charlie said, grinning. Hank's candidate's polling numbers had no doubt been bolstered by the recent revelation—this did not seem revelatory to me, but *revelation* was the word the local news programs used—that Olson, who was a white Democrat, had had a brief and childless first marriage to a black man in the late sixties. Olson was now remarried to a white lawyer with whom she had two teenage sons and a daughter, and I didn't see how her earlier marriage had much bearing on anything (the first husband had long since moved to Seattle, where he, too, was an attorney), but a series of ads was running that showed her and the groom holding hands at her first wedding, accompanied by ominous music and concluding with a question posed in stark red letters against a dark screen: IF SHARON OLSON HAS BEEN LYING TO US ABOUT THIS . . . WHAT ELSE HAS SHE BEEN LYING ABOUT?

Hank smirked. "A shame indeed. That poor gal."

I passed the water glass to Hank and said, "If you'll excuse me, I have some reading to do. Hank, nice to see you."

Over an hour later, after I'd heard the front door open and close and a car engine start, I returned to the first floor. "Are you thinking of running for office?"

"Jeepers creepers, woman, calm down." Charlie's voice was a little loose, and the whiskey bottle was, I noted, down to the dregs, but I couldn't remember how full it had been before.

"Given that it's almost June, what race could you realistically enter?"

"Seriously," Charlie said, "calm down."

"You know I've never trusted Hank."

"And anyone who runs for elected office is a pompous shyster—right, baby?"

"You're putting words in my mouth."

He leered. "I can think of something I'd like to put in your mouth."

"Can't you just give me a straight answer about why Hank was here?"

We faced each other, him still sitting on the couch, me standing a few feet away, and he said, "I got a call from Arthur before Ucker arrived—turns out I was right that we weren't to blame for the contamination. It wasn't the store the sports-banquet folks got the chuck from that had the problems, it was the basement fridge where one of the athlete's moms was storing it. Seems that a rat had gnawed the power cord." Charlie raised his glass. "Bon appétit."

"That poor woman—she must feel terrible."

"I'm just glad we recalled one-point-two million pounds of meat. Good thing the Upper Midwest region is safe tonight from the scourge of Blackwell beef."

"You did the right thing."

Charlie gestured toward the TV. "You just missed John on Channel Twelve news. He said, 'Our meat is not a crook.' " Charlie leaned back, chuckling at his own joke.

"I'm glad everything is cleared up." I took a seat and leaned forward to pull the latest issue of *The New Yorker* off the coffee table. "Did you know Yvonne Sutton had a baby?"

"Who's Yvonne Sutton?"

"Miss Ruby's daughter."

Charlie shook his head wonderingly. "You can't say those people aren't fertile."

"Charlie, Yvonne has two children. She's not exactly contributing to overpopulation."

"I assume it's a different father from Jessica's?"

"It's her husband, and he also works at St. Mary's." I closed the magazine, which I wasn't reading anyway. "I invited them over for lunch on Memorial Day."

"Wasn't that egalitarian of you? Maybe they can show our daughter how to grow dreadlocks." Several years before, for Ella's fifth birthday, she had requested a Barbie doll. We'd bought one for her—Dreamtime Barbie, who came with her own miniature peach-colored teddy bear—but when Ella unwrapped the box, she burst into tears. She wanted a Barbie "like Jessica's," she kept insisting, and eventually, I figured out she meant a black Barbie. I ended up exchanging Dreamtime Barbie for Day-to-Night Barbie, who came with a pink business suit and a pink dress that had a sparkly top and a sheer skirt, whose skin was dark brown, and whose hair was black. I felt almost proud of Ella, and I think Charlie was amused, though he did say, "Show that to Maj, and you and Ella will both be excommunicated." The irony was that while Charlie regularly remarked on his mother's racism, he made offensive comments more often than she did. That he made them with a wink, he seemed to think, meant he was less culpable and not more so, and although I disagreed and particularly disliked when he used slurs in front of Ella, I'd long ago given up trying to edit him.

In our den, I said, "Jessica is going to Stevens next year for junior high, which really makes me worry."

"I'm sure she'll be fine."

"It sounds like she's a great student and does lots of extracurricular activities."

"Did you run into her recently?"

"I saw Miss Ruby last night—when I was looking for you, I went by your parents' house." Mentioning that Miss Ruby had accompanied me to the play seemed unnecessary. I added, "I bet Jessica would thrive at a place like Biddle."

"Sounds like she's thriving already."

"Do you know which school Stevens is?"

Charlie grinned. "Where do you think I go to replenish my crack supply?" Then he said, "I'm not running for anything, okay? Hank came over so we could think about options for the future, but you're right—it's too late for this election year."

"Good," I said.

He extended one leg so his sock-encased foot was balanced on my knee. "I sure do love you, Lindy, even if you're a narrow-minded liberal who thinks I'm a conniving Republican."

I set my hand on top of his foot. "Sweetheart, if I were narrow-minded, I wouldn't love you back."

WHEN THE PHONE rang on Friday afternoon, it was one o'clock, and I was scrubbing the tiles in our master-bathroom shower (I had never hired a maid or housekeeper, which I knew Priscilla and my sisters-in-law considered odd, but I actually found it soothing to clean). I pulled the yellow rubber glove off my right hand as I walked into our bedroom, and after I'd lifted the receiver, I heard Lars Enderstraisse say, "Alice, I'm awful sorry to be the one calling you—"

Immediately, my heart stopped, it hung there unmoving inside my chest, and then, squeaking out the words, I said, "My mother?" and he said, "No, no, not Dorothy. It's Emilie. I'm afraid she took a spill, and there's been some internal bleeding, some bleeding in the brain, so we're over at Lutheran Hospital." This was the same hospital where I'd been born, the hospital where both Andrew Imhof and I had been taken that horrible night in September 1963.

"But she's not—" I paused. "She's alive?"

"She isn't conscious, but I know the doctors are working hard. Your mother's talking to one of them. Me and her are here outside the ICU, and we're hoping they'll let us see—"

"Granny's in the ICU?"

"Being that she's up there in years, they're taking every precaution."

"I'll get there as soon as I can," I said.

IT HAD HAPPENED late that morning, and not for any obvious reason—she had been walking from the dining room into the living room and had somehow landed on the floor, unconscious—and what the doctors were trying to figure out was whether the bleeding in my grandmother's brain had caused the fall or the fall had caused the bleeding. My mother had heard a thud, but not even a loud one, "like the mail dropping," she said, and she'd hurried out and seen my grandmother lying there. My mother tried unsuccessfully to revive her, and then she called an ambulance.

At the hospital, my mother kept apologizing, as if it were her fault, saying, "I'm just so sorry you had to come rushing out here."

"Mom, of course I came."

At some point late in the afternoon, Lars walked across the street to a convenience store and bought boxed cookies, which neither my mother nor I ate; he then offered them to the other people in the waiting room. A television sat in one corner, playing soap operas and then talk shows, and though no one seemed to be watching it, it appeared that everyone was too diffident to turn it off. The commercials, with their relentlessly zippy announcers and upbeat jingles, felt like a particular affront.

On the waiting-room pay phone, I had called Charlie, then I'd called Jadey to see if she could pick up Ella after school, and a few hours later, I'd called Jadey's house to talk to Ella, to explain what was happening. I'd hoped that hearing my voice would let her know I was fine and so was she, but instead, it was her voice that upset *me;* I so wanted to be beside Ella, holding her, that I had to blink back tears. In her serious, girlish voice, she said, "Is Granny going to die?" Granny was what Ella called my grandmother, just as I did; she called my mother Grandma, and she referred to Lars (he and my mother had quietly married in 1981) as Papa Lars.

I said, "I hope not, ladybug."

Around five, I called Charlie again at the office. "I'm still here, and there's no real news," I said. "Can you go get Ella?"

"You think Jadey would mind watching her a little while longer? I'm scheduled for a five-thirty squash match with Stuey Patrickson."

From the pay phone in the corner, I surveyed the room: a young husband sitting with one hand over his eyes, either resting or weeping; a small child running a truck along the carpet; my mother reading a months-old *McCall's* while Lars Enderstraisse sat beside her eating another cookie. (*My stepfather* was never how I thought of Lars. Not that I disliked him, I actually had developed a great deal of affection for him, and to my surprise, so had my grandmother; she had taught him to play Scrabble, and he'd become particularly knowledgeable about the tricky two-letter words, which meant he was a considerably more challenging opponent to my grandmother than my mother was. But still, I did not think of Lars as a father figure; he was simply my mother's husband, her companion.)

"Alice?" Charlie said, and I said, "I'd prefer for you to pick up Ella now. I don't want her to feel unsettled."

"Is she upset?"

"Well, I'm leaning toward staying at my mom's tonight. We haven't been allowed to see Granny, and I'm reluctant to come back to Milwaukee when everything is up in the air."

"You don't even have a toothbrush, do you?" he said.

"I can buy one."

"If you come home, you can jump in the car if you need to get back to Riley. It's, what, thirty-five minutes?"

The way Charlie drove, perhaps, but not the way I did. Besides, I knew that Charlie's eagerness to have me return to Milwaukee stemmed less from a particular wish to see me than from—it persisted—his fear of the dark; my husband was afraid to spend the night in our house without me. Depending on the circumstances, I found this phobia either cute or irritating. "How about this?" I said. "I'll call Jadey, and you and Ella can stay there."

"Remember how that fucking dog of theirs barked and slobbered in my face all night last time?"

"Charlie, my grandmother is in the intensive-care unit. Your options are to stay at home, go to Arthur and Jadey's, or you're welcome to drive out here with Ella and stay at my mom's. Why don't I give you a few minutes to make a decision, and I'll call back?"

He was quiet, and then he said, "No, you're right, you're right. I'll get Ella now, and if you wouldn't mind calling Jadey, I can cancel with Stuey. How're your mom and Lars?"

"They're fine."

"How are you?"

"I'm fine, too," I said, though at this moment, being asked, I felt a sadness overtake me.

Then Charlie said, "I know you think I hate spending the night apart because of not wanting to be in the house alone, but it's also because I miss you, Lindy."

"Do you and Ella want to come out here?" I realized this was unlikely. On his first visit to my family's house in Riley, Charlie had managed to conceal what I believe in retrospect was astonishment at how small the place was. In the years since, he'd become significantly less diplomatic. He'd say, "Sharing a bathroom with Lars is cruel and unusual punishment." Even on the holidays we spent there, we almost never stayed the night, and Charlie regularly lobbied for my mother, grandmother, and Lars to come to his parents' house for Easter or Christmas; they'd done so a few times early in our marriage, and I don't think any of them had felt particularly comfortable. I was pretty sure that neither Priscilla nor Harold Blackwell knew Lars had been a postal employee—he had retired in 1980—and while I wouldn't have denied it, I'd never made a point of telling them. The irony was that marrying Lars had no doubt made my mother far more financially secure. Since the episode with Pete Imhof, she had never mentioned money to me, and she and Lars had even gone on trips together to Myrtle Beach and Albuquerque.

"Honestly, it'd probably be better if we go to Jadey and Arthur's," Charlie was saying. "Ella and I would be underfoot at your mom's. Call me if you need anything, and call either way before you go to bed."

"Ella is supposed to go to Christine's house tomorrow, so make sure she's ready to be picked up by ten. Also, have her take her vitamin after breakfast."

"You'll be back in time for dinner at Maj and Dad's, won't you?"

I hesitated. "Let's cross that bridge when we come to it."

I could tell that Charlie was restraining himself from saying how important my attendance was, which it really wasn't except for the fact that the Blackwells took particular pride in their all-hands-on-deck dinners.

I said, "Charlie, I'm sure your family will understand."

AT SIX THAT evening, the ICU's last visiting hour, my mother and I were finally buzzed through the double doors to see my grandmother. Because only two people at a time were permitted, Lars remained in the waiting room.

She still was not conscious. She lay beneath a sheet in a white hospital gown with a pattern of small teal and navy snowflakes, and she was hooked up to several monitors, one of them beeping. A tube was taped to the crook of her arm, and two more emerged from her nostrils. "She's so little," my mother murmured. I had been thinking exactly the same thing. Against the backdrop of the oversize bed, my grandmother looked heartbreakingly old and heartbreakingly tiny.

I walked toward her, saying in a cheerful voice, "Hi, Granny. It's Alice and Mom—"

"It's Dorothy," my mother cut in. "Granny, boy, are we happy to see you. You gave us quite a scare today."

"You probably want to rest, so we won't stay long," I said. "But the doctor said you're stable now, which is wonderful news." It was impossible to know if she could hear us; the overwhelming likelihood was that she couldn't. "I don't know if you remember, but you fell this morning, so you're in the hospital. Now you're recovering"—this was my own wishful diagnosis, not the doctor's; he had used no word more encouraging than *stable*—"and the doctors and nurses are taking very good care of you." This also was optimistic inference; I didn't have much idea of what had transpired behind the closed double doors. Dr. Furnish, who was the attending physician, had explained a few minutes before to Lars, my mother, and me that my grandmother had had what was called a lobar intracerebral hemorrhage and they'd given her several blood transfusions so far but were hesitant to perform surgery, given her age and general frailness; he also warned that she might have brain damage. Dr. Furnish was not particularly warm, but he did seem competent. As he spoke, I took notes on the back of a receipt I'd found in my purse.

"Granny, I don't think the waiting room here would be much to your liking," my mother said. "The chairs are covered in an orange fabric you'd find very tacky."

"And Lars bought stale-looking cookies, which Mom and I were smart enough not to eat, but everyone else gobbled them up." I tried to sound jaunty and humorous.

"Emilie, you have to get better and come home in time for the season finale of *Murder, She Wrote,*" my mother said.

I added, "But if you get me out of dinner at Priscilla and Harold Blackwell's tomorrow night, I'll be in your debt."

"Alice!" my mother said.

"I'm teasing," I said. "Granny knows that."

We continued in this fashion, half talking to my grandmother and half talking to each other for the allotted thirty minutes, and the only response we got was the beeping of the monitor. As soon as we walked out the double doors leading back to the waiting room, my mother pulled a tissue from her pocket and dabbed at her eyes. "I know Granny's had a long life, and it's not for me to question God's plan," she said. "But, Alice, I'm not ready."

AND THEN, MIRACULOUSLY, my grandmother was awake. I called the hospital around seven the next morning, as soon as I'd gotten out of the shower, and they said she'd regained consciousness during the night. She was dozing again, a nurse said, and although she'd be woozy from the sedatives, she'd almost definitely be able to talk to us when we went in at nine o'clock.

My mother stopped in the gift shop on the lobby level to buy a balloon—flowers weren't allowed in the ICU—and so I entered my grandmother's room alone. Her eyes were closed, but when I said, "Knock, knock," she opened them immediately. "Granny, welcome back!" I said. "We missed you!" When I was beside her bed, I leaned in and kissed her cheek.

She blinked a few times, then said, "They've been feeding me very spicy chicken, and it's made my throat dry."

Did she even realize who I was? I said, "Can I give you some water?" A white plastic pitcher sat on the table beside her bed, and next to it was an avocado-colored plastic cup with a straw in it. I brought the straw to my grandmother's lips, and when she sucked on it, a tiny clear trickle dribbled out of the corner of her mouth. Though she was receiving fluids through an IV, I was certain my grandmother had eaten nothing, spicy chicken or otherwise, since her arrival at the hospital.

When she'd finished drinking and leaned her head back on the pillow, she said, "They're gambling on the roof, you know."

I hesitated. "Who?"

She nodded sagely. "*They* are."

I held my hand over my heart. "It's Alice, Granny. You're in the hospital, but you're getting better, and I've come to visit you."

She made an appalled expression. "Do you think I don't know who you are? I'm not *senile.*" She pointed at me. "Why are you wearing Dorothy's blouse? It makes you look frumpy."

I smiled. "I unexpectedly spent the night in Riley, so Mom let me borrow this."

"You should wear clothes more suited to your age."

"Granny, how do you feel? Be sure to let me know if you need to rest."

She didn't respond right away but looked around the room and then said, "I've been thinking of your father."

I felt a flare of anxiety. Although I wasn't at all sure I believed in heaven, it was hard not to imagine that by *thinking of,* she may have meant *communing with* or even *being beckoned by.* All I said, though, was "Oh?"

"He was very devoted to Dorothy," my grandmother said. "I had the opportunity to observe your parents' marriage closely over a number of years, and I saw how fond of each other they were." She peered at me. "What's your husband's name?"

I swallowed. "Charlie. Charlie Blackwell."

"That's right, the governor's son. You two are very devoted to each other as well."

I tried to smile. "Well, I hope so."

She regarded me shrewdly. "That sounded tepid."

"No, I didn't mean— I just— Lately, he's been drinking more than I think he should," I finally managed to say.

She made a pooh-poohing gesture, or tried to, though because of the IV inside her elbow, she didn't have full mobility. "Don't keep a tight leash on him, my dear. That always backfires."

"Oh, I don't—if anything, the opposite."

"You're not strict with him?"

I shook my head.

"Maybe that's the problem, then, that he'd like you to be stricter."

I hesitated—was this really the time or place to unburden myself?—but my grandmother had always enjoyed talking about people, and she did seem genuinely engaged. "This will sound ridiculous to you, but I think he's having some kind of midlife crisis. His twentieth college reunion is in a couple weeks, and he's obviously worried about not measuring up to his classmates."

"He went to Harvard University," my grandmother said, and her tone was strange—it was as if she were boasting to me about someone other than my own husband.

"You're right that he went to school on the East Coast, but it was Princeton. Anyway, I guess he had the idea that he'd have accomplished more by now. He comes from a line of successful men, his grandfather and father, and I'm sure you remember his brother Ed is a congressman." I wasn't at all sure she remembered, though she did nod as I spoke. "But I just don't think Charlie is meant to be a business titan or a politician. Not that I mind—I didn't marry him assuming he would be. He's so funny and lively, he has loads of friends, he's a terrific father, and I just— I don't understand why that's not enough, why our life isn't enough. It's enough for me, and I don't understand why it isn't enough for him."

"His ambitions exceed his talent."

I tried not to take offense. "I don't know if I'd go that far. He's very smart. And maybe it's me, it's that he finds me boring—" It was actually painful to remember the afternoon when Charlie and I had first said we loved each other—it had been the same day he'd met my mother and grandmother and Lars—and to remember how he'd prefaced it by saying he thought he'd always find me interesting. The reason it was painful was that I wondered with increasing frequency if it had remained true. What a wonderful compliment that had been, how unexpected, how *recognized* I had felt. I wasn't just a cute brunette to Charlie; he understood that I was a person who thought about things, who read and had opinions, even if I held them quietly, and all of these were qualities that made him value me. But did he ever wish, in retrospect, that he'd married someone more exciting, someone whose idea of a pleasant Saturday night wasn't eating dinner with our nine-year-old daughter and then reading forty pages of Eudora Welty before bed? Even the absence of real acrimony in our marriage, maybe that was disappointing—no opportunities for shouting or slamming doors, none of the delicious ugliness of rage, no fraught sexy reunions.

My grandmother said, "Everyone is boring some of the time. The most fascinating person I ever knew was a woman named Gladys Wycomb. Did I ever introduce you to my friend Gladys?"

I nodded.

"She was the eighth woman in the state of Wisconsin to earn her medical degree, truly a brilliant gal. But I'd go to visit her, and sure enough, within a few days, we'd both be reading a book at the dinner table. It didn't bother me a whit. What greater happiness is there than the privilege of being bored together?"

"I agree, but I'm not sure that Charlie would."

"Does he know you have doubts about him?"

"It's not me doubting him, it's him having doubts about his job and the path he's taken in life, which—" I broke off. Wasn't I lying, however inadvertently? It *was* me doubting him. I glanced at the floor, which was covered in white linoleum tiles. When I looked up again, I said, "I know you were impressed with Charlie when you first met, but are you still?" What was I doing asking this of my drugged grandmother, as if she were some sort of medium of marital wisdom? Or was I bold enough only because she was drugged? Even with Jadey, I was not quite this frank.

"I was impressed by him because I could tell he adored you, and you deserve to be adored," my grandmother said. "Frankly, what you're describing sounds like much ado about nothing. Go home, put on a pretty dress, some heels, and some lipstick, flirt with him, flatter him, and never forget how insecure men are. It's because they take themselves far too seriously."

In this moment, her instructions felt like a lifeline—so simple, so easily executed. What an immense relief to have someone tell me what to do! Then she said, "Get me some water, will you? They've been feeding me spicy chicken, and I don't care for the taste of it."

"Your cup is right here." I helped her sip again, and when she'd finished, I held up the book I'd brought in my bag. "I have your copy of *Anna Karenina.* Would you like me to read from it?"

"That would be lovely."

"From the section where she and Vronsky meet, or from the beginning?"

"When they meet."

As I opened the book, I said, "I hope I haven't made you think badly of Charlie. I'm sure you're right that I'm blowing things out of proportion."

She had already closed her eyes, and she shook her head. "Chapter Eighteen," I began, and I cleared my throat. " 'Vronsky followed the guard to the carriage, and had to stop at the entrance of the compartment to let a lady pass . . .' " When my mother arrived a few minutes later with the balloon, my grandmother had fallen back to sleep.

ON MY RETURN to Milwaukee, I stopped at a gas station. I'd already paid and was replacing the gas nozzle in the pump when a man's voice said, "Alice, what a coincidence."

I looked up, and just a few feet away, standing by a car on the opposite side of the concrete island, Joe Thayer held up a hand in greeting. He wore a yellow polo shirt tucked into madras shorts, and he looked characteristically handsome, but he also looked like he had recently lost weight he hadn't needed to lose: His cheekbones were more pronounced, and though he was well over six feet, there was a scrawniness to his shoulders. Not that I looked so hot myself—as my grandmother had observed, I had on my mother's "frumpy" blouse. Plus, because I hadn't brought the mousse that I used, my hair was a bit frizzy. I still was a good fifteen minutes from Maronee, and I hadn't expected to run into anybody I knew.

"Joe, how are you?" I glanced toward his car and, thinking I saw his son, said, "And is that Ben in the— Oh my goodness, that's Pancake!" Pancake was a black Lab famous in Halcyon for being able to stand on her hind legs and slow-dance with seventy-two-year-old Walt Thayer, Joe's father; this routine had never seemed entirely consensual to me, so I had trouble mustering the enthusiasm for it that everyone else demonstrated. "You must be gearing up for Princeton," I said. "Tell me what ludicrous uniform they have you wearing." Joe had graduated from Princeton in '63, five years before Charlie, which meant their major reunions were always on the same schedule.

Joe shook his head. "I'll be sitting this one out. Not quite the right time, if you get my meaning."

"I'm sure you'll be missed," I said.

"I tell you, Alice, I never thought I'd be a person who got a divorce."

"Oh—" I wasn't sure how to respond. Lamely, I said, "Well, it does happen."

"May I be candid?" he said.

"Of course."

"I find myself curious about how much of our family's trouble is out on the grapevine, if you will. I wouldn't want people to think— It seems that it's more commonly the husband leaving the wife in these situations, but that isn't what happened. I won't say Carolyn and I haven't had our problems, but I really was blindsided."

I feigned ignorance. "Joe, I'm so sorry. That sounds very difficult."

We looked at each other, and the thought crossed my mind that he might cry. He didn't have tears in his eyes, but it seemed he was holding his chin firm, possibly clenching his teeth. He and I had never spoken anywhere close to this personally. Between Milwaukee and Halcyon, I had been in his presence perhaps a hundred times—after our wedding, Priscilla and Harold had thrown an enormous cocktail party at the country club for all the family friends who hadn't been invited to the wedding, and I was pretty sure Joe had even been at that—but in eleven years he and I hadn't talked about anything more provocative than the new roundabout on Solveson Avenue, or the temperature of Lake Michigan.

I said, "Joe, I hope you realize that all families have problems, even in Maronee. You aren't the only ones. And I think everyone knows there's only so much we can control even in our own lives." I suspect it was less what I was saying than the mere fact of my continuing to talk that allowed Joe to pull himself back from the precipice of tears; already, he looked significantly less shaky.

"I appreciate that." His gas pump made a clicking noise, and he withdrew the nozzle. Gesturing to his car, he said, "I'm headed to Madison to spend the day with Martha." This was his younger sister, whom I knew from Halcyon. "I used to really crave free time," he continued, "and now I have more than I ever could have wanted. The weekends have become just brutal. Be careful what you wish for, I suppose."

"Well, you're welcome at our house anytime. If you'd like to come over and watch the ball game with Charlie, we'd be delighted to have you." This was probably not a wise offer—would Joe dropping by make Charlie even crankier?—but he seemed so despondent, and I didn't know what else to say. And really, the fact was that Joe and Charlie had known each other their entire lives; they were more like cousins than friends.

Joe pointed toward the interior of the gas station and said, "I'd better pay. It was good to see you, Alice. Thanks for listening to a sad sack."

I said, "You know, maybe you *should* go to Reunions. A change of scenery?"

"I'll think about it." He waved. "Give Chas my best."

WHEN CHARLIE, ELLA, and I arrived at Priscilla and Harold's for dinner, the house was alive with Blackwell energy. Our nephews Geoff and Drew were out on the front lawn playing ring toss, and Charlie couldn't resist stopping to join them, so Ella and I continued inside without him. It was hard to believe that Ella was the last of this generation of Blackwells; the next babies would be the children of her cousins. Harry, who was Ed and Ginger's oldest son, was now twenty-one and would graduate from Princeton a few days after Charlie's reunion; Liza, who was John and Nan's older daughter, was finishing up her junior year at Princeton and would be spending the summer interning at a fashion magazine in Manhattan; and Tommy, Ed and Ginger's middle son, was finishing his sophomore year but at Dartmouth rather than Princeton, which gave rise to much teasing about Dartmouth's general inferiority and the lack of activity in "Hangover," New Hampshire.

In the front hall, Ella hugged her grandparents, then immediately vanished with her cousin Winnie, presumably to the basement, which was where the cousins who still lived at home convened around a pool table, the older ones sharing various urban legends—after one such dinner, Ella had become briefly fixated on the idea of spontaneous human combustion—and also teaching the younger cousins dirty words. While riding back to our house at Thanksgiving, Ella had proudly announced, "I know what penis balls are."

Near the staircase where Charlie and I had married, I exchanged kisses on the cheek with my father-in-law, who said, "Alice, I'm terribly sorry to hear about your grandmother," and I said, "I'm happy to report she's much better today." I leaned in to greet Priscilla, who didn't so much air-kiss as not kiss at all; she simultaneously brought her chin toward you and angled it off to the side, never even puckering her lips, but I couldn't take it personally because she did it to everyone. This time, however, as I approached, she gripped my wrist, keeping me close. Against my ear, she murmured, "I'd like a word with you."

Harold went off to fix drinks just as Jadey emerged from the dining room carrying a marble tray of food, saying, "Maj, if I were a cheese knife, where would I be? Ooh, that scarf looks great, Alice. How's your grandma?" Jadey had picked out the scarf for me during a shopping expedition a few weeks before; it was from Marshall Field's and had a turquoise background with gold paisley.

"Jadey, surely you don't plan to put out all that cheese at once," Priscilla said. "You'll spoil everyone's appetite."

Breezily, Jadey said, "Oh, we'll save what doesn't get eaten, and the sirloins look super, so worry not, those'll be devoured in *half* a second." Over the years, Jadey had served as an example of how to behave with Priscilla—to be chipper and oblique, to sidestep questions without necessarily answering them, and to never directly challenge or contradict.

"My grandmother's had an amazing turnaround," I said. "She's almost her normal self."

"Oh, thank God," Jadey said. "Not that Chas and Ella aren't welcome at our house *any* time—I swear, having other people around makes us behave *slightly* better—but what a relief for you. Now, Maj, as for the cheese knives . . ."

"Second drawer to the right of the oven," Priscilla said, and I was surprised at how quickly she'd conceded. Then she said, "Jadey, I was under the impression you were watching your figure." She smiled. "I'd think these sorts of hors d'oeuvres would be very tempting." Nan and Ginger had entered the hall from the living room by this point, distracting somewhat from the unpleasantness of Priscilla's remark. Nan said, "Oh, Alice, we've been praying for your grandmother," and Jadey said, "No, she's on the mend," and Ginger said, "I love your scarf, Alice. Maj, tell us what we can do to help."

"You can get those barbarian sons of yours to quit tearing up my lawn." Priscilla laughed throatily. "At this rate, my foxgloves and irises won't live to see June."

A brief silence ensued, and Ginger said, "I'm sure the boys are ready to come in anyway." As she scurried out the front door, Jadey rolled her eyes at me before returning to the kitchen.

Priscilla said to Nan, "I'll steal Alice for a moment, if you don't mind."

I followed my mother-in-law to a little alcove on the far side of the powder room beneath the front staircase. Standing in the hall, I'd caught sight of Charlie's brothers congregated in the living room, and I'd thought that, recent tensions be damned, an evening of family boisterousness might be just the thing for both Charlie and me.

In the alcove, Priscilla said, "You had no business taking Ruby to the Performing Arts Center."

I blinked. What had I imagined Priscilla wanted to talk to me about? The strife among her sons, perhaps? Or something far more banal: that she needed me to fill the bird feeders while she and Harold were in Washington.

"It was extremely inappropriate," she was saying, and her voice was neither loud nor excited; it was merely frosty. "My household help is my concern."

"I didn't—" I hesitated. "I didn't realize it would offend you. I certainly didn't mean for it to." I would stop short of telling her I was sorry, I thought, because I wasn't. Miss Ruby was an adult, and so was I—both of us had the right to attend a play with whomever we pleased.

"You must imagine you're providing some sort of cultural edification for her, is that it?"

"Priscilla, it was a spur-of-the-moment invitation. I had no ulterior motive."

"Ruby has been in our employ for over forty-five years, and we've taken superb care of her during that time. Do you think she'd stay with us decade after decade if we hadn't? There are a number of things I'm quite sure you don't know about her, including that Harold and I helped her leave an unscrupulous husband. Is that something you were aware of?" Priscilla was almost six feet tall, but as she'd spoken, she'd leaned down so that mere inches separated our faces. I became aware of the fine lines around her lips, her mauve lipstick, her teeth, which, this close up, were smaller and a bit browner than I remembered; in addition, her crooked upper-left canine was prominent.

I opened my mouth to speak, but it was hard to know what to say.

"In the future, I'll thank you for not interfering," Priscilla said. "Have I made myself clear?"

"I hope you won't scold Miss Ruby," I said. "The outing was definitely my idea, not hers." Then—I couldn't help it—I added, "But with all due respect, I guess I still don't understand what you object to."

"Oh, Alice." Priscilla took a step back, chuckling. "I'm embarrassed for you that you'd have to ask."

I HAD A glass of wine before dinner, and for the meal, I managed to sit between Harold, benign as always, and John, who, despite the friction with Charlie, had never said an unkind word to me. As usual, Priscilla had designated seat assignments, but she'd essentially ignored me after our conversation behind the staircase. By dessert, my surprise over our exchange had subsided, and I was able to relax into the table's banter; at the outset, Priscilla had placed a moratorium on any discussion of Blackwell Meats, a wise move on her part. As we finished our butterhorn cookies and vanilla ice cream, Arthur, who, like most people present, seemed to have had quite a bit to drink, was giving Ed grief for his recent cosponsorship of a congressional bill with Judith Pigliozzi, a Democratic representative from northern California who was best known for her support of a failed medical marijuana bill. "Next thing you know, Eddie and Judith'll be smoking reefer in the Capitol," Arthur crowed, and Ginger, Ed's wife, said, "You know, some studies indicate that marijuana can be very helpful for migraine sufferers"—meek, mirthless Ginger, herself a migraine sufferer, said this, and it was so out of character that everyone exploded with laughter. "So *that's* how you can stand being married to Ed," Charlie said. "We always wondered." At the same time, John said, "Nothing like a hit of Mary Jane in the afternoon, eh, Ging?" Ginger was protesting, saying, "I didn't mean that *I've* tried it, no, it's just something I read about—" and Arthur and Charlie were miming inhaling joints. "Truly, I've never smoked marijuana," Ginger said, and she seemed very flustered. "It was in a magazine article."

"Alice, you ever smoked up?" Arthur asked, and Jadey said, "Don't put her on the spot," and Arthur said, "Then let's go around the table. Dad, it's safe to assume you're a no?"

Harold, with a weary smile on his face, shook his head. By this point, all the kids were back in the basement, and I gave thanks that Ella wasn't present; I wasn't in the mood to explain pot.

"We already have Ginger proclaiming her innocence," Arthur said. "Me, hell, yes. Nan?"

Nan wrinkled her nose. "I don't know if I like this game," she said, and Arthur said, "I'll take that as another yes. Ed?"

"I was too old," Ed said. "You have to remember that by the summer of love, I was already an associate at Holubasch and Whistler."

Arthur continued around the table. "Maj, I'm thinking no, but you're a sly one, so you want to confirm or deny?"

"Absolutely not," Priscilla said.

Arthur pointed at Charlie. "Chas, for you, the only mystery is, did you buy or sell more?"

Charlie grinned. "Hey, we all have to be good at something."

"You never dealt drugs, did you?" I said, and John said lightly, "Alice, don't ask questions you don't want to hear the answers to."

"Jadey, I know you're a yes, because I was there," Arthur said, and Jadey protested, "I was a teenager! That doesn't count!"

"If you were a teenager, then you must be almost twenty-five by now." Arthur smirked at his wife. (Were they really not having sex? They were so playful, or maybe there was more hostility in this exchange than I recognized.)

"John?" Arthur said.

"I gave it a whirl, sure, but it never did a heck of a lot for me."

"And now back to fair Alice." Arthur was across the table from me, between Ginger and Nan. "You're kind of the dark horse here. Chas, you want to place a bet on your better half?"

Charlie narrowed his eyes, scrutinizing me, and finally said, "Put me down for yes. Lindy's got more of an adventurous streak than you'd think."

I blushed—the comment seemed to have sexual undertones—and Arthur said, "Moment of truth, Alice."

"Just once," I said. "I think I'm in the same category as John, where it didn't do much for me." I thought of sitting in my grandmother's bedroom in the summer of 1968 with her and Dena Janaszewski, and then I thought of my grandmother in the hospital, and I did a mental finger-crossing that her condition would continue to improve.

"Alice, clearly, you didn't give it a chance," Arthur said. "Where's your stick-to-itiveness?" He was grinning the Blackwell grin, and he said to Charlie, "Why is your wife such a quitter?"

"Is it wrong that this conversation is starting to make me *crave* a joint?" Jadey said. "And I swear it's been about two decades."

Arthur raised his eyebrows at Charlie. "Chas, are you thinking what I'm thinking? But who do we know that—?"

Charlie tilted his head right, toward the swinging door that led to the kitchen. He said, "How about Leroy?" Dread seized me. Leroy was Miss Ruby's son, older than Yvonne. I had never met him, but I knew he'd had a few run-ins with the law.

"Brilliant!" Arthur reached over and lifted the small white porcelain bell Priscilla rang whenever she wanted to summon Miss Ruby. Right away, Priscilla snatched it back, and I was greatly relieved. "You will not implicate Ruby in your high jinks," she said.

"Don't try to tell me Big Leroy Sutton wouldn't know where in this city to find good herb," Arthur said, and John said, "Oh, I think he's well beyond that. Herb is child's play for a guy like him." (Did it occur to them Miss Ruby might be able to hear every word they were saying? It seemed not.)

"I believe this is when Ginger and I will make our graceful exit," Ed said, but he was smiling as he pushed his chair back. "Maj, Dad, thanks for a tremendous meal, as always."

"Stick in the mud, stick in the mud!" Arthur cried.

"Oh, it'd be *most* unsuitable for the representative from the Ninth District to get caught smoking weed five short months before he's up for reelection," Charlie said. "And in the home of the former governor, no less. Someone call *The Washington Post*!"

Wryly, Ed said to Ginger, "Come along, dear, and let's round up Geoff."

As Ginger rose from the table, Nan said, "I'm ready to call it a night as well." I saw her eye John meaningfully; they both stood, following Ed and Ginger.

When the four of them had disappeared, Harold cleared his throat, and we all turned toward him. "Allow me a bit of unsolicited advice," he said. "Nostalgia aside, this is an atrocious idea." He stood. "Would anyone care to join me in the living room for coffee?"

The table broke up then, the idea of buying marijuana either through Leroy Sutton or another source seeming to lose momentum—thank goodness, as far as I was concerned—and as the men accompanied Harold into the living room and the women cleared plates, Jadey whispered to me, "Now Maj probably thinks I'm a pig *and* a druggie." She did not seem terribly bothered.

When we all stood, Miss Ruby had magically appeared, along with a man named Bruce who helped serve and clear and acted as a bartender when the Blackwells held larger parties. Though I'd seen Miss Ruby several times over the course of the night, I had been able to greet her only briefly; she'd been busy preparing the meal, and other people had been in the vicinity. It was after the coffee was served, when Priscilla was in the living room, that I found an opportunity alone with Miss Ruby; she was setting silverware in the dishwasher. I said, "Has Mrs. Blackwell spoken to you about the play?"

Miss Ruby was hardly looking at me. She said, "That's fine."

"I want to apologize if I've created an awkward situation for you," I said.

We both were silent, and steam rose from the water gushing out of the faucet.

"Obviously, you didn't do anything wrong," I added. "I hope you all are still planning on lunch at our house a week from Monday. We're very excited about seeing Yvonne's baby."

Miss Ruby raised her eyebrows. "You told Mrs. about it?"

"I haven't, and if it's uncomfortable for you to come, I understand. But I hope you know we'd be delighted to have you. It'd just be Charlie and Ella and me." I paused. "We'll assume you'll be there, but should something come up, give me a call." Was I making a great mess of things, was I putting Miss Ruby's job at risk? But it seemed far more offensive to me to capitulate to Priscilla's whims than to defy them, and besides, she and Harold were returning to Washington in a few days. Bad enough that she should try to control our behavior while she was here, but it was simply absurd for her to attempt it long-distance.

Before I left the kitchen, I said, "Thank you for dinner. Everything was delicious."

ON THE CAR ride home—it was after ten when we left, and I drove—Charlie said, "There's a rumor going around that you socialized the other night with a Negress."

"Charlie, you know I don't like to make trouble, but for your mother to suggest that it's wrong to—"

"Don't blame me." He sounded amused. "You and Miss Ruby can prick your fingers and become blood sisters, for all I care. I'm just hoping I get good tickets for the Lindy-Maj showdown." He took on a sports announcer's tone. "In this corner, weighing one-thirty and wearing a pink tennis skirt . . ." Noticing that I hadn't laughed, he said, "Come on, this is good stuff. So you drove all the way into the core, huh? You're a brave lady."

The core was a derogatory name for Milwaukee's inner city, and not a term I used. I ignored Charlie, and from the backseat, Ella said, "Mommy, how many days left till we go to Princeton?"

Ella was excited about the reunion for the spectacle—Charlie had been teaching her the school's various fight songs and cheers, and I had done my best to describe the orange-and-black outfits, the bands in tents at night, the beauty of the campus (while Ella had gone with us to Charlie's fifteenth reunion in 1983, she'd been so young she had little memory of it)—and she also was excited because the trip would be an opportunity to see her cousins Harry and Liza. I said, "If today is May twenty-first, and we leave on June third, how many days is that? Do you remember how many days there are in May?"

"Thirty days hath September . . ." Ella began. She counted on her fingers. "Fourteen days?"

"Close," I said. "Thirteen."

"And that means my class party's in twelve days?"

"Exactly."

"Daddy?" Ella said.

Charlie turned to face the backseat.

"Your epidermis is showing," she said.

"Oh, yeah?" Charlie replied. "Well, there's life on Uranus."

Ella giggled. "Well, boys go to Jupiter to get more stupider."

"I remember my time on Jupiter fondly," Charlie said. "Your mother thought I was stupid to begin with, but when I came back, I'd even forgotten how to pick my nose." Then he said, "There's been a request for the world-famous opera singer Ella Blackwell to perform. The fans are clamoring. Will she disappoint, or will she rise to the occasion? Three, two, one, and hit it, Ella!" He was actually the one who began to sing: " 'Ohh, Princeton was Princeton when Eli was a pup. . . .' "

Ella replied in her own high, sweet voice: " 'And Princeton will be Princeton when Eli's days are up . . .' "

Together, rising in volume, they sang the last two lines, the ones I was not at all sure were appropriate for a nine-year-old: "So any Yalie son of a bitch who thinks he has the brass / Can pucker up his rosy red lips and kiss the Tiger's ass!' "

This was only one small piece of the Princeton propaganda my husband had pressed upon our daughter. There was also the outfit he'd been sent in advance of the reunion, which all the members of his class would wear for the campus parade and which, so far, Ella had tried on and Charlie hadn't: an orange warm-up suit with a black stripe running down the side of the pants and the jacket's zipper, and a floppy white hat with 68 printed in orange and black in a circle above the brim. (The outfit's theme was supposed to be tennis, or "Over-40 Love.") Then there was Ella's favorite cheer, known as a locomotive. At any moment—at dinner, or just as Ella was about to go to bed—Charlie would cry out, "Sixty-eight locomotive," and then they'd both chant, "Hip! Hip! Rah! Rah! Rah! Tiger! Tiger! Tiger! Sis! Sis! Sis! Boom! Boom! Boom! Bah! Sixty-eight! Sixty-eight! Sixty-eight!" Then they'd yell and clap and even dance; sometimes I found their routine charming and sometimes I found it exasperating. A Princeton reunion reminded me of an academic, institutional version of the Blackwell family, simultaneously impressive and self-regarding, overwhelming and intoxicating and marvelous and repugnant. This time around, I felt a particular concern about how much Charlie would drink; his fifteenth reunion had been the only time I'd seen him consume so much beer he vomited, and that had been in the days when he was drinking considerably less than he did now.

Charlie switched to a different song: " 'Tune every heart and every voice, / Bid every care withdraw—' " This was a song I liked, even though it concluded with a gesture that was uncomfortably close to the Nazi salute. But we were in the car, our little family, and I joined in, too: " 'Her sons shall give while we shall live / Three cheers for Old Nassau.' " And then, because we were a family, because in families you do the same things over and over, we sang the song a second time, a third, a fourth, and by the end of the fifth, we'd arrived home.

THE BREWERS WERE playing the Toronto Blue Jays that Sunday, and the game started at one-fifteen. The original plan was for Arthur and their son Drew to go with Charlie and Ella, but Arthur called that morning to say he'd been thinking it could look bad if, this soon after the meat scandal, he and Charlie showed up on TV, enjoying themselves at the ballpark (the Blackwells' seats were eight rows above the Brewers' dugout, between third base and home plate). "We were exonerated!" Charlie protested, but apparently, Arthur couldn't be dissuaded. When Charlie hung up, he said, "I smell John all over this."

I'd planned to spend the afternoon preparing for the upcoming week—the next day, I'd return to Riley to help my mother bring my grandmother home from the hospital, and on Tuesday, for a Garden Club luncheon at Sally Gilman's house, I was responsible for making potato salad for thirty—but I quickly agreed to go in Arthur's stead. We called Harold to see if he'd like to join us, but their flight back to Washington was at four.

I didn't really mind the change of plan; even before Charlie and I had Ella, attending baseball games was probably our best shared activity. I liked how you were part of a crowd, but an orderly crowd—there were seats and rows and sections so that even with tens of thousands of people, it wasn't chaotic, and if a fan became drunk and unruly, he was usually escorted away. I liked how the park was a setting where you could but didn't have to carry on a conversation, I liked the people-watching (the fans like us, families with children, and the adolescent or middle-aged couples on dates, the groups of friends in their late twenties or early thirties, the men who came alone, about whom there was something very moving to me, or at least there had been before Charlie became one of those men, at what I felt was my own and Ella's expense). But I liked the wholesome cheers and the corny traditions and the familiar songs and the basic tastiness of eating a hot dog and drinking a beer on a sunny afternoon or evening. The one part of a baseball game I didn't like was when a foul ball or a home run flew into the stands and people scrambled over it—when only one person got what so many wanted. But in general, baseball games kept Charlie sufficiently occupied, not bored, while also being calm enough for me. As for Ella, she liked games for her own reasons—her Japanese pen pal was a tremendous fan of the sport, which had increased Ella's interest in it, and she also loved that the frozen custard came in a small plastic Brewers cap that you could take home—but the important part was that she liked them, that we all did.

By the fourth inning, the score was 4–1 in the Brewers' favor, and Charlie seemed to have forgotten that he was freshly peeved with his brothers. This was when Zeke Langenbacher sidled up to us. Zeke was a man about twenty years older than Charlie and me, rumored to be the richest person in Milwaukee and possibly in Wisconsin—he was a high school dropout who'd started as a milk delivery boy and owned his own dairy by the age of twenty-five before diversifying into auto insurance, radio stations, and motels. I had met him a number of times, but I always imagined he wouldn't remember my name, and I was always pleasantly surprised when he did. He and Charlie occasionally played tennis together—on the court, Zeke was known to be both excellent and quite aggressive—and I think these matches, even losing them, gave Charlie a frisson of pride. "Zeke's a big fucking deal," he told me after one. "He's a captain of industry."

After greeting me and being introduced to Ella, Zeke gestured to the empty chair next to Charlie. "Anyone sitting here?"

Charlie patted the seat. "We were holding it open for you." Zeke had his own season tickets a few rows in front of ours—County Stadium never had luxury boxes, which to me was part of its charm—and earlier in the game, I'd noticed him down there with two other men.

Ella was sitting between Charlie and me, and Zeke was on Charlie's other side, so I couldn't hear what they were saying. I was surprised that he stayed into the seventh inning, by which point the Brewers had scored three more runs. I took Ella to the bathroom, then waited in line with her for french fries, and we were making our way back to our section when Ella and a little boy about her age collided. Almost half of Ella's french fries spilled from the paper cup onto the floor, and in a scolding tone, she said to the boy, "Look what you just did!"

The boy appeared frightened, and I said, "Ella, sweetie, it was an accident. It wasn't his fault any more than it was yours." The boy was accompanied by a man, and when I glanced up, anticipating an exchange of apologetic smiles, I saw that the man was Simon Törnkvist. I believe that we mutually considered pretending not to recognize each other—his glasses were different, with larger lenses, and he no longer had a beard, but his floppy blond hair was the same, his drooping left eye—and then I said, "My goodness, it's a small world, isn't it?" I set a hand on Ella's shoulder. "This is my daughter, Ella."

"My son, Kyle."

"It's sure a nice day for a ball game," I said.

"We live up in Oshkosh now, but we're here visiting some friends." Simon's tone was warmer than I would have anticipated.

"Isn't Oshkosh where you're from?" I said, and he said, "Good memory."

Good memory? I thought. *We dated for a year!*

"You might be surprised to know I ended up in the education field, too," he said. "I'm a high school history teacher."

"That's wonderful," I said. It seemed that he was waiting for me to provide a comparable update—*I'm still plugging away in the library*—and I found that I did not want to share with Simon that I no longer held a job. I realized I'd been wondering if he'd know whom I'd married, or at least know that it was one of the sons of the former governor, and I was glad he appeared to have no idea. How disapproving Simon Törnkvist would probably be, how pathetically bourgeois my life would seem to him. "We'll let you two get back to the game," I said. "It's good to see you."

"Maybe our families can get together when we're next down here," he said, and I smiled, banking on the fact that he'd never be able to track me down.

"Absolutely."

Back at our seats, Zeke Langenbacher was gone, and I said to Charlie, "You'll never believe who Ella and I just ran into—Simon Törnkvist."

"You mean Parsley, Sage, Rosemary, and Thyme?" This was the nickname that Charlie had made up for Simon years earlier, based on my brief descriptions. The two of them had never met, but Charlie had somehow gotten the impression that Simon was a long-haired guitar-strumming antiwar protestor; really, this said less about Charlie's idea of Simon than his idea of me. "He was with his son," I said, and Ella said, "He made me spill my fries!"

"Not all of them, by the looks of it," Charlie said, and reached out to take several. Indignantly, Ella hit his forearm.

"I thought old Parsley didn't want kids," Charlie said. "Isn't that why you broke up?"

It was my turn to feel surprised, pleasantly so, by someone else's ability to remember the past. "I guess people change," I said. I was aware that perhaps I should take Kyle's mere existence as an insult, and who knew whether Simon had other children? He probably did. But in fact, I felt an almost giddy gratitude that I was married to Charlie instead of Simon. How stiff and unaffectionate Simon had been when we were dating, how tedious, really, and I'd realized it only afterward; Charlie, even with his many flaws, was infinitely preferable. I reached over Ella to rub the back of Charlie's neck. "What did Zeke Langenbacher have to say?"

Charlie shrugged. "Just shooting the breeze."

The Brewers won 7–1, and we all were contentedly sun-saturated and tired driving home. As we pulled into the driveway, I glanced in the backseat. "Ladybug, I want you to pick up your toys by dinnertime."

"In case you're wondering where Barbie is, she's buck-naked and spread-eagle on the floor in the den," Charlie said. "Looks like she had a rough night."

"Charlie." I frowned at him.

"What does *spread-eagle* mean?" Ella asked.

"I'm just telling the truth," Charlie said.

To Ella, I said, "It means spread out. Why don't you put some clothes on her so she doesn't get cold?"

The phone was ringing as we entered the house, and my first impulse was to let the machine get it, but then I decided to answer because I thought it might be Jadey wanting to go for a walk.

"Hello?" I said. There was no immediate reply, then I heard the sound of a person sniffling, a sniffle I recognized, and my mother said, "Oh, Alice, I hate to have to tell you, but Granny has passed away."

I HAD NEVER bought Ella black clothing before. In fact, I'd told her it wasn't appropriate for little girls, a line she accusingly repeated back to me as I sat on a bench in the dressing room at Miss n' Master, Maronee's overpriced children's clothing boutique, and she wriggled into a gauzy black dress with ruffled sleeves and a sash across the midsection. She peered at herself in the mirror and said with unexpected pleasure, "I look like the girl from *The Addams Family.* For Granny's funeral, will you do my hair in braids?"

"Try this one." From a hanger, I removed a navy blue dress with a white Peter Pan collar. When Ella had pulled it over her head, she frowned at her reflection, and I said, "That's adorable. Why don't you like it?"

"I like the other one."

It was four o'clock on Thursday, four days since I'd received the call from my mother, and the funeral would be at eleven the next morning. I sighed. "Fine, we'll get the black one."

"Can I wear it for Christmas?"

"Christmas is in seven months, sweetheart."

"Can I wear it at Princeton?"

"We'll discuss it later. Turn around and let me unzip you."

At the cash register, Ella announced to the middle-aged woman ringing up the dress, "It's for my great-grandmother's funeral because she died of blood in her head."

The woman looked startled. "I'm sorry to hear that," she said.

IT WAS A strange thing to be in Riley without my grandmother. In the past, I'd been there when she was in Chicago with Gladys Wycomb, or I'd arrived for a visit when she was napping, but those times I had felt the force of her even in her absence, and now she was nowhere at all. Or who was I to say, what did I really know about the mysteries of the afterlife, and maybe she was right next to me, watching as I turned around to greet the people sitting in the pews behind the front one at Calvary Lutheran Church. A constricting band of sadness, like a belt that was too tight, was ever-present, but I also felt the tug toward social pleasantries that always surprised me at funerals—how the focused, mournful moments were the exception, the moments when you truly thought of the person who had died instead of being dimly aware of yourself in a church, part of a crowd, reciting prayers or talking to others. Perhaps sixty people had shown up for the service, primarily our neighbors as well as Ernie LeClef, who was now manager of Riley's branch of Wisconsin State Bank & Trust, and this turnout was higher than I'd expected, given that my grandmother had few close friends and had outlasted most of her peers and a fair number of people a generation younger, including, of course, my father.

The pastor was a man I hardly knew, Gordon Kluting, who opened the service by saying, "Blessed be the God and Father of our Lord Jesus Christ, the source of all mercy and the God of all consolations." After his greeting, we sang "Jesus, Lead Thou On," then there was the Litany and the Twenty-third Psalm, my mother reading from the book of Revelation (she was largely inaudible), and then it was my turn to read from the Beatitudes in Matthew 5: *Blessed are the poor in spirit: for theirs is the kingdom of heaven. Blessed are they that mourn: for they will be comforted . . .* I was glad to have been assigned this reading instead of my mother's, because of its tone of compassion rather than faith; after all these years, my faith remained decidedly shaky. That the world was miraculous, frequently in inexplicable ways, I would not argue. That these miracles had any relationship to the buildings we called churches, to the sequences of words we called prayers—that I was less sure of. Mostly, I found a place among believers, whether in Calvary Lutheran or at Christ the Redeemer, which was the Episcopal church we attended in Milwaukee, through isolated lines from the Bible, sometimes out of context. From the Letter of Paul to the Philippians, for example: *For I have learned in whatever state I am, to be content in it. I know how to be humbled, and I know also how to abound. In everything and in all things I have learned the secret both to be filled and to be hungry, both to abound and to be in need . . .* In simple ideas or graceful language, I felt a resonance that was absent when I took Communion or said most prayers. (The Nicene Creed, with its exclusionary, aggressive certainty, made me particularly uncomfortable, and sometimes, if I thought I could do so inconspicuously, I refrained from saying it; but if, for instance, it was Christmas Eve and I was in the pew next to Priscilla Blackwell, that simply wasn't a stand worth taking.) I considered it important to raise Ella in the church, if for no other reason than that years in the future, should she wish to take solace in religion, she would have a foundation for doing so; she would not need to seek it out as a stranger. The irony, then, was that on most weekends, I was the one who made sure we attended Christ the Redeemer. Early on in our time in Milwaukee, Charlie had been enthusiastic, but I think that had been related more to establishing us as a married couple in the community than to his faith, which was of the default variety. In Charlie's mind, of course there was a God; of course we ought to pray to Him, especially at Christmas and Easter and in times of unrest; and no, it was not wrong to impose on Him even with our smallest concerns (that was what, like a concierge at a fancy hotel, He was there for). In recent years, Charlie had become less diligent about going each Sunday to Christ the Redeemer, and sometimes Ella and I went without him; she attended Sunday school, which she loved because the teacher was a nineteen-year-old named Bonnie who had a prosthetic eye, and at the end of classes during which the children had behaved, she would remove it for them. Bonnie had lost the eye, Ella somberly informed me, when she was three and her older brother shot a rubber band at her, but Bonnie had long since forgiven her brother because, as Ella reminded me, quoting Jesus, "If you forgive men their trespasses, your heavenly Father will forgive you."

It was as I was concluding my reading of the Beatitudes that I looked out and caught sight of Harold Blackwell, sitting in the church's second-to-last occupied row. This was when I first felt tears well in my eyes. Even Jadey had not come—I had told her she didn't need to, and I'd had the sense she was relieved. Harold had made a special trip back to Wisconsin, I realized. And while my grandmother herself had been wary of Harold's political leanings, I was very moved. When I returned to my seat in the first pew, sliding past Lars and my mother into the space between Ella and Charlie, Charlie squeezed my hand and whispered, "Nice job."

After the homily, Pastor Kluting delivered a eulogy that I didn't think captured my grandmother—among other things, he referred to her as a pillar of the Riley community—and following the Apostle's Creed, the Lord's Prayer, and the Prayer of Commendation, the final hymn we sang was "Lift High the Cross." Again I became choked up. It wasn't that anything in the song reflected my grandmother, but it was a song I had heard and sung since I was a child, and as the organ played and the church was filled, or partially filled, by the voices of people who knew my family, there reared up in me a terrible sadness. Oh, how different my life would have been had I not grown up in the same house with my grandmother, how much narrower and blander! She was the reason I was a reader, and being a reader was what had made me most myself; it had given me the gifts of curiosity and sympathy, an awareness of the world as an odd and vibrant and contradictory place, and it had made me unafraid of its oddness and vibrancy and contradictions. And would I have married Charlie if not for my grandmother? Surely not, less because of her high opinion of him on their first meeting than because of the qualities they shared, the traits I valued in him because I'd valued them first in her: mischief and humor and irreverence, an implied intelligence rather than an asserted one. He stood beside me now, I could see his gray suit in my peripheral vision, and I thought, hadn't my grandmother been right about everything else? From fashion to education to helping me end my mistaken pregnancy, when had she not looked out for me, what had she ever misguessed? And must not she have been right, therefore, about him, too?

Her casket was on wheels, and the pallbearers were men from the funeral director's office. During the last verse of the song, they walked down the aisle first, then the pastor, then the family members, and I could tell that my mother was smiling at people hostess-style and also crying. In the car en route to the cemetery—we had not rented a limousine, even then, people in Riley didn't do such things—Ella leaned into the front seat and tapped my shoulder; Charlie was driving, and I was sitting in the passenger seat. When I turned, Ella seemed earnest, as if she'd been giving the subject serious thought. She said, "I think Granny would like my dress."

AT THE RECEPTION afterward, which was at our house on Amity Lane, I had just set a dish of Jell-O salad on the dining room table when Charlie slipped up behind me and said, "You think you'll want to linger here awhile or get on the road?" He was chewing the last of something—it appeared to be the cold bacon-cheese dip, served with potato chips, that I had only ever seen at funerals—and he swallowed and wiped his hands on a cocktail napkin.

"Are you in a hurry?" I asked.

"I don't want to make you feel pressed, so if you're trying to tie up loose ends here, maybe Ella and I should catch a ride back with Dad. Just a thought."

Nearly everyone from the funeral was sprinkled in the living room and dining room. The graveside ceremony had been short, and we'd arrived back at the house fifteen minutes earlier. Harold approached us then, standing between Charlie and me and setting a hand on each of our backs. (Since our arrival at the house, I'd sensed the other guests noticing Harold's presence, nudging one another and whispering—*I think that's Governor Blackwell.* But Harold either didn't realize it or was so accustomed to it, he paid no attention.) He said, "Alice, on behalf of the extended family, all of us are holding you and your grandmother in our hearts today."

"It was very good of you to come," I said.

"Where could I be that would be more important? I'm only sorry I have to take off now, but I'm due in San Diego for a speech this evening. As you can imagine, Priscilla was terribly sorry to miss being here."

I nodded. "Of course."

"We just couldn't love you one bit more," he said, and as we hugged, I thought how there was nothing else in the world as endearing to me as Harold Blackwell's sentimental streak. It was enough to make me wonder if there were other elected officials I was as wrong about as I'd been about him. Were there men (and it would be primarily men) who, instead of creating personas that were fakely righteous and honorable, were the opposite: fakely cruel, fakely callous? Men who, through the distortion of the media or a perceived pressure to act a certain way, sublimated, at least in public, their own decency and kindness?

When our embrace was finished, Harold patted Charlie on the shoulder. "Look after her, son," he said, and Charlie said, "Think you've got room in your Batmobile for two more?"

"Sweetheart, you can stay," I said. "You really won't be in the way."

Charlie didn't make eye contact with me as he said, "Yeah, see, I've got kind of a work thing that came up. Kind of a major thing, actually, otherwise you know I'd postpone it."

"Your brothers understand that you need to be with Alice today," Harold said, and I said, "What is it?"

Charlie hesitated. "I'd prefer not to get too specific. Word of honor, I'll tell you both the minute I can. Lindy, you're thinking you'll be home, what, around five or five-thirty?"

"Are you sure you can't say what it is?"

His lips stretched into an apologetic wince. "Give me a couple days, can you do that? It's come up all of a sudden, and I want to hold off on talking about it until it's more of a done deal." To his father, he said, "I'll collect Ella and meet you out front?" He leaned in and kissed me. "See you tonight by dinnertime?"

When Charlie was gone, I felt that Harold and I were implicated in a shared embarrassment—we were, after all, Charlie's father and wife.

In a tone of feigned lightheartedness, I said, "I fully expect you to get it out of him on the ride home and report back to me!" I expected no such thing.

"All very cloak-and-dagger, isn't it?" Harold shook his head. "Let us know if there's anything we can do."

ONE OF THE last people to leave the reception was Lillian Janaszewski, Dena's mother. I had already started carrying plates and glasses into the kitchen when she stopped me, saying, "Alice, you haven't sat still all afternoon. You're just like Dorothy."

"Thank you for coming," I said. "It's so nice to see you." I had repeated these words, or slight variations on them, so many times that day that they'd become automatic, as had the micro-update I provided on my life, as had the fleeting remembrances of my grandmother: *Yes, Charlie and I are still in Milwaukee. Ella's nine now, she's finishing up third grade. She's over there, yes, that's her with the long hair.* Or, *She just left—I know, I'm sorry you missed her. Charlie and I are very lucky.* Or, *I know, my grandmother was wonderful, wasn't she?* This part of the funerary proceedings also seemed to have far less to do with my grandmother as a person than with decorum, to the extent that, as I listened to myself chatter, I felt pangs of disloyalty. But what was the alternative? How could I bear to vividly and realistically remember her with everyone? *She found Riley somewhat dull. She was an excellent bridge player. She never lifted a finger to cook or clean, even when she was younger and more spry and easily could have done so, and she smoked constantly, including around her granddaughter. She liked* Anna Karenina *because she loved the characters, but she thought* War and Peace *was tediously political, and she stayed abreast of current fashion into her nineties, despairing of the trend toward wearing exercise clothes at all hours of the day; she also claimed Laura Ashley dresses looked like they were meant for peasants. She had a longtime love affair with another woman, which none of us really talked about, and then they broke up, and we hardly talked about that, either.* There was a way in which my grandmother's true self was not these guests' business; no one's true self was the business of more than a very small number of family members or close friends. In any case, I told myself, making superficial remarks didn't have the power to eclipse or insult the dead any more than missing them had the power to bring them back.

Mrs. Janaszewski took my hand, gripping it in hers, and her skin was unexpectedly cool, given that it was a warm May afternoon. "It just breaks my heart about you and Dena," she said. "She's living back here, you know."

"Is she not involved with D's anymore?"

Mrs. Janaszewski said ruefully, "Clothing stores are a difficult business, Alice. Customers are fickle, and in Madison, there's all the turnover with the students."

This surprised me, because D's had always been buzzing whenever I'd been by. Then I realized that my most recent visit to the store had been over a decade earlier; though I occasionally went back to Madison—to have lunch with Rita Alwin, my old friend from Liess, or to see an exhibit at the Elvehjem Museum—I avoided State Street because it made me sad.

"Dena's a hostess over at the steak house in the new mall, but the real news is she has a steady beau," Mrs. Janaszewski said. "You probably know him—Pete Imhof." I suppose an expression of alarm appeared on my face, because Mrs. Janaszewski brought her hand to her mouth, saying, "Oh, Alice, he's the brother— Oh, I'd forgotten all about— Forgive me."

"No, no, that was such a long time ago," I said, and I might have then felt the same disloyalty toward Andrew that I'd been feeling toward my grandmother—*I will minimize my grief for social pleasantries; this moment of small talk matters more than our history, your memory*—except that I was so disturbed by Mrs. Janaszewski's news. Dena was dating *Pete*? But Pete was awful! Dena was fun and cute and hardworking, and Pete was a dishonest layabout; he was a jerk. I even wondered, was she supporting him? How had they reconnected? Was it at all possible—for her sake, I hoped so—that he had changed since he'd swindled my mother? And then I thought, if Dena and Pete were dating, surely she'd have told him about my abortion. And my God, for him to find out all this time later that I'd been pregnant—would he be furious at me? Disgusted, or disappointed, or maybe just relieved I'd taken care of it? I said to Mrs. Janaszewski, "How long have they been together?"

"Oh, close to a year now. She says, 'Ma, quit asking when we're getting married. If I have something to tell you, you'll know.' "

So if Pete were going to track me down, to confront me, wouldn't he have done so months ago? Had Dena not told him, could it be that she didn't remember? This seemed unlikely but not impossible. After all these years, Dena and Charlie were still the only people whom I'd told; confiding in Jadey felt too risky.

I said, "That must be great for you, having Dena nearby."

"She just lives down on Colway Avenue," Mrs. Janaszewski said. "Now, I may not know the full story of what happened between you girls, but if I know Dena, I'm sure she'd love to hear from you. I'll give you her number, and she doesn't go into work until five—why, I'll bet she's home right now."

"Unfortunately, I'm headed back to Milwaukee shortly." I grimaced, as if I didn't yearn to return to my usual life, my own house and bed and kitchen and habits. "Ella and Charlie have taken off already. But I'm glad to hear Dena is doing well."

"You and I both know she can be stubborn, but you girls were so close. I used to think, Alice is like the fourth sister, if only my own daughters were half as well behaved."

I was surprised that Dena hadn't told her mother why our friendship had ended. But if she had, would Mrs. Janaszewski have treated me as warmly? I'd never felt that I was as much at fault as Dena had believed, but I also had never considered myself blameless; the flourishing of my relationship with Charlie at the expense of my friendship with Dena wasn't a subject I chose to recall with any frequency. Now, knowing she was dating Pete Imhof, I tried not to wonder whether, apart from the abortion, they'd ever compared notes on me.

I attempted to strike a regretful note as I said to Mrs. Janaszewski, "Maybe on another trip."

WHEN EVERYONE WAS gone, Lars and my mother and I sat in the living room, my mother sideways on the couch, her legs in black slacks extending in front of her and her feet, clad in sheer black stockings, on

Lars's lap, where he was absently rubbing them. I found the intimacy of the tableau both unsettling and sweet; certainly I had never felt Lars's presence more reassuring than on this day, knowing that when I drove back to Milwaukee, he would remain.

"I don't mean to be unkind, but did you see the nacho casserole that Helen Martin brought?" my mother said. "I've never heard of such a thing!" My mother was in a surprisingly upbeat mood; I suspect she was relieved that the guests had left.

"No, it was quite tasty," Lars said. "It had some kick to it, but not too much."

"It just *sounds* so funny." My mother looked across the room, where I sat in a recliner that had been one of Lars's few additions to the household when he moved in. "Did you try it, honey?" my mother asked.

I shook my head. "But I had more than my share of Mrs. Noffke's chocolate-chip cookies." The phone rang—my mother had finally replaced her black rotary ones with cream-colored push-button versions—and as I walked to the kitchen to answer it, I said, "I think she put walnuts in them. Hello?"

"You're still there?" Charlie said.

I looked at my watch. "It's not even five-thirty."

"Are you about to leave, or you think it'll be a while?"

"Charlie, I told you I'd be home by dinnertime."

"You happen to have Shannon's number on you? I'm gonna call and see if she can sit for Ella."

"I doubt she'll be free on such short notice."

My mother appeared in the doorway of the kitchen, frowning inquisitively. I set my hand over the receiver and shook my head. "Nothing's wrong. It's just Charlie."

"Just Charlie, huh?" Charlie said as my mother walked back out of the room.

"You know what I meant." A pause ensued, and I said, "I really wish you'd tell me what your mystery errand is."

He sighed. "You know how I was talking to Zeke Langenbacher at the game Sunday? Well, he's invited me to have a drink. This could be a huge opportunity—I can't say more right now, but trust me, it's big."

"Are you going to work for his company?"

"Not exactly. Listen, do you have Shannon's number? I promise I'll explain everything."

"Look on the fridge. No, you know what, don't call her. I'll get in the car now. What time are you and Zeke meeting?" I glanced at my watch; it was twenty past five, and it would take me fifty minutes to drive to Maronee.

"Six-thirty," Charlie said.

"Then that's fine—"

"No, but not at the country club, at Langenbacher's office downtown."

"Well, please don't leave Ella at home by herself. If you need to leave and I'm not back yet, take her to Jadey and Arthur's."

"I owe you," Charlie said. "Hey, how are things there?"

"They're fine."

"Are you mad?"

"I need to go."

"Drive fast, okay?" he said. "I'm not trying to be a total asshole, but this is important."

"I'll be there as quickly as I can." I could hear the tightness, almost a sarcasm, in my own voice, but this time Charlie did not remark on it.

I found my purse where I'd set it on a kitchen chair and carried it to the living room. "I think I'll be on my way," I said, and Lars said, "All's well on the home front?"

"Charlie wanted to know if I could smuggle the leftover nacho casserole back to Milwaukee," I said. "He claimed you two would never notice." Though Lars chuckled, my mother seemed somber; the mood of the room had changed while I was in the kitchen. "You all right, Mom?" I said.

My mother tilted her head to one side. "I keep thinking she's gone upstairs to read."

I understood perfectly; now that the distractions of planning for and enduring the funeral were finished, there was only the long future without my grandmother. Would Lars be enough to fill the house, to keep my mother company, after all?

With more confidence, more optimism, than I actually felt, I said, "Maybe she has."

OUR HOUSE IN Maronee was a 1922 Georgian colonial, the clapboard painted pale yellow—it had been white when we'd bought it, but we'd redone it about five years before, and I thought the yellow was softer—and on either side of the front door, two extremely tall Ionic columns supported a second-story pediment that was purely decorative. On most days, when I turned in to the driveway, our house struck me as ordinary, merely our house; but sometimes when I'd been away, especially when, as on this evening, I was returning from Riley, I realized again how large it was, especially for only three people. The house sat on an acre of zoysia grass (mowed on a weekly basis, except in winter, by Glienke & Sons landscapers), and tall oak and elm and poplar trees stood at irregular intervals, providing shade and a kind of buffer from the road. Our driveway was smoothly paved asphalt, our three-car garage freestanding and also yellow; though we had only two cars, we had managed to fill the extra space with bicycles, rakes, a stepladder, and an assortment of other domestic clutter. On this night, as I approached our property, I saw Charlie and Ella throwing a Frisbee in the front yard; Ella was barefoot but still wearing her dress from the funeral. As I pulled into the driveway, Charlie held up his left arm in a gesture that was half-wave, half-halt sign, and Ella began a dance that, as far as I knew, she'd made up: She set her hands on her head, index fingers up like antennae, and moved sideways in little hops. The early-evening sunlight through the trees was dappled gold, and in spite of my irritation with Charlie, I found myself thinking how lucky we were; really, I was not sure it was fair to be this lucky.

I set my foot on the brake and rolled down my window, and Ella called out, "Daddy threw me a bear claw, and I caught it!"

"Ladybug, your dress will last much longer if you don't play in it," I said. "Let's go inside and have you change."

"Thanks for coming back," Charlie said. "You're a lifesaver, Lindy."

"You're a Tootsie Roll, Lindy," Ella said, and Charlie laughed and swiped his hand against the top of her head.

To me, he said, "Mind if I take your car?" He opened the driver's-side door, extending his arm with an exaggerated flourish and saying, "Madame." I started to turn the car off, and he said, "Just leave the keys in the ignition."

When I stepped out, he very quickly kissed me on the lips, then slid into my seat. "Adios, amiga," he said to Ella, and to me, he said, "I should be home by ten." He was already backing up when I shouted, "My purse!" He reached over and tossed it out the window; improbably, I caught it, and he said, "Hey there, Johnny Bench." Then he reversed out of the driveway and disappeared down the street.

"Don't ever do that," I said to Ella.

"Drive fast?"

"That, too, but I meant don't throw Mommy's purse."

We went inside for her to put on shorts, then headed back out because she still wanted to play with the Frisbee. After we'd tossed it a few times, she said matter-of-factly, "You're not as good as Daddy."

"I haven't had as much practice," I replied.

When she'd tired herself out, we went in, and I ran a bath for her, and when it was time to wash her hair, she summoned me. For all that I had believed before the fact that I didn't want my daughter to have long hair, this was one of my favorite rituals. I still used Johnson's baby shampoo on her, with the pink droplet on the label that said NO MORE TEARS. Soon enough, I suspected, she'd take note of this label and be perturbed by the word *baby,* but so far she hadn't said anything. She sat naked and cross-legged with her back against the side of the tub, her head tilted forward, and I massaged her scalp in amiable silence; she occasionally flicked the surface of the water with her thumb and middle finger. I rinsed the shampoo out with the shower nozzle, and when she stepped from the tub, I was sitting on the toilet lid holding up a towel; she walked into it, and I wrapped her, holding her tight in my arms. "Mommy," she said.

"What?"

"I can lift a pencil with my toes."

I kept hugging her. "Since when?"

"Christine taught me. Want to see?"

"You can show me after you put on your pajamas."

The book I read to her that night, not for the first time, was *The Giving Tree.* We were at the part where the boy gathers the tree's apples to sell when I sensed that Ella had fallen asleep—both of us were leaning against the headboard of her bed—and after a few more pages, I shifted so I could look down at her eyes. They were indeed closed. I ought to have shut the book and turned out the light then, but I kept reading; I read until I'd reached the end.

IT WAS, I saw on the digital clock on my nightstand, after one when Charlie climbed into bed beside me. Groggily, I mumbled, "Did you have a flat tire?"

"Shh," he whispered. "Go back to sleep."

But as we lay there in the dark, instead of drifting off again, I became more alert. My mind pulled itself into focus, and I thought, *Where on earth could Charlie have been?* Surely this had been the longest day of my life.

When I spoke, it was in a normal volume. I said, "You need to tell me now."

Immediately, he rolled over and placed his arms around me, and when he spoke, his breath was warm against my face. I could tell he was excited. He said, "No, no, everything's good. Everything's *great.*" His happiness filled our darkened bedroom. He said, "I'm buying the Brewers."

THE COUNTRY CLUB pool opened that Saturday—it was Memorial Day weekend—and Ella insisted that we arrive right at nine o'clock. First, though, we picked up Jadey and Winnie. As they emerged from their house, a mammoth Tudor, I saw that Winnie was wearing a red bikini, the cups of it flat against her twelve-year-old chest, and Ella said to me from the backseat, "You said bikinis are inappropriate before you're sixteen!"

"Every family has its own rules."

"But Winnie is *our* family!"

"We'll talk about this later," I said, because Jadey and Winnie were almost to our car. Jadey, for all her talk about needing to lose weight, was wearing a bikini, too—*Bully for her,* I thought—which I could see under her sheer white linen cover-up. She also had sunglasses set on her head, pushing back her blond hair, and over one shoulder she carried a huge canvas bag with navy straps and a navy monogram. When they opened the car doors, I noticed that she and Winnie wore matching red toenail polish.

The girls immediately started talking in the back (Winnie was very sweet with Ella, very inclusive, which was part of how I knew Jadey and Arthur were good parents) and next to me, Jadey said, "How was the funeral? As funerals go, I mean."

"Not bad."

"Your grandma seems like she must have been such a cool lady." Jadey pulled a can of Diet Coke from her bag and popped it open. "I wish I'd gotten to know her better." As I turned out of their driveway onto Maronee Drive, Jadey rolled down the window on her side, then faced the backseat. "Ella, I hear you're joining the swim team this year. You will *love* Coach Missy. You girls are gonna have the best summer ever." Although we'd be spending July and part of August in Halcyon, missing half the swim season was considered acceptable because so many families who belonged to the country club also went away to vacation homes.

We weren't the only ones who'd come right on time for the pool's opening, and the lower parking lot was a chaos of children, mothers, a few fathers, and teenagers. The Maronee Country Club, really, was its own small nation, one of those tiny, slightly absurd kingdoms—Liechtenstein, perhaps. It took up two hundred acres, most of this land occupied by the eighteen-hole golf course. The clubhouse was an extremely long rectangle of white stucco—it always reminded me of a wedding cake—with a front porch full of oversize white rocking chairs and an American flag flying from the cupola. A valet took your car, though I always felt a little silly and would just as soon have parked myself. The main dining room was on the first floor, and this was where wedding receptions and debutante parties were held and where the tables and chairs were cleared out on alternating Fridays in the fall and winter for dancing school, which was open to children in sixth and seventh grade. On the lower level was a casual dining area known as the sports room, where, before my parents-in-law had moved east, Harold and Ella and I had met sometimes for a Saturday lunch of BLTs or Monte Cristos. In a building adjacent to the clubhouse were the weight room, squash courts, locker rooms, and lounge, and in the lounge, you were as likely to see a foursome of seventy-year-old matrons playing bridge as you were to see two male college students at the bar, outfitted in white, sweaty from a squash match (in the nation of the Maronee Country Club, a drinking age did not exist). The tennis courts sat between the clubhouse and the road, more than a dozen courts with a tennis shop in the middle where the pro had a desk and where one could get a cup of water, have one's racquet restrung, buy apparel, or argue about whether or not Björn Borg was the greatest player of all time (a comparable golf house existed, and there was a special section of the parking lot reserved for the fleet of golf carts). The tennis courts formed a barrier between the road and the clubhouse; the sandy green courts were enclosed by twenty-five-foot-high chain-link fences, and as you approached, you'd hear the hollow rubbery thwack of balls being hit.

Of course, the main attraction that morning was the pool—the enormous, majestic, glittery blue-tinted pool, which, between Memorial Day weekend and Labor Day weekend, exerted a magical pull not just for the children but for the adults as well. It was located behind the clubhouse, and six years earlier, at the wedding reception of Polly Blackwell (Polly was Charlie's first cousin), at dusk on a June evening, I'd looked out the window of the dining room, and it had been like gazing upon a lake in a fairy tale. The pool was Olympic-sized, with dark blue floating lane dividers, a deep end at the northwest corner, and a shallow end at the southeast (the shallow end was not the same as the baby pool, which was its own entity; predictably, its relative warmth was a source of endless jokes). One entered the pool area through a black-painted iron gate at the southeast tip; on the north side was a lawn of grass where the swim teams congregated during meets and where the rest of the time teenage girls sunned themselves; on the south side was the baby pool and the sign-in desk, which was also where you got towels (no one brought their own), and the concrete steps leading to the men's and women's locker rooms—every summer, a confused child would wander into the wrong one—and the snack bar. (Surely there are no smells and sounds more evocative for me than that particular combination of fried food being consumed under a midday sun, with a backdrop of splashing water and children's cries. To think of it now—normal life—fills me with nostalgia.) At neither the snack bar nor the clubhouse dining room nor the sports room nor the golf nor tennis stores nor anywhere on club grounds did you use cash. Rather, you were given a half-length forest-green pencil with no eraser that said MARONEE COUNTRY CLUB along the side, and you signed a bill that had a piece of carbon paper attached beneath it; I'd write *Mrs. Charles V. Blackwell.* At the end of the month, an itemized tab was sent to our house.

Either the best or worst part about the country club, depending upon how social I felt on a particular day, was that we knew nearly everyone who belonged; going for dinner there was like going to a restaurant where every face happened to be familiar. For the most part, this was comforting, giving me a stronger sense of community than I'd had even growing up in Riley. Sometimes, however, when I was in a hurry—if Ella had attended a friend's birthday party at the pool and I just wanted to pick her up quickly—it would not have been my preference to greet seven people, to have to say to Joannie Sacks, "Was France wonderful?" or to have Sandra Mahlberg announce, "Your sister-in-law made the most fabulous horseradish trout the other night!" And at rare moments, the insularity was downright unbearable—it made me ashamed of myself and everyone else at the club, ashamed of our wealth, our unthinking claims to privilege. The previous summer, I had brought that day's *Sentinel* with me to the pool, and I was sitting with Jadey on the flagstone terrace behind the diving boards when I read an article about a man living in the Walnut Hill area of the city who had hepatitis C and cirrhosis and who couldn't afford medication. And then I looked up and saw fifteen-year-old Melissa Pagenkopf rubbing oil on her belly, I heard a woman a few feet away say, "We never fly United if we can help it," and I felt a terrible sense of culpability. In this case, I couldn't simply write a check—there was no organization mentioned in the article, he was just an individual, and wouldn't he need medication for years to come? To send two hundred dollars would be a drop in the bucket. And I already knew I was not bold enough to seek him out (his name was Otis Donovan) without a charity acting as intermediary; I wouldn't want to write him a check that had my address on it, wouldn't want him to have a way of finding me.

At such moments, I felt that we were like the people in California who live in enormous houses on the sides of cliffs, that our lives were beautiful but precarious, their foundations vulnerable. And then I'd think, was it adolescent to become preoccupied with other people's problems, or to feel, while reading the newspaper or watching the local news, that if you didn't consciously will yourself not to, you might cry? Life was so hard for so many people, the odds were stacked so precipitously against them. The other adults I knew did not seem overly distressed about these imbalances, and certainly not surprised by them, whereas to me they were constantly surprising, they were never not upsetting.

I had turned to Jadey and gestured in front of us. "Do you ever feel guilty about all of this?"

"All of what?" she said.

"I'm reading an article about a man in Walnut Hill who has hepatitis, and then I think of how my worst problem is that I can't get my daughter to eat vegetables. Does it ever occur to you that you should be leading an entirely different life?"

"Oh, I know." Jadey was nodding sympathetically. "I used to want to join the Peace Corps. Can't you picture me in, you know, Zambia? How could I have made it ten minutes without my hair dryer?"

Although she spoke warmly, I knew not to push my point—she had sidestepped it the way she sidestepped our mother-in-law's insults and decrees—and I wondered if already I might have violated decorum, positing myself as ponderously thoughtful, as self-righteous. It was inappropriate to introduce poverty and woe while sunning yourself poolside; you either ought to be elsewhere, doing something about it, or you ought to sun yourself in the spirit that sunning requires. There was an older woman I knew in Garden Club, Mary Schmidbauer, with whom three or four years earlier, I'd been assigned to host a meeting, and when I'd suggested holding it in the country club's sports room, as was common, she'd said, "Don't take this the wrong way, Alice, dear, but I haven't been a member since my husband passed on. They're not crazy about having women belong by themselves, and of course they've never allowed Jews or blacks. When Kenneth died, I realized I'd had enough." I had been chastened, and Mary and I had ended up holding the meeting in my living room.

That Saturday of Memorial Day weekend, after Jadey, Ella, Winnie, and I had signed in—there was actually a line, which never happened on a normal day—we staked out lounge chairs on the southeast side of the pool, a little ways behind the lifeguard's chair, and Winnie and Ella obliged Jadey and me by letting us rub sunscreen on their backs. The second we were finished, Ella followed Winnie as her cousin darted toward the water, and they both dove in; they had the clean form of children who've taken lessons for such things. Jadey adjusted her lounge chair so it sloped farther back, then settled in, surveying the scene before her. "Is this a gorgeous day or what?"

It was indisputably a gorgeous day: sunny and still, the temperature in the low seventies. Leaning toward her bag, which was set on the flagstone between our chairs, Jadey extracted two magazines and held them up side by side: an issue of *People* and an issue of *Architectural Digest.* "Which one?"

I pointed at *Architectural Digest,* and she said, "I was hoping you'd say that, because I *need* to know what Princess Di is up to this week."

As we sat there, companionably turning pages, occasionally reading aloud a line or showing each other a picture—the ones I showed her were of fancy pillows or antique desks, and the ones she showed me were of Cher in some peculiar outfit, or Bruce Willis and Demi Moore holding hands—I was very tempted to repeat to her what Charlie had told me about buying the baseball team. I couldn't, though, because he'd explicitly asked me not to, and I didn't blame him. What I shared with Jadey she would surely share with Arthur, who would share it with John and their parents, and presumably all of Wisconsin and half of Washington, D.C., would soon know.

The night before, when Charlie had told me, I'd said, "You're not serious," and he'd said, "I am, but we can talk about it in the morning."

"We don't have enough money," I said. I didn't know how much it cost to buy a baseball team, but it had to be millions of dollars.

"Good God, not me alone," Charlie said. "It's an investment group, and I'll be managing partner. Managing partner of the Brewers has a nice ring to it, huh? I've just got to put up six or seven hundred grand, and the rest will come from the other fellows, namely Zeke Langenbacher and our very own Cliff Hicken. This is the opportunity of a lifetime, Lindy, it's what I was meant to do. My brothers'll eat their hearts out."

Only six or seven hundred grand? But I didn't respond—despite the surprising nature of what he was telling me, now that I knew his secret wasn't anything troubling, I found myself teetering again on the edge of sleep.

Sounding blissful, he said, "Think about going to all those games, and it counts as work."

Sleep was pulling me in, it was winning. I could hear him, but I was having difficulty forming a response. "Maybe you can find out what happened to Bernie Brewer," I said. Bernie was the lederhosen-wearing, mustachioed mascot who had been retired a few years earlier. Before his retirement, whenever there was a home run, he would slide into a large beer mug, which had delighted Ella.

Charlie chuckled, and I promptly fell asleep.

In the morning, I woke shortly after six, and Charlie was lying on his side, his eyes shut, his breathing rhythmic and untroubled. "Are you awake?" I said, which was a disingenuous trick I occasionally used. When he didn't respond, I asked again, and without opening his eyes, he shook his head. I said, "Did I dream that you and Zeke Langenbacher are buying the Brewers?"

Our real conversation had not taken place until a few hours later, at breakfast. Ella was also in the kitchen but on the phone, talking to her friend Christine (that she would soon see Christine at the pool apparently made a check-in more rather than less urgent), and Charlie explained the situation: Because Monday was Memorial Day, they'd be making the eighty-four-million-dollar offer Tuesday; the family who currently owned the Brewers, the Reismans, knew the offer was coming and were prepared to accept it.

Charlie was eating a piece of toast, and I was standing with my back to the sink. I said, "Well, congratulations."

"That sounded lukewarm."

"Not at all. I'm really excited for you, but what I don't understand—if your investment group is offering eighty-four million dollars, how many people are in it? I'm not suggesting you put up more, but how can six or seven hundred thousand be enough unless there are dozens and dozens of investors?"

In fact, parting with such a large portion of our savings did not seem insignificant. But it wasn't really my money, it never had been, and even if we lost it, we'd still have a cushion. We'd never had a mortgage or car payments, and some years our biggest annual expense was Ella's tuition—we'd be fine.

"Oh, they didn't come to me for my deep pockets," Charlie said. "Compared to some of these dudes, we might as well be in the poorhouse. No, a lot of what Langenbacher wants to do in bringing me on board is get the credibility and the connections of the Blackwell name, and frankly, I have no problem with that—I'm going into it with my eyes open. It'll be a synergistic type of situation, good for the team, good for me, good for our family. They know I went to B-school, and they recognize what I have to offer."

"So what will being managing partner entail?"

"Cheering for Robin Yount." Charlie grinned. "Booing when the White Sox come to town. Finally memorizing the national anthem. No, there's six other guys in Langenbacher's investment group, counting Cliff—you'd know most of these fellows by name—and they're all successful, obviously, but none of them are stars in the charisma department, if you catch my drift. They need a public face for the owners, whether it be with marketing or acting as a liaison to other leaders in the community. This is still top-secret, but one of the major goals is to build a new stadium ASAP, and you just know that'll necessitate a lot of kid-glove negotiations."

"And you're sure the Reisman family wants to sell the team?"

"Oh, Lloyd Reisman is thrilled that locals are prepared to pony up. It would be devastating for the morale of this city if the Brewers got relocated again. You're not worried about the money, are you? Because trust me, eighty-four million is a bargain. There's no way we won't get rich off the deal."

"I just never knew you had this kind of thing in mind," I said. "You're such an avid fan, obviously, but professional involvement—I'm surprised, is all."

"Now you know what Langenbacher and I were having our big talk about at the ballpark Sunday. You up for eighty-one games a year? Actually more, 'cause I'll travel with the team sometimes."

I smiled. "Sure." Could this be it, the thing that would bring Charlie peace? Being managing partner of a baseball team—and one that, for all Charlie's loyalty to it, wasn't particularly famous or winning—did not seem to me a recipe for a legacy. But given that I didn't understand why a legacy mattered in the first place, perhaps it was predictable that I didn't understand what might create one. If it was enough for Charlie, it was enough, more than enough, for me. Charlie was sitting at the kitchen table, and when I stepped toward him, he set his arms around my waist, hugging me. We were quiet, and Ella, who was still on the phone in the corner, said in an agitated tone, "But Bridget cheats at Marco Polo!"

Charlie said, "Which do you think most people would rather do: coach high school baseball or own a baseball team?"

"You're not doing this just to impress your Princeton classmates, are you?"

With his face pressed against my stomach, Charlie laughed. "Give me some fucking credit."

AT NOON, I walked around the perimeter of the pool to the snack bar to place our order for lunch: tuna sandwiches and Diet Cokes for Jadey and me, grilled cheeses and lemonade for Ella and Winnie. The snack bar was essentially a glorified shed with a kitchen in the back and a counter where you ordered; whenever an unexpected storm broke out, most people got in their cars and went home, but the most optimistic would cram into the front of the snack bar, hoping the rain would pass.

When I carried our tray of food back to the lounge chairs, Ella and Winnie were huddled together on mine, both soaking wet. Seeing me approach, Winnie called, "Step lively, Aunt Alice—we're starving!"

I distributed the food, and Winnie said, "Mom, when I'm finished, can I have an ice-cream bar?"

"Only if you bring me one, too," Jadey said.

We made the girls wait an hour before going back in the water, and they wandered off toward the grassy stretch at the north end of the pool; as soon as they were out of earshot, Jadey whispered, "When I was their age, I *never* waited." Jadey, like Charlie and Arthur, had grown up belonging to the country club, swimming in this pool. She'd told me that at her debutante ball, which had occurred at the club in June 1968, the theme had been "A Hawaiian Luau," and she'd worn a strapless Hawaiian print dress and an orchid lei around her neck; guests had drunk fruit cocktails, eaten pineapple-and-shrimp kebabs and pig from a spit (it had roasted for hours ahead of time), and while there was a traditional twelve-piece dance band in the dining room, outside, a man with a ukulele had sat strumming on the high diving board.

"You know who walked by when you were getting the food is Joe Thayer," Jadey said. "I was thinking I should have an affair with *him.*"

"Jadey, he's going through a divorce."

"Oh, I love wounded men. I've often wished Arthur were more bruised by life. But what makes me wonder about Joe is that their daughter turned out so creepy, and she had to get it from somewhere, right?"

"Megan's not creepy," I said. "She's nine years old."

"I can't *stand* that girl."

"Jadey!"

"Honest to God, last year at Halcyon, I was walking down to the dock and dropped this huge tray of snacks and drinks—everything went everywhere—and I'm cursing and picking it all back up, and then I look over and she's been watching me the whole time, not saying a word. She wasn't even laughing, she was just staring at me."

"She's a kid," I protested.

"She's a sociopath. Plus, Winnie said Megan once offered her a poop sandwich."

I suppressed the urge to repeat Ella's similar story. Poor Megan seemed to have enough problems without my gossiping about her, so I said, "I think you should talk to Arthur. I'm sure he knows you're mad at him, but he probably doesn't want to bring it up."

Jadey was adjusting the back of the lounge chair again, flattening it, and she made a harrumphing sound and rolled onto her stomach. Her face was turned to me, half of it pressed against the chair's vinyl straps. She said, "Did you have any idea marriage would be so damn much work? God almighty." She'd removed her sunglasses before lying down, and her eyes dropped shut. In a drowsy voice, she said, "You still worried about Chas and his whiskey?"

"I may have been overreacting."

"I forgot to watch him at Maj and Pee-Paw's, maybe 'cause I was so busy knocking back the vino myself. You have any of that merlot?"

"I had a glass of the chardonnay."

She opened her eyes, propping herself up on her elbows. "A glass?" she repeated. "As in one glass?" When I nodded, she said, "Honey, maybe it's not that Chas needs to drink less. Maybe it's that you need to drink more."

WHEN I REMINDED Charlie on Monday morning that the Suttons were coming for lunch—Miss Ruby had called the evening before to confirm, and when I offered to pick them up, she'd said Yvonne would drive—he was shaving in front of the sink in our bathroom, and I was standing in the doorway. "No can do," he said. "I've got an eleven o'clock tee time with Zeke and Cliff."

"Charlie, I told you about this over a week ago."

"Lindy, we're making the offer to the Reismans tomorrow. With eighty-four mill at stake, don't you think it'd be wise for us to dot some I's and cross some T's?"

"That's what you'll be doing on the golf course?" I folded my arms in front of me. "Don't make me be a nag."

He chortled. "Whether you're a nag is up to you, but I've got an eleven o'clock appointment, and it would be unprofessional to miss it."

I watched as he brought the razor down his right cheek, his mouth twisted to the left, and I felt such an intimate kind of anger. Was this what marriage was, the slow process of getting to know another individual far better than was advisable? Sometimes Charlie's gestures and inflections were so mercilessly familiar that it was as if he were an extension of me, an element of my own personality over which I had little control.

I said, "If you don't want to participate in social situations, then don't, but it's embarrassing to me and rude to other people when you say you will and then flake out."

When he glanced at me, I sensed that his mood had deflected my comments completely; my words were like pennies bouncing off him. He said, "But you don't want to be a nag, huh?"

"I'd think you'd try to go out of your way to be respectful toward Miss Ruby."

He held his razor under the faucet for a few seconds, then brought it back up to his face. "Who gave her the impression I'd be here? Wasn't me, darlin'. If this is so important to you, reschedule—see if they can do it next weekend. All's I know is I'm about to buy a baseball team."

"We'll be in Princeton next weekend." I took a step backward, into our bedroom. I would go downstairs and prepare lunch, and I'd welcome the Suttons to our home, I'd do this even if Charlie wouldn't deign to be there and his mother didn't approve. But first, in a voice so snippy I hardly recognized it, I said, "Don't leave your whiskers in the sink."

JESSICA SUTTON HAD grown probably a foot since the last time I'd seen her, and I knew as soon as we greeted the Suttons at the front door that she was, if not an adult, no longer a child. Some sixth-graders are still children—boys more than girls—but in other kids that age, you can see a new, unsettled awareness of themselves and the world. In the best cases, the awareness is also a politeness. When you ask them how they are, they reciprocate the question, and this was exactly what Jessica did, and then she said, "Thanks for having us over, Mrs. Blackwell," and I felt a small heartbreak for Ella, who was most definitely still a girl and would, I suspected, have difficulty keeping up with the poised, mature young woman Jessica had become. I realized that the default image of Jessica I'd been carrying in my head was from an Easter-egg hunt years before at Harold and Priscilla's (contrary to what Priscilla had implied, Blackwells did sometimes socialize with their hired help, but it was on the Blackwells' turf, under circumstances that highlighted their beneficence and largesse without implying that they spent time with these people because they actually enjoyed it). That Easter, Jessica had worn a red skirt with purple stars and a matching purple shirt with red stars, and even her barrettes had been color-coordinated. Her hair had been divided into little squares all over her head, each square gathered into a small ponytail, braided, and clipped with a red or purple plastic barrette; as she dashed about, accumulating eggs in her basket, the barrettes clicked together. Now Jessica was tall and serious, and she was pretty—she wore a pink tank top underneath a pink-and-white-striped dress shirt that she kept unbuttoned, and white slacks—but she was hardly girlish at all.

As soon as she, Miss Ruby, Yvonne, baby Antoine, Ella, and I were settled on the brick patio in our backyard, Ella said, "Can I show Jessica my pop bottle?" and I said, "Honey, they just got here."

Jessica said, "No, I'd love to see it." The pop bottle was a prize Ella had won at Biddle Academy's Harvest Fest the previous fall, a glass Pepsi bottle whose neck had been heated and stretched into distortion before the bottle, emptied of cola, was filled with a toxic-looking blue liquid. Though Ella had acquired this eyesore over six months earlier, it remained a fresh source of pride—when she was seeking to impress, she clearly considered it the most powerful weapon in her arsenal.

"Come back down in ten minutes to eat," I called after them as they headed inside, and when the girls were gone, I said, "I can't believe how much Jessica has grown up. And Antoine"—I leaned toward him, widening my eyes and opening my mouth —"I think maybe you're the sweetest baby ever." He wore a pale blue sleeper and had large brown eyes, a head of curly brown hair, and that perfectly smooth baby skin.

Sounding amused, Yvonne said, "Alice, you're welcome to hold him."

"Mind his head," Miss Ruby said gruffly as Yvonne passed him to me.

In my arms, Antoine was ridiculously light—at two months, he weighed perhaps ten or twelve pounds—and I found myself making all sorts of semi-involuntary coos and gasps and funny faces, no dispensation of dignity being too great for the reward of his tiny smile.

"Maybe you should have another, you ever think of that?" Yvonne said.

I laughed. "I'm too old."

Yvonne made a skeptical expression. "Oh, I bet you and Charlie B. still got some juice."

"Watch your mouth, Yvonne Patrice," Miss Ruby said, and at this, both Yvonne and I laughed. Miss Ruby had on turquoise linen pants, a turquoise short-sleeved sweater with scalloped sleeves, and flat sandals with turquoise straps, and Yvonne wore a flowered T-shirt and a long denim skirt. While Miss Ruby was slim, Yvonne had wide hips and thick upper arms, large teeth and lips, short hair that she fluffed up off her head, and, I noticed now, swollen nursing breasts.

"I'm sorry that Charlie isn't here today," I said. "We got our signals crossed, and he ended up scheduling a business meeting."

Yvonne waved away my apology. "Clyde's working at the hospital, so I know all about that. The doctors and nurses still gotta eat on Memorial Day."

"You and Clyde were married last summer?" I said.

"He's a real good guy." Yvonne leaned forward, to where I held Antoine on my lap. "Isn't that right, Baby A?" she cooed. "Papa's a good man." To me, she said, "Antoine looks just like his father, that's for sure."

"They always do at this age," Miss Ruby said.

A few minutes later, when Ella and Jessica returned, I brought out the cold pasta salad I'd made, which had asparagus and chicken in it. With her mouth full, Ella said to all of us, "Want to hear what Jessica taught me?"

"Swallow, honey," I said.

Ella had been sitting with one leg folded beneath her on a wrought-iron chair, and she stood, still holding her fork while she flung her arms in the air and twitched her hips:

"Basketball is what we do,
And we'll cheer it just for you.
Shake it high and shake it low,
In the hoop the ball will go."

"Impressive." I clapped a little, and Yvonne and Jessica did, too, but Miss Ruby didn't. I turned to Jessica. "Are you a cheerleader?"

"Nah, I just know that. Maybe in junior high, I'll do cheer."

"I hear from your grandmother that you're quite an English student. What books did you read this year?"

Jessica shook her head, smiling. "Grandma just likes to brag on me. No, let's see, we didn't read too many books for English, we did more workbooks. The only real book we read is *The Call of the Wild*—you know that one?"

I nodded. "Of course, where Buck goes to the Yukon." I turned to Ella. "It's a book about a dog who helped pull sleds when men went looking for gold."

Suddenly, and for the first time, Antoine began to cry, and Yvonne said to him in a singsong, "We'll never send *you* to the Yukon. No, we won't. So why are you crying, Baby A?"

"Pass him here," Miss Ruby said. Yvonne rolled her eyes but obeyed her mother, and Miss Ruby walked him around the edge of the patio, gently patting his back. Within a minute, he was quiet.

"Most stuff I read isn't for school, but I just like it," Jessica was saying. "I'm into Agatha Christie, you ever read Agatha Christie?"

"Oh, sure, Miss Marple and Hercule Poirot. I haven't read those for a long time, but I devoured them when I was a little older than you."

"I just finished *Murder on the Orient Express,*" Jessica said. "Ooh, I loved that one! You ever hear of V. C. Andrews?"

"Oh, Jessica!" I couldn't help voicing my disapproval, though I was laughing a little, too. "V. C. Andrews is so creepy."

"Yeah, but you can't put it down," Jessica said. "Grandma, remember you came in one night at three in the morning, there I was in bed, I couldn't stop reading. I just could *not* stop. Okay, Mrs. Blackwell, I bet you won't like this, either, but you know the Harlequin romances? Some of those are good, they really are. The one that's called *Storm Above the Clouds,* I'd say that's my favorite because the lady goes to Rome, Italy."

"You know I don't mean to pick on you, Jessica," I said. "It's great you read so much."

"My dad and me just finished *The BFG,*" Ella announced, and Yvonne indulgently asked, "Now, what does *BFG* stand for?"

"He only eats snozzcumbers, but he doesn't like them," Ella said, and I said, "Ella, maybe *you* should try eating things you don't like." To Yvonne, I said, "It stands for Big Friendly Giant—it's by Roald Dahl."

"Mommy, can Jessica go to the pool with us?" Ella asked.

"Oh, that water is way too cold," Jessica said. "I dipped my pinkie finger in one time, and I pulled it right back out!"

"Can she?" Ella persisted, and I hoped, with great uneasiness, that it was not evident to anyone else that Jessica was talking about the pool at Harold and Priscilla's—now that my parents-in-law were in Washington, they left the cover on it year-round—while Ella was talking about the pool at the Maronee Country Club. It wasn't that black people were officially barred from the club, at least not as far as I knew, but even in 1988, there were no black members; club trustees would have said it was because none applied, because so few blacks lived in Maronee. Even the staff, the waiters and waitresses and bartenders, the lifeguards and the trainers in the weight room, were all white, with the exception of one housekeeper who looked to be Latina. Perhaps twice a summer, you'd see a black person at the pool—it was usually a child who'd been invited to a class birthday party—and around the pool's perimeter, among the various swimmers and sunbathers, it was possible to feel a discomfited alertness; whether the discomfiture came from shame at the exclusivity of our club or outrage that the gates had been breached no doubt depended on the individual.

"And they have milk shakes, too," Ella was saying and Jessica said, "Grandma, you been making milk shakes for Ella Blackwell and not for me?"

"No, at the club," Ella said, and I was already talking over her, saying, "I don't think anyone will be swimming anywhere today." It had been sunny when we'd sat, but the sky had grown overcast, a washed-out gray. "Who wants to head inside for rhubarb pie?" I asked.

The Suttons had brought this dessert, and I'd exclaimed over it at length when Jessica handed it to me, then I'd hurried to hide the butterscotch cookies Ella and I had made that morning. We ate dessert in the dining room, and when we'd finished, Ella presented the gifts she and I had picked out the day before: for Antoine, from Miss n' Master, a yellow romper and a very silly pair of shoes, little red leather booties that had baseballs above the toes—an impractical present that Ella had insisted we buy. For Jessica (it was under the guise of a sixth-grade graduation present, though really I hadn't wanted her to feel left out when there were presents for Antoine), we'd gone to Marshall Field's at Mayfair Mall and selected a Swatch watch that had translucent pink plastic straps and a pink flower on the face. Jessica fastened it around her wrist and was holding out her arm for us to admire when I heard Charlie's voice in the front hall.

"Well, well, well," he said, and when we all turned to look at him, he was grinning. "Am I allowed to crash a ladies' lunch?"

"Look what the cat dragged in," Yvonne said. "We thought you were working, Charlie."

"How could I stay away?" he said. He had on pale blue shorts—not such a different shade from Antoine's sleeper—and a white polo shirt and white socks; he'd left his spiked golf shoes in the hall. If there was any doubt about where he'd come from, he still was carrying his clubs, and in that moment, he set the bag against one wall of the dining room. His hair and shirt were damp, I noticed, and when I looked out the window, I saw that it had started to rain. "And this must be the man of the hour," Charlie continued. He walked toward the car seat on the floor, where Antoine had fallen asleep. Leaning in, Charlie said, "That's a darn good-looking baby. Nice going, Yvonne. Put it here." He held up his hand for her to give him five, but before she could, he caught sight of the pie and exclaimed, "Vittles!" It was then that I realized he'd been drinking. After cutting himself a large slice of pie, he proceeded to scoop it up with his fingers. Silently, I stood and passed him my plate and fork, both of which he accepted, although he didn't use them.

"Charlie Blackwell, you don't have the manners of a barnyard animal," Miss Ruby said, which made Ella and Jessica titter.

Charlie, too, was smiling. "Yvonne, if I didn't have such an exalted mother of my own, I would have stolen yours years ago." He wiped his hands on someone else's napkin, then set a palm on Miss Ruby's shoulder. "Jessica, your grandmother is a national treasure," he said, and I wondered whether Miss Ruby could smell the alcohol on his breath.

"Daddy, listen to this." Ella, who, during the present-opening, had been standing close to Jessica in a self-appointed supervisory capacity, took a step back from the table, but when everyone was looking at her, she abruptly shifted modes, ducking her head to one side and looking at us from beneath her eyelashes. In a quiet voice, she said, "Never mind." This was a new affectation—there was a girl in her class named Mindy Keppen who would freeze when called on by a teacher, and when I'd explained to Ella what shyness was, it had captured her imagination. (Oh, my drunk husband and my darling, disingenuous daughter.)

"You want to show him the cheer, right?" Jessica said. "How about if I do it with you?"

Ella looked up, smiling and nodding rapidly. Jessica stood, and more or less in unison, they raised their arms and swiveled their hips from side to side.

"Basketball is what we do,
And we'll cheer it just for you.
Shake it high and shake it low,
In the hoop the ball will go."

For *shake it high* they rattled imaginary pom-poms above their heads, and for *shake it low* they brought them down to their knees.

"Outstanding," Charlie said when they were finished. "Superlative!" My heart sank as he walked around the table and took his place next to the girls, saying, "So it goes, *Basketball is what we do . . .*" Giggling, they taught him the words. Ella was purely ecstatic, possibly unable to imagine a better scenario—standing beside a cool older girl, teaching cheerleader cheers to her father, with an audience—whereas Jessica was a good-natured participant but was also, I suspected, analyzing the situation, trying to figure out Charlie's motives. Jessica and Charlie had known each other for her whole life and probably never had a real conversation.

When he'd memorized the words, the three of them recited the cheer together, and at the end, Charlie shouted, "Go, Brewers!"

Ella laughed and clutched at his belt, saying, "Not baseball, Daddy, *basketball.*" He lifted her into his arms, something I could no longer do, and the two of them grinned together. Clearly, this was the climax of the afternoon, and the Suttons sensed it; they soon stood to set their exit in motion, gathering Antoine's diaper bag and car seat, the presents and the pie dish. I put on a raincoat and walked out to the car with them. In the driveway, I said to Jessica, "Do you have plans for the summer?"

She was carrying Antoine, and she nodded down at him and said, "Here's my plans right here—Baby A and V. C. Andrews. No, I'm teasing about V. C. Andrews, Mrs. Blackwell."

"Well, we loved having you all here," I said. I thought of Ella's upcoming activities: swim team, the art camp she'd attend the last week in June, then in July, we'd be off to Halcyon.

When I reentered the house and closed the front door, Charlie was no longer in the dining room. I carried the plates and glasses into the kitchen, pushing back and forth through the swinging door, and I could hear the television in the den. As I loaded the dishwasher, I realized I had a headache. How large and empty our house abruptly felt.

I had squeezed the sponge a final time and set it in its spot next to the soap dish when Charlie came in and pulled a beer from the refrigerator. "That was one handsome Negro baby." He grinned, and I couldn't have said if he was trying to provoke me or if he was simply being himself.

We stood there facing each other, standing about five feet apart, and I thought of berating him, but I didn't have the will. I had the energy for a disagreement perhaps once every few months, not twice in one day.

"You're awfully quiet," he said.

"I have a headache. I'm about to go upstairs and read."

"Aren't you curious how golf went with Cliff and Langenbacher?"

"I assumed it got called off because of the weather." I could hear the rain outside, soft but steady.

"You wouldn't believe how pumped Langenbacher is to have me on board. It was Cliff who suggested me, which means I'm eternally indebted to him. But Langenbacher couldn't be happier with what I'm bringing to the table—I'm a huge fan, I don't have to fake that one bit, but I also have the business expertise." Charlie's cheeks were flushed, either with pleasure or with alcohol. "You're not mad because I missed lunch, are you?" he said. "I'd say by the end, they got their money's worth of the old Chas Blackwell charm. Come to think of it, maybe you were in cahoots with the meteorologists today."

"As a matter of fact, your showing up was awkward, because I'd told them you were at a meeting."

"I was."

"A real meeting."

"I *was.* Jesus, Lindy!"

"Then I guess I'm surprised Zeke Langenbacher doesn't mind people drinking so heavily on the job."

Charlie scowled. "What's your problem?" he said. "This is a professional dream come true, and I don't know why you're being such a goddamn killjoy."

"Of course I'm happy for you." As if balancing out his force and volume, I spoke more quietly than usual. I said, "But I told you I have a headache, and I don't feel very celebratory. My grandmother did just die."

I had almost felt that I shouldn't mention this, that however true, it was cheap, and the reminder would make him contrite but humiliated. I should not have worried. It is fair, I believe, to say that in that moment, he was glaring at me. He said, "For Christ's sake, Lindy, she was ninety years old. What'd you expect?"

AS WE'D PLANNED, I walked to Jadey and Arthur's house that evening before dinner, and as soon as she and I were a safe distance onto the golf course, she said, "Arthur came sniffing around my campsite this morning, but I ignored him."

"Jadey, maybe you should give him a break."

"Whose side are you on?"

"Both of yours," I said, but I wondered if I had it in me to have the conversation; I wondered if I should have canceled the walk. Since the Suttons had left our house a few hours earlier, I had been hovering between two possibilities: a torrent of tears or else—and I recognized this possibility as worse—a shutdown of all systems. It was the first time in over twenty years, the only time apart from Andrew Imhof's death, that I had felt the pull toward nothingness, and I knew the impulse was far more dangerous now; I had the responsibilities of an adult and above all was in charge of Ella's well-being. But how soothing it would be to give up, to sleepwalk—to quit trying with Charlie, or expecting him to try with me.

Jadey said, "You might disagree, but I think my husband needs to work a little harder to win back my affection."

We both were quiet—the storm clouds were long gone, sun shone through the leaves of the trees, the blades of grass glistened, and the locusts buzzed extravagantly—and I said, "Do you really enjoy playing these games with him?"

"Listen, not all of us have your perfect marriage."

"Are you being sarcastic?" This was a far sharper exchange than the ones Jadey and I usually had, and I think both of us were surprised that it was still gaining momentum.

Carefully—it was to Jadey's credit that the exchange did then begin to lose force—she said, "I didn't mean to step in a prickly patch. I just meant that you have it easier than some of us."

And then I did it, I burst into tears, and Jadey said, "God almighty, what did I say? Oh, sweet Jesus." I had stopped walking and brought my hands up to my face, and she patted my back. "Alice, you know I love you to pieces. Is this about your poor granny or what?"

I wiped my eyes. "You think I have it *easy*?"

"Your husband worships the ground you walk on. Yeah, so Chas probably does drink too much, but you've got to pick your poison. At least you're still hopelessly in love."

"Jadey, I'm— I'm thinking of leaving him. Our marriage is far from perfect."

"Leaving him like divorce?"

"I don't know. I don't even know how it works. Would I move out of the house or would he?" Speaking these words aloud to Jadey marked the first moment I had truly, realistically considered ending my marriage. For months, I had heard whispers—*separation, divorce*—and though it had seemed that they were carried to me on the wind, they were really coming from inside my own head. Even so: They'd been abstract ideas, escapes of last resort. "Or facing Maj, think about that," I added. (Though I did not, could not, call her Maj to her face, I was perfectly capable of using the nickname when discussing her with others. Not to would have been overly formal, drawing attention to myself.) "She'd be furious with me. I almost feel like she wouldn't let it happen, you know what I mean?"

"She doesn't control us," Jadey said. "Yeah, I know exactly what you mean, but when you get down to it, there's nothing she can do besides cut you out of her will." Was I even in Priscilla's will? I doubted it, though Jadey's point did raise the question of what shape my finances might take. Would I receive alimony? Would I be able to afford a house in this area, even a modest one, and in any case, how many modest houses existed in Maronee? Did anyone around here rent? I'd get a job, of course, and in some ways, that might be a good thing, but supporting myself and Ella (that I wouldn't have primary custody of her was unimaginable) when both of us were used to a decidedly privileged way of life would be a far cry from supporting myself as a single woman in Madison.

"Okay, what if Chas gets treatment for his drinking?" Jadey said. "What's that place in Minnesota called? He could go there."

"He won't do that." Would living the rest of my life with Charlie's moodiness be worse than splitting up? Divorce, when I thought it through, sounded dreadful—doable but dreadful. "We're going to Princeton on Friday," I said. "Maybe it'll help to get away from here for a few days."

"Oh, good God, you have Reunions?" Jadey looked horrified. "Alice, all anyone *does* there is drink. You know that. Don't make any decisions while you're there."

I gestured in front of us. "Should we keep walking?"

As we headed forward on the asphalt path, Jadey said, "Wait, it's his twentieth, isn't it? God almighty, Arthur's baby brother is twenty years out of college—when did we get so old?" Her voice contained the usual dose of Jadey hyperbole, but beneath it was a note of plaintive sincerity. Then she said, "Alice, you two can't divorce, you just can't." When I didn't respond, she said, "Because I don't think I can be a Blackwell without you."

ELLA AND I were in the kitchen when Charlie arrived home from work on Tuesday, and as soon as I heard him close the front door, I nudged her. "Go give Daddy a hug." In the twenty-four hours since the Suttons' departure, Charlie's and my interactions had been guarded but not outright hostile. We hadn't spoken on the phone during the day, which was unusual but not unprecedented; though he tended to call in the midafternoon, it was possible he'd been busy with the Brewers transaction. The thought had crossed my mind to do something festive for him, to make a cake in the shape of a baseball, perhaps, but I felt too stung by what had happened the day before to go to the trouble.

Ella took off at a gallop, shouting, "Oh, dearest Father, say hello to your wonderful and beautiful daughter."

This was just as I'd hoped—that her exuberance might compensate for my lack of it. But when Charlie entered the kitchen, I knew before he spoke a word that the deal hadn't gone through. "Lloyd Reisman's a fucking weasel," he said. He loosened his tie and took a seat, and Ella promptly sat on his lap and began pulling on his earlobes; she didn't react to his swearing, which had lost its novelty years before.

Charlie brushed Ella's hands away. "He's reneging on what he told Langenbacher, pulling this crap about how much we have to pay up front. Bunch of bullshit." Charlie shook his head. "I need a drink."

"So what happens next?"

"I have half a mind to tell him he can go fuck himself. He thinks he's getting another offer like this one, he's sorely mistaken."

"Do Zeke and Cliff agree?"

Charlie sneered. "Cliff is ready to bend over and spread his cheeks for Reisman. Langenbacher says we should wait a few days, starve him out, but I don't like having this stuff unresolved. Sell us the goddamn team or don't, but don't keep us in limbo."

"But Reisman's not the one delaying things, is he? If he's saying he wants you to pay more on signing, and Zeke Langenbacher is refusing to—"

Charlie waved a hand through the air, a signal I recognized to mean *This discussion has concluded.* "You want burgers for dinner?"

"Sure. I'll light the grill?"

In a robot voice, Ella said, "I will not eat a burger, please, thank you." She was still on Charlie's lap, and she poked the end of his nose. Could she not tell what a wretchedly bad mood he was in, or was it that her father's moods were beside the point, subordinate to her own? In moments like these, I envied her.

"Cut it out," Charlie said, and Ella-as-robot replied, "Will not cut it out. Do not know what *cut it out* means. Our planet is made of cotton candy, and we wear shoes on our ears."

Charlie looked at me. "Can you do something?"

"Ella, I need your help." I extended my hand, and she slid off Charlie and took it. Even standing that close, I did not kiss or embrace him, he did not kiss or embrace me, and I felt the shadow of my conversation with Jadey pass over us like an airplane on a sunny day. To Ella, I said, "Will you set the table?"

I DROPPED ELLA off at school the next morning, and I easily could have parked and walked over to see Nancy Dwyer—the admissions and financial aid office was down the hall from Ella's classroom—but I didn't want to go in without an appointment. Back at home, Charlie had left for work (he hadn't planned to tell Arthur, John, or the rest of his family about his plans with the Brewers until the deal was final, a decision that seemed smart now). I went upstairs and took a seat at my desk in the second-floor hallway. As I dialed Nancy's number, the ropy branches of a weeping willow outside stirred in the breeze, an enlarged reflection of the papier-mâché Giving Tree on my desk, and when

Nancy answered, I said, "It's Alice Blackwell. Am I catching you at a bad time?" The next day would be the last of the school year, though I knew that people in more administrative jobs tended not to abide by the same schedule as the teachers and students.

"Not at all," Nancy said. "What can I do for you?"

"I hope this won't seem too odd, but I—we—have some family friends, and there's a girl who's just finishing sixth grade—her grandmother is very close to Charlie's family—and she's quite smart, clearly a strong student, and I'm wondering if there'd be any way of squeezing her into the seventh-grade class for this fall."

"You mean this fall as in three months from now?" Nancy laughed, but not unkindly. She and I didn't know each other well. We had met when Ella was applying to Biddle as a three-year-old, an application that was a bit ridiculous in that it mostly entailed our confirming that she was potty-trained and wouldn't bite other children, and also in that John was head of the board of trustees. Charlie joked that Ella would have had to make a bowel movement on the floor of Nancy's office not to be accepted, and even then they probably still would have taken her.

"I realize it's a long shot," I said.

Nancy said, "But not necessarily impossible."

"There's more," I said. "I suspect she'd need full financial aid, or close to it."

"Oh, jeez, Alice."

"She's African-American," I added. "I'm imagining that might help? But really, she's just incredibly bright and nice, a leader in her church's youth group, she's on student council, and she's a voracious reader. She's graduating from Harrison Elementary, and she's supposed to enter Stevens, and, Nancy, between you and me, the thought of this really promising girl—"

"No, I know," Nancy said. "It's heartbreaking." She exhaled a long breath. "Let me have a think and get back to you. What I can already see that we'll run up against is the financial-aid factor. Even though the incoming seventh grade will be big, we can usually make room for another. But the aid was allotted months ago, and it's tight as a drum."

Biddle's endowment, I knew, was five million dollars, and I understood why it would be unwise to start draining it, but it was hard to imagine that fifty-five hundred dollars—the tuition for seventh grade—would make a difference.

"We could make her a top-priority candidate for the fall of '89," Nancy was saying. "But if the chance we can come through with aid is so slim this year, I'm hesitant to set the application process in motion—I don't want to get her to campus only to turn her away."

"No, of course," I said. "I appreciate you even considering the possibility."

"Give me her name." I could hear Nancy rustling through pieces of paper.

I said, "Jessica Sutton," going slowly enough for Nancy to spell it out.

"Now, Alice, I don't mean to be forward, but the obvious person to talk to about this is your brother-in-law John. Have you spoken with him?"

"I wanted to run the idea by you first."

"I'll be honest. On the one hand, I don't feel hopeful, given the timing. On the other hand"—Nancy chuckled a little—"we at Biddle do love the Blackwell family."

BIDDLE'S LAST DAY of school officially ended at noon, at which point the children in each class were loaded onto buses and shuttled off to their respective end-of-the-year parties. For the third-graders coming to our house, I'd gotten hamburger meat—not Blackwell brand—and a sheet cake that said HAVE A GREAT SUMMER! in unnatural-looking red icing, several tubs of ice cream, and balloons in maroon and navy, which were Biddle's colors. When I went to the party store to pick up the balloons, the clerk told me I was the second person that morning to request this color combination. Back at home, I called Jadey, who was hosting the seventh-grade party for Winnie's class, and said, "Did you also get blue and maroon balloons from Celebrations?"

She laughed. "As I was placing the order, I even thought of doubling it and giving half to you."

Two other mothers, Joyce Sutter and Susan Levin, came over to help with the party, bringing chips and condiments and two-liters of pop, and we unrolled the Slip 'n Slide in the backyard. Joyce positioned the hose nearby as Susan scooped the ground beef into hamburger patties. I was a little surprised to discover that neither of them knew how to grill, so I doused the charcoal in lighter fluid and dropped in a match myself.

We all hurried to the front lawn when we heard the bus, and we found third-graders everywhere, boisterous and disheveled. One boy tore his shirt off, shouting, "I call first on the Slip 'n Slide." Many of the children were already in their bathing suits, with towels around their necks; they tossed their bags and backpacks at will on the grass. "Everyone, please go around back," I kept repeating in my loudest and most authoritative voice. "The party's in the backyard."

Ella bounded over to me. "Where's my starfish towel?"

"It's in the kitchen. Remember, Ella—"

"Mother, I know," she interrupted. "I'll be a *very gracious hostess.*"

When she'd disappeared, Susan Levin stage-whispered, "Isn't she becoming a looker? Alice, she's the spitting image of you and Charlie."

In the backyard, I'd set the grill away from the patio but in a spot where I could still observe the children on the Slip 'n Slide: the running start, the belly flop onto the wet yellow plastic—Joyce Sutter stood there continuously spraying the hose for maximum slickness—and then the long skid forward, arms first. I desperately hoped that no one would knock out their front teeth on a root or rock.

Ella ate her burger standing next to me, shivering in her wet swimsuit, and I said, "Get your towel, ladybug," but she shook her head.

"I'm going again."

"Don't get a tummyache." I scanned the yard. "Honey, where's Megan Thayer?"

Ella shrugged.

"Did she come to school today?"

Ella thought about the question, then nodded.

"Was she on the bus?"

Ella shrugged again. "After this, can I wear my Addams Family dress?"

"Not while guests are still here." I nodded across the patio, where a girl named Stephanie Woo was sitting by herself. "Why don't you see if Stephanie wants to play a game of H-O-R-S-E?"

"I'm going back on the Slip 'n Slide."

"One game," I said. Ella was obviously about to protest, and I said, "I thought you wanted to wear the dress."

I set the top on the grill, closed the valve, and approached Joyce, who was standing by the pop table; Susan had taken over hose duty. "Would you mind keeping an eye on the grill while I run inside?"

In the house, I did a quick circuit of the first floor, which was empty except for the living room, where two boys—Ryan Wichinski and Jason Goodwin—were goofing around on the piano. Seeing them there brought me pleasure: Ella had so loathed the lessons I'd signed her up for that we'd let her quit after a year, and neither Charlie nor I could play at all. "You two are talented musicians," I said as I stepped into the front hall.

Upstairs, the doors to all the rooms were open, and in the last one, the master bedroom, Megan Thayer was sitting on the floor, impassively paging through an issue of *Penthouse* magazine. Several more issues were spread out around her, and before I was close enough to see what they were—oh, that she might have been perusing *The New Yorker,* or gleaning decorating tips from *House and Garden*!—I knew.

It seemed she had not found the magazines right away. First she had tried on a few pairs of my shoes, then a few pairs of Charlie's (they were scattered across the bedroom rug), and she'd sprayed herself with my lily-of-the-valley perfume—on my bureau, the cap was off the bottle, and the smell hung in the air—and she'd also dumped a jar of change Charlie kept on a windowsill onto the bedspread and separated out the quarters.

She looked up, and I am tempted to say the look she gave me was knowing, adult even, but to claim such a thing would only be an attempt to absolve myself. She was not knowing, she was not adult. She was nine years old, looking at photographs of women opening their legs, insolently thrusting out their abundant breasts.

I strode forward, swooping in to pull the magazine from her lap—she didn't resist—and I said, "Megan, honey, that's not appropriate for you."

She simply watched me, saying nothing, slumping there with her dark hair and her broad shoulders.

"Did you go in there?" I pointed to the bottom drawer of Charlie's nightstand, which, though it had a lock, he had apparently left open. "These kinds of magazines are for grown-ups, not children," I said. "They have pictures that can be very difficult to understand." (After the party, I started to page through a magazine, feeling that it would be responsible to know exactly what Megan had seen. I got to a spread of what I suppose was meant to be a "classy" woman: In the first shot, she was emerging from a limousine, wearing a fur coat and heels and nothing else; in the next, she was standing inside some sort of ballroom with her back to the camera, her buttocks on display, looking archly over one shoulder and holding up a flute of champagne. That was enough for me—I couldn't look at any more, and I shut the magazine. It was so silly, the model was so painted and plasticky, the magazine's notion of elegance was so *in*elegant, but it also seemed deeply strange, a violation of this woman's privacy that I should know what she looked like unclothed. I couldn't imagine why anyone would expose herself in such a way unless she was in the most desperate financial circumstances.)

Megan pointed to a magazine on the floor. "That one has a naked lady bowling."

What on earth was I supposed to say? When her mother came to pick her up, I would have to explain what had happened, and the idea of confessing to Carolyn Thayer that her daughter had stumbled on my husband's porn stash was about as unappealing a scenario as I could imagine.

"If you have questions about those magazines, Megan, I suggest you talk to your mom. I wish you hadn't looked through the drawers, because those are private, and they're not yours. But I'm also sorry about what you saw. It isn't meant for a nine-year-old." I hesitated. "And not all grown-ups look at these magazines. Personally, I don't care for them."

"Then why do you have so many?"

I'd asked for it, hadn't I? Stalling, I gathered the magazines into a stack and deposited them back in the nightstand; naturally, I didn't know where the key was. From outside, we could hear the sound of the kids shouting and playing in the yard. When I turned around, she still was sitting there. "I hope you won't discuss this with Ella or your other classmates, because it would make them uncomfortable. All right?" I gazed at her—I was a big believer in the power of eye contact, and not only with children.

"This is a stupid party," she said. "You don't even have a pool."

I forced a smile. "Well, isn't it lucky that you do?"

"Only at my mom's house."

"Why don't you come downstairs with me?" I said. "I'm about to cut the cake, and I could use your help."

She stood, adjusting her shorts. So she wasn't that uncooperative after all, I thought, and then she said, "I bet Mr. Blackwell likes those magazines because the ladies in them are prettier than you."

She was not a sociopath, as Jadey had claimed, but she was obviously a girl who made herself as hard to like as possible, and thinking this allowed me to feel sympathy for her rather than irritation. The likelihood was that she'd be fine, she'd grow up and have a normal life like anyone else, but what struck me as we stood in the bedroom was that middle school and even high school would probably be very rough for Megan.

I said, "Megan, our families are old friends, and that's how I know this hasn't been an easy year for you. But you're a very good, special person, and I hope fourth grade will be better. Now, I know Ella and some other girls are playing H-O-R-S-E, if that sounds like more fun than cutting cake."

We walked into the hall, and when we reached the top of the stairs, she said, "I made a three-point basket."

"That's terrific," I said.

"It was in our driveway, and my brother doesn't believe me, but I really did."

I patted her shoulder. "I believe you."

OVER THE PHONE, Charlie said, "Put on your dancing shoes. You're talking to the new managing partner of the Milwaukee Brewers."

"Congratulations. That's amazing, honey."

"I'm thinking dinner at the club. You want to make a reservation?"

"Charlie, this is great, but would you mind if we eat at home? I need to pack for Princeton, we had a big afternoon here with Ella's class party—"

"When's the last time I suggested a night out?" It was true. Besides attending baseball games, it must have been months. "It's time to celebrate, woman," Charlie said. "It's gonna be all over the papers tomorrow, but you heard it here first."

"I assume you've told your family?"

"Just got off the phone with Dad, and I'm about to break it to Arty and John. Ooh boy, but my brothers are gonna be jealous. Should we say seven-thirty?"

"I'm thrilled, sweetheart, I really am, but is there any way I can persuade you that we should eat here? I'm still cleaning up from the party, and— Well, there's something I want to discuss with you."

"What is it?"

"I'd prefer to wait until you're home." It had turned out that Carolyn Thayer hadn't picked up Megan, that Megan had left in a carpool driven by Joyce Sutter, which meant I'd had to call Carolyn. The conversation had proceeded about as disastrously as it could have—"I'm shocked that you of all people would let this happen," she'd said, and also, "I hope you know Megan won't be returning to your house." *And that's a threat?* I'd thought, but I'd been profusely apologetic. While talking to her, I'd realized, not having previously considered it, what a tasty morsel this could be for everyone we knew in Maronee. I might or might not have been able to prevent Megan from repeating to her peers what she'd seen (I shuddered at the thought of kids taunting Ella at swim practice), but would it be naive to hope for Carolyn's discretion? Perhaps, to protect Megan, she wouldn't share the story, but I knew that the pull toward gossip was difficult to resist. When I'd hung up the phone after talking to Carolyn, I'd felt the claustrophobia of Maronee, its intermittent oppressiveness.

"Is it something serious?" Charlie was asking.

"I promise we'll discuss it tonight."

"Gimme a clue. How many syllables? Rhymes with—"

"At the party, Megan Thayer went upstairs and looked at your copies of *Penthouse.*"

I cannot say I was entirely surprised when Charlie exploded with laughter. Didn't I want to be told it was no big deal, that in feeling remorseful, I was being silly? "You think she's a bull dyke?" he said. "She *is* built like a linebacker."

"Just so you know, I had a very unpleasant conversation with Carolyn this afternoon, and I hope this doesn't turn into some rumor that gets—"

He cut me off. "What conversation with Carolyn Thayer isn't unpleasant? And darlin', if word gets out that I look at *Penthouse,* it won't be a rumor. You know what? I don't give a rat's ass. You think half the men in Maronee don't beat off to girlie magazines?"

"So if Jadey found out, or Nan—"

He laughed again. "Their husbands are the ones who introduced me to porn. Calm down, all right? And call the club and tell them we want a table for seven-thirty."

I paused and then said, "No. I'm sorry, but no—we have a big weekend ahead of us, and I don't want to be frantic catching the plane in the morning. I need a quiet night at home so I can get organized."

"Lindy, I bought a fucking baseball team today!"

"Don't swear at me, Charlie."

"Then don't be such a bitch."

I held the receiver away from my ear, as if I'd received an electric shock. How had we devolved to this point? That Charlie was crude wasn't a surprise, but that he was crude toward me—it had not always been so. I had once believed he had a sweeter and more tender way with me than with anyone else, and it made all his vulgarity almost flattering by contrast. But now I was down in the frat house basement with everyone else, expected to chug beer and laugh at off-color jokes while my back was slapped a little too hard.

I thought he might be as disturbed as I was by what he'd just said, but when he spoke again, his voice contained not remorse but annoyance—*he* was annoyed with *me.* He said, "You enjoy your quiet night at home, all right? And I'll see if I can't find some folks more in the mood to celebrate."

WHEN THE PHONE rang again, I hoped it would be Charlie, having cooled off, but it was Joe Thayer who said, "I heard from Carolyn about what happened at the party, and I—"

"Joe, I'm mortified. I can't tell you how sorry I am. I hope you and Carolyn know—"

I had interrupted him, and now he interrupted me. He said, "I knew you'd be chastising yourself, and I'm sure Carolyn gave you an earful, but Alice, please don't worry. Take it from me, Caro's filled with a lot of anger these days. Now, everyone would prefer that this hadn't happened, you as much as us, but if that's the worst Megan ever gets exposed to, she'll be a lucky girl. It just flabbergasts me what's on television these days—have you seen the program *Married with Children?*"

"I've heard of it. Joe, thank you for understanding, but I hope you know I really am sorry."

"Surely the magazines aren't *yours,* Alice." In Joe's voice was a note of humor that I realized then had been there all along.

"Well, no," I said. "No, that's not the kind of thing I read."

"Don't forget how long I've known your husband," Joe said. "I remember when he was a kid up in Halcyon doing the old trick with the Indian girl on the Land O'Lakes package." I couldn't decide if it was cute or depressing that Charlie had shown this same trick to Ella just a few months before—cutting out the Indian maiden's knees and placing them at her chest so if you lifted a flap, it appeared she was propping up her own ample breasts. Apparently, even after three decades, some things never got stale.

"The first thing I thought when Carolyn told me, I have to confess," Joe was saying, "is, If I had a wife like Alice, I wouldn't be resorting to those rags. Charlie is a man who doesn't recognize what he has, and when we hang up, you tell him I said that."

Joe's tone was cheerful, and I tried to match it. I said, "You're kind."

"Much more important for our purposes," he said, "is that after I saw you at the gas station, I booked a ticket to Princeton for Reunions. I'd been so hung up on how discouraging it would be to go alone, and then I thought, That's silly. Being among friends could be just what the doctor ordered."

"Joe, that's wonderful. Bully for you. Now do they have you wearing some sort of crazy black-and-orange kimono?"

"I waited so long to register that I'm picking up the outfit on campus, and I can only imagine what it'll be. Let's make sure to look for each other at the P-rade, can we do that? I fear you might be the only other sane person there."

"Oh, you overestimate my sanity. I've been practicing my locomotive."

"You know, I could never get Carolyn to learn the cheers," Joe said. "Do you think I ought to have seen that as a sign?"

AS SOON AS we'd hung up, the phone rang again, and when I answered, Jadey said, "Did Chas buy the Brewers?"

I hesitated. "Sort of."

"When were you planning to tell me?"

"It wasn't final until today, so I just found out myself. You know it's not only Charlie, right? It's a whole group of investors, and his contribution— Well, I'm sure it's less than you'd think." The irony was that with Jadey's inherited money, she and Arthur probably would have been in a position to make a far more significant investment. Had it been only chance, Arthur's decision not to attend the game on that Sunday, that had excluded him from the deal?

Jadey said, "Are you gonna get us the best box seats ever?"

I laughed. "The ones we already have aren't so bad."

"Call me the minute you get back from Princeton, okay? I swear it was a hundred and fifty degrees at Arthur's twentieth, but we still had so much fun. And remember, Chas'll probably tie one on this weekend, but cut him some slack, because so will everyone else."

I thought of telling her about what had happened with Megan Thayer, and maybe also about Charlie calling me a bitch, but Jadey and I would have found ourselves in a forty-five-minute conversation and I had too much to do. Besides, I didn't want Ella to overhear. "I'll call you on Monday," I said.

FOR ELLA'S DINNER, I made toast with melted mozzarella cheese—pizza toast, we called it, though there was no tomato sauce involved, and its resemblance to pizza was rather fleeting—and for myself, I reheated a leftover burger from the class party and dipped it in Dijon mustard; if Charlie was hungry when he came home, he could eat a burger, too. Because it wasn't a school night, I let Ella watch *The Cosby Show*—she adored the character of Rudy, and Theo was her second favorite—and she lay on our bed in her ridiculous black dress while I packed, walking between her room and ours. I called to her, "I assume you want to bring Bear-Bear."

"Don't pack him yet!" she exclaimed. "I need him for tonight." Bear-Bear wasn't a conventional plush toy but more of a rag doll, covered in a patchwork of reddish fabrics. My mother had made him when Ella was born, and he was the only animal who still shared her bed every night.

A Different World came on after *The Cosby Show,* and after that *Cheers,* which I had never let Ella watch, and Charlie still wasn't home. How many nights would play out like this, how many nights would I *let* play out? When the phone rang yet again, I assumed once more it would be Charlie, and once more I was surprised. "Mrs. Blackwell?" said a female voice I knew but couldn't place immediately. The voice was not only female but also young and tentative. "It's Shannon."

"Of course," I said to our babysitter. "How are you?"

"Um, I'm sorry to bother you, but—"

"Is something wrong?" I asked, and Ella looked over from the bed. The phone was cordless, and I carried it into the hall.

"The reason I'm calling is, um, I just saw Mr. Blackwell." A spiral of anxiety began to uncoil inside me; it was like a warm, thin piece of wire. I thought what Shannon would say next was *with his car rammed into a telephone pole,* and what she actually said was not much more reassuring. She said, "Um, we were at Herman's?"

"What's Herman's?"

"It's a bar."

"And you ran into Mr. Blackwell there?"

"No, I, um, I went there with him. He called I guess a couple hours ago, and he said was I free, could he pick me up because he wanted to talk to me. I thought— I don't know, I just, um, assumed it was about Ella. And when I was in the car, he said did I want to, um, have a drink."

"Where is this Herman's place?"

"It's on Wells, near campus. I guess the reason I'm calling is, um, he had a few drinks, do you know what I mean?"

The wire spiral inside me exploded; little pieces raced in my bloodstream. So the rammed-into-a-telephone-pole possibility still existed; his date with the babysitter could be in addition to, not instead of, an accident. And campus—she meant Marquette, where she was a sophomore—was four miles from where we lived. I tried to sound calm as I said, "About how many drinks did he have?"

"Um—" She paused. "Um, five, maybe? Or six? We were only there for like an hour. Sorry, Mrs. Blackwell, but I just thought you should know."

"No, I appreciate your calling. When he left the bar, did he say if he was coming home?"

"I don't know, sorry. He said he bought the Brewers, so that's cool, I guess." She laughed in a small, awkward way.

"Did he—" I could hardly speak the words, but it would be unfair to make her speak them, even more unfair to force her to keep his secret. "Did he come on to you?" I asked, and my voice sounded strangled.

Quickly, she said, "No, no, he was just chatting. He was talking about baseball and stuff. He was in a good mood, and then he dropped me off back here."

He'd had five or six drinks in an hour, then gotten behind the wheel with Ella's babysitter beside him and driven her home?

"Shannon, I can't tell you how sorry I am. Mr. Blackwell acted very inappropriately, and you handled the situation exactly right."

"I wasn't, like, scared. I mean, I know Mr. Blackwell. I just hope he gets home okay."

Even as she said it, I heard him in the driveway, the engine and then seven or eight honks in a row. He sometimes did this, an announcement of his arrival.

"I promise it won't happen again," I said.

WHEN I REPLACED the telephone receiver in its cradle, my heart was beating rapidly.

"Who was that?" Ella asked, and I said, "A friend of Mommy's you don't know." A detergent commercial flashed on-screen, and downstairs, Charlie entered the house and then he was ascending the steps, singing. He was singing "When Johnny Comes Marching Home."

"When Johnny comes marching home again
Hurrah! Hurrah!
We'll give him a hearty welcome then
Hurrah! Hurrah!
The men will cheer and the boys will shout
The ladies they will all turn out
And we'll all feel gay when Johnny comes marching home."

He knew only the first verse, so he started it again as he entered the bedroom, leaning in to kiss me—my bitchiness had apparently been forgiven—and Ella leaped off the bed and proceeded to tackle him. He lifted her and turned her upside down, and when her dress fell over her head, he tickled her bare belly. She shrieked and writhed, clawing at him, and beneath the fabric, she, too, was attempting to sing: " 'The ladies they will all turn out . . .' "

Charlie made the last line operatic, elongating it, and then he tossed Ella on the bed, and she scrambled around until her dress was righted and immediately attempted to climb back up him. When this didn't work, she raised her arms, saying, "Lift me," and Charlie said, "You're breakin' my back, Ellarina. What do you weigh now, a million pounds?" He pushed her onto the bed again, tickling her, saying, "Someone's sure been eating a lot of hot-fudge sundaes! Someone's been chowing down on extra-large pizzas!" She laughed so hard that tears streamed out of her eyes, laughed a gaspy, screaming, red-faced laughter that even as a child, I had never been seized by. Under my anger toward Charlie, I felt impressed in a distant way I'd felt many times before—it was undeniably a talent to be able to change a house from sparsely inhabited and sedate to loud and raucous just by entering it, to be your own party, your own parade. And they were so happy, my husband and my daughter, that I couldn't reprimand him; I only watched as they goofed around. Charlie said, "Hey, Ella, you want to hear what I bought today?"

"A hot-air balloon!" she shouted.

"Even better." Charlie grinned. He actually didn't seem that drunk; cheerful, yes, but perfectly coherent. "I bought the Brewers baseball team," he said. "You ready to go to lots and lots of ball games?"

"Yay!" Ella cried.

Charlie looked at me. "Nice to see that someone appreciates it."

"Can Kioko Akatsu come?" Ella asked.

"Honey, Kioko would have to take a twelve-hour plane flight to get here," I said.

Ella began clapping and then held Charlie's hands with her own, trying to make him clap. In her imitation of an adult man, she intonated, "I am the best baseball player who ever lived. You are the stupidest person in the world."

Charlie broke his hands free of her hold and pressed them against the sides of her head. "I am the champion of Milwaukee, Wisconsin," he said. "You are the suckers with nine-to-five office jobs."

WHEN I CLIMBED into bed, it was a quarter to twelve, and Charlie was lying on his back with his eyes shut. I sensed he wasn't asleep, though, and I said, "I think we should pay for Jessica Sutton to go to Biddle."

His eyes opened, then scrunched into a squint. He sounded confused rather than confrontational when he said, "What the hell are you talking about?"

"I can't stand the idea of her being at Stevens. I called Nancy Dwyer in the admissions office to see if it's too late for Jessica to start in the fall, and it sounds like they can fit her in to the seventh grade, but they've already allotted all the financial aid."

"That just reminded me." He rolled onto his side. "Guess who I saw tonight?"

"If you don't mind, I'd like to focus on the conversation we're having."

"Just guess." He grinned.

Coldly, I said, "I know who you saw, and I don't think it's funny at all."

"You have no idea!" He still was jovial, pleased with himself.

"Charlie, Shannon called me as soon as you dropped her off, and she seemed very rattled, which I can't blame her for. Do you have any idea how you must have come across? You're twice her age, you're her *employer.* I don't know that we can ever ask her to sit for us again, and even if we do, I doubt she'll say yes. I wouldn't if I were her."

"You're nuts—she had a great time. She's a solid person, real salt-of-the-earth. Did you know her dad's a plumber?"

I was sitting up, leaning against the headboard of our bed, and I folded my arms in front of me. It was hard to know how to respond, hard to explain something so blazingly obvious. I took a deep breath. "She's our *sitter,*" I said. "You're forty-two years old, and you took her to a bar."

"But it's okay for you to take Miss Ruby to a play?" He smirked, and I understood: I'd been set up. He'd orchestrated his evening for the sole purpose of asking me this question. It was the reason he had picked Shannon, of all people—not because he'd enjoy her company but to teach me a lesson. And it was the same reason that since Shannon's call, I had felt deeply troubled without feeling romantically threatened or betrayed as a wife. Charlie just wasn't a philanderer. A flirt, yes, with men as well as women, but I couldn't picture him embarking on a real affair, the subterfuge and logistical complications. Though he might mock or humiliate me, he would not be unfaithful.

I said, "You know what the difference is."

He shrugged. "Housekeeper, babysitter—seems pretty similar to me."

Our eyes met, and I wanted to slap his face or shove his chest. Instead, I pushed back the covers and stood. "What's wrong with you? Can't you see this isn't a joke? And Shannon told me how much you drank—what if you'd been pulled over? What if you'd crashed your car and gotten yourself killed, or if you'd killed someone else?"

He rolled onto his back again, this time leaning on his elbows. Slowly, calmly, he said, "Alice, I'm not real sure you're in a position to be lecturing me on driving."

It was amazing—in the last few weeks, each time I thought Charlie had said the worst thing he possibly could, a few days would pass and he'd outdo himself. Furiously, I strode around the foot of the bed, and when I'd reached his nightstand, I yanked open the lower drawer, pulled out the issues of *Penthouse,* and flung them at him one after the other. "You're awful!" I said, and I had a dim knowledge that I was shouting, and that Ella was asleep a few doors down, but I felt powerless to quiet myself. "You're a spoiled brat, and you have no regard for anyone except yourself! You think that life is so amusing, so easy, and the only reason that's true is that you're insulated by being rich. You've always had people doing the dirty work for you, getting you in to schools, offering you a job at the family company, offering you a *baseball team,* for God's sake, and now you have me to smooth over all your odd, offensive behavior. But I'm tired of it, Charlie, do you understand? I've had enough. Just because you never get in trouble, it doesn't mean you haven't done anything wrong."

There were no magazines left. Charlie was shielding his face with his hands, a gesture of self-protection, and in the space between his fingers, his expression was surprised but still not entirely serious. It seemed he was holding out hope that I was kidding. I turned on my heel, walking toward the door.

"Lindy—" he said. "Jesus, will you calm down—"

I went to the guest room and shut the door behind me, and I was shaking. How could Charlie and I possibly remain married? And then I heard footsteps in the hall, and I was glad he had come to fight it out, it seemed somehow adult of him, or at least this was what I thought until I heard a tiny voice say, "Mommy?" When I opened the door, Ella began to cry.

WE ALL WERE quiet on the flight to Newark, just as we'd been quiet at the house in the morning and quiet driving to the airport, and the quiet continued as we picked up the rental car and merged onto I-95 South. Charlie seemed to be waiting for a sign from me, and I did not provide it; I barely met his eyes. Ella, too, was unusually watchful, looking tentatively between us. In the kitchen that morning, Charlie had shown Ella the article in the *Sentinel* about the Capital Group's purchase of the Brewers, and though his demonstration was subdued, I sensed that it was as much for my benefit as for hers. I didn't read the article myself.

Waiting for our plane, I had wondered if we might run into Joe Thayer, but it appeared we were on a different flight. Instead, we saw Norm and Patty Setterlee—Norm was a Princeton graduate from the class of '48, and he lightly punched Charlie's bicep and said, "Just promise we'll never let the White Sox win again."

On the plane, with Ella in the seat between us, Charlie had said to me, "I've given it some thought, and I wouldn't be a bit surprised if Jessica Sutton is eligible for a scholarship."

Ella looked up from the book she was reading, which was *Bunnicula.* "What does *eligible* mean?" When neither Charlie nor I responded, she pulled on my sleeve and said, "Why is Jessica eligible?"

"It means qualified for," I said. To Charlie, I said, "That's what I was trying to explain. She probably would be, but they've given out all the financial aid for the upcoming school year." I tried to sound matter-of-fact—calm and civil, not overheated, as I'd been the night before. If I was seriously thinking of leaving him, there was no reason to be anything but cordial.

Charlie said, "It's an admirable thought on your part, there's no doubt about that, but this isn't the ideal time for us. I'm unloading a huge chunk of our assets for the purchase of the team, and I want to be prudent in other areas."

I said—civilly, I hoped—"Do you know what the tuition for a seventh-grader at Biddle is?"

"Five grand? Six?"

My plan had backfired. "Fifty-five hundred," I said. "But"—*calmly, matter-of-factly*—"that's a fraction of the savings you're using for the Brewers. It's almost unnoticeable, isn't it?" Why was I still arguing for this? Even if I could convince him now, if I told Charlie I was leaving, there wasn't a chance he'd go through with it.

"We're not just talking for one year, though," Charlie said, and he, too, sounded like he was trying his utmost to be conciliatory. "Let's say she enrolls for the fall, we pony up the fifty-five hundred, and then Nancy Dwyer says, 'Whoops, clerical error, turns out there isn't money for her in next year's budget, either.' At that point, we're not going to yank Jessica out, are we? If we signed on, we'd have to assume we were signing on for the next six years."

He wasn't wrong, but still, he could spare what would amount to forty thousand dollars. It wasn't nothing, but we—he—could do it. Besides, wasn't part of the incentive of buying the Brewers the likelihood that eventually he and the other investors would make a profit? My impatience swelled; really, this conversation was only an opportunity for him to show his thoughtfulness. He'd ultimately reject the possibility, but he wanted credit for having examined it from all angles.

"I guess that's true," I said, and I went back to my *New Yorker.*

In the rental car, we hardly spoke until we were near campus. From the backseat, Ella said, "I'm hungry."

I turned. "They'll have food in the tent, but snack on these." I pulled a plastic bag of pretzels from my purse.

"I don't like pretzels."

"Since when?"

"Since always."

"That comes as news to me."

Charlie, who was driving, said, "Then I guess you won't mind if I have a few." He reached toward my lap, wriggled his hand into the bag, scooped up most of the pretzels at once, and shoved them into his mouth. His cheeks bulged, and crumbs collected on his shirt as he chewed and, his mouth still full, he made the Cookie Monster noise: "Nom, nom, nom." Ella giggled, and he grinned at her in the rearview mirror. Then he swallowed and glanced at me. "Hope you weren't saving those, 'cause if you were, I can give 'em back." He jerked forward and to the right, pretending to vomit: "Bleggggggh."

"That's *disgusting,*" Ella cried—the performance clearly pleased her—and I said, "Will you watch the road?"

We parked behind the New New Quad and made our way to the twentieth-reunion tent. I had accompanied Charlie to his tenth reunion, in '78, when we'd been married under a year, and to his fifteenth, in '83, when Ella was four, and both times my reaction to the campus was similar to the one I had now: that it looked, in its perfection, more like a movie set of a college campus than a real campus; that you initially resisted its charms as you'd resist the advances of a handsome, charismatic man at a party, knowing that he probably flirted with everyone.

Its buildings were Tudor or Victorian Gothic, brick and marble and ashlar blocks, with many-paned Palladian windows, with crockets and finials and coats of ivy (I had not realized prior to my visit in '78 that the ivy in the Ivy League was literal). There were towers and turrets and arches you walked under, arches that were shaded enchantingly, that *smelled* like learning and promise. There were the grassy quads bisected diagonally by walkways, and at the front of campus there was Nassau Hall, the first structure you saw upon entering FitzRandolph Gate, built of sandstone, grand and upright and sprawling; on either side of its front steps, bronze tigers whose coats were silvery-green from age and exposure sat guard. And then there were the students, the graduating seniors and also the underclassmen who'd stayed on to work at Reunions—among them our nephew Harry and our niece Liza—who were smart and sporty and privileged. Being at Princeton felt unfair in the way our lives in Milwaukee sometimes felt unfair, unfair in our favor. I could see Ella eyeing these nineteen- and twenty-year-olds, and I knew they were creating formative ideas for her of what it was to be a college student when, in fact, a student at Princeton University was as representative of a larger type as a thoroughbred racehorse or a Stradivarius violin.

The twentieth-reunion tent was in Holder Courtyard. Like the other reunion tents constructed at various locales around campus, it was massive—perhaps thirty by forty feet of white canvas supported by three interior poles—and at its entrance were black wooden signs with the class years in orange, and orange lightbulbs over the numbers: on top 1968, and below 1966, 1967, 1969, 1970. The tent held a wooden dance floor, a raised stage for the bands that would play that night and the next, a long buffet table covered in an orange paper tablecloth (I spotted some not terribly appetizing-looking turkey sandwiches as well as some cookies that were more tempting), and many round tables surrounded by folding chairs where, already, men in orange warm-up suits and floppy white hats sat drinking beer and laughing loudly. Besides the main tent, there were smaller tents where Bud and Bud Lite were free and on tap, along with water, all served up by student bartenders—at present, by a tanned, good-natured young man wearing an orange bandanna. Charlie had graduated from Princeton before it went coed, and a certain manly feeling pervaded the setting, despite the presence of wives in black-and-orange silk scarves, black or orange blouses or wraparound skirts, wives carrying purses made of woven orange grosgrain ribbons or, in one case, a wooden handbag, like a miniature picnic basket, on one side of which was painted Nassau Hall; I also saw two separate gold tiger pins with emeralds for eyes. The children wore university paraphernalia, and face-painting occurred in a corner of the tent, kids' cheeks being adorned with black and orange stripes and whiskers.

We walked to the registration booth, where a very pretty girl who had a long blond ponytail and wore an orange T-shirt gave us our room assignment in a dorm called Campbell (I'd previously sent in the reservation form—staying in a dorm would be much more fun for Ella, I thought, than staying at the Nassau Inn). She then directed us toward the pickup line for linens, which was overseen by another girl, also pretty, who was hanging out a first-floor window of Holder, distributing sheets and towels.

Already Charlie had said hello to perhaps twenty men, some of whom I recognized, some on their own and some accompanied by their wives. There were many warm exclamations, bear hugs, backslaps, mild bawdiness: "You're shitting me, right?" said a fellow named Dennis Goshen, grabbing the bottom hem of Charlie's jacket. "You still fit into this thing?" Since we'd left Milwaukee, Charlie had had on the so-called beer jacket from the year he graduated: a cotton jacket featuring an illustration of a tiger lying passed out atop an hourglass, its feet splayed, its curving tail forming a 6 and the top and bottom of the hourglass forming the 8; a mug of beer was slipping from its paw.

In greeting, Charlie's classmates would lean in and kiss me on the cheek, and to Ella, they'd make a pseudo-outrageous proclamation about Charlie. Tapping Charlie's shoulder with a pointer finger, Toby McKee said, "Spring of '68, for nothing but a cold six-pack, this guy got me to type his entire thesis. A hundred and twenty pages, and I even corrected his lousy spelling!" Or, courtesy of Kip Spencer: "Don't even get me started on the time your old man talked me into stealing the clapper from the bell on top of Nassau Hall!"

There'd be inquiries into our lives in Milwaukee, and eventually, I realized Charlie was prompting them, asking his classmates if they were still practicing medicine in Stamford, or still at that ad agency in New York. When they turned the question around, Charlie would say, "Matter of fact, I've got a new gig—just went in with a group of fellows to buy the Milwaukee Brewers."

"The baseball team?" a classmate might say in response. "Not bad!" Or "Holy smokes!" Or, in the case of a guy named Richard Gibbons, "Oh, man, I'm so fucking jealous!" Then Richard glanced at Ella and mouthed to me, *Sorry.* The more enthusiastic the reaction Charlie had elicited, the more modest he'd become. He'd say, "I was lucky to be in the right place at the right time" or "If you look at the ups and downs of our last few seasons, you know I've got my work cut out for me." Only one person called him on his false modesty. Theo Sheldon said, "Come off it, Blackwell, you'll be in pig heaven! When you're out there playing catch with Paul Molitor, you think of schmucks like me filing briefs, and that ought to alleviate your pain." I wondered again if Charlie had arranged the baseball deal in time to crow about it here, but it was hard to imagine he'd had that much control; it truly seemed, as events in Charlie's life often did, to be serendipitous.

We went to drop our suitcases in the dorm room, which was actually a suite and perfectly serviceable except that the bathroom was a floor below us, and though we'd been gone only a few minutes, the tent seemed twice as crowded on our return. I helped Ella get food. Kip Spencer and his wife, Abigail, had a daughter Ella's age named Becky, and the girls soon paired off and were racing around. They reappeared with their faces painted, then they appeared again with the paint smudged, and by that point they were part of a gang of ten or more children, and Ella seemed to be having a ball.

I was surprised to be able to relax, settling in to the afternoon. All around me the men in their ridiculous orange-and-black garb seemed to be getting drunk and jolly, Charlie himself was in high spirits, and the other wives and I would exchange indulgent smiles. By four P.M., the idea of ending my marriage seemed less a definite plan than a fragment of a dream. The tension between Charlie and me had dissolved, and though I was on the periphery of most conversations, this had never been a dynamic I minded; I'd always liked to be around loud, laughing, friendly people. When the men broke into a locomotive, or when they referred to Princeton as "the best damn place of all," which was a line from a school song, they seemed terribly sweet to me. And Charlie was solicitous in a way he rarely was anymore, asking whenever he went to get a refill of beer if I'd like one, too. (Everybody drank out of plastic cups whose tiger icon was different, depending on which tent you were in.)

Dinner was a pleasantly mediocre buffet in the tent, chicken and scalloped potatoes and salad and brownies, and then a Motown band got started, and they were terrific: seven black men in matching pale blue suits and one black woman in a white tank dress who sang "I Heard It Through the Grapevine" and "(Love Is Like a) Heat Wave" and "Ain't Too Proud to Beg."

The kids were the first to start dancing, Ella and Becky and the other children, mostly arhythmically but quite happily, punching the air and jumping up and down, and soon the adults had joined in. Charlie was a wonderful dancer; I hadn't discovered this until a few months into our marriage, when we attended his brother John's thirty-fifth birthday party, a black-tie gathering at the country club. It wasn't that Charlie was necessarily the best dancer in any setting, though he was good. But what made him so much fun to watch and to dance with was how uninhibited he was, how thoroughly he seemed to enjoy himself, how he was both confident and extremely silly at the same time. For "Ain't No Mountain High Enough," he shimmied several feet away, turned his back to me, bumped out his rear end, looked grinningly over his shoulder, and hopped backward, one hop for each line—"Ain't no mountain high enough / Ain't no valley low enough / Ain't no river wide enough." He soon was sweating profusely, and then he was dancing with Pam Sheldon, the wife of his classmate Theo, and I was dancing with Theo, and then Charlie was dancing with Theo, and Pam and I were standing there laughing. Around his peers, it was striking to me how fit and young-looking Charlie still was—many of them were bald or heavy or just seemed worn out beneath their cheer, but Charlie was as handsome as when we'd married. Really, his appearance had hardly changed.

Around nine-thirty, to Ella's delight, our nephew Harry and our niece Liza showed up, Harry in the beer jacket for that year's graduating class, and they both were festive and, I suspected, inebriated, Harry more so than Liza. Liza and Charlie danced while Harry and Ella danced, then Harry danced with me—like his uncle, Harry was deft on his feet (I'd have to tell Ed and Ginger that forcing him to attend dancing school had paid off), and he was flirtatious in the meaningless, endearing way that rich, handsome, self-assured twenty-two-year-old men can be. He would be spending the summer in Alaska, the bulk of it working at a hatchery (this was something else I hadn't been exposed to before marrying into the Blackwell family, the inclination to travel great distances and invest substantial amounts of money in order to do strenuous and possibly grubby work that subsequently would make for excellent storytelling: my nephew Tommy, Harry's brother, had spent a summer in high school in a program that built roads in Greece; Liza had volunteered at an orphanage in Honduras; and several of them had participated in Outward Bound or NOLS trips). After the hatchery, Harry would be met by his two brothers and Ed, and the four of them would go on a two-week chartered fishing expedition in northern Alaska; on their return, Harry would start a job as a researcher at Merrill Lynch in Manhattan. Given all this, of course the world looked to my nephew like a joyful and inviting place, of course he was drunk and happy on the eve of his Princeton graduation.

After Harry and Liza moved on, I was surprised to look at my watch and see that it was after eleven. I scanned the tent for Ella—she and a little boy were doing their nine-year-olds' approximation of a tango—and I told Charlie I was taking her to the dorm to go to bed. I felt a little negligent that it was as late as it was and tried to absolve myself by recalling that in Wisconsin, it would be an hour earlier.

"After you get her settled, come back out." Charlie almost had to yell to make himself audible above the music. "It's completely safe, you know that, right?"

I shook my head. "I'd rather not leave her alone, but stay out and enjoy yourself." I was sure this was what he'd do anyway, without my encouragement, but I wanted to be generous toward him for a change, to give his pleasure my blessings. I'd heard some of the men talking about heading over to the eating clubs—Charlie had belonged to one called Cottage—and I was just as happy to miss this portion of the evening. The eating clubs seemed to me like nothing more than pretentious fraternities (as the place where upperclassmen ate their meals and held parties, they occupied a row of mansions on Prospect Avenue, and to join, a student "bickered," a process that appeared negligibly different from rushing), but the clubs inspired such passionate feelings that surely I was missing something. As an undergraduate, Charlie had served as Cottage's bicker chair, and all this time later, the only bill in which he took real interest—he'd make a point of asking if I'd paid it—was the club's annual dues, then eighty-five dollars. Cottage had started admitting women in 1986, following a lawsuit filed by a female student, and while Charlie was disdainful of this woman's "strident feminism," he didn't seem to mind that Cottage had gone coed.

Standing beneath the twentieth-reunion tent while the band played "Dancing in the Street," Charlie said, "You sure you don't want to come back out? It'll be more fun with you around."

It was such a kind, plain statement that I felt my breath catch. I did not see myself as fun anymore, certainly not from Charlie's perspective. I stepped forward and kissed him on the lips. "I wish I could. Don't forget to pace yourself—there'll be a lot going on tomorrow, too."

He gave a salute. "Bring Ella over here to say good night."

Eventually, after I'd pried Ella from her new friends and she'd kissed

Charlie on the cheek, we walked back to the dorm. As we went down a flight of stairs and under an arch, she said dreamily, "I *love* Princeton."

THE P-RADE—the heart and soul of Reunions—started around two on Saturday. Thousands of us had lined up by class year on Cannon Green, and as we waited, there was much rowdiness, much drinking of beer (Princetonians are the only people I've ever encountered who can drink as much as Wisconsonians and still remain agreeable and upright), and classmates were constantly running into one another and exchanging excited greetings. It was a sunny day in the high seventies—the weather was always of great interest beforehand, whether it would be brutally hot or torrentially rainy—and by the time the parade finally started, the energy of the crowd was uncontainable. Leading the parade were members of the class of '63, who were celebrating their twenty-fifth reunion—the year considered to be a pinnacle of sorts, though really, I thought, these men were only forty-seven! I looked for Joe Thayer; amid the chaos of bodies and noise and sunshine, I didn't find him. Next came the oldest graduate who'd made it back—in this case, a gentleman named Edwin Parrish, from the class of 1910—who had the honor of holding a particular silver cane; Mr. Parrish rode in a golf cart driven by a current student, and as he passed, people roared their approval. After the oldest graduate, the order continued chronologically, oldest first, and each class was announced with a class-year banner that ran between poles, the fabric black with orange trim, the numbers orange. For the older classes, known as the Old Guard, the banners were carried by undergraduates or alumni's grandchildren; for the subsequent classes, they'd be carried by the alumni themselves. Many of the Old Guard were ferried by golf cart, and in some cases, it was not the men but their widows who rode, a sight that I was scarcely the only one to find poignant; I noticed people all around me tearing up. When a member of an older class was walking—a remarkably spry fellow from the class of 1916, who had to be well into his nineties, was practically tap-dancing—the crowd would cheer at a deafening level. In every direction, as far as you looked, there were orange warm-up suits, orange and black blazers and pants and T-shirts, baseball caps, straw boaters encircled by orange and black ribbons, children and adults alike wearing furry tiger tails. Some graduates drove antique cars that they honked jovially, and in celebration of themselves, the major reunion classes had arranged for special performers—brass bands from local high schools, a belly dancer, even a fire-eater—who preceded the class. Charlie leaned over, grinning, and said, "Rich people are bizarre, huh?" This was, of course, my drunken comment to him at Halcyon, and as he squeezed my hand then dropped it to applaud for the class of 1943, I thought that at least in one way, I had not been wrong when I agreed to marry him: He had made my life more colorful.

We waited, and waited some more, and then the class of '65 passed by, the class of '66, the class of '67—they were to our left, they'd been beside us all this time—and at last it was our turn. We fell into step behind them, and Ella got Charlie to start up a '68 locomotive: *Hip! Hip! Rah! Rah! Rah!* . . . All the classes younger than Charlie's cheered as we walked by, and we waved as if we were dignitaries. The parade route ended on the baseball field, where we stayed—Ella insisted, so that we could see Harry—until the last class, the graduating seniors, sprinted out and were officially decreed by the university president to be Princeton alumni. "When I go to Princeton, I want to live above Blair Arch," Ella said.

"Then you better get a good draw time," Charlie replied.

"And you better work hard in school," I added.

BECAUSE I TRIED to be an organized person, I had always appreciated organization in others, and I must say this: Princeton reunions were spectacularly well executed. All those tents and temporary fences and folding chairs and tables, the beer kegs and matching outfits, the academic talks and the a cappella groups performing around campus at thoughtfully scheduled intervals! The planning that went into the weekend boggled the mind, yet it all proceeded beautifully, seamlessly. For kids, two movies were being screened that night in McCosh 10, *Back to the Future* and *Splash,* while a Beatles cover band played in our tent for the adults. As we ate dinner—tonight it was barbecued pork, potato salad, corn on the cob, and corn bread—Charlie was both fidgety and extremely affectionate. I ended up in a long conversation with a classmate's wife, Mimi Bryce, whom I'd first met at the tenth reunion and who was a fourth-grade teacher at a private girls' school outside Boston; we spoke for probably forty minutes, during which Charlie approached me three separate times, saying, "Come on and shake your groove thing, Lindy" or "Charlie Blackwell waits for no one, and he won't wait for you." Finally, he just tugged at my hand, and I apologized to Mimi as I let him pull me toward the dance floor.

"I was enjoying talking to her," I said.

"They're playing 'Can't Buy Me Love,' and you'd rather discuss a fourth-grade curriculum?"

The band was actually near the end of "Can't Buy Me Love," and they segued into "Twist and Shout," which Charlie knew all the words to and animatedly serenaded me with, pointing at me, contorting his face into soulful expressions: "You know you twist so fine (twist so fine) / Come on and twist a little closer, now (twist a little closer)—" He beckoned with one finger, and when I stepped forward, he twirled me. For the "shake it up" part at the end, he raised his arms above his head and really shook them—he wore the orange warm-up pants and a white polo shirt, and there were large sweat spots beneath his arms. At the conclusion to the song, he pulled me to him, grabbing my rear end, kissing me hard on the mouth, and he said, "You want to go fuck in the dorm really fast before Ella gets back?"

"Charlie."

He grinned. "Why not? Won't take long, I promise." And then he reached up and squeezed my left breast. "It'll be fun." I took a step backward. The dance floor was crowded, the whole tent was crowded, and no one seemed to be paying attention to us, but still, I was stunned.

"Charlie, we're not animals," I said. "You can't do that in public."

"Maybe you're not an animal. I'm a tiger, baby." His face was flushed.

"I hope you won't drink anymore."

He smirked. "Why don't you go talk to Mimi again? I hear she has some fascinating insights on Dr. Seuss."

I took a deep breath. "I'll try not to ruin tonight for you if you try not to ruin it for me."

He still was smirking. "Lindy, you couldn't ruin it for me if you wanted to."

At that moment, a classmate of his named Wilbur Morgan approached us and jabbed his thumb toward Charlie—he seemed unaware we'd been arguing—and said to me, "Word on the street is that this guy just bought a major league baseball team." He turned to Charlie. "All right, Mr. Hotshot, true or false?"

"Morgy, I'm hoping you'll play shortstop." Charlie patted Wilbur's gut. "You need to start training, buddy."

"No fair!" Wilbur shook his head, smiling widely. "It is *no fair* that you ended up with the best freakin' job in the world. I'd give my left nut!"

"Funny, I never thought you had a left nut," Charlie said, and Wilbur said to me, "Has he changed one iota?"

I smiled wanly. "If you'll excuse me." I headed toward the water tent and had just accepted a plastic cup when I turned and found Holly Goshen, Dennis Goshen's wife, beside me. "You've got to stay hydrated on a night like this, huh?" she said. Dennis and Holly lived in New York, where Dennis was a trader on Wall Street and Holly was an aerobics instructor. We had been at their wedding in the early eighties, at the Rainbow Room, and Holly was, as one might predict of an aerobics instructor, thin and attractive, with wavy blond hair. We stood there sipping, observing the activity. To make conversation, I said, "I assume you two are headed back to New York in the morning?"

She nodded. "This is awful to say, but Alice, I'm so glad I'm not the only one here whose husband still does blow. You're such a nice, normal person that seeing you is really reassuring."

"Whose husband still what?" I repeated.

"I didn't mean it like—" She laughed nervously, and I could tell she thought she'd offended me. "Boys will be boys, that's all I meant. Some of the guys Dennis works with, they're freebasing every night of the week, and he can't do that anymore, thank God. He's forty-two!"

"Are you telling me that Dennis and Charlie used cocaine tonight?"

"I thought—" She seemed increasingly uneasy. "I saw them headed off together before dinner, so I just assumed— I've put my foot in my mouth, haven't I? Can we forget I said anything?"

I felt a strong desire to say, *Charlie wouldn't use cocaine,* but as soon as I thought it, I also thought of his odd behavior this evening, his physical forwardness.

And it wasn't Holly's fault, she had nothing to do with it, really, but I'd been drained of the energy necessary to smooth over this moment. I set down my plastic cup. "I have to go."

THOUGH I NEARLY collided with Joe Thayer outside the tent, I didn't recognize that it was him for several seconds, until after he'd said, "You're just the person I was looking for. I caught sight of you in the P-rade, but I was being carried along with the current and I didn't— Are you all right? Alice, my goodness, what's wrong?"

I'd been trying very hard not to cry, but I didn't succeed. It was the sympathetic expression on Joe's face, the kindness of his features. People were steadily entering and leaving the tent, and I probably knew many of them. Though a few tears had escaped already, I pressed my lips together and shook my head.

"How about humoring me by making me think I can help in some way?" Joe said. "Shall we stroll for a bit?"

I nodded, still unable to speak, and he set one hand lightly at my elbow, guiding me down the stairs and through the arch that led to the dorm where we were staying, except that in front of Campbell, we veered left, heading toward Nassau Hall. The campus was dark, the night air warm; it smelled like early summer. A good ten minutes must have elapsed before either of us spoke. Early on in the silence, I felt that I needed to pull myself together and say something, but I realized at some point that Joe wasn't waiting for an explanation—it was more that he was offering his presence, his company. I had stopped crying well before we reached Firestone Library when I said, "Have you ever tried cocaine?"

"I beg your pardon?"

"I realize it's trendy in certain places, but I just— I never thought—" Back in our twenties, Dena had told me that she'd done it a few times during her years as a flight attendant, but she and possibly her sister Marjorie were the only people I knew who had.

"Would it be forward of me to ask why this has come up?" Joe said.

We were between the library and the chapel, an imposing Gothic cathedral that looked a bit haunted in the dark, and I pointed at its steps. "Should we sit?" We took seats side by side. The moon was half full, the stars tiny and far above us. I said, "I think Charlie may be high right now, that he may have— You say *snorted,* that's the terminology, isn't it?"

"I believe it depends on the form of cocaine, but sure." If Joe was startled by what I'd told him, he didn't show it.

"You don't think he's in danger healthwise?" I said. "He isn't about to have a heart attack, I shouldn't call a doctor?"

"I'm out of my depth here, too, I admit." Joe crossed his ankles. "But as far as I know, the real threat is overdosing, and if he's upright and able to carry on a conversation—"

"He makes me feel so silly," I said, and Joe did not immediately respond.

After a while, he said, "I don't think you're silly for being concerned. Is this a habit with him?"

"I wish I knew. I found out about tonight a few minutes ago, and he wasn't the one who told me. I don't think—forgive me, Joe, for saying this to you of all people—but I don't think I can stay with him. Every day, every few hours, I go back and forth, as if everything he says or does is proof that I should either stick it out or leave. It's starting to make me fear for my sanity."

Again, Joe was quiet for over a minute before saying, "You never know the nature of another couple's marriage, do you? I've always thought the two of you seem wonderfully complementary. But I'll tell you what else—that weekend you and Charlie got engaged, we were stunned. My extended family, I mean. We heard about it, and we were only just getting to know you, but we thought, That sweet, sweet girl is marrying *Charlie?*"

Simultaneously, I felt my lips curve up and my eyes flood. With the back of my hand, I wiped my nose. "The engagement didn't happen in

Halcyon," I said. "We were already engaged, but we didn't tell people right away."

"I met you down on their dock, remember that?" Joe said. "I came back from fishing with Ed and John, we puttered up, and you were standing there in a yellow dress"—(he was right, that yellow knit dress with the collar, I had forgotten all about it)—"and I thought—I suppose I'm only admitting this because it was so long ago and because I've consumed more than my share of Bud Light tonight—but I thought, Who's that gorgeous girl? I was dumbstruck. Then Charlie took your hand."

The truth was that I didn't remember meeting Joe. I remembered meeting Charlie's parents that day, and Jadey later that night, when I'd foolishly allowed myself to get drunk, and I remembered knowing Joe later on, talking politely to him, when he seemed handsome and reserved and maybe the slightest bit dull, when it never occurred to me that I registered with him more than anyone else's wife. *Did* I register with him more than other wives?

"That was an overwhelming visit," I said. "God bless the Blackwells, but—I'm sure you understand. That's what's so nice about talking to you, Joe, that I don't have to explain."

Joe shook his head. "Look at us," he said. "Do you think we should find some undergraduates and warn them to be careful whom they pick to spend their lives with?"

"As if they'd listen."

We sat there on the steps in companionable silence; we could hear the distant songs of a few bands playing at once in different tents. "I suppose I've always nursed a small crush on you," Joe said. "In light of both our circumstances, it's made me stay away. Not literally, I don't mean, but to keep myself at a distance." When I didn't reply, he said, "I hope I'm not making you uncomfortable."

"Joe, I'm honored." I patted his knee in what I meant to be a friendly way, though as soon as I'd done it, I realized it might have seemed flirtatious, and in fact it may have *been* flirtatious. I had lost my bearings—I had started losing them before, at some indeterminate point, and now they were gone entirely.

"I won't try to advise you on what's happening with Charlie," Joe said. "That's none of my business. But if there was ever a chance, and I know, with Halcyon and my family and his family, I know we'd be opening a can of worms, I'm well aware, but if you ever thought the two of us—"

I cut him off by kissing him. I leaned forward abruptly—gracelessly, I suspect—and I pressed my mouth against his, and we kissed hungrily, and at first it was all-consuming, it was forbidden and wrong and exciting, but very little time had passed before I became aware of an unflattering comparison between the way he kissed and the way Charlie did. Joe was not as adept. It had been so long since I'd kissed anyone besides my husband that I'd forgotten there could be variations on it, or skill involved, but Joe—I felt cruel noticing this—drooled a bit, there was an excess of saliva that accompanied his tongue and lips. I pulled away and quickly stood. I brought a hand to my chest. "Joe, I— I don't— I need to find Ella."

He stared at me with passion.

At a loss as to what else to do or say, I made a gesture that was not unlike curtsying. "Forgive me," I said, and I hurried away. I did not even have the excuse of attributing my behavior to alcohol: Joe, by his own admission, had been tipsy, but I'd been perfectly sober.

BACK IN THE dorm, once Ella was asleep, I packed—our flight out of Newark was at one on Sunday—and the questions that sprang up in my head felt clichéd and overwrought, as if perhaps I'd heard them asked by a naive wife in a movie, or a public service announcement on TV about drug addiction: How many times before and how often and why? Maybe when I said *why* to Charlie, my voice would quaver, and that would reveal just how betrayed I felt.

But no—I did not want to be that wife, did not want to have that conversation. It was beneath me; it would give his worst behavior an attention it didn't deserve.

He returned to the dorm earlier than I expected, before midnight. More matter-of-factly than angrily, he said, "I didn't know where you'd gone," and I brought my finger to my lips, indicating Ella, now asleep. He lowered his voice. "Kind of a crappy band, if you ask me. Just the idea of a cover band is pathetic when you think about it, living off someone else's glory."

Did he have any idea? He had no idea. What other conclusion was there to draw? I was folding a pair of his pants, and I set them in our suitcase.

He stepped close to me, half whispering. "You're not pissed about before, are you?" So he had some idea, but such a narrow, watered-down one—it was close enough to having no idea. "You know how being around these goons gets me riled up." He leaned in to kiss me. "Brings out my inner eighteen-year-old." He grinned, and I felt both astonishment—how could our experiences of our relationship be so grossly different?—and also a relief at having chosen not to confront him. It was the right choice.

He kissed me some more, my cheeks and neck, he set his hands on my hips, and I realized he wanted us to have sex. I pointed to the wall and said, "Ella's on the other side."

"We can keep it down. Well, *you* might not be able to." He pulled the peach-colored blouse I was wearing (a nod to orange without being the real, aggressive thing) out of my white pants and stuck his hands beneath it. He reached around and unfastened my bra.

I acquiesced. It was easier than talking, it would be a balm to the discord of the weekend. The mattress springs were squeaky, which I found distracting, but I was distracted anyway. Lying on top of me, pumping in and out, Charlie gazed down and said, "You look beautiful, Lindy." He smelled of sweat and beer and some essential Charlieness, the smell of himself, that I was very accustomed to.

I thought with shame of kissing Joe Thayer. Already, I believed that I had kissed him less out of attraction than pity—I'd meant the kiss as a consolation prize, a way to spare him the embarrassment of having confessed to feelings that were one-sided. *Under different circumstances,* I'd meant to imply, and even if the implication was a lie, it seemed a decorous one, an extreme version of being a polite and considerate person. But perhaps this was only a convenient story. Perhaps I'd kissed him for more selfish reasons—simply because I wanted to—and when the experience was not as pleasurable as I'd anticipated, I'd changed my mind.

Charlie's breathing thickened, his mouth was next to my ear so I couldn't see his face, and then his movements slowed, and he moaned softly. He collapsed against me, and I held him. "You want me to . . . ?" he murmured (he always offered when I didn't come during penetration, he meant with his hand), and silently, I shook my head. I felt at once as if I were protecting him from and steeling myself for the destruction he didn't yet know that I would cause.

I WOULD GO to Riley, I had decided, and I would take Ella with me, but there was one errand I needed to run before leaving Milwaukee, and it entailed stopping by my favorite bookstore in the world, which was called Thea's. The owner, Thea Dengler, was about my age, a heavyset woman who paired loose black pants and sweaters with gauzy scarves or chunky turquoise necklaces, and her store was located in Mequon, two floors, with such tall shelves that even though it wasn't large, you always felt like you could browse in private. Plus, there was an excellent selection, Thea read constantly (there was rarely a book I picked up that wasn't on her radar), and if you wanted something she didn't have, she'd enthusiastically order it, as curious herself for it to arrive as you were. She also sold periodicals, but none of that clutter that seems mandatory in bookstores today: mugs and picture frames and greeting cards, magnets, calendars, fancy chocolates.

I'd planned to buy three books for Jessica Sutton, but as I stood in the young-adult section, stacking them in the crook of my arm, I decided five would be acceptable, and soon I was holding more than a dozen, balanced so precariously that I had to steady them with my chin. I propped them one by one, face out, on the shelves so I could more easily cull: *To Kill a Mockingbird* (that was definite, no question); *Deenie* (Jessica was twelve—how could I not give her a Judy Blume book, and this was less controversial than some of the others); *Roll of Thunder, Hear My Cry; A Wrinkle in Time; Anastasia Krupnik,* or else Lois Lowry's *Autumn Street,* which I also thought was quite wonderful; *The Westing*

Game (I imagined she'd like this, since she liked Agatha Christie); *The Outsiders; I Know Why the Caged Bird Sings; Homecoming;* and then I'd grabbed the two others from the Tillerman series, *Dicey's Song* and *A Solitary Blue; The Diary of Anne Frank;* and last, *Locked in Time* (I'd read Lois Duncan's older novels during my librarian days, but this new one looked intriguing). Besides the fact that this was nine more books than I'd intended to purchase, there was already one—Daphne du Maurier's *Rebecca*—that I knew I wanted to get her from the grown-up section, and I'd also considered *Pride and Prejudice.* I stood there trying to decide, and I eventually set back the Cynthia Voigt books; I also decided to forgo *Pride and Prejudice* and *Autumn Street* (maybe those could be saved for Christmas?). Was *Roll of Thunder, Hear My Cry* too young for Jessica? But it was so good! Then I realized I'd neglected to pull *A Tree Grows in Brooklyn* off the shelf, which was a must. I ended up carrying twelve books to the cash register. Eyeing them, Thea said, "That's some ambitious summer reading for Ella."

"No, no, they're for a family friend who's going into seventh grade."

"You want them wrapped?"

I declined, and she stacked the books in a large brown paper bag with string handles. When I left the store, I sat in the parking lot peeling off the price stickers—a useless act, given that the price was also printed on the back of the books, but decorum demanded it—and then I drove to the Suttons' house. It was Jessica who answered the door, holding Antoine. She stepped aside to let me in, and I said, "No, I'm just dropping something off. Jessica, as a former librarian, I feel compelled to introduce you to some writers other than V. C. Andrews. These are for you, but I promise you don't have to write any book reports." I extended the bag, holding it open to show her, and because Antoine was in her arms, I set it inside the house on the rug.

"Who is it, Jessie?" I heard Yvonne call, and Jessica called back, "It's Ella's mom." To me, she said, "Those are all for me?"

"We're so proud of how well you're doing in school. Now, I'd love to talk about any of these books with you, but again, you're not obligated to read them. Just if you want to, I think they might be fun."

"That's real nice." Jessica appeared confused but curious. "You want to come in?"

"I've got to run errands." I reached out my hand and rubbed Antoine's calf, which was bare; he had on a yellow terry-cloth onesie. "Say hi to your mom and grandma for me."

Walking back down the concrete steps to the car, I noticed two men sitting on the porch of the house across the street—young men, closer to Jessica's age than mine. One wore a black mesh tank shirt and the other, who had cornrows, wore no shirt at all. They watched me, and I nodded once without saying anything as I walked toward my car, my shiny suburban white-lady Volvo. As I drove away, the automatic locks clicked on, and I felt an uncomfortable relief.

I WAITED THAT night in the den while Charlie tucked Ella in, holding on my lap a copy of *The Economist* that I was too preoccupied to read. When he reentered the room, he said, "Do we have any ice cream? I've got a sweet tooth tonight."

"There's some caramel left," I said, but as he turned to go into the kitchen, I said, "Wait. Sit down." My voice had sounded more serious than I'd meant it to, except that this *was* serious—possibly the most serious conversation we'd ever had. He looked expectant as he perched on an arm of the couch.

My heart pounded. When had I last felt nervous with Charlie? Not about what he'd do, how he might transgress in front of other people and I might clean up after him, but nervous about how he'd react to me. "I want us to separate," I said.

"You what?"

Had he not heard or not understood? "A trial separation," I said. "Not a legal one—well, not yet."

"You want a divorce? Are you fucking kidding me?" He looked disbelieving, but this was the thing about Charlie—he also looked the tiniest, tiniest bit amused. I don't think he was, but he had such a mischievous face and such a tendency to revert to humor, whether or not it was appropriate, that I couldn't be sure.

"That's not what I said. I want us to live apart. I love you, Charlie, and I hope you'll always know that, but I can't live like this anymore."

There was a certain disintegration occurring in my chest, an increasing shakiness.

"I thought we were having a perfectly nice night."

"It's not— Tonight was fine." I had the strange impulse to stand and go to where he sat, to comfort him. Surely this would have been unwise? "I know you used cocaine in Princeton with Dennis Goshen," I said. "Holly told me. Or taking Shannon to a bar last week— I just— There are decisions you make that I can't live with. I can't be responsible for you, and if I'm your wife, I feel responsible. I'm terrified that you're going to hurt someone, either yourself or someone else, and it's going to destroy our lives. I know what that's like, and it's awful, and the worst part is that you'll make a mistake that can be prevented. That sickens me—the thought of you drinking a bunch of whiskey and getting in your car, it literally makes me nauseated, Charlie. I don't want to be around it, and I don't want Ella to, either."

"So you're not just leaving me, you're taking our daughter with you?"

"I thought initially—" Was he going to fight me on this? "I'm going to my mother's tomorrow," I said. "I thought Ella could come. It seems reasonable with your work schedule."

"I'm about to have a lot more flexibility."

I swallowed. "If I take Ella to my mother's, it can be like a trip, a vacation. We won't have to tell her anything yet. I don't want to unnecessarily disrupt her life or make her feel as if things are unstable. But you and I need to spend some time apart. Isn't that obvious to you, too?"

Charlie was silent, and then he said, "You ever hear of a warning signal?" I could sense his anger gathering force. "That's how it works in school, right? Teacher puts your name on the board, you get a check mark by it, *then* you get sent out in the hall. You don't get booted to the principal's office the first time you goof off."

"But Charlie—" Tears filled my eyes, and they were tears not of sadness but of frustration. I blinked them back. "That's just it," I said. "That's my point. I'm *not* your teacher. And I *have* told you that I don't like when you don't show up after you've said you'll be there, I don't like when you drink so much, I don't like when you insult me. If you've listened at all, I don't see how this could be a surprise."

"Sure, we fight, but you never mentioned separating."

"I'm mentioning it now."

"Before the other night, I hadn't done coke in years," Charlie said. "Goshen offered me some, I did a couple lines, and honestly, Lindy, if you weren't so freaking uptight, you might know that's really nothing. It wasn't going to kill me, it wasn't going to hurt anyone else, and I'm not planning to use it again anytime soon, all right?"

"It's not just the cocaine. It's everything. When Megan Thayer found those magazines, I didn't have the sense that you cared at all."

"So now it's my fault if I don't worry as much as you about what other people think?"

"It's no secret that we have different dispositions, Charlie." I wasn't yelling—though it was tempting to give in to rancor, no good would come of it. "For a long time, I've gotten a kick out of that. You have a lot of wonderful qualities, obviously, and if I didn't think that, I wouldn't have married you in the first place. But the whole rascally, naughty Charlie persona—I can't stand it anymore. It's not cute. We're forty-two years old, and I don't want to have to beg you to wear a tie."

"You think I don't respect you, is that what this is?"

I shrugged.

"There's nobody I respect more than you." Then he said, "I love you, Lindy," and his voice cracked.

Again, it was difficult not to stand and comfort him. I said, "I love you, too."

"I know I've tested your patience, but for Christ's sake, we're a family. You think Ella'll do better coming from a broken home—"

I cut him off. "A trial separation, Charlie, that's all I want. I want to see what it's like to not—"

"Who've you told about this? Have you told Jadey?"

I hesitated. "Not really."

"You want us to go to a shrink, we can go to a shrink. I'll get a referral."

"I appreciate the offer, and that's something we can consider in the future," I said. "For now, what I want is space."

"Where does that leave me?"

"I don't know," I said. "But I've become very unhappy." Then I began to cry—is it embarrassing to admit that I was moved by the simple truth of my own statement? My sobs were gulpy and undignified.

A minute passed, and when I looked at him again, he was watching me with an expression so strange that at first I had difficulty identifying it. Then I realized: He was frightened.

He said, "Fine, take Ella, but you have to promise to come back. I'll fix what's wrong, Lindy. I know you don't believe me right now, but I will."

I wiped my eyes, nodding without speaking. About this, he was right—I did not believe him.

ON OUR SECOND day in Riley, Lars drove Ella and me out to Fassbinder's, where ten or twelve years earlier, the factory founder's house had been converted into a cheese museum. The house was situated on the opposite side of the parking lot from the factory proper, and visitors to the museum could look through large windows and watch employees tending to vats of milk or cheese curd. You also got to sample the curds, still warm, and in the gift shop, you could buy various types of cheese as well as jellies, sausages, crackers, and little white porcelain thimbles with the Fassbinder's logo on them. I was examining a thimble when Ella nudged up against me and whispered, "This is boring." I shot her a look.

"I'll bet Dorothy will enjoy this with her morning toast," Lars said, and he held up a jar of gooseberry jam.

Beside me, Ella whined, "You said we could go swimming." I had indeed made this promise the day before, as we were driving into town, but at breakfast, when Lars proposed a visit to the cheese factory, I hadn't had the heart to turn him down.

I'd called my mother on Tuesday, prior to my conversation with Charlie, to ask if we might come stay with them for a couple weeks, though I hadn't told her the real reason. I'd said, "Charlie has a lot going on with the baseball team, and I think Ella is finally old enough to appreciate Riley's charms."

On Wednesday, we drove out around noon. I'd announced the plan to Ella only a few hours before, allowing enough time for her to pack and then for me to cajole her into repacking more realistically—two swimsuits instead of four, seven pairs of socks instead of one, no black dress. She seemed not particularly surprised by the abrupt announcement that we were leaving town, and even excited at the prospect. She said, "Will Papa Lars make me an egg with a top hat?" This was a breakfast that involved Lars placing a glass upside down on a slice of bread in order to cut out a perfect circle, toasting both the bread and the circle, preparing a fried egg, setting the toast over the fried egg with the yolky center peeking out the hole, and setting the toasted circle over the yolk—the top hat. I said, "If you ask him nicely, I bet he will."

When we arrived, my mother had made peanut-butter fudge, which Ella and I dipped into while Lars carried our suitcases upstairs. It wasn't until I made it to the second floor that I realized Lars had put Ella in my old room and me in my grandmother's. My heart clutched—it was one of those moments when you feel time is a rug that's been yanked out from under you; everything around you has changed so gradually that it is only all at once you look up and realize how different your life has become. There was my grandmother's single bed, though the spread on it was different—this one was striped. My mother had cleared the surfaces of my grandmother's bureau and nightstand of the cosmetics and perfume bottles, the ashtrays and cartons of tissue; she also had emptied the bureau's drawers, I saw when I opened them. But the Nefertiti bust was still there, set at an angle, and the bookshelves still were full. I ran a finger over the spines—the books were not alphabetized by author, as mine were, or in any other order that I could discern. *The Picture of Dorian Gray* and *The Group* and *Gone with the Wind, Frankenstein* and *Presumed Innocent* and *The Counte of Monte Cristo* and *The Golden Notebook, In Cold Blood, Lady Chatterley's Lover, The Great Santini, The Maltese Falcon, Native Son*—all those worlds, all the versions of myself I had been when I'd read these very copies, and all the versions of herself she had been. I pulled down *The Magnificent Ambersons* by Booth Tarkington (the title and author's name appeared in engraved gold on an otherwise blank cover of navy leather), and I opened to a random page, page 172, and smelled it, pressing my nose against the binding, but it smelled only like old paper, like an old house, and not like my grandmother.

At Fassbinder's, Lars said to Ella, "Did you hear the cheese squeak?"

"So what if it squeaks?" Ella said, and I said, "That's impolite, Ella."

Genially, over Ella's head—she was leaning against me, pulling on my blouse—Lars said, "I sense that someone's ready for a nap."

"I don't take naps anymore," Ella said.

This was not entirely true, but I simply said to her, "Do you think Grandma will like the jam Papa Lars picked out?" She didn't respond, and I flashed an apologetic smile at Lars. "We'll meet you in the car."

CHARLIE CALLED THAT night around eleven, when I was the only one awake. I was lying in bed reading *The Old Forest* by Peter Taylor, and as soon as I heard the phone—there was the extension in the room my mother and Lars shared, and the extension downstairs in the kitchen—I knew that it was Charlie, but there wasn't much I could do. I wasn't about to barge in on my mother and Lars, and there was no way I could get to the kitchen in time. Then my mother knocked on the door. She was wearing a beige rayon nightgown with a scalloped yoke and sleeves that ended just below her elbows, and her hair was askew. "Sweetheart, it's Charlie—"

I stood. "I'm so sorry, Mom. I'll take it downstairs."

In the kitchen, when I'd heard the click of the second-floor extension, I said, "Charlie, do you know what time it is?" and he said, "Just come home. Please. I'm begging you."

"You can't call like this," I said.

"I'm losing my fucking mind. You know I can't stay by myself. Want to know where I spent the night last night? At the Wauwatosa Ramada. The fucking Ramada, okay? You've called my bluff. I'm a lousy husband. But I *need* you, Lindy."

This is, almost without fail, a powerful thing to hear a person say. I sighed. "Charlie, if I came back, I can't see how anything would be different."

"I'll quit being an immature dick, that's how. Yeah, I *do* know what you were talking about—I've been selfish lately. But things have changed for me, this baseball stuff is really gonna be good, and I'm ready to turn over a new leaf."

"Are you going to keep drinking?" I could tell he'd been drinking in the last few hours. He wasn't slurring, but his voice had that looseness.

"Is that what this is about?"

"I don't know. Sometimes I *hope* it's the alcohol, but I'm not sure it is."

He was quiet, and then he said, "When did you turn against me?"

"That's not fair."

"May? January? Two years ago?"

I said, "I know you've struggled with getting older, your fortieth birthday, your twentieth college reunion, but I wish you hadn't been as— I guess what I'm trying to say is that there's such a thing as suffering quietly."

He laughed then, a dark chuckle. "Yeah, and apparently, you've cornered the market on it."

"I'm going to sleep," I said. "Everyone here is in bed, and I don't want to disturb them. If you'd like, we can talk tomorrow."

"Listen to yourself. You're a fucking ice queen."

"Please don't insult me."

"What do you want? What am I supposed to do?"

"I told you—I want space."

"Alice, you *know* I can't stay in this house alone. Come back here, that's all I'm asking, and we'll figure things out. I won't, you know, molest you at night—hell, I'll sleep in a different room. But this house gives me the fucking creeps."

"I thought you were at the Ramada Inn."

"That place gave me the creeps, too. I had to check out."

"So you're at home right now?"

"Where else would I be?"

"Our house isn't creepy, Charlie, and we live in a very safe area. Did you close the living room and dining room curtains?"

"What if I drive out there?"

I was sitting at the kitchen table, and I closed my eyes. "Why don't you call Arthur and Jadey? You should call soon, though, because I'm sure they're about to go to bed if they haven't already."

"Yeah, and then I can be humped by Lucky all night long."

"You could call John and Nan, or Ginger—"

"I don't want to stay with any of my brothers! I don't care to broadcast my personal business. I want to sleep at my own house, with my wife next to me, and my daughter down the hall. And you know what? Most people wouldn't think that's a whole hell of a lot to ask."

I said nothing, and for a while, he said nothing, either. At last, in a less combative tone, he said, "Is Ella asking about me?"

"She misses you. If you'd like to call during the day tomorrow, I'm sure she'd love to talk."

After a pause, he said, "Just so you know, you've sliced open my chest, you've pulled out my heart, and now you're squeezing it with your bare hands, so I hope this exercise in marital introspection, or whatever the fuck you're doing, I hope it's worth it."

"I'm going to bed, Charlie. I sincerely hope you can figure out a sleeping arrangement that makes you comfortable."

"Don't hang up on me."

"I'm not hanging up. I'm saying good night. Good night, okay? Good night. Are you going to say it back to me?"

"Does our marriage mean nothing to you?"

"Charlie, I'm not hanging up on you, but if you don't say good night back to me, I am going to hang up the phone. So for the last time, good night."

"Fuck you," he said, and then he was the one who ended the connection.

WE WERE AT Pine Lake when I heard the child crying—a girl, it sounded like, somewhere behind me—and I'd been aware of the crying for over a minute when I realized with a start that the child was Ella. I was sitting on a towel on the sand, my mother next to me in a folding chair, wearing not a bathing suit but slacks and a short-sleeved blouse; her one concession to the setting was that she was barefoot, holding her flats. She'd been telling me about the controversy over the location for

Riley's proposed statue to honor Korean War veterans—there was great disagreement about whether it ought to be on the shore of the Riley River or downtown on Commerce Street—and I turned, glancing over my shoulder, then jumped to my feet. "Mom, wait," I said. "I'll be back."

Pine Lake's beach wasn't large—perhaps a hundred yards across—and though this had not been the case in my youth, there were a lifeguard and ropes indicating the sanctioned area for swimming. The beach was part of Pine Park, and in the grassy area near the sand were picnic tables and grills. The beach's parking lot was gravel, and one corner was occupied by a frozen-custard truck whose side was a sliding window. Just outside this truck stood my daughter, wearing flip-flops and a bathing suit, her long hair wet and tangled, her face twisted and red as she sobbed hysterically. When I approached, she lunged toward me—she wailed, "Mommy!" and it was a heart-wrenching thing to hear—but her movement was stopped by a teenage boy who wore a white apron and was holding on to her wrist. Several people in the area, some snacking on candy bars or hamburgers, had stopped to watch.

"He's hurting me," Ella cried, and I said to the boy, "I'm her mother. What's going on here?"

"She stole an ice-cream cone!" The boy was irate. He was about five feet six and pale, with fair close-cropped hair and a wispy mustache.

I set my hand on Ella's wrist and nudged the boy's hand away—firmly but not aggressively, I hoped. "I'll take her," I said, and to my relief, he released her. Immediately, Ella buried her face against my waist. "If you'll tell me what happened, I'm sure we can solve the problem," I said.

"She stole!" he repeated, and he pointed to the gravel, where a melting blob of vanilla ice cream was loosely joined to a cake cone. "She tried to take it without paying."

Ella was mumbling against my stomach, protesting.

"What, sweetie?"

She pulled her head back, and her face remained tear-stained and flushed. "He wouldn't let me sign for it!" She quickly hid her face again.

I said to the boy, "There's been a misunderstanding. We don't live in

Riley, and where we live, we pay by—" It wasn't worth it; explaining the rules of a country club could only be more damning. "If you can wait, I'll get my wallet," I said. "Did she have anything besides the ice cream?"

Ella lifted her head. "I didn't even have the ice cream! He took it back!"

"You licked it," the boy retorted, and I said, "How much was it?"

"A dollar seventy-five."

"My wallet is in the car, which is over there." I pointed. "The blue Volvo station wagon, do you see it? You can watch me walk there, and then I'll come right back. Ella, will you come with me?" I smiled at the boy and at the other people who were observing us, then detached Ella from my torso and took her hand. As we headed in the direction of the car, she let her hair hang in front of her face. "I hate it here," she said softly.

WHEN WE GOT back to the house, Jadey had called three times; Lars had dutifully noted the time of each call, down to the minute, on the pad of paper by the kitchen phone.

I went upstairs to return the call; I didn't particularly want to talk to her, because I didn't know what there was to say about the situation, but if I didn't, it seemed clear she would keep trying, which would presumably increase my mother's suspicion. And my mother had to suspect already—it could only be her midwestern reticence that was preventing her from asking me outright why we had descended so abruptly on her household.

"So you did it," Jadey said. In the background, I could hear Lucky barking, and Jadey said to someone, "Put him in the yard." I heard Winnie protesting, and Jadey said, "I'm not asking your brother, I'm asking you." To me, she said, "Chas showed up here close to midnight last night."

"How did he seem?"

"I only saw him for about a minute, and he took off early this morning, but he told Arthur you're pissed at him. You didn't file for divorce, did you?"

"No," I said quickly. "No, we're just— Ella and I are spending some time here for a while."

"Alice, this is me you're talking to. I won't repeat what you say, especially to Chas, if that's what you're worried about."

I was more worried that she'd repeat it to Billy Torks or to one of her female friends.

"Were Reunions a disaster?" she said. "Remember what I told you—these guys set foot on campus and they go crazy. They get so caught up in the moment."

"It wasn't that," I said. "Not completely, anyway. Jadey, I appreciate your concern, I really do, but I just need some distance."

"No, do what you have to." She lowered her voice—perhaps Winnie had returned to the room. "When you're ready to come back, we'll be waiting for you."

THAT NIGHT, ELLA and Lars went to bed around the same time, and my mother and I watched *Knots Landing* together. I had assumed we'd be chatting while the show played, but to my surprise, I could tell from her body language that she'd become quite a devoted viewer, so I remained quiet except during commercials. When the program finished, she turned toward me, smiling in a shy way, and said, "I suppose it's a bit pulpy."

"Pulp has its charms."

"I'm so sorry about poor Ella at the beach today. Do you know, I believe that was Tim Ziemniak who scolded her. I peeked over at the ice-cream truck as we were leaving."

"Roy and Patty's son?" Roy had been my classmate all through school, and his father had been my dentist; Patty had also attended Benton County Central High but graduated a few years after us.

"I'm sure he didn't mean anything by it," my mother said. "He couldn't be but fourteen or fifteen, and I'll bet he takes his responsibilities awfully seriously."

"Ella will be all right," I said.

"Having her here, it makes me think of you at that age."

"Oh, Ella's a lot spunkier than I was," I said. "She's a real ball of energy."

"Well—" My mother paused, and her tone was reflective in that way that is inevitably sad, because the past is sad. "What I remember," she said, "is that you were always such a dear little girl."

I felt a great surge of affection for her in this moment; I had been so lucky to be raised, to be loved, by a calm, uncomplicated mother. I often had not appreciated her, I thought, overshadowed as she was by my more showy and entertaining grandmother. But really, the older I got, the more I observed the cruelties family members inflicted on one another, out of jealousy or ignorance or private despair, and sometimes for sport—people could be so savage in such banal, daily ways. This was what I didn't want for Ella: for nothing but chance, the chance of her birth, to put her at the mercy of Charlie's selfishness and immaturity. To be around an adult who acted thoughtlessly and impulsively and then to watch it go unchecked, unpunished—I felt that could give a child a misunderstanding of the world, hindering her ability to see logical patterns. I did not care if Ella went to Princeton, if she was exceptionally pretty, if she grew up to marry a rich man, or really, if she married at all—there were many incarnations of her I felt confident I could embrace, a hippie or a housewife or a career woman. But what I did care about, what I wanted most fervently, was for her to understand that hard work paid off, that decency begat decency, that humility was not a raincoat you occasionally pulled on when you thought conditions called for it, but rather a constant way of existing in the world, knowing that good and bad luck touched everyone and none of us was fully responsible for our fortunes or tragedies. Above all, I wanted my daughter to understand that many people *were* guided by bitterness and that it was best to avoid these individuals—their moods and behavior were a hornet's nest you had no possible reason to do anything other than bypass and ignore. And I loved Ella, I loved her immeasurably, but I wondered if she wasn't already being influenced by what was worst in Charlie and by my indulgence of his shortcomings. She would mimic us—surely she would, all children did—and would it be his entitled sulkiness or my martyrish passivity that she'd emulate? I didn't want her growing up thinking that I endorsed his choices; at the same time, I didn't know how to give voice to my dissent except by leaving him.

Beside me on the living room sofa, my mother said, "Will Charlie be calling again tonight, do you think? If he will, I might as well unplug the phone in our room."

"I hate to inconvenience you," I said, but she'd already stood.

"It won't take a minute."

In her absence, I looked around the living room, which still contained the broad square couch and chairs my parents had purchased in the early fifties, the maroon-spined *Encyclopaedia Britannica*s, Lars's recliner, the painting over the fireplace—a knockoff of Picasso's *Le Guitariste* that my grandmother had given them one Christmas and which I am pretty sure neither my mother nor my father had ever liked.

When my mother returned, I said, "I hope you weren't up for long after Charlie's call last night."

"Don't give it a thought. Will he be joining you here? Even if he'd just like to come for dinner, we'd be delighted to have him. Lars is very keen to give his suggestions for the baseball team."

"So I hear." We exchanged smiles. "Charlie has a lot keeping him busy in Milwaukee, so I don't know that he'll make it out, but that's kind." A little hesitantly, I said, "You and Dad never really quarreled, did you? You always seemed very compatible."

"Oh, heavens, all couples quarrel." My mother had sat again, and as she spoke, she picked up her needlepoint canvas, which had been resting since the previous night on the shelf beneath the coffee table. She was making a throw pillow cover with a rose on it.

"But you and Dad never had *serious* fights, did you? Where you considered ending the marriage?"

"That was much more unusual then." My mother was threading the needle, not looking at me, and her tone remained even. Still, I'm sure she understood exactly what we were talking about. "It's not so uncommon to get a divorce now, but years ago, I didn't know anyone who'd done it. I suppose the Conners were the first couple I knew—do you remember Hazel and William? People said he had a gambling problem. She was a nice lady, though." My mother turned the canvas over, peering at a particular stitch. "There were times when your father made me mad, but I can't say the thought of leaving him ever crossed my mind. I suppose I made a decision—" She paused. "There was a good deal of conflict in my family growing up, and it wasn't pleasant to be around. It only causes more of the same—once people work themselves up, it hardly matters what the disagreement was about, does it? After I married, I decided if ever your father and I had a cross word, I'd meet him with kindness. I decided, if I think he's wrong or if I think he's right, I won't try to prove it. I'll remind him that I care for him in the hope it reminds him he cares for me, too. I was fortunate, because your father had a gentle nature." She looked up, offering a willfully bland smile. "Not every man does."

I'm not encouraging you to divorce Charlie, but if you do, I'll understand—wasn't that what she was saying, more or less?

She had turned the canvas over again, she was stitching steadily, and I leaned in to look at it more closely. I said, "That's going to be a beautiful pillow."

AFTER I'D CHANGED into my nightgown and brushed my teeth, I returned to the kitchen with *The Old Forest,* waiting for the phone to ring. It was ten-thirty, then five after eleven, eleven-twenty, eleven-thirty, and I felt a growing irritation, thinking how inconsiderate it was for Charlie to call so late. By twenty to one, I knew he wasn't calling at all. My mother's house was very quiet, no cars passed outside on Amity Lane, and my irritation changed abruptly to a lonely disappointment.

WHEN THE PHONE rang in the morning, we were finishing breakfast, and Ella answered. After listening for a few seconds, she said, "Mommy's taking me ice-skating, and I know how to skate backwards." It was Charlie, wasn't it? "In the mall," Ella said. Then, practically shouting, "In the *mall*! Yeah, she's right here." Ella held out the receiver. "It's Grandmaj."

Without preamble, Priscilla said, "For crying out loud, Alice, get in your car and go back to Milwaukee. Chas sounds like a mess."

I might have been tongue-tied anyway, but with Ella, Lars, and my mother right there at the table, I couldn't think of a way to respond. Finally, I said, "If you wouldn't mind holding on for just a moment, Priscilla, I'll switch phones."

Upstairs, the phone was still unplugged from the night before, and I got on my knees to stick the cord back into the jack, then lifted the receiver. As I sat on the edge of the double bed, I heard the phone downstairs being hung up, and I said, "Hello?"

"This is simply nonsense," Priscilla said. "You knew he was a booze-hound when you married him. Now pull up your socks and fix things."

"Priscilla, I don't see Charlie's drinking as a personality quirk. It might be less obvious from Washington than it is living in the same house with him, but he's—" I hesitated, and then I went ahead and said it. "He's drunk almost every night of the week. He's an alcoholic."

Priscilla did not react as if I'd offered a revelation. She said, "Whose fault do you think that is?"

"If you're implying that I'm responsible for Charlie's drinking, I have to object. He's a grown—"

"Let me ask you this. What's your job?"

"I don't follow."

"Indeed you don't. You're a housewife, my dear. It is your *duty* to ensure that your house runs smoothly. Just whose income do you imagine it is that allows you the luxury of staying home?"

"Priscilla, it's not as if I'm sitting around eating bonbons and watching soap operas. But if I've disappointed you, I'm sorry."

"Oh, I'm not *surprised,*" Priscilla said. "Great heavens, I've been waiting for this day for over a decade. Everyone knew you'd married down."

I couldn't resist the grim satisfaction of correcting her. I said, "You mean that Charlie married down."

"Oh no, Chas married up. Why, Alice, he was a thirty-one-year-old wastrel, making that preposterous congressional run, no less, and he was dating waitresses. We couldn't imagine what you saw in him!" She chortled, and as I sat there on my mother's bed, bewilderment seized me.

"But—didn't you think I had somehow tricked him into marrying me? You said as much when we announced our engagement."

"I said nothing of the sort."

"You came up to me, and you told me how clever I was."

"You'd been so coy." Priscilla sounded—it was bizarre—almost admiring. "Here you'd been in Halcyon all weekend without giving a clue that you and Chas were engaged, and at just the right moment, you pulled a rabbit from your hat. It was a flawless piece of theater."

"I thought—" Had I misjudged her all these years? Or was she lying now? Or was it neither—perhaps it wasn't so much that she'd ever had a high opinion of me, only that she'd had, or still had, a low opinion of Charlie. "I thought you thought—" I began, but again I sputtered out.

Overriding me, Priscilla said, "What mystifies me is your timing, why you've chosen now to throw your little tantrum when Chas has just made the best move of his life. He'll be splendid with the Brewers, and Lord knows he's never been fit for anything else. Here he was running our company into the ground for years, Harold's intervention was the only thing that kept his brothers from firing him, and now that Zeke Langenbacher has done us all a great favor, the only thing for you and Chas to do is sit on your derrieres and clap for home runs. Surely you can manage *that*?"

My head was spinning: Did all the Blackwells think Charlie was incompetent and foolish? Did everyone? (The Thayers did, as I'd recently learned from Joe.) And was I, by extension, incompetent and foolish for having married him? In this moment, I felt defensive on Charlie's behalf—if he had a tendency toward swagger and raunch, Arthur did, too. Charlie wasn't the runt of the litter, he wasn't an idiot.

"It's neither here nor there why you want to abandon your marriage," Priscilla was saying. "I can imagine a dozen reasons, and frankly, none of them is very interesting. Nobody will dispute for a second that you're smarter and more refined than Chas, but you were smarter and more refined than him the day you met. At this point, that's your problem. It's not his, and it sure isn't mine. But you have a home together, and more important, you have a daughter. If you couldn't give her siblings, the least you can give her is two parents."

It was unclear to me if this had been the most illuminating conversation of my life, the most insulting, both, or neither. I took a deep breath—in general, the reason I tried to be diplomatic was that you might occasionally regret your diplomacy, but you'd more frequently regret having been snippy—and then I said to my mother-in-law, "Well, Priscilla, I have a lot to think about."

THE WAY WE'D decided to go to the skating rink at the Riley mall was process of elimination: Ella refused to return to Pine Lake, and we'd already visited Fassbinder's. Plus, she'd long wanted to try the skating rink at home, at the Mayfair Mall, and I'd never taken her; here, there wasn't much disincentive. Because summer was still new, because it was not yet horribly hot, the rink was mostly empty, and the pop music that blasted from enormous speakers just below the roof seemed aggressive. The last time I'd skated had been up in Halcyon one winter, before Ella was born, and it had never been a great talent of mine. We slipped and skidded along, and I watched her watching two other girls, sisters, it seemed, a few years older than Ella, who were quite skillful and who often called out to each other, arguing and laughing. "Do you want to go play with them?" I asked. When Ella vigorously shook her head, guilt billowed inside me. After we'd unlaced and returned our skates, we ate chicken tenders in the mall's food court, and in a store of cheap jewelry and accessories, I bought her a bracelet with a dolphin charm.

Walking down the mall's wide pink marble corridors (why did a mall in Riley, Wisconsin, need a marble floor?), I couldn't help wondering what I was doing to us. How long could Ella and I last in this town? Because it was easy to drive back and forth between Milwaukee and Riley in a single day, this was already the longest visit I'd made here in years, and while I had imagined it as a respite, what Ella had said in Fassbinder's had not been wrong: It was boring. I was of this place, and gratefully so, but each day here seemed three times as long as a day in Maronee. And yet if we went home, wouldn't it all be exactly the same? Charlie might be on his best behavior for a few weeks, a few months at most, and even that could be wishful thinking—he was as likely to be resentful as remorseful.

That afternoon, I called Jadey. (Looking back, this is what I most remember of that strange period in Riley—being on the phone. If my mother and Lars found the frequency with which I sequestered myself to call people or wait for calls to be reminiscent of a moody, inconsiderate teenager, I hardly could have blamed them.)

When Jadey answered, she said, "Please tell me you're calling to say you're home and you want to know if I can go for a walk, because the answer is yes. I've already gained four pounds from missing you—well, missing you, getting no exercise, and eating a tray of double fudge brownies."

"Does everyone in the family think Charlie is some sort of dimwit?"

"What are you talking about?"

"Maj called earlier today—she's none too pleased with me, as you can imagine—and she was implying— It was very strange. Have Arthur and John been wanting to fire Charlie?"

Jadey didn't reply immediately, which was an answer, and not the one I'd hoped for. Then she said, "He plays tennis in the middle of the day, I think that's the main thing. They don't know where he *is* a lot of the time, and if there's a distributor who's come in for a meeting that Chas set up . . ."

"Why didn't you tell me?"

"We can't babysit them, right? Don't be mad. Are you mad? Alice, he's always been like this. Nobody thinks he's stupid. He's just—maybe he's not the hardest-working guy ever, let's put it that way. But you know who the hardest-working guy ever is? Ed, and who'd want to be married to him?"

It was like the optical illusion of the hag and the elegant young woman—from this angle, my life was privileged and boisterous, containing its problems, certainly, but they were minor compared to its gifts; and from that angle, my marriage was a sham, my husband a laughingstock. I had long known how thin the line was that divided happiness and tragedy, tranquillity and chaos, but it had been many years since I'd walked it. "When you see him tonight, will you ask him to call me?" I said.

"Oh, Chas isn't staying with us anymore," Jadey said. "He was only here for the one night."

"Where's he staying?"

"I assume he decided to put on his big-boy underpants and go home."

I felt a prickly alertness, the sort that precedes goose bumps. He was not staying at home; I felt sure of it.

"Are you still there?" Jadey asked. "Say something."

I sighed. "I'm still here."

THAT SUNDAY, ELLA and I went to church with my mother and Lars, and Ella squirmed through the service, no doubt thinking longingly of Bonnie, the prosthetic-eye-removing Sunday-school teacher at Christ the Redeemer in Milwaukee. Back at the house, after lunch, Lars and I started a five-hundred-piece jigsaw puzzle of a train in the Swiss Alps—he'd set up the card table for this purpose—and in the front yard, my mother filled a clear glass salad bowl with water and a few squirts of Windex so that Ella could take Barbie swimming; if my mother or Lars had an opinion about Barbie's skin color, neither of them ever expressed it. After a while, my mother came inside, saying, "It wouldn't take five minutes for me to make a little towel for Barbie."

I looked up from the puzzle. "Or you could relax for a change."

But already, she had that musing, preoccupied look on her face: *a project.* She disappeared upstairs, where her sewing machine was in my old room.

Through the window screen, I occasionally could hear Ella talking to Barbie—"Now it's time to do backstroke"—and then she was quiet. When I went outside to check on her, she was squatting by the bowl of blue liquid. "Ladybug, how are—" I started to say, and when she looked up, I saw that she was wearing a glittery purple tiara and matching purple droplet earrings. "Oh my," I said. "Where did you get those?"

"From the lady." She pointed to the house directly across the street from ours, which was the Janaszewskis'.

"She gave them to you?" I said.

Ella nodded.

"Did she help you put them on?"

Ella nodded again. The plastic tiara was tucked behind her ears, the gaudy curlicues on either side of the front band rising to meet an oversize fake amethyst in the center, and above it, a sparkly star. The earrings were clip-ons, the amethyst droplets nickel-size and encrusted with ersatz diamonds. Immediately, I knew who would get a kick out of these types of accessories, but of course I couldn't be certain, and even if I were, I had even less idea of the gift's meaning. Was it a casual unanalyzed kindness to amuse a little girl, a playful peace offering, or was it the opposite, a mocking criticism with a pointed subtext: *Your daughter is a princess.*

"Did the lady say her name?" I asked.

Ella shrugged. "Grandma's making Barbie a towel."

"I know she is, and please be sure to thank her. Ella, did the lady who gave you this jewelry—did she know your name?"

Ella squinted, trying to remember. "I think so."

"What did she look like?"

"Mommy, she went right *there.* You can go see her yourself."

"Did she look closer to my age or Grandma's?"

Briefly, Ella scrutinized my face, and then she said, "She looked old, but like you."

I glanced again at the Janaszewskis' front porch. Was this an invitation, a challenge, or both? Or was it merely a toy Dena's mother had picked up at the drugstore and thought Ella would like?

I took a seat on the stoop, waiting to see if anyone would reemerge from their house, and soon my mother joined us—she'd even stitched a red B onto the miniature towel, which was clearly snipped from a worn-out full-size one—but she didn't ask about the origins of the tiara or earrings; she must have imagined they'd come from me. When we all went inside close to an hour later, we'd seen no other activity at the Janaszewskis'.

I'D TRIED CALLING our house in Maronee several times, at different hours of the day and evening, and Charlie had never answered; however, when I finally left a message, he called back within a few hours. We arranged that Ella and I would meet him the next day for a picnic lunch at a park off I-94, between Riley and Milwaukee. The picnic was my idea, and I thought it was better than a restaurant, in case he lost his temper and began to yell; also, it would allow him and Ella to run around. Our phone conversation was brief and not explicitly hostile—it wasn't emotional in one direction or the other—but it was definitely strained.

Ella and I made chicken-salad sandwiches, and my mother insisted on baking blondies, and Ella and I were about to leave the house when Arthur called. He said, "No one was hurt, Chas is fine, but he got a DUI last night, and he asked me to call to say he can't meet you. He knows you'll be furious, but Alice, I just saw him, and trust me, there's nothing you could say to him right now that he hasn't already thought of. A few hours in jail gives a man time for soul-searching, you know?"

"Is he—" Once again, I was in the kitchen, meaning I couldn't speak freely. "Is he still incapacitated, is that why he's not calling himself?"

"He's not still in the slammer, no—he's over at our lawyer's office. He's pretty frantic to keep this under wraps because it wouldn't look good to Zeke Langenbacher, so Dad and Ed are working the phones. Chas told me to see if tomorrow for lunch works for you instead, but maybe you can call him yourself later today? Not that I don't love being his secretary and all."

"When did—" But there was no question I could ask that would not include a word that would sound alarming to Ella and my mother: *injury* or *accident* or *lawyer* or *jail.* And then (it was oddly liberating), I thought, *He can clean it up.* I didn't need to intervene. If his car was totaled, if the newspaper caught wind of it, if he was kicking himself for risking his new job before it had even started—those were his problems. Arthur had said that no one was hurt, and that was all I cared about. I said, "Thank you for calling, but about tomorrow, the answer is no."

"Alice, he really feels bad for—"

"The answer is no," I said. "That's all you need to tell him."

When I'd hung up, I said brightly to Ella, "It turns out Daddy has a meeting for the baseball team today, and he can't get away. But he's so disappointed about not seeing you that he had an idea, and I'm only agreeing to it because you've been such a good girl. He wants me to buy you a tape of *Dirty Dancing.*"

Ella had been watching me suspiciously—I dared not even look at my mother—but when the words *Dirty Dancing* left my mouth, Ella squealed and threw her arms in the air. "Now?" she said. Her eyes were wide.

"Why don't we have our picnic in the backyard?" I said. "Mom, you should join us—there's an extra sandwich." I did look at her then, and her expression was optimistic in a guarded way; she didn't want to know the truth any more than I wanted to tell it. I said to Ella, "After lunch, ladybug, you and I will drive over to the mall."

My mother said, "Alice, we don't have a— What do they call the machines?"

"No, Charlie thought of that, too." I was smiling maniacally. "He's so appreciative for your hospitality to us that he asked me to buy you and Lars a VCR."

OVER THE NEXT two weeks, involuntarily, I memorized every line of *Dirty Dancing.* It was a different movie than I'd imagined—it was more nuanced, and it wasn't as risqué as I'd feared, though there was a scene in which, for under a second, the camera showed Patrick Swayze climbing naked out of bed after implied sex. To my surprise, there was also an abortion plotline that Ella seemed not to pick up on; mostly, she was focused on the dancing, which really was wonderful. It was set in 1963, and the main character was a year older than I'd been then, meaning many of the songs and references were evocative. I wouldn't necessarily have *chosen* to watch this same movie a dozen times, and we eventually started renting others, but I did, to my surprise, quite like *Dirty Dancing.*

During these days, sitting in the living room in front of the television, I felt as if I were waiting for something, but what? I did not call Charlie, and he did not call me. The start of Ella's art camp was approaching, and then it arrived; that morning, I phoned to let the director know she wouldn't be attending. There were decisions I needed to make, plans I needed to set in motion (how I wished that my grandmother were still there to advise me), but instead, I just kept stalling.

ON THE PHONE, Jadey said, "I don't know if I should tell you this or not," which is a preamble that surely has never been followed by the speaker not proceeding to share the information in question. "Chas has befriended some minister named Reverend Randy," she continued. "Nobody knows how they met, because if you ask, Chas deflects the question. Nan told me she and John saw them at dinner in the sports room last night, and I think he was with Chas at a baseball game, too."

"Who is he?"

"That's the thing—no one knows. No one has ever heard of him, although supposedly, he has some church over in Cudahy. Little Rose? Heavenly Flower? I'm probably making this sound more alarming than it is."

"How does Charlie seem?"

"Well, we invited him over for dinner, but I think he's afraid if he comes, I'll chew him out."

"Jadey, please don't."

"Believe me, Arthur has already given me the whole spiel about how you leaving and the DUI are punishment enough, blah blah blah."

This wasn't quite what I thought. It wasn't that I felt protective of Charlie as much as that I knew a lecture from Jadey would be wholly ineffective and only create a wedge between them. At the same time, as the days passed, I could feel the yielding of my own anger. I missed Charlie—I missed talking to him and sitting next to him, loading the dishwasher in the kitchen at night and knowing he was watching baseball in the den, joking around in bed after we'd turned out the lights and before we fell asleep. I missed his off-color remarks and the way that when he made damning comments about people we knew, it meant I didn't have to; I got to be the good guy and defend them.

To Jadey, I said, "I still don't get who this Reverend Randy person is."

"You and me both," she said.

AND THEN HE called; he called the next night, by which point we'd been in Riley for three and a half weeks. It was nine, and Lars and I had moved on to a puzzle of the Sydney Opera House. Charlie said, "It's all worked out. Jessica's enrolled for this coming year at Biddle, full ride—full ride from us, I mean, but none of the Suttons will know, because I assumed you'd think that's better. How's Ella?"

"You arranged for Jessica Sutton to go to Biddle?"

"Nancy Dwyer called the family, invited them to visit campus, she said the school had heard about Jessica from us—I figured Yvonne and Miss Ruby would have to be morons not to know we were involved, so why not 'fess up partway?—and Jessica passed all the tests today. It's a done deal. I'll write her tuition checks at the same time I write Ella's."

"Charlie, that's amazing. I'm not sure what to say. Thank you."

"You were right." He sounded better than he had in a long time, more energetic and upbeat, and he also didn't sound like he'd been drinking, or at least not much. "This is an opportunity for us to do a good thing, and who are we gonna open the coffers for if not Miss Ruby, you know? I'm glad you pushed me on it. All's well in Riley?"

It was as though Ella and I really were on vacation without him, as if Charlie and I were any married couple catching up at the end of a day apart. "We're fine." I lowered my voice—I was in the kitchen, and my mother and Lars were in the living room. "I think she's a little bored, to be honest."

Charlie chuckled. "Probably good for her."

"You sound great," I said. "You really— You sound wonderful."

"I've started running. You know, I made fun of John for wearing those faggoty spandex, but man, Lindy, the endorphins are something else. It's different from other sports."

"How long have you—"

"Just the last ten days or so, but I'm a new man. Getting up at six, heading over to the track in Cudahy, at the high school. A bit of a drive, but it's invigorating."

Charlie was getting up at six to drive to the south side and run on the track at a public high school?

"Listen," he said. "I don't want to keep you. Let me sign off, and I'll call Ella tomorrow from work."

"Where are you right now?" I asked.

"Just watching the game on TV—the Brewers are playing in Anaheim tonight. Hey, my new office at the stadium is great. You'll have to come see it." His tone was as friendly and unfraught as if I were a neighbor of whom he was genuinely fond. "Have a good night, Lindy," he said. "Love to you and El."

I had been on the cusp of asking again where exactly he was staying—at home, it seemed, except that I just couldn't believe it—and also who Reverend Randy was, but the conversation had gone so unexpectedly well that I gave in to its rhythms, its imminent conclusion. "Love to you, too," I said.

THE FOLLOWING NIGHT, Ella and I read a chapter of *Fantastic Mr. Fox* together before she went to bed, and after I'd stood to turn out the light, she said, "Mom, who's Andrew Christopher Imhof?"

I froze. Trying to keep my voice steady, I said, "Did someone mention him to you?" Could Dena have, when and if she'd given Ella the tiara? We'd also run into an old classmate of mine, Mary Hafliger, on Commerce Street, but surely Mary wouldn't have said anything about Andrew. And even if she had, or if someone else had, I'd have heard it.

From the nightstand, Ella lifted a large navy blue hardcover book. It was my high school yearbook, I quickly realized, seeing the embossed silver cursive on the cover: *The Zenith* 1964. "He's in here," she said, and she opened it, flipping the pages. Then she held out the "In Memoriam" page with Andrew's full name, his photo in black and white, his fair hair and long eyelashes, his heartbreakingly sweet smile. Beneath the photo were the dates of his birth and death: 1946–1963. They both seemed terribly long ago. The forties, that had been the decade of World War II and Sugar Ray Robinson and Rita Hayworth, but even the sixties, the early sixties especially, seemed very distant: a time when Jackie Kennedy wore a pillbox hat and chimps were sent into space.

Ella pointed to the dates and said, "Does that mean he died?"

I stepped toward the bed. "Andrew was a boy in my class, and he did die, when we were seniors in high school. It was very, very sad."

"How did he die?"

My heart had enlarged in my chest and was blocking my throat, making it difficult to speak or breathe. Was Ella old enough? She'd been in kindergarten when she asked where babies came from, and I had told her, simply and briefly but clearly; I'd used the words *vagina* and *penis,* which, when I repeated the story to her, Jadey couldn't believe—Drew was then twelve, and at their house, they all still called them *hoo-hoos* and *winkies.* But I believed that dodging children's questions wasn't necessarily good for them or you.

I took a deep breath. "He was in a car accident," I said.

"Was he wearing his seat belt?"

"A lot of cars back then didn't have them," I said. "They weren't as safe."

"Did you cry when he died?"

"Yes," I said. "I cried a lot." Then—I was not sure this wasn't an error in judgment, but I wasn't sure that staying quiet wouldn't be an error, too—I said, "I was involved in Andrew's accident. I was driving one car, and he was driving another car, and my car hit his."

Ella's eyes grew huge. "Did you go to the hospital?"

"Yes, I did, but I wasn't seriously hurt. I was lucky, and Andrew was unlucky. He was a wonderful person, and I liked him very much. I'd known him since both of us were younger than you. When he died, it was the saddest thing I had ever been through."

"Sadder than when your dad died and when Granny died?"

"It was different. When someone dies young—it doesn't happen often, and it's not something that will happen to you, although that's why you wear your seat belt, or it's why you look both ways before crossing the street, because you need to be careful—but when a young person dies, it's different from an older person dying. People are supposed to grow up and get married and have children, and when they don't, it feels like a mistake."

"Like Jesus?" Ella was possibly the most serious I had ever seen her—entirely focused, listening to every word I said.

"Well, Jesus was an adult when he died. But you're right that he didn't get married or have children, and his death was sad, too."

Ella was silent, pondering. "Do you think Andrew Christopher Imhof and Granny are together now?"

I smiled. "He was just called Andrew, or Andrew Imhof. You don't have to say his middle name. You know, he and Granny did know each other a little—as you've probably noticed, Riley is so small that everyone knows everyone else. When Andrew and I were a year younger than you are now, Granny and I ran into him and his mother at the grocery store, and Granny thought Andrew was a girl. His hair was a little bit long and curly then."

"She thought he was a *girl*?" Ella seemed both appalled and excited.

"I don't think he was too offended."

Beneath the sheets, Ella had propped her legs into a tent, the open yearbook resting against her thighs. She scrutinized the photo. "Did you love Andrew?"

"Yes," I said. "I did." In a way, it was nice to be able to talk about him—these were questions no one had ever asked me, questions no one besides a child would have dared—but it also was striking to think, standing there in my old bedroom, how far behind I had left him. I still dreamed of Andrew regularly, but in the dreams, a certain blurriness, an elasticity of facts, kept us peers, allowing me to ignore what was in this moment starkly obvious: I was twenty-five years older than he had been when he'd died; I had lived longer, by a significant margin, since the accident than he had lived before it; Ella was much closer to the age he'd died than I was. Was it disgusting, was it unseemly, that as a woman of forty-two, I could remember so clearly the anticipation of kissing him for the first time, how tan and handsome he had looked in his football uniform, how warm his skin would have been to touch? And now I dyed the gray from my hair, I had lines at my eyes and mouth, and my face was weathered—not in a terrible way, I wasn't someone greatly pained by my own aging, but no one would have thought I was any younger than I was. So much time had passed since Andrew's death. That was what was hard to believe, that so much time had passed and that the accident was no easier to understand than it ever had been. I could find words to describe it so that it sounded awful and faraway, tragic but long ago, when, really, if I thought about it, it was as difficult to comprehend as it had been in 1963. How could I have driven my car into Andrew's, and how could that have killed him?

Ella said, "Did you love him more than Daddy?"

I blinked. "Oh, sweetie, it's not like that. It's not— Andrew wasn't my boyfriend. We were friends, and I think we kept track of each other over the years, but we never dated. Because we came from the same place and were in the same grade, you could say we knew each other well, but that doesn't compare to the way you know someone when you live with them. We know almost everything about Daddy, don't we? What his snores sound like and which is his favorite shirt and how many ice cubes he likes in his glass of water at dinner."

Ella laughed—Charlie's snoring was a source of unfailing amusement to her.

"Just like I know almost everything about you," I said. "It's because I'm your mother and I love you and you're my favorite girl in the whole world." I leaned forward and kissed the top of her head, and as I did, I thought of what Charlie had said to me in the early morning after our wedding night, when I'd awakened from my dream of Andrew: *I want to be the love of your life.* He had gotten his way, hadn't he? Even with the two of us staying in different places, my moods were defined by him, by the latest thoughts I'd had about the hope or futility of our future together. Kissing Joe Thayer, however briefly and clumsily, had given me a glimpse of an idea that came back to me now—that I could not in my lifetime love another man. Not so much due to my loyalty to Charlie as due to a sort of weariness, a lack of interest in starting anew. I loved my husband out of affection and also out of habit, I loved him with my wife's heart, and with my secret heart, my dream heart, I loved Andrew Imhof. I had no other love to spare, not of the romantic variety. If I went through with divorcing Charlie, I wouldn't remarry; I simply couldn't envision it, and I found myself wondering then if living alone, being single again, would be harder than putting up with him. Even putting up with him might be easier than not putting up with him—being the beleaguered wife, propelled forward, given a sense of purpose, by my troublesome husband. Whereas if I were single, I would struggle financially, I would have to delicately navigate interacting with the Blackwells and with Charlie himself, and there would be acrimony of an explicit rather than a suppressed kind.

What I wanted to know (it was useless, and adolescent as well) was if I had left the house a little earlier or a little later that September night in 1963, or if Fred Zurbrugg's party had been called off, or if I hadn't argued with Dena and driven alone, or if our argument had left me so despondent I'd decided to skip the party altogether—if the accident had been prevented, would Andrew and I have become a couple, and if we'd become a couple would we have remained one, and would we eventually have married? This had long been the story I'd told myself, and if it was a fiction, it had nevertheless felt true—it had felt like the sort of truth you don't need to defend because, in spite of all arguments against it, it cannot be diminished. But now I was doubtful. I was sick of Riley after less than a month; I was ready to go home, because home wasn't here. If I had married Andrew, would I have been content to lead a smaller life, to stay forever in a place like this? Was it venturing into the world that had sharpened my appetite for what the world offered? Or if I'd stayed here, a farmer's wife, would I have felt stifled no matter what?

"I'm praying right now for Andrew Imhof," Ella said.

I switched off the light. "That's sweet of you, ladybug."

IN RILEY, THE Protestant cemetery and the Catholic cemetery were side by side, about a mile southwest of the river, and in the morning, I drove first to St. Mary's, the Catholic one. At Buhler's florist, I'd bought two bouquets of white tulips, and I placed one on Andrew's gravestone, which was a flat gray granite rectangle set into the grass. It was a beautiful late June morning, about seventy degrees with a light breeze, and no other visitors were in the cemetery, though a man on a riding lawn mower was cutting the grass in the distance. Looking for Andrew's grave, I had passed some headstones marked by dried flowers, fake flowers, whirligigs, or wind socks, though most, like his, were undecorated. I stood there looking down at his name and the dates. I hadn't attended his funeral, nor had I ever been to his grave—I probably wouldn't have come on this trip, if not for my conversation with

Ella—and it was jarring to see. I would say that it was like proof of something, except that there was nothing left to prove.

I wished in this moment for greater faith, for a prayer to recite that would feel sincere, but none came to me. I crouched, touching the cool stone as I had never really touched Andrew, and I thought, *I hope you're at peace. I'm so sorry.* The only answer that came back was the buzz of the lawn mower, but I hadn't expected otherwise.

I returned to where I'd parked and drove to Grace Cemetery, the Protestant one; it was probably half a mile from one entrance to another, and I could have gone on foot, but the roads here didn't have sidewalks, and it would be too darkly ironic to get hit crossing between two graveyards. In Grace, I knew where my father's and grandmother's headstones were: Unlike Andrew's, they were upright, my father's gray and slightly curved at the top like a headboard, my grandmother's similar in shape but a polished gray-mottled pink. PHILLIP WARREN LINDGREN, 1923–1976, BELOVED SON, HUSBAND, AND FATHER. And for my grandmother, EMILIE WARREN LINDGREN, 1896–1988. For my grandmother, my mother had selected a background that was like an open book with blank pages—generally meant to evoke a Bible, I assumed, but my mother had said to me, "Since Granny liked to read," and I knew she hadn't meant religious texts. The soil at my grandmother's grave was still dark and moist; she had been buried just over a month before, and I continued to feel that I was due to see her again shortly. I set the flowers between their headstones. Although I didn't know what I believed about souls or an afterlife, it comforted me that now they had each other for company. My grandmother had outlived her son, her only child, by twelve years, and I imagined outliving Ella; it was an unbearable thought.

I would not have asked my father, had he been alive, what I ought to do about my marriage; he wouldn't have liked such an intimate question. But I could guess what his advice would have been. As for my grandmother, no guesswork was necessary—she had told me straight out. And here in Grace Cemetery, it seemed shameful that I had ever considered otherwise, that I still was acting as if there was a choice to be made. Perhaps it was living around rich people—perhaps it was becoming a rich person myself—that had caused me to forget that life was hard work. Or perhaps it was the decade, the culture; it didn't matter. The fact was that I had forgotten. But almost eleven years earlier, I'd taken a vow, made a public promise. I thought of my father's motto—*Whatever you are, be a good one*—and though once my identity had been defined by being Phillip and Dorothy Lindgren's daughter, Emilie Lindgren's granddaughter, now I was Charlie Blackwell's wife, Ella Blackwell's mother. All of these people, each in a different way, would be deeply disappointed if I let my marriage fail. What choice did I have, really, except to go back—to try, as my mother had once made the decision to do with my father, to meet my husband with kindness?

BACK ON AMITY Lane, my mother passed me a note with Lars's handwriting on it: *Call Yvonne Sutton as soon as possible,* and then a seven-digit number. When I called, I could hear Antoine crying in the background. "Alice, we're thrilled about Jessica going to Ella's school," Yvonne said. "I don't know what you did to get them to give her that scholarship, but bless you."

"Don't think of Biddle as Ella's school—it's Jessica's now, too, and, Yvonne, she's the one who got herself in. We're so excited. If you have any questions about any of it, please feel free to call."

"That's real generous of you, and I almost forgot, thanks for the books, too—I don't think Jessie's looked up once since you dropped them off." I started to respond, but Yvonne continued, her tone changing. "Now, unfortunately, there's another reason I'm calling. Alice, Mama won't tell you herself, so I've got to be the one to say it—she can't stay another night in Maronee. God knows I don't mean to stick my nose in you two's personal business, but it just isn't right for a sixty-three-year-old lady to be babysitting a grown man."

"You mean that Miss Ruby—" I hesitated. "I'm embarrassed to say I'm not quite sure what's going on. Has Charlie asked Miss Ruby to stay with him at our house?"

"Not at your house—at Mr. and Mrs. Blackwell's. Alice, Mama would do anything for Charlie, he's had her wrapped around his little finger since way back, but she's too old for this. She needs to sleep in her own bed."

Of course—of course Charlie wasn't staying on Maronee Drive. He was staying at his parents', and Miss Ruby was staying with him in her room off the kitchen. She was probably also cooking him breakfast and dinner.

"You're absolutely right," I said. "I'm sorry, and I'm glad you called. I'm not sure if your mother has ever mentioned that Charlie— This will sound very silly, but he's afraid of the dark."

"Oh, I know." Yvonne laughed. "Believe me, we know all about the monsters under Charlie B's bed."

"I won't deny that he's unusual," I said.

"I try not to judge." Yvonne's tone implied that she wasn't succeeding, at least in this case. "I'm just concerned about Mama. Now, when I talked to Jadey, she said she doesn't know when you're coming home, but she's fine having Charlie there, so if you want to call him, or you want me to call him, either way. He'd probably listen more to you, but if—"

"I promise that I'll take care of it," I said. "Everyone will sleep in their own beds tonight."

BACK IN MARONEE, I dropped Ella at Jadey's—Jadey shrieked with joy when she saw me, and agreed to take the girls to the pool if I promised to go on a walk with her that evening—and then I went to our house to sort the mail and listen to the phone messages, to throw out the rotting food from the refrigerator and empty the trash and make our bed from what was, I presumed, the one night Charlie had slept, or tried to sleep, in it. Then I drove to Harold and Priscilla's, where Miss Ruby was watching *The People's Court* on the small television in the kitchen. I told her to go home and take the next week off—I would speak with Priscilla—and I collected Charlie's belongings. He had been sleeping not in an upstairs bedroom but on the couch in his father's study, which was nearer to Miss Ruby's room off the kitchen, and she had obviously been tidying his possessions. I took the alarm clock off the coffee table, folded the sleeping bag, which was from our house, and retrieved his toothbrush and toothpaste from the sink in the powder room under the stairs. I surveyed the second floor, but Charlie seemed to have been showering elsewhere—either at the country club or back at our house.

By this point, it was after four in the afternoon, and I drove to County Stadium. Finding an unlocked entrance, a non-game entrance, took some time, but eventually I saw a maintenance man leaving through nondescript metal double doors. He led me back in, and inside, I ran into another man, an older fellow who may have been the third-base coach, and that gentleman directed me to a third man, this one in a short-sleeved shirt and gray slacks, and after I'd explained separately to all of them who I was and asked where I might find my husband, at last I reached Charlie's office. It was smaller than I'd imagined, with windows onto the hallway but not to the outside; it was about the same size as the principal's anteroom, where the secretary sat, in the lower school of Biddle. Charlie had hung nothing on the walls, and the surface of his desk was mostly empty, with a few stacks of paper. He was sitting with his legs up on the desk and his ankles crossed—he wore black wing tips—and he held open a manila file folder and was reading.

The door was open, but I knocked on the aluminum frame. I said, "Am I interrupting?"

When he looked up, his expression was one of surprised pleasure, and also of wariness. He didn't stand, but he pulled his legs from the desk and set them on the floor. "This is unexpected."

Given how breezy he'd been when we'd spoken on the phone, the thought had crossed my mind that maybe he'd changed his mind about wanting us—wanting me—to return. I said, "How are you doing?" Before he could answer, I added, "I think it's time for Ella and me to come home. Do you agree?"

He bowed his head. Was he considering the question? A nervousness came over me. When almost a minute had passed in silence, I said, "Charlie?"

He lifted his head at last, and he seemed choked up. "You've caught me off guard, is all," he said. "Of course you should come home, absolutely. Lindy, I owe you a tremendous apology. I've behaved dishonorably as a husband."

"What? I— No, Charlie, that's not what I'm saying. Obviously, we both know that things can improve, but . . ." I trailed off; he was shaking his head.

"The Holy Spirit was working through you, Lindy. The Lord caused you to leave so that I'd see my sins and repent, and there's no doubt about it, I *have* sinned. But I'm a new man. I've been reborn, and if God can forgive me, I hope you can, too. I want you to know I haven't had a drop to drink in eight days."

I half expected him to smirk, to lapse into laughter, saying, *Just kidding—you fucking believed me! Admit it, you believed me!* Except that he didn't say it, and he wasn't kidding.

"Is this—" I paused. "Jadey told me you've been spending time with someone named Reverend Randy?"

"He's an extraordinary man, Lindy. You'll be very impressed when you meet him. He's thought long and hard about these issues, and he knows the struggle, he understands how hard it is *not* to sin, but boy, it's inspiring to hear him talk about the rewards of accepting Jesus as your Savior."

"How do you know him?"

"Funny thing, but it's Miss Ruby who introduced us."

"Oh, is he—is he black?"

Charlie grinned. "You ought to see the look on your face. No, Miss Racially Enlightened, he's not black."

"I didn't say it's bad if he is, I was just wondering. I assume, from the way you're talking, that he's a born-again Christian?"

Charlie looked amused. "Nothing wrong with glorifying God, sweetheart. When you're around Reverend Randy, you really feel the presence of Christ."

There were several possible ways Charlie might have reacted to my appearance at the ballpark, several moods I might have found him in—conciliatory or sulky, warm or blasé—but nothing, nothing in all the years I had known him, had prepared me for this. Charlie, my Charlie, had found religion? I knew it could happen to people, but he was the last one I'd have imagined. And yet if it was keeping him from drinking, if it was encouraging him to take responsibility for his own behavior . . . I do not deny that I felt a strong skepticism that afternoon, but I suppressed it, chalking it up to nothing more than my own snobbishness. Most people I knew attended church; no one I knew then was born-again. But hadn't I learned, over and over, that the world was larger and more complex than I'd once imagined, and wasn't this lesson an essentially positive one?

I said, "It wouldn't be a sin for a wife to kiss her husband right now, would it?" The question had hardly left my mouth when Charlie stood to embrace me. To have him back in my arms, that body I knew, the height, the scent, the skin and hair and clothes—what a great relief, how aligned my life felt for the first time not just in weeks but in years. Against my ear, Charlie whispered, "You have no idea how much I missed you."

I tilted my head back so we were looking at each other. I said, "Ella's swimming at the club with Winnie and Jadey. I don't suppose you could duck out early."

Charlie grinned. "Let me ask the managing partner." He cocked one ear, pretending to listen—there was no sound except, in the distance, the whirring of a very large fan—and then he nodded. "He says for a woman as good-looking as you, it'd be a crime to stay." Charlie gathered some of the papers from his desk, set them in his briefcase, and fastened the lock. Before we walked out, he took my hand.

Forty minutes later, we lay naked in our bed, I on my back and he on top, and just before he entered me, he paused—at this point, I was ready to take him in, more than ready—and he said seriously, "From now on, I'm going to be the man you deserve."

I nodded; I was breathless and flushed. I said, "Hurry."

ALL THESE YEARS later, they say I told him, "It's Jack Daniel's or me." Or in some versions, "It's Jim Beam or me." These ultimatums sound catchy, I suppose, but I didn't say them. I didn't even say, in a less pithy manner, that I'd leave him if he wouldn't stop drinking. I did leave him briefly, and he did stop drinking, and the events are connected, but not as cleanly or directly as anyone might imagine from the outside.

His critics are more fond of this false anecdote than his supporters, and what they think it illustrates, I gather, is that it's my fault—his election is my fault, his presidency is my fault, his war is my fault. Why couldn't I just have let him be an alcoholic? Plenty of wives put up with it every day!

But these accusations presuppose a consensus on the kind of president Charlie has been; a dreadful one, is what his critics believe. Do I think he has been a dreadful president? I think the story is always more complicated than people realize.

The accusations also presuppose that I knew, that any of us did. But I could not have imagined in 1988 how rapidly our lives would change, and if someone had told me, I'd have thought the prediction was as plausible as that of a man standing on a street corner, holding a sign that warns of the apocalypse. *Your husband will be president; the end is near.* I'd have smiled coolly and kept walking.

THE WEEKEND AFTER my return to Maronee, our friends the Laufs had an anniversary party that Joe Thayer also attended, and he approached me as I was walking toward the buffet dinner. I could tell from his posture, even before he spoke, that he was worked up—impassioned, I suppose. He said, "It's not my intent to pressure you, Alice, but have you given thought to what I said at Princeton?"

Surely he couldn't mean his suggestion that he and I embark on some type of long-term relationship, surely that had just been the alcohol speaking. But yes, clearly, that was what he meant. He gazed at me with such a fierce ardor that I might have laughed, if not for the very slightly threatening undercurrent that such ardor is always accompanied by.

In what I hoped was a firm but not unkind way, I said, "Joe, I'm not leaving my marriage."

"But in Princeton—"

I shook my head. "I ought to have been more discreet."

"Alice, you kissed me. I don't imagine you just *kiss* odd men all over the place! Or maybe I'm wrong, maybe you do!" He was as agitated as I'd ever seen him—perhaps he had the idea that he'd persuade me if not by flattery then by insistence and if not by insistence then by defamatory insinuation. I had the fleeting thought then that we are each of us pathetic in one way or another, and the trick is to marry a person whose patheticness you can tolerate; I never could have tolerated his. It occurred to me that Carolyn Thayer's behavior may not have been so egregious after all.

"It can't be," I said, and for the benefit of his ego, I tried to strike a note of regret. It may have been an ironic twist that it was Charlie who unwittingly saved me; he appeared at my elbow, setting a hand on my back and saying, "Joey T., when are you gonna come to a ball game with us? You pick the night, and we've got a ticket with your name on it."

Joe seemed to be gasping for air. He sounded accusatory as he said, "Aren't you generous."

"Heck, we ought to make it a men's night." Charlie nodded toward me. "This one is gonna be sitting through more games than she ever imagined in her wildest dreams, so we'll let her off the hook for once. But give your brother a jingle, see how everyone's schedule best coordinates, and we'll nail down a plan." Charlie leaned in, speaking more quietly. "Now, I don't know if you've taken the plunge back into the dating pool yet, but Zeke Langenbacher has a very attractive young lady working as his assistant, a super girl who comes from a real nice family in Louisville, and I'd love to set the two of you up. Alice, cover your ears." I didn't—he'd known that I wouldn't—and he said, "Not a bad rack on this gal, either."

"Charlie!" I swatted him, though I loved my husband very much in this moment. I was reminded of how, Joe's sarcasm aside, Charlie could be truly generous and kind. Joe glowered—I'm sure he currently despised Charlie as much as I adored him—and from then on, for the rest of our time in Maronee, Joe avoided me. He did it in such a way that I would notice, catching my eye when we found ourselves in the same place, then violently looking away and not talking to me. As far as I know, he and Charlie never attended a game together.

JADEY HADN'T TOLD me until my return to Milwaukee that my departure to Riley had greatly rattled Arthur; that the afternoon following Charlie's one ill-fated night at their house, Arthur had come home from work in the middle of the day, weeping, telling Jadey that if she ever left him, he would be completely lost and would rather be dead; that they had then proceeded to have stupendous sex; and that ever since, he had doted on her and had even, on two occasions, brought her flowers for no reason. ("One bouquet had carnations in it," she said, "but he's trying.") She revealed to him neither how hurt she had been by his comment about her weight nor with what enthusiasm she had considered an affair; she told me she'd decided to let sleeping dogs lie. She said, "Maybe you should skip town a little more often, because Arthur finds it to be a *powerful* aphrodisiac."

"I'm glad I could help," I said.

FOR CHARLIE AND Ella and me, the next five or six years were, I think, our happiest ones as a family. As everyone had anticipated, Charlie was perfectly suited to his new role with the Brewers. He attended just about all the home games and some of the away ones, and Ella and I attended quite a lot of them with him, though as she made her way through adolescence, the idea of spending an evening watching baseball with the two of us struck her as less and less appealing. But I remember all those weeknights and Saturday nights and Sunday afternoons with real nostalgia—the times it was windy and sunny, the times it was unbearably hot and we'd come home burned, the times we crouched together in raincoats, waiting for the umpires to call the game. We ate hot dogs and french fries, we chatted with the people in the seats around us, sometimes we even sat in mediocre seats for the purpose of Charlie mingling and signing autographs, which he loved being asked to do, taking particular delight in being asked to sign baseballs (I assumed at the time that sitting in the upper deck was something Zeke Langenbacher had suggested, but I later discovered Hank Ucker had), and I became genuinely invested in the team's wins and losses. Construction on the new stadium was completed in 1992, built on the same grounds as the old one, which was demolished; the new one has, among other features, luxury boxes and a retractable roof. I cannot say the fact that both stadiums turned out to be in Ed Blackwell's congressional district surprised me. Because the new stadium was publicly financed, a degree of controversy accompanied it, and I honestly believe that Charlie confronted the challenges with restraint and reason. He'd never worked harder in his life than he did during those years, and at the opening game in the new stadium, I was very proud of him.

It was in 1993 that Charlie made the decision to run for governor—at Hank Ucker's urging, needless to say—and he was elected in 1994. That, too, was a great turning point in our lives, though eventually dwarfed by the turning point that occurred in 2000.

We couldn't have guessed then what an asset Charlie's religiosity would turn out to be. Best of all was his sincerity. This, I suspect, has been a large part of Charlie's appeal to voters—if he can be petulant or sophomoric, he is never less than sincere. Even when called upon to act stately, he demonstrates, sincerely, that he's acting: He winks, he makes faces or at least conveys that he wishes he could. Often during his first presidential campaign, he'd say on the trail, when trying to contrast himself with the outgoing president, who was widely viewed as a slick panderer, "What you see is what you get." He'd grin impishly. I sometimes long to remind voters of this now; neither to them nor to me did Charlie ever conceal who he is.

Back before his gubernatorial bid, before our already not exactly average lives became as far-fetched as a fairy tale, his family thought it a hoot that he'd been born again. If Arthur said over dinner, about a recent Packers game, "It was a goddamm rout," Charlie might say, with jovial sternness, "You know I don't care for that kind of language," and Arthur would reply, "Jesus fucking Christ, Chas, get off your high horse." Or perhaps "Holy shit, you've lost your sense of humor!" (In fact, Charlie still enjoyed secular bawdiness and cursing—it was only people taking the Lord's name in vain that bothered him.) He also stopped purchasing pornography, which pleased me, though because I had a hunch he'd miss it, I bought him an artsy coffee table book of black-and-white photos of female nudes. Presumably, it was a poor substitute.

Charlie had joined a men's prayer group that met once a week, sometimes in our living room. Reverend Randy—now that he is director of the Multifaith Council, the public knows him as Randall Kniss—became a fixture in our lives. We never missed a Sunday at Heavenly Rose, we said grace before all meals (Charlie even said it at restaurants or dinner parties, which I found a tad ostentatious, but I bit my tongue), and Charlie read the Bible every night before bed.

That summer of 1988, we didn't end up spending much time in Halcyon, driving up just for a few weekends, both because Charlie was busy with the Brewers and because he feared that being around his brothers, particularly Arthur, would make it harder not to drink. Once, about a month after I'd returned from Riley, I awakened past midnight and found that Charlie was not beside me, though we'd gone to bed together almost two hours before. Thinking I heard voices downstairs, I walked into the hall and stood at the top of the steps; there definitely were people talking—chanting, it sounded like—in the den. It wasn't until I'd gone downstairs that I could hear clearly what they were saying, that I knew who it was, though I stopped short of entering the room. Through the doorway, I saw my husband and beefy, ruddy Reverend Randy on their knees, side by side, holding hands, their eyes shut, and Charlie weeping; over and over, they were reciting the sinner's prayer. I backed away.

He'd felt tempted to have a glass of whiskey, Charlie told me the next morning, so tempted he'd been unable to sleep. He had called Reverend Randy because Randy understood these desires, and they'd prayed together, and the urge had passed; Satan had gone elsewhere to do his bidding. This happened again, Reverend Randy's late-night appearances, but I never got out of bed for another one. I'm not proud to say that what I saw that night, looking into the den—it bothered me. It wasn't Reverend Randy as a person so much as the prayer as an experience, the fervor I would never share. Charlie had traveled outside my reach to a place I couldn't follow.

But I should note, for all my resistance to organized religion, that I don't believe Charlie could have quit drinking without it. It provided him with a way to structure his behavior, and a way to explain that behavior, both past and present, to himself. Perhaps fiction has, for me, served a similar purpose—what is a narrative arc if not the imposition of order on disparate events?—and perhaps it is my avid reading that has been my faith all along.

It wasn't until years later, until quite recently, in fact, that I learned exactly how Miss Ruby had managed to introduce Charlie and Reverend Randy: She had found the reverend by looking in the Yellow Pages under churches. Herself a faithful parishioner at Lord's Baptist in Harambee, Miss Ruby sensed that Charlie would benefit from spiritual uplift, and when she'd reached Reverend Randy on the phone, she'd requested that he make a house call. Jessica Sutton was the one who told me this, and I said, "But why didn't Miss Ruby ask her own minister to talk to Charlie?"

Jessica is thirty-one now, a tall, poised, whip-smart woman, a graduate of Yale and the Kennedy School at Harvard, and my chief of staff; during Charlie's first term in the White House, she was my deputy chief of staff, and at the start of his second term, when her predecessor left, I promoted her. I'm almost sure that Jessica is also a Democrat, though there are certain topics we do not broach. She laughed at my question, and though her words were damning, her tone was warm, as if she were teasing. She said, "Grandma thought he'd never listen to a black man."

PART IV

1600 Pennsylvania Avenue

TODAY, AS ON all mornings when we're in Washington, the phone on Charlie's side of the bed rings at a quarter to six. After answering it, he rises and walks to his bathroom (I'm half aware of this through the fog of my own sleep), and then he opens the door between our bedroom and the corridor, where a valet is waiting to pass him the newspapers. It's like at a hotel, except that instead of just the papers, you get a live person as well; heaven forbid the president of the United States should bend or reach.

Charlie carries them to my side of the bed: *The New York Times, The Washington Post, The Wall Street Journal.* He whistles as he approaches—he's whistling "Zip-a-Dee-Doo-Dah"—and when I prop myself up, I see that he is holding the newspapers out of my reach. He says, "You're only allowed to read them if you don't give me shit about Mr. Sympathy."

Mr. Sympathy is Charlie's nickname for Edgar Franklin, a retired colonel in the U.S. Army and the father of a soldier who was killed two years ago, at the age of twenty-one, by a roadside bomb. As of this morning, Colonel Franklin has spent one night sleeping in a tent on the Ellipse, the park directly south of the White House and north of the Washington Monument, and four more nights sleeping in the same tent on a two-hundred-square-foot lawn on Fourth Street SE, just beyond the Capitol and about three miles from the White House; he has been spending his days there, too, in the hope of talking to Charlie. It is the first week of June, and it was ninety-six degrees yesterday, the air thick with Washington's swampy humidity. I'd bet that outside, even this early, the temperature has passed eighty.

I extend both arms to take the newspapers, and Charlie shakes his head. "I didn't hear a promise."

"Are there new developments?"

He makes an expression of disgust. "Guy's a pawn of the Democrats. I guarantee he's on the payroll of some lefty kooks."

"I don't think he's being paid," I say.

"Give your word—no lobbying."

"I give my word," I say, and Charlie tosses the newspapers onto the duvet; they land with a thud. As he returns to the bathroom, he says over his shoulder, "Look in the business section, because I heard a rumor that General Electric and Alitalia are merging."

"Very funny." This is a joke I have heard so many times that the punch line—*And they're calling it Genitalia!*—can go unspoken. Charlie's second favorite joke on passing off the papers is stock-related: *Did you hear that Northern tissue touched a new bottom yesterday? Thousands were wiped clean.*

My usual pattern is to first scan the front page and then the editorial and op-ed pages of each paper, starting with the *Times,* and if there are no particularly alarming news articles, I go to the *Times*'s arts section, which I read in full. On the cover of today's *Times,* the headlines are about a helicopter crash yesterday afternoon that killed six marines; about the visits Charlie's Supreme Court nominee, Ingrid Sanchez, will make this afternoon to various senators in advance of her confirmation hearings; about Congress's vote on the new energy bill; about the damage caused by flash flooding in South Dakota; about Edgar Franklin; and finally, also on the front page, there's a feature on the increasingly popular cosmetic surgery procedure known as vaginal rejuvenation. After reading the Edgar Franklin piece, I skip to the arts: a profile of a nineteeen-year-old hip-hop artist named Shaneece, no surname; a review of a biography about Mary Cassatt; reviews of an opera in San Francisco, two plays in New York, and a ceramics exhibit in Santa Fe. When I'm finished with that section, I return to the hard news, which I also read thoroughly, at least in the *Times;* in the *Post,* I fully read only the articles pertaining to Charlie's administration and the style section, including, I admit it, "The Reliable Source."

Charlie and I sleep in what is technically the president's bedroom—many first couples have used separate rooms, and the adjacent first lady's bedroom is larger than the president's, with its own sitting room and bathroom, which I do use. (In the sitting room, I keep both my papier-mâché Giving Tree and the Nefertiti bust I inherited from my grandmother; Charlie decreed the bust too creepy for the room we share.) While I read, Charlie showers, shaves, and brushes his teeth as Mozart plays on a Bose stereo in a recessed section of his bathroom wall. Though he hasn't learned to distinguish baroque from romantic and isn't interested in which composer wrote what, classical music is something Charlie acquired a taste for during his governorship, when we attended symphonies at Madison's Oscar Mayer Theatre. I have mixed emotions about his late-in-life musical appreciation—I am glad that he enjoys it, but I can't help suspecting his enjoyment is tied directly to the hectic pace of his life, all the demands placed on him. He likes classical music, I'm almost certain, for what it doesn't contain, which is words or requests or criticism. It is only melody and mood, and so long as the mood doesn't become too somber, it soothes him.

When Edgar Franklin first staked his tent on the Ellipse, the *Times* buried the articles about him—they put them on A16 or A19—and the early pieces were less than a sixth of a page. Today's article, following two separate op-ed columns yesterday, is the most prominent yet: He has no plans to move, and he has been joined by supporters numbering in the hundreds, who stay overnight with friends or strangers in row houses or apartments all over the city, in hotels and motels, in tents of their own on campgrounds as far away as Millersville, Maryland, or Lake Fairfax Park in Virginia, then return each morning to Capitol Hill. Colonel Franklin has also received dozens of bouquets of flowers, hundreds of pounds of food, thousands of dollars in donations, and he has been joined by a Manhattan publicist who took leave of his job to work for free. In response, the *Times* quotes a White House spokeswoman, Margaret Carpeni (Maggie is thirty-one, an athletic young woman who has run two marathons and who just broke up with her boyfriend, a medical resident, though none of us is sure why) who said on Sunday, "The president continues to pray for our fallen soldiers and the loved ones they've left behind, recognizing the ultimate sacrifice these individuals have made to protect freedom and liberty in the United States and around the world."

He is a trim African-American man, Edgar Franklin, fifty-six years old, and for the last five days, he has worn not his army uniform—if he did, it would make me side more with Charlie, distrusting the staginess of it—but rather, khaki trousers and blue or white short-sleeved shirts, his sleeveless undershirts visible beneath them. He looks remarkably pulled together for having spent nights in a tent, although I assume he is showering each morning at the house belonging to the couple on whose lawn he sleeps. After originally setting up camp on the Ellipse, he was forced to move. Despite grounds for arrest, he was let off with a fine (he has told reporters he will pay it), and this was when a sympathetic couple in their late thirties who live on Capitol Hill offered to let him stay in their front yard. Whether Colonel Franklin is still in violation of an ordinance against camping is a question the advisory neighborhood commission, which is overwhelmingly liberal, appears uninterested in pursuing.

What Edgar Franklin wants is this: to meet with my husband in order to share his thoughts about why the war is futile and the United States ought to bring home the troops. It was in the spring of 2005 that Edgar Franklin's only child, Nathaniel "Nate" Franklin, was killed by a roadside bomb in a northern province. Already, Edgar was a widower, his wife, Wanda, having died of colon cancer in 1996. Edgar himself served in Vietnam—he was drafted at the age of nineteen—and he remained in the army for thirty years, ultimately being deployed to six combat zones and becoming an officer. In print and television interviews, of which there have been more with each passing day, he doesn't casually trash my husband. He isn't loquacious, or sloppy with words. He says, "I did not in good conscience feel that I could remain silent." Naturally, he has been censured by several former military colleagues.

His plaintiveness, his trim build and fastidious dress and terse commentary—they are haunting me. I asked one of my aides to find out if Colonel Franklin is, as his son was, an only child, and I was greatly relieved to learn he isn't. Raised in Valdosta, Georgia, Colonel Franklin is the second of five siblings, all the others sisters: Deborah, now fifty-eight, still in Valdosta and running a day care from her home; Pamela, who would be fifty-three but is deceased (she suffered from diabetes); Cynthia, fifty, a homemaker in Dallas; and Cheryl, forty-seven, a paralegal in Atlanta. Cynthia is also a military parent—her son is a Special Forces soldier serving overseas—and disavowed her brother's actions on Thursday in *The Dallas Morning News,* then refused to make further public comment; according to the article in today's *Times,* Cheryl joined Colonel Franklin yesterday in Washington.

When the story broke last Wednesday, Charlie told me, "You can't let the opposition dictate the terms of the conversation," and later that day, when Hank Ucker and I passed in the hallway outside the Map Room—Hank is now Charlie's chief of staff—he said, "The president tells me the Franklin fellow has gotten under your skin, but trust me, Alice, capitulating to his demands would set a dangerous precedent. You can't let the opposition dictate the terms of the conversation." There is no doubt in my mind which of them borrowed the phrasing from the other; we all have known one another far too long.

Charlie emerges from the bathroom with a towel wrapped around his waist, his torso bare. Although the presidency has aged him, as it has aged all the men who've held it—his hair is grayer now, his face more lined—he is still extraordinarily fit and handsome. He comes over and kisses me on the nose. "How'd I mess up the world today?"

"There's a Broadway production of *The Glass Menagerie* that got a great review," I say.

"What are they saying about Ingrid?"

In what I intend to be a neutral tone, I say, "They're mostly trying to gauge her stance on abortion." Ingrid Sanchez, Charlie's Supreme Court nominee, was a U.S. attorney in Michigan and then a judge for the U.S. Court of Appeals for the Sixth Circuit. She is a practicing Catholic and a lay ecclesial minister of her local church, and though she has made no official statement on the subject, she is widely assumed to be pro-life. She also appears to have an impeccable record, and the fact that she's female makes protesting her nomination trickier for women's groups, which isn't to say they're staying quiet. Charlie's last appointee, the new chief justice whose confirmation occurred in September 2006, is conservative as well, though his views on abortion, even after his first term, remain ambiguous. If Ingrid Sanchez is confirmed, it is possible that the Court will vote to overturn *Roe* v. *Wade.* While this makes me uncomfortable, the matter is not in my hands, and it's scarcely as if Charlie doesn't know my views; the whole country knows my views. Shortly before Charlie's first inauguration, the anchor of a national morning news show asked if I thought abortion should be legal, and I said, "Yes." Asked by the same anchor in 2004 whether I had changed my mind, I said, "No." Though I didn't expand on the topic in either instance, both times the question was one I had agreed in advance to answer.

"Typical of the *Times,*" Charlie says, and his nostrils flare in irritation. "Here Ingrid's got nearly three decades of legal and judicial experience, and they've got to reduce it to one issue."

"Sweetheart, I think that's to be expected. The Republicans are as curious as the Democrats." While Charlie reads no newspaper on a regular basis, relying instead on briefings from his staff, his contempt for *The New York Times* is particularly intense. This is ironic, given that in the eighties, when we were in Halcyon in the summers, he and Arthur would drive an hour and twenty-five minutes to Green Bay to buy the *Times* Sunday edition; they would call ahead to a grocery store to reserve their copy.

I push off the sheet and duvet and stand, wrapping my arms around Charlie and inhaling the scent of his neck and shoulders. "You smell very clean," I say. I reach for the slim leather folder on his nightstand and open it. These folders—an identical one is on my nightstand—contain our schedules for the day. Before we go to bed, we each receive both our own and each other's.

On his plate today: intelligence and FBI briefings, a late-morning speech at a conference for small-business leaders in Columbus, Ohio, a fund-raising luncheon in Buffalo, and a meeting with his economic advisers back in the Oval Office this afternoon, before and after which he'll make calls on Ingrid Sanchez's behalf. Tonight at eight o'clock there is a White House gala titled "Students and Teachers Salute Alice

Blackwell," which I find quite embarrassing. As Hank reminded me when he got me to agree to it in April, Charlie's approval ratings have dipped to 32 percent, while mine rest at 83 percent; I am allegedly the second most admired woman in the United States, just behind Oprah Winfrey. (Ridiculous as it is, this ranking is hardly the most ridiculous aspect of my life.) "Reminding Americans how much they love you reminds them they love the president," Hank told me. "You'll be taking one for the team, and all you have to do is show up and pretend you have an ego like the rest of us."

Charlie glances at his schedule, then pulls mine from beneath it. "You're not traveling today, are you?"

I shake my head. "The breast-cancer panel is in Arlington."

"A titty summit, huh?" Charlie grins. "Need any help performing a self-exam?"

"Get dressed." I push him away and turn to make our bed, a habit I've been told the maids find hilarious, but one I can't suppress. Prior to our arrival over six years ago, the sheets in the residence were changed daily, but I requested, so as not to waste water, that they be changed no more than once a week, even for Charlie and me.

He reappears a few minutes later in a white oxford shirt, a charcoal suit, and a red tie marked with tiny yellow dots. "You look nice," I say.

"You excited to be the belle of the ball tonight?"

Dryly, I say, "I'm beside myself."

"You're not dreading it, are you? Lindy, you deserve to be recognized. People have no idea how much you've done not just for the administration but for the country."

This is a way of talking I don't care for, talking as you'd hope others might talk about you, believing your press, or what you wish were your press. Though in public, I try to graciously accept both compliments and criticism, in the privacy of my head, I avoid giving myself credit for vague achievements tied to my position—for being a role model, for showing leadership—and at the same time, I don't blame myself for the broad general failures for which I am held responsible by my detractors. To others, I am a symbol; to myself, I have only ever been me.

I set my hands on Charlie's shoulders, and we lean in and give each other a minty, toothpastey kiss. "Ella gets in around four, and I have to give a tour to a third-grade choir after that, but otherwise, I hope she and I will get to relax," I say. (That our daughter is coming home for tonight's gala is, in my opinion, its main benefit; though I try not to crowd her, I adore when she visits.) "If you want us to come and say hi, if you have a spare minute, have Michael call up."

"Wyatt's not coming with her?" Wyatt is Ella's boyfriend of a year and a half. They both work as investment analysts at Goldman Sachs in Manhattan, and Charlie likes to play tennis with Wyatt because Wyatt is good enough to be challenging but not so good that Charlie can't have the pleasure of beating a man half his age.

I say, "Well, Ella leaves again tomorrow, so it's such a short visit. Will you have a good day today and be careful?" I say this to Charlie every morning. You would think—I would have thought—there would be an entirely different vocabulary that a president and a first lady would use, one that encompassed the constant possibility of national or international disaster, the weight of a country. And there's White House jargon—FLOTUS and pool spray and "the football"—but it turns out that for the most part, we make do with the same words we've always used.

"I love you, Lindy," Charlie says. It is six-twenty, and from here, he will go for breakfast in the Family Dining Room, where Hank and Debbie Bell, a senior adviser, will be waiting for him; they meet daily and call themselves the Oatmealers. From the dining room, Charlie will move on to the Oval Office for his briefings and then go directly to the South Lawn for the short ride on *Marine One* to Andrews Air Force Base and the longer plane flight to Columbus. (Punctuality has been a major point of pride with Charlie during both his administrations.)

He always reminds me in this early-morning moment of an actor going onstage, an insurance salesman, or perhaps the owner of the hardware store who landed the starring role in the community-theater production of *The Music Man.* Oh, how I want to protect him! Oh, the outlandishness of our lives, familiar now and routine, but still so deeply strange. "I love you, too," I say.

THIS IS THE part everyone already knows: that in the year 2000, Charlie won the presidential election by a narrower margin than any other candidate in U.S. history, that in fact his opponent received more popular votes while Charlie received more electoral ones; that the final decision was made by the Supreme Court, who voted 5–4 in Charlie's favor; that at his inauguration in January 2001, he made a pledge to work in an inclusive, bipartisan fashion, a pledge I believe he intended to keep; that eight months later, terrorist attacks occurred in New York and Washington, D.C., killing close to three thousand Americans; that, first in October 2001 and again in March 2003, the U.S. Congress authorized the use of force against countries thought to be harboring terrorist leaders and weapons of mass destruction; that Charlie's advisers and Charlie himself told the American people the war would be swift, that even as soon as six weeks after the March 2003 invasion, they assumed major combat operations were complete, as Charlie famously declared in a speech aboard a navy supercarrier, but that now, four years in, it is more bloody and chaotic than ever. Over three thousand American troops have died, the same number killed in the terrorist attacks, and close to twenty-five thousand have been wounded. As for foreign civilians, estimates range from seventy thousand deaths to ten times that. Every day, there are car bombs and suicide bombs, gunmen shooting police officers, mortar strikes on homes and schools, sniper fire outside mosques, decapitations at checkpoints. These days, Charlie and his defenders speak of freedom, of reshaping a region and shifting an ideology, of finishing what they started instead of cutting and running; his critics speak of quagmires and civil war. Some of those who were once his defenders have become his critics.

When we went to sleep at four A.M. on November 8, 2000, I didn't think Charlie had won the election, and I was both sorry for him and relieved for us, for our family. I hadn't wanted him to run for governor of Wisconsin in 1994, and I hadn't wanted him to run for president. What we'd mostly lost already—the option of shopping at the grocery store, quietly eating dinner at a restaurant, going for a walk alone or with a friend, or just spending a Saturday reading and cleaning the house, without obligations—I knew we'd lose completely if Charlie became president. I did not want the exposure, the forfeiture of our privacy and our last ties to ordinary life.

When the election wasn't decided for over a month, we laid low in the governor's mansion in Madison; I read, went to friends' houses for lunch, and attended a few gatherings for groups I'd become involved with as first lady of Wisconsin, while Charlie and Hank Ucker and various advisers and lawyers and relatives held urgent, secretive meetings and avoided the media. When, on December 12, after recounts and lawsuits, Charlie was declared president, I thought, *We will ride it out.* There would be risks, but we'd ride out the presidency as we'd ride out a tornado watch: Keep your head down, cross your arms over the crown of your skull. Not literally, of course—literally, what I'd do would be to comply with all that was public and obligatory, to show up when I was expected to show up—but that was how I'd think of it. For at least four years and likely for eight, I'd hold my breath, waiting for it to pass, and eventually, it would. A tornado is disruptive, but it never lasts.

But I hadn't considered—how could I not have?—the circumstances under which Charlie and I had gotten engaged. In the middle of a storm, he had left his apartment and climbed into his car and driven through the lightning and hail, he had swooped down the basement steps of the house I lived in and proposed marriage. He'd defied the tornado that day, not run from it. And look—it had worked. Here we were, still happily married all these years later.

What I had projected onto Charlie at the beginning of his presidency was my own wish not to cause a stir, not to attract undue attention or assert myself, when Charlie *enjoyed* asserting himself. I know there are those who suggest he, or some shadow entity of his administration, planned the terrorist attacks, and I consider such an idea ludicrous, unworthy of discussion. But it is indisputable that he responded; he took on the challenge. Did he conflate the terrorist attacks with the separate and lesser threats coming from the country we invaded in March 2003, when the attacks and the threats were then unconnected, and did he encourage the public to conflate them as well? Was the invasion only for oil, Charlie's vows to spread democracy mere lip service? Was he quicker to enter a war than he would have been if he'd had military experience himself instead of having spent the late sixties and early seventies working as a ski instructor? These are accusations his opponents level at him, and while they are fair questions, what I dislike most about the political conversation is its pretense that a correct answer exists for anything, that it's not all murkiness and subjectivity. I didn't know in the days leading up to the March 2003 invasion whether I thought invading was right or wrong, I didn't know if I agreed with the hawks or the protestors holding candlelight vigils. As in college, when I had neither supported nor condemned the Vietnam War, my inactivity stemmed from uncertainty rather than indifference. But not knowing what I thought, I did not try to influence my husband. There were plenty of people advising him, men and women (though mostly men) who'd spent decades as foreign policy experts, who in earlier times had traveled to this very country, met with this very dictator.

Now over four years have passed since the invasion. That a war once supported by 70 percent of Americans has become divisive and unpopular has served only to make Charlie more resolute; in the circular fashion of such things, it is about being resolute that he is most resolute of all. The average American doesn't have access to the intelligence Charlie does, he points out; the average American has become coddled and forgetful, unaccustomed to bloodshed or sacrifice. Think of the Revolutionary War, Charlie says, think of the Civil War, think of World War II. There is a price we must pay for democracy, and it has always been so. Nine months ago, in September 2006, Charlie said at a press conference, "To withdraw right now would be to surrender, and I wouldn't surrender even if Alice and Snowflake were the only ones left supporting me." (Snowflake is, of course, our cat; he was also my "coauthor" on *First Pet: What I've Seen from 1600 Pennsylvania Avenue,* an indignity either increased or lessened, I've never been sure which, by the fact that though we shared credit and all proceeds went to a national literacy program, I wrote no more of the book than Snowflake did.)

Since Charlie's inauguration, I have made endless calculations: We are 10 percent finished with his time in office. We have 394 weeks left.

We have five and a half years. From the beginning, I assumed his reelection not because I wanted it but the opposite. It is what we most desire that we're afraid to count on; it's always so much easier to believe in an eventuality you'd rather avoid.

The speeches Charlie gives, and my own as well, the fund-raisers and the funerals, the state visits and the balls, the ribbon cuttings and the receiving lines and the hundreds of letters that I write and receive every week—I am always checking them off a great list, counting down. It's not that I don't enjoy any of the responsibilities I bear as first lady. I do, and I feel grateful. I've met legends of art and literature, kings and queens and chieftains and an emperor, I've visited sixty-four countries, sampled beluga blinis on a ship on the Neva River, ridden a camel at the pyramids of Giza, waded in the waters of Pangkor Laut (I didn't swim, because I didn't wish to appear in a bathing suit before the cameras). At the airport in Asmara, Eritrea, where I had traveled without Charlie, local women threw popcorn at me as a welcoming gesture; at an orphanage in Bangalore, I donned a sari and read *The Giving Tree* to the children, accompanied by a Kannada translator; and in Helsinki, after a marvelous evening of conversation and a feast of crayfish, reindeer meat, and cloudberry layer cake, I committed a faux pas I could blame only on jet lag by saying, in a public toast to Finland's president, that I would always remember the kindness of the Swedish people. I have had the surreal experience of holding the Bible upon which my husband was sworn in as president (I was very moved, and at the same time, inappropriately, the line from the old folk song "Froggie Went A-Courtin'," which Ella had learned as a child, kept replaying in my head: "Without my Uncle Rat's consent, I wouldn't marry the president . . ."), and I have had the equally surreal experience of returning to Theodora Liess Elementary School, where I'd worked in Madison, for the school's rededication as the Alice Blackwell School. (I hoped that Theodora, the nineteenth-century daughter of a director of the Milwaukee and Mississippi Railroad and herself an outspoken advocate of educating Ojibwe girls, would forgive me; to decline the school's honor seemed impolite.)

I have often felt a pang at not being able to share the more colorful of my experiences with my grandmother; what a hoot she would find my life, how she'd relish the gossipy details. But Charlie and I have included many of our relatives and longtime friends in the pleasures of our unexpected circumstances: For the eightieth birthday of my Madison friend Rita Alwin, I flew her to Washington and had her stay in the Lincoln Bedroom (on the plane out, she wore my mother's garnet brooch, which touched me). One Christmas Day, Charlie, Ella, my mother, Jadey, Arthur, their two grown children, and I spent a delightfully raucous afternoon in the White House bowling alley (we don't travel for the actual holiday to Wisconsin because we don't want our Secret Service agents to be away from their families). And, among other political appointees, Charlie made our friend Cliff Hicken—a steadfast campaign fund-raiser—ambassador of France, so I've ended up having several wonderful visits in Paris with Kathleen, the two of us jaunting around to restaurants and museums and fashionable shops.

If the life Charlie and I share is prescribed and demanding, it is also privileged and fascinating. We are now and will always be members of a tiny club. And really, my own pleasure in or aversion to our status is irrelevant; it exists and cannot be unmade. We are famous, and when Charlie leaves office, we'll be famous emeritus.

Today will, no doubt, be a day of drama and obligations, but it will be a day like any other; all our days now are days of drama and obligations. Three miles away, Edgar Franklin waits—futilely, I fear—to talk to Charlie; also nearby, Ingrid Sanchez prepares to visit senators; aboard *Air Force One,* en route to Columbus, Charlie might be vetoing a bill, deciding to increase or decrease spending or taxes by billions of dollars, conferring on the phone with the prime minister of the U.K. Later this morning, at the breast-cancer panel in a hotel ballroom in Arlington, Virginia, I'll wear a red linen suit and encourage women to quit smoking, exercise regularly, and schedule yearly mammograms after the age of forty. This afternoon, I will visit with my daughter and give a tour of the White House to a group of forty third-graders who in turn will perform "God Bless America" at tonight's gala in my honor. I wasn't born to stand before crowds, to dispense advice or exhort, and after much coaching, I'd say I am only slightly better than adequate as a public speaker. Nevertheless, I attempt to rise to the occasion—I am the wife of the president of the United States, and I try to be a good one.

Charlie will be in office for nineteen more months.

IT IS AT the end of the breast-cancer panel, during the part when the panelists and audience members have their picture taken with me—I greet the individual, we pose in front of a flag, the photographer's flash goes off, and we're on to the next person, all within a matter of seconds—that I see Hank Ucker leaning against the wall near the stage. I feel a flare-up of the fear that accompanies me everywhere, a fear whose omnipresence I recognize by the ease with which it sparks. Just once, in September 2001, was the fear truly justified, and even now I quickly realize that whatever is wrong, whatever has made Hank Ucker show up at a ballroom in Arlington, can't be life-threatening to Charlie. If it were, I'd be whisked away immediately, shuttled to a bunker, outfitted in a bulletproof vest. (I've worn them more than once; above all, they are heavy.)

I glance at the line of people waiting to have their picture taken and try to count how many remain—more than forty—and I gesture to Ashley Obernauer, who is my personal aide. (Ashley is twenty-five and dazzlingly competent.) When she leans in, I say, "Ask Hank why he's here."

She soon returns. "He says he wants to chat—his word—with you on the ride back. He didn't say about what."

"Your husband is doing such a wonderful job," a short woman in white polyester slacks, with wavy gray hair, says as we shake hands. "We pray for both of you every night."

"Thank you." I turn toward the camera, nudging her a bit as I do, so she's facing forward, too.

"I'm so honored to—" she starts to say but is cut off by an advance person moving her along.

"Thank you for coming," I call after her.

Another older woman is next (perhaps a nursing home was bused in?), and she says, "You tell President Blackwell that Mrs. Mabel Fulford says don't back down one inch from the terrorists."

"Will do," I say, and the flash goes off, and I am on to the next person, a woman closer to my own age who says, "I skipped work to hear you today."

"Your secret is safe with me," I say. There can be a Potemkin feel to these events, the contrast between the enthusiasm and warmth of the people we meet and the overwhelmingly negative coverage from the media of anything having to do with Charlie's administration. Many constituents also hold a negative view, of course, but they tend not to come to such events unless it's to protest, and the precautions taken to keep them out are ever more elaborate. For safety reasons, I entered this hotel through the service entrance in the back, but as we drove in, I still glimpsed today's protestors standing across the street, holding signs and chanting. Usually, they're chanting antiwar slogans, but I believe that today there were also some placards opposing Ingrid Sanchez's Supreme Court nomination.

The next woman says, "When is Ella going to marry that boyfriend of hers?"

I laugh. "I'll let you know when I do." Camera flash, camera flash, camera flash, and finally, we're at the end of the line. The event organizers are thanking me profusely, bestowing on me a gift bag that Ashley accepts, and we all are headed out the back doors to the motorcade—Ashley; a deputy press secretary named Sandy; Bill Rawson, who is one of the official White House photographers; a woman named Zinia who is a health policy expert; and six Secret Service agents (more agents wait outside). As we walk, Ashley says, "Alice?" and I hold out my palms; she squirts Purell on them, and I rub my hands together.

Hank has materialized beside me. He says, "America does love its first lady." My dislike of the term *first lady* is well established (though I use it sometimes myself for lack of an alternative, I find it fussy and antiquated), and everyone within the White House calls me simply Alice or Mrs. Blackwell. I give Hank a tight smile. Outside, the June heat assaults us even on the ten-foot walk from the service entrance to the motorcade; a Secret Service agent named Cal holds open the rear door in the third SUV for me. (I avoid motorcades when possible, preferring a few Town Cars, but the breast-cancer summit was a highly publicized event. Before September 2001, I used three cars and six agents for public events; now, in addition to the police escorts, I use five cars and nine agents, an extravagance that no longer seems bizarre. Also after September 2001, my motorcade was granted "intersection control" in Washington, meaning we need not stop at lights.) Hank climbs in after me, and Ashley is about to follow him when Hank says to her, "Ride behind us, will you, Ash? We'll all powwow back in the East Wing."

Ashley glances at me, and I think of objecting, but something in Hank's tone stops me. Fastening my seat belt, I say, "Hank, I thought you'd gone to Ohio."

"Change of plans."

"I assume Charlie's all right?"

"The president's fine." Visibly, Hank roots with the tip of his tongue in a molar; above all, he likes to appear unruffled, so his studied casualness in this moment means that *something* must be wrong. Sure enough, he says, "I got a call this morning. Does the name Norene Davis ring a bell?"

I shuffle through my memory, though the problem is that I no longer know everyone I know. I often feel that I do nothing except meet people; it is fully possible I spoke to someone for fifteen minutes at an event, that I even sat next to him or her for the duration of a meal and we had a pleasant conversation, and that I have no recollection of it. At functions, a person might say, "I treasure the picture I had taken with you at our annual banquet last spring" or "My wife and I often talk about meeting you at the Republican Convention in '96," and I nod in a friendly fashion. Sometimes these hints prod my brain—I *have* seen this person before—but I never would have made the realization on my own, and I could sooner levitate right there on the spot than tell you his or her name. I say, "I don't remember a Norene Davis, but it's possible."

Hank clears his throat. "She's alleging you had an abortion in October of '63."

I gasp; I hear the intake of breath before I realize it was mine. *Expect the unexpected* is an apt if clichéd guideline for life in the White House, but I did not expect this. I half expected it once, back when Charlie first ran for governor, and then again when he ran for president, and I worried about the damage it would do to Charlie's candidacy more than the violation of my own privacy, though I would not have relished either. But what could have happened didn't, and it seemed that the revelation's potency could only dwindle. If I was going to be exposed—if Dena Janaszewski, or whatever name she went by now, was going to sell me out—it would have happened already. Thus I shelved this particular worry; there are always more than enough to choose from.

"Can you think of any reason Ms. Davis would make that claim?" Hank asks, and his tone is deliberately empty. No one else in the car reacts, not Cal, who sits in the front passenger seat, nor the other Secret Service agent, Walter, who's driving. (Cal, who is currently my lead agent, played football at ASU; Walter is the father of twins—because they know far too much about us, both Charlie and I have made an effort to get to know our agents, and Charlie has personally shown the Oval Office to many of their family members.) I can see only the back of Walter's head and some of Cal's profile, but I'm confident both that they're listening and that they'll say nothing during this car ride, nothing when we're back at the White House; they almost never speak first unless it's an issue of safety. In crowds, I sometimes hear one beside me, having floated up without my noticing, murmuring, "Veer left," or "Hold up, ma'am." For men generally weighing over two hundred and fifty pounds, they are remarkably graceful.

To Hank, I say, "Are you sure this woman's name is Norene Davis?"

Hank removes a BlackBerry from the inner pocket of his blazer and reads from the screen. "Age thirty-six, current address 5147 Manchester Street in Cicero, Illinois, although we have reason to believe she's no longer living there. Divorced, no kids, employed as a home health aide by a rinky-dink-sounding organization called Glenview Health Service."

"Is it possible she used to go by a different name?"

"Anything's possible. My impression is she's fronting for someone, but the question is who. While our tireless investigators figure that out, I wanted to check with you. Now, here's where the plot thickens: This gal isn't interested in blackmail, at least not in the conventional sense. Instead, she's threatening to go public unless you speak out against Ingrid Sanchez as a Supreme Court nominee."

Confused, I repeat, "Unless I—" But even before I finish the question, I understand. The brevity of the two answers I gave about my stance on abortion on the morning news show in 2000 and 2004 did not pacify pro-choice activists; in fact, it seems they might have preferred a pro-life first lady—a clear adversary—to one who quietly believes in reproductive freedom. As I said, the interview question was essentially staged both times, Charlie had given his blessings, which meant Hank had, which meant it served the administration, which it did because many Republicans are, after all, pro-choice themselves. The anchor had agreed in advance to ask no follow-up questions, and that first time, the next thing he said was "Now, on a less heavy topic, there's one member of the Blackwell family known to be even more press-shy than you. Can you tell viewers a bit about the elusive Snowflake?" After that television program aired, Jeanette Werden in Madison, who had so annoyed me all those years ago at the cookout where I'd met Charlie by prattling on about her marriage and children, and who had been pregnant at the time with her third child, wrote me a letter saying she'd terminated an earlier pregnancy at the age of twenty-eight—she had given birth to Katie, their daughter, just six months before, and was struggling with what today would be called postpartum depression. When Jeanette wrote about how glad she was I'd spoken out, I longed to call and tell her the rest. I didn't, though; I couldn't.

During Charlie's first gubernatorial campaign, one of Hank's minions interviewed me extensively; he had me walk him through every stage of my life, trawling for secrets or controversy. We spoke extensively about Andrew Imhof—it was a tabloid that first broke that story a few years later, in 2000, and I had the campaign press secretary confirm its accuracy as quickly as possible—and I answered every question the minion asked. But I did not volunteer extra information. Charlie and I had discussed it the night before, and he had said it was fine with him if I didn't mention my abortion. If it never came out, then there would have been no need, and if it did come out, it could be dealt with then. But to preemptively divulge it—the minion's questions were designed to elicit just such bombshells—seemed to me the surest way, through one person in the campaign confiding in another and another and eventually in a journalist, of making it public.

In this moment in the SUV, however, the *then* of *it could be dealt with then* has arrived—the *then* is now, it is today. I say to Hank, "Isn't this kind of threat illegal?"

Hank actually smiles. "We'll take down Norene Davis easy, don't worry, but what I'm curious about is why you think she'd level this particular charge."

What Hank isn't saying—he can't because I'm first lady—is that he either suspects or knows the charge is true. (Sometimes the etiquette with which he must comply cruelly amuses me, the fact that he has to call Charlie Mr. President, or stand when I enter the room. *You made us,* I think, *and now you must worship at our feet.*) If Hank didn't find the charge credible, he wouldn't be here; after all, the White House receives dozens of letters, e-mails, and calls a day from delusional individuals: "Tell Alice Blackwell to quit sending my dog messages through the TV!" Or "I'm the president's secret half brother from his father's affair in 1950, but for two million dollars, I promise to keep quiet." These accusations, like the threats to our lives, are constant, yet we learn the specifics of very few.

"Charlie knows what's going on?" I ask.

Hank nods. "He said I should come to you directly." Did Charlie tell Hank the charge is true? I doubt he said it outright, but he may have hinted.

I look out the window; we're heading east on Arlington Boulevard, the other cars on their way to Washington pulled over as we whiz past.

"Listen," Hank says. "This is a solvable problem. If Norene Davis is operating on her own, she's in way over her head. The likelihood that she'll back down with a little intimidation is high. Now let's say for the sake of argument that she's worked herself up and decides she'll go to jail before she'll be silenced, so she goes ahead and talks to a reporter, or let's say she does shut her trap, but oops, wait a second, she's already told her sister, she's told her boyfriend, whoever it is—either way, the allegation is out there. In that case, I'm thinking *Larry King.* Not an immediate booking, we don't want to go on the defensive right away. We wait ten days or two weeks, we fold it into another appearance—literacy, breast cancer, you pick the topic—and we let him ask you point-blank. You categorically deny it." There is a question mark implied in this scenario, and I allow the question to hang there in the air.

I say, "And when the press corps asks Maggie or Doug about it?"

" 'While we'd normally consider it beneath us to acknowledge such outrageous and false accusations, Mrs. Blackwell's respect for this sensitive and controversial issue blah blah blah . . .' Then, you know, lather, rinse, repeat."

"Just don't say 'sanctity of life.' "

"This isn't the time to fly your pro-choice flag, Alice."

"You've told me yourself the public accepts—"

Unusually, Hank interrupts me; he has turned in his seat so we're face-to-face. "The public accepts a first lady who supports the right to choose. Don't kid yourself that that's the same as accepting a first lady who had an abortion."

So he believes the allegation; he should, and I already knew he did, but there's a bitter satisfaction in forcing him to say it aloud. In the front seat, Walter and Cal are as alert and impassive as sphinxes.

I look Hank in the eye. "I'm not sure who Norene Davis is, but the person behind this is a former friend of mine named Dena Janaszewski. I haven't spoken to her in thirty years, and I haven't heard anything about her in probably fifteen, but she—she and maybe her boyfriend—are the only ones besides Charlie who've ever known about my abortion."

"Can you spell her last name?" Hank has his BlackBerry out again; if he's shocked by my admission, he has the restraint not to show it, and no one else says anything, either.

I say, "I'm not sure what name she goes by now, but she's much older than thirty-six—she's my age. She was married, and her name was Cimino, and then she was divorced, and she might be remarried, possibly to—" I pause. "Back in the late eighties, she was dating a man named Pete Imhof, so they might have broken up, or they might still be together. He's the brother of Andrew, the boy who—"

"Right." Hank nods.

"And also he—Pete—he's the one I got pregnant by, but he never knew."

"Dena would have told him." Hank isn't asking; he's making a statement.

The SUV is quiet except for the sirens of the police motorcycles escorting us, though even those sound distant because of the Doppler effect.

"Please have the investigators who talk to Dena be careful," I say to Hank. "I wish she weren't doing this, but I don't want her life to be ruined, and I don't want her going to prison."

"The pregnancy was before or after Andrew's death?" Hank is, I can see, imagining how to spin this, wondering if somehow the death can cancel out the abortion. I could spare him the trouble and tell him it can't.

"After," I say.

For a moment, Hank is silent, absorbing the information, and then he says, "Well, we've got our work cut out for us." (On second thought, perhaps he doesn't worship at our feet at all. That he is eating this up, luxuriating in the sordidness, is undeniable—it is not so much that Hank loves nothing more than a crisis but that he loves nothing more than his own indispensability to my husband in the face of one; there is a reason Charlie's nickname for Hank is Shit Storm.)

"Don't let the investigators physically threaten Dena," I say. "Do you hear me, Hank? I want them to be respectful."

"Alice, she's trying to thwart a Supreme Court nomination and lead a smear campaign against the president and the first lady of the United States."

I frown at him. "Don't be melodramatic." Before turning again to look out the window, I say, "She was once a close friend."

THE WAY FAME works is that people start to see your name in the news, whether on television or in the paper or a magazine. Something has just occurred (your husband has, with seven other men, bought a baseball team) or something is about to occur (your husband is on the verge of announcing he'll run for governor of Wisconsin, or he's on the verge of being elected), and people you know, though not necessarily well, contact you. People from the country club, whose house you have never been inside, who have never been inside yours—they call and leave joking messages, saying, "Don't forget us little people." Or "I saw you on Channel Four, and I had to get in touch while you still remember that you know me." Whatever the thing is that has just occurred or is about to occur, it's time-consuming; your life has never been more hectic, nor have there ever been more people contacting you for essentially pointless reasons, yet you feel compelled to respond, lest they think the attention has gone to your head. You hear from your dentist, your daughter's high school math teacher, people from your past: childhood friends, old classmates, former coworkers. They are surprisingly skilled at tracking you down. Sometimes they merely want acknowledgment, but increasingly, they want favors, and then strangers want favors, too. They ask you to speak at events, to be an honorary host, to be a member of their board of trustees, to auction off an evening with yourself; they want tickets to baseball games, tickets to the World Series, permission to get married on the baseball field, tickets to tour the governor's mansion; then they want you to help them gain access or entry to places to which you have no connection whatsoever, a fancy restaurant in New York, a golf course in North Carolina; they want you to help their nephew obtain a summer internship at a talent agency in Los Angeles. Before your fame extends beyond the state, they are already sure that it does. It would be impossible to say yes to all of these requests, though again, saying no increases the likelihood that you'll be viewed as rude; almost every person who asks a favor appears unaware of the existence of every other person doing the same. You realize that anyone can create an obligation for you just by wanting something; they write you a letter or an e-mail, they leave you a phone message, and while not granting their wish is bad enough, to ignore them would be unforgivable. In this way, they determine your schedule and duties; you have become public property.

Gradually, your fame settles on you, it's like a new coat or a new car that you become used to, but it continues to provoke odd and awkward behavior in others. At your public events, people you *never* knew, friends of friends of friends, your college boyfriend's aunt, the neighbor of your plumber—they, too, claim you, reciting the few degrees of separation between you and them. At private events unrelated to you or the reason you've become famous, the weddings or cocktail parties or school fund-raisers you still attend to try to convince yourself you remain a regular person, other people eye you heavily. You try to be modest by not assuming anyone recognizes or is looking at you; if you're meeting a person for the first time, you introduce yourself, you remark on the flowers or the food or the weather. But really, all they want to talk about is you: how they are connected to you (the more tenuous the connection, the more they insist on establishing it), or where they were when they saw an article or television segment featuring you, or what they overheard people on the street saying about you. They want to talk to you about how strange it must be, being famous; they don't realize they are even now creating the strangeness.

And then you become truly famous—not locally or regionally famous, but famous famous—and of all things, your burden lightens. Steadily, your entourage has been growing, and now it is large enough and professional enough that there is a buffer between you and the rest of the world. In public, you're flanked by aides; either visibly or invisibly, you're accompanied by a security detail. You can't just be approached, and the situations in which you can be approached are controlled and systematic. This is why it's harder to be moderately famous than very famous; when you're moderately famous, you still go to the grocery store, you still do the things you did before, while at any moment, you might be noticed and accosted. When you're very famous, you don't go to the grocery store unless it's for a photo op, and you know that wherever you do go, you'll be recognized at once. Any environment you set foot in will be altered, your presence will mean that everyone must start talking about you, taking your picture with their cell phones. This is why, during Charlie's presidency, we have hardly eaten at restaurants in Washington except during events organized around our attendance; we've been criticized for being aloof when the reality is that I feel it's unfair to all the other diners. They've gone out, perhaps to celebrate a job promotion or a birthday; they are buttering their bread and we appear, unsettling the equilibrium of the room. If this was to be the dinner where you celebrated your promotion, it has become instead the dinner where the president and the first lady showed up. It is selfish, really; we take up more than our fair share of oxygen.

Early on, at moments when I felt most overwhelmed by my new role as first lady, I'd tell myself that I was surely the most famous person in the country, and probably in the world, who had not sought her fame. This was a lie. Who did not *want* her fame would have been more accurate. I sought fame with a reluctant heart, with great reservations, yet I granted interviews and posed for photographs and rode with Charlie on buses and planes, I gave speeches of my own and cheered for his, I visited churches and hospitals and fish fries. Like every famous person, I was complicit in my fame. Yes, a few times a year, a handful of ordinary citizens become the focus of a media frenzy—a victim of a particularly grisly crime, or the kid who reaches over the stands to catch a home-run ball in a play-off game—but that fame passes. The true enduring kind must be constantly burnished and enhanced. It never happens by chance.

Perhaps it started back in 1977, with Charlie's first congressional campaign, or perhaps well before that, when Harold Blackwell ran for attorney general of Wisconsin in 1954. We threw ourselves at people—there are more savory ways to say it, but really, that's what we did. We searched them out, we left leaflets at the front doors of their houses and under the windshields of their cars, we spoke to them through ads on television, we went to their schools and town halls and farmers' markets. We begged them to listen, we bombarded them with promises and plans, but all along we were selling ourselves—selling him.

We did everything we could to get as many people as possible to pay attention to us, and it worked, and now we complain. *Leave us alone,* we say. *Just like you, we're entitled to privacy.*

BEFORE DELIVERING HIS speech in Columbus, Charlie calls to say that he thinks Dena is a credibility-lacking piece of trailer trash. "Go easy," I say. I am, as much as possible, trying to suspend panic. This scandal, if a scandal is what it will be, is in such an early stage; I need to better know the shape of it before allotting my anxious energy.

My personal aide, Ashley, and I are walking from the South Lawn into the Diplomatic Reception Room when Nicole Hethcote, another aide, says, "Mrs. Blackwell, your daughter's on the phone. Are you available?"

"I'll get it at my desk," I say. In my office in the East Wing, as soon as the phone rings, I pick it up.

"Can you please make Dad go talk to that Franklin guy?" Ella says. "Just for five minutes?"

"Honey, you can't let the opposition dictate the terms of the conversation."

"You sound like Uncle Hank."

Ah, my Ella. She is twenty-eight now, and her schedule at Goldman Sachs is worse than Charlie's, ninety hours a week on a regular basis. Magazines sometimes run pictures of Ella and her boyfriend, Wyatt, entering or leaving fancy restaurants (their main form of recreation besides working out, which they both do avidly), and while the exposure doesn't please me and I admit to being a bit thrown by the idea of my daughter spending more on a bottle of wine than I used to pay for a month's rent in my twenties, I never worry that Ella will be caught behaving inappropriately. She is our miracle, smart and levelheaded and joyful, inheritor of an improbable combination of my calmness and Charlie's mischief. Perhaps most extraordinary to me is her apparent lack of resentment toward either of us. Mundane bickering and disagreements have always arisen with us, as with any family, but even those scuffles, which peaked when she was in high school (over atypical issues such as the ubiquity of her security detail, and more mundane ones such as the lengths of her skirts, the hour of her curfew, and the urgent necessity of there being two piercings rather than one in her left ear), have all faded. While I doubt she would have chosen this path for our family—she was in eighth grade when we told her Charlie was going to run for governor of Wisconsin, which prompted her to accuse her father of trying to ruin her life—it would appear she has forgiven us.

In June 2001, she graduated from Princeton, an event where Charlie's appearance created a bit of a ruckus on campus; knowing we'd force all the other families to walk through metal detectors, among other inconveniences, we'd considered skipping the ceremony, but neither Charlie nor I could bear to do it. (Sitting in the front row, facing Nassau Hall, I did think uncomfortably of Joe Thayer, who, over ten years earlier, had married a younger, gentle-seeming music teacher at Biddle Academy with whom he has had two more children. In a pleasant turn of events, his once-troubled daughter Megan is also married and living in Maronee with two young children.) Ella again followed in Charlie's footsteps by attending Wharton, though, as Charlie quipped in the commencement address he delivered two years ago, the school has become so competitive that if he'd been applying when Ella did, he wouldn't have gotten in.

At this point, Ella is neither in thrall to nor disdainful of politics: When she was younger, we shielded her, never allowing her to speak to the press, and although she attended both of Charlie's inaugurations, the first time she participated in any campaigning was when she held a BLACKWELL/PROUHET sign on a street corner in Manchester, New Hampshire, in January 2004. She still has never granted an interview, and while she would prefer, as I think most twenty-eight-year-old women living in Manhattan would, to spend more time with her friends and her boyfriend than with her parents, she always comes home for holidays and surprised me on my sixtieth birthday last year. I can't imagine she herself will ever run for elected office, but once I couldn't have imagined that I would be the wife of our country's president.

"Seriously," Ella says, "the dude must be roasting out there."

"I know, ladybug, but the situation isn't as simple as it looks."

"Mom, believe me, it's not that I agree with him about withdrawing the troops." At Princeton, Ella majored in public and international affairs, and she was a vocal supporter of the war from the beginning. "A regime change is the only way to eliminate the Islamic jihadists," she'd say, and I would be awed by her intelligence and confidence. What would my own father have made of such an educated, opinionated young woman? Expounding on the Middle East, no less! (For that matter, what would my father have made of Charlie's presidency? He was such an uncynical man, patriotic in the most old-fashioned sense, and I like to think he'd have respected Charlie and been proud of me by extension. But perhaps it is for the best that my father didn't live to see this part of our lives. In light of his belief about fools' names and fools' faces, I can only guess at his reaction to an article *Esquire*—a magazine my father subscribed to—made waves with last month: "Ten Reasons Why Charlie Blackwell Is a Shit-Eating Bastard." Whereas my father, when referring to the presidents of my youth, called them Mr. Truman or Mr. Eisenhower; he even called the janitor at the bank Mr. White.)

"It just makes Dad seem heartless," Ella is saying. "I hate giving ammunition to his critics. How will it look when this old man has a heatstroke?"

"Sweetie, Edgar Franklin is younger than your father or me."

"You know what I mean. Anyway, you guys aren't spending the day in the sun. Hey, you're wearing sexy heels tonight, right?" In the late nineties, Ella converted me, at least for formal events, from what she calls "blocky heels" to "sexy heels." She said, "They're slimming," and while, thanks to being prodded and encouraged by two personal trainers, I now weigh less than I have since I turned thirty, the camera adding twenty pounds is no myth; I accept whatever help I can get.

"Signs point to yes," I say. This is when Hank appears outside my office; through the open door, I can see him talking to Jessica Sutton, my chief of staff. If Ella finds out I had an abortion, *when* she finds out, how will she react? On the one hand, I like to think she's an essentially compassionate person; she is also, presumably, sexually active herself. On the other hand, like Charlie, Ella considers herself a born-again Christian, and as an adolescent, she stuck a bumper sticker to her dressing table mirror that read, IT'S NOT A CHOICE, IT'S A CHILD; she'd acquired the sticker from the leader of her youth group. When I noticed it, I said, "I don't think any woman wants to have an abortion, honey, but some of them feel that it's more responsible than giving birth to a baby they aren't prepared to take care of." Ella looked at me in horror and said, "That's what *adoption* is for." More recently, after the two times I stated my stance on abortion on the morning news shows, Ella made no mention of either, though I don't think she was unaware of them.

Jessica knocks gently on my open door, and when our eyes meet, she says, "Hank has an update." She takes a step toward me, lowering her voice to a whisper. "Are you okay?" I called Jessica from the car to tell her what's going on, and asked her not to mention it to anyone else yet. Although I have an excellent staff, Jessica is the person I trust most—

given that I've known her for her entire life, perhaps this is not surprising.

"I'd better go, sweetie," I say into the phone. "Will you call me from the airport?" To Jessica, I say, "Send him in, but stay."

When they reenter my office, Hank closes the door behind him, meaning the Secret Service agents are on its other side. "So far the trail doesn't lead to your friend Dena," he says. "Do you recall a doctor named Gladys Wycomb?"

I stare at him. Gladys Wycomb? Dr. Wycomb, my grandmother's paramour? "But wouldn't she have—" I try to pull together my disparate thoughts. "She must be a hundred years old."

"A hundred and four, still living at home in Chicago, and taken care of by an aide named Norene Davis." Hank rolls his eyes. "They weren't exactly trying to cover their tracks—hoping for some attention is more like it. I just got off the phone with Gladys, and I swear I'm not being arrogant when I say that receiving a call from evil incarnate might have been the most exciting thing that's ever happened to the old crone."

"You spoke to her directly?"

Hank nods. "She's feisty for a centenarian, I'll give her that. She says you had the procedure under the name Alice Warren."

"Isn't this a violation of patient confidentiality or the Hippocratic Oath?"

"Funny you should ask." I know from Hank's glib tone that I'll be unlikely to see the humor in what he's about to say. "As a matter of fact, it's abortion that's a violation of the Hippocratic Oath. Granted, it advocates confidentiality, too, but you know what? When you're a hundred and four years old, you do what you damn well please."

I think then of Gladys Wycomb's white cat's-eye glasses, her heavyset build, her chauffeur and her fancy apartment and the gold fleurs-de-lis on the wallpaper in the hall outside it, the hall where, over four decades ago, I vomited into the Christmas vase. Slowly, I say, "And what she wants from me is to publicly malign Ingrid Sanchez?"

"Yeah, no biggie—just that, and while you're at it, you can remind Americans how enthusiastically you support a woman's right to choose."

"Does Dr. Wycomb know I *have* said I'm pro-choice?"

"Not for three years, and apparently, your brevity both times was unsatisfying. I get the feeling this gal knows she's about to kick the bucket, she's spending a little too much time watching C-SPAN, and she's had an eleventh-hour vision that she should intervene. She's framing it as a matter of conscience."

"By blackmailing me."

"Again, let me emphasize: She's a hundred and four, and she probably figures she'll croak before she sees any legal repercussions. She doesn't give a"—Hank pauses—"a hoot." (A perk of being first lady: I've never been crazy about swearing, and now the only ones who feel comfortable doing it in my presence are Charlie and Ella.)

"Isn't she putting Norene Davis at risk of imprisonment, too?" I say.

"The bottom line is you had an abortion. I'm not judging you, Alice, but the American people will. If Norene Davis goes to the clink, she'll serve a few years, and then think of the media exposure, the book deals. She gets heralded as a champion of women's rights, and the conservative base is cleaning up the mess for years to come."

"So instead what? I deny the charge and call Dr. Wycomb a liar?"

"You don't have to be the one to do it." He turns to Jessica. "Can you help me out here?"

"What are our other options?" Jessica asks. Jessica is tall and lean, wearing black pants and a yellow silk sleeveless blouse. There is a good deal I admire about my chief of staff, but perhaps most of all her combination of unflappability and warmth; I've often found calmness and professionalism to go with an emotional remoteness, but this is not the case with her.

Hank says, "I'm not wild about this idea, and I don't think the president will be, either, but we can schedule an interview where, in the most oblique way, you go ahead and criticize Ingrid Sanchez. We'll set it up like it was an unexpected tough question, and if we go this route, woman-to-woman will work best—you're showing Diane Sawyer how beautiful the Rose Garden is this time of year, she surprises you by asking what you think of the Supreme Court nominee, and you blurt out that you wish Sanchez showed clearer signs of supporting a woman's right to—"

Jessica is shaking her head. "And what if that's not enough for Gladys Wycomb? That'll be the worst of both worlds, if we've capitulated and she still talks."

"I want to go see her." I stand; the idea has come to me abruptly, but I am certain. "If I leave immediately, I'll be back in time to do the tour for the children's choir. I'd like to talk to Dr. Wycomb in person. She was—" I break off. "She was my grandmother's dear friend."

"Her loyalty to your family is touching." Hank looks at his watch. "If there's nothing you need to do before you leave, the plane's ready when you are."

"You already scheduled it?"

Hank smiles. He delights in knowing what a person will want even before the person herself. "For obvious reasons, it's got to be a baseball cap trip, and we'll put the word out here that you went to see your mom." *Baseball cap* is our term for trips that are off-the-record—OTR—or at least ahead of time, and that involve as few people as possible. The phrase has its origins in the way Charlie has traveled twice to the war zones overseas: In the dark of night, he left once from the White House and once from Camp David and rode to Andrews Air Force Base in a single tinted SUV, no motorcade, sitting in the back wearing a baseball cap, accompanied by his secretary of state and just two Secret Service agents; even the tiny press pool who joined him aboard *Air Force One* wasn't told where they were going until midflight. "Jessica, I'm thinking you're the only one who accompanies her, plus whoever Cal thinks is necessary securitywise," Hank says. He turns back toward me. "If anyone can sweet-talk this woman out of coming forward, I'm sure it's you. You go out to Chicago, trade on your personal relationship, flatter her, and ooze sincerity. The disadvantage is if she can't be sweet-talked, you may have given her credibility by paying a visit, but we can spin that into her being an Alzheimer's-addled crackpot: She's right that she saw you, but she invented this abortion business."

"Hank." I wait until he's looking at me directly. "I don't ooze sincerity. I *am* sincere."

Hank's smirk is slow and closed-lipped. "It's your Achilles' heel," he says.

THE PART ABOUT being famous that nobody who hasn't been famous can understand is the criticism. Sure, sticks and stones and all of that, but the fact is that many people have probably wished at least once or twice that someone would be completely honest with them. How does this dress or this haircut really look? What do you truly think of my wife or my son, the house I built, the memo I wrote, the cake I baked?

In reality, they don't want to know. What they want is to be complimented and for the compliments to be completely honest; they want all-encompassing affirmation that's also true. That isn't how unvarnished opinions work. People's unvarnished opinions are devastating, or they are at first. As one of my predecessors, Eleanor Roosevelt, wrote, "Every woman in public life needs to develop skin as tough as rhinoceros hide."

There are two ways of being criticized: neutrally and intentionally. The neutral criticism comes, for example, in an ostensibly objective article, in a throwaway line: *Mrs. Blackwell, who has never been known for her fashion acumen . . . Asked about her husband's low approval ratings, Alice Blackwell stiffens and becomes defensive . . . Though insiders claim she has a sense of humor, Alice Blackwell rarely shows it in public . . . Unlike the first couple before them, who were warm and frequent hosts . . .* You have spent an hour in the presence of a reporter, you were guarded, especially at first, but you got along perfectly well and shared a few laughs (yes, laughs, in spite of your alleged humorlessness), you thought the interview went well, and then—this? The neutral criticisms sting more because of how casual they are; although they aren't necessarily the truth, they feel like it, like the reporter isn't *trying* to be mean but is simply stating facts.

And then there are the outright attacks, which appear mostly on cable television or blogs; in the case of blogs, they are vehement in ways that evoke spittle and flushed faces and the pounding of keyboards: *What a traitor to feminism . . . How much Valium do you think she has to take to forget she's married to the Antichrist? . . . OH MY GOD she's SUCH a Stepford wife!!!* Once or twice a year, I type my name into an Internet search engine—I don't want to be overly sheltered from what's out there—and skimming the results makes me feel as if someone is turning a doorknob inside my stomach; each time I've done it, I've thought afterward that it was a mistake, and then enough time has passed that I've forgotten. To be lambasted by strangers is not only painful but so pronounced a reversal of the usual social code that it's also quite astonishing. Unfamous people imagine that famous people are endlessly pleased with themselves and their exposure, and I suppose some are, but far from all. These online rants also feel, in a different way, deceptively like the truth, unguarded and without the filters of the mainstream media. Although my critics are in the minority, how can I listen to praise when the faultfinders are so aggressive, so aggrieved, and so certain?

In addition, there are vast quantities of distorted or flat-out wrong information, motives or emotions that are incorrectly ascribed: about Andrew Imhof's death (*Isn't it lucky Alice Blackwell was white and rich and didn't have to go to prison after murdering her boyfriend?*), about my supposed Christian evangelism (a cartoon ran in many newspapers of me reading the Bible to a group of Muslim children, saying, "Now, now, boys and girls, if you just pray to Jesus Christ, everything will be all right"), about my supposed intellectual superiority in comparison to Charlie (another cartoon: Charlie and I are lying in bed at night, and I am absorbed in *War and Peace,* while he pages through *The Cat in the Hat*). One year Jadey sent me a birthday card—apparently, a popular one—which had a smiling photo of me in which I wore a navy suit and an eagle pin. (I was never very fond of that pin, but it had been given to me by the wife of Charlie's secretary of defense, and I felt obligated to wear it a few times.) On the front of the card, it said, *Some things are worse than another birthday . . .* and inside, it said, *You could be married to HIM*. Underneath, Jadey had scrawled, *Don't be offended, also don't show C!*

Some of the misinformation out there about us, about me, is more factual and insignificant—how old I was when Charlie and I got married, the spelling of my childhood neighbor Mrs. Falke's last name—but no matter the tone or type of error, it is very rarely worth it to have my press secretary request a correction. I also must accept that some errors have been propagated by Charlie's inner circle, specifically by Hank: that I am the daughter of a postal carrier was a widespread one during the first presidential campaign. (It is a great irony that my middle-class roots have proved, from a political standpoint, to be my most valuable asset. The whiffs of East Coast Ivy League dynastic privilege that cling to Charlie—I dispel them with my humble Wisconsin authenticity.)

Even as my approval ratings have remained high, a public idea of me has formed that has little relationship to who I am, what I think, or even how I spend my time. Hank once commissioned a poll that found the majority of Americans believe I'm a devout Christian who has never held a paying job. Perhaps this is *why* my approval ratings have remained high.

I don't imagine any person could remain entirely impervious to her own public distortion, and I won't claim it doesn't bother me, but I made a decision in Charlie's first gubernatorial campaign not to devote my energy to correcting misinterpretations. A press secretary had arranged for a reporter from the *Sentinel* to come for tea with me at home (how I hated having reporters in our house, knowing they were scrutinizing our family pictures, our magazines and knickknacks and refrigerator magnets, when we'd never meant for them to be scrutinized, we'd only acquired them in the course of living—it was easier after we moved to the governor's mansion and then to the White House, because I always knew that if the reporters were interlopers, so were we). During this *Sentinel* interview, the reporter asked me about gardening, baking, and children's books; I provided my tips for growing delphiniums, my recipe for molasses cookies, and a list of my favorite titles, starting with *The Giving Tree.*

Despite the family she married into, Alice Blackwell is avowedly apolitical, the article began. *Social security and health care? No thanks, she'd rather talk about how she gets her molasses cookies so darn chewy . . .*

I was mortified; Charlie thought it was hilarious; and Hank was thrilled by the article, in large part because Charlie's Democratic opponent, the incumbent, had recently divorced his wife of thirty-three years, married a suspiciously attractive and much younger lobbyist, and couldn't hope to compete with our sugary domesticity. For a twenty-four-hour period after the article ran, I was tense and jumpy, continuously composing letters to the editor in my head. I had gone for a walk alone—we no longer belonged to the Maronee Country Club, Charlie had had to resign given the awkward fact of the club having no black members, and so now, if I wasn't with Jadey, I walked along our street—and all at once, a notion lodged itself in my head, a notion I've come back to again and again in the years since: Although Charlie was running for office, I was not. The fact that I was represented in an article in a particular way made it neither true nor untrue; the way I lived my life, the way I conducted myself, wasn't just the only truth but also the only reality I could control. I wouldn't stretch or stoop to accommodate the media, I decided. I would be accountable to myself, and I would always know whether I'd met or fallen short of my own expectations. How much distress I'd avoid this way, how much calmer I would feel. Since that afternoon, I have always tried to be polite with members of the media, though I realize I haven't always been forthcoming in the way they'd like. I attempt to express myself as simply as possible, I respond to what they ask rather than promoting my own particular interests, I don't share personal details or vulnerabilities. When I met Charlie, I fell for him, I say, because he was fun; when Andrew Imhof died, I say, it was incredibly sad; and when I think about the troops, I say, I am concerned for them and admire their bravery and sacrifice. I don't bend over backward to convince reporters that everything I say is heartfelt (after all, they don't determine whether it's heartfelt) or to proffer clever sound bites; I don't disparage Charlie's opponents. That I'm not particularly quotable and am often a bit dull, optimistically dull, I consider a minor victory.

When Ella was in college, she was in an eating club—not the one Charlie belonged to but a different one, Ivy—and this was the bulk of what the public knew about her: that she attended Princeton, that she belonged to an exclusive club whose members drank often and zealously. As it happened, she also was a volunteer in an on-campus Christian organization that on the weekends organized soccer and basketball tournaments for children from low-income neighborhoods in Trenton, and the White House press secretary, at that time a fellow named Travis Sykes, tried hard to persuade me to allow an article about Ella's participation in the organization. I declined. I know that some people feel that if it isn't documented, it didn't happen, but I disagree. It is not a camera, or a reporter, that makes something real and genuine; more often, a camera or a reporter does the opposite.

It's no secret that in many individuals, attention tends to create an appetite for more of the same. Because of this phenomenon, I consider myself lucky never to have felt the hunger. If you don't want attention but must put up with it nevertheless, it's a nuisance. But if you do want it, no amount will sate you; I've observed this truth over and over in both Wisconsin and Washington. I sometimes wish I could talk openly about this subject to Oprah, the one woman in the country more visible than I am, and even more a canvas onto which Americans project their dreams, wishes, and fears; really, what a burden being Oprah must be, though she handles it graciously. While I've appeared on her program twice, I'm sure that a tête-à-tête won't happen because I suspect she's a Democrat who doesn't approve of my husband.

In any case: Dispatches and warnings from this side of the fame fence tend to go ignored, dismissed as either whining or false modesty; if they weren't ignored, if people listened, no one would ever again seek attention. But they always do, they strive and strive, hoping one day they, too, will have the luxury of lamenting their high profile. *It will make me content at last,* they think, and only if they successfully achieve the celebrity they were pursuing will they realize they were mistaken.

Or perhaps I am wrong. Perhaps most people would be like Charlie—they'd enjoy fame's perks without feeling unduly burdened by its costs and responsibilities.

GLADYS WYCOMB LIVES in a different apartment, a different building; this one is a few blocks from the one where I stayed during the last days of 1962 and the first days of 1963, equally fancy but smaller. Upon being led into Dr. Wycomb's living room by Norene Davis (it seems increasingly clear that Ms. Davis is more an employee than a co-conspirator), I remember some of Dr. Wycomb's paintings from all those years ago, though now I recognize their provenance: They are by New York School artists, and I'm almost sure one is a de

Kooning. By this point, I have been inside countless lavish houses and hotels, I live in a museum, for heaven's sake, but it strikes me that Dr. Wycomb's was the first elegant home I ever visited, and that it had something money alone couldn't buy—it had style. No wonder my grandmother was so taken with her.

Dr. Wycomb herself sits in a parlor chair upholstered in olive-colored velvet and though it is warm in her apartment, a blanket covers her lower half. She wears unfashionably large plastic glasses (not cat's-eye) and a silk muumuu, though she is no longer a large woman; she probably weighs half of what she did when I last saw her. Her face is extremely wrinkled, her hair short and gray, and her eyes behind their glasses are alert. A walker is positioned next to her, between her chair and a revolving walnut bookcase, and there's a small black-and-white television of perhaps thirteen inches (I haven't seen a black-and-white television in years), which rests on a marble-top round table a few feet in front of her. Though she reached forward to turn down the volume knob as I walked in, the TV is, as Hank predicted, turned to C-SPAN.

She didn't stand when Norene Davis announced my arrival—I had the impression it would be a good deal of trouble for her, but she also may have been making a point—and I approach her now, bending. "Dr. Wycomb, it's been a long time," I say in an overly loud and cheery way. I extend my hand, and when she doesn't extend hers, I pat her forearm. "Your apartment is lovely."

The hint of a smile crosses her lips. In a slow and quiet but perfectly audible voice, she says, "Alice, not all of us who are old are also deaf."

Immediately, I feel a relieved recognition. With people who knew you before you were famous, you can tell within the first few seconds who you are to them now—whether they understand that you're still you and that they can treat you as such, or whether you have been transformed in their eyes, requiring toadying and deference. I suppose it's not surprising, given how much all humans are primed and influenced by one another, that these two types of behavior tend to be self-fulfilling. When old friends or acquaintances act as if I'm worthy of great respect, I tend to pull back (I'm uncomfortable, but no doubt it comes across as aloofness), which seems to reinforce their sense that they dare not relax around me the way they once did; but if they are relaxed from the start, I am, too. It's obvious that to Gladys Wycomb, I am less the first lady of the United States than the granddaughter of Emilie Lindgren.

I gesture to a gold-leaf armchair. "May I sit?"

"I'm glad we finally got through to you," Dr. Wycomb says. "Norene attempted to reach someone in your office repeatedly, but she kept being rebuffed. That's when I thought for her to try Mr. Ucker."

"Oh, I'm sorry." Just how many people did Norene talk to? I wonder. And what did she say?

Again, that faint smile. "Mr. Ucker was quite interested once his people realized we weren't batty." She pauses. "Norene and I think Mr. Ucker resembles a troll."

Hank is the most visible member of the administration besides Charlie and the vice president, and he therefore has both a cult following and legions of detractors. Seen by the public as a Svengali, Hank is credited with Charlie's election and reelection, as well as with many of his most conservative policies. Knowing Hank as I do makes him less intriguing and mysterious than he must seem from a distance, but I don't disagree with the view that Charlie probably wouldn't be president if Hank hadn't urged him to run for governor and engineered the subsequent campaigns. (Hank was delighted when Charlie became managing partner of the Brewers because at last Charlie had an identity apart from his family, a track record he could point to when voters in Wisconsin asked what he'd done for the state. The difference between Hank and Charlie was that Hank saw the job as an ideal steppingstone, whereas Charlie saw it as an ideal job; without Hank's prodding and ego pumping, I think Charlie would not have minded remaining in the role indefinitely.)

"Now, where did your henchmen go?" Dr. Wycomb asks. "Would they like a beverage?"

"They're fine," I say. Cal, my lead agent, insisted that three of them come to Chicago and that three more local agents meet us here; on our arrival at Dr. Wycomb's building, Walter and the third fellow from Washington, José, did a walk-through before I entered. Now José and Cal are stationed in the hall, Walter is back by the Town Car at the curb

(Jessica sits inside the car), and the three local agents are patrolling the outside of the building.

I say, "Dr. Wycomb, when my grandmother and I came and stayed with you, it was the first time I'd been to a big city, and ever since then, I've had a place in my heart for Chicago." As I say it, I have the unsettling realization that I must now be the age Dr. Wycomb was during that visit.

"I never thought of living anywhere else," she says.

I hesitate, then I say, "Obviously, we both know why I'm here. I understand your concerns, I really do, and I want to make it clear that I respect your opinion. But for you to talk about my medical procedure with members of the media would be a serious mistake. I won't pretend that it wouldn't be damaging to me, but I strongly suspect it would be damaging to you, too."

"If it's damage you're worried about, Alice, look around you." Dr. Wycomb's tone is abruptly different than it was when we were making small talk. "Your husband and the vice president should be tried as war criminals." I'm about to respond when she continues, "I suppose the president's excuse is that he was born a fool, but I've wondered for the last six years what yours is. I don't know how you sleep at night."

It's not that I'm unaware people think this, but the sentiments are rarely expressed at such close range. Also, they don't emerge from the mouths of people I know, or people so old.

I say, "Aren't we both lucky to live in a country that allows the expression of this kind of criticism? Dr. Wycomb, it's your right to disagree with any or all of the president's choices, but please remember that his administration is a different entity from me personally."

"How convenient." She is looking straight ahead. "But the personal is political, or did you miss the women's movement?" She turns her head so our eyes meet. "Many times, I've had the notion to write you a letter, and I've told myself, Gladys, it won't make it to her. She'll never see it. But I still thought you'd intervene. I kept waiting for evidence that you were reining him in and speaking as a voice of reason."

"Not every conversation I have is public, Dr. Wycomb."

"Are you telling me that you have confronted your husband?"

"I answer to my own conscience. That's as much as I want to say."

"And I answer to mine," she says. "Lest you think I have misgivings about sharing your secret, my only regret is that I didn't speak out years ago."

We both are quiet, and I can hear another television—a soap opera, it sounds like—somewhere else in the apartment. Norene Davis, I saw when she let me in, has black hair pulled back in a low ponytail and is wearing scrubs with teddy bears.

"Who do you think will be hurt by overturning *Roe*?" Dr. Wycomb says. "Not women we know—they'll go to their doctors like you came to me, very hush-hush but perfectly clean and professional. But the poor women, where do they go? Every doctor knows outlawing abortion doesn't make it less common, it just makes it less safe. Before '73, I had patients who found me after botched procedures. They'd show up with cases of sepsis and bacteremia that would give you nightmares, and these were the lucky ones—the others died before they could get help. I should stand by and say nothing as our country returns to that?" She is shaking, a mild tremble throughout her body. "What I can no longer abide with this administration is the attitude that if it doesn't affect them personally, it doesn't matter. *I* was never going to need an abortion, was I? Now I'm so old that come what may, I won't be around to see it. But that doesn't mean I say, 'To hell with the rest of you, and so long.' "

"Dr. Wycomb, it's important to remember that the American people elected President Blackwell. Even if you don't agree with him, a lot of citizens do. It's impossible to satisfy everyone."

"Those elections were fixed." Her thin lips are drawn together; she is furious with me, truly furious.

I say, "I'm sympathetic to your frustrations, but—"

"You're a puppet. Even the words you use, it sounds like a speechwriter told you to say them."

This isn't the way people talk to the first lady—no one does, except for a protestor at a speech, and if that happens, he is quickly quarantined. Dr. Wycomb's comments are insulting and irritating, they are patronizing, but there also is something pure and true in her anger, like a winter wind. It's almost refreshing, almost a relief, to be berated face-to-face.

Although I already know the answer, I say, "I trust that you're aware I've said in two separate interviews that I'm pro-choice?"

"The times you gave one-word answers?"

"I'd like for us to come to a mutually agreeable resolution," I say. "Do you think we can?"

"Keep Judge Sanchez off the Supreme Court."

"That isn't an area where I have any control."

"For crying out loud, you're married to the president of the United States! Who does he listen to if not you?"

Could I convince Charlie to retract Ingrid Sanchez's nomination—or, as protocol would have it, convince Charlie to convince Ingrid Sanchez to withdraw herself as a nominee? Even if it were possible, it seems so sleazy, a way of sparing myself public humiliation rather than a real political stand. It's not that I wouldn't strongly prefer for abortion to remain legal, not that I don't understand that with Judge Sanchez's confirmation, it might not. Nor is it that I don't see how I come across as a hypocrite here, although I would disagree with the characterization; I actually haven't said one thing and done another. It's that I honestly don't believe it's my responsibility or even my right to try to legislate. No matter how many times I say it, people are unwilling to accept the fact that *I* was not elected. Have I tried to encourage Charlie in certain directions? Of course. A program on early education, increased funding for the arts, a literacy initiative—issues that inspire little controversy, issues on which he *seeks* my input.

I say, "Dr. Wycomb, I admit that I don't know yet if what you're proposing is blackmail, but it certainly comes close, and Norene Davis is implicated. Please know I'm not threatening you when I say that striking a deal could only end badly for all of us. I can't try to bar a Supreme Court nominee to protect myself—that's not something I'm willing to do, and I don't think I'm capable of it anyway. That puts the decision back in your hands in terms of how you want to go forward, but for you to tell a reporter about a medical procedure you performed on me seems a clear violation of patient confidentiality."

"The word is *abortion.*" Again, she is not looking at me. "And you didn't mind breaking the law when it suited you. For you people, it's only a crime if someone else commits it."

She's really going to do it, I realize—she's fearless. She doesn't care what the consequences are, even, apparently, for Norene. Her life of over a century has been distilled to this: She hates Charlie, she hates everything she thinks he represents, and possibly she hates me more. And she doesn't just hate me by proxy—no, she thinks I am worse than he is. She subscribes to the belief, widespread among Democrats and shared by some Republicans, that he's a moron, an evil moron, and to a certain extent, that lets him off the hook. But I—I should know better.

Unexpectedly, I think, *Okay. Okay, announce that I had an abortion; let the world know, let them hear about it in Missouri and Utah and Louisiana, in Ireland and Egypt and El Salvador.* It's not inaccurate; I did have one. I will be judged, I will be criticized, I will be dissected on talk shows, joked about on late-night TV, excoriated or defended (though mostly excoriated) in op-eds. The Sunday after the news breaks, in *The New York Times*'s "Week in Review," three separate articles about me will make variations on the same point. Even those who are pro-choice will denounce me as a dissembler; women's groups will use me as proof of something, or as a cautionary tale about something else. In every interview from now until the end of my life, I'll be asked to explain why I had an abortion and why I was silent for so long afterward, asked to reconcile the inconsistencies between my private experience and my husband's policies and legislation. Anything I say in reply will boil down to this: *I did not contradict myself; I live a life that contains contradictions. Don't you?*

Pete Imhof will know, if Dena hasn't already told him. My mother will know, my poor mother, if, in her present state of senility, she is cognizant enough to absorb the news. The silver lining, such as it is, is that other women who have had abortions might feel—what?—less alone? Less guilty? But that's to assume they feel alone and guilty now, which I generally doubt. Personally, I've never regretted having an abortion; I've regretted the circumstances that led to its necessity, but I maintain that it *was* a necessity, that it was, however cowardly Dr. Wycomb thinks I am to lean on the phrase, a medical procedure. Would I feel more uncomfortable if it had occurred in the twelfth week or the sixteenth instead of what was likely the fifth or sixth? Yes, I would. But the debate about when life begins seems to me misguided; I made a private, personal decision related to my own health.

When it becomes public, it's difficult to know how adversely the news will affect Charlie. His administration has proved resilient at weathering scandals, but he is a lame duck at this point, obstructed by Democrats in the majority in both the House and Senate—the '06 elections were when Hank's supposed political sorcery faltered at last—and Charlie's focus has returned after all these years to his legacy, the topic that so used to rankle me. I suppose the preoccupation is more justified now, but I still silently resist it. Viewing a legacy as a few grand acts seems reductive. Isn't your legacy not the one or two exceptional gestures of your life but the way you conducted yourself every day, year after year? Either way, Charlie personally will forgive me, I feel confident. To lobby him to withdraw Ingrid Sanchez's nomination would be a betrayal in his eyes; to be outed as the first lady who had an abortion would merely make me a victim. In order to placate his conservative Christian base, it's likely he'll want me to grant an interview in which I condemn my behavior, to say, *I am a sinner,* but when I decline, he won't push me. This is our implicit agreement, that we can suggest or recommend but that we never force, never make ultimatums; it's why we don't resent each other.

And perhaps in some secluded part of my conscience, I even welcome the disclosure, just as I welcome the scolding from Gladys Wycomb. The Lutherans I was raised among believed less in a vengeful God than a disciplining one: If we had faith in Jesus, we'd find eternal salvation, but in the meantime, here on earth, we might encounter obstacles or tests intended to help us grow. Many years have passed since I've had faith in Jesus, but it is undeniable that the framework of our upbringing stays with us, and it's entirely plausible to me I'm now being "disciplined" for past transgressions: not for Andrew (in that case, the mistake and the punishment were one and the same) but for the life I've lived in spite of that terrible early error. It all could have unraveled for me, couldn't it? But it didn't, and I became lucky—I was allowed the felicities of marriage and motherhood, the comforts of wealth, and ultimately, the exorbitant privileges available at the highest level of politics. Since Charlie entered public office, I have felt an amplified version of what I used to feel at the Maronee Country Club, the fear that we were like the Californians who live in beautiful houses overhanging cliffs.

In my expectation that good fortune will lead inextricably to its reversal, I should note that I don't think I'm less deserving of happiness than anyone else; it is that in an unequal world, nobody deserves the privileges I enjoy. I've thought often since Charlie became governor that it isn't a surprise so many famous people seem mentally unstable. As their celebrity grows and they're increasingly deferred to and accommodated, they can believe one of two things: either that they're deserving, in which case they will become unreasonable and insufferable; or that they're not deserving, in which case they will be wracked with doubt, plagued by a sense of themselves as imposters. I suppose this is why I've tried mightily to lead a "regular" life—why I still make our bed, why I stay at Jadey and Arthur's house instead of at a hotel when I'm traveling in Wisconsin without Charlie, why I read the newspaper instead of relying on briefings, why I shop myself, albeit with agents, at Hallmark, where I pick out birthday or anniversary cards (never ones featuring us) because how can you rely on an aide to know what kind of birthday card to get for your own friend or brother-in-law? If I can remain a normal person, I hope to share my normalcy with Charlie; I realize my attempts are inadequate, but they are better than nothing.

In Dr. Wycomb's living room, I say, "It doesn't seem as if either of us will be able to persuade the other to come around, does it?"

"All those women who'll have to have back-alley abortions—you'll be able to live with that?" She still is shaking.

"Dr. Wycomb, I know you feel passionately—"

"You have the power to change history, and you don't care. Reproductive rights don't strike your fancy? Well, how about gay marriage? I can think of at least one reason that ought to be close to your heart. How about the environment, how about civil liberties, how about this godforsaken war, or do the two of you plan to sit there with your blinders on until he's out of office and his successor can clean up the mess?"

"You've made your point." I stand; I have had enough. "I'm going to leave, Dr. Wycomb. I wish you well." I can't imagine touching her in goodbye, I can't imagine she'd want it. I begin walking toward the foyer.

I've reached the threshold when Dr. Wycomb says, "Your grandmother would be so disappointed in you." The part that stings most is that her voice in this moment is less angry than wonderingly sad.

I turn, and though I remind myself that Gladys Wycomb is no different from a journalist who writes an article about me, that her saying something doesn't make it true, I can't help responding. "I don't agree," I say.

"Emilie may not have been a political person, but she knew right from wrong."

"*You* disappointed her," I reply, and I can hear in my own voice an unattractive note of ferocity. "She told me herself that you tried to make her choose between you and us, and she chose us. That's all I need to know—she chose us."

"You and your parents practically held her prisoner in that dumpy little house. And the way you all tried to whitewash her sexuality, I shouldn't be surprised by what kind of person you've become."

Is this accurate? Either way, is it what my grandmother believed, what she told Dr. Wycomb, or is it what Dr. Wycomb decided on her own?

"I loved my grandmother, and my grandmother loved me." Before continuing into the foyer and out the door of the apartment, I say, "You can't poison that."

ONE SATURDAY EVENING in October 1994, by the time it was clear Charlie was likely to win the gubernatorial election in Wisconsin, our old friend Howard from Madison drove to Maronee for an overnight visit with his wife, Petal. (Howard and Petal had gotten back together, and married, over a decade after I'd met her on Union Terrace as a pretty young college graduate.) This was an exhausting time for our family—on many nights, Ella slept at Arthur and Jadey's while Charlie and I and Hank and other members of the campaign staff wound our way among the tiny towns up in the northern part of the state, Cornucopia and Moose Junction and Manitowish; if we stayed in a Holiday Inn as opposed to a no-name motel, it seemed like a luxury. (Early in the campaign, Charlie had started traveling with his own down pillow, which I folded in half each morning and set in my canvas bag.) Given our schedule, the opportunity to visit with friends was rare, and I felt that it would be restorative for all of us and especially for Charlie. I'd noticed that the more days in a row he spent campaigning, the more impatient and cranky he became—that morning at a power plant in New Richmond when a single mother of three asked him why she should believe he knew anything about working families, he'd snapped, "If you don't think I do, then maybe you shouldn't vote for me"—but even just a short break could do him a world of good. That Saturday afternoon, we'd flown back to Milwaukee from Eau Claire on an eight-seat prop plane. Though initially I'd had grand plans of making a real meal, all I had the energy for was spaghetti, but the evening turned out to be great fun, Howard and Petal and Charlie and Ella and I sitting in the kitchen instead of the dining room, talking and laughing.

Ella was in the middle of reading *The Odyssey* for English, and I was rereading it myself—I took it with me as we campaigned, and I'd made a copy of her syllabus so that I could read the same pages each night that she did and we could discuss them on the phone if I wasn't there (I had always loved *The Odyssey*). It turned out that when Howard had read it in ninth grade, he'd been required to memorize the first five lines in Greek and still remembered them: *Andra moy ennepay moosa / polutropon hos mala polla . . .* Then they announced that Petal was thirteen weeks pregnant—they'd been trying for years—and we were, they said, the only ones they'd told besides their families; they didn't know yet if it was a boy or girl, so we debated names for both. Ella suggested Ella, Charlie suggested Charles, and when I didn't suggest Alice, Howard said, "Why so bashful, Al? Can't you keep up with these egomaniacs?" After dinner, we went into the den to play hearts, and Ella shot the moon; the night had taken on the festive air of a slumber party. Charlie was the first to turn in—ever since he'd started jogging in the morning, he went to bed by ten if he could—and when he was asleep, Petal and Ella and I went to the attic so I could find my old maternity clothes to give Petal. Most were hopelessly outdated.

The next morning, Howard went running with Charlie, and then Howard and Petal took off for Madison around the same time we left for church. Not for the first time, there turned out to be a local news camera waiting for us after the service at Heavenly Rose—this was in October—and Charlie stopped and spoke to the reporter for a few minutes while Ella and I waited in the car. That evening, Charlie was giving a speech in Green Bay, and I was staying in Milwaukee but meeting up with him Monday in Sheboygan, where six hundred area Republicans had paid a hundred dollars each to attend a luncheon with us. It was following the lunch, over twenty-four hours after it had happened, that Charlie told me: During their Sunday-morning run, Howard had said it would be a huge favor if he could set up a meeting between Charlie and his brother, Dave, who was the CEO of a large engineering firm hoping to win a contract with the state. Between the two of them, Howard said, Dave's firm was vastly more qualified than any of the ones currently doing business with Wisconsin's Department of Transportation. "You think that's why they came to see us?" Charlie asked.

"I'm sure it's not," I said, though I wasn't sure at all. Charlie and I were sitting in the first row of the conversion van, headed to the town of Little Chute, where Charlie was to give a speech to a bunch of dairy farmers, and I told myself that no one else in the van was listening to us. At that moment, our driver, Kenny, was in the front seat; a speechwriter named Sean O'Fallon was in the back row, wearing headphones and typing on his laptop; and Hank and Debbie Bell, a strategist, were in the second row, having a noisy and impassioned debate about whether the Garth Brooks song "Friends in Low Places," which had just come on the radio, would be a good one to play before Charlie's rallies. With the song's reference to places "where the whiskey drowns and the beer chases my blues away," it seemed clear to me that using it would be a disastrous idea, which was the argument Hank was making—he said it was practically baiting the media to uncover Charlie's 1988 DUI, then still a secret—while Debbie was insisting that it was such a beloved song and so perfectly captured Charlie's unpretentious personality, as well as the Wisconsin way of life, that the alcohol references didn't matter; plenty of voters liked Charlie better because of his struggles.

Sitting next to me, ignoring the Garth Brooks argument, Charlie seemed melancholy rather than irritated when he said, "I guess this is how it works now, huh? We ask everyone we know for money, and everyone we know asks us for favors." He chuckled, though not happily. "I'm a high-class hooker."

"If that's how you see yourself, I don't know why you're running," I said. "A governor can be a great force for good, and anyway, *high-class hooker* is an oxymoron."

"Now, hold on just a second." Charlie grinned, this time for real. "Who're you calling an oxymoron?"

"Seriously," I said, "if you get elected, and it looks like you will"—this was not simply optimism on my part; his polling numbers were in the high fifties—"you'll have the opportunity to improve the lives of lots of people. Isn't that why you're running?"

All these years later, I see the question of why Charlie ran for governor, or for president, as moot—our lives have become what they've become—but at the time, it mattered to me, it felt like an important puzzle that could be solved if I examined it thoroughly. I suppose I believed that if I understood Charlie's impetus, I might agree that running for election was a good idea. "Because he feels called to lead," Hank would tell reporters. Charlie himself, refusing to be serious, would say to me, "For the same reason a dog licks his balls—because I can." Because he wanted to prove that he was as smart and ambitious as his brothers, journalists speculated, or because he wanted to avenge his father's own humiliating presidential run in 1968, and while neither of these possibilities reflected particularly well on Charlie, they were more flattering than my own theory, which I shared with no one: because of his fear of the dark. Because if he were governor, and then president, he'd be guarded by state troopers and later by agents, he'd never be far from people specifically assigned to watch out for him; he might be assassinated, but he wouldn't have to walk down a shadowy hallway by himself. (Indeed it seems clear that I fear Charlie's assassination more than he does. Before he officially entered the presidential race the first time, I felt compelled to tell him about my peculiar, guilt-ridden relief when Kennedy was shot. Wouldn't it be a perfectly symmetrical kind of punishment for having had such thoughts, I said, if my own husband became president and was killed similarly? To which Charlie replied, without a second's hesitation, "You know that's bullshit, right? That's hocus-pocus teenage-girl thinking.")

The reality of why Charlie ran, I imagine, was a combination of factors, including ego: He did feel some sense of public service, as he defined it; he did feel some sense of "why not?"; he did want to prove himself to his family and to prove his family to the world; he did want the perks. Such motives, inglorious as they are, do not offend me; they never persuaded me that Charlie's entry into politics was wise, but I wonder if anyone else's motives are nobler.

For his first presidential campaign, in 2000, Charlie ran as a "tolerant traditionalist," a bit of alliteration that was Debbie Bell's brainchild. Ironically, Charlie's avowals of sympathy for the marginalized and the underclasses, and his credibility with more left-leaning voters, were bolstered not only by his centrist record as a governor but also, predating his public life by over a decade, by his consistent history of donating to organizations such as food pantries, after-school centers, shelters for women and children affected by domestic violence, and AIDS clinics. These were, of course, the modest donations I had made surreptitiously; when our financial records were first vetted and this bit of duplicity emerged, Charlie and Hank were both thrilled. "God bless your sneaky liberal ways!" Charlie exclaimed.

Another irony when it came to Charlie's tolerant traditionalism was that the tolerance did not seem to extend to sexual orientation, yet I had never doubted that Debbie Bell was a lesbian. I didn't know whether she had romantic involvements—she never referred to any and hadn't been married—but she had a certain comradely air with men and a more flirtatious way with women. She was tall, with short blond hair, and even when she wasn't wearing a pantsuit, she carried herself as if she were; in everything about her, her voice and posture and opinions, there was a briskly athletic confidence that unfortunately you rarely see in heterosexual women. It was on the infrequent occasions when she'd remark on a man's handsomeness, or lament her unmarried status, that she seemed most obviously gay to me—the comments came off as forced and unpersuasive. I discussed my view with Jadey and later with Jessica, both of whom agreed, but I never mentioned it to Charlie because I thought he'd be distracted by it, he might start acting strange around Debbie, teasing her outright or making jokes behind her back. I was surprised Charlie didn't pick up anyway on her mysterious sexuality, but I think he was so gratified by Debbie's unswerving devotion to him that he may not have wanted to analyze it for fear of finding something psychologically iffy. And in fact, I suspect Debbie has spent her interior reservoirs of love, the ones most people save for a partner or children, on Charlie. (Many times, I've longed to pull her aside and whisper, *You deserve better than a mere surrogate; you, too, are entitled to the real thing and not just scraps from my husband.* Needless to say, I have bitten my tongue and hoped she leads a private life about which we know nothing.)

Debbie had worked as a publicist for the Brewers—she was as passionate a baseball fan as Charlie, herself a former softball star at UW, and she also, with Charlie's encouragement, had joined Heavenly Rose Church and been born again in 1990—and when Charlie had left the Brewers, she'd gone with him. In those early days of Charlie's political climb, I was sometimes surprised by how willingly and even ardently people followed him. Because he did not, as I had learned over time, inspire much confidence among his own parents, brothers, and sisters-in-law, it was hard for me not to see him as a bit of an underdog. But particularly during and after his stint with the Brewers, others saw an idealized version, as if Charlie were the star of a movie about his own life: a handsome, funny, good-natured guy who'd graduated from prestigious schools, had a prominent and successful career (was he the son of privilege? Sure, but with baseball, he'd gone in a different direction, and within a minute of meeting him, you could tell how unaffected he was—he preferred burger joints to fancy restaurants, he'd joke around with your kid, he was impishly self-effacing). He was confident and fit and religious, with a marriage that bore no trace of scandal, and a close relationship to his only child. In this narrative, he was the kind of guy whom men wanted to be friends with and women wished their husbands were more like. While my proximity to Charlie is undoubtedly part of the reason for my own less worshipful perspective, I can say sincerely that the single most astonishing fact of political life to me has been the gullibility of the American people. Even in our cynical age, the percentage of the population who is told something and therefore believes it to be true—it's staggering. In a way, it's also touching; it makes me feel protective. (To be a person who sees a political ad on television and takes the statements in it as fact, how can you exist in this world? How is it you're not robbed daily by charlatans who knock at your door?)

I had assumed everyone and particularly political insiders harbored the same private skepticism that I did, especially about the discrepancy between an individual's words and actions, and that decorum made all of us conceal this skepticism; I was evidently wrong. I love Charlie as much as—or, I should hope, more than—someone like Debbie, but I love him differently, with a sharper understanding of his faults. If I believe he ran for president because it was a way of allaying his fear of the dark, then I am able, on my most generous days, to see this motive as endearing. Debbie, on the other hand, believes Charlie ran for president because God summoned him, and she sees him as heroic.

As I sat in the van next to Charlie, heading toward Little Chute, what came on the radio after "Friends in Low Places" was "Achy Breaky Heart," a song that had become a joke during that campaign because no one would admit to liking it, yet we all knew all the words, and we ended up hearing it on the radio everywhere we went, particularly in the staticky backwaters. Hank called to Kenny in the front seat to turn up the volume, and Hank and Debbie sang jubilantly, their Garth Brooks argument suspended. Next to me, quietly and seriously, Charlie said, "You think I'm up to the task of being governor, don't you?"

"I think you'll be wonderful." I wasn't lying. When Charlie had decided to run over a year earlier, he'd known little about our state that hadn't been filtered through family lore or his own experience as a congressional candidate in '78, but he had diligently immersed himself in the history and politics of Wisconsin. Hank had arranged for experts in economics and education and health care to come in and brief him, usually confidentially, and Charlie had worked on memorizing facts and statistics until he could recite them fluently.

Hank tapped my shoulder. "Why aren't you two singing? 'You can tell your ma I moved to Arkansas / You can tell your dog to bite my leg . . .' "

I flashed him a smile. "Looks like you've got this verse covered, Hank." When he had leaned back again, I said softly to Charlie, "I'm sure there'll be plenty of challenges, but if you stay focused on what you're trying to achieve, you'll be great."

"You know what I realized today?" Charlie said. "Shaking hands with people at lunch, I thought, I'll never make another friend. Assuming I'm elected, I mean—from here on out, it'll only be people wanting favors and access."

I couldn't disagree. "You're lucky, though, that you already have so many friends," I said. "We're both lucky."

"But that's the thing." He was very reflective in this moment, especially in contrast to Hank and Debbie hamming it up behind us. "After Howard asked me about the engineering contracts, I'm not faulting him, but I better always be ready for that from now on. I shouldn't let down my guard and assume any get-together is just fun and games when even people we know—heck, Arthur or John or Ed—a lot of them will have an agenda. When I think of it this way, I nagged Ed about the baseball stadium."

"You should talk to him about this, or your dad. I bet they'd have good insights." Ed was still a congressman, and though there had been discussion of his running for Senate in the '92 election, he hadn't, and I wasn't sure why.

"You know the one person who'll never use me?" Charlie pointed at me.

"Sweetheart, I'm sure I'm not the only one. It might be a transition for some of our friends, but I wouldn't underestimate them."

"People get funny, though. I'd forgotten about this until earlier today, but when my dad was governor, there was an old friend of the family who ran afoul of the law, I think for embezzling, and he wanted Dad to intervene. When Dad refused, this guy's kids—fellows I knew well from the country club—they quit speaking to me. The man didn't end up going to prison, either, so I don't know what the family had to be so sour about."

From the seat behind us, Hank leaned forward again—the song was nearing the end, with the chorus repeating several times—and called, "Last chance. Chuckles, you're lucky you chose politics, because you'd never have made it in a traveling minstrel show." (Chuckles was Hank's nickname for Charlie, payback for Shit Storm. Of course, while Charlie is now Mr. President, the Shit Storm moniker has endured.)

Agreeably, Charlie joined in: " 'Don't tell my heart, my achy breaky heart . . .' "

I took his hand, lacing my fingers through his, and I leaned in so my mouth was by his ear. "I love you very much," I whispered.

IN THE TOWN car, Jessica is on the phone with Hank. "She'd prefer not to," Jessica keeps saying in a level tone—she has impeccable manners—and I can hear fragments of Hank's voice, wheedling but insistent; he wants to talk to me directly. "No, she wasn't," Jessica says. "She doesn't think Gladys Wycomb is concerned about that. No. No. All right. I'll call you from the plane." She presses the red "end" button on her cell phone, folds it shut, and immediately reaches for her BlackBerry and starts typing with her thumbs.

We are two miles from Midway Airport, Jessica and Cal and I in this car, which is driven by a local agent. I say, "I'd like to make a stop in Wisconsin before we return to Washington."

Jessica raises her eyebrows. "Your mother?"

My mother outlasted her second husband, too (Lars, who was perhaps the only person in either Charlie's or my family to take unequivocal delight in Charlie's political rise, died of acute renal failure in 1996), and my mother now resides in an assisted-living facility in an area outside Riley that was a pasture when I was growing up. She has Alzheimer's, but the blessing is that she remains both good-natured and seemingly happy; given how many of the people who have neurodegenerative diseases are depressed or violent, I am grateful. However, even as we're using my mother as the pretext for my traveling today, she isn't the one I wish to see.

This morning, when I assumed that it was Dena Janaszewski who had contacted Hank's office, it made a sort of sense—there was unfinished business between Dena and me, and this would be a reckoning. Learning, then, that the blackmail threat had nothing to do with her was almost a disappointment. I've often recalled that afternoon in Riley when she gave Ella the tiara—the more time has passed, the surer I have become that it was Dena and not her mother who did it, and that the gesture was a peace offering as opposed to a taunt—and I've regretted that I didn't reciprocate in some way. But that happened during such a topsy-turvy episode in my life, when every relationship other than the one I had with Charlie felt peripheral. All these years later, I am afraid I missed an opportunity, and I'm increasingly aware that if I don't initiate it, I might not have another. Like most people, I've always been able to reassure myself, on entering a new decade, that I'm still not old, that my previous sense of this age, thirty or forty or fifty, was skewed by my own youth. I even managed this feat of self-persuasion after turning sixty—sixty-year-olds bungee jump and swim the English Channel!—but at this point, I've reached the age when, if something happened to me, it would be sad but not tragic. I would be slightly young, but only slightly. In the same vein, if I were to hear someday that Dena had died—it's hard to know how the news would make its way to me, with my mother in her condition and both Dena's parents deceased, but surely I'd find out eventually—I could not be shocked. Other peers have passed on, Rose Trommler from Madison died of breast cancer in 2003, and last year my high school classmate Betty Bridges Scannell's husband had a brain aneurysm while they were on a cruise in the Caribbean. The sadness of these deaths clung to me for several days after I received word of them, but it would be remorse, a deep remorse, rather than mere sorrow I'd feel about Dena. For the first three decades of my life—for half of it—I didn't have a closer friend. Sure, she had her shortcomings, but who doesn't? She was lively and funny, she was much more daring than I was, and we knew each other so well; friendships have survived on far less.

It is strange to realize that at this point, my closest friend is probably Jessica. Jadey and I still speak once a week, and she visits us in Washington, sometimes with Arthur and sometimes without him, several times a year. Having her in the White House is always a tremendous breath of fresh air—she'll say to Charlie, "I'm only calling you Mr. President if you call me Dame Jadey," and she complains that visiting us makes her constipated because she can't comfortably go to the bathroom in such a historic setting—but there is an unspoken wedge between us that has grown over time. Although she's a Republican, she took it hard when Charlie supported the amendment to ban gay marriage; she remains tight with her interior-decorator friend Billy Torks, whom I always got a kick out of but haven't seen for years. While that was a passing tension, I think this is the ongoing problem for Jadey and me: Once our lives were alike, and now they're not. She still attends Garden Club meetings, she's joined the board of the Milwaukee Art Museum, she fund-raises for Biddle even though both Drew and Winnie graduated years ago, and all these activities are parts of her life I envy, I feel a great pull of sentimentality when she mentions them, but she has made it clear that she thinks I must find it boring and provincial when she tells stories about Maronee. Despite my repeated efforts to convince her otherwise, she refuses to believe I'd far prefer discussing her life to mine. She says, "No, no, tell me what the king and queen of Spain were like."

It feels unseemly to complain to my extended family or to friends from Wisconsin, so I don't. Early on in Charlie's political career, I once mentioned to another of my sisters-in-law, Ginger, that I was worried about the floral arrangements for a ball we were hosting in Madison, and she said, "I think it takes real nerve for you to complain about anything like that when Ed deserved to be governor a lot more than Chas." I found this to be a breathtaking comment not least because of Ginger's usual meekness, but perhaps even more surprising than the shift in Ginger was the one in Priscilla, who was the last person I'd have expected to be swayed by our fame: Shortly after Charlie was elected governor, she confided in me that I had always been her favorite daughter-in-law; she'd long believed we shared a similar sensibility. When Charlie was elected president, she began telling not just me but our relatives and also the media that I was her favorite *person.*

As for the other women I knew in Maronee or Madison, my friends from Garden Club or the mothers of Ella's classmates, so colorful and distracting is the pageantry of my life now that I think they have trouble remembering I am still myself, that my concerns are often mundane—my favorite shampoo has been discontinued, my husband snores, I struggle to find time to exercise—and that when my concerns aren't mundane, when I'm worried about war or terrorism, the grandiosity of my anxiety doesn't vault it into another category of emotion unimaginable to them; they'd be able to imagine it just fine if they could stop being impressed.

These all are reasons I so value Jessica, though I recognize that because I am her employer, ours is not a pure friendship. But the fact that we aren't peers makes things easier, I think; unlike Jadey, she is not comparing herself to me or her husband to mine. (In 2002, Jessica married a lovely man named Keith who works for the World Bank; Charlie and I attended the wedding at the Washington Club on Dupont Circle, and at the reception, Charlie danced with Miss Ruby, now retired and in her eighties but still energetically grumpy, and I danced with Jessica's younger brother, Antoine, then a six-foot-tall freshman at Biddle Academy.) Jessica and I have formed a two-woman book club; we switch off picking titles, and though there are no official rules other than that the books must be fiction, we tend to read translations of ones by authors from countries we've either just visited or are about to visit. In general, it's not that I can explain to Jessica my first-lady angst—it's that I don't have to. She is part of everything that happens, she knows exactly how scripted and confined and luxurious my life is, how the strangest parts are what the public *doesn't* see: that when Ella and I traveled to Peru, the hotel pool was drained as a safety precaution and filled with bottled water so we could swim in it; that I am called on by the White House's chief usher to start preparing for Christmas—the parties and cards and decorations—every April.

"I'll visit my mother on the next trip," I say to Jessica. "It's Dena Janaszewski I'd like to see, if we could arrange it."

If Jessica is caught off guard, she doesn't show it, a mark of her professionalism being that she expresses surprise only over minor matters and never over significant ones. I had an abortion? She simply nods. But I'm wearing magenta high heels? "Whoa!" she'll exclaim. "Hey there, Mrs. Fashionista!"

She looks at her watch and says in an even tone, "It's now one-twenty Central time, meaning two-twenty in D.C. Assuming it takes us an hour and forty minutes to fly back and then twenty minutes to get to the residence, that puts us at four-twenty without the stop in Riley, and the choir tour is scheduled for five-fifteen. Would you like me to delay the tour, cancel it, or find a substitute?"

The punctuality Charlie's administration is known for is not something his own family was stringent about when he was growing up, but it's another of the ways he sought to impose discipline on himself after he quit drinking. Following his example, I, too, strive to be on time; to do otherwise seems a form of arrogance. Furthermore, while it rarely bothers me to decline requests or invitations, it weighs on me when I make a commitment and am unable to honor it, and it weighs most heavily when that commitment involves children. And yet I want to see Dena today; I want to see her, and I want to see Pete, too, if they're still together.

When the abortion story comes out, Dena and perhaps Pete will be the only people who can confirm its veracity. But I don't hope to silence them. Rather, I see a visit as an opportunity to clear the air after far too long. In theory, I could go to Riley another day, I drop in every six weeks to check on my mother, but if I wait, won't the moment have passed? Won't I lose my nerve if I don't do it now?

"Let's find a substitute for the tour," I say, and then, inspired, "Ella! Children love Ella!"

"Will she be offended if I get a docent to accompany her?"

"She'll be relieved. Oh, if she'll agree to it, this could be perfect." It occurs to me that this could be the last favor I ask Ella for a long while. Once she learns of my abortion, I expect she might distance herself from me. As Jessica types on her BlackBerry, I say, "I think Hank's office at least started tracking Dena down this morning, but her surname could also be Cimino and maybe Imhof, although I don't know if they stayed together. If she's gotten married to someone else, then I have no idea. But her date of birth is 6/16/46." This, I suppose, is a sign of childhood friends, that you never forget their birthdays, whereas for the friends you make in adulthood, you never quite remember; I like to send birthday cards, but if I didn't mark my personal calendar, I'd miss them.

Jessica says, "Are you envisioning that Dena comes to the plane, you go to her house, or you meet at a public place?" The airfield we land on in Riley is tiny, used only by private planes and the fleet for White River Dairy.

"I'll go to her house," I say. I experience a vestigial impulse to add that I don't want to inconvenience Dena, that we should find out first if she's free today, but inconveniencing people is beside the point. From one perspective, I have for the last six years been nothing but an inconvenience, causing traffic to be stopped and streets closed, buildings locked, manhole covers sealed; from another perspective, many Americans and many people in the world, even now, wouldn't mind having their day turned upside down for the "privilege" of meeting me.

Jessica says, "While the office finds Dena, would you like to ask Ella or shall I?"

"I'll do it."

Jessica reaches into her pocketbook for a second cell phone, opens it, and dials. "It's Jessica. Hold for your mother?" Jessica is silent, then says, "In how long?" Again, a pause. "Perfect. We'll look forward to it." When she hangs up, she says, "Ella will call back in five minutes." Oh, thank heavens for Ella Blackwell, the only person who habitually rebuffs the president and first lady of the United States. I mean it not facetiously but sincerely when I say, what would we do without her to keep us humble?

Using her first cell phone, the one she was on earlier, Jessica presses a single button and, after a few seconds, says, "Belinda, I've sent messages to you and Ashley, but I need a home address and phone number for an individual in Riley. This is high priority." Jessica relays the information about Dena that I've provided then suggests Belinda try Lori in Hank's office, and when she hangs up again, she says to me, "So that I know when to schedule wheels up from Riley, how long do you anticipate meeting with Dena?"

"Half an hour? But let's not leave Chicago until we confirm that she's available. For all I know, she doesn't live in Riley anymore—I can imagine her having moved to someplace like New Mexico."

"If it's impossible to arrange the visit in time to be back for the gala, I'm certain we can find her phone number and you can still talk to her tonight. But we'll see if we can't set up an in-person meeting. You want to listen to the radio while I hop back on the phone?" Jessica's tone and expression are sympathetic; I haven't told her the details of my conversation with Gladys Wycomb, only the end result, but I think she can tell I feel fragile.

"Sure," I say. As it happens, we left on such short notice that I didn't bring a book.

Jessica says, "Cal, will you turn on NPR?"

I recognize the show that becomes audible as *Day to Day* before I recognize the subject of the current interview: It is Edgar Franklin, the man camped out on Capitol Hill, the father of the dead soldier. Jessica realizes who it is at the same time I do, even though she's already talking to someone else on the phone. To that person, she says, "Hang on," holds her palm over the mouth area of her cell, and says to me, "Want him to change it?"

I shake my head.

On the radio, the interviewer, who is male, says, "It seems you plan to stay here indefinitely—is that correct?"

"I plan to stay here until the president will see me," Edgar Franklin says.

"And if that doesn't happen?"

"I plan to stay here until the president will see me," Edgar Franklin repeats. His voice is firm but not belligerent—he speaks more quietly than the reporter, and he has a mild southern accent.

"Do you really believe you can convince President Blackwell to start bringing home the troops, or would you view a conversation as a symbolic act?"

"Too many young men and women have lost their lives, and I don't believe the president has ever been able to justify our presence there," Edgar Franklin says. "My impression is he hears selective intelligence, and it makes it hard for him to understand the personal toll this is taking."

"Although you yourself haven't had the opportunity to meet with the president, the White House has made a point in the last several days of mentioning his frequent visits with family members of the fallen, including two weeks ago in southern California. What do you hope to tell him that he wouldn't have heard from others whose situations are painfully similar to yours?"

"After your son dies this way, you look for a reason his death meant something. You hope he made a sacrifice he believed in, and that's why it's tempting to accept"—Edgar Franklin hesitates—"the rhetoric of war, is I guess how to put it. If I thought Nate's death was a waste, wouldn't that be disloyal to my son and my country? It would mean I wasn't patriotic, is what I thought at first, but I've come to see it that bringing our troops home would be the patriotic thing. A lot of families just now going through what I experienced two years ago, just starting to grieve, maybe they're not thinking about the political side yet."

"What do you make of the outpouring of support you've received since your arrival in Washington last Wednesday?"

"The tide has turned. Americans know it's time for an honest conversation."

"Colonel Edgar Franklin, thank you for speaking with me."

"Thank you, sir."

"You're listening to member-supported WBEZ," a female voice says as our police-escorted Town Car is waved through the gates leading to the private section of the airport. We cross the tarmac, and in the overcast heat of the Midwest, a glare bounces off the Gulfstream parked two hundred feet away; the steps are already pulled down, awaiting us.

CHARLIE USED TO have a line he'd tease me with before dinners on the rubber-chicken circuit; he'd say, "Don't forget that *fund-raiser* starts with *fun.*" He said this because he knew I loathed them—the repetition, the forced greetings and stilted conversations, the endless photo ops, and above all, the uncomfortably transactional feeling that people were literally buying us. I've always found the thousand-dollar dinners more unsettling than the twenty-five-thousand-dollar ones—if someone pays the Republican National Committee twenty-five thousand dollars (or, more likely, fifty per couple) to breathe the same air as Charlie for an hour or two, then it's clear the person has money to spare. What breaks my heart is when it's apparent through their accent or attire that a person isn't well off but has scrimped to attend an event with us. *We're not worth it!* I want to say. *You should have paid off your credit-card bill, invested in your grandchild's college fund, taken a vacation to the Ozarks.* Instead, in a few weeks, they receive in the mail a photo with one or both of us, signed by an autopen, which they can frame so that we might grin out into their living room for years to come.

But there was one fund-raiser that, to my own surprise, I did find fun. This was a million-dollar dinner held at a former plantation in Mobile, Alabama, in July 2000. Charlie and I always ate at separate tables, and that night I was assigned to be with the wife of the chairman of the Alabama Republican Party, two well-dressed middle-aged couples who looked like variations of the people we knew in Maronee, and a father-and-son duo. Before an event, an aide provides a paragraph or two describing each of the bigwigs who will be in attendance, and that evening, the original plan had been that I'd be sitting between a man named Beau Phillips, who owned a regional chain of fast-food restaurants, and a man named Leon Tasket, who was the CFO of the largest producer of industrial machinery in Alabama. As it turned out, Leon Tasket's wife had come down with the flu, and in her stead—it's hard to imagine this last-minute switch happening now or at any point after Charlie became president—Mr. Tasket had brought his adult son Dale, a tall, heavy, mentally disabled fellow. Though I suspect Dale had the intellectual aptitude of a nine- or ten-year-old, I wouldn't have guessed this if I'd been observing him from any distance—his features weren't irregular, except perhaps that he looked friendlier than most other guests. When it was time to sit for dinner, the men at the table remained standing while I and the other wives found our places, and Dale, to whom I had been briefly introduced a minute before, plopped next to me in the seat that had a place card for his father; Mrs. Tasket's place card was one more over. "Oh, no, you don't," Leon Tasket said immediately. Mr. Tasket was shorter and wirier than his son, with a well-trimmed white beard and mustache and a three-piece suit. "Boy, if Miss Alice Blackwell saw the way you ate, she'd be scared half to death."

I smiled, shaking my head. "It's fine with me if he stays there—if it's all right with you, that is."

"That's an awful brave lady who doesn't mind sitting in the vicinity of a black bear, isn't it, Dale? You think we should call her bluff?"

On the stage just above our heads, a man in a flag tie was tapping the microphone, saying, "If you'll all take your seats . . ." At another table, Charlie sat between the governor and the state's Republican Party chair.

"Really," I said. "It's fine."

As waiters brought our salads, Beau Phillips, the fast-food honcho on my right, said, "Your husband is on a sure path to victory," and simultaneously, on my left, Dale said, "My favorite actress is Drew Barrymore, do you know who Drew Barrymore is?" Both men had endearingly thick southern accents, though only one of them—Dale—was talking with his mouth full; he had torn into his salad with gusto. To Mr. Phillips, I said, "Thank you," and then I turned toward Dale. "I do know who she is."

"The liberal elite has lost touch with real American values," Mr. Phillips said. "We need someone to stand up to those activist judges pushing for the homosexual agenda. That lifestyle might cut it in the Northeast, but I'll tell you what, it sure doesn't fly down here."

Mildly, I said, "I know Charlie likes to focus on what we as Americans have in common."

"Did you see her in *The Wedding Singer?*" Dale was asking.

I turned back. "I didn't, but I've heard of it."

"She's the most pretty and talented actress there is," Dale said, and his father, who'd been talking to the chairman's wife on his other side, chuckled and said, "If I were a bettin' man, I'd say we must be discussin' Drew Barrymore."

"I saw her when she was a little girl in *E.T.,*" I said. "Oh, and you know what, Dale—my daughter and I recently watched a movie she was in called *Never Been Kissed.* Have you seen that?"

It was Mr. Tasket who said, "Have we seen *Never Been Kissed?* Only three times a week do we see *Never Been Kissed* at our house. I've watched that little movie more times than I've watched the evenin' news."

"Mr. Coulson thinks Josie's a student, but when he finds out she works for the newspaper, they can fall in love," Dale said.

"I remember that part," I said.

"Drew's birthday is February twenty-second, 1975," Dale said. "That means she's twenty-five and seven months and three days, and she's a Pisces, and I'm a Gemini, but I'm older than her because I'm forty."

Dale's father had faded again from the conversation, but on my right, Mr. Phillips said, "This election will be a real comeuppance for the Democrats. You mark my words, we'll have payback after eight years of them running roughshod."

"Charlie and I are as curious about what will happen as you are," I said. To Dale, I said, "If you're a Gemini, that must mean you were born in May or June."

"I was born on June third, 1960. What are your hobbies?" Dale had a dab of salad dressing on the outer corner of his lips. "Mine are Nintendo, stamps, and the zoo."

I couldn't resist. I said, "It sounds like Drew Barrymore is a hobby of yours, too."

Dale smiled slyly and said, "A girl can't be a hobby!" Then he said, "When you come to our house, I'll show you my Classic American Aircraft stamps. I have all of them, but the best is the Northrop YB-49 Flying Wing."

"Mrs. Blackwell, are you and your husband in the area for long?" This came from a wife across the table, but Dale preempted my response by saying, "And the Thunderbolt is real cool, too."

I said to the woman (I already couldn't remember her name), "Unfortunately, we fly out tonight, and I'm sorry, because it would be fun to explore. I was just reading about the Bellingrath Gardens."

"When you're next here, you ought to go over to the Eastern Shore. We all have places there"—she gestured to the other couples at the table—"and it's a wonderful place to relax, very quiet. Campaigning must be tiring."

They were polite, all of them, and they also were clearly irritated that Dale was monopolizing my attention, and that his father and I were allowing it. And I was fully complicit—what could have been more delightful than to sit beside someone brimming with his own interests and enthusiasms, none of which was political, a person who neither knew nor cared who I was beyond the fact that I'd heard of Drew Barrymore and was willing to talk about her? No one else at the table could compete with Dale's volubility, his lusty and fearless ingestion of the food on his plate, his ingenuous questions and announcements; I was enchanted. The others at the table soon gave up on me, and several times after I'd been left to conspire with Dale, I noticed his father glancing with amusement at us, and I wondered if he hadn't brought his son as a sort of joke, an antidote to the stuffiness rampant at these fund-raisers. There was something fearless about Mr. Tasket, too; despite his earlier demurrals when Dale had sat by me, he seemed unapologetic about having brought his mentally disabled adult son to a fancy dinner.

When our entrées came, I wasn't particularly hungry and ended up offering my sirloin to Dale, which he accepted with great pleasure. He said, "Are you sure?" He ate my dessert, too, a strawberry shortcake.

It was about ten minutes into Charlie's speech when Dale patted my arm and said, "Miss Alice, do you like tic-tac-toe?" He was speaking in a normal volume, not whispering, and at our table and the tables near ours, people looked at him. Leon Tasket, appearing not particularly perturbed, leaned in from Dale's other side and murmured something to his son. Dale's expression became big-eyed and chastened, and he sat back in his chair, crossing his arms over his substantial belly.

I reached into my purse and found a paper napkin and a blue ballpoint pen. I drew a crosshatch, placed an X in the upper-right square, and nudged the napkin toward Dale. His face lit up, and when it seemed he might speak again, I brought my finger to my lips. Onstage, Charlie was saying, "As I travel around this great land of ours, I hear a consistent refrain: *Bring integrity back to the White House.*" As always, on each word, he pounded the podium once, and as always, loud applause followed. Dale drew an O in the center square. "*Bring integrity back to the White House,*" Charlie repeated. "Now, everyone here knows what that means, but I'd like to illustrate the principle by telling y'all a story." I drew an X in the lower-right square, and Dale blocked me by placing an O between my two X's. "Not long ago, I visited a school in Ocala, Florida. A fifth-grade boy, a little guy named Timmy Murphy, raised his hand and said to me, 'Governor Blackwell, isn't the president of the United States supposed to be a hero? But my parents say the man currently occupying the Oval Office isn't heroic at all.' " Again, sustained applause. I drew an X in the middle of the right column, and Dale made a frustrated exhalation; this time, I'd blocked him. I especially detested this part of Charlie's stump speech both because of how self-aggrandizing it was and because it was so improbable that a fifth-grader would use the words *currently* or *occupying.* "Well, Timmy," Charlie said, and Dale drew an O in the top box of the center column, "I'm not Superman, and I'm not Spider-Man, but if your mom and dad vote for me, I promise you that courage and morality will reign again in Washington, D.C." Here, the applause was thunderous. Our game had ended in a stalemate, and Dale quickly drew another crosshatch. The next game also ended in a stalemate, as did the three after that—by this point, Charlie was deep into talking about being a tolerant traditionalist—and then Dale beat me, four more stalemates occurred, and I beat him; the paper napkin was by then more blue than white, and our crosshatches had shrunk with each round to fit in the limited space. Charlie was finished speaking, and the local party chair was emphasizing the importance of supporting all Republicans in this year's tight races. A standing ovation concluded the speeches, and as it tapered off, Dale said, "You should give me your address, and I'll write you letters."

"Miss Alice is a busy lady," Leon Tasket protested, and I said, "I'd love it if you wrote to me."

I printed my first and last name and the address for the governor's mansion in Madison on the back of one of Mr. Tasket's business cards. Just before I was pulled away for photos, Dale hugged me. He said, "After you and your daughter rent *The Wedding Singer,* then you need to rent *Poison Ivy.* Drew is only seventeen in that, but it's a real good one. You have pretty blue eyes, Miss Alice."

"Why, thank you," I said.

I did indeed receive a letter from Dale after two weeks, written on lined paper from a spiral notebook, the fringy edge still attached. Despite being punctuation-free and erratically capitalized, it was perfectly comprehensible: *Only three Months until Charlie's Angels Movie comes out are you Excited cause I am you should Come Back to Alabama you could go Alligator Hunting with Me and Dad . . .* I wrote a reply by hand the next day, on the stationery that had my name embossed at the top; I mentioned that I had been traveling with my husband, that we had most recently visited Ohio and Pennsylvania, that I was reading a biography of former first lady Abigail Adams, and that although I hadn't had an opportunity to rent *The Wedding Singer,* I was looking forward to seeing it. After returning from Mobile, I'd told my staff in Madison to watch for any correspondence from Dale and to make sure I personally saw it rather than it being answered with the standard letter and a black-and-white photo of Snowflake and me. Because I'd made a point of explaining to my aides who Dale was, when no follow-up letter from him arrived, I had to conclude that it was less likely it had been lost than that he'd never written it. I was disappointed, and I have since wondered several times how he's doing; whenever I see that Drew Barrymore has a new movie out, I think of him.

That evening in Mobile, in the van headed to the airport, Hank, who'd been sitting at the table adjacent to ours, said, "The retard took a real shine to you, huh, Alice?"

"What retard?" Charlie asked.

A few weeks later, Leon Tasket made a donation of eight hundred thousand dollars to the RNC, but rather than feeling triumphant about this development, I was a little sad—it was as if my delight in Mr. Tasket's son had, like so much else in politics, merely been for show. That I had played tic-tac-toe with a fellow audience member during my husband's stump speech was written up in *Time* magazine and has been repeated in many articles since, a little nugget about me that, in the absence of more substantive disclosures, is assumed to reveal something meaningful about my personality.

"SO EXPLAIN TO me why it is you're going to see your wacko former friend who you haven't laid eyes on in thirty years when it turns out she had nothing to do with this shit," Charlie says over the phone. In the Gulfstream, we are flying above the Illinois-Wisconsin border, and Charlie is en route to a remote park along the Potomac for an afternoon bike ride; in other words, three vehicles containing him, his mountain bike, assorted agents and their bikes, and even a physician are making their way south.

I say, "It turns out Dena's still dating Pete Imhof, so this is really about seeing both of them. I guess I just feel the need." Belinda in my office confirmed to Jessica that Dena and Pete do live together, though Belinda said Dena was uncertain whether Pete would be present when I arrived.

"I thought you and Ella were planning on a girls' afternoon," Charlie says.

"Well, I'm excited to see her tonight, and I hope she's not offended by my change of plans. I'll be back an hour before the gala. Did you ask Ella if she wanted to bike with you?"

"She said it's too hot."

I hesitate, and then I say, "I'm worried about how she'll react to this abortion story. Hank has gotten Dr. Wycomb to promise not to come forward before tomorrow—I think he must be pretending there's still a chance I'll speak out against Ingrid Sanchez—so I'm planning to tell Ella tonight in person. After I do, will you make sure you're around? I have a feeling she'll need someone to talk to, but she'll be angry with me."

"Is that why you're avoiding coming home?"

"Honey, I'm not avoiding anything. Seeing Dena is a chance to tie up loose ends."

"Well, Ella's a tough cookie," Charlie says. "She'll be fine."

"But from a religious standpoint—"

"You think any Christian worth their salt can't get their head around the idea of sinning? So you messed up forty years ago—that doesn't mean you never walked with God again."

I knew he'd say this, even though surely he's aware I don't consider abortion a sin (unfortunate, yes, but immoral, no), just as he's aware that I do not share his Christian convictions. Our unspoken deal regarding religion is similar to our deal about politics: I don't object when he talks about God, and he doesn't insist that I proclaim myself a believer. I have spoken of my agnosticism to as few people as I've spoken of my abortion, so I understand the widespread assumption, among both friends and strangers, of my faith.

As for the Christian right, the traditional-values advocates—whatever name you call them by, they are the ones who believe Charlie is a Messianic figure. So untenable a hypothesis is this to me that I can only squelch in my mind any consideration of it. That Charlie, encouraged by his advisers, Hank foremost among them, has promoted this preposterous notion is an act of either such cynicism or such bottomless hubris that it would be impossible to say which is worse. My suspicion is that for Charlie, the vision of himself as messiah-like is sincere (how else to explain his rise from floundering alcoholic to president?), and for Hank, it is insincere, though I do not doubt the sincerity of Hank's belief in Charlie. I might say that I don't understand that belief, since Hank is clearly the more intellectual and ambitious of the two men, except that I do understand: Hank recognized early on that Charlie could be his charismatic proxy. And didn't I, too, hitch my life to Charlie's, allowing myself to be guided and defined by him? So why wouldn't I understand the impulse in someone else?

Charlie sounds upbeat when he says, "Once the mudslinging starts, remember that I'm never running for anything again, so you don't need to feel guilty on my account."

I look out the window; the captain's chair I am seated in faces sideways, perpendicular to the walled-off cockpit, so I can see the blue sky outside. This jet, which I prefer to the Boeing 757s I must use when accompanied by larger groups, seats sixteen, and the fabric covering all the chairs is white leather, the carpet cream; the decor has always reminded me a bit of a tacky person's idea of heaven. I say, "Sweetheart, I appreciate your support, but before we start calling my abortion a sin—doesn't that imply you wish I hadn't had it? And we'd never have married, would we, if I were the mother of a thirteen-year-old when we met?" He's quiet, and I say, "It's not uncomplicated. That's all I'm trying to point out. And I hope this is a story that blows over, but my fear is that Ingrid Sanchez's nomination will keep it in the news."

"You're not suggesting I give her the boot?"

"No, but I wouldn't underestimate how much the press will relish the irony."

"What really chaps my ass," Charlie says, "is the idea of this bitter witch doctor deciding she's going to expose you, and everyone rolls over and plays dead. Could there be a clearer case of blackmail?"

"She's a hundred and four, Charlie."

"Yeah, so everyone keeps saying. Kept alive by good old-fashioned liberal rage, huh?" He chuckles. "Hey, if that's all it takes, you might outlast me yet."

We both are silent; outside the cabin of the plane, the engines hum.

Jessica sits a few feet away in her own white leather seat, eating a sandwich prepared for her by one of the two flight attendants; Cal and José are chatting in the plane's rear while Walter reads a thriller. I try to keep my voice low as I say, "I don't agree with Dr. Wycomb's methods, but you do remember that I'm pro-choice, don't you?"

"See, that's what makes America great—room for all kinds of opposing viewpoints." I can tell Charlie's grinning, then I hear an unmistakable noise, a bubbly blurt of sound, and I know he's just broken wind. Though I've told him it's inconsiderate, I think he does it as much as possible in front of his agents. He'll say, "They think it's hilarious when the leader of the free world toots his own horn!"

"I heard that," I say.

"I don't know what you're talking about." Before ending the call, he adds, "Give my regards to the divorcée."

IF A REPORTER or stranger asks what in my life I never imagined I'd find myself doing, I say, "Giving speeches!" Invariably, it's an answer that elicits laughter. If friends ask, I say, "Having a cat." That was Hank's doing—a poll he commissioned in the early nineties revealed that the voters of Wisconsin would have a more favorable idea of our family if we owned a pet, ideally a dog. I protested because of Ella's allergies, and this is how we came to own Snowflake, our allegedly hypoallergenic Russian Blue.

That our cat is standoffish is, as far as I'm concerned, all the better; I have shed no tears over her apparent aversion to sitting on our laps or even anywhere near us. Charlie sometimes lifts her up and smashes his face against her ribs, rubbing his nose in her fur, saying, "You're the only one who really loves me, aren't you, Snowflake? Yes, you are, you good Republican cat." Maids feed Snowflake and change her litter box, and a vet makes house calls for her annual checkup; if she has her way with birds or mice on the White House grounds, I'm not privy to it. My dislike of cats, cemented when I was scratched on the cheek by one as a five-year-old, isn't public (with something like seventy million cat owners in this country, Charlie joked, I could have sabotaged the election with that admission alone), but the fact that it isn't public is why, when I am called upon by friends to share some morsel of my private life, I can trot it out. It is, of course, a fake revelation, a pseudo-intimacy, which is a trick I've learned from White House press secretaries; on a regular basis, they dispense pieces of information about us that are true but absurdly trivial, that masquerade as sharing—these are humanizing, they tell us. *Charlie Blackwell loves the movie* Anchorman. *Alice Blackwell gave the president a digital camera and a biking jersey for Christmas. Ella Blackwell's favorite food is fajitas.*

The real answer to the question of what in my life I never imagined I'd find myself doing is this: having a face-lift. And though there has been plenty of media speculation on the topic, it will never be confirmed either by me or by any staff members, in part because few of them know for certain. Charlie had decided as early as 1997, before his gubernatorial reelection, that he'd run for president in 2000. In 1998, at a Super Bowl party we were hosting at the governor's mansion for staff and close friends, I was standing with Debbie Bell; Hank's wife, Brenda; and Kathleen Hicken. Debbie, who was at that point Charlie's director of communications, said, "Between us girls, have any of you ever considered plastic surgery? I was in Ann Taylor the other day, and those dressing-room mirrors are *not* forgiving."

"Debbie, you're young still!" I said. She was about a decade behind Charlie and me—this would have meant she was then in her early forties—so I wanted to think this.

"See, but I keep hearing how easy the procedures are these days," Debbie said. "I'm not talking about, you know, implants or a nose job, just—" She held her hands up on either side of her face and pulled back. "Eliminate a few wrinkles," she said. She turned to me. "Would you do it?" (I should have known—oh, I was a terrible dupe, but I didn't get it.)

"Doesn't a face-lift take months to recover from?" Kathleen said.

Debbie shook her head. "Maybe it used to be like that, but doctors have made a ton of advances. If I schedule an appointment, Alice, will you come with me for moral support?" This struck me as an odd request, because I wasn't close to Debbie. We knew each other well, she was part of Charlie's inner circle, but she and I never spent time together one-on-one.

"I think I'll pass, but I'll be curious to hear what the doctor tells you," I said. "I'll bet you anything he turns you away for being far too youthful."

That, it turned out, was Phase One. Phase Two was Jadey calling and saying, "I'm not supposed to tell you this, but Hank wants you to get a face-lift, so I'm supposed to suggest we go to Florida and get them together, like it's my own idea, but then I thought about it, and I'm kind of intrigued."

"*Hank* wants me to get a face-lift?"

"I know it's real manipulative—"

"And he called you?"

"Debbie called me."

"I'll call you back in a second," I said, and when I'd hung up, I dialed the direct line to Charlie's office. His secretary Marsha answered, saying, "He's meeting with the Board of Regents right now, but I'd be happy to—"

"Please tell him it's urgent," I said.

When Charlie picked up, he said in a breathless voice, "Ella—" and I said, "No, she's fine, nothing bad happened, except apparently, Hank is going around telling people I need a face-lift."

"I warned him you wouldn't like this."

"You knew?"

"It's for TV, Lindy, that's all. You know I think you're beautiful, but he has the idea that when we're on more of a national stage—"

"Are *you* planning to have a face-lift?"

"I don't have to tell you there's a double standard. Listen, they should have been more straightforward with you—"

"They?"

"We—we should have. Hank's logic is that if you want to do it, do it now. You can't have that kind of surgery in the middle of a campaign."

"Where is this coming from? Did Hank run a poll on my appearance?"

Charlie hesitated, and I said, "Is he there with you now?"

"He's in with the Regents, which is where I should be. It's your decision, Lindy. I'm sorry if you're offended. You're still the prettiest of all my wives."

"This is incredibly insulting."

"When I get home tonight, I'll show you how attractive I find you. Now I've gotta go before I get a woody just thinking about it."

I suppose I was offended not only because the thought of Charlie's staff discussing my appearance—and finding it lacking—was humiliating but also because the suggestion reinforced my own self-doubt. Although I'd never been insecure about my looks, it hadn't escaped my attention that the lines at the corners of my mouth and across my forehead were deeper, that the skin on my neck was not as smooth as it had once been, and that when I appeared on television, these flaws were more obvious than in person. Still, I hadn't thought the situation required more than some experimenting with makeup.

For three days I fumed, on the fourth day I had my assistant Cheryl go buy a book about plastic surgery, and on the fifth day I went to see a doctor. He was not the one who performed the procedure; a month later, Jadey and I did go to a clinic in Naples, Florida, to a surgeon reputed to be the best in the field, and afterward, we stayed for two weeks at a secluded house overlooking a canal. Unfortunately, the setting was wasted on us because we weren't supposed to swim or expose ourselves to the sun; Cheryl, who was thirty, had accompanied us, and we encouraged her to drive to the beach and even snorkel one afternoon. Meanwhile, Jadey and I lay around reading, watching television, complaining, and making fun of ourselves. We'd been instructed to keep our heads elevated—Jadey was more bandaged than I was, though we were both simultaneously numb and tender, and my face became quite puffy—and six days after the procedure, we went to have the stitches removed from the incisions at our hairlines (before the operation, a nurse had complimented me on how beautifully my haircut would hide any mild scarring). Jadey and I made a pact to never tell anyone—our husbands knew, and Cheryl, but we'd say nothing to our other sisters-in-law or to Priscilla or our children. It was thinking of Ella, actually, that gave me pause: What a negative role model I would be if she knew, how vain and unaccepting of the aging process. Conveniently, however, she was away at Princeton, and the story we told everyone else in Madison and Milwaukee was that we were taking a painting class, an intensive study of watercolor. ("What do we do when they ask to see our work?" I said, and Jadey said, "We say it's being shipped back." As it turned out, no one ever asked.)

Especially in the first few days after our twin surgeries, Jadey and I looked so banged up that we questioned, out loud and at regular intervals, whether we'd made a mistake, and it crossed my mind (this part I did not express aloud) that we were like characters in a fairy tale, narcissistic hags grasping at our lost youth. But we weren't, in the end, punished for overreaching; even a week after the surgery, the bruising had faded, the swelling had shrunk, and on the night before our return to Wisconsin, we joined Cheryl for dinner at a wonderful and very festive Mexican restaurant; we weren't supposed to drink, but Jadey sneaked a few sips of Cheryl's margarita. Upon our arrival home, we kept calling each other to compare notes on how many compliments we'd received, how rested people said we looked from the fresh sea air. Of all the unfortunate facts about plastic surgery, perhaps the hardest to accept is this: If it's done well, it works. Once you've had it, you realize how many other people must have also, and while there are plenty of inept examples where the surgery is obvious, there are many more women and men, especially in the public eye, about whom we haven't a clue, even as we admire their healthy and youthful glow.

I had learned in the book I'd read that the benefits of a rhytidectomy, as it is formally called, tend to last for five to ten years, at which point a repeat performance is recommended. That means that even by the most optimistic calculation, my face-lift has expired. I don't plan to have another, not because my vanity has disappeared but because now Jadey and I prefer Botox treatments, an option that didn't exist in the late nineties. Every three months, she flies to Washington, and Charlie's private physician, Dr. Subramanium, performs the treatments on us in the privacy of his White House office; the procedure takes ten minutes and involves no anesthesia. I would like to think that part of the reason I stick so assiduously to this routine is that it's a source of bonding for Jadey and me, a way for us to maintain our closeness, but this is only partly true. I also do it because I don't want bloggers and late-night talk-show hosts to make fun of the way I look. That I routinely submit to having poisonous bacterium injected into my face is flabbergasting to me, but no more flabbergasting than my marriage to the president of the United States, my residence in the White House, my ridiculous title of first lady. As far as I know, Debbie Bell has never had plastic surgery of any kind.

Back in 1998, after I returned to Madison from Naples, Ella came home for spring break a few weeks later, and I went to pick her up at the airport; though I had security detail as Wisconsin's first lady, I still occasionally drove. Ella's spring break was two weeks long, and she and a bunch of friends had spent the first half in Turks and Caicos, at the vacation home of a classmate named Alessandra Caterina Laroche de Fournier (she went by Alex). The trip had become a little boring by the end, Ella said; she'd felt self-indulgent, and this week, she wanted to drop by the soup kitchen where she had volunteered during high school. I'd cleared my schedule in anticipation of her being home, and I told her that if she wanted to see any movies, or if she needed to shop for clothes, especially for her upcoming summer internship at Microsoft, I was flexible. In a neutral tone, she said, "Yeah, maybe."

We were back at the mansion, and I'd parked when she said, "Mom, by the way?"

I turned to look at her.

"Nice face-lift," she said.

THEY LIVE ON the first floor of a house on Adelphia Street. With my heart thudding against my chest, I climb the porch steps and knock on the door, though knocking is a bit of a formality given that both their apartment and the one above it, accessed through a door next to theirs, have already been inspected by the Secret Service agents. An air-conditioned coolness, infused with cigarette smoke, comes out to meet me from inside when Dena appears behind her screen door. She is a lean woman with a stringy neck and thin lips, her face lined, her once light brown hair now blondish-gray and dry-looking, still wavy but clipped just beneath her ears. She is old, Dena's *old,* but she's also unmistakably herself, and I begin to cry. She opens the door, an amused look creeping onto her face, and she says, "Well, you don't need to be a drama queen about it." When we embrace, I cling to her.

We step into the living room, which holds a black leather couch and matching chair as well as a low coffee table, all facing an entertainment system—a triptych of shelves whose centerpiece is an enormous television set, flanked on one side by a stereo, speakers, and CD and DVD cases, and on the other side by several rows of propped-up collector plates featuring either horses (they gallop against the backdrop of western landscapes, their bodies at sharp sideways angles, their manes and tails blown fiercely by the wind) or else American Indians (a chieftain gripping a tomahawk with an eagle perched on his shoulder, a woman in long black braids and a fringed leather dress kneeling devotedly over a papoose). Has Dena's taste changed, has mine, or have the times? Perhaps some combination. The walls of the living room are covered in wood paneling, the carpet is mauve, and a doorway leads to an overcast narrow hall at the end of which another doorway opens onto, from my vantage point, a strip of a sunny room with a black-and-white checkerboard floor—the kitchen, I assume. The television is on, set to *Dr. Phil.*

"You thirsty?" Dena asks. "I'd offer you a real drink, but we quit years ago, so about the most interesting thing we have is Diet Coke."

"That sounds perfect." When she starts down the hall, I look around for tissue—there's a box on an end table—and blow my nose. On the coffee table is a bowl of rose potpourri, an issue of *People* magazine, and a pack of Merit cigarettes. From the kitchen, I hear water running, and as Dena returns to the living room, she talks to someone in one of the rooms along the way, but I can't make out the words over the television. It must be Pete; I know from my agents that I am now sitting in the same apartment as Pete Imhof. Outside, through the front window, I see José, one of the agents, standing on the porch with his arms folded, surveying the street.

Dena carries two glasses, one with dark, fizzy liquid in it and one with water; she passes the Diet Coke to me, turns off the TV, sits in the chair, and gestures for me to sit on the couch. "I've gotta say, when the girl from your office called to announce you were on your way, I thought someone was playing a joke." Dena's tone is neither cold nor fawning but simply normal; for the second time today, I am not Alice

Blackwell but Alice Lindgren. Or I am both, because she says, "So what's it like being married to the president?"

In what I hope is a light voice, I say, "It depends on the day."

Dena crosses one leg over the other. She's wearing jeans and a sleeveless black V-necked shirt that shows her cleavage to such flattering effect, I can't help wondering if she's either wearing a padded bra or has had implants. She also wears dangly silver earrings, a silver chain necklace, and two silver rings, neither on the ring finger of her left hand: One, with a moonstone affixed to it, is on her left middle finger, and the other, a band imprinted with tiny peace signs, is on her right thumb. The peace signs give an extra weight to what she says next, or maybe it's my imagination. She says, "I never knew you were a Republican."

"I wasn't."

"Yeah?" She smiles. "How's that worked out?"

We are quiet, and I say, "I've thought of you a lot over the years, Dena. I wish—" *I wish our friendship hadn't imploded, I wish it hadn't been three decades since we last spoke.*

But she says, "I know. I wish it, too." She laughs a little. "I'd say I've thought of you, but it's more like I've *seen* you. That cashmere coat you wore at Charlie's inauguration, at the second one, that was gorgeous. I thought, When I knew Alice, she was such a penny-pincher about clothes, but that must have cost a fortune. I was glad to see you'd loosened up." *Charlie's inauguration*—this is how the public refers to him, as Charlie, or more sarcastically, as Chuck or Chuckie B. In Washington, I am the only person who directly interacts with him who could get away with such informality. "That's a nice suit, too. What designer is it?" Dena nods toward my increasingly wrinkled red linen jacket and skirt, which I donned for the breast cancer summit this morning—a lifetime ago. When I'm in the residence, I dress casually, much the way Dena's dressed, albeit in more modest shirts.

"It's de la Renta," I say.

She nods approvingly. "I was gonna guess him or Carolina Herrera." She gestures out the window at the agent on the porch. "Do those guys listen when you pee?"

I laugh. "They don't go into the bathroom with me, no. They wait outside. A few of them are female—no one who's traveling with us today but some of the others—so if there's a situation where it might be awkward to have a man present, a woman can step in."

Dena shakes her head. "Better you than me."

"It's a strange life." I pause. "Dena, Pete's here, isn't he?"

"And I thought I was the main attraction."

"No, you are, but if it's possible, I'd like to talk to both of you at the same time."

She turns her head toward the hall and calls out, "Babe, she wants to see you, too!" Looking back at me, she says, "He thinks you don't like him. I told him you wouldn't make a personal trip here just to scold us, the first lady has bigger fish to fry, but you know Pete."

Not really, of course—I don't know Pete Imhof anymore, if I ever did.

Again, more impatiently, she yells, "Babe!"

After another minute, he materializes: He, too, wears jeans, and a gray Badgers T-shirt and brown leather flip-flops. (The dark hair on his toes! With a jolt, I remember it from when I was seventeen. How strange that I once, briefly, was well acquainted with Pete Imhof's body.) When I last saw him, after that infuriating pyramid scheme, he had gained a good deal of weight, and he has gained a good deal since then. He's not enormous, but he's more than big, and both his hair and beard are silver. He's actually a handsome man in an earthily sexual sort of way. I stand, and we exchange a clumsy handshake; I don't mean to be cruel when I say that the clumsiness is his, that his discomfort is clear. God knows I have many shortcomings, but at this point, managing a handshake isn't one of them. "You sure surprised Dena today," he says as he steps backward so he's next to her chair. He perches in a not particularly comfortable-looking way on an arm of it while I sit back down on the couch.

"Babe, get a chair from the kitchen," Dena says, and he does, setting it close to hers.

"I hope I didn't pull the two of you away from other obligations," I say when Pete has sat. I know, through Belinda telling Jessica, what their jobs are—Pete is a night security guard at White River Dairy, and Dena is a part-time massage therapist at a chiropractor's office.

Wryly, Dena says, "We managed to make time for you."

"I bet you both are wondering why I dropped in out of the blue."

Neither of them replies, and then Dena says, "Yeah, you could say that."

"Well, first, I wanted to see you—I wanted to know what had become of you, Dena. But also, a news story is about to break that's indirectly related to you, Pete. I'm not sure whether it will be a television program or a newspaper that will report it first, but in the next day or so, it'll become public that I—that in 1963, I had an abortion. And I'm telling you because, although the media won't have any idea of this part, Pete, it was you I'd gotten pregnant by. I don't know if Dena ever mentioned—"

"He knows." Dena says this matter-of-factly, and when I glance at Pete, he does not contradict her; he watches me with little emotion. (Would Andrew have become so heavyset as he aged? I doubt it, because they had different builds.)

"If I had it to do over again, obviously, it would have been more respectful to have told you at the time," I say.

"Who's spilling the beans?" Dena says. "Someone you know?"

"It's—" There are several ways to describe Gladys Wycomb, but I decide to leave my grandmother out of it. "It's the doctor who performed the procedure," I say. "She's very old now, and she's doing it to protest— I don't know if you two have been following the Supreme Court nomination of Ingrid Sanchez, but that's what the doctor is protesting." I look at Pete. "I hope this isn't a news story that will have legs, but it's possible some reporters will get it into their mind to try to figure out who I was involved with at the time, and I don't think they'll be able to except through one of us. But I wanted to warn you. I'd prefer that you don't talk to reporters if you hear from them, but it's your decision, and if you'd like, someone in my office can connect you with a media coach." Lest this sound condescending, I add, "Although I've had loads of coaching, and I still haven't learned all the tricks."

Dena and Pete exchange a look, and Dena says, "Yep, we hear from your friends at the tabloids on a regular basis. Well, not just the tabloids—babe, where was that guy calling from a few weeks ago, was it Croatia? It was a country I wouldn't be able to find on the map, I'll tell you that much."

This should not surprise me—exposés and tell-alls about Charlie's administration or his family or his early years are published on a weekly basis, both articles and books, in tabloids and reputable magazines alike, and during the 2000 campaign, when the first reporter discovered the accident that killed Andrew Imhof, that was big news that I addressed by giving an interview to a *USA Today* reporter. I said, "It was incredibly sad. I know it was very hard for his family and our classmates and really the whole community, including me." In all the times I've been asked about it since, I have repeated these comments without expanding on them. To pad out the various books and articles, therefore, the writers must find more loquacious subjects, so they talk to anyone we ever so much as passed on the sidewalk. I know of at least one biography of me that identifies Dena as my childhood best friend, which must be how other journalists know to track her down. The biographer's source for this information was our old classmate Mary Petschel née Hafliger, she of the hairy forearms, she who kicked me off Spirit Club after Andrew's death, and she whom Ella and I ran into when I fled to Riley in 1988; since that encounter, I haven't seen Mary.

And I realize in this moment that neither Dena nor Pete has ever spoken about me to the media. For so long, I was so sure Dena would that it felt like she already had. Even earlier today, she was the first person I thought of when Hank came to tell me the abortion story was going to break, but she'd had nothing to do with it. That Dena and Pete have stayed quiet even though they've been together all these years, even though they've each had separate reasons for wishing me ill, and even though surely they could have reinforced each other's antipathy, justifying their right to get back at me—I haven't been sufficiently grateful, it occurs to me, I have never properly appreciated a thing that hasn't happened. I haven't thought of them as having opportunities they declined when clearly that's been the case, clearly the opportunities have been plentiful.

I say, "So when the journalists call and you say no—why do you?"

"Are you kidding? You think we'd talk about you to some sleazy reporter?" Dena scoffs. "We were raised better than that, and hell, we didn't even vote for your husband!" She leans forward, extracting a cigarette from the pack, and after she's lit it and taken a puff, she says, "At least I sure didn't. Pete here just doesn't vote."

Pete smiles the way Charlie does when he's broken wind particularly loudly, as if he's half sheepish and half pleased with himself. Fleetingly—I don't want to think this—I wonder if Pete is brain-damaged. Not that any single terrible event necessarily happened, but it could be that alcohol and perhaps drugs have had a cumulative effect.

"Hey, why won't Charlie talk to that black guy?" Dena says. "You tell him old Dena thinks he should." She means Edgar Franklin, I'm pretty sure, though unlike Gladys Wycomb, Dena does not use an accusatory tone; instead, she sounds self-effacing, as if she doesn't really believe her opinion could matter. Or maybe it's that, having once been married herself, she knows regulating one's husband's behavior is no small feat, so she doesn't hold me accountable for Charlie's decisions. She lifts a clear glass ashtray from a shelf beneath the coffee table and taps her cigarette into it. "Now, am I allowed to get a picture, Alice, or will your goons freak out?"

"Of course," I say.

"Otherwise my sisters will never believe me you were here." She stands.

"How are your sisters doing?"

"They're plugging along. Marjorie's oldest son's over in the first of the 158th Infantry, so that's hard." Again, there is a notable lack of blame in Dena's voice. How is it that she's forgiven me for both the past and the present? "Peggy's living in Mom and Dad's old house, which you couldn't pay me enough to do. The place is falling down around her, not to mention she's due to have hip surgery, so I don't know how she plans to get to the second floor."

"Maybe she can have one of those chairs put in like my grandmother had," I say, and Dena chortles, though I wasn't kidding. It is sobering to think of Peggy Janaszewski needing hip surgery when, as little girls, she and Marjorie were our students the times that Dena and I played school and pretended to be teachers named Miss Clougherty.

Dena disappears down the hall, to find her camera, presumably, and Pete and I are left alone. The room is silent except for the whir of the air conditioner, and then Pete says, "A lot of water under the bridge, isn't there?"

"There sure is." We both start to speak at the same time, and I say, "Go ahead."

"When I look back, I don't feel real good about everything," he says. "That was a tough time."

Is he referring to after Andrew's death or to the pyramid scheme?

"And the papers, they can't leave it be. Every time it goes away, someone brings it up again, but they don't care what he was like—they act like he didn't do anything his whole life but get in the car and drive to that intersection."

"I hope you know that I still think of him," I say. "I still wish I could change what happened."

But Pete does not seem angry. He says, "I always knew you were a nice person. I probably didn't show it, but I knew."

Unexpectedly, my eyes fill with tears; they are close to the surface, I suppose, given that I sobbed immediately upon my arrival. I swallow, keeping the tears at bay, and say, "I had no idea how to act back then, and I bet you didn't, either."

"He had a real big crush on you," Pete says. "You could probably tell. I remember the time we saw you downtown, and you two were flirting like crazy." (That afternoon just before my senior year of high school, when I'd been buying ground beef for my mother—the sunlight and Andrew's eyelashes and Pete in the driver's seat of the mint-green Thunderbird.) "If I'd found out you were pregnant," Pete is saying, "I like to think I'd have done the right thing and married you, but it was probably for the best I didn't know. I was too immature."

Married me? I can truly say the thought never crossed my mind; it is far likelier I'd have had the baby and given it up for adoption—I couldn't have kept it, the disgrace would have been too great for my family—but the circumstances under which I'd have married Pete Imhof are unimaginable.

He says, "What if we let Andrew be the father instead of me? That seems more like what it was supposed to be—revisionist history, isn't that what they call it?"

Except that if Andrew had been the father, I wouldn't have had an abortion, at least not if I'd learned I was pregnant after his death. And Andrew wouldn't have been the father anyway, because we wouldn't have had that rash, impulsive sex. But Pete Imhof is trying to offer me a kindness, so all I do is smile sadly at him.

From the pocket of his jeans, Pete withdraws his own pack of cigarettes; they are Camels. He pulls one from the pack but doesn't light it. He says, "I would never have gotten my shit together without Dena. I kept showing up at the steak house where she was working until she finally took me home with her and saved me from myself, you know?" He leans in and adds, "Don't tell her I told you, but I did vote for your husband. I like how he's tough on terror." Pete winks. "Dena has no idea." As he lights his cigarette (it no longer seems like he's brain-damaged), he says, "You want something to eat? Did she offer you anything?"

"I'm fine," I say, and I hear Dena approaching from the hall. She says, "It won't go on," and when she's in the living room, she hands a digital camera to Pete. "What am I doing wrong?" He fiddles with it, and the camera makes a zooming sound, the lens emerging.

Pete says, "You two stand together," and I join Dena in front of the shelf of decorative plates. The lighting would be better outside, obviously, but I say nothing. Dena sets her arm around me, a gesture I am moved by, and I do the same for her.

After Pete has taken several shots, Dena says, "Now you guys." Pete and I stand side by side, smiling and not touching; this isn't a photo I ever imagined posing for. After the pictures are taken, they look at the tiny versions on the screen. "Isn't technology today amazing?" Dena says.

"I'm sorry to rush out, but I have an obligation back in Washington," I say. "It was very good to see both of you, and let's stay in touch as things unfold. Did you keep Belinda's number?"

"It's in the kitchen," Dena says.

"Call if anything comes up, or if you have questions."

Dena lightly punches my upper arm. She says, "Don't look so grim, First Lady. We'll be fine, and so will you."

"Hold on, Alice," Pete says. "I have something for you." He lumbers into the hall, and when he's gone, I say to Dena, "I'm here visiting my mother every couple months, so maybe we could have lunch next time."

"That'd be a kick," she says. "You just say the word." Then she adds, "You know it was me that gave Ella the tiara that time, don't you? I thought you'd come over and say hi."

"I wish I had." Charlie and I are currently having a house built in Maronee, the place we'll live when we leave Washington. Is it possible, back in relative proximity to Dena, that she and I might become friends again, real friends? Are our situations too different? It is such a comfort to see her, to be linked to a life all but lost to me now.

When Pete returns, he passes me an envelope.

"What is it?" Dena asks, but he shakes his head. In a not entirely joking tone, she says, "It better not be a love letter." She turns back to me, her expression mischievous. "If anyone was ever watching you and me, they'd have thought there were only three men to date in the whole world, and we just kept trading them back and forth." I laugh, and Dena links her arm through Pete's. She says, "But it looks like we both ended up with the ones who were right for us all along."

AMONG THE PEOPLE whom I'm aware have been quoted on television or in print on the subject of Charlie and me are about a third of my classmates from elementary school, junior high, and high school, including Mary Hafliger Petschel and my junior-year prom date, Larry Nagel; the daughter of the former owner of Tatty's (Tatty's itself no longer exists); Marvin Benheimer, my New Year's Eve date in 1962, when I had to dash from the restaurant as soon as the food came in order to vomit, a fact that has not stopped Marvin from appearing on a recurring basis on CNN, always identified as "Childhood Friend of Alice Blackwell"; several of my sorority sisters in Kappa Alpha Theta, a few of my aged professors, and many university classmates whom I never met; my thesis adviser from library school; Lydia Bianchi, the principal at Liess Elementary, and my colleague Maggie Stenta, a first-grade teacher; Nadine Patora, the Madison realtor from whom I didn't buy a house in 1977; Ja-hoon Choi, the Ph.D. candidate who lived downstairs from me in my apartment on Sproule Street; and two men with whom I went on blind dates in, respectively, 1969 and 1974, whom I truly have no recollection of, though I believe that the dates occurred. "She was pretty but seemed like a prude" was one fellow's assessment, and the other's was "She wasn't interested in current events—she mostly just wanted to talk about her students." These remarks at least had brevity on their side and were nothing compared to the entire memoir published by Simon Törnkvist, *I Knew Her When: My Love Affair with Alice Blackwell Before She Became First Lady.* With the help of a ghostwriter, Simon chronicled our long-ago relationship: my alleged desperation to get married and have children, and his extensive reservations about me that apparently stemmed from what he recognized even then as my conservative leanings. *Here she was, living in a vibrant and liberal college town, but she led an incredibly staid, sheltered life,* he wrote. *It was obvious she was afraid of talking to me about my experiences in 'Nam, and she avoided any confrontation. I knew from the get-go she was aiming for the white-picket-fence, 2.5 kids lifestyle, and if it wasn't happening with me, she'd make it happen with someone else. When I heard that she'd married one of Governor Blackwell's draft-dodging sons, I knew her wildest dreams must have come true.* Also, humiliatingly, there was this: *She was very vanilla when it came to sex. The thing I never understood was that it was easier for her to climax when she was on top, but she preferred missionary-style.* I had been skimming the book for about half an hour when I got to those lines; I snapped it shut, gave it to my personal aide, Ashley, and told her to get rid of it as she saw fit. I felt particularly offended, as I actually had had indirect contact with Simon since we'd run into each other at the Brewers' game in 1988; in 1995, he'd requested six VIP tickets for himself, his wife, his two children, and his parents to take a Christmas-lights tour of the governor's mansion. The request had come through my office, and while I hadn't spoken to Simon, I had been the one who signed off on the dispensation of the tickets. He never thanked me or anybody else—I had only two aides then, and I asked them—and the next I heard of him was when my White House press secretary alerted me to the existence of his book a few months in advance of publication. "I always had a hunch that Parsley, Sage was a low-rent hippie" was Charlie's take on the matter.

Generally, there tends to be an inverse correlation between how well someone knew you and his or her willingness to talk; there also seems to be a link between discretion and class, or so I've always thought until seeing Dena and Pete. The people we know, or knew, in Maronee, the people from the country club, have been the most tight-lipped. The notable exception was that early in Charlie's first administration, Carolyn Thayer (she has not remarried and still has the same surname) sat for an interview with *60 Minutes* for a segment they were doing about Charlie's past struggles with alcohol. "We all knew, everyone talked about it," she said. "It was common knowledge when he got the DUI, and more than a year before that, at a Christmas party, I saw him fall flat on his face. I said to him, 'Do you need help?' but he just laughed it off." It must have been the Hickens' party, I thought, because I remembered Charlie cheerfully walking toward me with tissue stuffed in both his nostrils, and when I asked why, he said he'd gotten a nosebleed. I didn't watch the *60 Minutes* episode when it ran, but after it aired, I heard from several of our old friends about how appalled they were, what a breach of etiquette they considered Carolyn's behavior, so I had an aide obtain a copy. Because Carolyn had moved from Maronee to Chicago ten years before, it wasn't as if she could be shunned from the community, and for this, I was glad. I'd have preferred that she hadn't spoken to the program, but the fact was, she hadn't said anything untrue. Regardless, Carolyn was the exception who proved the rule—she is the only person from Maronee who has spoken on the record and without our blessings to a media outlet, and very few people have spoken anonymously, either. I suspect the ones who have are people we hardly knew.

Simon's was not the only tell-all memoir—there was also the one written by my first cousin on my mother's side, Patty Lazechko, who is the daughter of my Uncle Herman, and I'm under the impression that the gist of her tale was that marrying up runs in my blood, that after meeting my father, my mother turned her back on her own siblings and parents. When the book was published two years ago, I hadn't seen

Patty since childhood, and I confess I bypassed that one; there are too many accounts, and they are too demoralizing to keep up with. Of late, there have been a few contributions to the exposé library from people who have worked for Charlie and me, campaign consultants and a fellow who was a deputy White House press secretary in the first administration, and while it's always disappointing to feel that a person you trusted has violated that trust, such transgressions are standard in politics and have occurred to a lesser extent under Charlie than they did under his predecessor.

Charlie has become inured; he has never been interested in what his critics have to say except insofar as Hank can strategically deflect it. Obviously, I'm not as impervious, but I almost never try to have anything refuted, and a quote or observation in a newspaper article that once would have bothered me for days now bothers me for ten minutes, or for two. The last time I was particularly ruffled was over a year ago, when I opened the *Times* one morning in May to find an op-ed by Thea Dengler, the owner of the bookstore in Mequon that I used to love. Thea's bookstore still exists at a time when fewer and fewer independents can make a go of it, and for people who follow such things, Thea has risen to greater prominence and is regularly quoted in articles about the bookselling industry. But that was not the topic of her op-ed; the topic was me, and the headline was DO SOMETHING, ALICE BLACKWELL! It began, *Those of us who knew Alice Blackwell in Wisconsin have been doing an awful lot of head-scratching during the past five years. As a frequent customer at my bookstore throughout the eighties and early nineties, Mrs. Blackwell was inquisitive, compassionate, and open-minded. How, then, can she be—or so it seems—happily married to a man hell-bent on weakening civil liberties? Although Mrs. Blackwell is sometimes made out to be nothing but the First Lady Who Lunches, she's a former librarian who knows just how crucial privacy and intellectual freedom are to a democracy.*

Sitting in bed reading this, I had felt a rise of the sort of anger that I experience infrequently. It wasn't the sentiment Thea was expressing, which I had heard often enough, but the source—unlike Carolyn Thayer, or my cousin Patty, or even Simon Törnkvist, Thea was a person with whom I'd once felt great kinship. And why couldn't she give me the benefit of the doubt, why couldn't she assume I was doing the best I could under the circumstances? Who was Thea to decide the exact quantity or nature of what I ought to say, and to whom, and how? I reminded myself of the decision I'd made years before, walking alone on Maronee Drive after the ridiculous *Milwaukee Sentinel* article about my molasses cookies—that I could not be defined by others from the outside, and that the fact of something being printed didn't make it true. Still, this was Thea and the *Times.*

They think they'll sway you, but they do the opposite—the more people there are exerting pressure, the more they are part of a pattern. There is also the fact of each individual who lobbies you having a pet issue—Thea objected specifically to the reauthorization of the Patriot Act—and how even in their national concerns, people are driven by a sort of altruistic self-interest. *This* is what I have done most wrong, *this* is how I have fallen short. While the criticism I receive can be discouraging, the variations on it negate one another. Whatever I have accomplished that was positive, it wasn't enough. What's important is what I've overlooked or ignored. (And again: I'm popular, my approval ratings are twice Charlie's. It doesn't surprise me that he ignores his critics altogether.)

These are my "issues": breast-cancer awareness and detection; historic preservation of art and buildings; pediatric AIDS prevention here and abroad, especially in Africa; and literacy. If the issues on which I've focused are noncontroversial, I believe they're legitimately worthy. What has been most wrenching as first lady, however, is that the old sense of obligation, guilt, and sadness I used to get when I read the newspaper in Milwaukee has been dramatically compounded. Though I resist the notion shared by Gladys Wycomb, Thea Dengler, and many others that I ought to lobby my husband, it's true that if I visit an organization or invite its members to the White House—a veterinary clinic that spays pets for people who can't afford it, a program that tries to decrease gang violence, an orphanage for homeless children in Addis Ababa—that organization will receive an influx of donations, a shower of publicity. I *can* change people's lives, and many times, although it is cowardly, I have wished I didn't have that ability. The pressure is too great, and the hardest part is not that what I do is insufficient in others' eyes but that it's insufficient in my own. I stay busy, I travel, I try with my visits—with my actions, that is, more than my words—to support other people's good work, but I don't doubt that I'd have felt better about my contributions to the world if my power were more modest. If I had remained a single woman, a teacher, I have the idea that I might have begun, at the age of forty or so, to take in foster children, and not necessarily white ones; I'd compost, and perhaps by now I'd have purchased a Prius, though I still don't think I'd have affixed an antiwar bumper sticker to it. In whatever way such things are measured, I probably would have done less, but I wouldn't have had to face the reality that I could have done far more.

As for those who hate me because they hate Charlie, hate me by extension, I am curious of this: At what point, in their opinion, should I have done something, and what should that something have been? Should I not have married him? Should I not have discouraged his drinking? ("Jim Beam *and* me, have us both"—is that what I ought to have said?) When he told me that he wanted to run for governor and I told him I'd prefer he didn't (though I foolishly thought at least it was better than congressman or senator, at least it would keep us in Wisconsin)—when he decided that in spite of my stated preference, he was indeed going to run, should I have left him? Should I have stayed with him but not campaigned for him? Should I have stated explicitly to the public when my views differed from his? Should I have left him when he decided, also against my wishes, to run for president? Anyone who has been married, and especially anyone married for several decades, knows the union is a series of compromises; to judge the compromises I have made is, I take it, easy to do from far away.

If I am diffident, then my diffidence stems in part from my aversion to arriving hastily at decisions. During the lead-up to the war, I sincerely didn't know what I thought the right course of action was; I read articles for both sides, and I found convincing arguments in each. Because the stakes were so high, I did have an uneasy feeling during the early months of 2003, but Charlie and I talked about the situation less than one might imagine, or I should say we talked logistically more than we discussed the philosophical or historical implications. He'd call from the Oval Office and say, "I've got to go to a meeting in the Sit Room, so how about if we watch that movie tomorrow night instead?"

Or, as he once put it about the secretary of state, "We've been pumping up Stanley for his talk to the UN Security Council on Wednesday, and I think he's really gonna hit this one out of the park."

These days, it is common for people in both political parties, for people who don't consider themselves members of any party at all, to say Charlie's administration bungled the war and we should bring the troops home. And Charlie's administration *did* underestimate how neglected the country's infrastructure was, how likely an insurgency would be, and how many weapons the insurgents had. All of that is now clear; the question is how to proceed. For America, it would be advantageous to leave, but what about *them,* the country we invaded?

When Ella was in Montessori at Biddle Academy, the classroom activities included building blocks, wooden puzzles, and, to Charlie's great amusement, a sink filled with plastic cups and dishes ("So she can learn to be a scullery maid," he'd joke). The guiding principles of the classroom activities were these: Finish one task before you start another, and clean up after yourself. In the midst of our war in a hot, sandy country over six thousand miles away, a country whose art and culture and language and science stretch back to the beginning of human civilization, I keep returning to these ideas, that it is our responsibility to clean up the mess we made. For the last four years, I've wondered if we'll make things worse by withdrawing, and I've remained confused about whether it was right to invade in the first place. If we invaded as a democracy unseating a dictator, does the fact that there were more deaths than Americans expected mean invading was wrong? If we were right to invade but it was sloppily executed, does *that* make it wrong?

When I see political pundits on television, or meet the Republican ones at events in or outside the White House, what strikes me most is their certainty. Is it exaggerated for the cameras, and do they in the privacy of their homes, at the end of the day, remove it along with their socks or stockings? Or are they always so bombastic and assured? I envy them as I envy the deeply religious, including my husband, but I have felt incapable of joining their ranks. I've never tried to assert my views unless they are self-evident, not reliant on an argument from me to prove or disprove them: Breast-cancer awareness and AIDS prevention are good. Illiteracy is bad. Historic preservation will allow future generations to understand what life used to be like and in so doing will help Americans chart a path forward. The issues and decisions that are more complex I have left to others, to those confident of their own rightness. I have imagined that I'll know what I think of this war when Charlie is long out of office, but that I don't know now—it is a novel I haven't reached the end of.

Or so I have often told myself.

And yet if Andrew Imhof's death was the singular tragedy of my life, if in some ways I have lived since then trying to compensate for my error, trying to be worthy of having survived—if his death was the worst thing I could have imagined, then what words are there, what space in my imagination, for the deaths of thousands of American troops and foreign civilians? If my critics are right that I share responsibility for Charlie's administrative policies, including the decision to go to war, then Andrew Imhof's death is the least of what I have caused; it is nothing, and utterly insignificant. What if I believed the consequences of the war were also my fault? The twenty-nine-year-old former high school athlete from Hot Springs, Arkansas, killed by small-arms fire while searching a house in a southern neighborhood of the capital city; the twenty-five-year-old sergeant from Ogden, Utah, killed on his third tour of duty a month after his daughter was born, who didn't want to reenlist but needed the twenty-four-thousand-dollar bonus for a down payment on a house; the nineteen-year-old from Cape Girardeau, Missouri, who joined the army on his eighteenth birthday and was killed in a marketplace explosion; and the tens of thousands, or likelier hundreds of thousands, of civilians, a member of a local city council, a shopkeeper and his wife and three daughters, journalists and cameramen and translators working with the American military or the media, a bride and her new mother-in-law and twelve of the guests celebrating a wedding attended by a suicide bomber—killed and killed and killed and killed. If the blood of these people were on my hands, if there were something I personally could have done to prevent such carnage, the loss of so many adults and teenagers and children who presumably wanted, just as I always have, to live an ordinary life—if I believed I could have made a difference but instead remained silent, then how could I bear it?

"OKAY, THOSE THIRD-GRADERS are terrors," Ella is saying. "Can we just establish that you're eternally in my debt?"

"Belinda says you did a fabulous job," I say. "She told Jessica you had them spellbound."

"Seriously, this one boy tried to climb over the rope in the Red Room, and then this other kid pushed a girl into the wall in the Vermeil Room. You'd think they'd have some reverence for this place, but they were like animals. I can't wait to see what they do onstage tonight."

It is just past six on the East Coast, and I'm back on the jet, above the cloud cover; we're half an hour from Washington, meaning that after the motorcade ride back to the residence, I'll have an hour to dress for the gala. "Thank you for standing in for me," I say. "You did your good deed for the day. Ladybug, there's something I want to talk to you about tonight when I get home."

Immediately, accusingly, she says, "Do you have breast cancer?"

"What on earth— No, honey, I don't have cancer."

"You just sounded so serious. Okay, so I picked out which shoes you should wear tonight—are you ready?"

Jessica passes me a note: *Hank on hold, says urgent.*

"Mom?" Ella says.

"Let me call you back in a minute." When I've pressed the "end" button on one phone, Jessica passes me another, and I cover the mouthpiece. "He won't say what it's about?"

"He wants to talk to you directly," Jessica says.

I hold the phone to my ear. "This is Alice."

"Ding dong, the witch is dead." Hank's voice is unmistakably gleeful. "Gladys Wycomb bought the ranch an hour ago."

"What are you talking about?"

Jessica mouths, "*What?*" I hold up a finger.

Hank says, "The old ticker gave out, and no, I didn't have her offed, if that's what you're wondering."

"Did you?" A wave of horror passes over me. I'm not a conspiracy buff, but I'm quite sure things take place in any presidency that would shock most voters; I've never dwelled on what those things might be in Charlie's case, because I am conflicted enough about the controversies that are known and legal.

"Alice, I swear to you I had nothing to do with it, and neither did anyone else except Mother Nature. Now, tell me this isn't the best news you've heard since Van Halen announced their reunion tour."

"But her helper, Norene—"

"Not a chance. Turns out in the mid-nineties, she was the go-to girl for dime bags in Cicero, Illinois, and she's got a police record longer than your arm. The geriatric feminist avenger had nothing to lose, but Norene has plenty."

"You're telling me that Dr. Wycomb died of completely natural causes?"

Jessica is still standing in front of me, and her jaw drops. "Gladys Wycomb *died*?" she whispers, and I nod.

"She was a hundred and four, Alice," Hank is saying. "There doesn't need to be foul play—unless it was you who slipped a wee thimbleful of arsenic in her afternoon tea."

"I don't find that funny."

"In all seriousness, blackmailing you was probably physically draining. I've got to hand it to her that she went out with a bang and not a whimper, but the good news for us is it's over—the abortion story is off the table. You ready to come home and be saluted by students and teachers?"

"How can you be sure she didn't tell anyone besides Norene?"

"So what if she did? It'll be hearsay, nothing but another urban legend. You've got a former physician claiming *she* performed the abortion, the press is going to sit up and take notice. You've got a friend of a friend of an aide of a dead lady, and if you seriously think that'll fly, well, then wait till you hear the one about Richard Gere and the gerbil."

"I'm assuming you've told Charlie?" I say.

"He said to tell you congratulations."

When I've hung up, Jessica says jokingly, "What, he took out a hit on her?"

"I know. Maybe she sensed the end was near and that's what made her act, but it's awfully unsettling. Hank is dancing a jig because he thinks this gets me off the hook."

Jessica is quiet, musing, and then she says, "It probably does."

WHEN I CONSIDER the trajectory of Charlie's presidency, when I try to pinpoint the moment its tone and direction were established irrevocably, I keep revisiting his choice of vice president. In the summer of 2000, the decision had to be made in time for the Republican National Convention, and it came down to two candidates: Arnold Prouhet and Frank Logan. Frank was two years younger than Charlie, a Colorado senator who was serving his third term, came from a wealthy Baptist family, was a father of eight, and was a vocal critic of homosexuality and abortion. (I have always found it peculiar, to say the least, when conservatives, especially conservative men, make these particular issues their ideological focus; there is something suspect to me about individuals who devote enormous amounts of time and attention to subjects they profess to find repugnant.) I was opposed to Charlie selecting Frank as his running mate, and I also didn't relish the idea of spending time with Frank's wife, Donna Sue, who had self-published several books proffering tips on raising a traditional Christian family.

Meanwhile, Arnold Prouhet had been a congressman from Nevada in the seventies and early eighties who subsequently served under two presidents as a security adviser. As far as I knew, Arnold was more a fiscal conservative than a social one, he was eleven years Charlie's senior, and on the few occasions I'd met him, he'd seemed serious and taciturn; I imagined these would be qualities that might help balance Charlie's playfulness. (While Charlie had, under Hank's tutelage, become a disciplined student of policy and government, I knew, and I think everyone knew, that he was in it for the power and adventure and human connection and not because of any wonkish devotion to or interest in the issues. The problem that has ensued is that wonkish devotion cannot be faked. The fever isn't in Charlie's blood, as it is in Hank's—Charlie would never read a book about the First Amendment for pleasure—and this is why so often in the years since, when there has been a deviation from the public script or when, as at a debate or a press conference, there isn't a script, Charlie falters. Being president is for him like taking a ninth-grade English test on *The Odyssey,* and he's the kid who did most of the reading, he studied for an hour the night before, but he's not one of the people who loved the book. Besides, he'd always rather crack a funny joke in class than offer a genuine insight.)

Hank objected to the selection of Arnold Prouhet, saying that where Frank Logan shared Charlie's youthful energy, Arnold seemed old and dour. Arnold also could make Charlie appear insecure, as if he were seeking a father figure. But Arnold's foreign policy expertise was significant, I countered when I was asked to weigh in (which was never by Hank and occasionally by Charlie, though usually he wanted to vent more than he wanted input). I also worried that Frank Logan's own ambitions might hinder his work with Charlie; if he became vice president, he'd probably run for president afterward, whereas if Charlie served two terms, Arnold Prouhet would be seventy-three when they left office, and unlikely to embark on a presidential campaign. Charlie's advisers besides Hank—among them Debbie Bell, a consultant named Bruce Kettman, and a frighteningly smart twenty-six-year-old protégé of Hank named Scott Taico whom Charlie called "Taco"—had mixed opinions, and I felt fairly sure Charlie would pick Frank Logan, but he didn't. He picked Arnold. The night before he made the announcement in July 2000, he said to me, "I think you might be right about Logan, that he's too focused on peering into people's bedrooms and not enough of a visionary."

Again, then, I find myself wondering if I am partly to blame for what has happened since. Would Frank Logan in fact have been a better vice president, would there have been less bloodshed under his watch? More homophobia, a sharper curtailing of reproductive rights, but not the unilateral use of military force, the defiant enthusiasm for preemptive war? It is indisputable that Charlie has been greatly influenced by Arnold Prouhet, and indeed it seems to be *because* Arnold has been so influential that Charlie insists as relentlessly as he does that he believes in the war, that he won't back down. How embarrassing it would be not only to rely on the guidance of one's hierarchical inferior but to rely on the wrong guidance—how unsophisticated Charlie would seem to himself and everyone else. And so rather than consider this possibility, he forces it to be untrue, he continues down the path he chose.

Years ago, shortly after Charlie and I moved to Milwaukee and joined the country club in the late seventies, we went there for dinner one night, to the main dining room on the first floor, and I excused myself from the table to use the ladies' room. There was a lounge-like anteroom, a pretty area with couches and a dressing table and walk-in closets for hanging coats, a place where, sometimes at large parties, you'd find women chatting or applying their makeup. This was the first time I'd ever been in it, and once you entered the anteroom, you saw two more gold-handled doors: one directly across from the one you'd just come through and one to your left. I was trying to find the toilet stalls, and rather than asking one of the three older women then sitting on the couches—I say older, though they were no doubt younger than I am now, and stylishly dressed—I took a guess and walked forward to the door that was farther away. When I opened it and stepped through, I found myself back in the dining room where Charlie and I had been eating. I immediately realized there were two separate ladies'-room entrances; obviously, the toilets were behind the door I hadn't tried. The logical thing at that point would have been to turn around, but I felt self-conscious. I was unaccustomed to country clubs, I imagined the women in the anteroom would notice and think me silly, and so, with a full bladder, I rejoined Charlie and didn't urinate until we arrived home over an hour later. What I mean to say is that a part of me understands Charlie's behavior. I understand it because I love him, because I am predisposed to sympathize, but I also think that, unlike many in government or the media, I don't ascribe to people loftier motives just because they're in a loftier place.

It seems to me that after the terrorist attacks in 2001, Charlie panicked. And Arnold, who had a professional history with these countries, who had already sparred a decade before with the dictator of one, swiftly stepped in with recommendations. He was hawkish, he believed in America protecting its superpower status, and he was confident of victory. He convinced Charlie, or Charlie convinced himself—establishing democracy in the Middle East, what a legacy *that* would be—and the rest has followed. The part that caught me by surprise was how the

American people and the American media egged him on, how complicit they were in Charlie's cultivation of a war-president persona. *The terrorist attacks have given President Blackwell a heretofore undemonstrated seriousness of purpose,* averred *Time.* Or, as *The Washington Post* put it, *If there is a silver lining to these tragic events, it's that President Blackwell has risen to the occasion as a leader . . .* In the *Times,* an unsigned editorial was titled simply "Blackwell's Finest Hour." Had none of these people ever taken Psychology 101? Did they honestly believe Charlie, or anybody, changed in a matter of days? Did they think because, amid the rubble in lower Manhattan, he climbed atop a fire truck and spoke into a megaphone with resolve and sympathy, he was a new man? Charlie had *always* had the capacity for resolve and sympathy, which had nothing to do with whether invading other countries was a good idea.

I don't mean to minimize how frightening the terrorist attacks were, how confused everything seemed in their aftermath. We all thought, of course, that the fourth plane was headed for the White House that day, and so they hurried me and Arnold Prouhet to Camp David on helicopters (Charlie was giving a speech in Ohio to a real estate association, a speech he famously declined to interrupt, and I didn't see him until that night; when we hugged, when I had him in my arms, it was the first time since learning of the attacks that I wept). Even after we returned to the White House, we were evacuated several more times during the next few days, and once, in the middle of the night, we were rushed by agents from our bedroom to the Emergency Operations Center, an underground bunker beneath the White House. Then there were anthrax spores being sent through the mail, the threat of smallpox bombs. Charlie and I visited Pentagon burn victims, and later we met family members of men and women killed in New York, among them young children, and every morning I read the *Times*'s "Portraits of Grief"—I read them all, and they were devastating. So it was a strange, difficult time, and we were in the thick of it. I don't doubt that both Arnold and Charlie had to harden in certain ways during this period, that their toughness wasn't just masculine bluster; it was interior as well, and for the benefit of others.

Nevertheless, I feel a growing suspicion that Charlie continues to fight this war for much the same reason I couldn't bring myself to reenter the ladies' room at the Maronee Country Club, and he even has my compassion, except for this—that night at the club, when I needed to urinate and hadn't, the only one who suffered for my foolishness was me.

RIGHT BEFORE OUR plane landed at Andrews Air Force Base, I said to Jessica, "I have one more stop for us before going home. I'd like to go talk to Edgar Franklin."

Jessica's eyes widened. "Now?"

"I promise this'll be it."

"It's just that, I don't know how long you'd envision talking to him, but the gala starts an hour and a half from *now.* As it is, you'll have to get dressed at warp speed."

"Are you trying to tell me you think going to see him is a bad idea?"

"No—no, I—" She broke off. The two of us were sitting with our seat belts fastened for landing. "Hank will kill me for saying this, but I think it's a great idea. I just think tomorrow is better than today."

"He's spent five nights out there. That's long enough."

Jessica looked at me for several seconds, and then she said, "Okay."

"Only tell the agents. I don't want to try getting Charlie's blessing, or Hank's, because we both know they'll try to talk me out of it."

And this is how we've found ourselves racing up Suitland Parkway in our caravan of armored limousines. (Although I prefer the SUVs to the limos because they seem slightly less ostentatious, limos are what the White House sent; that I could have gone to Edgar Franklin in a Town Car was, I knew, out of the question, far too great a security risk.) The flickering lights and blasting sirens create the usual mortifying theatricality, but I don't see another option. I would not be authorized on my own to invite Edgar Franklin to the White House, and if I suggested it, even if I could convince Charlie and his advisers that it was the right thing, it would have to be elaborately choreographed.

I got off easy—that's what it feels like. That Gladys Wycomb's threat was a false alarm has left me relieved but also disappointed. I wouldn't say that I'm compelled to go see Colonel Franklin because of a need to exchange one revelation for another—so the American public can learn today not about my abortion but instead about my sympathies for an antiwar activist—but being forced to consider Gladys Wycomb's threat made the threat less ominous than it would have appeared in the abstract; it made it almost enticing. I have felt so strongly since Charlie entered public office that my foremost duty is to take care of him, to be the one person he sees on a daily basis who's not paid to agree or disagree with him, who really is just a friend. Is it startling, then, that I wasn't altogether displeased by an event that would draw attention to my disagreement with his stance on a particular issue without my being the one who'd revealed our conflicting views? Could that have been the best of both worlds, that I could publicly and even privately lament Dr. Wycomb's indiscretion while feeling a silent gratitude?

Such circuitous conjecture! If, for example, Ella came to me explaining herself in this way, wouldn't I say to her, "For heaven's sake, you're allowed to hold opinions." Wouldn't I say, "A relationship for which you suppress and censor your beliefs is no relationship at all." Wouldn't I say, "There are perfectly ladylike and respectable ways of expressing yourself, no matter the subject, no matter the context, and though in some cases, biting your tongue *is* the most dignified course, if it's a matter of conscience, then to speak out is not just optional but necessary"—wouldn't this be what I thought if the person in question were someone other than me?

The motorcade pauses when we're still over two blocks from the yard on Fourth Street SE, and via earpieces, there is much conferring among the agents in our limousine, the agents in the others, and the police escorts; I can hear the word *Banjo,* which is their code name for me (Charlie's is *Brass,* Ella's *Braid*—the Secret Service gave us the letter, and we picked our own names, though I let Ella pick mine). In our car, it's still Cal and Walter who are with us in the back, plus José and another agent in the front seat. Both Jessica's phones ring at once—she has already called to tell her assistant Belinda to put out the word that we're running late but on our way—and then I glimpse, even from this distance, the television news vans, their satellite uplinks reaching high above the roofs of the row houses. Cars are parked tightly on either side of the street, and up ahead, I see that the sidewalks are dense with people, some of them holding signs.

Cal says, "Ma'am, we can't recommend going farther. There's too much congestion. With your approval, we'd like to return to the residence."

Jessica and I look at each other.

"Isn't there any way—" I begin, and Jessica says to Cal, "What about inviting Edgar Franklin into the car?"

Speaking in a low voice into his lapel, Cal says, "We're turning onto D Street."

"What about Jessica's idea?" I ask.

"The risk of a mob is too great," Cal says, and we're already on D Street, the police sirens still blaring.

I say, "No, stop. Cal, I insist. We can park on another block, and you can barricade the whole street, but if he'd consider coming to the car, I want to try."

Somehow I hadn't realized what a circus it would be—it doesn't look as crowded on television, or maybe more supporters have arrived today. In my fantasy, it was the two of us, Edgar Franklin and me, strolling down the sidewalk, which was delusional in any case, because for years, I have rarely strolled down a sidewalk unless it has been cordoned off, sniffed for bombs by German shepherds.

Jessica is the one who climbs from the limousine to issue the invitation; agents from the other cars flank her as she walks the two blocks to the yard where Edgar Franklin has pitched his tent. Brave Jessica Sutton, the little girl who played with Barbies on the kitchen floor at Harold and Priscilla's house, who read Harlequin romances when she was in sixth grade, who went on to graduate second in her class at Biddle Academy and Phi Beta Kappa from Yale, who has traveled with me to Israel and South Africa, who is my most steadfast colleague, my truest friend. She retrieves Edgar Franklin, and she brings him back to me; then, as he is patted down by Walter before climbing through the limo door, Jessica says, "I'll be right over there," and gestures to the limousine behind mine.

He sits perpendicular to me, our knees only inches apart, the soupy outside heat emanating from him. At the far end of the limousine, facing us with his back to the front seat, Cal watches. It would surely be too much to hope that this conversation could go entirely unobserved.

I say, "Colonel Franklin, I'm Alice Blackwell."

"Edgar Franklin."

We extend our hands and shake.

"I wanted to come out and talk to you, but unfortunately, that wasn't going to work," I say.

With a vaguely amused look, he surveys the interior of the limousine and says, "This isn't so bad." (I again wish it were an SUV.)

"Would you like some water?" I lift an unopened bottle from the holder beside me, and he accepts it. "Colonel Franklin, I'm not authorized to speak on behalf of President Blackwell's administration, I need to make that clear. I'm here only as myself. But I want you to know that I'm terribly sorry for your loss. I'm aware that your son—that Nate was an only child. I'm also the parent of an only child, and I can't begin to guess how difficult it must be for you."

Matter-of-factly, not snidely, he says, "No, ma'am, I don't imagine that you can."

"He was twenty-one?"

Edgar Franklin nods. "Planning to be a pharmacy technician after his tour."

"My grandfather worked in a pharmacy," I say. "I never knew him, unfortunately, but this was in Milwaukee, Wisconsin. I understand that you're from Georgia?"

"We moved around when Nate was growing up, including a couple years each in Germany and Panama, but he went to high school in Columbus, Georgia. I'm retired now and live in Decatur." Edgar Franklin clears his throat. "Mrs. Blackwell, I'm a quiet man. It was never my plan to draw attention to myself, but this war is the worst mistake I've seen the United States make in my lifetime."

"Obviously, it's caused a great deal of controversy."

"Why are we fighting, Mrs. Blackwell? What is it we're fighting for?"

"Again, I don't speak for the administration, but if you asked my husband, I think he'd say for democracy."

"Is that what you'd say?"

I swallow. "I'm not a military analyst, but— Yes. I'd say the same thing."

"They don't want us in their country any more than we want to be there." He speaks calmly. "They don't think we make them more secure, they don't say we've improved their lives. They see us as occupiers. I've been in battle, Mrs. Blackwell, and I know it's messy, but that's not the problem here. Our troops are caught in the middle of tribal factions, in a place they have no business fighting. The president says the way to honor the memory of the fallen is to complete the mission, but if the war was wrong to begin with, it won't become right by going forward in the same direction."

What can I say in reply, what is there for me to tell him? I can maintain eye contact; I can show him that I'm listening.

He says, "President Blackwell won't be out of office for nineteen months"—*I know,* I want to tell him. *Believe me, I know exactly*—"and how many soldiers will die in that time? Two thousand, three thousand? I think we honor the memory of the fallen by preventing more senseless deaths."

I say, "Our country is so indebted to you and families like yours, and I know there's no way to repay Nate's sacrifice. But the situation is extremely complicated, and if the United States were to—"

"Mrs. Blackwell!" His interruption surprises both of us, it seems. He gives the impression of a very polite person straining against the confines, the straitjacket, of his own politeness; he is saying more than he thinks he should, in a sharper tone (I am, after all, the first lady, and he is, after all, sitting in my armored limousine), but less than what he actually feels (I am, after all, the first lady, and he is, after all, sitting in my armored limousine). He says, "I beg your pardon, but you *can* repay my sacrifice. You can't bring back Nate, no, but there are a hundred and forty-five thousand American troops still over there, and all of them have people who love them, who worry and pray every day for their safety. You can tell your husband, 'These people have families.' "

What was it I said to Gladys Wycomb earlier today? *My husband's administration is different from me.* Also: *He is the one the American people elected.*

"I saw you interviewed a few months back," Edgar Franklin says. "The lady who talked to you, she said, 'How do you and your husband spend your quiet time?' And you said, 'We read, we play Scrabble, the president watches sports.' Mrs. Blackwell, that's all anyone wants."

"I'm sorry," I say. "I'm very sorry."

"Nate's mother passed on in 1996," Edgar Franklin says. "She was a wonderful cook, and she never had to follow a recipe. Meat loaf, black-eyed peas, macaroni and cheese, everything she made was delicious. Well, after she was gone, it was just Nate and me, and he was still a youngster. I hired a lady to help take care of him and make our meals during the week, and come the weekend, Nate and I had spaghetti with sauce and called it a bachelor dinner. We'd say if we turned on the stove, it counted as cooking." We exchange a wry smile; Edgar Franklin does not hate me, at least not the way Gladys Wycomb did.

"Now, after I retired," he continues, "a few years passed, and I thought, It's about time I learn to cook. I bought cookbooks, and I read through them, and at first there were only a few recipes I could try—there were words I didn't even know the meaning of, *parboil* and *braise* and what have you. But I improved. I had some humble moments that no one but me ever needs to hear about, but I improved. I had a plan that when Nate got back, I would make him a full dinner, and wouldn't he be surprised: pork tenderloin with mushrooms and olives, a fresh salad, some homemade bread. I'd ordered a breadmaker from the Internet—people are very impressed by homemade bread if they don't know all you do is put in the ingredients and press a button. I tried the different kinds to find the best one, because Nate didn't care for raisins, but you could do herb bread or sourdough or any number of them." I know what Edgar Franklin will say next, and I'm not wrong, though the way he says it is more restrained, less maudlin, than it could be. He says, "I never did make that dinner for my son."

The limousine is quiet—outside, agents stand on all four sides—and after a minute, I say, "I've been close to people who died young, and I know it's terrible in a way that's different from other deaths. It feels like it's unendurable, but you endure it because you don't have a choice." I pause. "If there were anything I could do to bring back your son, to change what happened, I would."

"It'd be rough no matter how he was taken, that much I know,"

Edgar Franklin says. "But it wasn't a cause worth dying for. Weapons of mass destruction that were never found? Access to oil fields? Politicians playing cowboys and Indians? I guess those sound like good reasons when it's not your son."

Edgar Franklin is wearing khaki pants and a white short-sleeved button-down shirt beneath which I see the shadow of a sleeveless undershirt. He also wears a watch with a black leather strap, a plain gold wedding band on his left hand, and brown leather loafers with tassels. The tassels are what do it; they break my heart. I look directly at him and say, "I think you're right. It's time for us to end the war and bring home the troops."

ON NOVEMBER 7, 2000, which was Election Day, we voted when the polls opened in Madison; Charlie and I voted at the same time, and outside the curtained booths at the elementary school near the governor's mansion, we joined hands and, with our free outer arms, waved to the assembled journalists, photographers, cameramen, and well-wishers. We then boarded a plane and traveled to our final campaign stops, a rally in Portland, Oregon—Oregon was known to be a close race—and another in Minneapolis before we flew back to Wisconsin and rode to the hotel, where we were planning to watch the election returns in a suite with various staff members and relatives, including Arnold Prouhet and his wife and family, and all the Blackwells. Our nephews Harry and Drew had been campaigning full-time on Charlie's behalf since the beginning, and Harold and Ed had also done extensive fund-raising. That night, in addition to Ella, Harold, and Priscilla, every single one of Charlie's brothers, their wives, and their children, most of them married with children of their own, had come into town, and this all-hands-on-deck representation was quite touching to both Charlie and me. Someone had ordered dozens of pizzas, and the suite was a chaos of nerves and excitement; the only calm moment, which I appreciated, was when Reverend Randy led us in prayer before we ate. That the election would be tight was no secret, but Hank was confident Charlie would win, and Charlie was confident, too. Not because of anything we ever said to each other but due more to our exchanged glances, due to what we *didn't* say, I was pretty sure that my father-in-law and I were the only ones who had serious doubts about Charlie's victory. Harold was retired, or "actively retired," as he liked to say, but he still had many close ties inside the Republican National Committee, and his seeming skepticism struck me as informed, whereas mine was based more on intuition. Whether I wanted Charlie to win felt beside the point by then. Sure I did, and of course I didn't. I wanted him to win the way you want your hometown baseball team to win, or your daughter's high school soccer team. I wanted that in-the-moment triumph, wanted our emotions to build to celebration rather than sink into disappointment, which was not the same as wanting the triumph's long-term consequences. I wanted Charlie to win the election, but I didn't want him to be president. For eighteen months, we'd been caught up, both of us, in a great tumult of chanting crowds holding red and blue signs, of strategizing advisers and pollsters and reporters, of waving flags, brass bands, planes and airports and hotels, schools and county fairs and nursing homes. It had been fun sometimes and exhausting more often, and now it was almost finished. The hotel ballroom was reserved for the victory party, and one of the reasons I still knew that I wasn't cut out for politics was the built-in mortification of a victory party when there was a perfectly good chance there wouldn't be a victory.

As the hours passed, it became clear that the entire election came down to the state of Florida—it reminded me of baseball games, how all nine innings could somehow shrink to one final pitch—and just before seven our time, eight on the East Coast, the networks announced that Florida's twenty-five electoral votes would go to Charlie's opponent. The suite became quiet except for our niece Liza's three-month-old son, Parker, who was wailing inconsolably. Everyone looked at Charlie, or they tried not to look at him—he was sitting on a sofa near the large television, Ella on one side and Hank on the other—and I wasn't surprised when, within a few minutes, Ella whispered in my ear, "Dad wants to leave."

Harold, Priscilla, Hank, and Debbie Bell accompanied us back to the governor's mansion, but everyone else stayed behind. As we walked through the lobby and climbed in the SUVs that would take us home, none of us spoke to the hordes of media who called out, though I smiled at a few of them; there were many we knew well by this point. It wasn't as if they'd need encouragement—they were following us back to the mansion no matter what, and the reality was that we'd have to let them inside, Charlie would have to talk to them, before the end of the night.

At the mansion, we congregated in the second-floor living room, and I was tempted to suggest a game of Scrabble or euchre, but I don't think anything could have distracted us. Everyone's personalities seemed in this moment both reduced and magnified, distilled to some essential quality: Debbie Bell was angry, Hank was insisting that Florida couldn't have gone to Charlie's opponent and there must have been an error, Harold was stoic, Priscilla was disdainful of Charlie's opponent and the fools who would elect him, Ella was sweetly protective of her father, I was quiet, and Charlie was wounded—boyishly so, it seemed. He was speaking less than anyone else, and Priscilla was speaking the most. "That smug, sanctimonious tree-hugger," she'd say when images of Charlie's opponent flashed on-screen. "If that's the man the American people want for president, then they deserve him." I think election nights were particularly evocative and fraught for Priscilla and Harold—we were, of course, sitting in the governor's mansion they had occupied for eight years, where Charlie himself had spent most of his adolescence.

I had a maid bring out some peanuts and popcorn, and two televisions were playing—the one in the wooden cabinet, and another that had been brought in so we could watch more than one channel simultaneously, though we turned off the sound on both—and Charlie was preparing to call his opponent and concede the race when his and Hank's and Debbie's and Harold's cell phones all started ringing at once, and less than three minutes later, the networks reported that they were placing Florida back in the undecided category. By one-thirty A.M., Charlie was leading in Florida with a hundred thousand votes, and by three-thirty A.M., he was leading with fewer than two thousand, with most of the votes in the uncounted precincts expected to go to his opponent. When we went to bed just after four, it was impossible to know what to think; the only consensus by then was that the results would be so close there'd have to be a recount, and it might be several days before anyone knew the outcome. I wouldn't have believed my fatigue could be so overwhelming on such a nerve-racking night, but the last few days of campaigning had been especially wearying, and I felt that my body was begging me to lie down. Equally surprising was that Charlie seemed to feel the same. As the night had worn on, we'd been rejoined by several family members, we'd been paid a visit by a group of television and newspaper reporters and their attendant cameramen and photographers, and I'd noticed that increasingly, Charlie stuck close to me. Once, when I stood up to use the powder room, he asked where I was going. "And you're coming right back?" he said. I nodded. At close to four, when I said, "Will you forgive me if I turn in?" he said, "As a matter of fact, I'll join you." The thirty or so people in the living room applauded as Charlie walked out, and he looked sheepish when he paused and grinned.

In bed, after we'd brushed our teeth and turned out the light, he set his head sideways on my chest, and I ran my fingers through his hair. He said, "So what's gonna happen?"

"Oh, honey, I don't know any more than anyone else."

"But what's your hunch?"

"Honestly, sweetheart, I don't—"

He interrupted me. He said, "I've been thinking what I should do is be baseball commissioner. I'd be perfect, right?"

It was the first I'd heard of this idea, but it sounded plausible enough. I said, "Okay."

"It'd be fun—challenging but not a total pain in the ass, and a good way to utilize all the skills I've acquired. But this state-government shit, the three-hour meetings about groundwater or labor relations or some dairy law from 1850, I've had my fill."

"Is the baseball-commissioner position going to open soon? It's Wynne Smith now, isn't it?"

"I'll put out a few feelers. Smith's pushing seventy, so I'll bet they're ready for new blood."

"Just don't forget you have two years left of being governor."

Charlie was quiet, and then he said, "If I resigned, would you think that was terrible? Monty is up to the challenge, no question." Monty was Ralph Montanetti, the lieutenant governor.

"You wouldn't want to see this term through to the end?" I said.

"This campaign has been brutal—I don't have to tell you that, but between the two of us, I'm starting to feel like the thrill is gone. I already know Hank's gonna be gunning for '04, but I'm not sure it's worth it. The idea of winning a presidential election, lately, it's been reminding me of— What's that line about making partner at a law firm? You've won a pie-eating contest, and your prize is more pie."

"Will you do me a favor?" I said. "Will you try to remember that whatever happens, we'll be okay? If you want to stay in politics, if you want to get out and go back to baseball, if you just want to relax—" Charlie was fifty-four by then, and it wouldn't be embarrassing if he no longer worked; he could take early retirement, we could travel, we could even buy our own second home somewhere other than Halcyon, in Minnesota or Michigan, and he could fish and I could read. "You're lucky that you have so many options, and so many supporters and admirers," I said. "That's what's important."

Charlie lifted his head and turned it so that, in the dark, we were face-to-face. From the far side of the second floor, we could hear the televisions and the people still awake in the living room. He said, "When they announced I hadn't gotten Florida, that pissed me off. We've been down there, what, fifteen times in the last year? And I'll bet you right now everyone in the liberal media is shitting their pants with excitement—they get to say I lost, then they say, 'No, wait, you didn't,' and then they'll say, 'Oh yeah, you did.' Twice the fun, right? Over at the hotel, that wasn't my idea of a good time, to have to smile like a gracious loser while everyone I've ever known sits around staring at me. But then I thought, If everything happens for a reason, God must know what He's doing. What kind of believer would I be if I only trusted in Him when life goes my way?"

"There's still the possibility that you won," I said. "The election's not over yet."

He shook his head. "You know I lost, and I do, too. I feel it in my bones. But Lindy, I'm at peace." He kissed my lips and said, "This might sound crazy, but I'm already starting to think I dodged a bullet."

I THOUGHT WE'D ride back to the White House in the cars we were in—I was looking forward to a moment alone, or alone with three agents, to absorb what just took place—but the minute Edgar Franklin leaves my car, Jessica reappears, climbing in as she holds out a phone. "It's the president."

If it were anyone other than Charlie, even Ella, even my mother, I'd refuse. But I raise the phone to my ear, and when I say hello, Charlie says, "When did aliens kidnap my wife and replace her with you?"

He sounds boisterous, and he also sounds like he's walking somewhere—possibly toward the residence elevator to change for the gala, which is in a rather alarming twenty minutes.

"Charlie, I didn't intend to catch you off guard, but I couldn't let another—"

"No, it was brilliant. Hank is only pissed he didn't think of it himself. One parent to another, that was definitely the way to go."

"You're not upset?"

"I just hope Mr. Sympathy appreciated how generous it was of you to make time for him, especially since the word on the street is that now you won't have a chance to freshen up. But don't worry, I promise not to tell the students and teachers saluting you that you're wearing stinky underpants."

Uneasily, I realize he thinks I spoke to Edgar Franklin in his stead, less as myself than as a presidential surrogate, the way I sometimes attend funerals of foreign leaders. I say, "Charlie, I told Edgar Franklin I support ending the war and bringing home the troops."

For ten seconds, Charlie is silent, and then, in a bewildered voice, he says, "You support ending the war and bringing home the troops?"

"I made it clear I don't speak for the administration, I don't speak for you, and it's not as if he and I had an elaborate discussion about foreign policy. It was mostly him expressing his views and me listening."

"I'm sorry, but I think our connection must be messed up. It sounded like you just said that you told an antiwar activist surrounded by TV cameras that you side with him over me." I am quiet, and Charlie says, "Good God, Lindy."

"Sweetheart, you and I can have differing opinions. The abortion issue—"

"Is that what this is about? You were determined to cause a huge controversy today, so after the witch doctor croaked, you cooked up another one?"

I feel a great urge to be in the same physical place he is, to set my hand on his cheek, to embrace him—to show him that though I've done something uncharacteristic, I'm still his loyal wife.

"I'm walking toward a TV right now," he says, and then, to someone else, he says, "Yeah, while she was just talking to him." To me, he says, "Yep, it's on every station. Way to go, baby. You want to torpedo my immigration bill while you're at it? Sabotage Social Security reform?"

It's already on every station? Edgar Franklin climbed from my car minutes ago. But the newscasters must have figured it out while he was still in the limousine, they must be reporting live in their urgently speculative way.

"I'll be home in five minutes," I say. "Will you wait for me to get there before you become wound up?"

"See, I always forget this about you," he says, and even now, long after we first lost our privacy, I can't help wondering who's overhearing him. "Every decade, you like to pin me to the ground, pull open my mouth, and take a shit right into it."

I ONCE THOUGHT, when I was thirty-one and Charlie was running for Congress, that with practice I might learn to hold a novel in my purse and read it during his speeches, but I was wrong; reporters and audience members often glance at a candidate's wife while he speaks, gauging her reaction. Also around this time, which was when Charlie and I were falling in love, I thought that I could support him not as a politician but as a person, and I told him this, and he thought it, too. "I can assure you I'll never *tell* anyone if I disagree with you," I said to him. "That's no one's business but ours."

THE GALA IN my honor, attended by more than three hundred guests, is pleasant and crowded and a bit over-the-top. Charlie and I sit side by side in the front row, and after the third-graders sing "God Bless America" and a tiny twelve-year-old boy in a wheelchair is pushed onstage by his mother to lead us all in the Pledge of Allegiance, there are speeches by a principal at a public high school in Anacostia, a fifth-grader at a school in Bethesda, Maryland, and a Democratic senator known for his sponsorship of education-related bills (though he and I have gotten along well over the years, it's no secret he despises Charlie; however, he's hoping for support for his housing-voucher program). There is then a baton-twirling routine performed to R. Kelly's "I Believe I Can Fly" by a trio of nine-year-olds in leotards, a scene from the play *The Miracle Worker* in which two respected Broadway actresses play the parts of Helen Keller and Annie Sullivan, and a reading of the Langston Hughes poem "Theme for English B" by a high school senior, an African-American girl who is probably fifty pounds overweight, quite pretty, and in possession of undeniable stage presence.

At this point, three teachers receive awards: chrome apples affixed to wooden tablets, each presented by the student who nominated the teacher. The evening culminates with the reappearance onstage of all the earlier performers, two of whom unfurl a banner that has to be forty feet long and says THANK YOU FOR BEING OUR ADVOCATE MRS. BLACKWELL. During the teacher awards, I slipped backstage, and as planned, I walk out from the wings, smiling and waving. At the podium, two ninth-graders present me with my own chrome apple that's a foot in diameter (if my apple were life-size, as the teachers' apples are, it wouldn't provide the requisite photo op, and the flashbulbs are indeed blinding in this moment). I don't give a real speech but simply say, "Thank you very much, and thank you all for coming tonight. This has been an extraordinary evening, and I'm honored to be in the presence of so much talent. I hope each one of you will remember that wherever you want to go in life, education is the ticket. And now, in light of the fact that it's a school night, I recommend that you all go home, make sure your homework is finished, and get a good night's sleep." (Not a speech, but still—even these aren't words I wrote.) While normally, I'd be embarrassed at having such a fuss made over me, after all the drama of today, these proceedings are a giddy distraction. Onstage, I pose for photos with the students and teachers; several students not waiting in line have formed a circle around one of the "God Bless America" third-graders, who is vigorously break-dancing. Charlie is gone, I note. We have acted our parts tonight, sitting next to each other with pleasant expressions, Charlie smiling gamely whenever someone onstage said something kind about me, but he gave me no nonmandatory attention, no whisper or hand squeeze or knee pat.

After I returned to the White House from my conversation with Edgar Franklin, there wasn't time for me to find Charlie—as he had predicted, there wasn't even time for me to change clothes, but I did hurry to the residence to use my own bathroom and saw Ella. We hugged, and I said, "We should head down there now," and she said, "Aren't you going to refresh your makeup?"

"Honey, we're running late."

She smirked. "You think they'll start without you?" Although Mirel, a lovely young woman who acts as my makeup artist, and Kim, who does my hair, were waiting in the beauty salon (a room installed by Pat Nixon), it was Ella who, using Mirel's supplies, dabbed gloss onto my lips, rubbed the brush over my cheeks, said, "Look up," and ran the mascara wand through my eyelashes. "Now look down." I obeyed, and she said, "Now blink." Then she said, "Mom, I'm glad you talked to the Franklin dude, but if the troops were withdrawn right away, there'd be a domino effect of lawlessness across the Middle East."

Her tone was reminiscent of when she was a teenager, explaining to me something she thought I ought to already know—diplomatic enough not to offend me but confident that logic was on her side. (*Obviously* she should be able to stay out until two in the morning because she was extremely responsible, because none of her classmates had a midnight curfew, and because it wasn't like she drank.) In a strange way, I was caught off guard and touched by Ella's directness, her willingness to talk about the war itself rather than about how to fix my supposed slip of the tongue. This, I knew already, would be the approach of everyone else. Just in the time it had taken Jessica and me to get back to the White House, Jessica's two phones had rung six times (and those were only the rings I heard—there were probably many more beeps for calls interrupting the calls she was in the middle of), and apparently, Hank had spoken to several reporters. I'm not sure if he'd have skipped the gala anyway, but this was what he did, no doubt to continue setting the record straight. When Jessica, Ella, and I met Charlie in the Family Dining Room, Debbie Bell and Hank were both with him, perhaps to serve as a buffer between Charlie and me, perhaps at Charlie's request, and so were Charlie's personal aide, Michael, and my personal aide, Ashley, and Charlie didn't kiss me hello but instead embraced Ella and more or less ignored me; I also could tell that Debbie was fuming. The eight of us walked together through Cross Hall, and just before we entered the East Room, Hank peeled off, and Charlie took my hand and forced a grin onto his face. Subtext: Nothing is wrong, and no one at the White House is concerned about the first lady going off-message.

When I've shaken hands and been photographed with everyone onstage who's lined up, Ella, Jessica, and I are ushered out by Cal—Ashley squirts Purell for me—and we head toward the residence without speaking to the few dozen journalists in attendance at the gala; they are kept at bay by the press secretaries. "Here's Hank's plan," Jessica says in a low voice as we walk to the elevator. "No interviews for several weeks, and you don't take questions from the media at public events. Then we see where things stand and ease back in."

I nod. This doesn't seem so bad; silence on my part is far preferable to the sort of verbal acrobatics I'd need to engage in if I were trying not to either reinforce or undermine what I'd told Edgar Franklin. Not that I'll be off the hook altogether, obviously—whenever I am interviewed again, I'll be asked about my comments (which Edgar repeated immediately to the assembled reporters, which I knew he would), but I plan to be terse.

Though she rides the elevator upstairs with us, Jessica doesn't step out; instead, the elevator attendant, a spry senior citizen named Nicholas, holds open the door as Jessica bids Ella and me farewell, acting as if she's going home herself, though I'm fairly sure she's planning to return to the East Wing to keep working. "Thank you for everything," I say to Jessica. "You deserve a medal for today."

"You deserve a gigantic apple plaque," Ella says. Ella is merely making a joke; she thinks I went to see my mother this afternoon and doesn't know about Gladys Wycomb's threat, doesn't know what a long day it's been. In any case, I've already lost track of the chrome apple. I believe Jessica's assistant Belinda carried it away.

Jessica says to me, "Take it easy tonight, okay?" She looks at Ella. "Make her relax."

"The same to you," I say.

"I'm not the one in the eye of the storm," Jessica says. Abruptly, she jumps out of the elevator and hugs me, and as she does, she whispers in my ear so Ella can't hear, "You did the right thing."

Ella and I sit in the Family Kitchen, and Ella pulls cheese, hummus, and baby carrots out of the refrigerator. She isn't a fan of the food here—even though downstairs the chefs will fix anything we want exactly to our specifications—so I always make sure we're stocked in the residence when she visits. I call down to ask for a Cobb salad for myself, and Ella and I analyze the evening for a while, discussing the impressive delivery of the girl who recited "Theme for English B," the vaguely and uncomfortably sexual overtones of the baton-twirling fourth-graders, and Ella says, "Did you talk to Senator Zimon tonight? I think he's had hair implants." She adds, "Does Jessica ever annoy you because she's so perfect?"

I smile. "Does that mean Jessica annoys you because she's perfect?"

"Not at all!" Ella grins her father's grin. "No, I'm totally not threatened by this woman who's close to my own age, who you spend all your time with and like better than me. Not one little bit!"

"I think the world of Jessica, but I only have one daughter, and there's no one I love more. Would you like to sit on my lap?" I am mostly teasing, as Ella is, too, but she rises, turns, and lowers her rear end onto my thighs for a second. I run my palm down her back, over her still-long caramel-colored hair. Then she stands, reaching forward for a carrot that she dips in the hummus. She bites into it and says over one shoulder, with her mouth full, "What I'm really hungry for right now is a poop sandwich."

"You're a class act," I say. This is an old joke between us, a requirement whenever eating a meal together after time apart. (Needless to say, *I* never make the joke, but Ella can be counted on.)

"Are you and Dad in a huge fight?" Ella asks.

"Why would you think that?"

"There has to be some fallout from your heart-to-heart with that Franklin guy."

"Don't worry about Dad and me. We'll be just fine."

"So what's the thing you wanted to tell me?"

"Oh—" Should I do it? I no longer need to, now that I've been spared by Gladys Wycomb's death, but I still could. What is the difference between giving voice to an overdue truth and being a parent who indulgently unburdens herself? Telling Ella wouldn't be fair to her, I realize, it would be unsettling—not just because of her religious convictions but also because (I know Ella, and I, too, was an only child) it will make her think she could have had a brother or sister. I say, "It was nothing."

Ella leans over and kisses my cheek. "Then I'm going to go call Wyatt. Tell Dad when he gets up here that I have something hilarious to show him on YouTube."

I lightly swat her rear end. "Put your plate in the sink."

When Ella is gone, I move to the West Sitting Hall, which has a beautiful lunette window overlooking the Old Executive Office Building, the Rose Garden, and the West Wing. I take a seat on a sofa and remain there for an hour and a half, reading. The book I left here yesterday, *Stop-Time* by Frank Conroy, has been waiting for me for twenty-four hours—all night last night and all day today, while I hopped from Arlington to Chicago to Riley. I enter it, and it welcomes me back.

Just before eleven, I set down the book and stand, and when I do, I remember Pete Imhof's envelope, folded into the pocket of my linen jacket. I lift it out, and before I reach inside—the envelope is not sealed but already torn open—I see that on the back, in my own seventeen-year-old handwriting, it says, *Mr. and Mrs. Imhof.* Right away, I know exactly what it is, and with the tip of my thumb, I press against the envelope's uneven bump, confirming its outline. (It's so small! Not over half an inch at its widest point.) I pull out the note.

I will never be able to express to you how sorry I am, my seventeen-year-old self explains in blue ink. *I know that I have caused you great pain. If there was anything in the world I could do to change what happened, I would.*

This pendant is something of mine Andrew once told me he liked, so I thought it might comfort you to have it. My pulse is racing as I withdraw the pendant, and it is very tarnished—I will never polish it—and I look at it in my palm: my silver heart. This is what Andrew leaned in to touch that afternoon before he went to football practice, the gift my grandmother gave me for my sixteenth birthday. (Oh, the past, the past—how the memories of the people I loved sear me.)

I'm not sure what I'll do with the pendant; it's obviously an inexpensive piece of jewelry, not particularly suitable for a sixty-one-year-old woman and even less so for the first lady, but maybe I can wear it on such a long cord that it won't be visible beneath my shirts. No object in the world could be dearer to me, and I marvel at the strangeness of its source. Perhaps, though I didn't yet know I had it, this is what nudged me to go talk to Edgar Franklin—that Pete Imhof had given me back my heart.

I MEET CHARLIE in the hall outside our bedroom. He is walking from the opposite direction, and I can tell that he's trying to decide how friendly or unfriendly to be—after we make eye contact, he immediately looks away, then seems to realize how absurd it would be to pretend not to see me when it's only the two of us, or only the two of us and Snowflake, who scampers off as soon as he notices me. A valet hovers outside our bedroom and opens the door as we approach, nodding once at Charlie. "Good night, Mr. President," and then to me, "Good night, ma'am."

"'Night, Roger," Charlie says as we walk by, and I smile without speaking.

When the door closes behind us, I say, "Please don't give me the silent treatment. If you're angry, let's talk about it."

"*If* I'm angry? Lindy, how the fuck could you blindside me like this? You know how it looks if there's not even unified support for the war in my own marriage? I'm the laughingstock of the world tonight, and I have to sit there clapping for baton twirlers."

"Sweetheart, I think you're overreacting. What I said to Edgar Franklin wasn't a political statement."

"What planet are you living on? When the first lady of the United States talks, it's always political!" Between our bed and the flat-screen television above the fireplace is a sitting area: two wingback chairs, a sofa, and a wooden table off which Charlie grabs the remote control. "Hmm, I wonder what they're saying on TV. I'm sure this isn't all over the networks, because obviously, it was just you speaking as a private citizen, it wasn't a political statement, and the media fully understands those subtle distinctions." When the screen comes to life—it's Fox News—there's a clip of Charlie's press secretary, Maggie Carpeni, saying this evening, "Listen, we *all* want to bring the troops home, every person in America does. The question isn't if, it's when, but the first lady knows as well as anyone else that a precipitous withdrawal would have disastrous consequences. She and the president stand united in their certainty that victory will come when stability and freedom have been achieved."

"I don't think that makes you look like a laughingstock at all," I say. That Maggie is misrepresenting my own remarks doesn't particularly bother me—first because of my belief that the fact of someone saying something about me, even when the someone is in my husband's inner circle, cannot make it true or untrue, but also because I didn't realistically imagine that the White House would leave my statements to Edgar Franklin untouched. That I said them once, in earshot of only Colonel Franklin and my agent Cal, has to be enough, at least for now—if I ever expect to reaffirm or expand on them, or to reassert my pro-choice stance, I will have to do so with great care. And Maggie or Hank can minimize what I said, but they can't erase it. It exists. While I often have been surprised by the trusting nature of the American public, people clearly have become more wary during Charlie's presidency, and so I can hope that at least some of them will assume the truth: that Edgar Franklin quoted me accurately, and that I meant exactly what it sounded like. Whether my words will have any positive effect, including on my husband, remains to be seen.

Charlie clicks to CNN, where the caption at the bottom of the screen says ANTIWAR FATHER RETURNS TO GEORGIA. Edgar Franklin stands before an electronic bouquet of no fewer than a dozen microphones; beside him is a plump woman identified as his sister

Cheryl. It is still light out, which means the press conference must have been filmed several hours ago. "I believe that I've gotten as close as I will to the president," he says. "Today I spoke from the heart to Mrs. Blackwell, and I choose to think she heard me and will act as a conduit to her husband. Whether he will listen is up to him. Although I'm going home tonight, I know that for as long as the war continues, it's my responsibility to protest it."

There is then a jump away from Edgar Franklin and back to the commentators in the studio—now the caption across the bottom reads ET TU, ALICE?—and one of the pundits, a man in a bow tie, says, "I'm sure all our viewers remember President Blackwell's claim that he wouldn't withdraw the troops even if Alice and Snowflake are the only ones left who support him—well, Mr. President, you may want to keep a very close watch on the first cat!" (This is yet another strangeness of being a famous person—that sometimes, on television or a website or in an article, a person addresses you directly but rhetorically directly, seemingly never imagining that you might see or read what they're saying.)

The four commentators sit at a long, narrow triangle of a table, and they all chuckle at the bow-tied fellow's quip. The show's host says, "The big question now is whether the Dems will see this as an opportunity to kick Blackwell while he's down vis-à-vis his Supreme Court nominee, Ingrid Sanchez."

"Do you really want to watch this?" I ask. Charlie usually stays away from television news, believing the vast majority of producers and reporters have a liberal bias. Fox, obviously, gives him the most favorable coverage, but even with them, he gets fidgety after a couple minutes.

"Just don't act like your betrayal isn't the topic on everyone's lips tonight." Charlie raises the remote control and clicks off the TV. "If you think that, you're kidding yourself."

"Aren't you at least happy that Edgar Franklin has gone home?"

"You mean because you sold me out and gave him what he'd come for?"

I sit on the brocade-covered bench at the end of our bed (the bed frame is French walnut, acquired by Theodore and Edith Roosevelt; the mattress is a custom-fitted Simmons Beautyrest World Class with memory foam and pillow top). Charlie is still standing behind one of the wingback chairs eight or nine feet away from me.

"I love you," I say.

"Maybe you should sleep in the other room."

"Did you hear what I just said?"

"You want us to kiss and make up, and then what will you do tomorrow, join Greenpeace? I still don't know what the hell got into you."

"Charlie, talking to Colonel Franklin wasn't out of character for me. He's a father, and his son died, and the fact that the White House was ignoring him made me very uncomfortable."

"Then you should have said something to me, or to Hank, or to—"

"I *did* say something to you! Or I tried to, but you might recall that as recently as this morning, when you brought over the newspapers, you'd only give them to me if I didn't mention him."

"So I left you with no choice but to slam my foreign policy?" His expression is skeptical. He is wearing the charcoal suit, white shirt, and red tie from earlier—neither of us, it turns out, changed for the gala, though by now he has unbuttoned the top button of the shirt and loosened the tie. Perhaps I'm a pushover, but I've always found this to be an endearing style in any man and especially in my husband. He says, "You ever think the time has come for you to forgive me for being elected president?"

We watch each other, and I say nothing. Then—a lump has formed in my throat—I say, "The reason I didn't want you to be president is that I was afraid it would turn out like this."

"Like what? You mean you and me?"

I shake my head. "Not us. Just the—the responsibility. How much is at stake when you decide something." This is a way we never talk, Charlie and I. We speak of when he is giving a speech where, when he is traveling where, or when I am. We discuss in small, momentary ways how the State of the Union went, whether an airplane flight was bumpy, if his cold is any better. It would be crushing, I think, for us to analyze the enormity of our lives now, their meaning and repercussions, yet surely it is this very reticence, our workaday manner of communicating, one foot in front of the other, that has landed us in a place we wouldn't thinkingly have gone. This has been Charlie's presidency: episodes of experience, choices he's made based on the input of advisers reluctant to tell him anything he doesn't want to hear; he has prayed, but I've often worried that the voice of guidance he's heard has been not God's but Hank's, or possibly Charlie's own, echoing back at him.

But he doesn't see it this way. He looks incredulous as he says, "Do you think I'm not aware of the responsibility of being leader of the free world every minute of every day? Lindy, if at this point it's news to you that the president is under tremendous pressure, then I don't know where you've been for the last six and a half years."

"But aren't you—" I pause, start again. "Don't you feel guilty?"

He stares at me. "For what?"

"A lot of the soldiers who are dying are younger than Ella. They're younger, but some are married, they have kids of their own. Or they come back, and what if you're twenty-six years old and both your legs were blown off and you never had a college education? We met a fellow like that at Walter Reed, remember? What's he supposed to do now?"

Charlie's nostrils flare even more than usual. He is—it's unmistakable—disgusted. "Did you attend some peacenik workshop in Chicago today? Lindy, grow up. Freedom has a price, and you know what? A lot of people consider it an honor to pay it."

"Sweetheart, I'm not trying to bait you—I'm not a journalist at a press conference. Can't we talk sincerely?"

"About what?" His face is scrunched up in a sneer, his eyes squinty. "I don't know where this is coming from, but frankly, I don't need it from you, of all people."

Isn't he right in a way, that it's far too late to change the rules? Our predecessors—Democrats—were known for being a team of sorts. "Two for the price of one" was a campaign slogan, and the first lady had an accomplished law career behind her. But he was adulterous, and she was ultimately a divisive figure among both men and women (Jadey professed to hate her, though I secretly always admired her), and when Charlie ran largely in contrast to that administration, the differences between me and her were not a political creation; they were real. I moved the first lady's office back from the West Wing to the East Wing, I have until today avoided controversy, I have not tried to convince my husband of much of anything. Isn't it indeed unfair, then, to start confronting Charlie with my opinions and criticisms? And isn't it cowardly, aren't the consequences too serious, not to?

I say, "One time, this was probably twenty years ago, I was with Jadey at the country club, and I was reading an article in the paper about a man who was sick with hepatitis C and cirrhosis and couldn't afford his medication. The article was just incredibly sad. I looked up from reading it, and people were, you know, splashing in the pool, Jadey and I were lying on those recliners, and I asked her if she ever felt like she should be leading an entirely different life."

Almost imperceptibly, Charlie's face softens; his nostrils shrink, they are no longer at full flare.

"I guess I wonder if I should have been an entirely different first lady," I say. "Yes, I realize it's been six years, but I finally feel like, Oh, *this* is how it works. When I was a librarian, every time I read a new book to the children, it was only after the class was finished that I knew how I should have led the discussion, what the activities should have been. It was as if I knew how to do it right in the future from having done it wrong."

"Lindy—" He folds his arms across his chest. "You're a great first lady. Your approval ratings are sky-high."

"Those numbers don't mean anything."

He shrugs. "You're preaching to the choir on that front, but come on—America loves you. The applause you got tonight—"

"You don't have to tell me how great I am," I say.

"Really? Because I'd be thrilled if you'd do that for me." For the first time since we entered our bedroom, he grins—not a thousand-watt grin, but still a real one.

I glance at the fireplace, where porcelain vases that once belonged to Dolly Madison flank the TV, then I look again at my husband. "On the plane today, I was thinking about how, after Andrew Imhof died, from then on, anything in my life that wasn't bad felt like a pardon. Especially meeting you, marrying you—I wasn't sure if I deserved to be so lucky. And when you wanted to run for governor and president, even though I had such doubts, I didn't put my foot down because I thought it wasn't my right. Who am I to tell other people, including you, how to live? I'm not such a paragon of perfection." I pause; I have gotten to the part that's harder to say, where I incriminate not just myself but him as well. Slowly, I say, "But if you've made certain choices and I've stood by, aren't I responsible, too, indirectly? If you look at it like that, then the car accident pales in comparison to the deaths since the war started. I almost couldn't survive the guilt of killing one person and now how many thousands—and not just Americans but—"

"This is crazy talk!" Charlie strides toward me, he pulls me up from the bench, and he places his palms on either side of my head, gazing at me intently. He seems fierce, fiercely determined, but not hostile. "You're being nuts, do you hear me? There are casualties under every president, every single one without exception. You're so good-hearted that you feel personally responsible, but Lindy, it has nothing to do with you. When it comes to spreading democracy, yeah, there's some collateral damage, and that might sound callous, but the casualties so far, no matter how you tally them, it's nowhere close to Vietnam or World War II—this doesn't hold a candle. And believe me, those wars had their critics, too, but no one looks back and thinks, Yeah, we really should have let Hitler go ahead and rule Europe. You're in the thick of things, and that's why it's hard to maintain perspective—I struggle, too—but future generations will thank us. They will, Lindy. There's no doubt in my mind."

Did I bare my soul to him of all people—not to Jessica or Jadey or even to my father-in-law—precisely so that he could comfort me with passionate disagreement? Who would be more assured of, more invested in, my blamelessness than Charlie? In a similar fashion, I once allowed him to convince me that dating him against Dena's wishes was no big deal.

He says, "They got to you today, didn't they? The witch doctor and Mr. Sympathy, they gave you hell because you're too nice to put them in their place. But just because they talk a good game doesn't mean they're right."

Oh, Charlie. Oh, my dear and cherished husband in your white shirt and your loosened red tie, standing before me warm and fervent and familiar, my husband whose every expression and gesture and inch of skin are known to me, my partner in the strange circumstances of our lives, the man whom I have endlessly wished to make happy, endlessly been amused by, endlessly loved—do you not imagine I know all too well that just because people talk a good game doesn't mean they're right?

I have often felt, observing the world, like a solitary person in a small cottage looking out a window at a vast dark forest. Since I was a little girl, I have lived inside this cottage, sheltered by its roof and walls. I have known of people suffering—I have not been blind to them in the way that privilege allows, the way my own husband and now my daughter are blind. It is a statement of fact and not a judgment to say Charlie and Ella's minds aren't oriented in that direction; in a way, it absolves them, whereas the unlucky have knocked on the door of my consciousness, they have emerged from the forest and knocked many times over the course of my life, and I have only occasionally allowed them entry. I've done more than nothing and much less than I could have. I have laid inside, beneath a quilt on a comfortable couch, in a kind of reverie, and when I heard the unlucky outside my cottage, sometimes I passed them coins or scraps of food, and sometimes I ignored them altogether; if I ignored them, they had no choice but to walk back into the woods, and when they grew weak or got lost or were circled by wolves, I pretended I couldn't hear them calling my name. In my twenties, when I was a teacher and a librarian working with children from poor families, I thought it was the beginning, that my contributions to society would increase and continue, but in fact that was my deepest involvement; in the years since, I have only extended myself from higher and higher perches, in increasingly perfunctory ways, with more cameras to chronicle my virtue.

I could have lived a different life, but I lived this one. And perhaps it is not a coincidence that I married a man who would neither fault me nor even be aware of my failings. I married a man to whom I would compare favorably because if I have done little, he has done less, or perhaps more; if I have caused harm accidentally and indirectly, he has done so with qualmless intent and total confidence.

The tears that have been welling in my eyes over the course of the conversation spill out at last, and Charlie wipes them with the pads of his thumbs. He leans in and kisses my right eyebrow. He murmurs,

"Come on, baby." If he hasn't yet forgiven me completely, then it's only a matter of time; he will forgive me so long as my behavior today remains an anomaly. He says, "Lindy, both of us—we're instruments of God's will."

HAVE I MADE terrible mistakes?

In bed beside me, my husband sleeps, his breathing deep and steady. Before I awakened, I was dreaming of Andrew Imhof, the old dream: the two of us standing in different places, with different groups of people, in a large and badly lit room, my constant awareness of him. But in tonight's dream, there was a startling change: After decades of elusion, we find each other. What happiness! We both are shy, we both are young, we make our way toward each other awkwardly but with a shared understanding, a certainty. He is strong and sweet and golden, and I am wearing a red dress that I never in reality owned. We don't say much because it's not necessary. And then—a miracle—we kiss, we are kissing. This is all I ever wanted, to come back to you, to be held by you, for what existed between us not to be cut short, and especially not at my hand. Your lips are soft and tentative, without the pushy sureness of a husband's tongue. It is enough, just this—your hand at the small of my back, the heat of your chest beneath your shirt, our faces close together, and a cloak of privacy surrounding us. Could I have been your wife after all, might we have made a life together on your parents' farm or one of our own? Once, on that extended visit back to Riley, I decided not, but now that we're together, our compatibility makes me think of course we could have. We can talk to each other, we make each other laugh, there is between us a common sensibility, a wordless affection whose subtext is a single question: *What took us so long?*

And then I awakened, a sixty-one-year-old woman in a big, grand, shadowy bedroom in Washington, D.C., the wife of the president of the United States. Can Charlie and I not also talk to each other, do we not make each other laugh, is there not between us a common sensibility? It isn't necessary for me to insist to myself that I love Charlie; I know that I do. But that dewy certainty I felt for Andrew, the lightness of our lives then—it is long gone. I have never experienced it with anyone else.

I didn't vote for Charlie for president. I did vote for him both times for governor, but when he ran for president, I didn't want the upheaval or the burdens, and I also believed sincerely that his opponent would do a better job. He had more experience, a more nuanced view of the issues; he was a lifelong public servant rather than an intermittent dabbler. I wondered, exiting the voting booth in 2000 and again in 2004, if my expression might give away my actions, but my vote was apparently so inevitable that no one ever asked me about it, no reporter or campaign staffer. I suppose it would have been disrespectful. In the photo taken of us that morning in 2000, Charlie and I pause outside the curtained booths at the elementary school in Madison, simultaneously holding hands and waving. What does the photo show, I've wondered since—my treachery or his? During the periods when I've been the most frustrated by our lives, or by what is happening in this country, I've looked outside at the cars and pedestrians our motorcades pass, and I've thought, *All I did is marry him. You are the ones who gave him power.* At other times, I have felt both a sense of regret for deceiving him and an oppressive awareness of my complicity in his elections.

Did I betray Charlie, or did I act on principle? Has he betrayed the American people, or has he acted on principle? Perhaps the answer is all of the above. If the many novels I've read are an accurate indicator, I have to assume there are betrayals in most marriages. The goal, I suppose, is not to allow any that are larger than the strength of the partnership.

While I don't imagine that I'll ever be able to reveal to Charlie this particular betrayal, the future is difficult to predict, and perhaps there will come a time when even having voted for his opponent might seem an amusing anecdote. I doubt it, but it's possible. For now I will say nothing; amid the glaring exposure, there must remain secrets that are mine alone.

ACKNOWLEDGMENTS

In researching the life of a first lady, I relied on many books, articles, and websites. I drew particular inspiration from the facts and insights of *The Perfect Wife: The Life and Choices of Laura Bush,* by Ann Gerhart. I also must acknowledge my debt to four other books: *Laura Bush: An Intimate Portrait of the First Lady,* by Ronald Kessler; *Ambling into History: The Unlikely Odyssey of George W. Bush,* by Frank Bruni; *Living History,* by Hillary Rodham Clinton; and *For Love of Politics: Inside the Clinton White House,* by Sally Bedell Smith. I am grateful to all these authors and would encourage anyone interested in nonfiction accounts of life on the campaign trail or in the White House to seek out their work.

In addition, my gratitude and affection go to my editor, Laura Ford, my publicist, Jynne Martin, and my agent, Jennifer Rudolph Walsh. I'm lucky to have many other advocates and allies in publishing, including Gina Centrello, Jennifer Hershey, Tom Perry, Sanyu Dillon, Sally Marvin, Avideh Bashirrad, Janet Wygal, Victoria Wong, Robbin Schiff, Amanda Ice, Suzanne Gluck, Tracy Fisher, Raffaella DeAngelis, Michelle Feehan, Lisa Grubka, and Alicia Gordon. For her years of steadfast support, there will always be a place in my heart for Shana Kelly.

For being smart and supportive, I thank my early readers: Susanna Daniel, Cammie McGovern, Samuel Park, Brian Weinberg, Shauna Seliy, Emily Miller, Jennifer Weiner, Lewis Robinson, Katie Brandi, and Susan Marrs.

For helping me figure out particular details, I thank James R. Ketchum, Marisa Luzzatto, Katie Riley, Jo Sittenfeld, Ellen Battistelli, Darren Speece, Jennie Cole, Joe Litvin, Marc Miller, Chris Thomforde, Susan Brown, Marcie Roahen, Susan Schultz, Jeanne Stewart, John Stewart, Sr., John Stewart, Jr., Mikey Stewart, Nick Stanton, and once again, Susanna Daniel. Any errors in the book of either fact or judgment are my own.

As always, I thank my parents and siblings for being my parents and siblings, and I'm especially appreciative to my father for his feedback and input. Finally, I thank Matt Carlson, who read each section as I finished it and encouraged me to keep writing because he wanted to find out what would happen next.

American Wife

Curtis Sittenfeld

RANDOM HOUSE READER'S CIRCLE

A Reader's Guide

A CONVERSATION WITH THE AUTHOR

Grateful acknowledgment is made to *Time* for permission to reprint an interview with Curtis Sittenfeld by Radhika Jones, senior arts editor, *Time,* copyright © 2008 by *Time*. Reprinted by permission of Time Inc.

***Time*: How did this idea come to you?**

Curtis Sittenfeld: Soon after George W. Bush was elected I read a few articles about Laura Bush that made her seem different from what I would have expected. I learned that she's a big reader, and that she would invite people who had political opinions different from her husband's to events at the governor's mansion and then events at the White House. And then I read a biography of her in 2004 by Ann Gerhart called *The Perfect Wife: The Life and Choices of Laura Bush*. That reinforced the sense I had that she had led a really complex and interesting life. So I wrote this article for Salon—which I would not have written if I'd known that I would end up writing this book—that was basically about being a liberal who has this weird admiration for Laura Bush. In that article I said that her life resembled a novel. And then two years later it occurred to me, I should write that novel.

It's clear when you read the book that it's about the first couple, but it feels equally like a book about relationships and how you fall in love and how your character forms.

I agree one hundred percent. And if I'd wanted to write a book that was a hatchet job on Laura Bush—if that was my big goal—I could have made it two hundred pages. But I wanted to explore the human heart much more than I wanted to explore politics. Some people have said to me, Why did you not write more about Charlie Blackwell's political ascension and his becoming governor, and the campaign, and I feel like there are excellent books out there on political campaigns and mine wouldn't add anything to the mix. There are so many people who are so much better qualified to write about politics than I am.

I understand that plot is very important to you; you have literary concerns but you also want to keep people turning the pages. And that happens in *American Wife*. But in this case, unlike your earlier novels, many of the elements of the plot came to you ready-made. Did that affect the way you worked?

The book has four sections, and in each section there's a major plot twist that has a strong resemblance to an event in the real life of Laura Bush. But then everything else is made up. There's a chapter where Charlie Blackwell is drinking heavily, and he buys the baseball team and gives up drinking and finds religion, and obviously those have George Bush parallels. But there's all this other stuff that has to do with a Princeton reunion, and Alice Blackwell's sister-in-law having doubts about her own marriage. So even in the sections that borrow most heavily from real life, almost everything is made up. And of course, literally, every scene is made up—because even if we all know that there's a point when George Bush became religious, I sure wasn't there!

How long ago did you start working on it?

It's been two years in the making. When I was writing my first two books I was also freelancing and teaching and doing other odd jobs. For this one I pretty much just wrote. And I wrote much longer hours than I had in the past. I worked more intensively on this book than I plan to for any future book. I don't think I'll have another book for four or five years, and that's fine with me. In some ways I think it would be very dignified if I went away for twenty years and then wrote my fourth book.

Can you describe the research you did? You mentioned *The Perfect Wife*.

That was my biggest influence, and that's the book I recommend to people. If someone says, Oh, *American Wife* makes me curious to learn more about Laura Bush, I would definitely urge them to read Ann Gerhart. I read another biography of Laura Bush by Ronald Kessler. I read a book by Frank Bruni called *Ambling into History: The Unlikely Odyssey of George W. Bush* about Bush's first presidential campaign. I read Hillary Rodham Clinton's autobiography, which I enjoyed much more than I thought I would. I read a book called *For Love of Politics: Inside the Clinton White House* by Sally Bedell Smith. I interviewed some people who worked in the White House. Because the book takes place primarily in Wisconsin, I ordered 1960s Wisconsin yearbooks off eBay, and I interviewed people from Wisconsin. For the Princeton stuff I talked to Princeton librarians. And I interviewed friends and family members who I thought had expertise on any topic that might be relevant to the book.

How about the sex in the book? I was reminded of something you said about *Prep,* that it might not be your parents' cup of tea for various reasons, and the graphic sex was part of that. It's quite a visual, the sex in *American Wife*.

Actually, for Christmas last year I gave my parents a special copy of the book that had all the sex scenes cut out. Then when some of the sex scenes were put up by websites in July—which was very misrepresentative of the book—my dad stumbled upon them and I basically said, You know, I tried to protect you from that, and if you sought it out on your own, that has to be your concern, not mine. I mean, the book is about a thirty-year marriage, so of course there's sex.

And realistically, there's less of it as it goes on.

Exactly. And I know the distinction is hard for people to make, but I do not feel like I wrote a novel about Laura and George Bush. I feel like I read things about them that inspired me to create fictional characters, and then these fictional characters lead their own lives and have their own interactions. So this is not a book about Laura Bush's sex life.

I've read that you didn't expect *Prep* to get the kind of reception that it did. But *American Wife* was coming into an environment where it would get a lot of attention precisely because it is so relevant. Was the run-up to publication different? Did it feel different as you were writing?

To me the question when I was writing was, one, will I finish it, ever? That's a question that a lot of novelists ask themselves while writing. And, two, will I feel like it's good enough that I'll want it to be published? Those were the questions I was focused on. The fact is that in this day and age I don't think any novelist can assume that a book will get attention. There are books that have pretty provocative subjects that disappear without a trace. I would say that already it's gotten more attention than I anticipated. At the same time I think it's probably the most commercial book that I'll ever write. It has the most obvious hook of any book that I'll write.

QUESTIONS FOR DISCUSSION

1. The novel opens and closes with Alice wondering if she's made terrible mistakes. Do you think she has? If so, what are they?

2. Alice's grandmother passes down her love of reading. How else is Alice influenced by her grandmother?

3. Why does Andrew remain such an important figure to Alice, even decades later? Do you think they would have ended up together under different circumstances?

4. To what do you attribute Dena's anger at what she calls Alice's betrayal? Do you believe her anger is justified?

5. Is Charlie a likable character? Can you understand Alice's attraction to him?

6. Does Alice compromise herself and her ideals during her marriage, or does she realistically alter her behavior and expectations in order to preserve the most important relationship in her life?

7. Were you surprised by the scene between Alice and Joe at the Princeton reunion? Why do you think it happened?

8. What would you have done in Alice's situation at the end of the novel? Do you think it was wrong of her to take the stance she did?

9. How do you think Laura Bush would react to this novel if she read it?

PHOTO: © JERRY BAUER

CURTIS SITTENFELD is the author of *The Man of My Dreams* and *Prep,* which was chosen by *The New York Times* as one of the Ten Best Books of 2005. Her nonfiction has appeared in *The New York Times, The Atlantic Monthly,* Salon.com, *Allure, Glamour,* and on public radio's *This American Life.* Her books have been translated into twenty-five languages. Visit her website at www.curtissittenfeld.com.

ABOUT THE TYPE

This book was set in Garamond No. 3, a variation of the classic Garamond typeface originally designed by the Parisian type cutter Claude Garamond (1480–1561).

Claude Garamond's distinguished romans and italics first appeared in *Opera Ciceronis* in 1543–44. The Garamond types are clear, open, and elegant.